SUN & MOON ACADEMY
BOOK TWO: SPRING
SEMESTER

KRISTIE COOK   TISH THAWER   BELINDA BORING

ROSE GARCIA   E.J. FECHENDA   AMY RICHIE

JUSTINE WINTER   VICTORIA FLYNN

HAVENWOOD FALLS COLLECTIVE

TO OUR READERS

While the Havenwood Falls world has been free from the Covid-19 pandemic, we noticed it's pretty obvious the authors wrote this during the crazy times of 2020: we've dropped a helluva a lot of F-bombs throughout these pages. We'd apologize, but who are we kidding? It's been that kind of year. We think you'll understand, but for our parents and others who may be sensitive, please just skim right on past those. We're just glad we were able to get this book done at all. Thank you for your patience! We hope it's worth the wait.

PROLOGUE

RHIAN

A mild shock rippled through me as I entered my dorm room in Muninn Tower at Sun & Moon Academy College of Supernatural Guardians, the school under the mountain. I didn't know what I expected, because it looked just as I had left it that night in December after an insane battle of fighting animated statues and re-animated corpses. Perhaps I expected it to be tainted by lingering horrors of that day, settling in while I was gone. I shook the memory away. It was a pleasant surprise to see my lovely room again, and there was no need to ruin it. The bed, with its canopy of tapestries and fairy lights, still stood in the center of the room, a throw pillow with *Rhian* embroidered on it sitting at the top. A shaggy purple rug lay on the smooth wood floor. On the far side was my favorite part of the room—the window seat that looked down on campus. *Home Sweet Home*, I thought with a happy sigh.

Winter break had been fun, full of holiday cheer in Havenwood Falls, probably one of the best places on Earth to spend the winter holidays. The small town seated in a box canyon of the Colorado Rockies had felt like a winter wonderland under a Christmas-themed snow globe. Elliana and Brielle Knight and their BFF Charleigh Wotsit had rented a condo with me, and we'd spent the last month skiing, drinking coffee, and celebrating the multitude of holidays that were crammed into the last four weeks.

The dark energy I'd sensed around the Knight twins at the beginning of last semester—the energy that drove me away from making Modi Tower my home—had weakened after Brielle's challenge last semester, although I'd felt it building again already by the end of break. It was a good thing for us to be separated now. Even though we were underground, I was happy to be back on campus and in the sweet room that felt more like home than anywhere I'd been in this life.

Even when I knew this semester would be no better—perhaps even worse—than last.

Everything I owned fit in my backpack (though it was admittedly charmed to hold much more than a normal school bag), so I figured I'd unpack before crashing into bed. Just like last semester, the portals to campus had reopened at midnight, but this time we had three days to settle in before classes started on Monday, rather than over a week, as we had in the fall. At least this time I already knew where I belonged.

I'd barely begun unpacking when a handwritten note floated in the air and landed on my bed:

Rhian, Board of Regents is meeting now and asks for your audience.
- Addie

"So much for being a normal student this semester," I muttered to myself as I dropped a hoodie into the armoire that served as my dresser, among other things.

My secret had been revealed during that battle that ended last semester. Well, one of many, anyway. Before then, only Addie Beaumont had known I was Rhiannon, a goddess of the moon and night and death. My power over death had been altered ages ago, though, turning it dark and sinister—giving me the curse of raising the dead when my power transferred to their corpses. Thus the zombies that started last term's battle. I'd had to come clean and reveal my true self to put a stop to it all. Up until then, I'd been living life as any other SMA student.

Well, except for the part where I'd been asked to observe the students and take notes for an old acquaintance.

I quickly changed out of my jeans and sweater, pulling on

black leather pants and a black leather jacket that made me look more my part—at least, the part the Board expected of me. Not my full-on goddess look, but more of a warrior than a teenaged university student. My long blond braids and dreadlocks were pulled up into a massive bun on the top of my head, and I fixed the stray locks that had fallen loose. With my slight frame and impish facial features—particularly my big blue eyes—I still looked deceptively innocent. I kind of liked it that way, though. I preferred melting into the background, but it was always fun to surprise people when they underestimated me.

Another note appeared:

We're waiting.

"Gods and goddesses," I muttered as I hurried out of the room. I couldn't imagine what couldn't wait until tomorrow, let alone another few minutes for me to change and get across campus. Much of the Board consisted of creatures of the night, so their midnight meeting wasn't too surprising. The urgency, though …

But I should have known.

My old, so-called friend who'd basically asked me to spy on the students and faculty here was likely the reason for the Board's urgent demand. They knew her as Kialah Tursten, who'd once lived in Havenwood Falls for a brief time over a century ago and had guided the Court of the Sun and the Moon—the supernatural leaders of Havenwood Falls—to the Harvard palace under their Mount Alexa. The site that became the campus for the new college. They believed her to be a friend—an ally.

I knew her as Kialah, but also by many other names and identities over our lifetimes together. Her true one was Zandra, a Vanir goddess. The Court and town of Havenwood Falls had met her authentic self a little over a year ago. Over break, Addie had told me some of the horrors she'd inflicted on the local residents when she'd gone by the title of the Collector. They'd presumably won their battle against her, but I couldn't be sure. Although I hadn't personally been in contact with her since before then—all of her communication had come by messenger or magic—I knew Zandra too well. She'd never be so easily defeated.

3

I hadn't told anyone about Kialah's true identity. She was playing some kind of two-faced game with the Court and now SMA's Board of Regents. Ally or foe? I wasn't sure yet. But I did know if they had any idea who Kialah really was, they'd shut down SMA, and that was the last thing this town and the world needed. Especially if her recent message held any truth.

I jogged through the tunnel that connected Muninn Tower to the library and rushed through the dark mezzanine to the doors leading to Halstein Hall—the largest building on campus that housed the student union, dining hall, classrooms, and administration offices. The whole way, I wondered if they'd received a new message, or even better, discovered the pieces to the weapon Kialah had mentioned in her last note. The weapon that could destroy a god who was even more dangerous than her.

Hermod.

I had a pretty large grudge against that fucker, and the thought that we'd be able to finally end him had my feet rushing faster up the stone stairs of Halstein, the way lit by fire sconces and magic orbs. I passed the Valkyrie statue at the entry to the admin offices and burst into the Board's conference room unceremoniously.

My gaze swung around the dark stone cavern with its long wooden conference table and the trickling water that fell down the side of the far wall. In the flickering firelight of the wall sconces, I didn't see a weapon or even its pieces, and the Regents weren't sitting around the table, either. Rather, they were gathered at one end of it, their heads bent together until they all looked up at me.

Addie Beaumont, witch-hellhound hybrid, liaison and business manager for the Court of the Sun and the Moon, part-time SMA professor, and member of the Board of Regents, smiled at me, the diamond in the side of her nose winking in the dim light.

"It's about time," Elsmed Fairchild, an ancient Seelie fae, murmured, barely glancing at me before returning his attention to whatever had had them all enraptured before I'd entered.

"I take it you haven't found any of the pieces?" I asked.

"We've searched and searched this entire campus—physically, magically, every possible way we could imagine—since we received the last message on New Year's Eve," Addie said. "The one you helped us with. There are so many artifacts and so many chambers we could detect but couldn't figure out access to—the possibilities are endless, and since we don't know what exactly we're looking for ..." She gave me an exasperated look, her brown eyes wide behind her glasses, and shrugged.

"It's been utterly impossible," Gabriel Doyle snapped, the vampire's patience obviously thin.

"Until now," Saundra Beaumont, Addie's grandmother and one of the high priestesses of the Luna Coven in town, said.

Addie waved me over to the table. "We think this book might be a piece?"

Elsmed's long white fingers flipped the front cover closed to show a large and quite ancient looking leather-bound book.

"A grimoire?" I asked.

"We're not sure that's what it is," Saundra said. "Although it's definitely soaked in ancient magic."

"I received this book two days ago," Elsmed said. "Another delivery from Kialah. But the pages were blank until tonight, just after the campus portals re-opened and the students returned."

"Is it a piece of the weapon?" Gabriel demanded, his blue eyes piercing me as he tried to read my mind. I already had my defenses up, though, against him and Elsmed both.

Still, I had to be careful with how I worded things. "As I told you before, I don't know what all the pieces look like or what exactly they do. I just know that they had to be co—" I almost said *collected*. That might hint at too much for them. "Gathered from various places, and once they were, they could be assembled to become a god-killing weapon. Specifically, one that would end Hermod."

"The god who's supposedly headed for our world to destroy our magic," Saundra clarified.

"That was Kialah's warning," Elsmed said, his faith in her even stronger than before. If he only knew...but then the search would be over, and if she was telling the truth about Hermod's approach, this world would be doomed. We needed to piece together the weapon.

"So what does the book say?" I asked as I stepped up next to Elsmed.

He opened the cover, revealing a reiteration of the message they'd received and shared with me on New Year's Eve:

The destroyer of magic
  Comes our way
  Bringing death and destruction
  And a world of decay

But my friends,
  Do not fret
  Within the rock guardian
  Our hope is kept

Entombed in stone
  Difficult to find
  Is the weapon of the gods
  Broken in nine

Together with their staff
  The nine become ten
  And hope for our world
  Will be restored again

May the lady of the moon
  The ruler of night
  The protector of magic
  Bring you her light

We'd already discussed that Halvard meant "rock guardian" in Norse, so the *where* was clear—SMA's campus. I'd warned them before that the pieces would be difficult to find and protected by strong magic and who knew what else.

"Is that it?" I asked.

"That's it," Elsmed said, flipping the page to a blank one.

"Since we've been unable to find any of the pieces on our own, we thought we'd take advantage of the two hundred students here on campus," Addie said.

"It seems the campus likes to test them anyway," Elsmed

added. "Finding the weapon's pieces will be a perfect way to do so and hopefully please the campus's magic in that regard."

"We're hoping this isn't as dangerous as the trials the campus put them through last semester," Saundra said.

I suppressed a harrumph. I was pretty sure last semester was only a taste of what came next.

"We've created a class with ten teams of students—one team for each piece," Gabriel continued. "They'll have the semester to find and retrieve it. Those who find their piece will be rewarded with a good grade."

"But we're starting them off with practically nothing to go on," Addie said. "They have no idea what they're looking for or where exactly. And they can't know that it's part of a weapon. That's the last thing we need leaked within the student body."

I nodded in agreement but frowned. "So you're giving them a project they're more than likely to fail. That hardly seems fair."

Elsmed turned fully toward me, crossing his arms over his chest. His thin form towered over me, and his frosty eyes gazed down his long nose and chin at me. "We were hoping you'd be able to help us with some clues."

I threw my hands into the air with exasperation. "Don't you think if I knew anything I'd tell you? I want Hermod ended more than anyone in this universe. There must be more to that book, is all I can say." I gestured at the tome, my gaze falling on its pages. My brow furrowed. "What's that?"

We all stepped closer, watching as the page that had just been blank began to reveal a colorful image set within a rectangle. Addie and Saundra both gasped as the image filled in.

"Is that a tarot card?" Addie said as she gripped the corner of the book and pulled it closer to her and her grandmother.

"Not traditional Rider-Waite, but it does look like it could be a High Priestess card," Saundra confirmed as the colors darkened. Her fingers trailed over the beautiful though haunting image—the colors were dark, the image more fantastical and quite eerie, hardly anything like the more commonly known decks. Yet I couldn't help but think the witches were right. As Saundra pulled her fingers back, the image peeled away from the page.

A collective gasp filled the room.

She now held the card in her hand.

"There's writing on the back," Elsmed pointed out, and Saundra flipped it over.

"I think we have our clue," I said after we all read it.

"So a tarot card and a poem—that's it?" Gabriel asked.

Nobody had an answer, but more pages started filling in with gorgeous dark images. Ten of them in total.

Then one of those maddening gongs from last term rang out through campus.

"Let the new semester begin," Saundra declared.

"And may the odds be ever in our favor," Addie muttered, her tone dripping with a mixture of sarcasm and dread.

I knew exactly how she felt.

THE HIGH PRIESTESS

KRISTIE COOK

To My Fellow SMA Authors
Who helped me find my fucks when 2020 tried to take them all

CHAPTER 1

emons and darkness.

The energy radiated from the couple in front of me, sliding over my skin and penetrating deep within, down to my soul. All at once, I wanted to bask in their dark power like a cat in the sun and tear their hearts out, sending them back to Hell where they belonged.

Well, at least the male half of the couple. I wasn't sure about the girl. I just knew my natural instincts had my body reacting in conflicting ways that set my jaw on edge and lifted my shoulders to my ears while I forced myself to stay back a step and lean away before I inappropriately invaded their personal space.

Charleigh stood in line next to me, and I knew the witch could sense my tension. I should probably leave the line and let her get our order, but the couple was almost done and they'd be on their way. I could surely maintain control for another minute or two. Cups in hands, they finally turned to leave, and my shoulders dropped an inch.

Right before I was doused in hot coffee.

"Dude!" I screeched, jumping backward as the hot liquid splashed on my chest and down the front of my turquoise blouse. "What the fu—"

"Oh, my goddess! So sorry." The girl began patting my chest with napkins as I stood there, clutching my last remnants of control while dark energy pumped through my veins. I didn't know why she was apologizing when the guy standing next to her had been the one who'd just dumped the contents of his cup all over me. His green eyes almost seemed to glow under a flop of raven-black hair as I glared at him while visions of ripping his head off danced in my mind. When I tore my gaze away to look at her, her blue eyes caught mine, but they weren't the ones I'd been searching for since arriving back at campus after winter break. Still, there was something about them—both of them—that made my breath catch.

I didn't know what she was, but the Darkness in me sensed some in her, too. The demon that was apparently her boyfriend repulsed me, though. My spine tingled, my wings wanting to come out and end him with one slice through his neck. But I was still drawn to him. To both of them. And it pissed me off.

"Don't *ever* apologize for a guy's fuck-up," I snarled, snatching the napkins out of her grip.

A familiar hand landed on my forearm, sending a burst of warm energy into me as Charleigh quietly warned, "Elliana."

"It was my fault, though," the blond girl insisted. "I distracted Torent—"

My nostrils flared, and Charleigh stepped between us, facing me but talking to them as her brown eyes, so light they were almost orange, held mine. "Don't worry about it," she said. "Shit happens. I'll take care of this."

She waved her hand in front of me, muttering a spell, and the coffee stain disappeared from one of my favorite tops. I could have fixed it myself with my own brand of magic—fae, sorceress, and angel blood were just part of my mixed DNA—but the Darkness in me was bubbling up, calling to them as theirs called to me. I loved the power of it, but it was a dangerous energy. It was taking every bit of focus I had to keep control of what I referred to as the beast inside me. Charleigh knew it, which was why she'd stepped in.

"Are you hurt, though?" the girl asked.

"I'm fine," I said through gritted teeth. Luckily, it took a lot more than scalding coffee to harm me. I breathed out, "Just. Go."

"I need a new cup—" the guy started to say, but his girlfriend smartly pushed him away from the Coffee Haven counter.

My gaze followed them as they left, something deep within reaching out, wanting to go with them while that tingle between my shoulder blades finally began to ease. I called on my Amadis power—the power given to us by the angels, which was the most dominant part of our DNA. Ours, as in my twin sister, Brielle, and mine. Charleigh, our BFF and cousin by life though not by blood, was a witch. A powerful one and assigned to us as our protector. She had Amadis power, too, but not like mine and Brie's. It was the power of angels and goodness that I needed to suppress the Dark beast that always threatened to rise.

From what sounded like a great distance but was only a couple of feet away, I could hear Roxy McCabe, the cougar shifter, asking for our order. Charleigh gave me another shot of her power, an extra boost, before finally releasing my arm, and her orange hair whipped in my face as she turned toward the counter of Coffee Haven's campus location.

"Are you okay?" Brielle asked as she hurried up to me. "What happened?"

I closed my eyes briefly, mentally shaking it all off, before opening them again and forcing a smile for my identical twin. "Nothing. I'm good."

Her mahogany gaze drifted over me from forehead to feet before coming back up to my face, a brow lifted. "Are you sure?"

"If you don't let it go, I may not be," I warned.

She threw her hands up in surrender. "Okay, okay. Letting it go."

Maybe she'd finally learned something after last semester's chaos—the more focus we gave the dark energy within us, the more powerful it became. The best way to control it was to acknowledge its existence as part of us but otherwise pay it no attention, as though it was nothing more than a freckle or mole. Easier said than done.

Charleigh turned just then—carefully, unlike some people—and held out a cup of steaming hot joe to each of us.

"Unicorn Farts for you, Miss Elli," she said, "because you need some rainbow sprinkles right about now. Your favorite java chip mocha, Miss Brie, and Witch's Brew for me."

Leaving the long line of Coffee Haven on this first morning back to campus after winter break, we searched for an empty table in the busy Student Union. I felt the eyes on us, as if the many gazes were tangible strokes over my skin. I'd become somewhat used to it—my love for fashion, including low cut tops and high-heeled shoes and boots, tended to draw attention. Not all of the wanted kind—aka, boys. I didn't wear it for them and not even for girls, although I didn't mind when certain ones noticed me. I mean, come on. There were a lot of hot girls here. I chose my clothes for me, because they made me feel good. We didn't have such luxuries as fashion in our home world, which had been in a post-apocalyptic era since before we were born.

As I glanced around, I realized more gazes than usual were on my twin. Although we were identical, our fashion choices were on opposite ends of the spectrum, making us easy to tell apart. She couldn't care any less about what she wore, her makeup, or hair style, and she'd spent last semester blending into the background as much as possible, more concerned about what was going on in her head than outside of it. While her outfit today wasn't quite up to my standards, the knee-high boots, leggings, and tunic were definitely a step up from her usual jeans and hoodies, and they brought out her best features. I had a pretty good idea about the why behind the change, although I didn't see Aithan Lanrete's copper curls anywhere in the Student Union.

"Why don't we just head back to Modi?" Charleigh suggested, referring to our dorm tower and giving up on finding an open table. "We can see what everyone's up to and who's in our classes. Our schedules should be available by now."

The three of us crossed the white marble floor of the Student Union, passed the fountain with the Valkyrie statue, and exited out the double doors to the quad. The underground campus was unusually dark for this time of day, looking more like late afternoon than mid-morning, as snow fell through the skylight at the top of the mountain, blanketing the ground, bridges, and buildings that had been carved into the stone or created by the stalagmites. The first skybridge on the right of the quad led us to the teal and silver door of Modi Tower. The slickness from the snow made the many skybridges around campus extra precarious. It was a good thing we were all supernatural and had our own defenses. Otherwise, I couldn't fathom how many students would slip off and fall the several stories to their deaths.

I envisioned the new powder on the mountains outside and imagined the ski slopes were busy with tourists today. I already missed them. We'd had a killer time over winter break, milking the experience of Havenwood Falls during the holidays for all it was worth. I'd felt Brielle's guilt—it was a twin thing—for enjoying all of the luxuries of this world while our families were likely in the midst of another war in our world. Charleigh and I had to remind her that our parents brought us here. And knowing our mothers, they'd want us to make the most of being here, in a world that was much like ours had been when they'd been our age. I'd been angry about coming here to hide from our reality for a while, but then decided I wasn't about to let myself feel guilty for indulging in the life we should have had at home, if not for the demons who destroyed our world. Life had handed us a box of lemons—we could pucker up and pout or add vodka and have one hell of a party. I was all about the party.

With a wave of Charleigh's hand, the door to Modi Tower opened, and we entered onto the balcony that curved around to the right, following the building's outer wall about halfway around. Seating areas were scattered about in front of the bookcases along the wall. To the left was open to below and above, the outer wall on that side punctuated with a series of three-story windows that started a floor below, providing a view of the quad, the river, and the lake. We headed straight, over the bridge that connected to the central spiral staircase, and skipped down a flight to the main floor of the common room.

A dozen or so people were sprawled on the groupings of furniture between the windows and the vast fireplace that butted up to the stairwell in the center of the room. More were on the other side of the stairwell, under the balcony of the floor above. During the first week of last semester, the common room's décor had changed almost every hour as witches and fae tested out different looks, but once we selected our tower colors of teal, silver, and black, the theme settled. Now the room was only in those colors, with images of Pegasus, our chosen mascot, everywhere, including on the huge tapestry that hung over the hearth.

Aithan sat in one of the cushy couches by the windows and waved us over. I didn't miss the smile that spread across my twin's face. I was happy she'd finally opened her eyes to see what was right in front of her since the trials last summer—the demigod who even I had to admit had a perfect ass. And he seemed to be a decent guy, though not quite as ambitious as Brielle and me. Nobody would ever be good enough for my sister, but if I had to choose anyone on this campus, I supposed Aithan would do. With his laid-back attitude, he had a way of removing the stick that was constantly up her ass.

I couldn't help myself from looking around for what had been right in front of my own face all last semester—although not quite in the same way. The electric blue eyes had caught my attention on our first day in Modi Tower, but I hadn't thought their owner was my type. I still wasn't sure if she was, even after what we'd shared on Halloween and New Year's Eve. Okay, she was definitely my type. I just wasn't sure if I was hers. The elven girl seemed to have issues, and I didn't know if I really wanted to deal with them. Still, my gaze swung around the room, hoping to find those enrapturing blue eyes staring back at me.

There.

My heart stuttered as our gazes locked from across the room. Sadie Angrec sat in a dark corner under the balcony, as usual surrounded by her elven friends. Her lips pursed for a moment before she looked away and pulled her blond hair in a curtain around her face, breaking the contact.

No, I really didn't need to deal with her shit. If only my heart didn't react the way it did every time I saw those electric blues.

"Elliana?" Brielle's voice held the same annoyance I felt. Her finger jabbed into my ribs.

"What?" I snapped, then I sighed. "Sorry." I stepped around the low table and sank into a chair across from Aithan and Brielle, who were quite noticeably close to each other. In fact, any closer and she'd be in his lap. Charleigh sat in the chair perpendicular to all of us.

"We were comparing schedules," Aithan said, holding his phone up. "They came in about ten minutes ago."

Crossing one booted leg over the other as I leaned back in the chair, I pulled my phone out of the pocket of my leather jacket, not that I really needed to check. We'd picked classes at the end of last semester, and I already had my schedule memorized. As I glanced over the email, though, my brows pinched together.

"What in the actual fuck?" I studied the schedule harder, shaking my head. "This isn't right. What the hell is this shit?"

"What's wrong?" Charleigh leaned over, her head close to mine as we both stared at my screen. "You signed up for . . . what even is that? I don't remember a Task Force being an offering."

"I did not sign up for that!" I huffed. "Eight a.m. on a freaking *Monday*? You know me better than that. Hold up. And then nine at night on Wednesday? And three in the afternoon on Friday? That's sleep time, party time, and chill time! Could this be any more messed up?" I shook my head again, then stood.

"Where are you going?" Brie asked, barely glancing up as she and Aithan compared their schedules.

"I obviously need to see my advisor and get this changed. I don't want to take this Interdisciplinary Task Force, whatever the hell that even is. It sounds awful. Are any of you in it?"

They all shook their heads. Without another word, I strode out of Modi, back across the quad and into Halstein Hall, the biggest building on campus that housed the Student Union, dining hall, classrooms, and admin offices, where I headed to now.

"I'm sorry, Ms. Knight," my advisor said after I'd waited what felt like a week. Apparently I wasn't the only one with schedule issues. Her waiting area was packed. "If you'd read the email, you'd see that it's a mandatory class. I can't change it. You should be honored to be selected for the first one."

"But—"

She shook her head, her dark frizz sparking with static, before calling the next student.

With a sharp exhale, I spun on my heel and nearly collided with Electric Blues.

"I guess that answers that," Sadie muttered as she turned back for the door.

"They put you in this Task Force class, too?" I asked.

"Yep. Not exactly my thing."

We jogged down the stairs, our steps in synch.

"Sadie," I started when we hit the bottom.

"I have to go," she said, before hurrying over to her friends, who were watching us.

"Okay, then. I can take a hint," I said to no one.

Apparently, I wasn't exactly her thing, either.

CHAPTER 2

Grumbling all the way to Halstein Hall for having to be awake at this ungodly hour, let alone in class, I entered the lecture-style classroom at precisely one minute before eight a.m. on Monday, our first day of classes for Spring Semester at Sun & Moon Academy College of Supernatural Guardians. Entering at the back of the room, I went down the left aisle between the rows of theater-style seats to the first one that was empty and slid into a hard chair. There were thirty, maybe forty students already seated, most talking to others around them, creating quite the din. How can they be social this early? Of course, most, including myself, had Coffee Haven to-go cups sitting on the wooden slab that served as a desk in front of each chair.

Natalie Putnam, a witch and friend of Charleigh's, sat a couple of rows down with her bestie Tempest and a guy whose name I believed was Eryx. Timber Greenwood, a Seelie fae who'd also helped with the big battle at the end of last semester, was a few rows in front of them with Cole Silver, an Unseelie fae, an unlikely duo. Infiniti Clausman sat a few seats down from them. I glanced over my shoulder, where Marina Del Mar, Vanna Shaw's roommate, sat by herself behind me, and to my right, at the other end of her row, was the jerk who'd spilled coffee all over me, his girlfriend next to him. *Great.* Then at the last minute, someone slid into the seat next to me, and my whole body went on alert.

"Hey," Sadie breathed.

Double great.

"Fancy meeting you here," she teased, her elbow knocking into mine for a brief moment, sending an electric zap through my veins.

What the hell was she doing? There were more than enough empty seats she could have chosen, but she finally decided to acknowledge me?

"Are you talking to me? Actually *talking* to me?" I snapped.

"Please don't be that way," she said, her voice low.

I snorted. "Sorry, but I honestly don't know *how* to be with you."

The words came out harsher and louder than I meant at the exact same time Saundra Beaumont had entered the front of the room and the whole class had fallen silent. My face heated, and I slid down into my seat, wishing I could disappear into the floor. Sadie blew out a sigh, her only response as Professor Beaumont began to speak.

"Welcome to Interdisciplinary Task Force," she said, striding purposely across the front of the whiteboard at the head of the room as she spoke. Her silver hair was in its usual twist on the back of her head. Saundra Beaumont's fashion style was elegant but incredibly boring—always a blue or black suit and white blouse, though sometimes she wore a skirt and other times pants. Pants today. At least her clothing was of the highest quality, and her shoes probably cost a small fortune.

"You all have been selected as our inaugural class for this special style of education that will give you hands-on, real-world type experience," she continued as she crossed the room to the other side now, before turning back again. "The Task Force will be intense and immersive, requiring more from you than all of your other classes combined. If you're already taking a heavy workload, you may want to consider dropping another class. No, you may not drop this one. We chose you for a reason, but don't worry. All Halvard students will have to take ITF before they can graduate. You just happen to be the first group."

She stopped pacing, leaning against the front of the desk on the right side of the room. Her legs crossed in front of her at the ankle, she folded her arms over her chest, her gaze continuously sweeping over us. While I'd glimpsed a softer, almost grandmotherly side to her in the past, the woman was intimidating, her magical power pouring off of her.

"As you have noticed on your schedules, the classroom part of ITF takes place at different times throughout the week. Your instructors will vary, as well, teaching a wide range of topics that will give you a well-rounded education in subjects that you may otherwise not take for your major. You will also participate in more in-depth small group learning in the classroom and beyond. Attendance and participation is mandatory, and it is your responsibility to know where you need to be at any given time, as is expected in the real world. Supernatural or otherwise," she added as though an afterthought. "In addition to teacher-led classes and workshops, you will be working with a team on assigned missions. There are several of these missions to span the semester. Your team can decide what order you want to do them in, and which team member will serve as lead for that mission. Each member must serve as leader on at least one mission."

With a flick of her hand, a paper suddenly appeared on each of our desks, and writing began to magically fill the whiteboard behind her. She verbally recounted what was on both the paper and the board, going over the various missions we'd be doing for the next twelve weeks. *Missions.* I snorted internally. An exciting word for group projects, and we all knew how those usually went. I had a couple in my classes last semester, and everyone always had their excuses for not doing their share. If it weren't for Brielle, we all would have failed. And I didn't have Brie with me this time. I was hating this class more and more each minute.

"Your teams have been assigned, indicated by color. There will be no changes, so learn to work together. You may recruit the assistance of others, both faculty and other students. However, faculty can only serve as a resource of knowledge, information, and guidance. They cannot work on the actual mission. Other students may participate, but only the students in this class receive the credit. You may need to use your leadership and team-building skills to encourage others to assist, if you need it." She straightened up and walked back to the center of the room. "You'll spend the rest of this first class session getting to know each other and deciding on your first mission. You'll also need to select a card up here that provides the clues for The Hunt mission." She indicated an arc of cards that appeared before her, spread out like a magician would do, but hanging in the air rather than laid out on a table. *Pick a card, any card,* I could almost hear her saying. "It's one of the more challenging missions. I do not recommend putting it off too long, but that is up to each team."

With a clap of her hands, we each lit up with various colored glows surrounding our bodies. Mine was dark blue.

So was Sadie's.

I wasn't sure how I felt about that. She'd have no choice but to speak to me, yet it's not like I wanted to force her into anything. In fact, she'd been the one to start the whole thing between us. I was just trying to keep up.

A long, lithe body sauntered over to us from behind. And here I thought the class couldn't get any worse.

"Midnight blue," demon-boy said, his green-eyed gaze traveling over Sadie and me and then to something behind us. He nodded and gave a crooked smile. "Seems appropriate."

I had no idea what that meant. I looked over my shoulder at another guy who glowed the same dark blue as us. I didn't know him, but I smelled the animal that was part of him. As he took a seat, he introduced himself as Slaine. Demon-boy's name was Torent Stark, a Havenwood Falls local. Within minutes, he dropped his girlfriend's name (Mallory), as though warning Sadie and me that he was taken. As if either of us cared. Although, maybe Sadie did. Maybe she was bi or pan, and that was her issue —she had a boyfriend. I honestly didn't know with the girl. I honestly needed to stop caring.

"So what's our first mission going to be?" I picked up the paper, needing to focus on something else. Everyone studied the projects' descriptions, nobody seeming to want to take the lead. I sighed and spoke up. "The Hunt mission—it says here the card contains our clues for finding an artifact hidden somewhere on campus. Maybe we should see what that's about and then decide?"

Torent shrugged. Slaine grunted in agreement. Sadie said, "Sure."

But nobody moved.

Internally rolling my eyes, I stood and strode down to the front of the room. Professor Beaumont smiled in greeting.

"I'm not surprised to see you taking the lead," she said.

Duh. My major was Leadership, which she'd been partially responsible for putting me in. She and the rest of the Court of the Sun and the Moon, along with our parents. After all, someday Brielle and I would be leading our world.

"You're the first one down here, so you get first choice." She motioned at the arc of cards, the side facing us a dark blue with the image of a golden sun and silver moon in the center. "Close your eyes and use your intuition to select the one that feels right to you. You'll know it when you feel it."

I stepped up to the cards hanging in the air, closed my eyes, and lifted my left hand, palm out. The energies pulsing off the cards varied, and I did indeed know exactly which one called to me. I plucked it from the arc and flipped it over.

"Interesting," the professor said, but nothing more.

When I returned to the group, I placed the card on my desk front up so we could all study the image on it. A woman with long silvery hair waving in the air around her seemed to float above a violent sea, her long teal and blue robes flowing into the waves. Tendrils of her robes trailed over a crescent moon at her feet, as though cradled by the rocking sea. At the top of her head appeared to be horns or a two-pronged crown, with a glowing orb between the points. Behind her hung a purplish, transparent curtain draped over a rod hanging in the air, a dark, star-filled sky and still water in the background. She held an unrolled scroll in front of her. The image was darkly beautiful, the lighter colors on it almost seeming to glow against the dark blues and purples.

"Any ideas?" I asked the group.

"She could be a witch," Slaine suggested. "With the moon and the scroll. Maybe we have to find a spell?"

"There's like a thousand grimoires on this campus," I said. "We need more to go on than that."

Torent's long fingers snatched the card off my desk. The

closeness of his being to mine made my wings prickle under my skin. I'd hated demons for as long as I could remember, but even more so as I grew older and learned all that they'd done to our world. What they were still doing to it. For years, I'd planned to be a demon assassin when I grew up. Then shit happened, and we ended up here, in this world where demons lived as a part of society—not trying to destroy it. Some even contributed to it. Even wanted to be a part of the army that would protect it. Like Torent here. I'd done my best to accept that not all demons were like the ones at home, but I'd have to get better at it if Torent and I were both going to survive the semester.

As he studied the artwork closer, I noticed the back of the card had changed. The sun and moon had faded into the background, and words now scrolled across the surface.

I read them aloud.

Pulp and leather, words in ink,
Their collection, their meaning
Have more power than you think.

Within, without, above, below,
Way up high is where to go.

There you'll find the portals of four
But if it does not open
It's not your door.

"Move your finger, demon-boy," I ordered. Torent lifted his middle one. "Funny. Not that one." He adjusted his grip on the card, and I continued reading the rest.

A single tome reveals the way
But beware: with blood
You'll surely pay.

Through planes of darkness
And realms of light,
You'll find what you seek

Behind the veil of night.

"What does that even mean?" Sadie asked.

Ignoring her question, Torent flipped the card back onto my desk. "Looks like some kind of tarot card, if you ask me."

"Yeah, I can kind of see that." Slaine nodded as he studied it. "But no idea which one. Anybody know anything about tarot?"

Our blank expressions were answer enough.

"We need a witch," Sadie declared.

Of course, I first thought of Charleigh, but she didn't know a lot about tarot.

"We could just ask Professor Beaumont," Torent suggested.

We all glanced at the front of the room.

"Why don't we look at these other missions first," Slaine quickly said. I bit my lip to keep from laughing at his obvious intimidation by the witch. I couldn't blame him. Saundra Beaumont was a high priestess of the most powerful coven in town. For all I knew, the most powerful in the country or even world. Of course, I didn't really know much about any of that, so that was simply speculation.

We spent the rest of class reviewing the other missions, but I couldn't tear my gaze away from the card. Well, I could, but if I didn't purposely focus on it, my eyes would inevitably drift to the gorgeous blonde next to me. As it was, I kept sneaking glances, watching those full lips curve up and down with the conversation and the pointed tips of her ears peak out of white-blond locks that felt like silk between my fingers. The memory of New Year's Eve played vividly over and over in my mind.

"What's your vote, Elliana?" Torent asked.

I glanced around at the three faces staring at me. Shit. *Busted.* "Um . . . for what?"

He rolled his green eyes. "Which mission to do first."

"Oh . . . uh . . . The Hunt." I tapped the card. "Definitely The Hunt. If it's our most challenging one, we may as well get it over with."

"It's unanimous. And we already voted you as leader," demon-boy announced with a smirk.

27

CHAPTER 3

"The portals of four—that has to mean the portals to leave campus, right?" Slaine asked. "Maybe go up high means out of the mountain. Like the top of the mountain?"

"There are only three portals in the vestibule to leave campus," I pointed out.

"Besides, it's obviously in a library," Sadie added, and I nodded in agreement.

"Could be the library on Falls Campus, for the lower Academy in Havenwood Falls," Slaine still argued.

"There are only three portals," I repeated.

"Oh. Right."

With the chaos of the beginning of the semester and starting classes, our team didn't have a chance to meet again until Wednesday night, right before our next ITF class. We gathered in a seating alcove down the hall from tonight's classroom— Addie Beaumont's—to discuss the clues. I'd hoped someone had some great ideas because I had few. The references to books and the library in the written clue was obvious, but I hadn't had a chance to even look into tarot or try to decipher the card's image.

"It has to be our library here on campus," I said.

"That place is scary as hell," Sadie said with a shiver.

I was surprised to see Torent nod in agreement. "Not exactly my favorite place. Especially high up in the stacks, which is where this clue apparently wants us to go."

"Wasn't Shirley Velisk attacked up there?" Slaine asked, referring to an incident last semester. We all fell silent in respect for the dead.

"Regardless, unless we want to fail this mission and possibly this class, we have to go up there," I said. "We'll just have to make sure we're prepared."

"And that we touch nothing we're not supposed to," Sadie added. Most students ran into danger in the library when they touched books and other objects when explicitly warned against it. The library and its stacks, even many of the actual books, seemed to be sentient beings, and they didn't much like to be bothered.

"So before we even try, we need to know what we're looking for," I said, motioning to the card that lay face-up on the low wooden table centered between our seats. "Do we know for sure it's a tarot card?"

"According to Mallory, it's a tarot card, and her team has the Moon one," Torent said. "Natalie Putnam's on her team, so I'm pretty sure she would know."

"Then my vote is that it's a tarot card," Sadie said. "But I have no idea which one."

"Anybody have a chance to look more into it than that?" I asked, and they all shook their heads.

"Class is in five minutes," Addie Beaumont said as she strode past us, toward her room. "You get me as your instructor tonight," she reminded over her shoulder.

Everyone immediately jumped to their feet, eagerly following her. Addie was much cooler and quite a bit less intimidating than her grandmother, although at least as powerful. She was only about five or six years older than us, making her much easier to relate to, and she really knew her shit. Well, except potions. I'd heard that wasn't exactly her strong point, so Charleigh said they brought in a new teacher this semester, Madame Tahini, to take over Addie's Intro to Potions class. Charleigh and the other witches did say Addie was excellent at magical combat—even better than Charleigh herself, which was saying a lot, considering how we grew up. I wondered what she'd be teaching us tonight as I followed the young woman dressed in her usual black hoodie and black, ripped up jeans, her always present bracelets jangling as she walked.

"Tonight we'll be discussing intuition," she announced after starting class. I stifled a groan, hoping for something more exciting. Intuition wasn't exactly *my* strong point. "We all have it and to a much higher degree than humans. Shifters have their animal instincts. Vampires have their own special sixth senses. Witches rely on intuition to work much of our magic. Each and every one us should always be developing and honing this very special sense, if for no other reason than because it's highly useful in combat."

Now I and many others perked up a little as she went on to describe how sensing an opponent's next move even before they decided on it provided a major fighting advantage and then went into other benefits.

"Knowing what's coming before it happens, sensing what's beyond that in front of us or even in the physical realm, feeling and following our guts, our hearts, our *souls* is critical during a fight. I'd go so far as to say that it's even more important than understanding and knowing what's physically happening around us. The warrior with a highly developed intuition and connection to the energy of this world and beyond will always have an advantage over those without."

For the next hour, she taught techniques and tips for honing our intuition, giving us exercises to practice. While I appreciated some of them, I also had to keep from squirming in my seat. Tapping into my inner-self—that otherworldly energy that courses through all of us—meant tapping into the Dark stuff. It was just as much a part of my connection to the Creator as the Light. Giving it extra attention defied my need for control, which was why I tended to rely on my physical senses more than intuition. I mean, I had very well developed instincts and those physical senses were far beyond any human and even most supernaturals', so why tempt the dark beast that lived inside me?

"One way to hone your intuition is to practice reading signs and symbols all around you," Addie said as the class began to come to a close. "Look for them in the world—they're everywhere. Especially on this campus. Your assignment is to write a one-thousand-word essay about using intuition to read signs and symbolism. You can choose anything relevant to the topic, but if you're struggling with a starting point, I suggest looking into tarot. The tarot is all about intuition and symbolism. Your assignment is to be submitted to my inbox—email or physical—by Friday noon. Class dismissed."

"My intuition says we should learn more about tarot," Sadie said as we walked back to Modi Tower together. Although there were a handful of night classes to accommodate those students with more nocturnal tendencies, the campus was dark and quiet.

"All signs seem to point that way," I said with a snort.

She giggled and bumped my shoulder with hers. "Who knew Elliana Knight had a dorky sense of humor?"

"Who knew Sadie Angrec was just as dorky?"

"Um . . . I think a lot of people do," she quipped as we reached the teal and silver door.

I looked at her as she held the door for me, giving her a lingering and appreciative once-over. "I don't think dork is ever, in any way, used to describe you."

Pink flooded her cheeks, which made me feel giddy. "Nor you."

Perhaps the communication lines were finally beginning to open. I opened my mouth to clear the air—

"You're back!" declared a high-pitched voice. Fig, another elf, emerged from the dark stairwell we were headed toward. A couple of other elves followed right after her, and the next thing I knew, Sadie was gone, swept away by her friends.

Pursing my lips, I inhaled a deep breath, then trudged up the spiral staircase to the top floor, where my own posse waited for me. Except Brielle had earbuds stuck in her ears as she sat cocooned in a blanket on her bed, studying and barely acknowledging my return with a brief wave of her fingers, and Charleigh was passed out in her own bed, mouth open, snoring away. She'd apparently fallen asleep while studying, considering the books spread out on her blankets and the one that had fallen to the floor next to the bed.

I loved our dorm room. Not too much larger than the double and single rooms on lower floors, it allowed the three full-sized beds due to the alcoves in the walls that were perfectly sized for them. That also gave us enough room in the center for a small seating area with a loveseat and chair, a low table squatting in front of them. When we wanted to watch a movie or TV show, Charleigh magically projected the image from one of our laptops or phones to the one blank wall in the room. Tapestries covered the arched ceiling and walls of my bed alcove, making it feel like a fortune teller's tent. The only lighting came from candles and the fire in the hearth, completing the cozy ambiance.

My favorite place, though, was the seat in the high, arched window that looked over the quad and part of the lake below. It was the favorite of all of us, so we often had to fight over it. This cold winter night, however, was made for snuggling under the covers in bed, just as Brie was.

After changing into pajamas that included a hoodie and thick flannel pants, I gathered two blankets around me and leaned back against a wall of pillows before opening my computer and starting a search on tarot cards.

"I think it's the High Priestess," I said to Addie the next afternoon during a break between classes.

Addie studied my team's card from The Hunt mission and nodded. "Tell me why you think so."

"Well, that's what I'd planned to make my essay about."

"Excellent choice. Drawing the High Priestess card means to trust your intuition and senses beyond what you see, hear, and physically feel before you. A perfect topic for your essay, but it might help to talk it out first."

"Am I wrong?"

She smiled, the clear crystal in the side of her nose twinkling in the light. "That's not what I said. But since getting this right is for two assignments, that's a double whammy if you're off."

"Okay." I gestured at the card. "I think the biggest giveaway is the moon at her feet, which is like the traditional Waite deck and many others. The way her hair on top of her head forms to look like horns or a crown, with that orb in the middle, looks like the triple-moon crown on the woman in the Waite deck." Addie nodded, encouraging me to go on. "There's a scroll, and there's a veil behind her. Some important parts are missing, though. Like the two pillars and the pomegranate symbolism."

"True, but I think the contrast of the light and dark in the imagery itself preclude the need for the black and white pillars."

"Did you do the artwork?" I asked, something I'd wondered since the first day of class.

Addie laughed. "I wish I was that talented. No, not my work. It's beautiful, isn't it?"

"It is. Dark but gorgeous."

"As many things are." She gave me a pointed look. "So what do the symbols of the card tell you?"

I bit my lip. "I still need to research that more. I wanted to make sure I was on the right track first."

She nodded. "Do you know how it works as the clue for The Hunt?"

"Would you tell me if I'm right?" I asked hopefully.

"I would if I knew. You are allowed to ask for help with that, but I'm not privy to the answer. I can only give you my own thoughts. Tell me yours first."

"Based on the clue on the back, we're supposed to go to the library and find a book. I think the scroll reinforces that—maybe it's ancient or written on parchment or something."

"Hmm." Addie tilted her head side to side. "I can see that. What really stood out to me, though, is her pendant. Look closely. I've been reading tarot since I was a kid, so I'm familiar with many decks. Usually the High Priestess wears a cross, if anything at all."

I picked up the card and peered more closely at it. You could barely see the woman's pendant behind the top hand holding the scroll. "But that's not a cross."

"Nope." She popped the *p*. "It's an ankh. Which is very interesting."

"Do you think that's what we're looking for? An ankh?"

She shrugged. "It stands out as an anomaly, so possibly. But as you're hopefully learning, these cards are full of all kinds of symbolism. It may end up being something completely different— the scroll, the triple-moon crown, even a curtain or veil."

I groaned. "How are we supposed to find the object if it could be so many things?"

"If it were too easy, would you learn?" She gave me a wink. "I think you're on the right path. Keep going. I look forward to reading your essay about the High Priestess. She's one of my favorites."

Saturday, after the first full week of classes and a mountain of homework piled on us, Sadie, Torent, Slaine, and I agreed to meet in the library and figure this thing out. We had too many projects —sorry, *missions*—to get bogged down on this one for too long. I'd gone over my thoughts about the High Priestess and what Addie and I discussed after Friday's class. Sadie had pretty much decided the same thing. It would have been nice to have worked together on that, but she'd been elusive, as usual. Not surprisingly, the guys didn't really contribute much else, so we went with the High Priestess and that we were looking for something that resembled any of the many objects on the card. Yeah, ambiguous as fuck, but what else could we do?

"Ugh, I can't believe they allow this thing to be operational," Sadie said as we boarded what was supposed to be an elevator, though it was much more like a death trap.

"We don't have to take it. We can hike up to the top floors," Torent teased.

At once, all of our heads fell back as we tried to peer up into the darkness above. Nobody was really sure how many stories up the library went. The higher levels were pitch-black and full of noises that often sounded like bones crunching, but some students reported hearing other things—a woman's wail, a baby's cry, pain-filled moans, and what had once been described as the sound of flesh tearing. How much of it was real and how much had been figments of the imagination by overstressed students' minds was unknown. The library simply held too many secrets.

"I can always fly," I said, my spine and shoulders tingling at the thought, my wings anxious to come out. It'd been a while since I'd indulged in a nice flight.

"Actually, this ancient contraption could take forever," Slaine said. "You could go ahead for us. At least let us know what floor to get off at."

I looked at Sadie, wondering if she'd be okay with that. Like I needed her permission or something. Ridiculous. I supposed it was more that I wanted her to tell me to stay with her—protect her from the scary library or elevator—or at least be able to stand close to her in the small space. She shrugged, and her lack of interest was all I needed. A flight would be much more fun.

Using glamour to adjust my top so it could accommodate my wings without ripping to shreds and exposing myself, I snapped the black and purple appendages out and let them spread behind and to the sides of me. I couldn't open them fully —they were large and I didn't want even the purple tips of the feathers to come too close to any books. We had too much to do to have to deal with any mishaps before we even left the mezzanine.

Sadie's eyes twinkled as she gazed at me with admiration, and at least there was that. I launched myself upward, keeping an eye ahead to ensure I avoided slamming into the labyrinth of bridges and passages that crisscrossed the center of the library. The cool air blew my hair back as my wings carried me upward. When the light dimmed to nothing and the darkness seemed impenetrable, I slowed and began circling the floors, using my heightened vision to watch out for portals or an ankh or something that looked like the triple moon.

Many stories up—perhaps ten or twelve—my wing tips brushed against a wall here, and a few moments later, I gave them a flap and felt the books fall over before hearing the crash. *Shit.* I held my breath, pausing in midair, waiting for the ramifications, but nothing happened. The books didn't scream or fight back, and nothing tried to chase me down. Not that I could tell, anyway.

When I moved again, my face slammed into something I hadn't even sensed there. The darkness was too thick for me to be trying to fly. I reached out, and my fingers found stone—the top of the bridge I'd just flown into. I pulled myself up and decided I'd stay on foot now. Hiding my wings, I crept along the bridge and through the stacks, searching for the elevator. It wasn't where I expected it to be. A search of the whole floor made me realize the elevator didn't open on this level.

I went up a floor, to see if it just skipped that one, but couldn't find the lift there either, so then I headed downward, finally finding the last floor of the elevator as my team-mates stepped off.

"So this is the top?" Torent asked, squinting into the darkness.

"Nope," I said. "It's just where the elevator stops. We'll have to climb the rest. I can't even fly up there. Too dark and too tight."

We checked out the current floor before taking a narrow set of stairs upward, stopping at each level to search for anything that matched our clues. The books were thick, and several moaned and groaned. On one floor, I caught movement out of the corner of my eye, and some kind of small creature—but not a mouse or even a rat—skittered around the corner of a shelf. A few more stories up and the walls were so close that the bookshelves were crammed together, the rows between them barely wide enough for us to squeeze through.

Sadie kept so close to me, she was nearly on my back. At one point, we had to sidestep along a ledge around a bookcase, our backs pressed against the stone as we slid sideways. A screech sounded from close overhead, and Sadie grabbed my hand in a death grip, nearly slipping off the edge as she did.

"I got you," I said, pulling her back.

As we ascended to a new level, the air opened around us, where there were no rows of shelves, only cases lining three walls. Near the fourth wall, an orb of orange light danced in front of four closed doors. They were each a different shape and color, and when Torent rushed to check, he found all of them locked.

"The four portals," Sadie breathed over my shoulder, her breath soft and sweet on my cheek. As though realizing how close our lips were, she quickly stepped away.

"I don't know," Slaine said, then he quoted the clue. "'If it does not open, it's not your door.'"

"Four doors and four of us," I said. "Maybe we should each try them all?" I knew the logic wasn't fully there—Torent should have been able to open one of them—but we all tried, just in case. The doors remained steadfast. I mentally recalled the rest of the message. "'A single tome reveals the way.' So we have to find a book."

"In a library," Torent quipped.

"Where there are literally thousands of books," Sadie added.

We all looked around at the bookcases lining the walls surrounding us. Just in this one area were hundreds of books, if not thousands.

"Any ideas which one it might be? Maybe a grimoire with a spell that opens one of these doors?" Slaine asked.

Torent's head tilted, and he strode over to the far wall, facing a bookshelf. "Or maybe it's this one."

He reached up for a book on the top shelf, and the rest of us yelled in unison, "STOP!"

"You can't just go around touching whatever you want," I reminded him.

He looked over his shoulder and gave us a cocky grin. "I'm trusting my intuition, like Addie said, and it says this one."

He grabbed the book by the spine before any of us could stop him and slid the book from its place. We all froze. I couldn't even hear a heart beat. When nothing happened after several seconds, we released the collective breath we'd been holding. Torent strode back over to us.

"Look familiar?" he asked, showing us the spine. There was a Roman numeral II—the number of the High Priestess—and the same symbols as on the scroll she held on our card of clues. The front cover depicted a replica of the full imagery. When he tried to lift it, though, the whole book turned over. "The cover's stuck."

Torent tried using force to pry it away from the pages, but it wouldn't budge.

"Let me try." I snatched it from him, but I couldn't open it either. Murmuring a few words, I tried a spell, but to no avail. Placing it on the floor, I warned everyone to stand back before I blasted a harder shot of energy at it. The book flipped over, the covers tight as ever.

Slaine leaned over and picked it up. Lifting the cover from the pages.

"'If it doesn't open, it's not your door,'" Sadie murmured. "It must be your door, Slaine."

Slaine's eyes roamed over the interior cover page before he looked up at us. "So this is the door? Not those?"

He lifted his chin to indicate the four doors.

We gathered closer as he flipped through the pages. We all gasped when he turned a page about a third of the way in. The remainder of the pages were all stuck together with the center hollowed out. Someone had created a hiding place. Nestled inside was a key. When Slaine picked it up, the red wooden door began to glow.

"I'd say that's our door," I said. As the others simply stared at it, I plucked the key from Slaine's loose hold and strode over to it. The key wouldn't even fit in the hole. I tried the other doors but no dice. "Here, Slaine. It really is *your* door."

The key slid right into the hole for him, and the red door swung open. I led the way into a pitch-black room of undeterminable size. As soon as we were all inside, the door slammed shut, and the floor fell out from beneath us.

We plunged into a never-ending freefall.

CHAPTER 4

I snapped out my wings and reached for both Sadie and Torent, who were closest to me, but we suddenly slammed into solid rock ground that seemed to come from nowhere. The rough surface tore through my jeans and sweater, scraping up my side from knee to shoulder. The pain and injuries were short-lived as my body immediately healed itself. I used glamour to fix my clothes as I spun for Sadie.

"Are you okay?"

"I'll live." She grunted, her eyes squeezing shut as she shoved on her own misshapen shoulder until it popped back into place.

"Torent? Slaine?" I turned for them. Torent was nearby, shaking off the impact. Slaine was several yards away, pushing himself to his feet.

"That was wicked," he muttered.

We were all a little worse for the wear, but realizing we'd survived, I took in our surroundings. "What the hell?"

"I don't think we're in the library anymore," Sadie said.

No, we most definitely were not. Rather, we were on a small rocky island in the middle of an angry sea. Waves crashed against black boulders, sending spray high into the air, droplets falling on us in a light mist. Overhead, a storm churned in what seemed to be a late afternoon sky, wind gusts picking up and whipping my hair against my face. Strange contraptions were scattered across the landscape. But no ankh or curtain, veil, crescent moon, or anything else from the clues except the churning sea.

"Where are we?" Torent had to shout to be heard over the growing raucous of wind and thunder.

"I know!" Slaine shouted as he jogged toward us. But when he was about ten feet away, the ground around us shuddered and opened, and steel poles shot upward, surrounding us—Sadie, Torent, and me encircled with Slaine on the outside. Rising dozens of feet up, the poles narrowed to sharp points at their tips, and what looked like rows of razors lined the rods' sides. The poles were only inches apart, leaving just enough space to see through. I reached out and touched one and was zapped with a strong current of electricity.

"My clan came here long ago to train," Slaine yelled. "It's an obstacle course."

I looked up to find the space above open. Grabbing Sadie's and Torent's arms, I sprang into the air, but as I came level to the tips of the poles, another strong current charged through me and into the others, knocking us to the ground. I fell on my ass, swearing. Jumping to my feet, I hardened my wings so the feathers became like steel themselves, the edges razor-sharp. Arcing one out, I skated the blades across the poles. Sparks flew as metal screeched against metal, but no damage was done. Not even a scratch. Torent and Sadie both tried their own abilities against the steel fence, but we appeared to be locked in.

"Look!" Sadie pointed toward the far end of the obstacle course. A key dangled in mid-air about six or seven feet from the ground.

"That must be our way out," I yelled. "Slaine, it looks like it's up to you to get it."

He stared at me with black eyes, his nostrils flaring. "I've never done the course before! It's meant to maim and even kill—only the best warriors survive."

With a groan, the ground shifted, and the poles all moved inward, tightening our circle.

"Dude, you don't have a choice," Torent shouted. "Just fucking do it!"

Slaine looked at the course again, then back at me. Fear shone brightly in his eyes. The poles tightened again, reducing our space to about a six foot diameter now. Torent let out a string of profanities, and I heard his heartrate climb. Heat poured off his body. Fire was one of my elements—it didn't scare me. But I worried about Sadie if Torent's demon side took over.

"He's right," I yelled to Slaine. "You don't have a choice. If you don't, we'll die!"

"If I do and I fail, we'll still die."

I stepped up to the poles and grabbed one in each hand, ignoring the cuts of the razors into my palms and the electricity shooting through me. "The only failure is if you give up. Or if you do nothing at all. You were chosen to become a guardian, for fuck's sake. You got this!"

His jaw muscle popped, and he nodded. Then he began to strip. Our circle tightened again.

"Hurry!" Sadie hollered as she pressed up against me.

"I'll be faster in my kelpie form," Slaine yelled before his human shape morphed and grew, until a large black horse replaced him.

The kelpie took off in a gallop, and it wasn't long before I realized the course was much more dangerous than it first appeared. As he jumped a rock fence, flames erupted, singeing his tail and legs. He kept going, though, even as an axe dropped from a post and swung out, slicing across his back. More steel spears shot out of the ground in his path, and the horse cried out as one pierced its underside. He managed to free himself, but his gallop slowed to a canter as blood poured from his wounds. A shower of stones pelted him as he weaved through a copse of trees. The farther he went, the slower he became, stumbling several times.

"Keep going!" I yelled when he fell to the ground. "You can do this!"

The poles surrounding us closed in once more. Torent and Sadie also cheered Slaine on. He pushed himself up and continued, unstable as he was on his hooves. He was only a few yards from the key when there was a loud boom and a large boulder slammed into the kelpie's side, knocking him back to the ground. This time he didn't get back up, no matter how loud we yelled. The poles were moving in closer and faster now until all three of us were pressed into each other. The electricity zinged around us, our hairs lifting into the air.

"Come on, Slaine!" I yelled. "Don't. Give. Up! That is the *only* failure!"

The horse shrunk in size, transforming back into Slaine's naked human shape. Blood oozed out of several places, and dark bruises already blossomed over almost every inch of his skin. One leg was twisted out at an unnatural angle. Pushing his shoulders off the ground, he half-crawled, half-dragged himself toward the key. With what had to have been a final burst of strength and energy, he lunged upward and closed his fingers.

All light and sound suddenly disappeared.

Then reappeared a moment later—but different. We were back in the library in the area outside of the four doors, lit by the orange orb.

Sadie and I dropped to our knees next to Slaine's prone form. He was unconscious, his body trembling.

"He's in shock," Sadie said as she began to go to work on treating his many wounds. "His pulse is weak, and he's barely breathing. Hurry! Go get help!"

I sprang to my feet and ran past Torent who stood dumbfounded, staring at the key—in his own palm.

"It just appeared in my hand," Torent said the next day when he, Sadie, and I met in the library again, facing the four doors. Our artifact *had* to be behind one of them. "I don't know how, but it was there as soon as we returned here."

"Then you must be up next," I said, gesturing at the doors.

"Slaine woke this morning, but he's out of commission for a while," Sadie said. "It's up to the three of us. Let's hope yesterday was a fluke."

"Yeah, right, as fucked up as this school is?" Torent said with a chuckle as he strode over to the first door on the left—the black one with silver vines crawling up it. "I'm pretty sure the campus is intent on killing us, and anyone left standing by graduation will be the true warriors."

"Guess it's one way to weed out the weak," I muttered, then I frowned when Torent's key didn't fit in the black door's lock. "Huh. I was pretty sure the black one was yours, demon-boy."

Torent snorted. "It's probably yours. As black as your soul."

Ouch. I opened my mouth for a comeback when Torent unlocked the green door, and it swung open. Beyond it was a black, wrought-iron gate set into two tall pillars of foliage, and beyond that appeared to be some kind of garden. As soon as all three of us crossed the threshold, the door slammed shut behind us and the gate creaked open ahead.

"Here we go again," Sadie said as we inched our way forward.

The tall bushes on each side of the gate stretched forward for hundreds of yards, creating two walls on each side of a pathway. The green expanse was broken up only by colorful flowers dotting it in clusters. At the far end, straight in front of us, appeared to be another wall of foliage. Overhead, the branches reached up and over, intertwining to create an arched ceiling. Faint light filtered through the branches and leaves, dappling the dirt path ahead of us.

It looked as though the walls on each side ended before the wall on the far end, creating what I hoped to be two exits, so I led the other two into the tunnel.

"This is interesting," Sadie mused from behind me as we walked.

"Understatement," Torent said, walking along her side. "But what exactly are you thinking?"

"Yesterday, Slaine opened the door, and we ended up in a place relevant to him, and he had to do the dirty work. Today, you opened the door, but I'm pretty sure this is nothing like Hell. In fact, if anything, all the greenery is a lot like the elves' homeland in Faerie. I'd kind of hoped this was going to be your challenge to face, but that theory's shot. It must be mine."

I glanced over my shoulder at her, impressed that she didn't sound scared or even worried, just as she reached up and picked a flower from the wall. When she lifted it toward her mouth, I knocked her hand away.

"Are you crazy?" I hissed, noticing more flowers cupped in her palm.

She shrugged. "I'm an elf. Can't help it. That's like you trying to say no to tacos growing all around you."

Dismissing the fact that she even knew how much I loved tacos, I slapped her hand, the petals falling to the ground. "You have no idea where we are or *what* they are! They could be poisonous!"

She rolled her eyes and touched her nose. "How stupid do you think I am? I can detect poisons, venoms, anything harmful. Lots of elves can, but I'm especially tuned in. It's what makes me a good healer."

She picked another flower and popped it into her mouth, then pulled a face, spitting it back out.

"See!" I said, alarm making my heart skip.

"It's . . . not . . . poisonous," she insisted between spits. "It's . . . nothing. Not even like paper or cardboard. More like it's not even real."

Wiping the back of her hand over her tongue, she gave the flowers growing out of the wall a dirty look, as though they'd deeply offended her. I couldn't imagine eating a bad taco, so I supposed I'd feel the same way if I bit into a tasteless one.

We continued on, reaching the far wall with an opening on each side of the junction, but no clue which way to go next.

"Maybe we should split up," Torent suggested.

I nodded. "Good idea. You go that way, and Sadie and I will go this one. Holler if you find anything."

Sadie and I went right and took off in a jog between more bushy walls before we were forced to turn right again. The path twisted and turned, sometimes coming to a fork or a T and making us choose. I thought I saw something ahead when we broke through a small opening in the wall.

"Well, shit," Sadie swore. "We're right back where we started."

I cupped my hands around my mouth and yelled, "Torent! Did you find anything?"

"No," came an answer in the far distance. How large was this place, anyway?

"Let's try again," Sadie said. "Let's go to the left at that first fork instead of right."

I nodded before jogging off again. The new path turned darker and darker as we went. I couldn't tell if it was from night falling, a denser coverage overhead, or a kind of haze that was thickening into fog. I swore something huge and hairy crossed the path more than once but was gone before I got a good look.

"This way," I said, when I saw the dappled yellowish-green light of daytime again. We broke through—right back where we began.

"Now what?" Sadie asked, throwing her arms up in exasperation.

I called for Torent again, but only heard some distant sound that could have been him . . . or something else.

"Do you think he's okay?" Sadie asked with concern.

"I'm sure he's fine. He can handle himself." I turned toward the right. "Let's try this way one more time. There's that other turn we can try. If we end up here again, we'll go find Torent."

When we made the new turn, we followed the ever-narrowing path until we had to slow to a walk in a single file. Branches scratched along my cheek and shoulders, grabbing at my hair like skeletal fingers. Sadie stayed close behind me as the light again darkened.

"Elli, I need to tell you something," she whispered, grabbing my hand and pulling me to a stop. I turned to face her, catching her chewing on her bottom lip. I ached to reach up and free her lip with my thumb, but worry shone in her electric blue eyes. So I fisted my hands at my sides, trying not to think about how that bottom lip tasted.

"Not now," I said quietly. "Whatever it is can wait."

She blinked, then nodded. And the next thing I knew, her hands were on my face pulling me to her as her lips crushed against mine. They were soft and hot and urgently demanding, her tongue sweeping over the crease of my lips, parting them. She tasted like strawberries and cream, just as I remembered from our time together on New Year's Eve, when she'd snuck away from her friends after midnight and found me alone in the hot tub. That night had been incredible as we spent hours together talking and kissing and talking some more. We'd done little more than kiss— not even our bikini tops came off—but it was the most intimate I'd ever been with anyone. I mean, I'd been with others before, but it just wasn't the same. The intimacy was more than physical. We shared things I hadn't even told my twin or Charleigh.

We'd both been raised in different realms—her in the elven lands in Faerie—and we talked about what it was like coming to this one and feeling so out of place. We laughed and bonded over the silly and indulgent things we adored here, like makeup and music and superheroes. We were each considered royalty in our own worlds, and we both faced high expectations and intense pressure when we finished at SMA and returned home. We quietly admitted to feeling torn between the need to serve our duties in our home worlds and the desire to stay in this one, which was far from perfect but so much better than our own. Especially mine. We secretly vowed to each other that we'd make the most of our time here—together.

Then the next morning, she'd gone back to pretending like she didn't know me.

With that memory clear, I broke the kiss and stepped back. My body screamed, already missing the feel of her so close.

"No," I said, shaking my head. "Not again."

She blinked as tears filled her electric blues. The skin over her throat moved as she swallowed and averted her eyes. Her voice came out thick and husky and full of a sadness I not only heard but felt deep in my soul. "I know. You're right. I really can't do this. I'm so sorry, Elliana. I really am."

Her hand landed on my forearm, but I shook her off. "Just leave me the hell alone."

"Okay," she whispered.

She stepped around me and continued the way we'd been going. Closing my eyes, I inhaled a few deep breaths to calm my heart and my emotions. This wasn't the time or place to address the cracks I felt splintering within my chest. The Dark energy coursing through my veins gathered and grew, and I leaned into it as I'd done many times before, letting my old friend bring a bit of comfort before pushing it back.

Feeling better, I took off after Sadie just as she turned a corner. When I rounded it myself only moments later, she was nowhere to be seen, though there was nowhere for her to have gone either—just another alley surrounded by greenery.

"Sadie?" I called.

A scream came from my right.

"Sadie!" I shouted as I saw her hand jut out of the leafy wall several yards ahead.

"Elli!" she cried out, but her screams became muffled, then silent.

"Sadie!" I ran to the place where she'd disappeared, but it was completely closed up. Not even a broken branch or bent leaf out of place. "Sadie!"

I kicked and chopped at the foliage, but it was thick and strong. Calling a ball of flames into my palm, I threw it. The fire blazed a small hole, but I saw no signs of Sadie anywhere. No signs that anyone or anything had been there at all except for leaves and branches. Bringing my wings out, I hardened the feathers to steel again and sliced through more branches. After several rounds of burning and slicing, I finally broke through to the other side.

And found myself in another lane between walls of bushes.

"Sadie!" I yelled, but there was no answer. "Torent!"

Again, no response.

I turned around, but the hole I'd come through had already closed up. Overhead, however, was open, revealing a dark, cloudy night sky. Spreading my wings, I sprang into the air.

Walls of greenery spread out for as far as I could see. Just as I suspected, we were in a maze. Sadie was nowhere to be seen, and night was definitely descending everywhere. I made a tight circle then spiraled outward, but it was as if the maze had swallowed the elf girl up whole.

In the distance, an orange glow hovered over a section of the maze. I flew that way to investigate, then realized it was fire. But not normal fire. There was something strange about it, and when I uttered a spell to control it—I had power over all the elements, but thanks to my dad, I was particularly strong with fire—it didn't respond. A large, weird shadow danced in the light. As I came closer, I realized the shadow was a beast—the same big, hairy thing I'd caught glimpses of before. Below it was a much smaller figure fighting it.

I gasped. "Torent!"

With a flap of my wings, I soared over to them. It only took one swipe of my hardened feathers to decapitate the beast.

To save a demon.

Who would have ever thought?

"Elliana, I can't get out of here," Torent yelled. He was surrounded by walls of fire. Hellfire. It had to have been. He'd said he could create and control it. Had he done this to himself? But why couldn't he pass through it?

I circled over him, debating. I didn't know how to help him since I evidently had no power over this kind of fire. And Sadie was out there, somewhere. What if that beast had a mate? What if that was what took her?

My eyes scanned over the top of the maze, looking for any evidence, when my gaze fell on something glowing not too far away.

A key!

I yelled down at Torent, "I see our way out! Hold on!"

I flew for the key, another skeleton key, but this one gold. When I was close enough, I reached out for it and hit an invisible wall.

Bouncing off, I somehow landed right next to Torent, in his circle of fire.

"I found the key, but it won't let me get it. I think you have to." I looked at him for the first time and saw panic in his eyes.

"I can't! I can't get out of here. I'm trapped. We're trapped!" He pushed his hand through the mop of black hair on his head, his green eyes glowing. "I can't believe this is how I'm going to die." He shook his head. "No, I always knew I'd die like this."

My brows lifted. My hands reached up and grabbed his shoulders, giving him a shake. "Dude! Chill the eff out! Nobody's dying here."

He froze, looked at me, and nodded, his nostrils flaring and his jaw muscle twitching. "Right. We're not going to die. I can't do that to Mallory."

"Exactly. Think of Mallory. We're going to get you back to Mallory."

The flames around us flared up as panic once again sparked in his eyes. My brow furrowed.

48

"Torent . . . do you feel trapped with Mallory?" I hedged.

His wild eyes turned on me. "Hell the fuck no! Mallory's my . . . my everything. My freedom. When I'm with her is when I *don't* feel trapped."

I glanced around, noticing the hellfire dying down now. I'd misunderstood his first reaction. From the little bit I'd seen of the two of them, this made more sense. "Then Mallory's our way out. Think of her, Torent."

"Of course she is." He dropped his hands to his hips and nodded. "As long as I'm with her, everything's good."

The flames dimmed then extinguished themselves. "See? We're not trapped. Lookie there."

I gestured at a break in the wall, beyond it a golden glow. We pushed through, and Torent rushed over to the key, reaching for it.

"Wait!" I barked. "We need to find Sadie!"

But it was too late.

We were back in the library.

CHAPTER 5

I lunged at the green door, trying to force it open with all means at my disposal—brute force, magic, fire, ice . . . nothing worked. Torent tried to help but he wasn't strong enough either, and both keys were gone. The one that had opened it had disappeared in the lock when we went in, and the one he grabbed inside had vanished when we returned. He took off, presumably for help, as I proceeded to pound on the wooden planks, alternating between demanding the door to open and yelling for Sadie. After a while, I leaned my back against the door and slid to the floor, dropping my head in my hands.

Addie and a couple of the school's Regents eventually showed up, but their magic didn't open the door either. After what might have been hours or days, I could no longer tell, they began to leave, all but Addie.

"You're just going to leave her in there?" I demanded.

"We don't know how to open it. *Yet*," Addie added quickly. "We need to do some research. This place, though . . . it has a mind of its own. We'll keep trying. In the meantime, you need to get some rest."

I didn't want to go with them, so I stayed behind a while longer. The guilt of leaving things like I had with Sadie weighed heavily, while at the same time, the Darkness tried to take over. It'd be so easy to give into it completely. Part of me wanted to so badly.

I'd lost someone special already, right before we came to this world, all because I couldn't be there for her when she'd needed me most. Now here I was again. Sadie needed me, and I couldn't do a damn thing for her. The cracks she'd made by rejecting me were nothing compared to what the guilt was doing to me now.

And the Darkness could take it all away if I let it.

I finally forced myself up and away from the door. At the ledge that led downward, I leaned forward and plunged. The heaviness within me sank me like a stone as I passed floor after dark floor of the library. When the space opened up more, I let my wings out and drifted in circles toward the bottom.

I had no idea what time it was. It had been early afternoon when we'd passed through the door, but I didn't know how long we were in the maze or how long I had sat outside the door, hanging on to the bit of hope that Sadie would be spit back out. Still, I was mildly surprised to find bright daylight shining down through the skylight, making the snow on the ground sparkle like an array of diamonds.

Anger built within me as I made my way across the quad, avoiding snowball fights and ignoring the laughter coming from small groups of students I passed. How could they be so lighthearted in this terrible place? Havenwood Falls itself was lovely. This campus, though. It was like the charming town's ugly underbelly, bringing death and destruction to all who entered, whether they deserved it—like me—or not, like Sadie.

The Darkness strengthened, pressing at my resolve.

I trudged up the spiral staircase of Modi Tower toward the top floor. Brielle flew at me as soon as I stepped inside our room.

"Elliana Katerina Ames Knight! I was so scared!" she cried as she held me tightly.

"Why? *I'm* fine," I bit out, pushing her off. "Which is more than I can say for others."

"You've been gone for three days," Charleigh said, hanging back. She was always a good gauge of my mood and knew I didn't want or need a hug right now. Brielle did, too, but her hug was for herself.

"We had no idea what happened to you!" she accused.

"Three days?" The Regents had failed to mention that part. Of course, I hadn't really been interested in anything they had to say that didn't have to do with opening that damn door. "Well, like I said, I'm fine. I just need a shower and maybe some sleep." Though the thought of actually being able to sleep was pretty laughable.

I stood in the stone shower, letting the hot water pour over me, wishing it would wash away my guilt and pain, but alas, life was never so kind.

But I am, the Darkness whispered in my mind, continuing to tempt me to give in once and for all. *I can ensure you never feel anything again.*

I did my best to ignore it—for Brielle's and Charleigh's sakes, if no other reason—and forced myself out of the shower. As I made my way down the hall between the floor's communal bathroom and our dorm room, I heard a great deal of commotion echoing up the spiral staircase. Brielle threw the door open before I even reached it.

"Sadie's back!" she squealed.

I nearly dropped my towel as I ran into our room. The normal human eye probably would have lost track of my movement, I dressed so fast and then flew down the stairs to the eighth floor. A small crowd was gathered around Sadie's door, mostly elves, but I pushed my way through. Fig and her other closest friends hovered around her as usual. Those electric blues locked on me right away, though, and Sadie came to the door, pushing a lock of her light blond hair behind her ear.

"I'm okay," she said quietly, before she shut the door as she was tugged back inside.

I stood there stupidly for the blink of an eye. Before I could be humiliated any further, I turned and headed back upstairs. The crowd was already dispersing.

She's okay. That's all that matters. I repeated the words to myself over and over as I brushed my long, dark hair until it dried, went through my emails, and determined what classes I'd missed and what studying I needed to do. Unable to focus, though, I sat in the window seat and watched the campus far below. The light from the opening in the top of the mountain dimmed from dusk to full on night. Students came back from classes then left their towers again for dinner at Halstein Hall. I watched as Fig, Paisley Underwood, and others left for dinner, then returned with a to-go carton, probably for Sadie. Brielle and Charleigh brought me dinner back, too, but I couldn't stomach the idea of food.

After a trip to the bathroom, I decided to change my location and crawled under my covers in bed instead of going back to the window seat. Although I knew better, I hoped sleep would come and carry me off to oblivion. It might be the only thing to stave off the Darkness that was becoming more and more enticing.

Then my phone dinged with a text.

Come to my room?

I didn't recognize the number. It wasn't one already stored in my phone. Yet I knew. I had half a mind to text back, "Who dis?" and be a bitch about it, but instead, I found myself knocking on Sadie's door without further thought.

The door opened slowly, and Sadie's face peeked around the corner. She saw me and immediately averted her eyes.

"Come in," she whispered.

Stepping inside, my gaze swept over the room as she closed the door behind me. It was like I'd stepped into an enchanted forest. Trees were painted on a sage green background of the curved walls and up the ceiling, with two three-dimensional trees that appeared so real, my hand twitched, wanting to reach out and make sure they weren't. Their trunks had little doors in the bottoms, and lining the ceiling, branches reached out into the room, colorful lanterns dangling from them. Very real vines dotted with flowers grew around the four posters of her bed and along the top of the wall behind it, fairy lights glowing everywhere. It smelled like earth and plants and sunshine with a hint of strawberries and cream that was all Sadie.

"Is this what your home world is like?" I whispered, fearing anything louder would ruin the magical feel.

"Yeah, Makenna did a great job at the illusion, with Fig's help. Mak's fae, but she's never been to the elven lands, so Fig told her about our homes in the massive trees. She wanted me to feel like I was there. Thought it would help me recover faster."

"Did it?" I asked, turning around to finally face her. I couldn't help but notice the purple half-moons under her eyes, nor how the hollows of her cheeks seemed deeper. Her blond locks were piled on her head in a messy bun, and she wore a loose tank top and flannel pajama pants with puppies printed all over them. I had to avert my own eyes when I noticed her nipples poking through the thin material of her top. Damn it, she was too sexy for my own good. I lifted my gaze up to lock on her tired, but still beautiful face.

She pressed her full lips together and gave a tiny shake of her head. "Not as much as seeing you here. In my room. The two of us alone."

She took a step closer to me. I backed up a step. "You said—"

"I know what I said." She moved another pace closer. When I backed up, I hit the bed and had to stop myself from plopping down on it because I knew that would lead into dangerous terrain. Her hand grabbed mine, and when I tried to pull free, she held tighter. "I'm sorry for being so weird. I really am, Elli. It's just . . ." She bit her bottom lip and looked away for a moment before turning that electric blue gaze back on me. "I know in my head that it's best for this not to happen. There's so much you don't know about me, and it seems all I know how to do is break people's hearts. And that breaks mine. So I've just been trying to protect both of us from all that pain. But especially you."

"Me?" I chuckled with the irony and gave her a small smile. "I know pain too well. Inflicting it and receiving it."

She nodded. "I know. I can see it in you, ever since I first laid eyes on you at the trials last summer. Which is exactly why I told myself to stay away."

I swallowed as I waited for her to continue, but she didn't.

"But?" I finally asked, hearing the word in her tone, though she didn't actually say it.

"But . . ." She hesitated before taking another step closer to me while at the same time releasing my hand and fisting my shirt in both of hers. "But I can't fucking stay away from you, Elliana Knight."

She yanked me into her and claimed my mouth with hers. Those full, luscious lips urged mine to part, and when they did, her tongue swept in, flicking against mine. The kiss deepened, and hot desire zinged throughout my body, especially when she pressed herself fully against me, her hands flattening between us. When one moved up my ribs to explore, I had to break the kiss and gently push her back.

"Sadie—" She looked at me with such heat in her eyes, I almost gave in. I shook my head, trying to clear the haze of my own desire, and blew out a sigh. "I can't keep doing this hot and cold, mood swing, whiplash kind of BS. I have to know where we stand. What exactly do you want?"

Her head lowered, and she looked up at me through long lashes. "You, Elli. I just want you."

My heart stuttered at the sincerity in her voice. But I needed more than that. "For how long, though? Are you going to act like you don't know me as soon as we're around your friends?"

She grimaced. "I'm not really the PDA type. You know how it is."

I had to nod. I did know how it was. Unlike hetero couples, we often became an unwitting and unwilling show. "That's not the same thing as completely ignoring someone, though. Or kissing them and then running away. Or having a really spectacular night together and then pretending like it never happened."

"I know. I won't push you away anymore." Her hand lifted to cup the side of my face. "I promise you that, Elliana. I want this. I want us. I want *you*. If you'll have me . . ." She trailed off, watching me with expectation.

Even if she kept her promise and stopped flipping the switch between us as though our connection were nothing more than electricity flowing to a light bulb, I knew this would eventually end in heartache. We were from two completely different worlds, and we'd both have to return to our respective homes at some point. I had no idea when that would be for either of us. And we'd agreed that night in the hot tub that we'd make the most of our time here, in this world, with all it had to offer.

For me, that included her. And apparently, she felt the same.

Whatever grew between us was guaranteed to end in pain.

But it just might be worth it.

I fell onto the bed, pulling her with me.

"So the plant wall tried to eat you?" I asked later as we lay together in her bed, snuggled under her thick duvet. Our lips were swollen and our legs entwined, but our clothes remained. We'd agreed to take this one step at a time, but at least I knew she actually wanted to go down that path together. "Talk about tables turning. I guess that's what you get for eating its flowers."

"Funny." She reached over me and snagged a petal from a pile of "snacks" on her nightstand and popped it in her mouth.

"And then it spit you out in the forest here?"

"I guess elves don't taste all that good. But yeah, I was suddenly in the middle of the woods, disoriented and with no clue where I was. Then I recognized the scents from cultivating herbs in that forest, and something pulled me in the right direction, straight to the clearing on Clifftop. I'd never been so relieved to see the opening into the mountain."

I twirled a finger in a curl that had fallen loose from her bun. "I was so worried. I waited outside that door for hours."

"I figured you'd try to find me. Even after . . . after what I said to you. I know how you are, that you wouldn't give up. Which was why I tried to get back here as fast as I could."

"I'm just glad you're safe."

"And I'm glad you and Torent are. Oh!" She reached over me again, I thought to pluck another petal from her nightstand, but her fingers dangled something else between them—the golden key from the maze. "This was in my hand. Guess this means the next door is mine."

A bad feeling swept over me, and I snatched the key out of her hand and tossed it on the floor. "I don't want to even think about that stupid mission right now."

She smiled, a twinkle in her eye. "Oh? And what do you want to think about?"

"Nothing," I breathed, closing my eyes as she leaned in, brushing her lips over mine.

Being with Sadie was like nothing I'd ever experienced before. The girl I'd left behind in my home world—we'd never had the chance to have this. And before her were only a few stolen kisses, usually with girls who weren't sure what they actually wanted and I was their experiment. With Sadie, though, I already knew that if given the chance, we could meld together completely—in mind, body, and soul. I'd felt it New Year's Eve, and it was even stronger now. The deepness of the connection between us was unfathomable to me, feeling almost unreal. It was different than I had even with my twin, though we seemed to be quite opposites.

"We're not, you know," she whispered after I mentioned this while observing her nearly white hair intermingling with my nearly black locks on the pillow. Her pale finger traced a pattern on my olive-toned, Mediterranean skin.

"I don't just mean our coloring," I said pointedly.

One side of her mouth lifted. "Oh, I know exactly what you mean. But I believe there's a darkness in me, too, Elli. I've always been attracted to it."

I rolled my eyes. "You are all that is light, Sadie. That's what you should be attracted to."

"But am I?" she asked. She rolled over on to her back and sighed as she stared up at the branches and leaves decorating her ceiling. "In the elven lands, there's rumor of the dark elves. Some call them night elves or blood elves. Most think they're mythological, stories told to scare the young into minding their parents. Others say they're as real as the shadow fae and just as awful."

My brows pulled together. "I've never heard of the shadow fae. My grandmother, she's a light fae, never mentioned them."

"Nobody ever talks about them. I've heard rumors of some courts using them as slaves and others that they're locked away in The Vault or that they even control it."

"The Vault?" The tiniest hint of recognition niggled in the deep recesses of my mind, but it slipped away before I could latch onto it.

"A supernatural prison with some of the worst of the worst." She paused. "My mother once said something . . . something unbefitting of royalty, mind you . . . that makes me think she has some kind of connection with The Vault. Or with the shadow fae or dark elves or . . . I don't know. She'd never elaborate, but I can't help but feel that connection, too. I see the beauty in the dark. Thus, my attraction to you."

"You like me for my Darkness?"

She turned her head to look over at me. "I admire you for being able to control it. For not shying away from it, but not letting it rule you, either. I hope . . . I hope if I'm right about something with my mother—with her past, my father—that's how I'd be."

My eyes widened, understanding. She obviously didn't want to say it out loud, and I wouldn't force her to, but I got it. She questioned who her real father was, and if she was right about who her mother had been with in the past, he had dark tendencies.

I rolled over on my side to face her and pushed a lock of hair behind her pointed ear. "Regardless of what flows in your blood, you can choose how you want to be, Sadie. I hope you will always choose light."

She sucked her bottom lip between her teeth, nodding as she looked at me in earnest. "But I've already chosen you, Elli."

CHAPTER 6

"What I told you about my mother," Sadie began the next afternoon when I checked in on her after classes. We sat on her bed, me on the edge in a cropped maroon mock turtleneck, short black skirt, and thigh-high boots, and her sitting cross-legged up by the pillows. She'd changed her pajamas into leggings and an oversized hoodie with the word COEXIST formed by the shapes of supernatural creatures across the front. "I've never told anybody that. Not Fig or anyone. Nobody can know. It would ruin . . . everything."

I gave her a reassuring smile—this girl made me smile much more than I was used to—and trailed my fingers over her thigh. "Don't worry. I'm very good at keeping secrets."

"Thank you." Her return smile was shy at first but quickly became mischievous as her electric blues twinkled. "I missed you today. I should have gone to classes."

"Enjoy your extra day off. Trust me—you'll be back in the thick of things too soon. We have to finish this mission, after all, or we're going to get further behind than we already are."

Her gaze flickered over to the golden key back on her nightstand before returning to me. She nodded. "Yeah. Tomorrow, okay?"

"I'll let Torent know. Slaine still isn't up to par."

"And tonight?" she asked, wrapping her pinky finger around

mine and pulling until I leaned closer to her, our faces only inches apart. Just as I was about to kiss her, she frowned. "Oh, wait. I promised Fig and the others I'd have dinner with them."

We stared into each other's eyes for a long moment. I tried to hide it, but I wondered if she saw the hope in mine. Hope that she would invite me along for once and stop shutting me out.

"Maybe later?" she suggested instead. "We can study together."

One side of her mouth curled up in a smirk, and I didn't miss the air quotes around the word *study*.

I supposed I could accept that, and I returned the smirk. "Yes, I'd like to *study* with you."

She pulled me in for that kiss.

If I'd had any doubts about her feelings for me, they were cleared now. She'd been hurt before and was scared. I could understand that. She'd been brave to reach out to me last Halloween, overcoming her fears. She'd tried again at New Year's. It'd just taken a while for her to get all the way here. Here as in together, Sadie and me, perhaps even as a couple.

The kiss became many more strung together, with bursts of conversations in between. I caught her up on the latest gossip, and we joked about instructors and particularly a certain professor and his student lover who were all the talk. Dinner time came around too quickly.

"I guess I should go," I said, pulling away from another lingering kiss and standing from the bed.

"You know what?" she said, picking up her phone from the nightstand. "I'm going to cancel with them."

"No, you—"

"Elliana, I eat with them all the time. Tonight I want to spend with you."

I wasn't about to argue further, but bit my lip instead, trying to keep the giddiness from pouring out. Who was I? I didn't get giddy. Never. What was this girl doing to me?

"But we do have to study," she said after texting a message. "Go change and get your books."

I looked down at myself. "I thought I looked pretty hot today."

She laughed as she trailed a finger along the tops of my boots.

"You most certainly do. But like I said—I really do have to study. You've already distracted me all afternoon."

We managed to get some actual studying done, but I didn't know how much I'd retain. We couldn't sit on her bed together without touching—because of physical space, not just desire—and each time sent a jolt of excitement through me. We took frequent breaks, too, as a question about a class easily slipped into long and lively conversations that traveled over a variety of subjects before returning to the one at hand. I may not have learned everything I needed to for class, but each time, I learned a little more about Sadie. A little more about how her mind worked, what she believed in, how her heart felt.

But not enough. I didn't know if I could ever learn everything I wanted to. If I could ever get enough of her. We didn't have that kind of time. After all, our days together were numbered. It was too easy to forget that.

The next day, the two of us stood outside the four doors in the library, waiting on Torent.

"Where is he?" I asked, losing my patience. "We only have a couple of hours before our IAF class. I want to get this done." We both knew I meant ITF class, but we'd dubbed it IAF—Insane As Fuck.

"Maybe we should wait?" Sadie suggested, studying the key in her hand. "What if we're in there for days again? I should at least go to class once before that."

"Or maybe this one will finally have what we're looking for and we can turn it in at class," I pointed out. I was pretty sure that wasn't the case. I had a feeling we had to go through all four doors first, but there was a possibility I was wrong. The campus surely liked to mess with us like that.

We waited another five minutes, but still no sign of Torent and not even a text message with an excuse.

"Let's just do it ourselves," I said, gesturing toward the doors.

With one more glance around for Torent, Sadie turned to the

door that was as blue as her eyes. I sidled up next to her as she slipped in the key and turned the knob.

The door opened to a long hallway lined with dozens, perhaps hundreds of mirrors on each side. The floor, ceiling, and what could be seen of the walls behind the mirrors were all black as ink.

Sadie hesitated. "Maybe we should wait. Just in case."

"I think we just go in. Who knows what's keeping him. Probably Mallory."

She looked over her shoulder behind us once more, but there was still no sign of Torent. She finally nodded.

"Let's just do it. I have too much work to catch up on over the weekend to be worrying about this project." She paused, then added, "If we get out of this alive, anyway."

One side of my mouth curled up. "I'd never let anything hurt you, Sadie."

She gave me a small smile. "Nor I you."

Squaring our shoulders and straightening our spines, we both walked in. At the same time, footsteps drummed behind us.

"Wait!" Torent yelled, but on its own volition, the door slammed shut in his face with a loud clang that probably rang throughout the library, annoying the librarians, books, and other creatures among the stacks. He didn't seem to care, though—he made more of a ruckus, pounding on the door. Sadie tried to open it, but it wouldn't budge.

"Just you and me, all alone again," I teased, and she turned around, gazing at me for a long moment.

"In here?" she whispered.

And while I was only joking, hunger shone in her eyes, and an aching desire suddenly swept over me.

Her tongue swiped over her bottom lip as she took a step forward. At the same time, we reached for each other's faces. My hand slid across her jaw and up into her hair, pulling her close as she did the same with me. Our lips nearly touching, we both paused, more energy than ever crackling between us as we looked into each other's eyes. This was different than before, than those hours in her room while she was recovering. Even different than New Year's Eve. Perhaps it had something to do with this weird room, but it was like we couldn't stop ourselves.

Her lids fell, and I closed my own eyes as we leaned into each other. Our lips pressed together, the kiss starting off soft and tentative, but instantly deepening into something of hunger and fire. Our lips parted. Our tongues met. Heat flooded my body as we moved into each other, eliminating any space between us, but every part of me ached for more.

And I could tell she felt the same. Her body thrummed against mine, begging for more, as our mouths continued to devour each other. A part of me knew this was the wrong time and place, that we shouldn't be so stupidly blissed out when danger likely lurked somewhere in these mirrors. But I wanted her more than anything else in this moment, and I could tell she wanted the same.

Focus, you idiot! Are you trying to get both of you killed?

I forced myself to slow the kiss, then pulled back. She leaned in closer.

"I'm not done kissing you," she said, her voice husky and sexy as fuck.

"Not here." I ran my thumb over her bottom lip. "But later," I promised.

I glanced around at the Hall of Mirrors, seeing our still entwined bodies reflected back at us. Except . . . not us now, standing there and looking in the surfaces, but as if we'd continued making out.

"We look hot together," I said.

Sadie frowned before taking my hand and pulling us farther down the hall. As we walked, the images of us in the mirrors grew hotter and heavier, clothes beginning to fall away. I was now very glad Torent had been locked out.

"We thought the maze had been about fears," I said, "but this seems to be quite the opposite."

"Um . . . I don't know about that," Sadie murmured.

"What does that mean? You fear me? Us?" My head tilted as I looked sideways at her. "You don't need to, Sadie. I won't—"

"Oh shit," she said on a heavy sigh as she came to a stop.

Our images in the mirrors were no longer alone. Sadie's friends and other elves surrounded us. Her reflected self suddenly broke away from our embrace, her eyes filled with fear as she looked from me to the others, shaking her head in denial. My brows furrowed as I turned toward the real Sadie, studying her face, which was just as fear-filled as her reflection. On a mirror behind her, her reflection shoved me away, tears streaming down her face as she seemed to silently plea with the others.

Realization dawned on me.

"You fear us, but not in the way I thought." My heart, which had been bursting with fullness just moments ago, shrunk and hardened, falling to the pit of my stomach like a stone. "Holy hell. And now it all makes sense." I ripped my hand from her grasp.

"Elli—"

I shook my head, blinking against the burn in my eyes. "You're *ashamed* of us! Of me! That's why you don't ever want to be seen with me. Am I not good enough for you? Is that it?"

"Elli, please," she begged. "Let me explain."

"No explanation necessary. I deserve better."

She reached for me as I turned and strode back for the door. I'd find a way to open it, because I couldn't stay here with her a moment longer.

"You're right. You do," she called out after me.

The knob wouldn't turn, so I put all of my supernatural strength into busting the door down. To no avail, of course.

"Then why would you do this to me?" I demanded. "You started this whole thing, but you're ashamed of it? Talk about fucking with someone's emotions!" I directed my anger into my magic, throwing a pulse of energy at the door. Nothing.

"I'm so sorry." Her words were strangled as though she choked with emotion. "You deserve to be treated like a princess. You're intelligent and beautiful. So brave and courageous. You don't care what anyone else thinks. You embrace who you are, even the Darkness, and that authenticity makes you so much more alive than most people. Makes you more understanding and caring, kinder than you probably realize. More than you give yourself credit for. You're everything I've ever wanted, Elliana. I wish—" She drew in a stuttered breath. "I wish I could walk proudly with you on my arm."

I spun around, finding her still several paces away, standing in the middle of the Hall of Mirrors, tears rolling down her cheeks.

Her reflections were true now—hundreds of Sadies staring at me with pleading blue eyes.

"But you don't," I accused as I strode toward her. Angry energy flickered over my fingers and palms, and I fisted my hands to keep fire from spewing from them. "You hide me. You play with my emotions, making me think you care and want to be with me one moment, but then barely acknowledge me as soon as we're in public. So what the hell, Sadie? You say all these things, but you don't mean them. You say what I deserve, but it's still not good enough for you. You think you deserve better than me?"

She dropped her eyes, shaking her head. "No. I don't even deserve you."

I stopped a few feet in front of her and folded my arms over my chest, keeping my hands fisted under my biceps. The Dark energy lit up within me, begging to let loose. Breathing deeply, I called on my Amadis power, calming myself and the beast within me.

"Then why are you so ashamed of me? Of us?" I asked quietly.

She didn't respond at first, but eventually lifted her lids, looking at me through her lashes. Our eyes locked for a long moment, and I watched as something shifted in her.

"I'm not ashamed of you," she said. "Not at all. I just . . ." She hesitated again, her gaze bouncing around before coming back to me. "Elli . . . I haven't come out. I can *never* come out. My friends and family can never know I'm gay."

Shock trapped my breath in my lungs. Why had I never considered that? My mouth hung open as thoughts and emotions swirled through me.

"You can't live your life like that," I finally said. "That's not fair to you. Or to those you love."

She blinked, more tears filling her eyes. "I *have* to. I'm not like other elves. There are expectations of me. My family and our people need me to carry on our bloodline and power. I'm betrothed and everything. They can never know I'm anything but committed fully to the cause, or it will destroy us all. It's the same reason my mother can't say what I know to be true. There are too many lives depending on us."

Now my heart morphed from feeling like a cold rock to filling with sadness. "You deserve to be happy, and you never will be if you pretend you're someone you're not."

Her shoulder lifted in a shrug. "I have no choice. My family and my people need me."

"They need this so much that they don't care about you? About *your* feelings and *your* needs?" Renewed anger rose, but aimed at another target.

"My feelings and needs—my happiness—they can't matter."

"Bullshit," I snarled. "That's crap, Sadie. What kind of family would make such demands of someone they supposedly love?"

"The royal kind," she whispered, turning away from me.

My brows pinched together, and my head shook. "Nope. I don't buy it. My family is royalty. We have a ton of expectations. But they would never expect me to be someone I'm not, especially when it comes to love."

"Then you're lucky. Besides, they still have Brielle. Would they be so accepting if they only relied on *you* to carry on their bloodline and power?" Her words were tight and cold and felt like a slap in the face.

My anger turned once again. "You know what? I call bullshit again. Your friends aren't like that. I know them. Fig—Fig is awesome. I can't believe she would want you to be anything but happy. So either it's all in your head or you're just making up lies to push me away. Well, congratulations. You've done it. I won't be with someone who can't truly be with me."

I waved my hand at the mirrors as I strode toward the door again. They all cracked and shards of glass fell to the floor, shattering the illusion of Sadie and me—the illusion of us.

The door opened when I tried it.

I sat in the window seat of our dorm room, gazing down at the campus below blanketed in a fresh layer of snow and thinking about what had happened in the Hall of Mirrors. My chest ached —for Sadie, for me, for everyone who felt the need to hide who they truly were and whom they loved because of others' expectations. I'd been awful to Sadie, but at the same time, I knew

I couldn't be in a relationship based on lies and secrets. That just wasn't me. The Darkness bubbled within as I thought about how terrible people were for making such demands on the people they supposedly cared for.

"You okay?" Brielle asked, coming over to the window and sliding her arm over my shoulder. She must have sensed that Darkness when she came into the room.

I tamped it down as I watched Infiniti Clausman and Joe Greg making out in the quad below. Did they appreciate the freedom they had to show their love so openly? Or did they take it for granted as most people did?

"Do you think Mom and Dad would be so accepting of me if you didn't exist?" I asked as I still stared out the window.

"Why? You planning my murder?" she teased as she pushed me closer to the window with her butt and slid in next to me. Her arm tightened around me as she rested her chin on my shoulder, gazing down at the scene below. "They love you and accept you, no matter what, Elli."

"But would they if you weren't here to continue the bloodline? You know how the Amadis are."

"And so does Mom. She would never put on either of us the demands they put on her. She didn't let them dictate whom she would love and whom she would be with. Thank God and the angels or Dad wouldn't be our dad. Neither of them would do that to us." She paused, then added, "As long as whoever it is doesn't hurt us—I can't imagine what Dad or Mom would do, but it wouldn't be pretty!"

She was right. I'd always known that, but I'd let Sadie's words get to me, creating unnecessary doubt.

We sat quietly together, lost in our thoughts about our parents and home. The familiar ache in my chest rose, bringing tears to my eyes.

"I miss them so much," I whispered.

"Me, too, Els. Me, too."

Silence stretched out once again as we leaned our heads together. Joe and Infiniti below headed toward Halstein Hall, arms around each other.

"Besides, there are other ways to continue a bloodline," Brie finally said. "And Mom and Dad always say there's too much hate and fear in our world as it is, especially in the Before time, and look what happened as a result." Everyone at home who'd lived before the War of Armageddon referred to then as the Before time —Before the war, Before the end of the world. All because of hate and fear, created and nourished by the demons. "They'd never condemn love in any of its forms," she continued. "We need more of it, not less. Something this world needs to realize before it's too late and it ends up like ours."

"No shit," I muttered. *And apparently the Faerie realm, too. Or, at least, the elves.*

Of course, Brielle was right again. In fact, Mom and Dad had both said the same thing pretty much word for word when I'd first told them about my attraction to girls and not boys. Even long before then, they'd made it very clear to everyone they ruled that they wouldn't stand for bigotry and behavior that condemned love in any way. I hadn't appreciated enough their own unconditional love. I'd apparently taken for granted what I thought all parents would be like with their children.

Poor Sadie.

My already heavy heart hurt even more for her. And anger simmered under the surface. How dare anyone dictate to someone else something so personal and individual as who they loved!

How fucking dare they.

CHAPTER 7

I stood in front of the black door, staring at the wrought iron key that had appeared in my hand when I'd left Sadie yesterday. Torent had been right—the black door was mine. As black as my soul, he'd said. He wasn't completely wrong, and Sadie wasn't totally right. The Dark energy within me hadn't blackened my soul, but it sure as hell tried. And I didn't own it and embrace it as well as Sadie thought. I don't think anyone understood just how dark and powerful the beast within me was. *I* didn't know, and I was honestly afraid to find out. I kept her locked up a lot tighter than anyone could ever realize, even my twin. Because if I let her loose? I shuddered at the thought. They all believed I had dark tendencies now—they had no idea what truly lurked deep below. Hopefully they'd never find out.

Which was one reason I stood alone right now. If the doors opened to what we feared most, then that would be myself, and I couldn't unleash that on anybody else. Not even Torent—in fact, if the Darkness overcame me and took me out of my right mind, he would probably be my first target, his kind being my sworn enemy and all. Slaine was still out of sorts, and I had no idea what to do about Sadie. I didn't want to deal with that right now. I just wanted to finish this first mission so we could move on, however that might be.

Inhaling a deep breath, I stepped up to the black door and inserted the key. On the exhale, I twisted the knob and pushed.

My brows pulled together. I looked over at the blue door, which was tightly shut again, just to make sure—because mine hung open to show the exact same Hall of Mirrors.

"Not what I expected," I muttered as I stepped inside, the door slamming shut behind me.

The ambient lighting—from where it came, I couldn't tell—dimmed as I walked forward, coming even with the first mirrors. At first, they reflected back my image in the fighting leathers I'd donned just in case things went wonky in here—the black leather corset, pants, and knee-high boots were specially enchanted to protect me. With the way the mirrors were set and angled, I could see my backside and admired my ass for a moment before calling on my wings and admiring them. I only had an idea of what they looked like from behind because I'd seen my twin's. I was glad to see mine were just as impressive. Pleased, I hid them again.

As I shifted my weight to take a step, the image began to change. Though the lighting in the hall remained the same, it changed in the mirrors, bringing a harsher effect to my skin, highlighting angles in my cheekbones, browbone, and jawline that weren't so hard and sharp in real life. My upper lip curled in a smirk, and my eyes changed, too, darkening and glinting, making my overall expression look arrogant and threatening. Dangerous and . . . dark.

I moved on, my reflection following me to the next mirrors, still morphing, becoming a monster of nightmares. I only looked at her from the corner of my eye, because I knew what she really was—the beast inside of me. I didn't want to see her fully. I didn't want to know what she might look like. I didn't want to risk seeing that she was beautiful.

A large paw with sharp claws longer than my fingers swiped at the surface, and for a second I thought she was going to come through. At the same time, the real beast inside me whined and mewled to be free.

"No," I said aloud, my voice loud and firm. Thank the angels it didn't sound as freaked out as I felt. "You stay."

The image in the mirror dissipated into a black fog, and the beast within me quieted, though she still didn't settle down. I moved on.

The next mirrors were like windows into my home world—I saw my parents and extended family that made up my mom's council huddled over a table, studying something. As though an invisible hand swiped through a wet painting, the image distorted and then disappeared. Now I saw them outside at night, taking off hurriedly toward something in the next mirrors. I ran to keep up with them, only to see them ambushed by a cluster of demons.

"No!" I shouted. "Mom! Dad!"

Of course, they couldn't hear me. I glanced around, looking at the other mirrors. Only I couldn't really see the Hall of Mirrors anymore—I'd been transported to join them. The air was acrid with smoke and sulfur and brimstone. Large plumes of flames licked the sky from a town in the distance, but between here and there, Mom, Dad, and our people fought the demons. No, not just demons, for they weren't our only enemies. All kind of supernaturals and humans, too, were fighting each other as the world burned around them.

Was this the past, during the war? Or the present or the future? I had no way of knowing for sure. When we'd left to come to this world, our own had been on the brink of another world war. Our mother might have even started it. Was this what was happening while we were here, safe and sound? It made sense that the mission would bring me here. Besides myself, my next biggest fear was that we'd left our parents and our people to fight another war because of us, because of Brielle and me and the power we possessed that others wanted to use—or to destroy. The power I kept locked up tightly.

I took to the air and soared toward them to join in the fighting, but before I could reach them, a plume of black smoke blossomed and surrounded me. I tumbled in the air for a moment before aiming for the ground and crash landing as I heaved and choked. Magic darker than even what lived inside me permeated the air, even as the smoke cleared.

Transported from the scene of the battle, I stood to find myself near the dimensional gate my sister and I had unintentionally opened when we were little. Our brother had opened a gate that crossed dimensions to this alternate version of our world, the one of Havenwood Falls that we called the shiny place. It was how we'd come here. Brielle and I, though, opened a gate to a world of blackness and death and unadulterated evil.

And it was swarming through.

"NO!" I screamed, spinning around, looking for help, but I was alone in the dead, black forest surrounding the portal.

Not counting the dark creatures charging into my world. They took off as soon as they came through, scattering to all ends of the earth, I imagined, and I didn't know what to do to stop them. My beast came fully alert again, the dark energy calling to her, and I wondered if she could help—and if that was a good idea.

Come join us, a voice hissed, the sound coming from everywhere around me. *You brought us here, young one. Now come join us.*

I spun again, but saw nobody. Until I faced the gate again. Black fog poured out and began to take the shape of four massive horses standing at least three or four stories high. On top of each sat a figure of proportionate size. I could see no features, but could tell they wore some kind of armor, including helmets with spiked crowns. Neither the figures nor the horses solidified, as though they were formed only of black energy. The riders' vaporous legs blended into the horses and the smoke surrounding them. Their eyes, though, glowed a bright red like laser beams, and they were all trained on me, boring into me as though they were, indeed, laser beams aiming for my soul.

My beast reared up and shoved against the internal cage I kept her in.

You called. We are here. Though the voice still came from all around me, I knew they had spoken. All of them, as one.

I shook my head. "I did not. Go back where you came from!"

Too late.

The humongous horses charged forward, and before I could do anything, one of the figures swept its arm down, grabbed me, and threw me on the back of the ephemeral horse. I tried to fight and shout and even fly off the horse's back, but the dark energy stilled and silenced me, locking me in place. All I could do was watch in horror as the horses galloped across the lands, decimating everything in their path to black ash.

We came upon the burning town and my people still in battle, but didn't stop. As we passed them by, they were obliterated too.

No. No, no, no. This can't be happening.

Tears streamed down my cheeks as I looked over my shoulder at what was left in the wake of these four horsemen—nothing but smoke and ash. When I turned back to see where we headed, I saw the familiar black sand beach where our brother Dorian had taken us for our escape, where he'd opened his gate. And there it was—the gate to this world, to Havenwood Falls.

"NO!" I yelled at the top of my lungs. "YOU CAN'T GO THERE!"

I was suddenly falling and landed hard on my ass, back in the Hall of Mirrors. My breath came in pants as I jumped to my feet and looked around. The glass surfaces reflected back dozens of me and their own images, like normal mirrors again.

"What the fuck," I muttered as I tried to calm my heart and breathing. What had been the point of all that if I was right back where I started—and no artifact in hand?

Swearing in all kinds of ways, I walked up and down the long hall, watching the mirrors for some kind of hint, but they remained normal. Not knowing what else to do, I went for the door, but there was no knob, no way to open it. I knocked my fists on it a few times, in case someone was on the other side, though I knew that was futile. Turning back to the mirrors, all I could think to do was to start shattering them. Just as I began to gather my magic while trying to decide on the proper intent for a quick spell, pounding came from behind me.

"Elliana!" Sadie's voice shouted from the other side.

"Elli, are you in there?" Brielle was with her.

I lunged for the door and banged on it again. "I'm here! But I can't get out!"

"Elliana?" Sadie said again, her pitch rising, sounding almost panicked. "Elli, please! Stop!"

Not panicked. Scared. She continued to cry out, as though begging for her life.

"Help us!" Brie screamed, adding to it. "No! *Please!*"

Other voices shouted and shrieked, all of them filled with fear and pleas. What the hell was going on out there?

I moved my hands over the plane of the door, trying to feel for the magical energy keeping it closed. The ruckus on the other side grew louder, the despair intensifying. My heart pounded as their panic and fear washed through me. Then I felt it—the magic.

Dark. Terrifyingly dark.

The same energy of the four horsemen.

Movement in the closest mirror caught my eye, and I rounded on it. All of the mirrors filled with images of the Halvard campus. It was like last semester, when Brielle's Darkness had leaked out and tried to take over all of the students. But this was worse. So much worse. The four horsemen were out there, destroying everything in their wake again, the beautiful towers reduced to smoke and ash . . . and they headed for the portals that would take them out of the mountain, into Havenwood Falls, into this shiny world.

No. We weren't supposed to let this happen.

"Elliana!" Brielle yelled, still on the other side of the door. "You have the power to end this!"

"You can do this, Elli," Sadie joined her. "Let it out! All of it out!"

My beast—that Darkness within—threw herself against my hold on her. She thrashed and kicked, begging me to let her free. Could she end this? Or would she only add to it?

There was only one way to find out. I internally reached for the hold I had on her.

No. You've done it before with terrible consequences. This is not the way. My own voice spoke to me from somewhere within, perhaps from my soul. I didn't fully understand—I'd never unleashed my full power before. Had I? But then Addie's voice slid in, a memory from class, about tapping into our intuition.

"The world is not always as it seems. Things around you are not what they appear to be," she'd said in class. And then what she'd said about the High Priestess . . .

The card—the poem and the image, the mission. I'd nearly forgotten that was why I was even here, swallowed up by the illusions around me.

74

Illusions.

"These are only illusions," I said aloud. The High Priestess symbolized illusions and using intuition to pierce the veil and reveal what was beyond.

My gaze swept over the mirrors, the horrifying images continuing to play out around campus as people yelled from the other side of the door. I saw and heard it all, as though it was truly happening in the physical world around me, but I felt in my gut, in my soul that none of it was real. Knowing the proper intent now, I gathered my magic inside me—the good, not the Darkness —and let it build, warming my chest and tingling along my arms, down to my fingers. I lifted my hands, palms out toward the mirrors on each side of the hall.

"This is not real. Reveal the truth," I ordered as I pushed the power outward.

Glass exploded and shattered down the hall, the mirrors breaking one by one until a deafening silence fell. There was no more pounding or screaming from the other side of the door. No knob yet, either, so I wasn't done. Which was apparent by the new arrival at the far end of the hall.

It looked like a curtain made of the night sky, similar to the one hanging behind the High Priestess on our card. On the card, however, the smooth water and background could be seen through the star-dusted curtain. This one was opaque, whatever was beyond it indecipherable. I tried to swipe the curtain to the side, but there was no edge to it, and my hand went right through it. I jerked it back to me, holding my fist to my chest.

The last lines of the poem came to me, and I recited them out loud. "Through planes of darkness and realms of light, you'll find what you seek behind the veil of night." I blew out a heavy breath. "Okay, then. Here goes nothing."

I jumped through the veil.

My wings snapped out, though I didn't really need them. I wasn't on the ground, but gravity didn't pull me down either, as though it didn't even exist wherever I was. Starlight and colorful clouds surrounded me, but at a distance. In my immediate space was a whole lot of nothing, as though I was in the space between planes and realms.

And there—there was an ankh, about six inches tall with various symbols and runes etched into the silver, hanging in midair. My hand closed around it, and a bodiless female voice rang around me.

"What you saw will come to pass if you do not do what needs to be done. You must close what you have opened. You must stop what you have started. You must return where you began. Or all worlds will end."

The female's voice was otherworldly. Angelic. Divine. I wondered if she was one of my ancestors, if the angels had bothered to finally communicate with us again—or if it was just another illusion.

At least it's better than the horsemen, I thought as the stars faded and I was returned to the Hall of Mirrors, the ankh in my hand.

"Elliana!" Sadie's voice came from the other side, still panicked.

I ran for the door, and it opened just before I reached it. For some reason, though, there was a pile of rocks in front of it, a small opening at the top.

"Elli?" Brielle's face popped into the space above, Sadie's peeking behind her. Smudges of dirt marred their otherwise perfect features. "Stand back." Then they both disappeared.

"I'll do it," Sadie said.

"I don't think so," Charleigh said from somewhere up there. "That affliction power of yours nearly destroyed the whole library and created this mess." Her faced popped into view. "Hold on, Elli. We're coming."

Magic zinged downward, and the pile of stones disintegrated into a mound of sand. I climbed up it as Brie and Sadie reached down, each gripping one of my wrists. They hauled me up to a small crowd of our friends, including Fig and the other elves. Brie and Charleigh gave me a quick group hug, but Sadie's hand on my wrist hadn't released, and she tugged me around.

Her electric blue gaze traveled from my head to my feet, lingering on the ankh briefly, before coming back to my face. Her lips stretched into a smile filled with relief. "You're okay."

"I—" I started, but she didn't let me finish. She pulled me into her, her free hand slipping around my waist and her mouth crashing on mine.

"Woowoo!" Fig teased as others whistled and cat-called.

Sadie and I broke apart to see her friends cheering us on.

"You were right," she said. "They just want me to be happy."

"Congratulations to the first team to complete The Hunt mission," Addie said at our next ITF class, holding up the ankh. "I believe it was harder than they expected, so the rest of you be warned. Now back to our regular scheduled programming." She turned the class over to Professor Timothy Wu, who was new to the school and taught healing arts.

After class, Sadie and I returned to Modi together.

"I need to talk to you about something," she said as we began climbing the spiral staircase. "Something really important that you need to know. Important as in, well, kind of life-changing."

My heart sank. I didn't know what she had to say, but I had a feeling she wanted to take our relationship to the next level now that she knew she had support among her own people.

"I need to talk to you, too," I admitted, internally cussing because I so was not ready for this. But I had to, and probably the sooner the better. We exited the stairs on her floor. "And I should probably go first because it might change whatever you have to tell me."

She snorted as she opened her door. "I don't think this is something that can be changed, but okay."

I waited until we dropped our book bags and we both sat on the edge of her bed. My stomach churned and my heart already hurt as I prepared to deliver the speech I'd recited numerous times in my head the last couple of days. After I told Brielle and Charleigh about the visions and the divine voice in the Hall of Mirrors, we'd agreed on what needed to be done.

When I looked into those expectant electric blues, though, I nearly chickened out.

"Fuck," I breathed, averting my eyes as I pushed a hand through my hair.

"Are you . . . breaking up with me?" Alarm filled her voice, and when I looked back at her, she was blinking back tears. Damn, she was making this so hard. I needed to just do it.

"Not exactly," I started, and she pulled away, scooting up on her pillows and grabbing one to hold to her chest.

"What does that mean?" she whispered.

"We might have to go home," I blurted, the words coming out in a rush before I changed my mind. "Brie and Charleigh and me. We might have to go home sooner than expected. I don't know when. Charleigh's trying to reach our parents, but it's magic crossing dimensions, so who the hell knows how that's working. But I learned something during that mission, and I don't know if it's true or not, but if we find out that it is—or worse, we don't get an answer—we need to go back."

I wanted to blame Addie for insisting that I trust my intuition, but it wasn't her fault. In fact, if it weren't for her, I probably would have blown off the voice behind the veil or this persistent feeling that could mean life or death for our loved ones there and maybe even here. I just hated the not knowing part and had already decided that if we didn't hear anything by the end of the semester, we needed to act.

Sadie blew out a breath, her head bobbing up and down and one shoulder lifting and dropping. "Okay. Well, we knew this was going to happen sooner or later, right? For either of us or both. But we still have right now, yeah?"

Hope replaced the fear in her face of moments ago, and all I could do was smile and nod. "Yeah, we have right now."

I grabbed her hands and pulled her to me, wrapping my arms around her slender figure, and she returned the embrace before pulling slightly away to kiss me. For a very long time.

"So what did you want to tell me?" I asked when we finally broke apart.

"Oh, um . . ." She hesitated, her gaze darting about before coming back to me. "Kind of the same thing, really. That I'll have to go home this summer. I have to talk to my parents and the elders, and I honestly don't know if they'll let me come back for next semester."

"So . . . you were going to break up with me?"

"No, no. There was something . . . never mind, that part's not important right now. I was going to see if you wanted to come to Faerie with me, though, for a visit. I know that won't be possible now, but maybe some time in the future?"

I blinked in shock, a thrill running through me for the briefest of moments until reality hit. "I'd love that. I really would. Unfortunately, now—"

She squeezed my hands. "That's the thing, Elliana. The Faerie realms are connected to each other. You're part fae, so you can get in. All you have to do is get to Faerie, and we should be able to find each other again."

"Seriously?"

"Seriously. All hope for us is not lost, Elliana Knight. But in the meantime . . . we still have right now."

I nodded. "Let's make the most of it."

And so we did.

THE HANGED MAN

BELINDA BORING

To my sweet niece, Maisie. My world is more magical with you in it. Thank you for all the kisses you blow me when we video chat. Love you 3000!

CHAPTER 1

$\mathcal{H}$er pitiful sobs tugged sharply on my heartstrings, drawing me closer as if there were a thread of suffering that connected us intimately.

I hadn't seen her face yet, but I knew that her tears were those of pure, unadulterated grief and sorrow. No, that was wrong. I didn't know—I *felt* them, understanding them so absolutely like they were my own.

Her long blond hair fell loosely like a curtain that hid her features from onlookers. The palms of her hands curved over her cheeks, and her slender fingers held a constant tremble as they hovered over her eyes. I wanted to gather the miserable creature into my arms and shield her from the pains of the world—to protect her as though she was mine to cherish.

What kind of misery and Hell had she faced? More importantly, was she still trapped there in an endless spiral of suffering?

My chest constricted, making it almost impossible to draw in each breath.

"Hello?" I whispered. White puffs of air escaped my mouth. The strange woman seemed oblivious to the cold—the thin shift-like dress barely covering her. In fact, the night chill was biting at my own exposed skin. "Miss, can I help you?"

Nothing. Not even a break in her whimpers. If anything, her

body shudders grew stronger as a new wave of sobs coursed through her.

I stepped closer and looked around, desperately trying to find some kind of clue. Was she hurt? Lost? Why wouldn't she answer?

Somewhere in the distance, a wolf howled, baying at the moon that illuminated the night sky.

"Please, let me help you. You're not safe here." My boot struck the concrete ledge she was sitting on, and now that I could see better, I realized it was a stoned tomb.

Grief. The beautiful stranger was lost in heartache and mourning.

I dragged my fingers through my hair, nervous—my tongue darting out to wet my lips. I sat down beside her, hoping she'd start to sense my presence when I bumped into something and sent it clattering to the hard ground.

Shit. A chalice. I scrambled to place the dusty and neglected object back beside her, but instantly dropped it again because suddenly a cacophony of loud hissing filled the air. As if through magic, the cup overflowed with angry serpents, weaving back and forth, their bodies tangling with each other. Snakes didn't normally scare me. Since my birth I'd felt an affinity with the creatures, but that wasn't the emotion bubbling up inside me—banging hard against my mind as they demanded attention.

They knew me.

They sensed my innate connection with them—an all too familiar tug of kinship.

What the fuck was happening here?

Abandoning the cup, one serpent slithered its way toward me, slowly curling its cool scaled body around my wrist. All the while, the stranger continued to bury her face in her hands, oblivious to my presence. No matter how gently and then hard I tried to shake the reptile loose, it had fully encircled my arm now with its forked tongue testing the air. I was missing something—something important, but for the life of me I didn't know what.

The only certainty I had was that I was meant to be here in this precise moment and that it held some kind of meaning.

Eryx, the soft voice whispered. Cold-laced dread filled my heart as sweat trickled down my back. It couldn't be. Not her.

You can't remain hidden forever. I will find you, boy.

A gruesome specter appeared above us with tendrils of ghostly hair spreading out across the breeze. While she didn't reveal her true form, I would've known that cruel voice anywhere. Poets and minstrels might have sung ballads in her praise and worship, but I was all too aware of the darker side to the goddess.

There was always a flip side to every emotion and intention, so while others focused more on her beauty and love, I saw her for what she truly was.

A monster.

Always drawn to the tears of the victim, Eryx, crooned the specter seductively. *So pathetically like your mother. Return to me, boy, so I may end your suffering. Succumb to the emptiness you crave.*

Lies. Her tongue was more barbed than the serpents hissing beside me. Despite being distracted, I could still feel the snake that now rested on my shoulder, its head next to my hair. Comfort infused me, as though the slight weight from its body acted like a mother's touch.

My mother's touch.

I stood and faced the ghost down, refusing to crumble with fear. "Be gone, demon," I yelled. "Accept you hold no power."

Her response was a tinkling, hollow sound that failed to support her confidence. I'd expected her to throw more threats my way and remind me of the torture that awaited me once she found where I was hiding. Instead, she pointed out into the distance toward the grove of trees.

There, hanging from a branch, was a man suspended by one foot.

"Heed the signs," came a new voice. Her voice. The young woman with the endless sobs. "Pay attention, Eryx. Tears demand vengeance."

A snake's head escaped from between her lips, and it was only then I realized that I was encased by countless serpents, each one constricting around my body.

The specter laughed again, further witness that she'd never stop hunting me.

All I could do was scream, and scream, and scream.

"Eryx. Wake up!"

Jolting up from my bed, it took me a few seconds to realize where I was. Instead of being confronted by the now fading scene of depression and darkness, I found myself staring into the concerned eyes of my girlfriend, Tempest. The relief I felt at seeing her was almost crushing, and without thinking, I drew her into me, wrapping my arms around her body.

"My god," I uttered, fully aware of how weird I sounded. Last thing I remembered was sitting on the bed while we both studied and finished up assignments for class. Her presence in my room was starting to become a welcomed sight—even though it was also an incredible distraction. One moment I'd be reviewing class notes for potions, and next I'd be wondering what it would be like to throw my work to the side and spend the rest of the afternoon making out with her.

Damn could Tempest kiss. In all my life, I'd never met anyone who could set my blood on fire and addle my thoughts like her. Even I knew she was a once-in-a-lifetime woman, and it had killed me to keep her at arms-length for so long.

I'd never felt my curse and innate power so keenly. I'd have sold my soul to Hades himself if it hadn't been for the fact that somehow, by some incredible miracle, Tempest remained unaffected by the mistakes I'd made.

I still couldn't believe that revelation.

"Ssshh," she whispered, realizing that something had shaken me to my core. I knew that I'd been caught up in a dream—a nightmare—but my body hadn't quite caught up to that truth, and I still shook. Her hand rubbed up and down my back, her other arm tightening around me. "You're safe, Eryx. I promise you. Whatever it was, it's not real."

Why did her kindness prickle tears in the back of my eyes? Was I that bereft of tenderness and comfort that the simplest of affection touched me so deeply?

I pushed the thoughts away. My past was exactly that, and for right now, this was all that mattered—being in her arms.

"What can I say?" I chuckled softly, hoping to diffuse the

heaviness in the air to something lighter. The last thing I wanted to do was talk about my dream, and I knew my girlfriend well—she would be relentless in trying to drag the truth out of me. Hell, it was her persistence and tenacity that had broken down my resistance to a relationship. God, I loved her for that. "This semester is already messing with my mind!"

She gave me the look—the one that said she knew I was full of shit. "Seriously? Is that the story you're going with, Strathos?" Her eyebrow arched as she waited.

I had to think fast. I didn't want to try to explain why I was dreaming about the card we'd chosen for the Hunt mission in the new task force class we shared, and I sure as hell didn't want to talk about how the voice that tormented me might be connected.

I'd run long and far from any enemies that might still be searching for me. Sun & Moon Academy was supposed to be my sanctuary from all that.

Trouble was . . . you can't always hide from your problems.

I pulled her into me, flipped her over so I was now spread out across her, and lowered my lips to hers. "Yep," I murmured as I brushed away a strand of her hair that had caught on her long eyelashes. "That and I plead the fifth."

My gaze dropped to her mouth as she slowly smiled back up at me.

"On the grounds that it might incriminate you? Now I'm even more curious." She dragged her fingernails up and down over my bare arms, and I shuddered in pleasure. "I have ways of making you talk . . . skills."

Shit. She shifted beneath me, and the subtle movement made me a believer. I didn't think she realized just how crazy she drove me. Not that I would ever complain.

Two could play at that game, however, and I wasn't ready to yield. "I have my own talents, Tempest." Licking my lips, I leaned in ever-so-slightly until my face barely hovered over hers. "I can make you forget your name."

Her eyes flashed with surprise that I'd make such a claim and then smoldered. "Is that so?" She hooked her leg around mine as a way to bring us closer. "Prove it."

Tempest didn't need to repeat her challenge. I crushed my

mouth down over hers and kissed her with everything I had, savoring the way she tasted when our tongues touched.

All that mattered was her.

Being with her.

Drowning in her.

Feeling safe from my past.

Tempest was a goddess in her own right.

I didn't know who groaned first—me or her—but there was one thing blatantly obvious, and that was the dream was forgotten.

CHAPTER 2

"Can I confess something completely cheesy?" Tempest's voice was soft and languid.

We'd both spent the last few minutes staring up at my room's ceiling, cuddled up with each other. I wanted to answer her—I really did—but somewhere between the endless kissing and breathing, I'd lost the ability to form a cohesive thought. All I could do was grunt and kind of nod my head.

I was rewarded with one of those laughs she gave that filled me with a wicked sense of pride knowing I'd caused it. Fuck, if I was going to be one hundred percent honest here, my ego was also inflated because the last time I snuck a peek at the beautiful girl in my arms, she looked thoroughly ravished—with tell-tale whisker burn from my stubbled jawline rubbing against her sensitive skin.

Tempest cleared her throat and then whispered into my chest as though she was embarrassed. "I could spend forever right here, right now, the world be damned."

That comment sent my thoughts straight to the bloody gutter.

"Well," I started, making the effort to speak so she knew exactly what I'd do to her if we had that kind of time. "I have a few ideas, sweetheart. Just say the word, and I'll pick up where we stopped."

I lazily trailed my finger down over her arm and watched as

goosebumps erupted. Tempest was definitely reactive, and I couldn't wait to see how else her body responded to my touch.

Unfortunately, our forever would have to wait. A loud beeping sounded, followed by an equally annoying moan from Tempest.

She slipped out from under my arm and padded over to where her phone rested with her bag and homework.

"What do you call it when you kill your alarm? Clock-icide? Buzz-tricide?" With deft fingers, she silenced the alert and looked over at me forlornly. "Explain to me the importance of going to class, Eryx, please. I'm sure I'd learn more staying with you." She kicked her bag in protest only to bend over and start filling it with her stuff.

I propped myself up on my elbows and watched her. I wanted to agree with her and throw responsibility out the window. Screw class and trying to be adults. What was life if we didn't make a few mistakes along the way, right?

I knew my girlfriend, though, or at least I thought I did. Tempest liked to talk a good game, but her education was important to her. Last semester had thoroughly kicked her ass— her words—and she'd spent most of the time convinced she was about to be booted out by the Board of Regents. Working in her favor was a literal guardian angel in her corner, fighting on her behalf. Micah Westbrook, one of the academy's professors, had taken it upon himself to be her benefactor and was a pretty decent guy. There was a lot to respect about him.

"Let me walk you to class, okay?" I added, tugging on my shoes. "I can finish up my studying at the library before heading to my later class." I didn't tell her that I'd found an even quieter place to hang out when not together. I liked to think of it as my own private oasis. One day I'd share it with her, but for right now, I didn't have many things that I could call exclusively mine. It felt good. "Then maybe we can catch up for something to eat?"

Tempest nodded, her bag already slung over her shoulder. She peered into one of the mirrors I had hung on the wall and tried to smooth out her hair. While I thought bedhead was sexy as fuck, I knew she didn't want to traipse around campus looking disheveled. With a quick layer of lip gloss, she puckered her lips, and turned back to face me. "Sounds perfect."

Everything was going fine, I was almost ready myself, when something caught her attention, and her smile turned into a frown.

"Eryx?" she asked, pointing over to the pile of schoolwork on my desk. "You've already started working on the card assignment?" Sure enough, she now held the notes I'd jotted down. Shit.

We were both enrolled in the Interdisciplinary Task Force and had luckily been assigned into the same group of four. One of the assignments was to search for some kind of artifact, clues for it given on a card with images that we needed to decipher and solve. The card we'd chosen was actually quite beautiful in design and reminded us of a tarot card when we'd first discussed it. Because it seemed the most complicated out of the four projects for the semester, we'd placed it at the bottom of our priority list. Without much argument, everyone also allowed me to be the team leader.

In their minds, it was simply a divvying up of responsibility, and I'd volunteered to spearhead that particular task. To me, though, the second I'd seen the images, I felt sucker-punched and couldn't claim it fast enough.

My dreams—my nightmares.

They were the same images from the card.

Holding it in my hand that first time, I felt nothing but unadulterated paranoia. Somehow, *she* had not only found me through the countless wardings and protective spells I'd cast, but she was toying with me—her sick game she loved to play throughout the centuries.

In my naivety, I'd hoped that she'd give up and forget my *almost* deadly kiss eons ago, but her threats still echoed in my ears. She wasn't used to being vulnerable or hurt, and somehow, I'd managed to do that. The goddess hated to feel powerless, and she'd been quite descriptive with how she'd punish me once she was done playing her cat and mouse game. Her pride had been attacked, but I couldn't let her win, that much was obvious. I'd run that night and hadn't stopped since. Now that I had Tempest in my life, I couldn't let the goddess hurt the one person who meant the world to me.

Especially if my paranoia proved correct and Aphrodite was involved.

Tempest coughed, clearly annoyed that I wasn't answering her quickly enough. "Care to explain?" She held my notes up in her hand. "This is a team project, Eryx. Not some solo mission."

She glanced down at the paper and began to skim read, her lips moving along with her gaze.

"I know, I know," I countered, careful not to rip them as I extracted the notes from her grasp. I did need them back from her because I couldn't remember if I'd included thoughts about my secret. "It wasn't intentional. I had a quick thought, so I jotted it down so I wouldn't forget it. Promise." Folding the paper in half, I slipped it into my own messenger bag. "Now come on. Let's get you to class."

As I guided her to the door, Tempest half pouted for a moment before placing her hand on my chest, stopping me. "Fine. You're forgiven. Truth be told, out of all the missions we were given, the card's the one that intrigues me the most." She rose up on her tiptoes and feathered a light kiss on my lips then winked. "I would've done the exact same thing as you."

I burst out laughing and shoved her through the door. "Ahhh, so that's the reason for the pout! You're just upset I beat you to it?"

"Beat who to what?" came a new voice to the left. For the most part, the hallways here in Modi were quiet, and I'd lucked out in not having to deal with a roommate, but since classes had started again, I kept bumping into one of the other students, Calix.

Turned out he was also a Greek descendant—the very image of some Adonis all chiseled and gorgeous, according to Natalie, Tempest's roommate. Frankly, I tuned them both out whenever they discussed how "dreamy" he was with Marina. It was either that or vomit. Marina could be pretty graphic about what she'd like to do to him.

He was the third member of our task force team. We hadn't had much of a chance to get to know one another but there was something . . . different about him. I couldn't quite put my finger on it, either. It was just a weird feeling I got whenever I saw him.

Tempest liked to tease me and ask if I'd been bitten by a radioactive spider growing up and it was just my Spidey-senses tingling. I'd fire right back that for all she knew I could be Superman or Batman in disguise, so she'd better show more respect for her super-hero boyfriend. She snorted and leveled me with a glare before adding that she was a Marvel girl all the way and I should take my DC Comics references out of her presence.

She chimed in and answered Calix before I could. "This guy's already sneaking in notes for the card assignment." She elbowed me extra hard. "Can you believe it?"

Calix gave me a look as if to say he wasn't quite sure he wanted to get in the middle of this. I didn't blame him. Tempest had the ability to eat him alive if he wasn't careful.

"Hey, why are you complaining? If he finishes it before we get a chance to look at it, it's one less stress for us in that class." He shrugged and slid his hands into the pockets of his black jeans. "It's a win-win if you ask me."

Tempest eyed him closely before chuckling. "I like how you think, Pareias!" She turned to me with a wide smirk. "As you were, Eryx. Don't let us stop you!"

Calix followed us down the hallway to the staircase that led downstairs.

"Before I forget," he chimed in, keeping up pace. He leaned in as if he was sharing some major conspiracy. Guy was too freaking chatty and just needed to go away. "Did you see that Slaine's been given the green light to return to I.T.F. class finally? He's been gone . . . what? One or two weeks?"

We rounded the bend in the descending staircase. Tempest's curiosity was instantly roused. "Something like that. I figured he must've got a nasty case of campus crud. That shit can be brutal and sometimes spell resistant."

I merely grunted my semi-interest and picked up the pace.

Calix briskly shook his head before lowering his voice. "I heard it was because of that Hunt mission. I saw him earlier, and man, the dude looks like crap!" He blew out a low whistle of sympathy. "That and with the explosion the other week—why are we here again?"

"Because we want to be all that we can be and save the world!" Tempest chuckled.

I snorted. "That or we're gluttons for punishment." It hadn't skipped my attention that Sadie and Elli's group had looked pretty banged up. I was hoping it was some kind of training mishap, but Calix's giving voice to the rumors piqued my worry again.

We couldn't have another repeat of last semester with hour glasses and death and chaos.

"Well, what's life if it doesn't test your courage," Calix quipped. He let out a quick sigh before dazzling Tempest with a grin. Ass. "I gotta run and get to my next class. No rest for the wicked." He didn't wait for us to respond.

We were finally outside.

"What an ass," I murmured beneath my breath.

Once he was out of sight, Tempest turned and slapped my arm. "It wouldn't hurt you to be nicer to him. Cut him some slack. You don't want to be known as a mean girl."

I almost choked on my spit. "Are you expecting me to bake him a friendship cake or something? Perhaps invite him over for a late-night hair braiding session?"

I was being ridiculous, but as far as I was concerned, I'd been perfectly fine.

She threw me a sidelong glance filled with disbelief. "I don't find your sarcasm adorable, Mister. I'm not asking you to go out of your way, but he's in our group, and you're practically neighbors. Would it kill you to at least appear like you tolerate him?" She pulled a grumpy face that made me laugh. "That's exactly what you looked like the entire time he walked with us. He probably thinks you want to pee in his Wheaties or something."

Now I couldn't stop laughing. "You got all that from that brief little conversation?"

Tempest tapped her temple lightly with her finger. "Never underestimate the power of a woman's intuition, Eryx. We know things that would make you men weep and cower in fear."

"Duly noted," I answered. Grabbing her hand, I squeezed her fingers before kissing them. "Good thing I have you around to educate me on manners." I bit my tongue from adding that I couldn't pretend that Calix bothered me. Maybe she was right and all I needed to do was put in an effort and those apprehensions would disappear. I didn't tell her that though.

"What can I say? I'm a joy and blessing." Her phone began buzzing again as her alarm rang loudly. "Crap, now I'm really going to be late. Do you mind if we cut this short and I leave you here? If I run non-stop, I should get to class in time for Natalie to roll her eyes at my tardiness."

Being late was one of her superpowers and a constant thorn in her side. Setting alarms was her latest attempt at breaking the habit, and so far, the jury was still out over whether it worked.

"Go." I kissed her, waving her on. "Say hello to your roommate for me as well. Tell her I miss her."

I didn't hear Tempest's response but watched as she waved over her shoulder goodbye. Life was definitely better with her firmly in it.

Letting out a sigh, I looked around and didn't see anyone I knew. I'd told her I was going to the library, but my oasis beckoned, and I knew I wouldn't be interrupted there. I turned around and headed toward Clifftop, where the school's greenhouse was just outside.

Each step I took told me another truth.

What I really wanted was to study the card again, especially after the dream I just had. There was a reason I'd been given it—something beyond Sun & Moon Academy.

My past was knocking on the door again, and if I didn't figure out why, we were all in for a world of hurt.

CHAPTER 3

*T*he peace I felt here was unlike any I'd ever experienced before—and that said something because I'd been alive for an insanely long time. I was born when the Greek gods were at their zenith, experiencing the birth and death of civilizations.

The small private grotto was hidden along a path that led through and past the academy's greenhouse, and it still struck me as odd that I'd been the only one to discover it. I knew no one else came because there was never any evidence to the contrary. The air remained still and undisturbed, welcoming me whenever I stopped by to study or think.

I did that a lot—think. Here I was able to be myself without constantly worrying someone would uncover who I was, revealing the identity I'd spent lifetimes protecting.

It was filled with greenery that clung to the stones, reminding me of a childhood I'd spent surrounded with nature. I assumed that the magic that helped nurture the plants needed for classes spilled outward, so the grotto was filled with small bushes and elegant trees. The place existed in hushed tones and whispers—a reverence that suited my needs.

I thought a lot about my mother and how life would've been different had she lived. From the moment I understood her fate and what she'd been forced to endure, I made it my mission to honor her shortened legacy. While the world and history viewed her as a monster, I knew better.

My mother was a victim of circumstance—of the cruelty that fell upon women of the time. While I couldn't go back and alter time, I would make sure that I held myself to a higher standard. Of course, my curse made that goal a little easy.

Kissing had been impossible, that was until I met Tempest and discovered she was immune.

Whoever heard of a centuries old virgin?

Entering the grotto now, I sat down in my regular spot, my back up against a stone. In front of me, a familiar grave marker stood with designs etched into the granite. I liked to think that it represented all those I'd lost. As I did every time I came, I closed my eyes slowly and offered up a silent supplication that those who suffered would find the mercy and help they needed.

"*Geiá, sou mitéra,*" I greeted, knowing that wherever she was, my mother could hear me. It was a belief I clung to tightly—the image of my mother watching over me with love, proud of what I'd accomplished. "I wish you were here to meet Tempest," I added. My cheeks warmed with the admission, but I didn't care whether I blushed. It was important that I share these things with my mother. "I really think she's the one. Not just because . . . you know, I can kiss her, but she makes me so unbelievably happy."

I slipped my homework out of my bag while I continued to talk, and when my gaze caught hold of my notes, I reached for the card that was tucked away inside my binder. Just like my girlfriend, I couldn't resist the images—couldn't keep their meanings far from my mind.

"I have this assignment, *mitéra*, that has me worried. I've been dreaming about it for the past few weeks, and earlier, *she* appeared to antagonize." Flashes of the specter entered my head, causing knots to tighten in my stomach. "I've spent my whole life running, keeping myself hidden like you'd want, but what if she's found me? I have so much to lose now." The very thought of Tempest being hurt in any way brought bile up my throat, filling my mouth with a bitter acidic taste.

My fingers brushed over the task card. I had so many unanswered questions, and part of me wished I could simply take the assignment back to Professor Beaumont and ask for a different one. I was in no way a coward, but this felt a lot like messing with fire. Blistering, dangerous, world scorching fire.

The sobbing woman from my dream intrigued me. I couldn't shake the feeling that she meant something and was pivotal to solving the project. We were meant to find something important, and by studying the clues contained in the image, we'd be able to solve the puzzle. Problem was, this hit too close to home. Even if there was a mere sliver of a chance that I was being overly paranoid, I couldn't risk being exposed.

Sun & Moon Academy was my chance to breathe without constantly looking over my shoulder for attacks. I deserved this opportunity to be normal—well as normal as I could be, considering. I was hidden, protected, and finally falling in love.

It was with that motive that I planned on solving the problem before my teammates had the chance. They could be pissed off at me all they wanted. If it all went to hell like I worried it might, then they could thank me for taking one for the team.

"Tell me what it means," I whispered. Emotions choked my voice, and a reluctant tear escaped from my eyes. This was another reason why the grotto was precious to me—I could have moments of weakness like this without fear. "Help me, *mitéra*. I need your guidance. Am I right to be worried or am I overreacting because I'm falling . . ." I stopped myself from finishing the sentence. I hadn't admitted my feelings for Tempest out loud.

I listened to the air, hoping to catch even a hint of her voice—the sound I'd long ago forgotten. There was the faintest swell of magic as though, somehow, she was trying to answer, but that ebbed away as quickly as it had risen. I was alone in the grotto. I was alone in facing whatever stirred.

With the pen in my hand, I tapped it against my notebook, studying the thoughts I'd already jotted down. Slowly I began adding the insights I'd received via the dream, including the specter's taunts. Even though the tree was in the background, I wondered if the figure hanging upside-down was important. Generally, I'd assume it wasn't, that the man was simply part of the scenery, but my gut warned me that everything mattered.

I'd also heard that Elliana's and Natalie's teams decided their cards were tarot or tarot-related, at least, making my first inclination to assume all of ours were as well. Maybe it was the fact I'd lived for so long, but I'd been burned before when I jumped in without researching. I had to make sure we weren't dealing with something else.

Better to be safe than sorry was my motto.

I snapped a photo with my camera, and then enlarged it so I could see the hanging figure better. The image pixelated the bigger I made it, but something tugged at my memories. I'd seen something like this before. It was significant.

My phone buzzed with an incoming text, and I welcomed the interruption. It was Tempest, and when I opened the message, I saw she'd sent me a selfie of her blowing me a kiss with the comment that she was missing me.

I keyed back my response and pocketed my phone. I was getting nowhere sitting here, stewing in my thoughts. There were still a few hours before my next class, and maybe that time was better spent at the library. With all the books there, maybe I could find something to shed some light on the assignment.

Quickly returning my things to my bag, I said my goodbyes, and gave one last look at the grotto. I'd be back soon. The peace I felt here was too alluring to ignore.

CHAPTER 4

One of the things I loved about campus was how grand and magnificent everything was. It was like there was no expense spared when designing each structure, tower, and accommodations—the sole goal being to make life as comfortable as possible for the students and faculty.

I'd experienced the full spectrum from opulence and wealth to squalor and poverty. It drove home the lesson that life could change in the blink of an eye, and the key to survival was to be grateful and appreciate wherever I found myself.

Entering Halstein Hall pulled the same reaction out of me every single time—awe and amazement that this was the place I called my home. From white marble floors to crystal chandeliers that illuminated the space—I viewed the hall as a one-stop shop for anything a student might need. There was no need for frantic Google searches, scrolling through Amazon, or venturing out of the mountain to Havenwood Falls, even though I enjoyed visiting the small town.

I loved it.

There was one store I especially liked because it always caught Tempest's attention. She was forever dragging me into Howe's Herbal Shoppe and talking my ear off about the different crystals and trinkets they sold. Even though I hadn't taken a potions class yet, I felt I'd already received a crash course because she'd tell me about different properties of plants and what she was learning.

I approached the window and peered inside at the display. Right now, my sole focus was on the beautiful labradorite wand for sale—Tempest's favorite stone. I knew instantly that I was smitten with her when I vowed to surprise her with it.

The whole reason I took this detour through Halstein instead of going the side way to the library tower was so I could finally buy it. Yet as soon as I stepped inside the store, the soft scent of burning incense tickling my nose, something else caught my eye.

There was a shelf of oracle and tarot decks, each box neatly lined up except for one deck where the shop had showcased a few of the cards. While I wouldn't say I was an expert at using these tools for divination, I knew what they were.

"Can I help you?" Scarlett Howe asked, approaching me from around one of the displays. "Looking for a deck for class or for fun?" I could feel her studying me, but I couldn't pull my gaze away from one of the decks.

"Just looking," I murmured, transfixed. I pulled one of the cards down from the shelf and held it up to my face. Holy shit.

"Ah, yes. This is one of our most popular items. We're always selling out of them because the artist definitely has a gift with design."

I'd already started tuning the poor girl out because there in my hand, in a much clearer image, was the Hanged Man card—a man suspended upside down from a tree. Like in my dream. Like in the task force assignment.

My assumption had been right after all. We were all given tarot cards, and here was the proof. I'd been overthinking it.

"I . . . um," I started and placed the card back on the shelf. "I actually came in for the labradorite wand you have in the window." I pointed over my shoulder and chuckled. "Then totally got sidetracked over here."

Scarlett smiled knowingly as though she heard customers say the same thing all day every day.

"It's an easy thing to do in here, trust me." She stepped back and gestured me toward the window. "Let me grab the wand for you, and maybe . . . tempt you with a tarot deck?" She sounded hopeful. I hated to disappoint her. I'd overheard Tempest talking with Natalie, who also worked here at the store, and they both really liked the witch.

"Maybe next time. I'm kinda pressed for time and wanted to make sure I got Tempest a gift." I offered her a genuine smile, winking as though she was now in on a secret, and followed Scarlett to the counter where she started to wrap the stone and ring up the sale. Maybe later I'd come back and choose a deck for myself, but for the moment, I could research the card at the library for free—putting my brain to work.

The transaction complete, Scarlett gushed over how much Tempest would love my surprise and then slipped a flyer in my bag about an upcoming sale, suggesting once again that the tarot decks were a popular item and to not miss out on them.

Escaping out into the main thoroughfare in Halstein, I followed the familiar path to the library entrance, Tempest's gift in my bag, and my thoughts now focused on one thing . . . a lead.

Excitement bubbled inside my chest.

Thankfully the library was still standing after Sadie Angrec, one of my tower-mates, almost caved it in a couple of weeks ago when her team was working on The Hunt mission. They'd been the first to complete it and not without consequences, as Calix had been gossiping about earlier. I still didn't know all the details, but the campus had shaken after a deafening boom filled the air.

I'd like to say it was a rare occurrence that something huge was happening at the Academy, but you could never quite predict what each day would bring. I still stand by my comment to Tempest that the Board of Regents needed to include some kind of stipend for hazard pay because simply walking into class at times was a risk.

She rolled her eyes at me and laughed. She thought I was adorable.

As I finally entered the library, I let go of all thoughts about my gorgeous girlfriend, and refocused. Catching a glimpse of Vidar at the counter helping another student, I made my way over to an empty desk.

I was grateful to be one step closer to uncovering some answers.

The Hanged Man.

Major Arcana.

Suspending certain action.

Sacrifice.

Hanging by his own free will.

It was that last piece of information that struck me hard because I'd automatically assumed that he was being hurt by someone else—that the actions of someone else was influencing his ability to live.

Part of me keenly identified with that. While I sometimes gave into the illusion, ultimately, my life had never been my own. There were greater powers out there who could swoop in at any time and obliterate me. I guessed that most mortals felt that way—that their destinies weren't truly in their hands to decide. They could step outside and be struck dead by lightning or cross the road to be hit by traffic. Death and disease were part of life—we all accepted that truth.

The fact that the tarot card depicted a man *choosing* to hang upside down by the world—sacrificing immediate action so he could wait patiently for the appropriate time to respond— definitely had me scribbling that down in my notes. Electricity sizzled through me, reinforcing that I'd stumbled upon an important piece of the puzzle.

The thought reminded me of a favorite saying I'd picked up somewhere along the way—that we each had the choice to act or react to any given situation. Sometimes the greatest strength lay in exercising patience and allowing events to unfold and reveal more information.

Was that what the card wanted me to know?

I sat back in my seat, mindful of my surroundings. I'd already spent an hour in the library, most of that walking through the book stacks for answers, and now I felt like I had even more to think about. The more I dove into solving this task, the more I realized I was dealing with a figurative onion—as each layer was peeled away, the more the center eluded me.

I huffed out a frustrated breath and rubbed my tired eyes.

What I needed was sleep and a chance to recharge. The brief nap I'd stolen earlier had been filled with the nightmare, and I could feel the weariness in my bones. There just weren't enough hours in the day to get shit done.

"Hey, teammate." Calix slid into the chair across from me. He placed his books on the desk and let out an equally tired breath. "Tell me classes get easier, man. I thought learning magic and shit would be a piece of cake."

Despite my misgivings, I had to laugh. "Hate to break it to you, but this school is pretty much going to kick your ass and expect you to smile while accepting it. I thought you'd figured that out from last semester."

Gossip was still circulating about the hourglass that had been a constant presence in the courtyard and the craziness that surrounded it. Tempest had been dragged into that mess, and I'd watched it test her sanity and abilities.

For the tenth or twentieth time, I wondered whether attending Sun & Moon Academy had been a wise choice. Here I'd assumed I could hide away from the world and immerse myself in academia, and instead the new semester had already seen students nearly die from completing class assignments. We were all here to learn how to be supernatural guardians armed with the skills to protect our communities, but where would the Regents draw the line? They couldn't exactly train us, if they killed us all off in the process.

I'm doing the right thing, I silently reminded myself, watching Calix flip his binder open and twirl a pen between his fingers. I have to keep Tempest safe at all costs. I wasn't going to lose her just as things were getting good between us.

All the more reason to figure this shit out.

Calix opened his mouth, ready to add something, but instead he smiled, his eyes sparkling. "You. Are. A. Goddess. In. Disguise."

Before I could turn about and see whom he meant, a tray of insulated cups with the Coffee Haven logo on the side appeared.

Tempest.

And yes, Calix was right. Caffeine was exactly what I needed at the moment.

"I like the way you think," she countered before handing us each a drink. "Although, I'm a little disappointed that you share the same abysmal taste in coffee as my boyfriend here." She leaned over and kissed my cheek. "Would it kill you to live a little and add some flavor or even milk to this sludge?"

Popping the lid open and taking that first delicious inhale of fresh coffee, I shrugged. "Why mess with perfection. Black coffee is the elixir of the gods."

Tempest rolled her eyes when Calix nodded. She was positively disgusted when we both answered that first sip with a loud, obnoxious groan of pleasure. "You guys are freaking heathens."

"Let me guess?" Calix countered, and resting on his elbows, he bent forward as if he could see through the cup to the ingredients. "You've got about ten pumps of vanilla or cinnamon or mocha. Non-fat milk. No . . . almond milk. Something that feigns healthiness but is crushed beneath the calories involved with syrup."

Tempest didn't give him a chance to finish. Instead, she swatted him and threatened to take back his drink. "Don't make me hurt you, Calix. You don't want to get on my bad side."

All I could do was sit back and grin, watching him squirm in his seat beneath her scrutiny. I'd been on the receiving end of her laser-like focus. "Say thank you. Trust me. It won't end well for you if you don't."

Wisely, he threw up his hands in surrender. "Thanks, Tempest. It's greatly appreciated."

She nodded and came to sit beside me. "It's always nice to see a guy that can be taught." Bumping shoulders with me, Tempest added, "Isn't that right, lover?"

Calix almost choked on his mouthful, earning himself a loud shush from neighboring students. My girlfriend said nothing, instead handing him a napkin and pointing to her chin.

"Were we meant to meet today to discuss the other projects for I.T.F.?" I asked, scrambling to remember the schedule we'd set up at the beginning of the semester. We were only a few weeks in, but with the course load getting heavier, I was lucky to remember whether I'd eaten or not. "Is Felicia coming?"

Felicia Coates was the fourth member of our team, and her specialty was as a psychic medium who was spookily good with communicating with the dead. We'd joked that should the semester kill us, she could still help us submit our assignments for a grade. Well, partly joked. You never knew around here.

Tempest shook her head. "Nope, that's on Friday. You told me you'd be here before class, and I had a few minutes, so I thought I'd bring you some sustenance." Tilting her head slightly, she gestured toward Calix. "I don't know about this one. So forgetful."

I saw the moment her eyes landed on the book spread in front of me. Up until now, she'd been focused on drinking her coffee, but now she was flicking through one of the books, eyebrows cocked. "Research?"

I nodded. "Who says studying had to be boring?"

Calix joined in, reaching for a book, and almost tipped his half-full coffee over.

"Fuck!" he exclaimed loudly, forgetting where he was. He fumbled with the cup a little before finally getting a tight grip. I was pretty sure it was a universal rule in all libraries that you faced the unholy wrath of the librarians should you desecrate any of their precious volumes of knowledge. Humans were known to be scary, so magical ones were nightmare inducing.

Tempest snorted. "Do you really think I'd bring you klutzes something you'd easily spill?"

I narrowly stopped myself from reminding her that out of the three of us, she was the one most likely to set something on fire or trip over her feet. I said nothing, however, choosing self-preservation instead.

Having a witch as a girlfriend had all kinds of perks, and she demonstrated one as she tipped the cup upside-down—the hot liquid staying in place, no matter how much she tried to pour it out.

"Magic's your friend. Anywho, as much as I want to stay, I gotta get to my next class. You coming?" She looked at me pointedly.

Shit. I was going to be late myself.

"Yep, give me a second to put these books away first." I stood abruptly and scrambled to gather them into a manageable pile.

Calix shoved my hands away and slid the pile to him. "I got this. I'm done for the day, and maybe this'll give me a chance to flirt with the hot chick over there."

"Deal!" Tempest answered hurriedly. She grabbed my hand. "Come on. I can't be late for my next class, and I gotta tell you something as well."

I was lucky to escape the library with my arm still attached to my shoulder socket. Whatever was on her mind, it had Tempest excited, and I was curious.

"Hey, slow down. Tell me what's so important."

I expected her to launch into some story about class or her latest plan to help cheer up her best friend and roommate, Natalie. The poor girl had lost her mother last semester and was grieving pretty hard. Tempest spent most of her time trying to wrack her brain with ideas to help her.

Instead, she stopped abruptly, threw her arms around my neck, and crushed her mouth over mine. The kiss she leveled me with was hot and intense, sending jolts of lust down through my body. Encircling her waist with my arms, I pulled her hard against me, and deepened the kiss. Fuck, she tasted so good, and I reacted like I was starving for affection. A lifetime without this kind of intimacy had taken its toll, and now that I knew it was safe with her, I couldn't get enough.

Ever.

Time stood still.

I didn't give a shit if that was a cliché or not.

This girl turned my word upside down, and I loved every single second of it.

CHAPTER 5

*T*he next day found me back at the grotto, and for once I wasn't obsessed in figuring out the card.

Instead, I pulled out the lunch I'd grabbed from the cafeteria—a club sandwich, red apple, and a packet of potato chips. It was a meal fit for champions.

The grotto held a softer sense of energy today. Whatever magic stirred through the air seemed to stroke against me, lulling me into a peaceful state of mind. Everything looked like it glowed somewhat, and the green of the foliage appeared more vibrant than usual. Almost as though something deep within the ground was preparing to be born and the world around it trembled slightly in anticipation.

If Tempest had been here, or her bestie Natalie, maybe they'd figure out what was happening, but for right now, I was more content to sit here eating my food and soaking up the calming vibes.

A soft meow came up beside me, followed by the sleek body of the most unique looking cats I'd ever seen. Half black, half ginger, Mystic was the familiar to Natalie and Tempest, and had somehow roamed this far from Hel Tower. Peering up at me with her one blue and one green eye, Mystic rubbed herself against my leg in greeting.

"Hello, pretty girl," I cooed, scratching her gently behind her ear. That earned me the loudest purr of pleasure, and I chuckled over how it made me think of Tempest. She made a similar noise whenever I kissed her *just* right. "Do they know you're having an adventure?"

I picked the kitty up and let her sit on my chest. Within seconds she began kneading me with her small paws, her body thrumming as she hummed.

I tore a small piece of ham out of my sandwich and offered it to her. She promptly sniffed the meat, stuck her nose up at it, and turned about so she could curl into a ball.

"Ham's not your thing, huh?" I murmured. "Good to know. Maybe I'll start carrying around kitty treats for whenever you come to visit me." One green eye opened, and I swore I saw Mystic smile at my comment.

We sat in silence and before long, she was faintly snoring, and I'd polished off the last of my potato chips. I knew I should probably gather the cat up and return her to Hel Tower, but watching how serene Mystic looked, I couldn't bring myself to move. As carefully as possible, I reached into my pocket and pulled out my phone, choosing instead to read a few chapters from the book I'd started.

I was a huge history nerd, which wasn't really surprising considering I'd lived through most of it and had seen events unfold firsthand. I'd gone through a period where I devoured every epic high fantasy novel and series I could get my hands on.

I loved a good story I could escape into—especially when my reality became stranger than fiction.

I'd almost missed the sound, dismissing it as Mystic quietly stirring in her sleep. But, despite being distracted by tales from the American Revolutionary War, there was no denying the noise was real. Pausing and holding my breath, I tilted my head and strained to see if I could hear it.

There it was again—this time clearer and louder than before. I dropped my phone to the ground in shock. The sound was a voice . . . sobs. Claws dug into me, breaking through my shirt to the skin below. Mystic was now awake, and each inch of her fur stood on end.

"Hello?" I called out, curling my hand around Mystic protectively. "Is someone there?"

The crying became more forceful as though the owner was doubled over in full-body, gut-wrenching weeping.

My dream. It was the young woman from my nightmare, and while I still couldn't see her, there was no mistaking the familiarity. "Please. Show yourself. You're safe. I promise I won't hurt you." I rose to my feet and turned slowly in a circle. Nothing. Mystic and I were still all alone in the grotto, and nothing had magically appeared. All I could do was try to convince whoever remained hidden that they could trust me.

Something flickered from the corner of my eye, yet when I stared in that direction, all I saw was the same old grave marker that had been there. Nothing had changed, yet there was no denying the crying was growing louder.

Then, finally, the sobbing turned into words.

"Help me," the woman begged. "Free me. Free us."

I whipped about, trying to locate where she was, much to Mystic's disgust. The poor kitten hissed and growled in response, which made me wonder if it was magic she was reacting to.

Tempest and Natalie had claimed Mystic as their familiar, and while I wasn't a witch, that didn't mean I couldn't try to read the cues. Clearly the cat was unsettled. Did she sense a threat? Was I wrong in somehow believing that the woman had no ill-intent and actually needed my help?

"Give me some kind of sign, Mystic. What are you sensing?" No sooner had I uttered the question than she leapt from my arms and scurried over to the gravestone, using her tiny paws to scratch at the ground. All the while, her loud meow filled the air, mingling with the now softer pleas for help.

The hairs on my arms prickled, and an overwhelming feeling to leave took over. I didn't like how Mystic was almost frantic in her digging, and I'd never forgive myself if something happened to her. Without another thought, I scooped her up and grabbed my stuff, hastily shoving my empty wrappers into my bag. Gone was the peaceful energy in the grotto, and in its place a wildness spiraled.

Free us.

Free us.

Free us.

Those two words repeated in a desperate mantra, and as I ran from my safe haven, they continued to echo in my ear.

Free us.

Who the hell was *us?*

CHAPTER 6

I practically fell into bed. I was beyond exhausted.
Modi Tower was all abuzz with activity, but I was in
no condition to go celebrate and join in with the others. There was
always something happening on campus—a way to blow off steam
and have a little fun to balance out the grueling schedules most of
us had. Practicing magic, learning a variety of fighting techniques,
and then trying to cram in every bit of information imparted by
professors was enough to turn my brain to gray mush, but I
fucking loved it.

Some may call me a masochist for knowledge, and they'd be
right. It was the blessing that came with living for centuries where
the greatest power someone could possess was understanding the
way the world and humanity worked. If you knew what made
someone tick, you could use that to your advantage.

That wasn't why I was here, however. I would do my part to
help protect my world, but I had a far more superior and devious
enemy to contend with. I worked hard so I'd be ready for our
inevitable confrontation.

My aching body slowly relaxed into my soft mattress—eliciting
a deep and guttural groan. Thank the goddess for Tempur-Pedic
bedding and all the creature comforts that came with the twenty-
first century.

Gradually everything fell away—the noise, the nagging

thoughts and reminders, images of Tempest smiling up at me as I leaned in to kiss her gently. We'd spent a glorious hour or two making out in her room while Natalie was gone.

My eyelids grew heavier, and then I was finally asleep. I knew that because in the space of a breath, new images surfaced, and I was standing once again beside the sobbing woman in my grotto. Only this time, her tears were filled with anger and accusation.

You, she yelled, her finger pointing at me. *Why won't you help me?*

Her hair fanned out around her like a majestic crown of twigs and flowers. Beside her stood a small fawn—the same critter that featured on the card. There was no sign of the specter, and for at least that I was grateful.

I opened my mouth to utter my apologies and beg for her to explain what she needed. I hated seeing anyone cry or in pain, so if it was within my power, I would do what I could.

Free me, Eryx. Free me from my prison.

The second I heard her utter *free*, realization jolted through me. I'd heard that voice before.

"How," I finally answered her, sputtering from the force it took to speak. My mouth felt like it was filled with wet sand, and no amount of swallowing could remove the sensation. "Tell me what to do. Please."

Her eyes flared and widened, fiery flecks of gold burning within their depths. With her hands now fisted at her side to keep the length of her sheer blue dress from flying up and out with the wind, the woman took a step toward me. She was barefoot.

Avenge me, she commanded.

I couldn't move. "At least tell me who you are?"

My muscles trembled with exertion, and I was finally able to move my arms. I reached for her, hoping that at least my touch could help soothe her.

I am all of us.

Lightning sizzled through the night sky followed shortly by the sharp crack of thunder. The wind whipped into a greater frenzy as though the weather existed solely to punctuate her demands.

I am all those who scream for vengeance.

It wasn't a name, but it was something. This woman was

somehow a victim and spoke on behalf of others. Was that what the card referred to? Was the woman demanding the hanged man cease his waiting and act?

A million thoughts exploded in my mind like a filing system that had sprung open and the contents spilled out. My heart pounded strongly in my chest, and my mouth became drier than the Sahara Desert. Words failed me solely because I had no clue which question to ask first.

Where is your loyalty, Eryx, son of she who represents us all? Have you forgotten your oath to honor her legacy?

My mother. I was right. This was connected to my mother, and if that was the case, it was also linked to the events that followed her death.

"Tell me what to do? Show me!" I fired back. "Let me be the instrument in freeing you."

A wailing sound began filling the air until it reached an almost deafening crescendo. Terror filled the woman's features, and she lunged forward to grab hold of me.

The moment she passed through me, her body without solid form, a blinding pain took over, and to my complete horror, my limbs began to turn to stone. I was being slowly paralyzed, and with each creeping inch upward, the feeling of panic struck harder. It would only take seconds before the paralysis hit my lungs and stopped me from breathing—until it hit my heart and forced it to cease beating.

Adrenaline kicked in, and my desire to survive obliterated any fear or thought I had. The woman had resumed sobbing, and I willed myself to wake up. I refused to die in my sleep. This was not going to be how my life ended.

Thunder roared overhead, and with one final crack of lightning, I jolted awake, but instead of being safe in my room, I was somewhere else.

Cold darkness sent chills through me, and my knees ached from kneeling on the hard ground. I didn't need to open my eyes, however, to know where I was. I'd have recognized the place solely by smell and hearing alone.

I was in my grotto, kneeling by the grave marker, my hands curled into claws as I dug frantically into the dirt. Pain emanated from beneath my fingernails from the sharp rocks and gnarled bush roots. If I was able to look closer at my hands, I just knew there'd be blood.

"What. The. Fuck!" I exclaimed, trying to stop but unable to. A reassuring meow answered, and to my surprise, I found Mystic perched on the top of the marker, standing guard while I'd dug in my sleep.

I glanced around for Tempest, praying to whoever was listening, that my girlfriend was here, that through whatever magic brought her familiar, the same had led her to the grotto to help me. I was alone, however, and that awareness was devastating. While I'd initially wanted to keep this all a secret, part of me longed to share this burden with someone—with her. Even the secrets of my past felt unbearable now. I was drowning— suffocating from the weight that pressed constantly down on me. Vulnerable, desperate, and borderline hysterical, there was no slowing my racing heart or breath. I wanted to scream out in frustration as the terror of being paralyzed still felt fresh in my body and mind.

It's only a nightmare, I silently muttered over and over again. Yes, I'd managed to sleepwalk to the grotto, but I wasn't in any imminent danger. Finally, free to move, I tumbled back onto my backside and cradled my injured hands in my lap.

Tears fell, and I didn't stop them.

Long-contained mourning burst out from my lips, and for the next few minutes, I sobbed. I couldn't withhold the pain I still felt over losing my mother and the torment I'd had to endure ever since. On and on the anguish bubbled forth. The locked box I'd kept the emotions buried in had flown open, and I didn't have the will or strength to fight it.

I wept for her.

I wept for myself.

I wept until there were no more tears, and I slouched forward, exhausted.

Mystic brushed her soft body back and forth against the side of my leg, her way of grounding me back to the here and now. With the help of her insistent purring, I was able to regulate my breathing so all that was left was going back to my room to clean and wrap my hands.

The cat had other plans, however, as she began digging in the same hole I'd just made.

"Mystic," I said, trying to pick her up. "I need to get you back home. Come on, it's late." Yet when I reached to scoop her up, she hissed and swatted at me. Jumping into the hole, she continued meowing louder. Something was wrong.

I peered at the dirt that had been moved and saw a rocky surface peeking out from the soil. Nothing seemed out of the ordinary. The ground was filled with pockets of rock like this, but Mystic was persistent in touching it with her claws. With each strike of her nails, the kitty looked up at me as if to say the rock was important.

I let out a tired sigh. All I could think about now was washing my hands, changing clothes, and climbing into bed to catch a few hours of sleep before my alarm went off. It was tempting to ignore my morning classes and sleep in, but I hated being behind. A cup or two of black coffee from Coffee Haven would perk me right up. Hell, maybe I'd have an espresso instead. Nothing screamed wake up than a hard-hitting jolt of caffeine.

"It's just a rock, little one," I answered and attempted to pick her up again. This time I was rewarded with a sharp swipe of her paws and an angry scratch that was already beading with fresh blood. "Ouch, you brat. What are you expecting me to do?"

Heaven help me, but Mystic tapped the rock again, staring at me.

"Fine," I grumbled, quickly licking away the blood at my wrist. "If I do this, will you quit attacking me?" With sore fingers, I slowly began wiping away the surrounding dirt and seeing if I could pry the rock out of the ground. The second my skin came in contact with it, however, a blast of magic zapped my fingers.

Holy. Shit.

Like a radio switching on and filling a quiet room with loud and boisterous music, the sobbing woman's voice rang out. Over and over she cried for help and that I free her—free them. Whatever lay hidden within the rock, it was linked to the card and this whole nightmare.

Content that I was finally listening, Mystic allowed me to lift her up and out of the way. It took a few solid minutes of manipulating the soil, but eventually the rock broke loose and I was able to hold it in the palm of my hand.

I turned it about to see if there were any cracks—anything that might help me crumble away the hardened dirt.

"What do you think it is, Mystic?" I asked. When there was no answer, I looked down, and sure enough, the cat had already left— her mission accomplished.

I slowly stood and brushed away the debris and dust that covered my pants and picked the stone up. I could still hear the voice faintly in my head, but the loudness diminished the longer it remained unearthed.

This was definitely a piece of the puzzle.

Gripping it tightly, I left the grotto and made my way back to Modi Tower. It would be dawn soon, and I needed a shower now.

I needed a lot of things, but as I got closer to my dorm, I managed to complete one important task. I boxed back those emotions and the grief that had all but consumed me moments ago. I didn't have time to fall apart now, and the tears that I shed would have to be enough to alleviate the pressure inside.

Something told me that once I figured out the task force assignment, I'd have some of the answers I needed. The rock was just one clue, and I was committed to see this through alone.

I had people to protect.

I had a legacy to honor.

CHAPTER 7

"*H*ey, Eryx, wait up!"

It was Felicia calling out to me as I passed one of the potion labs. Jogging to catch up, her ginger hair was pulled into a ponytail that swished back and forth in the air.

I tried not to groan like an asshole, but I was totally dragging ass. I was so tired, and I still needed to get to my weaponry class. When I'd gotten home from the grotto this morning, sleep had eluded me, and I was surviving solely on energy drinks and sheer will. Class was getting in the way of me trying to figure out the rock, and I didn't have time to stop and chit chat.

Thing was, Felicia was one of my task force teammates, and if I was a jerk to her, I was pretty sure I'd hear it from Tempest.

"What's up?" I answered. I waited for her to start walking beside me and threw her a friendly smile. Hopefully it didn't look more like an exhausted grimace. "You just finish Potions?"

Felicia nodded and let out a frustrated groan. "I understand the necessity of learning all this, but do you ever get the feeling the Regents are trying to cram so much stuff inside our brains that there just doesn't seem like there's enough room? I keep thinking my skull's going to explode from all the pressure."

I had to laugh. "And they promise that it'll get easier to retain and that we'll have a lifetime to put it all into practice," I added, totally agreeing with her sentiment.

Felicia grinned. "But sometimes I wonder if they've overestimated our ability to assimilate every. Damn. Detail. Perfectly." Each word was punctuated by our steps.

"Or," I chuckled, "they've underestimated the importance of knowing how to exact venom from a ridged back, striped newt or conjure lightning with a glass tumbler, paperclip, and twine string." I cast her a side-long glance and saw she was grinning.

"Like MacGyver!"

She clapped her hands, startling a student who was passing by. "Yes, like freaking MacGyver! I thought magic was meant to be easy."

We'd reached the doors that led to the outside, and I held one open for her. "I guess that's the hope. Anyway, did you need me for something?"

I studied the young psychic, noting the freckles that were scattered across her nose and cheeks. I'd heard that every freckle a ginger had represented a soul they'd taken, which was ironic considering Felicia dealt with the dead.

"I just wanted to make sure we're good for tomorrow. I was thinking we might also want to pick Sadie's brain about how her group dealt with the card they picked."

My forehead furrowed in confusion. "Huh?"

It was her turn to look at me strangely. "The library. Tomorrow night. We're meeting to talk about the task force assignments." Felicia shook her head and rolled her eyes. "Because god knows we need to cram more meetings and shit into our day."

Damn, I liked how this chick thought. "I'll be there." I leaned in and lowered my voice to a hush. "Unless my head explodes and all that's left is my poor body convulsing where I stood."

She punched my arm and snorted. "Good thing I could still talk to you then. You can never have too many ghosts for friends. Makes things interesting." Before I could retort, she looked at her wrist and noticed the time. "Ugh, this pace is going to kill me! I gotta run. No freaking rest for the wicked."

I watched as she waved over her shoulder and raced off to her next appointment, leaving me to make my own way to my next class.

I wasn't meant to be by the potion's lab right now. I'd actually gone searching for answers, because every attempt I'd made to break away the dirt encasing the rock to see if anything was inside had ended in failure. I was hoping I'd find some kind of spell or concoction to make the task easier but that had led me to a dead end. Addie Beaumont had offered a few suggestions and with her permission, I'd taken one of the back desks and ran a few experiments.

Straight acid had only resulted in a toxic plume of smoke.

A mixture Addie swore would work simply ran off the surface like it was water on a duck's back. She even performed a few spells, and they all kind of fizzled. By the end, Addie was just as baffled as I was, but promised she'd look more into it if I needed her to. I didn't explain that it was for an assignment, otherwise she'd have given me a lecture about cheating or something similar.

With the promise that I'd keep her posted and let her know if I found a solution, I'd quickly escaped the lab and bumped into Felicia. Thankfully she had no clue that I was acting alone on our card assignment.

Another trip to the library was in order, and I was confident that there had to be some spell or piece of magic that could penetrate the stone. I just needed to find it.

But before that could happen, I had a class to attend.

Magical weaponry.

Fun.

Every inch of my body hurt, and my muscles felt like they were in open rebellion against me.

Even though part of the class was theory, we were able to touch some of the weapons and try to wield them with the limited skills we had. Well, some of us had. Most of the items on the syllabus were swords and armaments I was acquainted with.

In fact, as I handled the broad sword and hefted its familiar weight in my hand, an idea formed. If magic couldn't penetrate the rock, there was nothing stopping good old-fashioned steel and iron from breaking it apart.

I waited until the end of class and for most of the students to leave before I started tentatively swinging the sword about me, slipping easily into the formations I'd been taught so long ago from a tutor. I almost didn't hear Professor Beltaine approach because I was so absorbed in the flow and motion of the magnificent weapon.

"Something tells me that you're no stranger to that beauty." There was definitely a hint of excitement in his eyes as he watched me come to a finish. It wasn't hard to see that I had impressed him with my sword skills.

Wiping the sweat from my brow, I grinned. "I'm no master like you, but I've had some experience. Thanks for letting me play with her a little."

I loved how the hilt felt as though the sword was made especially for me. I was reluctant to let the blade go.

He nodded and offered me a cleaning rag. "Feel free to come practice with her whenever you'd like. You have great form, and it'd be a shame for you to let your talent for swordsmanship go to waste." He gestured to the cloth. "Continue and clean her up when you're done. The space is yours."

With a quick nod, I was left alone, and all I could think about was the new idea begging to be focused on.

Double checking that no one was watching, I slipped the rock out of my bag and brought it over to the stone bench we sometimes sat on while we watched a demonstration. I carefully placed it in the middle, and with the sword back in my hand, I measured my steps backward, so I had ample room to swing.

For a split second, I felt guilty for using such a pristine and well-loved weapon. It felt a little like butchery to hack away at the geode when so much care had been taken to keep the blade sharp and nick-free.

I gazed over to the armory where I knew there might be better options—perhaps an axe with a blunter edge. I'd have to return the sword there once I was done so what was a few extra minutes to swap the weapons out.

Time. That was the issue. There were always students coming in and out, and there was no guarantee I'd be left alone for long. If I was going to see whether I could slice the geode open, it was now. The voice still echoed in my head whenever I came in contact with it, and it was beginning to wear on my nerves.

Taking in a deep breath, I raised the sword over my head and took careful aim. Then with one hard thrust downward, the blade whizzed through the air before striking the target perfectly. Strong vibrations flowed up through my arms and pulsed through my body, rattling my teeth.

The stone remained perfectly still and intact.

The bloody thing looked like it hadn't just been hit with as much force as I could muster.

Cussing beneath my breath, I was tempted to try again but my gut told me that it would be in vain. So far, this rock proved impenetrable. I would need to figure something else out.

Whatever contained and controlled the voice I'd heard would have to remain a mystery a little longer.

CHAPTER 8

o matter how hard I tried to sleep, the rock continued to call to me, the voice driving me to the point of paranoia.

I lived in a tower filled with magical users of all kinds. Hell, the entire fucking mountain was a mecca of energy and powers—someone had to be hearing the same woman begging over and over again to help free her.

The longer I lay in bed, the more my skin itched, and every sound I heard sent thoughts tumbling of my door being kicked open, windows shattering from outside attackers, or worse . . . people from my past arriving to demand the pound of flesh. Paranoia was winning. I couldn't sleep like this. I had to take the rock somewhere safer—anywhere but here.

Pacing back and forth over the soft carpet I'd lain over my floor, the motion did little to settle my nerves. When I heard someone racing past my door to their own room, I knew I couldn't stay here—I needed fresh air or something before I lost my freaking mind.

I wrapped the stone in a piece of fabric I'd found in my suitcase—a memento from some past vacation—and shoved it into the bottom of my backpack. I'd take it to the grotto. That place was private, and no one would suspect me walking about campus with my bag. I'm sure I wasn't the only night owl desperate to find a quiet place to study.

Two steps out into the hallway and I ran into Calix. Seeing him did little to stifle my growing mistrust. There was no surprise on his face either, which made me wonder if he was lingering outside my door—perhaps listening in.

My shoulder bumped his, but I didn't wait to hear whatever explanation he had for being there so late. All I could focus on was getting the rock some place safe, and only then would I address whatever it was between us.

"No worries, Eryx," he called out to me. "No harm done."

I was already gone, my feet hurriedly clattering down the stairs. Damn, this tower had way too many bloody levels.

The night air was brisk, and I pulled my hoodie up over my head, casting furtive glances about. For the most part, campus was pretty quiet, and I didn't cross paths with anyone as I made my way to the grotto. If there were any creatures working under the guise of darkness, they kept to themselves, and I did the same.

The greenhouse was empty, which I took as a good sign. For once, luck was on my side. It was only when I entered my beloved grotto that I finally took a deep and calming breath. The rock had been buried here for who knew how long, so logic dictated that this was the best place to keep it.

Without reburying it, I placed it back in the hole by the grave marker, and spent a few added seconds looking at it, judging whether I was making the right decision. The voice was still there —a gentle whisper now—and I crumpled to the ground exhausted.

I couldn't keep up this pace. It had only been forty-eight hours at the most, and I felt like I was coming apart at the seams. Closing my eyes, I bowed my head, and sent out a heartfelt prayer to my mother—begging her to watch over me and give me the strength to see this task through. When at last a peaceful feeling permeated my body, I got up on my feet, grabbed my bag, and slipped away from the grotto.

Tempest was still eyeing me with concern whenever we met up. She saw how distracted I was, and despite my best efforts in giving her my full attention, there was always some part of me occupied with the task.

My thoughts were still there as I passed through the greenhouse, but unlike earlier, something moved quickly within the shadows, and the hair on the back on my neck prickled. With each step I took, the feeling of being watched grew stronger.

Without a sound or warning, I spun around and grabbed hold of the person behind me. My fists crumpled the front of the sweater tightly, and with one powerful motion, I slammed them against the stone wall beside us.

"Who the hell are you?" I demanded. "And why are you following me?" The lack of sleep had robbed me of my filter, and I was aware of the possibility that I was manhandling campus staff, or even worse, a professor. But I didn't give a shit. I shoved them again into the wall, demanding an answer.

"You need to let me go, man, before this escalates further."

Calix. My instinct had been right. The asshole was completely untrustworthy and had followed me from Modi Tower.

"Or what?" I uttered angrily. There was no valid excuse for him to be here this late.

Slowly he raised his hands in submission. "Listen, I'm not your enemy, Eryx. I promise. I realized I didn't have a specific ingredient for class tomorrow, so I figured I'd come straight to the source." He jerked his head toward the greenhouse.

I stared deep into his eyes, searching for the truth. I couldn't shake the paranoia I felt, though. His explanation seemed too convenient.

I shook my head, still gripping his own hoodie tightly. "And it had to be done at two a.m. in the morning." It was a statement, not a question.

He chuckled with surprise. "Says the guy who's roaming campus alone with his face hidden. I could say the same thing about you. What trouble are *you* getting into? Why would you attack some stranger if you weren't guilty of something?"

I refused to let him twist this around on me. He'd been lurking in the shadows.

"I'm going to ask you once, and so help me, if I find out you're lying . . ." I let my words trail off as my unspoken threat hung between us. "Who are you working for? Did. She. Send. You?"

Confusion clouded his features. "Who? Eryx, I don't know whether you need to be medicated or something, but you need to dial yourself down a notch or two. Last time I checked, we were freaking classmates. We're working on assignments together, and that's it. Is this about your girl? Tempest?" When my hands went back for him, this time his throat, he back pedaled. "I'm just trying to understand what the hell your damage is here. I'm not working for anyone. I don't know who *she* is. I just want some damn pennyroyal, and figured if I got it from the greenhouse, I wouldn't have to dig into my budget and get it from Howe's." He stared back at me calmly. "I swear it. I have no issue with you."

I staggered back as my surroundings became clearer, and I realized what I'd just done.

I'd attacked a student.

That was a punishable offense that could get me kicked out. I needed to stay here within the Academy's protective wardings. I wasn't ready to face Aphrodite yet. Had I just completely fucked things up because I'd let this task get the best of me?

"Shit," I uttered, stepping farther away so there was more space and Calix could see I was no longer a threat. "I'm sorry," I repeated over and over. Scrubbing my face, all I could do was look at Calix and try to at least judge whether he was mad enough to report me.

The fact he still stood there was a good sign. "At the risk of pissing you off again, what's going on with you?" He straightened his clothes and ran his fingers through his dark curls.

There was a very strong possibility that I'd totally misjudged this guy.

Excuses vied for my attention, but I decided to keep it simple. "I'm not sleeping. I saw you in the shadows and jumped to conclusions. I know it doesn't make up for it, but I really am sorry. I shouldn't have accused you. Hell, I'm surprised you didn't start swinging."

Seeing that the situation was diffused, Calix appeared to relax somewhat. "Trust me, I almost did, but I like you, Eryx. I'm hoping we can be friends because I'm not embarrassed to admit that I'm having a hard time here." A smile finally broke across his face. "You actually caught me walking past your door earlier because I wanted to talk."

My eyes widened. Damn, I'd really messed up. "Then I definitely feel like an asshole." I stuck out my hand as a gesture of peace. "I wouldn't blame you if you told me to get lost, but how about we start again? Hey. I'm Eryx. Generally good guy, but sometimes a jerk."

Calix gripped my hand tightly and shook it. "Hi. I'm Calix, and I need to learn how to not hide in shadows obviously." He waved his hand to the side. "Shall we head back?"

I nodded but stopped as a thought came to my mind. "Wait, did you end up getting the pennyroyal?" Calix groaned which was all the answer I needed. "Come on, I know a secret way in. Consider this my way of making it up to you."

Our stealth mission was a success, and as we parted ways, my body tumbling forward onto my bed, I couldn't tell whether this morning was a good thing or not. The voice was quiet, and I managed not to almost kill someone.

It was a win.

I needed one.

I just didn't like how close I'd come to losing control.

CHAPTER 9

"*I*t's like you're not even trying!" Tempest's disgusted snort spoke volumes. "You keep bragging how easy these moves are, but then you act like a limp freaking noodle!" She clapped her hands in front of my face. "Wake up!"

I wiped the sweat from my brow with the back of my wrist. "Considering I'm not even taking the class, you should at least pretend to be a little more gracious."

Her idea of showing gratitude was a swift sweep of her leg that sent me flying onto my back. A second later, she straddled my hips. Hmmm, maybe this wasn't as bad as I thought. In fact, as I grabbed her hips with my hands, holding her there, I was perfectly content to stay like this for the next thirty minutes.

"We don't have time for that, Mister. If I don't nail these moves in time for the next class, I'm going to look bad in front of everyone." She pinned my hands beside my head and stared down at me. Her ponytail draped by her ear, and I itched to tug on the dark brown strands. "Don't make me and Natalie concoct a hex to punish you, Eryx. I wouldn't want to ruin those pretty boy features of yours."

Her threat fell hollow, however, because distracted or not, I easily outweighed her. Flipping her off, and ensuring she was now beneath me. I repeated her move and secured her own arms beside her head.

"You'd miss me," I teased, feathering a soft kiss over her lips. I could feel her resistance melt away, her legs and hips no longer flailing to regain control. "Plus, would you rather this kissing you?" I contorted my features, crossed my eyes, and gave myself a goofy overbite. "You still love me, right?" I buried my face into her neck and snuffed like a pig burrowing for truffles. I threw a few oinks in just because I loved the way she sounded when she laughed.

"You're impossible!" She gasped, unable to catch her breath. "You won't have anyone to make out with if I fail and the Regents kick me out for laziness. What are you going to do then?"

I drew her close. "I don't know." I somehow managed to shrug while trying to maintain a serious expression. "Maybe I'll hide you in my dorm room and sneak food and books to you. You're stuck with me, sweetheart."

I'd obviously given the right answer because she stretched upward, connecting our lips. Gone was any focus I'd managed to hold onto, and I released her hands. Cradling her face, I deepened the kiss, opening my mouth so I could taste her.

She was pure addiction and sin.

I prided myself on being a gentleman, but this feeling she stirred within me was hard to ignore. I wanted to explore more than just her mouth, stripping us both down until we were skin to skin—heated touches and completely intimate.

"Where did your mind just go?" she asked, breathlessly. Her eyes were practically glowing with desire.

I grazed the tip of my nose softly across hers, before taking her bottom lip between my teeth and gently tugged. "The exact same place yours went."

This was all unchartered territory for me. After the first time I'd kissed someone, and they'd almost died, I'd spent my entire existence denying myself any form of sexual connection with someone. Tempest had been a god damn miracle when she'd shown no reaction to my first moment of weakness. The fact I was lying here, kissing her, contemplating taking our relationship to the next level was huge.

If I could kiss her, surely making love would be okay.

Fuck, I hoped so.

"Eryx," Tempest whispered, trying to pull my ear closer to her

mouth. "I don't have class for the rest of the day. We could always .
. ."

"Take this somewhere more private?" I chuckled, fully aware
that if things got any hotter, we'd begin drawing a crowd. "That
would be a good idea." Sliding off her, I stood and offered my
hand to help her up.

She slapped my hand, and before I could register what she was
doing, Tempest screamed out "*Sucker!*" and twisted her legs around
mine again, forcing me to fall forward and hit the ground. This
time, she straddled me from behind so there'd be no distracting her
with kisses.

She'd used my hormones against me.

I couldn't even fault her because that was part of our training
throughout our classes—that sometimes the element of surprise
was more successful than a head filled with knowledge or an
armament of weapons.

"Do you yield?" she asked, pinning my arm behind my back.
"Have I paralyzed you with fear at my strength?"

I'd heard the word a million times before, but there was
something about hearing it from her mouth. I shook my head,
trying to clear the thoughts that already started rushing in, but all I
could hear was that one word.

Paralyzed.

Someone had used that same phrase a long time ago, and there
was no stopping my reaction. I tensed up to the point of being
rigid, and then I bucked her off me, scrambling away, getting to
my feet. I couldn't look at Tempest or gauge how she was reacting.
All I could think was how many times had I risked her life by
kissing her.

I'd just been imagining us snuggled in my bed after hours of
lovemaking. What if I was wrong? What if the effect temporary and I was foolishly ignoring how dangerous I was?

"What the heck, Eryx?" she asked, letting out a hurt breath.
"Was it something I said?" She was being sarcastic in an attempt to
disguise how my sudden cold feet wounded her, but I still heard
the emotion underneath.

"Sorry," I muttered, staring at the ground as I tried to regain my composure. With my hands planted on my hips, I turned about in half circles, silently begging the ground to open up and swallow me whole. All I could see was her lying beneath me rigid as stone—a literal statue. "You just caught me by surprise."

Gone was the sarcasm as she came closer and rested her hand tenderly on my arm. "By what? The fighting techniques we've been practicing?" She now stood in front of me, both her hands forcing me to stop and look her in the face. "What's going on? And don't say nothing, Eryx, because then you'd be a liar. Something's been bothering you all week, and for the life of me, I can't figure out how to make you trust me."

I didn't like that I was making her doubt herself. That was the last thing I intended so instead, I gave her the same lame excuse I'd given Calix, knowing I was a coward. "I've been having a hard time sleeping, is all."

Understanding slowly dawned across her features. "The same nightmare as before?"

I nodded and gathered her to my body as she stepped in and wrapped her arms tightly around me. "It's kicking my ass, and nothing I've done has helped."

She kissed me beneath my chin, and the gesture wasn't lost on me. "Would it help if I mixed up a sleeping elixir for you, maybe? Natalie's been struggling with the same thing and made a nighttime drink that's helped. I could ask her for the recipe and make you some."

God, I didn't deserve her.

What Tempest needed was the truth, not some half-assed lie wrapped up in a fact.

"Just know I'm worried about you. I feel like the two most important people in my life are in trouble, and I'm helpless to do anything." The sadness in her voice was heartbreaking.

I took a step back and nodded. "Then let's see if we can at least solve the problem of my insomnia. Cross that off your list of things to worry about."

I wasn't sure whether she truly believed me, but it seemed to distract her from probing deeper. Sooner or later we'd have to talk, but only when the timing was better. She had a best friend who was deeply grieving over her mother's recent death. Natalie needed her support more.

"Let's go," she answered.

I let out a mental sigh.

Crisis averted.

CHAPTER 10

I still hadn't solved how to open the rock. I couldn't shake the feeling that the stone held answers inside it that were connected to the Hunt, and whenever my intuition acted this way, I tried not to ignore it. That was something I'd taken away from Addie's task force class earlier this semester—the importance of acknowledging our instincts and how using our intuition went hand-in-hand with being a good guardian. The list I created for the different methods I'd attempted was growing longer and longer by the minute. There was only one idea I had left, and that was a long shot as well.

Approaching Professor Knox's door, I smiled at the memories I'd made with him. I'd struck up a friendship with the man over Christmas when I'd volunteered to help him play Secret Santa. One of the things I remembered from our conversation was he'd studied alchemy and was here at the Academy to teach it to us.

Perhaps that was the key here. I'd been so focused on trying to smash open the rock or alter it with magic that maybe transforming the matter into something different would work. I'd be a liar if I said I understood the principles behind the precursor to modern chemistry, but I was desperate. I needed whatever lay inside the stone—the voice of the woman echoing in my head.

I knocked on the door and entered once I heard him answer. It still struck me how young Phineas Knox looked—that he'd somehow managed to find the fountain of youth. I knew he was at least a century old because he'd shared a little of his history, including his friendship with Marcus St. James. Hearing some of their stories had left me wondering what it would be like to claim a vampire as a brother.

As far as I knew, I was an only child, and I was my own family. Maybe I needed to claim someone who wasn't blood like Knox had.

"What can I do for you, Eryx?" he greeted, sitting behind his desk that was stacked high with paperwork and opened books. This was a man who was always eager to learn, so it didn't surprise me that he'd taken advantage of the wealth of knowledge the Academy hoarded away in the library. "I was just thinking of you today. Are you surviving the semester so far?"

I took one of the winged leather chairs opposite him and let out a groan as I sank into the cushion. "What did Aristotle say . . . that the roots of education were bitter, but the fruit is sweet?" I shrugged and tried to stifle a yawn. "I wonder if he was referring to the obscene amount of coffee someone has to ingest in order to get to the good bits."

Knox leaned back in his own chair and threw his head back in laughter. "Who knows, but I'm sure the philosopher would've had a word or two to say about it." He fell quiet and watched me. "You didn't come here for idle chit chat, though, did you?" I could feel him studying my reaction, and it was hard not to squirm beneath his scrutiny.

"That obvious is it?" This time I didn't bother hiding my yawn. "I've got a problem that refuses to be solved, and I was hoping to pick your brain about it. Do you have time?"

Knox's gaze strayed to the clock behind me on the wall. "I'm all yours for the next fifteen minutes. Is that enough or do we need to schedule an appointment?" He scooped up the papers in front of him and placed them in a neat pile to the side of the desk. I had his sole attention.

I paused and wondered if I should take up the offer so I could bring the geode to him. It might be better if he could actually see what I was dealing with. "Actually, maybe an appointment would work. I have a rock that I'm pretty sure is hiding something inside it. I've tried everything to break it apart, but it's being stubborn."

Knox cocked his eyebrows, intrigued. "Homework or personal?"

Not that it would've mattered to the professor. I had a feeling he was just like me and enjoyed a good puzzle.

I wanted to tell him that it was for the task force class assignment, but I found myself answering personal.

"Liar," came an accusation from behind me.

Tempest.

"Eryx?" Knox interrupted, his gaze jumping from me to Tempest who stood angrily at the door with her hands on her hips. "Do I need to give you two a minute?"

Tempest shook her head. "I have a feeling this is going to take a little longer than that, Professor." She glowered at me, and in that second, I knew that time had run out. She'd be demanding answers, and I knew I couldn't keep things secret for much longer. She deserved the truth. "I'm sorry to barge in like this, but I'm going to need to take Eryx with me. He's got some explaining to do."

I didn't resist. I offered my apologies and let Knox know that I'd come back later if needed.

Tempest refused to look at me as we left the office. I could see that she had a small grasp on her frustration, judging by how tightly she clenched her teeth.

"Imagine my surprise when Professor Beaumont told me she might've figured out a way to open your rock, Eryx, and I had no freaking clue what she was talking about. So, I decide to see what my sneaky boyfriend is hiding and discover you here . . . talking with *another* professor. Considering we share a lot of the same classes, I wanted to see what you were up to." It was never a good thing when Tempest used air quotes to emphasize her anger.

"Follow me," I said, resigned to the situation.

"Where?"

"It's time you knew the truth."

I took her to the grotto.

There, surrounded by the reverence and peace I frequently enjoyed, I led her over to the grave marker, and handed her the small geode.

"This is what I've uncovered so far with the assignment. The dreams I've been having were connected to it, and a voice led me to the stone." I stopped when I remembered another piece of the puzzle. "Actually, Mystic was the one who was with me when I found it."

Tempest stood with the stone resting in her palm, staring at it, when she registered that I'd mentioned her familiar. "My Mystic?" she asked. "My sweet little bundle of black and ginger fur?"

I nodded, and gesturing to where I usually sat whenever I came here, I led her over to the spot. Once we were both as comfortable as we could be, I started. I began with why I'd been so adamant about being the leader of the Hunt, how I'd felt an intense connection to it. Next I shared the elements of my dreams, how the woman had at first only spoken to me there, asking me to help free her.

"Who is she, Eryx?" Tempest asked, no longer angry about finding that I'd kept this a secret. "And why did she pick you?"

I gulped nervously, because the connection I'd finally accepted came with a larger, more complex explanation. "I'll get to that part next." Ignoring her questioning look, I went on to share that I now heard the voice while I was awake, and that the effects had made me act paranoid. I wasn't proud of having to confess my attacking Calix, and when Tempest went to interrupt, I shook my head, and stopped her with my raised hand. "I know how crazy I sound, but I swear, I felt one hundred percent justified in doing this alone. All I wanted to do was keep you safe and protected."

I could see she was trying to understand, to grasp at the straws I was offering. "Protect me from what? Aside from constantly risking our lives over the tasks the Regents sent us, I'm pretty sure we're in the safest place in the world. No one can get in without them knowing."

I nodded in agreement. "I know. I went the other day to discuss the wardings and magic that keeps the campus a secret, just to be sure no one could infiltrate the barriers without them knowing." I was lucky the Regents hadn't kicked me out of the room when I'd asked, but I had to make sure for my own peace of mind.

"Who the hell do you think's coming for you, Eryx? Seriously, enough with the secrecy. If you don't know by now that I love you and you can trust me, what does that say about us?"

She'd said she loved me.

She'd actually said it.

It was time to show her that I felt the same by telling her the truth.

"It's because of who my mother was . . . is." Saying it out loud didn't feel as dire as I'd expected. "She made a lot of enemies throughout her life, and as her son, I've kind of inherited them."

Tempest blinked. Then blinked again. "What? You're protecting me from your mom's enemies?" Repeating back what I said didn't seem to help her digest the new information. "Eryx, please stop. I can't take you lying to me."

She pulled her hand out from mine, and I grabbed it back, needing her to believe me. "You asked me to trust you so I am. You know I'm from Ancient Greece and that my past has been complicated. There's a reason why I've evaded all your questions, because I know how this might sound. Just please, give me a chance to tell you everything. If you decide then that it's too much, I'll step aside."

Tempest weighed my words carefully and then nodded. "I asked for the truth, didn't I? Okay, what else have you been keeping to yourself? You're the heir to your mom's drama. Who isn't? What else?"

I took in a deep breath and squeezed her hand. "The reason why I was so adamant we could never be together and why I react whenever we first kissed was because of who I am . . . of who my mother is."

Tempest flinched. "Oh shit, don't tell me she's like mine and is a mother from hell. I'm not sure whether I can handle two of them."

I shouldn't have laughed, but I did. "No. You don't have to worry about that. My mother's dead." It was now or never. "My mother is . . . was Medusa."

139

Her gaze rose to my head, and I instantly knew what she was thinking.

"No snakes. In fact, her power manifested differently in me. Where she could turn people to stone with a mere glance, I paralyze . . . kill with my kiss. Imagine discovering that the first time."

She touched her lips gingerly. "But we kiss just fine."

And there was the one ray of sunshine. "And I have no idea how that's possible. That's why I freaked out the other day. I remembered that I still had no clue and that I was being selfish with you."

"So you've been worried about hurting me?" It was her turn to trail her finger lightly down the side of my face. The sorrow that filled her voice also caused tears to trickle from her eyes. "Oh, Eryx."

The air was heavy, and I was grateful I'd brought her to the grotto. I knew there was bound to be more questions—many, many more because I'd only barely grazed the tip of the iceberg. I'd answer them all as well, as honestly as I could. Part of me was afraid that the second I closed my mouth, Tempest would've turned about and ran.

"I almost killed someone once." Now that the truth was out in the open, it was time to come clean with it all. "Not just someone, but a goddess."

Tempest cocked her brow in surprise. "Damn, you aim pretty high. Who was she?" When I didn't answer, her eyes grew wider, her mouth forming a soft *o*. "Nooooo."

I nodded. "Yep. Aphrodite. I was young and foolish and didn't realize that my curse went beyond affecting humans. Things got hot and heavy between us one night, and before I knew it, she was being turned to stone."

I still remembered how terrifying that scene had been to watch —as her soft porcelain skin slowly turned into a dull, stone appearance.

"So, she's dead?" She laid her hand on my arm as a way to comfort me.

Shaking my head, I let out a loud breath. "No, she survived, although it might've been better for me had she turned into an eternal statue. She was beyond pissed after she recovered and has sworn to torment me forever. She's the reason why I'm here actually . . . I got tired of always looking over my shoulder."

The room became silent as my words began to slowly sink in with her. "Is she a better kisser than me?"

My brow furrowed in confusion. Did she really just ask me that?

"Seriously?"

She laughed. "Sorry, just a small moment of insecurity. Can't blame a girl for being curious." The room went quiet again. "So," she finally spoke, shaking her head slightly. "I don't know what to say, Eryx . . . other than . . ." She paused as if searching for the right words.

"I get it if this is too much." I'd grabbed hold of her hands and now took the opportunity to squeeze them reassuringly before letting them fall away. This was the moment. That part of me had been right and this was way too much to expect someone to accept. "I'll walk you back to Hel Tower if you'd like."

Tempest reached for me—stopping me dead in my tracks. "What are you talking about? I'm not scared of you or who lurks in your family tree, Eryx. I'm not afraid to get my hands a little dirty and kick someone's ass if needed. I've got your back." She then raised her fists as though she was ready to start throwing punches. My god, she was beautiful.

My jaw dropped, and I simply stood there, watching her. I could hear her words tumbling about inside my brain, but they seemed too good to be true. "What?"

She chuckled and rolled her eyes. "If you think I'm going to give up on you now, after all the work I've put in, you're smoking some serious crack, Strathos." Tempest grasped my face between her hands and pulled my face to hers, our foreheads touching. "I don't think you've noticed, but I'm falling in love with you. I have a bazillion questions, of course, but we've got time, and I'm not about to let you off so easily."

I crushed her to me, kissing her hard and fast. The world could've ended right that second, and I'd have been happy.

We were going to be fine.

More than fine.

CHAPTER 11

There was no time for celebrating. Once I was positive Tempest and I would be okay, we took the rock and called for an emergency meeting of the group. I wasn't ready to share the grotto's location with anyone other than my girlfriend, so we arranged to go to Clifftop and talk there.

Thirty minutes later and the four of us were together—Felicia and Calix were bundled up in coats and sweaters to ward off the wintery cold and confused over why there was so much urgency. Their gazes kept furtively dropping to the rock Tempest held, and when I finally saw we were alone, I guided them over to a more private cluster of benches.

I let out a quick puff of breath, distracted momentarily by the white fog that appeared from my lips. An icy chill had colored Tempest's cheeks red, and poor Felicia couldn't get her nose to stop dripping as she wiped it furiously.

Damn, Colorado was a frigid nightmare during the winter, and I added the need to pack an extra scarf in my backpack to my mental to-do list.

I didn't think anyone would pay much attention to us—students came and went, the semester in full swing, and most were busy studying or practicing the skills they were learning in class.

"Okay, so are you two going to fill Felicia and me in?" Calix started, his impatience wearing thin. He stomped his feet in an attempt to keep warm. "What couldn't wait until tomorrow or in the very least some place that didn't threaten to freeze my balls off?" He glanced at Felicia and found her nodding in agreement.

"This," Tempest exclaimed, ignoring him and jutting out her hands. With a quick nod, I followed it up with the card we'd been given as the task force assignment. "And that."

They both came closer, and Felicia tilted her head to the side. "Oka-ay," she drew out. "I'm still confused. Didn't we decide to wait until we finished the other tasks and leave this to last?"

Calix smirked like he understood. He elbowed Felicia and pointed to me. "Eryx has already started working on the assignment, and I'm gathering that the rock is a major clue."

He cocked his brow as if challenging me to deny it.

I was done lying. "I didn't tell you guys at first because I was worried what you'd think, and honestly, there's been something about this task that said it was solely for me." I shook my head quickly so they wouldn't interrupt. "Hear me out. I wish I could explain it all to you, but this task also has something to do with my past. I was scared that involving you all before I understood what meant risking your safety."

Felicia wasn't buying any of it. She crossed her arms over her chest and jutted her hip to the side. Tempest liked to call it the 'oh-shit-you-didn't-just-say-that' stance. To me, it looked more like that 'you-better-not-be-inferring-I-need-protecting-because-I'm-a-girl' stance.

"I can take care of myself, Strathos. We're a team. If you're in trouble, we're all in trouble. Just tell us what you need, and we'll get it done." She looked over at Calix to see whether he agreed. He nodded immediately. Perhaps he also interpreted her stance the same way.

Tempest just smiled like she desperately wanted to tell me *I told you so*. While walking to the clifftop, she'd told me I'd underestimated how much people would want to help.

"So let's figure this out." Tempest handed the rock to Felicia and took the card from me. "From what we've been able to figure out—what we need to finish the task lies inside that." She pointed to the stone. "Eryx has been dreaming about this card from the moment we were given it. He believes that the woman is crying because she needs to be freed, which also makes me think it symbolizes the rock. The answer is inside."

"That seems like a long stretch," Calix said, his brow scrunched in concentration. He took the card and peered at it. "What about these other things . . . the chalice of snakes, the ghost thing in the corner."

This was when I chimed in. "The ghost I know is tied with me and my past. I'm not sure that it really factors though. The snakes are also related to me. Along with the dreams, that's why I felt this was mine, and mine alone to solve."

Tempest's finger landed over the grave marker. "The rock was found buried in front of an identical stone."

She looked at me for confirmation, and I nodded.

There was still one more thing I hadn't shared. Slipping my hand into my pocket, I pulled out a coin. "Then there's this. This is a keepsake I've had for as long as I can remember. It's kind of a family heirloom."

Felicia made a face. "Unless you have two of those, Eryx, it's not enough." We all studied the image, and sure enough, there were two coins.

Well, shit.

I wracked my brain, trying to remember if I somehow had a second coin. The one in my hand had particular sentimental value because it had the image of my mother embossed on the face. I had the odd coin from the different places I'd lived, but nothing like this one.

"I don't. Do you think it'll matter?" I scanned the group to see what they thought.

Tempest shrugged, and then shook her head. "They kind of look identical, don't they?" We all studied closer this time, and sure enough, they were. "Do you think the library might have a similar piece? Who could we ask?"

Calix cleared his throat, slowly reaching into his backpack. When he pulled out a coin, those old suspicious thoughts came flying back, larger and more persistent than before.

I instantly lunged for him. "Where did you get this?"

The coin fell to the ground, but not before I caught a glimpse of the face . . . my mother's image peered up at me.

He shoved me off, pissed that I'd once again tried to attack him. "I'm fucking Greek as well, asshat!" he thundered. "Calix Pareias. My freaking name means chalice!"

He paced back and forth, watching to see if I'd come at him again. Tempest had placed herself between us while Felicia appeared ready to do the same.

"We don't have time for this!" Tempest said, staring straight at me. "Focus. If she's using this task to come for you, we need to figure out how to solve it."

I knew what she was saying made sense, but I couldn't stop looking at Calix and the coin that lay between us.

"We're going to talk about this later," I snapped, not bothering to hide my annoyance. Taking a few steps back and letting out a pent-up breath, I desperately tried to refocus. "So I guess we know all the pieces. Even he's represented as the damn chalice in the card. Now what?"

We were stuck once again. What good were pieces if we didn't know how to use them?

"Wasn't there a clue or something that came with the card, Eryx? Everything was given to you, remember?"

All eyes turned to me. Shit. Did I overlook a vital part of the assignment?

I crouched on the ground and went through my backpack. I rarely went anywhere without it now and pulled out all the notes I'd taken.

"Well, shit. You definitely did start it," Calix murmured looking at all the papers covered with my scribbles and doodles. "I thought Tempest was kidding."

I ignored him and finally pulled out the card. There was writing on the back. "Here."

I passed it to Felicia, and she read it out loud.

Contained in this image the pieces you'll find
Look inward for power, share it in kind.
A body of water to contain what is shed
Sacrifice then action to your answer be led.

First blood, trinkets, then sacred wine,

Lift up your voice, call on goddesses divine.
Devil's flame with pure magic, unite as one.
Call for what is hidden, let secrets be undone.

"Well, that makes it clearer," I moaned, kicking myself for not knowing this already. "Just when I think we're a step closer, we actually get forced five steps backward like a blood cha-cha."

Felicia didn't answer, and instead, her mouth moved silently as she reread the clue. Her fingers gripped the paper, making it hard for anyone else to look.

"What are you thinking?" Tempest asked, staring at the ginger. The girl held up her finger, gesturing for one more second. She was wearing a huge grin.

"That it's a brilliant thing I know how to dance, because I'm pretty sure I know what we now need."

A demigod, a witch, and a girl who talks to dead people walked alongside a lake sounded like the beginning of some corny joke, but it wasn't far from the truth. Only in this case, throw in two extra witches, a hellhound, and a guy I still didn't trust, and you'd get the complete picture.

It had taken another two hours for everyone to get on the same page and gather their parts for the ritual. Tempest had instantly texted her besties and asked for their magical help. Natalie and Marina hadn't required any convincing, and after reading through the clues again, the three of them figured that the devil's flame was just the same as Vanna's hellfire.

"Is anyone else freaking out here?" I asked, my stomach in knots. I'd fully intended to work this all by myself, but now we were here—a larger group than anticipated—I worried things might backfire.

"Have a little faith, lover," Tempest encouraged, fixing her long hair back into a bun with one of her favorite crystal hair sticks. "The Fab Four have looked over the magic required, and it seems pretty routine."

Calix looked at the four girls skeptically. "Excuse me for not jumping on the band wagon just yet, but is this something you do every day?"

I wondered what he saw when he looked at Tempest, Natalie,

Marina, and Vanna, and had he been here last semester, would he have even uttered a breath of disbelief in their powers.

Felicia wrapped her arm around his shoulder and pulled him in. "Oh, my sweet boy. Weren't you paying attention last semester? These chicks are as badass as they come. If they say this is easy-peasy, then smile and be grateful you get to witness something incredible."

Vanna didn't say it out loud, but I heard her whisper softly to Marina. "Damn, maybe we should consider expanding the girl band to the Fab Five. She's good for my ego."

Marina chuckled and shushed her.

Felicia must've had the ears of a hawk because she winked and shrugged. "Just tell me where to audition, and I'll bring my resume. It might not be as epic as all of yours, but I do all right for myself."

I cleared my throat, bringing the focus back to the moment. "So, are we agreed? Vanna will create a pillar of hellhound fire and encase the rock in the center. That's where the four of us will form the four elemental points, and then Natalie and Marina will surround us to finish the call of a witch's circle, asking their patron goddesses to come and assist."

Everyone nodded.

"Next," Tempest continued, "once the circle is made sacred, we'll each toss a chosen token to represent our innate powers as an offering and also give a few drops of our blood to amplify the magic. I'll step back and join with Natalie and Marina to say the spell. If all goes well, the hellfire will consume the items and reward us by opening the stone and revealing what's inside." I loved that she also trusted my intuition about the rock.

"Assignment completed and we can then go celebrate for being overachievers and getting it done so quickly!" Felicia exclaimed, blushing when she realized how loudly she'd said it. "Sorry, I guess I am a little nervous. Don't mind me."

There it was. Our plan. To everyone, it was a way to get to the grade, and for me, it was a chance to put my past and fears behind me.

"Why do I feel like we're missing something?" Tempest asked.

Her eyes were cast to the side like she was trying to rifle through her thoughts. "Felicia, read the clue out loud again."

We all listened quietly.

"Well, shit," Marina murmured. "I've got the magic, but I wouldn't exactly call myself pure. Although, I've had a few guys use some choice words to praise me with."

It was Vanna who groaned and apologized for her roomie. "Chica, it's about your intent. Not your virginity."

"Or lack thereof," Natalie added, surprising the others.

Things were starting to get off track, and based on Calix's foot that hadn't stopped tapping since we'd stopped to get prepared, we needed to refocus and get down to business.

"Guys," I exclaimed, not hiding my growing frustration. "Can we save the confessions until afterward?" I hated being the buzzkill, but the quicker this was done, hopefully the sooner I'd be able to sleep.

It was like someone had flipped a switch. Instantly the air above the group changed—becoming more charged and centered. As everyone assumed their positions, I cast a glance over to Tempest. Her smile did a lot to settle my nerves, and I sent her one back. This would work. Any doubt I felt was slowly slipping away.

One by one, each member performed their part.

Hellfire.

Rock.

Summoning of powerful goddesses.

Tempest offered the magical wine from the cellar she'd found last semester.

Felicia offered a resin skull from her medium toolkit.

Calix kissed his coin and added it to the pile.

I said a silent prayer to my mother and tossed mine in as well.

Wind started to whip about us as the three witches began reciting the spell they'd written especially for the task, and flickers of electricity danced over my skin, leaving a trail. A rushing sound emerged from the pillar of flame, and I could feel the vibrations pressing hard against my chest as if it was trying to measure my worth.

I glanced around and saw everyone else was feeling the same

effects. Right when I thought I might fall to my knees from the pressure, there was a flare of bright light and then nothing.

Calix gasped as he bent over, hands on his knees. "Well, did it work?"

I waited for someone to say the spell had been successful, but no one did. In fact, when I turned to look at Tempest, she was busy whispering to Natalie and Marina—all three of their features clouded and apprehensive.

Felicia stretched her back from side to side. Her hair was a mess from leaving it out in the wind. "I'm gathering you were right, and there was something we forgot." She started to pull out the clue again, but got distracted by something else. "Umm, Calix? Wasn't your hair black before?"

"Yeah," he answered, running his fingers through it. "Why?"

Something had happened through the spell, but not what we expected.

Calix stood there now with blond curls, much like the color of mine. The more I stared at him, however, the more I noticed a different kind of aura about him—as though magic was malfunctioning. It flickered a few times rapidly until finally it stopped completely.

Everyone but Calix gasped, but not as loud as me.

"I think we figured out why the spell didn't work," Tempest said, stepping toward me as if she wanted to shield me.

She didn't need to worry about me moving. My feet were rooted to the ground in utter disbelief. All semester Calix Pareias had been this Greek guy with dark curls and scruffy dark facial hair. He was kinda smaller build to me and about two inches shorter.

That was all gone now.

Whatever glamour he'd used to disguise his true self had been incinerated by the spell and hellfire.

"How?" I asked.

Calix must've realized that he was discovered, because after touching his face, he then raised his hands as if to calm me. "Eryx, it's not what you think. Give me a chance. Please."

I was pretty sure there wouldn't be enough words in the

universe for him to explain, and frankly, I didn't think I wanted to hear them.

This had to be a trick.

It was like looking in a mirror.

"Why the fuck do you look like me?"

"*E*ryx," he answered, taking a slow step toward me before stopping abruptly. "I wanted to tell you the instant I saw you that first day we met. I've thought about this moment ever since, and it's killed me to keep hidden from you."

Everyone else was ignored. All I could see was this threat before me who'd been masquerading about as a potential friend.

"So you lied when I asked if you were working for her. You stood there and bold-faced lied. Give me one good reason why I shouldn't break your neck right here and now." My hands clenched at the thought. My gut had warned me something wasn't right about this guy, and I'd foolishly ignored my better judgment—instinct that had kept me alive all this time. "Aphrodite is a bitch who should've just let me go after our last encounter."

"What has she got to do with anything? It was Athena who sent me to Sun & Moon Academy to be with you." The wildness that I saw reflected in Calix's eyes was the same that was tearing my insides apart.

His admission sent me reeling.

"Athena sent you?" That was a betrayal that hurt more than I expected. The Greek pantheon were fickle at the best of times, but the Goddess of Wisdom and War had been my ally and mentor—or so I'd thought. It was under her protection that I shrouded myself from prying eyes and spies. She'd been the one to tutor me in ways of fighting and strategy. That she'd sent this imposter to me hurt deeply. "Am I to trust no one?" I wheeled about as I looked to the heavens.

I knew that the others were still there, watching as all my secrets came to the surface. I just didn't have the mental capacity to contain the explosion. Everything I'd held so tightly had just been eviscerated in the blink of an eye.

"Eryx." Calix's voice sounded nearer. He'd managed to close the distance between us and was now within arm's reach. "You. Can. Trust. Me."

I almost choked on my fury. "You are the last person on this earth I'd ever trust." My mind was swirling and tumbling and frantically trying to grasp some thread of reason. "Why? Please, tell me why?"

He grabbed my arms and looked straight into my eyes. "Because I am your brother."

Everything became deathly quiet.

"What?" I whispered, making barely a sound.

"I'm your twin brother, and I'm here to stand with you. We were separated at birth, but Athena stopped them from tossing me away like second-born trash. She's kept me hidden until the right time. Now." Despite that this echoed in my head like madness, there was no ignoring the gentle reassurances that he was being honest.

Tempest finally came to stand beside me. "He's your family, Eryx. I know it's a lot for you right now, but remember what you told me. You've got time and nothing to lose by hearing him out."

Indecision warred within me. I desperately wanted to believe him—to know that I truly wasn't alone in the world. But I hadn't survived this long by unwisely agreeing with every revelation thrown my way. I'd need some kind of evidence to digest it.

A hissing sound suddenly replaced the silence, and there curled about Calix's shoulders was a serpent—one from my dream—and that peaceful feeling I often had after talking with my mother filled me.

She was claiming her son before me.

My twin.

Holy. Shit.

153

We'd undone the circle, closing it properly, before gathering all the items. It was time to retry the ritual now that we'd figured out with Calix being glamoured by a powerful enchantment, the magic hadn't been pure. Intentions hadn't been upfront and open.

There was a numbness that had crept over me, and I still wasn't sure whether I was in the right frame of mind to be a part of this. Casting glances over to Calix, it was incredible to think that he really was my brother.

"Are you okay to do this?" Tempest asked, and Felicia approached, nodding in agreement. "No one's going to be upset if you need some time to process before we perform the spell again."

"Exactly. The assignment's not even due until the end of the semester so we have plenty of time, Eryx. Seriously, there's no rush." I really liked Felicia. I hoped once the task force class was over, we'd get to hang out more. She definitely fit in with this group.

Calix stood back in his position, and I could tell he wanted to say something, but didn't want to intrude. I studied him for a moment and tried to get around the fact we looked the same, to see if there was anything else I could sense from him.

My coin burned inside my pocket, and I pulled it out quickly, carefully holding the edges between my fingers. Whether it was real or imagined, I didn't care—I could've sworn I saw the snakes on my mother's head slither a little before going back to normal.

If there was anything I knew with any surety right now, it was that I could trust her, and she approved of Calix. We'd somehow get to the bottom of everything and answer each other's questions.

I walked to Calix and extended my arm, offering him the warrior's greeting. He didn't hesitate, and then took another risk. He drew me in and embraced me, slapping his hand against my back.

"I know this doesn't make things magically perfect, and we still need to get to know one another, but I'm grateful to at least have the opportunity."

This time I didn't duck my head or look away. "Me too. This is a lot to swallow, but I imagine it hasn't been easy for you either." I wiped the back of my wrist against my face and let out a tired sigh. "Once this is done, let's go eat or something." It seemed like the best step forward.

"Okay."

Tempest wore an expression of pride when I rejoined her. "I'm proud of you."

Releasing the tightness in my jaw, I nodded. "I love you." She gasped, but I didn't give her a chance to react past that. "Let's try again, shall we? I've got things to do and a brother to get to know."

In silence, we began the spell again, repeating the steps the ritual demanded.

Hellfire.

Rock.

Summoning of powerful goddesses.

Tempest offered the wine.

Felicia's resin skull.

Calix's coin and then finally mine.

Electricity crackled once more, and the wind began whipping about our bodies. I closed my eyes as Natalie, Tempest, and Marina began chanting their incantation, and this time I just knew that the ritual would be successful.

Where before there had been a flare of bright light and then nothing—a loud crack split the air and the sobbing from my dreams burst into reality.

Except, this time it wasn't just the familiar woman who emerged from the pillar of hellfire, but a chorus of wailing and tear-filled cries from countless bodies that then swirled above the now broken rock. As the flames diminished, we could see that there had been something inside—the most beautiful, iridescent crystal in the shape of a tear.

The magic had been successful.

The spell, however, was still in effect as more and more spirits burst free from the crystal. The more I watched in awe, the more it reminded me of looking at a tornado, only this time it was made from ghosts who'd been trapped for who knew how long.

When the last of the beings had escaped, the sandy ground around the crystal became soaked with water, and they formed a crowd over the lake, each one staring back at us.

The woman who had been shown on the card and had appeared in my dream stepped forward—the allocated spokesman to the group.

"Thank you," her voice called out, growing stronger with each passing second. Gone were the tears of grief and mourning. Her smile was softer, kinder, and one filled with a gentle kind of happiness. "You have freed us from our prison, and for that we will forever be grateful."

We huddled together, holding each other's hands for support. Never in our wildest dreams had we thought this would be the result. We'd talked about what to do once the spell was performed, but it hadn't gone any further than picking up whatever remained from the rock and then turning it in to Addie Beaumont.

Instead, we were on the receiving end of something sacred.

"Who are you?" I asked, respectfully.

"We are like your mother, Son of Medusa. Human females who were caught by the cruel and deceptive webs of the gods to be used and discarded as playthings. We are their victims. It will be our tears for vengeance and justice that fuel the power remaining in that crystal." She next turned and focused on Felicia. "Please send us to our afterlife, medium. We have been restless for far too long."

Perhaps it was an occupational hazard and part of her magic, but Felicia pulled out a small brass bell from her pocket and nodded. "It would be my honor."

As she recited the words of her craft, the spirits rose into the air until all but the woman remained.

"The crystal in the wrong hands poses a great threat. I trust that you will ensure its safety, Sons of Medusa."

Silence returned, and the ritual was declared complete.

No one spoke a word.

What would we have said anyway?

CHAPTER 14

$\mathcal{N}$ ow this was my idea of heaven.

Back when I'd gone to Athena for protection from Aphrodite, she'd promised me eternal life, or until I'd at least found a way to overcome my paralyzing power and discover true, heartfelt happiness. She'd taken pity on me.

In this moment, I'd almost be tempted to claim I'd found it.

Wrapped up in Tempest's arms, alone in my room, we'd spent the last few hours kissing and melting into each other—the kind of make out session that addles your brain and robs you of breath.

God, I loved this woman. I loved everything about her, and it was safe to finally accept that she was in fact mine. There'd be no more secrets and pushing her away, no more fear that I'd be the one to someday kill her from being careless. She soothed that ragged part of me that had experienced too much cruelty and found it hard to trust.

I couldn't get enough of her—her smile, her sass, and definitely not of the way her heart seemed to beat in time with mine. She understood my hesitancy in fully embracing Calix and supported the small steps we were starting to take. There was no pressure from her, despite how slowly I felt things were going between us. For now, we were exactly as we should be—blissfully in love and figuring out what that meant.

"Eryx," she murmured softly. "Don't think I've forgotten that you said you loved me."

I kissed the top of her head and pulled her in closer to my body. Her hand was now draped over my chest as she lay on her side.

Absolutely, undeniably in love.

"And I meant it. Never going to take it back, just in case you're worried. I say what I mean and mean what I say."

The contented sigh she released bypassed my heart and shot straight to my crotch. We hadn't discussed sex yet, but sooner or later that would be the next thing up for discussion.

"Then say it again . . . loudly. Shout it to the world."

I laughed as I reached around so I could cup my hands in front of my mouth. "I love you, Tempest Bell!"

As far as being a shout, my attempt barely reached the walls of my room.

She rolled her gorgeous brown eyes and rested up on one elbow. "I doubt just this floor heard that, Eryx. I guess I was wrong."

"That's because my whole world is in this room with me." I'd seen some cheesy meme on the Internet and couldn't resist using the sentiment on her. It earned me the reward I wanted—a goofy grin that made me lean in and steal another kiss.

"I wish everyone could be as happy as I feel right now, Eryx. I hate that I can't fix everything." Her voice had taken on a sad tone, and I knew exactly who she was referring to.

"You can't force Natalie to be cheerful, sweetheart. Some people, most people need to time to process, to grieve, to figure out their next move. The best thing you can do for her is to let her know you're there when she needs you without smothering her with love. You don't have to fill the silence with words. She knows you care. She'll let you know when she needs something."

"So me trying to fill every moment with something to take her mind off her mom's death isn't really what she needs right now." I could see the guilt beginning to creep across her face. This girl had such a good heart.

"What does your gut say?" I countered softly, knowing she already knew the answer.

Tempest chuckled low and drew in a deep breath. "That there's such thing as overkill and that I wouldn't blame my bestie if she felt she needed to smother me with my pillow in my sleep." A softness filled her features as she watched me. "How the hell did you get so wise?"

The truth was it came from having to survive the death of my own mother and the avalanche that followed. I didn't confess that maybe for Natalie, time wouldn't be the all-healing grace people professed it to be, that maybe she'd simply learn to function with the pain and settle into a new form of normal.

Like I had.

"What doesn't kill you makes you stronger, right? Even as it leaves a giant empty hole in your heart," I joked.

Natalie and I now had that in common.

Death was a mighty changer of souls.

"Speaking of hearts, what does this mean for you and Calix? How does it feel knowing you not only have a brother, but a twin?"

"Can we just go back to kissing?" I asked, more serious than I was teasing. I still couldn't quite wrap my mind around the bombshell he'd dropped at my feet, but I couldn't ignore the fact he existed forever. Athena had kept him hidden for a reason, choosing now as the time to reunite us. I didn't always understand her methods, or agree with them, but she'd done right by me in the past. I was currently alive because of her and given the chance to find love and happiness despite Aphrodite. It had always felt like a curse until Tempest. Falling in love with her and knowing she felt the same about me made the endless centuries alone worth it.

Who knew, maybe having Calix now would give me the family I'd always craved.

"Just promise me you'll give him . . . the both of you a real chance."

It was my turn to look at her questioningly. "And if I don't?"

She shrugged and tapped her finger lightly over my lips. "Then it's going to be a really long rest of the semester. Reeaaallly long."

I shifted on the bed, so I was back to leaning over her. I loved the way she stared up at me—trusting that I wouldn't break her heart. "You'll be by my side, though, right?"

"Absolutely. Especially if you need your stubborn ass kicked. I take my girlfriend responsibilities seriously." She squirmed beneath me, knowing that it got a rise out of me.

I feathered a light kiss over both her eyes before stopping right above her mouth. "As I take mine."

"Remind me," she murmured.

She didn't need to ask me twice.

"With pleasure."

CHAPTER 15

"Well, I'd like to say I'm glad that's over with, but who am I kidding? Something tells me that the Regents will continue to give us assignments from Hell." Dusting off his hands, Calix glanced at me, waiting to see if I agreed with his sentiments.

I'd volunteered to be the one to deliver the crystal to Addie and he'd spoken up about joining me. It was still weird looking at him and seeing my own reflection. He'd dropped the glamour now the truth was out, and things had been tentative between us ever since.

I had a twin.

I wasn't alone in the world.

And surprise, surprise, we were both fellow students at the academy.

I smirked in agreement. It was a bullshit way to learn, but damned if it wasn't effective. "I'd like to say it's all smooth sailing from here on out, but I'd be lying."

With the door to the boardroom closed, and the crystal finally delivered into the Regents' hands, our assignment was officially completed. If I didn't get an A for all the shit we went through, I'd be pissed.

"So," Calix added, falling into step beside me, "where does that leave us?"

For someone I'd been so skeptical and cautious about, I wasn't quite sure how to answer. He wasn't some guy following me around after hours or always seeming to lurk about. He wasn't even just some student. He was my brother, and we shared a history together that needed to be explored.

Where had he been all this time? Why hadn't he tried to find me? Was he clueless to my existence like I had been to his? Had he faced any of our mother's enemies?

But most importantly—how did our mother's curse afflict him?

I had more questions than answers.

"I think we take it one step at a time and get to know one another," I replied, my hand keeping the strap from my backpack on my shoulder. "I think we hang out and see how it goes."

"That simple, huh?" he countered. "If I remember right, you threatened to kick my ass."

I chuckled at the memory. "And I'm not promising I won't do it again, but the point is," I came to a stop so I could talk face-to-face, "I've never had a brother before, and I'd like to see what that feels like. As long as we're upfront and honest, we'll be just fine."

A wave of relief crashed over my brother's face. "I can do that." He slapped the side of my arm. "Brother."

I liked how that sounded.

Brother.

Sun & Moon Academy may try to kill me every semester, but I couldn't ignore the gifts it had granted.

Tempest.

Friends.

And now, family.

THREE OF PENTACLES

E.J. FECHENDA

Havenwoodies, you're the best!

CHAPTER 1

*M*ovement out of the corner of my eye distracted me, and I looked up from my sketchpad to see Timber Greenwood pacing a few feet away from where I was sitting. I had found a table in Halstein Hall, tucked in the corner, away from the food court and main entrance. I tensed and immediately looked around for Timber's best friend, who also happened to be my ex-boyfriend. I didn't see Cole anywhere and let out a breath. We weren't like enemies or anything, but our relationship didn't end well. In fact, it almost killed me.

Timber hadn't seen me yet, and my lips twitched with amusement as I watched him pace. *What is he doing?* I thought to myself and took advantage of his being unaware of my attention. Timber was what my best friend Makenna and I considered a fabe. He was a fae and a babe—a golden prince straight out of a fairy tale, as cliché as it may sound. Timber was all cheekbones, refined jawbone, muscles for days, and had the most intense green eyes. Add in his flawless, pearlescent skin and his thick, white blond hair, and he practically glowed. Timber was the total fabe package and put any human male model to shame. While Cole had the same appeal, and was the dark to Timber's light, Timber's looks weren't dangerous. Unlike Cole who was a Gancanagh, an Unseelie fae variety of incubus, who had a fatal allure for human women. Timber had caught my eye last semester, but he was best friends with my ex, an unlikely friendship they had developed when Cole was exiled to Faerie. Despite my physical attraction to Timber, I considered him off limits. I had spotted them in Havenwood Falls over winter break, and they were always together. But here he was without Cole.

Timber hadn't really been on my radar until late last semester. At the time I had been dating Orion, a lion shifter who had recently moved to my hometown, Havenwood Falls. Then one day in early November, I stumbled upon Timber while he was alone. He'd been perched on a boulder that suspended out over the lake, playing the violin. Timber's hiking boots were on the rock next to him beside an open violin case. The water was warmer than the air outside, and his bare feet disappeared into the mist that rose up from the lake's surface like smoke. He played with such emotion. Every glide of his bow across the strings spoke of sadness, longing, heartache, and joy. Such complexity. His back was to me, and he'd appeared to be lost in the music. His long fingers coaxed out notes as he cradled the violin between his shoulder and jaw. His silvery blond hair moved as he rocked gently to the song. I noticed that plants had sprouted up along the water's edge and from in between cracks in the rock. These swayed in sync with Timber's movements.

I'd felt like an intruder. This was his own private moment, and I was a voyeur, but I couldn't look away. I was captivated by him. The music stopped, and Timber set his violin down on his lap to gaze out across the water. I should have slipped silently away then, but I didn't.

"Do you want to join me? There's room," Timber's deep voice broke the silence. He patted the empty space next to him.

"Uh. Um." A flush crept up my neck and bloomed on my cheeks when I realized he knew I had been creeping on him the entire time. "I have to go."

I turned around and ran. Why? Because I was an awkward asshole, that's why. From that point on, I was hyperaware of the Seelie fae, but always kept a safe distance for where Timber was,

Cole was sure to be near, and I couldn't allow myself to get close to him.

"Timber, are you looking for something or someone?" I called out, and he stopped pacing immediately, turning to face me, and my breath caught when my eyes met his. They were bright green, like emeralds glittering in a sunbeam. Then he smiled, and my heart literally broke in half. His smile softened the hard lines of his jaw and lit up his eyes even more. *Holy faeries, I'm going to need to change my panties.*

"I noticed you were alone, and I was wondering if I may join you?" Timber had a subtle accent and spoke like he was from a different century. I bet he had never said OMG or WTF in his entire life. His old fashioned mannerisms were endearing and added to his fabeness.

"Funny, I was thinking the same thing...that you were alone, I mean. Not about joining you." I tripped over my words and warmth flooded my cheeks.

"Oh, I see." Timber lowered his gaze and started to step away.

"Wait! You're more than welcome to sit with me. I'm just chilling. If this semester is anything like last semester, once classes start tomorrow I won't have time to draw." I moved my bag off the other chair at the table and gestured for him to take a seat. I smiled at Timber and took a few deep, centering breaths to help settle the flutter of nerves that erupted when he smiled in return and sat down.

"Why is it that on Earth, the females always seem to travel in packs?" he asked.

"What?" I responded with a laugh.

"It's just that I noticed females aren't often alone."

I cocked an eyebrow at this statement. "Honestly, it's safety in numbers. Women are horribly victimized. You should look at the statistics some time. Is it not like that in Faerie?"

"Fairies, no!" Timber answered, appalled. "The queen punishes crimes like that so severely that no one dares."

"The pluses of living under matriarchal rule, I guess." I tucked a chunk of loose hair behind my ear and leaned forward. "Tell me more about Faerie. I've never been."

"I think I would remember you if you had," Timber said with

a smile. "Your cousin Julia has. I met her at Court in Tír na nÓg once." Timber started telling me about his life in a different realm, and I was enthralled. We spent the next two hours talking.

Later that afternoon, I went back to my room in Modi Tower to drop off books and to get ready to meet Makenna and Taylor for dinner. My roommate, Fig, looked up from her corner of our room when I walked in. She pointed at my dresser to an enormous bouquet of flowers. They were Calla lilies, my favorite. These particular ones were a light aqua blue on the outside of the tubular petal and the inside a dark purple. I could smell the lilies from across the room and grinned at the reminder of home. My mom owned a florist shop in Havenwood Falls, so I automatically thought she had sent them.

Thanks for the flowers! I texted to my mom, and she replied almost immediately.

Mom: What flowers?

I took a picture of the bouquet and sent it to her. It miraculously went through. Sometimes I had to wait an hour for a text to send or sometimes they never delivered at all.

Mom: Not from me or the store. No deliveries from here to campus. Who is sending you flowers??

Me: IDK

"Hey, Fig, who delivered these?"

"There's a card," she said with a shrug.

I poked around the flowers, but couldn't find an envelope.

"Where?" I asked, growing annoyed.

Fig was painfully shy and getting information out of her was like pulling teeth. With a huff she looked up from the book she was reading. "Underneath."

The bouquet wasn't in a vase, but tied up with a teal and silver bow, which happened to be the Modi Tower colors. I lifted the bundle, and that's when I saw the note. It was on some sort of vellum, and the slanted handwriting looked like it was written with a fountain pen. There were heavier spots of ink absorbed into the fibrous paper.

Paisley – I look forward to next time. X

"Who is X?" Fig asked, revealing that she had snooped and read the note.

"I don't know." I flipped the paper over to see if there was anything written on the back, but it was blank. I wasn't exactly lying to Fig. I mean, being fae, I couldn't lie to her. I didn't know exactly, but had my suspicions. There was one guy in particular who could grow flowers, vines, even a whole forest with a thought —a fae ability identical to my mom's. A guy I had spent the last two hours with: Timber. *Was he into me like that, though?* The thought made me flush. We had exchanged numbers, so I reached for my phone and sent him a text.

And that's how it all began.

CHAPTER 2

ONE MONTH LATER

*L*amps lit the courtyard as I crossed over to the library, the flickering light from their flames creating an illusion that the shadows were moving. I spotted Amaruq, Vanna, and Timber walking together. Using my preternatural speed, something I couldn't do in Havenwood Falls because there were too many people around, I caught up to them and was tempted to smack Timber on his delicious ass, but had to act normal.

Sneaking around and keeping a relationship secret when you're a fae was so hard. You see, fae can't lie. We could be pretty adept at twisting the truth or giving vague enough responses, though, which was how Timber and I had kept our relationship on the down low. Fortunately, my roommate, Fig, could give two figs where I went and with whom. If I was roommates with my best friend, Makenna, she would know my prolonged and unexplained absences were suspicious. It was a lot harder for Timber to keep Cole in the dark and explain his sudden unavailability since they were best friends *and* roommates. We promised each other we would go public soon, when we were ready, on our terms.

What helped was that we were on the same team for the Interdisciplinary Task Force or ITF, which, in my opinion, stood for Isn't This Fucked? Because it was. Each team had been given several missions that needed to be completed by the end of the semester. The extra class added more work, and the missions weren't easy. So, yeah, it was stressful. The only consolation was Timber. Since we were on the same team, it meant more time spent together and provided the perfect cover for us.

"Hi, guys!" I said and fell into step beside Vanna. The tattoos on her arms were a blur of color as we walked. She wore a short sleeve shirt even though living inside Mount Alexa was like always being inside a refrigerator. Vanna's Hellhound blood meant she always ran hot and that she always had to wear sunglasses. Hellhounds' eyes were fatal to other species who gaze upon them. The campus was fairly quiet. Most students were done with classes for the night, except for those signed up for Professor Shimizu's Combat and Defense class, and for ITF, which included a lesson every Wednesday night. We had finally completed our first mission. It had taken almost a month. Like I said, they weren't easy.

"Are you ready?" I asked Amaruq, looking over at him. He was tall and moved with purpose, his long legs eating up the ground with his stride. Thick, dark hair hung over his almond shaped eyes. His face was angular, all sharp cheekbones and a strong jaw.

"Yeah, I'm turning the report in before class. Piece of cake, eh?" Amaruq, an Inuit from Northwestern Canada, had a strong accent, and he ended most of his questions with eh.

For each task, one of us had to be the team leader. At our first class, when the missions were handed out, we decided it'd be easier to go alphabetically, so Amaruq was the leader for our first mission, which required us to locate ingredients for and to make a detoxifying potion. This wasn't going to be the only potion we were required to make this semester, but it was intended to be the most challenging. It wasn't like we could just go shopping at Howe's and buy all the stuff needed; no, the list contained obscure items, like a scale from a siren and venom from a Malayan pit viper, which aren't native to Colorado. None of us on our team were witches, either. Amaruq was a grey wolf shifter, Vanna a hellhound, with Timber and I being Seelie fae. Fortunately, we were able to ask for help and seek outside resources. One of my good friends, Taylor Augustine, was a witch and a student at SMA. Once we acquired the venom, she helped us finish the potion, which we were supposed to keep on us for emergencies. Moments like this reminded me that SMA was not an ordinary college. I thought college was supposed to be easy, like beer bongs and eating shitty food at three in the morning. Not here. Here we were being trained to be supernatural guardians.

Other teams were already working on their second mission, and I was beginning to feel the pressure. We were almost halfway through February and with mid-terms right around the corner, I didn't know how much time we would have to devote to the task force.

We reached the classroom in Eirhal and filed in with the other students. The classroom was set up like an amphitheater with four rows of seats in a tier that looked down on the lecture area. Dark wood paneling lined the walls and made the atmosphere almost cozy. Amaruq split off to set his report on the table in the lecture area. I spotted Roxy McCabe across the room, and we waved to each other as I climbed the stairs to an empty row. Timber sat down next to me and moved so his thigh was flush with mine. I set my bag down on the floor by my feet and on the way up, briefly touched his leg and gave it a quick squeeze. I looked around to make sure no one saw.

Fortunately, Cole was sitting in the front row with his team, which was made up of Fin, D, and Fin's sometimes nemesis, Cat. He had his laptop set on the small desk and sat ready to take notes. This was one of the noticeable changes I'd observed from afar since Cole had returned from Faerie. In high school, he was always chill and spent most of his time doodling in his sketchbook. Now he was focused and driven. I mentioned this change to Timber when we first started dating, and he offered an explanation.

"Cole sees SMA as a second chance—a way to prove he's not a monster."

"But he's not one," I had protested. For the longest time I hated Cole, but that had faded over time, and I understood what had happened wasn't his fault.

"You and I both know that, but he thinks he is after what he did to you and the other girls. He wants to learn to be a force for good. But enough about Cole." Timber had ended the conversation by kissing me. He gave expert-level, distracting kisses. One of the paneled walls opened, and Elsmed Fairchild entered the room, pulling me out of the memory. Everyone went quiet, so quiet you could hear the rustle of his robes. Not only was Elsmed on the Board of Regents for SMA, he also sat on the Court of the Sun and the Moon, the supernatural governing body of Havenwood Falls. He could also read minds and was over a thousand years old. His frosty blue eyes scanned the room and paused on me briefly. I stopped breathing and immediately cleared my head of my thoughts about Timber's kiss and the dirty things I wanted to do with him after class. Elsmed scowled and shook his head before moving on. *Shit, too late.*

"Good evening, young academics. For those of you who don't know me, I am Elsmed Fairchild, and I am one of your Regents. It's been a few centuries since I taught in a classroom. Now, before we get to tonight's lesson, I understand that one of the teams has completed a mission." He held our team's report in his hand, and Elsmed's frosty gaze landed on Amaruq. "Please stand young man."

Amaruq, who was sitting directly in front of me, peered over his shoulder at us, wearing a slightly panicked expression.

"You got this," Vanna elbowed his side, spurring him into action. Amaruq rose to his feet.

"Tell me, Mr. Kasook," Elsmed said. "How did you go about completing this mission?"

After clearing his throat, Amaruq explained the process of finding the ingredients and how we worked together to create the potion.

"And are you positive the potion works?" Elsmed asked.

"Um, yeah. Pretty sure, eh?"

"Pretty sure? Let's test it out. We can't have you out in the field with a faulty antidote. That can mean the difference between life and death. Come on down here, young wolf. You and your teammates."

We all looked at each other in confusion. This hadn't happened before where a team was called up for a demonstration. Apparently Elsmed's methods were more hands-on. I shrugged and proceeded down the steps that led to the lecture area. Elsmed dug into a pocket in his robe and pulled out a test tube sized vial, he held it out toward Amaruq who took it hesitantly.

"What is this, Sir?" he asked, eyeing the murky dark purple liquid with a raised eyebrow.

"It's Acotinum napellus, also known as monkshood, but you probably know it as wolfsbane. Drink it."

"What?" The color drained from Amaruq's face, and he dropped the vial like it burned him. I wasn't surprised. Wolfsbane was highly toxic for wolf shifters. It was essentially rat poison for them. Before the vial hit the ground, Elsmed caught it in mid-air, displaying moves that belied his elderly appearance.

"I don't understand. The other teams didn't have to test out their potions like this." Amaruq's dark eyes met Elsmed's frosty blue ones, and I gasped at my teammate's balls to challenge the ancient fae.

"Yes, well, I believe in hands-on education," Elsmed said and nodded in my direction. Son of a faerie! He plucked that straight from my mind. "Now bottoms up, lad, we don't have all night." Elsmed held the vial out again.

"It's okay, Amaruq. I'm a healer, remember? I got your back if the potion fails," I said in what I hoped was a reassuring tone. Vanna came to stand beside me, moving closer to the action.

"This better fucking work," she whispered, and I nodded in agreement, not taking my eyes off of Amaruq as he tilted his head back and swallowed. His Adam's apple bobbed up and down, and we could all tell the moment the wolfsbane hit his system. A guttural howl erupted from his throat before he dropped to the floor. The vial of detoxifying potion that he had been holding in his other hand fell and rolled, coming to a stop when it hit the steps. Fortunately, the glass didn't break. His veins became visibly black beneath his skin and purplish gray foam began to bubble out of his mouth.

Timber moved into action and knelt on one side, holding Amaruq down. The rest of the class stood up to watch the horrific spectacle unfold. I held my hand out and focused on the vial. Telekinesis was one of my latent abilities that I had been developing since my awakening. Shaving off a few seconds meant the potion could be administered sooner. The vial skipped along the concrete floor before it became airborne. It flew across the lecture area and landed in my palm.

"Hold his mouth open," I ordered Timber who carefully avoided sharp canines that appeared. Amaruq was getting ready to shift, and we couldn't let that happen. He had a better chance of fighting off the toxin in his human form. If he achieved full shift, it could be fatal. I had learned this in the field medicine class I took last semester.

Vanna had taken up position at Amaruq's feet and held him down to control his thrashing. I poured half of the potion into his mouth, and Timber held it closed, forcing him to swallow. Almost instantly Amaruq stopped convulsing and his veins faded to normal, like ink being washed away. Within minutes he was sitting up and wiping sweat from his brow as color slowly returned to his face, restoring the ruddy olive complexion.

"Excellent work! You have successfully completed this mission." Elsmed breezed nonchalantly to the front of the lecture area as if poisoning a student happened every day and was no big deal. "Now take your seats and let's move on to tonight's lesson—shielding your minds from telepaths—like me."

"Are you all right, man?" Timber asked when he helped hoist a shaky Amaruq to his feet.

"Yeah. Thank fuck that potion worked."

We walked close to Amaruq as we climbed the stairs to go back to our seats.

"No kidding. Here." Vanna reached into her bag and handed him a bottle of water before we all sat down. It was hard to focus after that, but somehow we managed.

After class, we walked to Halstein Hall, where the food court was located, to get some food in Amaruq's stomach. The smell of greasy fries from Blazed Burgers hit my nose the moment Timber opened the door.

"After you, milady," he said with a wink as I walked past him.

It seemed like almost everyone else from ITF had the same idea, and voices bounced around the hall, the cathedral ceiling amplifying everything. As I was waiting in line behind Amaruq for a vanilla milkshake, Joe Greg approached him.

"Dude, Fin told me what happened!" He slapped Amaruq on the back. "Wolfsbane is no joke."

"Right, eh? I don't ever want to experience that again." Amaruq grabbed his order of five venison burgers and walked off with Joe to go sit at a table with other wolf shifters.

"You were pretty amazing in class, you know," Timber said, coming to stand next to me. "You acted quickly and took charge."

"Thanks." My major was Emergency Medicine, and it was a boost to my confidence knowing I responded quickly and with a clear head. I gave him a shy smile when all I really wanted to do was throw my arms around his neck and kiss him. I started to move closer then I saw Cole approaching and took a step back.

"Hi, Paisley," he said when he reached us. Cole's long fingers rubbed a cuff wrapped around his left wrist, something I noticed he did a lot, like he was reassuring himself that it was still on. I had undergone my awakening when Cole and I were dating. That was over two years ago, and at the time, the very sight of Cole's beauty would render me breathless. His dark hair and sea glass green eyes stood out against his flawless pale skin. Fortunately, the cuffs he wore were made of a special fae alloy that suppressed his toxin and his allure.

"Hey," I responded and was relieved that it was my turn to pick up my order so I wasn't expected to continue the conversation. Cole and I weren't on bad terms, but not great either. Despite knowing how bad he was for me, there was still a part of me that longed for him. I was addicted to his toxin, and I think a part of him would always be inside me, nestled deep and eager for another taste. Perhaps I should drink some of that detoxifying potion.

"Here you go, Paisley," Bale Grayson handed me my milkshake and scanned my SMA tattoo for payment. Whatever I owed would be billed to my student account. Bale hadn't changed much since high school. His brown hair was still on the long side and hung in his dark eyes. He was more the quiet and observant type, which was why I was surprised to find him working the register. He was usually behind the scenes manning the grill, like Simon at Fallview Tavern & Grille in Havenwood Falls. Perhaps it had to do with breathing fire, but apparently dragon shifters knew how to barbecue.

I was putting a straw through the hole in the lid when Timber tapped me on the shoulder. "Hey, Paisley, I'll catch you later. Cole and I are heading back to our room."

"Oh, okay. See ya." I stood there with my shake in hand watching them leave, frustrated and disappointed that our goodbye had to be so platonic.

"Stop it, Paisley Violet Underwood! You do not look longingly after your ex-boyfriend! That's like, rule number one. You're over him. He's bad for you. Move on." Makenna appeared in a blur of energy, coming to stand in front of me in order to block my view. She grabbed my shake and took a sip. I rolled my eyes and reclaimed it.

"I was not looking at Cole."

"Good. He practically killed you, and I'd have to kill you if you were even considering..." Her brown eyes grew wide then she squealed. "Holy faeries, you were checking out Timber! Can't say I blame you girl, as we have discussed his faebeliciousness. Questionable judgment though, if he's friends with what's-his-face."

"Cole isn't some evil serial killer, Mak. He didn't know I'd react to his toxin like I did. Hell, how could any of us know? Had he known, he would have kept away. I feel bad for him. It's not like he chose to be born a Gancanagh." I started to walk away from the crowded area for more privacy.

"No, no, nope, you are not changing the subject. Back to Timber, the man who knows his way around wood, if you know what I mean?" Mak wiggled her eyebrows suggestively, and I snorted.

"Stop!" I said with a laugh and swatted at her arm. "I'm going to spew milkshake out of my nose. That would be wasteful and nasty."

"This is true." She snagged the cup again and took another long sip before handing it back. "So are you going to spill or what? I can tell by how red your cheeks are that there is more to this story."

I couldn't lie, and this was my best friend. Not telling her had been torture. We shared everything. "Fine, let's go somewhere private."

The great room was busy, and I spotted Fig sitting with her friend Sadie and Sadie's new girlfriend, Elliana, around the huge hearth, so I knew our dorm room was available. We took the spiral stairs to the eighth floor, and when we reached my room, the magical lock read the magic in my tattoo, causing the door to click open. The portals to get into campus were set up in a similar way. You had to have a special SMA tattoo to gain access. Magical infused tech, when it worked, was pretty cool.

Makenna flopped down on my queen bed, and her red hair fanned out against my white comforter. I set my bag down on my desk chair and paused to sniff the bouquet Timber had anonymously sent me at the beginning of the semester. The lilies hadn't aged or faded and smelled as sweet as the first day. The lighting in the room suddenly dimmed, and a breeze caressed my cheek. Being that we were inside a mountain, beyond the reach of any breeze, I turned my head in the direction and was surprised to see a set of French doors wide open framed by gauzy white curtains that fluttered in a gentle wind. Instead of a view of stalactites and the dark gray stone walls that made up the inside of Mount Alexa, the glittering lights of Paris at night stretched out before me, the Eiffel Tower in the distance, glowing like a giant beacon. The doors led out to a small balcony that held two chairs.

"Wow, Mak! This is your best glamour yet," I said as I stepped out onto the balcony. The sounds of traffic swirled up from below, the scent of coffee and sweetness of fresh baked pastries hung in the air. Looking down, I saw a patisserie on the corner. I placed my hands on the balcony railing that had a dull shine like old pennies, and the cold of the metal seeped into my skin. "It's not iron," I commented. Typically, this would be a wrought iron balcony, but fae were highly allergic to that metal, which was one of the few weaknesses to our immortal race.

"Copper," Makenna said from behind, and she stepped out to join me. "I've been practicing. Pretty cool, huh?"

"Amazing!" All fae had the ability to create glamours, but Mak's talent was exceptional and her superpower. I could change my appearance and create some illusions, but could never conjure up something so real like this.

"I don't know how long it will hold, so you better spill the tea about Timber, Paise." Mak came to stand beside me, and we both looked out at the skyline. I was quiet for a few seconds, taking in the sight of the Eiffel Tower, while I contemplated how to tell her about my secret romance.

"First, I need you to make two promises."

"I'd help you kill someone and hide the body, you know that. What am I promising to do?"

"Okay, first promise me you won't freak out, and secondly, you can't tell anyone. Not a soul. This stays strictly between you and me."

"Now you're beginning to freak me out." Makenna turned to face me, leaning one elbow on the railing.

"Just promise, okay?"

"Fine, I promise. Pinky swear." She held her pinky out toward me, and I grinned. We had been making pinkie swears since the first grade. With her promises sealed, I took a deep breath.

"Timber and I have been secretly seeing each other for almost a month," I blurted, basically just ripping the band-aid off and putting the truth out there.

"What!" Her eyes grew wide and reflected the Paris lights. "Are you serious?"

I nodded and chewed on my bottom lip in an effort to contain my grin. I was relieved to finally share this with my best friend, and being able to shock her added to the joy.

"For almost a month?"

I nodded again, and this time I couldn't hold back my smile. "He's incredible, Mak, and I hated not telling you."

"Why keep it a secret?" She had stood up straight and crossed her arms over her chest. Based on her tone, I could tell she was a little more than pissed.

"Because of Cole. I don't want it to be awkward or weird. Plus, I'd feel terrible if Cole got pissed at Timber. They're best friends, and I don't want to come between them."

"Unbelievable!" Mak threw her hands up in the air and spun around. As she walked, the glamour shadowed her, and the Paris backdrop started to shrink. As the edges approached the balcony, like a wave creeping on shore, I followed her inside my room.

"I thought you'd be annoyed, but didn't expect you to be this mad, and you promised not to freak out," I said to her back. She spun around to face me.

"For faeries sake, Paisley, do you even hear yourself? You've been sneaking around behind all of your friends' backs to protect Cole? The guy who almost killed you?" Her voice grew louder and her face redder with each question. Makenna rarely became angry, but when she did, she had the temper of a hungry giant. Any earlier joy I had experienced at finally telling her had been extinguished.

"It's not like that!" I shouted back, instantly regretting rising to her anger. I took a deep, steadying breath, reminding myself that Makenna was my best friend and her reaction came from a place of love—of concern for me. My next words were said in a calm voice. "Mak, what Timber and I have is so different than my relationship with Cole. I hope you know me well enough that I'm not going to allow myself to get caught up like that again."

It had been over two years since Cole and I split up. I'd done a lot of reflecting since then. "I realize that the euphoria I felt when I was with Cole, and how terrible I felt when we were apart, was my reaction to his toxin. I recognize that wasn't normal, and I was displaying all the traits of an addict. With Timber, our connection is deeper."

Makenna sighed and sat down on the edge of my bed. "I just worry about you."

She looked up at me, her blue eyes glistening with tears.

"Oh, Mak, I know." I sat down next to her and took her hand in mine. "I'm really okay—I promise. And I'm glad you know now. It's up to Timber to tell Cole, since they're best friends."

"I don't like it, but your secret is safe with me."

"And that's why you're my bestie." I smiled at Mak, and she squeezed my hand before releasing it and standing up. She tossed her hair out of the way before lifting her bag to her shoulder. She smoothed the short navy blue skirt she wore, erasing any wrinkles with magic.

"I have a test in Magical Combat tomorrow that I have to prepare for, so I'm going to head out. No more secrets, okay?"

"No more secrets," I promised.

"Let me know the moment Timber tells Cole and he better do it sooner than later or I'm going to think he's playing games with you."

"I will."

She left, and I sunk back against my pillows. I stared up at the strands of tiny white lights that were strung across the ceiling. With Mak now in the know, part of the weight I had been carrying from not saying anything lifted.

CHAPTER 3

*B*ecause, apparently, I was a glutton for punishment, I picked classes that started at either 8:00 or 9:00 am every day of the school week. No sleeping in for me. Thank the faeries Willow had opened a location of Coffee Haven on campus. On mornings where I didn't get a lot of sleep the night before, the dark roast with an added boost of energy tincture, what I jokingly referred to as my special fairy dust, saved my ass.

Cup in hand, I walked into my Interpersonal Communications class. Professor Cece Amundson, who owned Havenwood Falls Music & More, stood in the front of the room. She wore black leggings with boots that came up to her knees. A soft blue sweater complimented her blue-gray eyes and blond hair. For an angel, she looked like a regular human. Scanning the room, I spotted Natalie Putnam and starting walking toward her, but then I saw Amaruq sitting toward the back and went to join him instead.

"Hey, any complications from last night?" I asked him.

He ran a hand through his dark hair and sat back in his chair. "Nah. Nothing some burgers and beer couldn't cure, eh?" He winked at me and cocked a grin, which made me laugh. "Now it's your turn. Are you ready for the next mission?"

"Nope," I said, and it was his turn to laugh. "Maybe we can all meet tonight for dinner and discuss. I don't want to waste any time. Are you available?"

"Yeah, the party at Hel Tower isn't until later. It is Thirsty Thursday." Amaruq was one of the resident bartenders at Hel Tower's now legendary rooftop parties, and his services were in demand, especially since he liked to bartend shirtless.

"Great. I'll send a text to the group chat." I pulled my phone out of my bag and typed a message.

"Good morning, everyone," Professor Amundson said in a soothing voice and with a reassuring smile. The class immediately ceased their chattering, and I turned to face the front of the room, setting my phone down on my lap. Cece exuded calm and warmth, which were part of her angelic qualities. Out of all the classes this semester, this one was my favorite. She was teaching us the importance of listening as well as communicating. If I planned on being a healer, these were two valuable skills to master. "Let's pick up where we left off on Tuesday. We had a good conversation going about overcoming language and species' cultural barriers." A silver cross hung around her neck and caught the light when she moved, more like glided, over to the chalkboard.

The next hour and a half flew by, and since I had a break before my next class, I decided to kill time in Halstein Hall. My first stop was Coffee Haven.

"Back again?" Harlow Augustine asked. Harlow was my friend Taylor's older sister, and we used to work together when I worked at Coffee Haven. In fact, Harlow was a huge help when I went through my awakening and accidentally used my healing powers in public, and on a human, which was a big no-no. Harlow helped minimize the damage and basically saved my ass from getting in serious trouble with the Court. I think having Harlow's grandmother on the Court helped too.

"You know me—I can't get enough!"

Harlow laughed. "What can I get you? Wait, let me guess, a large hot dark roast with energy tincture plus a blueberry scone."

"Am I that predictable?"

"Nah, you're just a girl who knows what she wants." Harlow winked and set about making my coffee. I watched as she added the energy tincture, the blue liquid glowing briefly before disappearing into the dark brew. The only visible sign that something special had been added was a shimmer on the surface of my coffee, similar to that of an oil slick. Harlow handed me the coffee and a paper bag with my scone. "Need anything else?" she asked. Aware of the line forming, I made it quick.

"Actually, there is. When you have a few minutes, can you find me? I'll be sitting over there." I pointed to a section of tables to the left of the Valkyrie fountain that dominated the front entrance to Halstein Hall.

"You got it. Roxy should be here soon. Once she's here, I'll find you."

I thanked her and found an empty table. My phone had been vibrating like mad in my pocket, and I unlocked it to find several messages in the group chat. The team confirmed to meet at 5:00 to grab dinner and talk while we ate.

The timing with Harlow worked out perfectly. From the outside pocket of my bag, I pulled out the card that supposedly contained clues to our next mission, the one I had to lead. We had all looked at it briefly when we first received our assignments, and we all agreed it looked like a tarot card, which none of us knew anything about. Harlow was a witch and the perfect person to ask. Ordinarily I'd go to her sister, Taylor, for help, but she had just helped us with the potion and Harlow knew more about tarot.

The main image was one of a woman who, coincidentally, resembled me. She had fae-like features and silver hair threaded with purple. I had grown tired of my pixie cut and magically grew it out so now my hair brushed my shoulders, almost identical to the woman in the picture. She was wrapped in what looked like a bed sheet and a man was suspended just below her, also wrapped in a sheet. They weren't clothed, and there was a sense of intimacy, like I was gazing upon two lovers. It immediately made me think of Timber, and heat flared my cheeks. Next to the man was a butterfly, but it wasn't colorful like a Monarch. Rather, the wings were all black and edged with red. The bottoms of the wings were long, tapered, giving the effect of dripping blood. Above the people and butterfly, were three pentagrams on what looked like coins, encased in spheres. The background was an overlay of trees and plants, indicating growth—at least, that's how I interpreted it.

On the back of the card was a cipher that was supposed to

provide clues as to what artifact we had to find and where it was located. I read the poem again, to see if it made any more sense:

Be careful what you seek
  Reward doesn't come without sacrifice
  And is not for the weak
  Instinct will guide you, beware of false advice
  All journeys lead to enlightenment;
  Transformation and truth lie ahead
  If that's your intent.
  A test of wills and strength at its core.
  What you unearth can destroy or restore.

I took a bite of scone and read the words again. They still didn't make any sense. Were they supposed to be prophetic or code for the actual location of the artifact? I still had no idea what that artifact was. How were we supposed to find something when we didn't even know what we were looking for?

The chair across from me squeaked on the stone floor, and I looked up to see Harlow sitting down.

"Keep furrowing your brow like that and you might actually develop a wrinkle," she teased. Fae were known to not age and look younger than their actual years. Elsmed Fairchild had the appearance of an elderly man with the gray hair, cane, age spots and all, but that's all it was—an appearance. Underneath his glamour, the ancient fae looked around fifty human years old. When I hit eighteen, my aging started to slow down considerably. "So, what did you need to talk about?"

I handed her the card and explained what it was for. After tossing her long, dark hair over her shoulder, Harlow studied it and traced her fingers over the illustration. "Oh, this is definitely magical in origin, and it looks similar to the Three of Pentacles card, which is associated with the earth element." She flipped that card over and read the poem, nodding as her eyes scanned the words. "The transformation part makes sense. The butterfly is a symbol of transformation. Which could mean personal transformation or...hmmm. Do you have any shifters on your team?"

"Yeah, Amaruq is a wolf shifter, and you know Vanna. She's a Hellhound." Vanna's brother was a member of the SIN MC, and Harlow's mate, Ryker, was the club's enforcer.

"The woman in this picture looks a lot like you," Harlow said, glancing up and studying my face. "If this is magically altered to reflect your team, who's the guy?"

I felt my cheeks flush, and I broke eye contact, which caused Harlow to chuckle. "Okay, now I really need to know."

"Timber Greenwood. He's from Faerie. You probably don't know him."

"I know him. He's a fan of Unicorn Farts." Not literally Unicorn Farts—Harlow was referencing a specialty coffee drink on the Coffee Haven menu. "Interesting. The Three of Pentacles is also connected to new relationships." She gave me a knowing look.

"You can't say anything," I whispered, leaning forward to close the gap between us. There were way too many supes in the hall with preternatural hearing. "We're keeping it on the low."

"Of course. Now, back to the card." She studied it some more. "These discs with the pentagrams, I think they're either stone or metal because they resemble ancient coins or medallions, which makes sense because both are rooted in earth. I think that's literally what your artifact is going to look like, and there are three of them. There are powers in three—like the maiden, mother, and crone. In this case, I think it's past, present, and future. Unearth? Well, we're in a mountain, and closer to the center of earth—to the core. Perhaps it's literally buried somewhere. Your team will be tested. Whatever this artifact is, it could have ramifications on the future, hence all the caution."

"Holy faeries," I whispered. A weight settled in my stomach, and my mouth went dry. "Like how your sister was tested last semester?" Taylor was forced to contend with a breach from the spirit realm, where dark spirits possessed faculty and staff. Not everyone survived. Taylor's special mixed heritage of witch and Itako, a rare kind of medium from Japan, meant she was the only one able to seal the breach and literally drag the spirits back to the spirit realm. The word "sacrifice" jumped out at me. I sure hoped that didn't mean someone had to die. The task suddenly became a lot more serious.

"Paise, please be careful, okay?" Harlow handed the card back and stood. "I have to go, let me know if you have any more questions."

"I will. Thanks, Harlow."

I looked at the time and noticed it was almost time for my next class. Gathering up my things, I rushed out of Halstein Hall, hyperaware of the card tucked away in the front pocket of my bag.

CHAPTER 4

*L*ater that day, Timber and I joined Amaruq in the dining hall. He had a tray piled high with food and was already shoving forkfuls into his mouth. I looked around for Vanna and noticed her outside the main entrance with Professor Asher Kinkaid. Professor Kincaid taught several of the technology courses. They appeared to be arguing, which wasn't a surprise. They had an illicit relationship that ran hot and cold, kind of what you'd expect with a pairing of a Hellhound and a vampire.

Professor Kincaid said something, and Vanna shook her head then crossed her arms over her chest. He said something else and reached for her. She lowered her arms and stepped into his embrace. They held each other for a few seconds before separating. Vanna tilted her head, and the professor leaned down, placing a gentle kiss on her lips. For someone usually hard edged and guarded, she seemed to soften under his touch. Her shoulders dropping and her whole body swaying toward him, she set her hands on his hips. Any earlier defensiveness melted away. Once again, envy tugged at me. They were open and public about their relationship. I thought about what Mak said, that she would begin to suspect Timber was playing games with me if he didn't tell Cole. I hated that she had planted a seed of doubt. With a sigh, I looked away and turned my attention back to the team. Underneath the table, Timber placed his hand on my thigh and began to draw tiny circles with his thumb. I dropped my hand over his and gave it a squeeze, grateful for the reassurance.

"I still think it's weird that a teacher is allowed to date a student. Most universities frown upon that," Amaruq said between bites of food.

"Well, SMA isn't your typical school," I responded.

"That's for damn sure," he agreed.

"Sorry I'm late. What did I miss?" Vanna appeared suddenly and plopped down in the empty seat next to Amaruq and across from Timber.

"Nothing much. We saw why you were late." Amaruq winked at Vanna. "Trouble in paradise, eh, Shaw?"

"No. Vampires are so dramatic," she said and stole a tater tot off of his tray. Since she was wearing sunglasses, I couldn't see her eyes, but imagined she had rolled them.

"I met with Harlow today and she gave me some insight on the card's meaning," I said, getting down to business. I retrieved the card from my bag and set it in the center of the table, illustration side up. I relayed Harlow's interpretation, leaving out the part about Timber. "What do you guys think?" My question was answered with silence.

"It could literally be anywhere," Vanna said.

"Right. We need to look for a stone or a coin or something with the pentagram."

"You mean three of them, right?" Amaruq asked.

"Maybe. Harlow seems to think so."

"Can Harlow perform a locating spell for us?" Vanna chimed in. "Or I can ask Natalie or Tempest to do one?"

"That would be cheating," Timber responded. "Besides, that would be too easy, and every team would be doing it. This mission is called The Hunt for a reason. What do you recommend, Paisley, since you're the team leader this round?" Timber directed his gaze at me, and I got lost for a moment in his eyes.

Amaruq cleared his throat, and I quickly looked away as heat rushed to my cheeks.

"Geez, you two. Get a room. Your pheromones are going to

choke me out." He touched his nose. *Pheromones, really?* I knew I was feeling all sorts of ways from sitting so close to Timber.

I opened my mouth to deny it, but was unable to. That part of my fae nature refused to let the lie form on my tongue. Instead I stayed quiet, and so did Timber, but I could feel myself blushing. Vanna just smiled at me and thankfully changed the subject.

She tucked a chunk of blond hair behind her ear and leaned forward, flipping the card over to the poem side. "We'll cover more ground if we split up and do a cursory search. We each check our towers and then we should divvy up the public buildings. From there, we search the grounds and other areas. What do you think?"

"I agree. That's a good plan. We'll check in on the group text if we come across anything. Let's plan to meet again—say Sunday for breakfast?" I asked.

Everyone agreed, and while we finished eating dinner, I pulled out my sketchpad and drew a map of the campus, drawing a giant plus sign down the middle to divide the campus into four regions that I assigned one per team member. Vanna and Amaruq left soon after that, leaving Timber and me alone. He covered my hand with his. My breath caught at this public display, and I looked at him with an eyebrow raised in question. He flashed me a lopsided grin before popping an apple slice into his mouth with his other hand.

"Walk with me to class?" he asked when he was done chewing.

"Sure. I'm still amazed that you have to take Faerie Geography. I mean, you were born and raised there."

"I know. I could teach the class, but as you know, it's a requirement for graduation."

Timber stood and gathered up my trash and his, breaking our brief moment of contact. Once outside, we walked close enough together that our arms brushed against each other. Timber's class, which was taught by Willow's husband, Chase MacElvoy, was held in Haldor Hall, across the Courtyard from Halstein and practically next door to my tower. A footbridge spanned the wide chasm that separated the two-story building from the courtyard. We quickly crossed it and caught up to Chase, who happened to be arriving at the same time as us. Like Timber, Chase spoke in an antiquated fashion, the only difference being he had a strong Scottish brogue.

"Paisley lass, you're not giving away any of my secrets from last semester, are you?" he asked with a wink of a startling blue eye. I had taken his class already and struggled. I discovered early on that geography, especially that of a foreign land, was not my strong suit.

I shook my head and laughed. "You're hilarious. Timber is probably your star student."

Chase just smiled. "Aye, he does have a wee advantage." He turned and waved his hand in front of the tall stained-glass doors to the building, and they parted on demand. "I must depart and prepare for class. I'll let Willow know I saw you."

"Please tell her hi and give Arabella a hug from me."

"I will. She's in what the humans call her 'terrible twos' and they truly are terrible. Timber, I'll see you inside shortly. Don't be late!" With that final warning, the tall fae glided into Haldor, and the doors closed silently behind him.

We were alone again, for the most part. There were a few students hanging in the courtyard, so Timber pulled me around the side of the building that faced the river. The roar of the rapids filled the air like distant thunder. Here we were safe from prying eyes.

He cupped my face, tracing my bottom lip with his thumb.

"I need to kiss you," he whispered before lowering his lips to mine. I reached up and threaded my fingers through his hair. We moved backward in a clumsy dance until my back was against the building, and Timber leaned into me. I groaned into his mouth when a hand slipped underneath my jacket. His touch was hot against my cool skin, and I practically melted.

I wanted to keep going. I wanted him to continue exploring my body. He made me forget we were outside and that he had class. Timber proved to have more restraint than I as he broke the kiss after I reached for the button on his jeans. We were both panting when he pressed his forehead to mine, and I let out another groan, one of frustration and desperation.

"I have to go. I don't want to, but Professor MacElvoy already saw me." Timber let out a sigh and started to move away, but I fisted his jacket so he couldn't.

"Call or text me later, okay?" I hadn't told him yet that I told Mak about us but this wasn't the right time.

"I promise," he said and delivered another searing kiss that left me breathless, long after he had gone inside.

Needing a few moments to collect myself, I took the long way back to Modi. Once on ground level, I walked along a stone path that led from Haldor to my tower. My phone started chirping in my bag. Cell service was intermittent in Havenwood Falls and was even worse inside Mount Alexa, so when I pulled out my phone, it alerted me to a bunch of texts from Makenna and Taylor that had been sent hours earlier.

Mak: Galentine's movie night in my room at 9:00!

Taylor: I'll bring my Practical Magic DVD. Anything else?

Mak: Ohhh, you're ditching Clay?

T: He gets me tomorrow night. Paise, are you in?

Mak: Helloooooo

Taylor: Where are yooouuu?

Mak: ...

Holy faeries, they were impatient and a pain in my ass, which was why I adored them.

Me: Just getting messages. I'm in. Where's Cat?

Mak's roommate could be a real bitch sometimes, especially about sharing her space.

Mak: Finally! Cat is going to the Hel party.

Me: Taylor, where's Fin? Is she coming too?

Taylor: Where do you think?

Me: With Joe?

Taylor: Yup. It's just going to be the 3 of us tonight.

The number "3" jumped out at me and reminded me of Harlow's interpretation of the card and that I needed to be out searching for the artifact. I stood outside Modi Tower, my thumb hovering over the keyboard as I debated being responsible and canceling on the girls. In addition to my task force duties, I had a full morning of classes that started at 9:00.

"Fuck it, I'll start looking for the artifact tomorrow," I muttered to myself as I opened the door on the ground floor level, which wasn't the main entrance and not heavily used.

I did a double-take when I bumped into Eryx Stathos as he was walking out at the same time. At first I thought it was his twin brother Calix, since they looked so much alike, but Eryx had a slightly bigger build. He held the heavy wooden door open, giving me a weird look when he caught me talking to myself.

I ignored him and continued up the eight flights of stairs to my room. Fig wasn't there. Her running shoes were on the stone floor by her bed, one knocked over on its side, fresh mud clinging to the tread, and her bath towel plus basket she kept her toiletries in was gone from where she kept it on her dresser. She liked to run in the evenings, up on Clifftop and closer to nature. Fig was an elf, and like the fae, elves recharged when surrounded by the energy nature emitted. I tried to spend time at Clifftop at least twice a week, especially when the sun was shining. The extra boost of vitamin D was fantastic.

I set my bag on my bed and with a wave of my hand, changed my outfit. The jeans and sweater I wore to classes morphed into black leggings and a baggy purple sweatshirt. I didn't change my favorite boots, which were Doc Martens with a floral pattern that I bought during the summer before my senior year in high school. That was my first big purchase with money I earned working at Coffee Haven. After graduation, I spent a year at Colorado College and couldn't use my abilities there at all. I was forced to change clothes like a human. Being able to be myself and to develop my healing skills were the two main reasons why I decided to attend SMA. Constantly suppressing my true self in order to blend in among humans grew tiresome after a while. Here I was free to use magic and to let my pointy ears show.

A few minutes later, I left to walk over to Heimdall Tower where Mak lived. This time I left through the main entrance, which was located on the fourth floor, and took the skybridge that led to the courtyard. From there, I cut through Halstein Hall.

There was a small line outside the movie theater. I spotted Fin and Joe at the concessions counter. The buttery smell of popcorn hung in the air and lured me in. Fin and I chatted for a bit while Joe balanced their snacks and drinks on a tray. Then it was my turn to order popcorn. They said goodbye and continued on inside. We could have had movie night here, but Mak's version was so much better. She used her glamour skills to transform her side of the room into a mini movie theater, complete with a screen and everything.

"So you and Orion are really done?" Taylor asked later, once we were settled and the movie started. "No plans for hot Valentine's Day booty?"

"Oh yeah, they are definitely done. Right, Paise?" Makenna gave me a knowing look and smirked. I shot daggers back at her with my eyes.

Taylor snapped her fingers, and the movie paused. She turned to face Mak and me.

"Okay, what's going on?" She looked at me, then Mak with her eyebrows raised in question.

"It's not my story to tell," Mak said, popping a jellybean in her mouth and giving me another significant look.

"Real subtle, you brat." I pegged Mak in the head with a piece of popcorn, which got snared in her red curls like a bug in a spider web. She laughed and shook her head, knocking the kernel loose.

"Clearly you're not telling me something, and that's just plain rude." Taylor flipped us both off, and Mak laughed even harder.

"Ugh! Fine. It's supposed to be a secret, but big mouth over there couldn't keep quiet."

"Hey, I haven't said anything!"

I cocked an eyebrow at her, and Mak grinned before eating another jellybean. She always had a stash on hand.

"What's the secret? Now you have to tell me. If you don't, I'll cast a truth spell," Taylor warned, wiggling her fingers. "Or I'll just wait until later and do some light scrying." And she would too. Taylor had really come into her witchiness at SMA and learned she had quite the gift for spellcasting and divination.

"You must swear yourself to secrecy and really, really swear unlike a certain fae in this room." I glared at Mak who attempted to look contrite, but her lips twitched the entire time, and I knew she was trying not to laugh. Her brown eyes twinkled with amusement.

"Of course. I solemnly swear." Taylor's expression was serious, her dark eyes focused on mine, so I could see the truth. I nodded in acceptance of her oath.

"Timber and I are kind of together. We have been for over a

month, but we're not going public until Timber has a chance to talk to Cole."

Taylor didn't say anything at first. Her mouth hung open briefly before she snapped it closed. A frown formed, followed by a crease in her brow. "You're keeping this secret because of Cole? Why? He doesn't deserve any kind of consideration."

"Exactly what I said!" Mak chimed in, throwing her hands in the air.

"Are you two like exclusive? Most guys want to stake their claim, especially supes. It's just odd. Clay very openly pursued me," Taylor said, referring to her boyfriend. They had started dating last semester.

"Yes, we're exclusive." My voice pitched up at the end, making my statement sound like more of a question.

"You don't sound too sure."

"If Timber was seeing someone else, I would have heard about it. It's a small campus."

"Well, you two have been successful in keeping your relationship secret. He could be doing that with someone else," Taylor said.

"He wouldn't do that. Timber is too kind and considerate. It's not in his nature." But it was too late. Taylor had planted another seed of doubt, right next to the one Mak had planted the day before. I thought they were wrong, but what if they weren't? What if not telling Cole was just an excuse? People had been cheating on each other for centuries.

"Mak and I will always have your back, so if you find out he's stringing you along, let us know. It will be fun playing with him. Like, I learned this new transformation spell, and I can turn him into a cockroach." Her face lit up with a grin at the idea.

"You're kind of freaking me out," I said with a laugh. Taylor winked at me and grabbed a handful of popcorn before unpausing the movie. Soon they were lost in the world of the Owen sisters and their witchy ways, but not me. I sat ruminating over the possibility that Timber was keeping me secret for nefarious reasons. With a sigh, I pulled out my phone and typed a text.

Me: Can you talk?

I hit send, and the message failed.

"Son of a bitch," I muttered and hit send again. This time failed as well. I heard Dillys, who lived in my tower, had created tech to boost cell service that was constantly being disrupted by the magical protective wards surrounding Havenwood Falls. I needed to hit her up one of these days to see if it was true. Finally, ten minutes later, my text sent. An hour later, after the movie was over and as I was getting ready to head back to my dorm, Timber responded.

Timber: Sorry, love. At the Hel party with Cole, can't talk.

My mind immediately questioned it. Was he really with Cole? The doubt literally made me feel ill. I huffed across campus with my unsettled mind and stomach, half tempted to march over to Hel Tower and confront Timber. I didn't have the greatest experience with relationships, and I knew that added to my suspicions.

Cole was my first boyfriend, and I fell hard for him. Then I almost died. During my freshman year at Colorado College, I dated a human, thinking he'd be safe, but I didn't feel a connection with him and it was hard hiding my true identity. Orion was safe too, because I knew it wasn't serious and there weren't any expectations. We were basically friends with benefits, and whew, he had A LOT to offer in the benefits department.

Timber was different. He was far from safe because from that moment I encountered him playing violin by the lake, I started to fall. I let him in and really liked him. I left myself open for the potential to be hurt again, and that was terrifying.

The rush of the river grew louder as I walked closer to Modi. In the distance, wolf howls echoed, their cries bouncing off the mountain walls. Amaruq and Joe weren't the only wolf shifters on campus, and most shifters preferred to run, hunt, and even patrol during the night. Not everyone was at the party.

When I opened the door to my room, the only light came from the bedside lamp next to Fig's bed. She was asleep, a textbook open and face down on her chest that rose and fell with her deep breathing. Using my telekinesis, I focused on the book. Seconds later, it lifted off of Fig's chest, and I moved it to her bedside table. Next, I focused on her comforter and pulled that up over her body. She mumbled something in her sleep and rolled over, away from the light, her long brown hair fanning out behind her. I plugged in the white lights over my bed before turning off her lamp. Later, after climbing into bed, sleep refused to come. Thoughts of Timber and finding the artifact kept me awake. Fig slept like the dead while I tossed and turned.

CHAPTER 5

*T*he next morning, I was grumpier than usual. If I didn't have fae genetics working for me, I probably would have looked like a train wreck. Fortunately, bloodshot or baggy eyes weren't something I had to worry about. While I didn't look like I hadn't slept, I sure felt it. Every movement was sluggish, as though I was moving through quicksand. This morning was going to require a double shot of energy tincture at Coffee Haven just to make it through my first class.

Fig, on the other hand, had a full night's sleep and was bouncing around our room. After getting dressed, I crawled back into bed with my sketchpad and watched her comb her long hair, which hung down past her waist. She created a few braids and clipped them together with a barrette shaped like a butterfly. I had just started to sketch her profile when she put her comb down on her dresser and moved across the room.

"Okay, I'm off to grab breakfast," she said as she put her gray wool peacoat on.

"Cool. See you later."

She opened the door and paused. "Your secret admirer made another delivery." Fig bent over to pick up something and came back into the room with an armful of red roses. There had to have been two dozen. The stems were wrapped with twine and attached to the bow was a note written on vellum paper. I set my sketchpad down, and Fig handed the bouquet to me.

"Can I have one?" she asked, eyeing the red petals hungrily. "They smell so good and are really fresh."

"Get your own," I said with a laugh, holding the flowers protectively against my chest. Being an elf, Fig loved to eat fresh flowers, and I caught her once eating sunflowers Timber had sent me.

"It was worth a shot." Fig shrugged before she left. As soon as I was by myself, I removed the note.

I love making you flush as red as these roses when we kiss. This is my first Valentine's Day and our first together. You have my heart. X

Valentine's Day wasn't a thing in Faerie, and Timber had been fascinated by the concept of a holiday that celebrated love. As much as I loved the roses and his note, the fact that he didn't deliver them himself or sign his name to the note made it seem fake. A secret romance can be thrilling at first but that thrill was wearing off.

As I walked across campus, couples were on display everywhere. Fin and Joe were walking so close together, they might as well be one person. Sadie and Elliana were kissing outside of Halstein Hall when I jerked the front door open. I couldn't begrudge their happiness, and they were absolutely adorable together, but a part of me was envious. Sadie had not come out to her friends and had been secretly seeing Elli until recently, and they had gone really public with their relationship ever since. Inside, Taylor and Clay sat holding hands, cups of coffee in front of them. I longed for the day when Timber and I could be open like all these couples.

Then I spotted Timber and Cole in line at Coffee Haven. They were laughing about something. At the sight of them, I spun around on my heel and went back outside. I was jealous of my ex-boyfriend and his relationship with my current boyfriend. How fucked was that?

I arrived at class early and minus a coffee. My stomach was already growling. I had been anticipating a blueberry scone. My mood soured even more when Scottlin Glover, the instructor for my Basic Healing class, walked in the door carrying a large coffee from Coffee Haven.

"Good morning, Paisley," she said and set her stuff down on the desk at the front of the room. She tossed her strawberry blond braids over her shoulder and took off her puffy parka, revealing light blue scrubs. "There was an emergency at the medical center this morning, so I didn't get a chance to change," she explained, pointing at her clothes. Scottlin was a nurse practitioner and worked with my dad at the Havenwood Falls Medical Center. She was also half witch.

"I bet they're comfortable," I said, and she agreed.

"Like wearing pajamas."

It was only a fifty-minute class, which went by quickly, and I had a class immediately after that in one of the classrooms in Halstein Hall. My hopes to grab a coffee were dashed when I saw the line at Coffee Haven. Hungrier than ever, and in desperate need of caffeine, I was not in the mood to be greeted by a smiling Clay in our Introduction to Supernatural Culture class.

"Paisely, did Taylor show you the necklace I gave her for Valentine's Day?"

For faeries sake! I wanted to scream, but just shook my head and found a seat in the corner, away from everyone else. I did not like feeling this way. I was usually a cheerful and upbeat fae. Not today. I was in a mood. I hurt, but it was my own fault. I let it happen by trying to be so understanding in regards to Timber and his friendship with Cole, and not being assertive with my needs— my wants. So in addition to being mad at the world, I was mad at myself most of all.

My next class was Basic Survival, and it wasn't held in a classroom, but on Clifftop. Being out in the open and close to nature improved my mood a little bit, until Timber arrived. My heart skipped when I saw him step into the clearing. His hair gleamed in the sunlight, and his eyes shone brightly. He walked over and stood next to me, but not as close as a boyfriend would. I was so done with this keeping up appearances shit that I wanted to make a public announcement right there that Timber and I were dating, but the part of me that cared about Timber's feelings made me stop.

He leaned over and whispered in my ear. "Did you get the roses?"

"I did. Thank you."

He quirked an eyebrow at my unenthusiastic response. "I wrote a song for you. I'll play it for you the next time we're alone."

"And when will that be? When we're sneaking around somewhere?" I crossed my arms and tilted my head back, glaring up at him. "You know, normal couples go on dates for Valentine's Day," I hissed.

"Paisley," Timber started to say, but Clay approached and asked us if everything was okay. Apparently, our whispered exchange hadn't gone unnoticed.

"No, Clay. Everything is not okay!" I yelled and stormed off, ignoring the professor who called after me.

I made a beeline for Coffee Haven. I needed to eat something before my stomach digested itself. I was surprised to see Willow standing behind the counter.

"Willow! What are you doing here?"

My cousin smiled at me and walked around to the front, pulling me into a much-needed hug.

"I sensed a disturbance in the force," she teased. She stepped away, placing her hands on my shoulders and looking me in the eyes. She had gorgeous turquoise eyes that, like her great-grandfather Elsmed, peered deep into one's soul. "What's going on, Paise? You're a jumble of emotional knots." Willow was a powerful empath, so I shouldn't have been surprised that she sensed my emotions.

With that one simple question, I burst into tears. Willow didn't say anything. She just guided me to the side and hugged me. As she held me, she absorbed my emotions. I felt them being drawn out of me and pulled into her.

"Shhhh," Willow whispered and stroked my back, comforting me like she did her daughter when Arabella was having a meltdown. After a few minutes, I had calmed down and moved away, wiping my eyes. My cheeks flared with embarrassment at my outburst. "You have nothing to be embarrassed about," she reassured me.

"Emotions are hard," I said.

Willow laughed. "Yes. Yes, they are. When you stop feeling them, that's when you need to worry. Want to talk about it?"

I shook my head. "I do want a scone, though. And coffee."

"Sure thing!" Willow flicked her wrist, and her long, silvery blond hair twisted into a chignon at the nape of her slender neck. She tightened her apron strings as she walked back around behind the counter. She didn't take my order as she knew what I needed. She placed a plate with two blueberry scones in front of me and then went to make my coffee. I noticed she added the energy tincture as well as a mood enhancer tincture made with St. John's wart. I took a bite out of one of the scones and groaned in pleasure. Before Willow was finished making my coffee, I had inhaled the scone.

"Feel better?" she asked and handed me the coffee.

"I do. Thanks." I went to pay for my order, but she waved me off.

"Family discount," she said with a wink. "I'm always here for you, Paise."

Feeling better after food, coffee, and a good cry session, I spent the time I would have been in class searching for the artifact. I went back to Modi Tower and started from the ground floor, working my way up. I made notes of anything that contained a pentagram, which, surprisingly, there were a lot of, such as paintings and tapestries on the stone walls. Some of the walls even had pentagrams engraved in them, which I never noticed before. I searched the common areas, taking advantage of them being practically unoccupied since a majority of students were in class or eating lunch. In one of the side rooms, I came across Elliana's twin sister, Brielle, and their friend Charleigh. They were leaning close to each other and seemed to be having an intense conversation, but they jumped and fell silent when I opened the door.

"Sorry!" I said and quickly left, making a note to search that room later.

During this time, my phone had been vibrating in my pocket, but I kept ignoring it. Finally, right before heading to Halstein Hall for the task force class, where I would see Timber again, I checked my messages.

There were new messages in the group chat with Taylor and Mak.

Taylor: Look at this necklace Clay got me. Isn't it gorg?

A picture followed of a silver sun and moon pendant that sat just below Taylor's collar bone.

Mak: Holy faeries that's beautiful! <3

Mak: Garrett surprised me and will be in HWF tonight. He's taking me to dinner at Whisper Falls Inn and even got us a room.

Taylor: Ohhh! Bow chicka wow wow!

Ugh. I couldn't respond. Mak was dating my cousin, Garrett, and I didn't want the visual of them having sex. No thank you!

There were several messages from Timber.

Timber: What did I do wrong?

Timber: We need to sort this out.

Timber: Are you ignoring me? I hate this technology. It's no way to correspond. Can we just talk?

I was tempted to not respond, but I was going to be seeing him at the task force class. If he asked me if I saw his texts, I wouldn't be able to lie or pretend I didn't. Sometimes being a fae had its drawbacks.

Me: See you in class.

It was with trepidation that I entered the classroom. This one was set up with tables surrounded by chairs, like pods. Timber, Amaruq, and Vanna were all sitting together as were most of the other teams. Destiny Nelson and her teammates made up the pod next to us. I deliberately sat down next to Vanna and not in the empty seat next to Timber. He furrowed his brow and gave me a questioning look. I responded with a shake of my head and looked away, distracting myself by pulling my notebook out of my bag.

Saundra Beaumont walked in, and everyone drew quiet—that's the kind of respect this witch commanded. The rap of her high heels against the wood floor was amplified by the sudden silence. Her brown eyes scanned the room, and I could imagine her mentally taking attendance.

"Congratulations! Each team has successfully completed at least one mission. Please continue your efforts. Now for a little housekeeping. I understand that some of you found Wednesday's class a tad unorthodox. Rest assured, the faculty and Board of Regents will never deliberately put you at risk. Your safety is of upmost importance. Now, for today's lesson, you're going to have to rely on your senses. I've hidden a diamond in the room and you have to find it. The only catch?" The entire class seemed to be leaning forward in their seats, waiting for the challenge. Professor Beaumont raised her hands in the air and clapped. The sound ricocheted off the walls, louder than a normal clap should have, and suddenly I couldn't see. A chorus of gasps and cries filled the room. "You need to find it while blind."

In the end, Elliana Knight's team found the diamond. I'm not sure how since it was wedged in between two floorboards. As soon as it was discovered, everyone's eyesight returned. Being rendered blind was a sobering experience and left several of my classmates shaken, including me. I understood the importance of the lesson. If we were to be disabled in any way, we needed to know how to be proactive and work together. Perhaps that was Elliana's strength? I had heard that the realm where the Knight twins and their friend, Charleigh Wotsit, came from was basically a dystopian society. They were already used to surviving and succeeding under dire circumstances.

We didn't have any class time to meet as a team and provide any updates, but we did confirm to meet Sunday morning for breakfast as our next check-in. Timber walked out beside me, but Cole soon caught up, and we strolled out of the building together. They talked about the class while I listened, hoping to find an opening where I could get Timber alone to talk. As we were approaching the point where they would split off to go to their tower and I'd go to mine, I decided to create an opening, but Timber beat me to it.

"Paisley, I need to talk to you about the task force. Do you have a few minutes?" He looked at Cole. "I'll catch up to you later."

Cole didn't look happy at being dismissed, but he got the hint and left. Timber and I didn't speak as we crossed the courtyard. I led him across the bridge that vibrated with the power of the river rushing below, past two Valkyrie statues that stood like sentries guarding the bridge. We turned to the right and wandered down to a secluded part of the lake. This area wasn't cleared out like the two beach sections and rarely used. In fact, it was the same spot where I had stumbled upon Timber playing his violin. The shadows were dense here away from the campus lights, but with our enhanced vision, it was easy to see.

"Why are you mad at me, my love? What have I done?" Timber asked, not wasting any time. He tried to take my hand, and I pulled away from his touch.

"First, since you couldn't lie to Cole about talking to me about the task force, I did some searching around Modi today for the artifact and didn't find anything. You?"

"I haven't even begun to start searching,"

"There. We spoke about it. Now, to answer your questions, I'm tired of sneaking around. I want us to be a real couple. When are you going to tell Cole about us? It's been a month since we started seeing each other."

Timber placed a hand on the back of his neck and bowed his head slightly. Looking at the ground, he kicked at a rock with the toe of his boot.

"I know," he said. "Cole has been asking more questions lately, too. It's becoming harder to come up with answers. If he gets mad and makes me choose, I choose you. I'll always choose you." He looked up at me then, his green eyes shining in the dim light.

And there was the issue. While it warmed my heart to know he'd choose me, I didn't want Timber to have to face that choice. "I hope it doesn't come to that. I don't want to come between your friendship."

"You know him—he doesn't seem the jealous type. I think he'll be angry I didn't tell him, but I don't think he'll be mad I've been seeing you."

"I know. Why we even started sneaking around seems stupid now. I thought maybe you were seeing someone else."

"What? Never! You're my only. Where did you get that idea?"

"Well, I kind of told Mak and Taylor about us, and they weren't happy. They think it's weird we're being secretive because of Cole. I tried to explain, but..."

Timber's arms circled my waist, and he pulled me into a hug. Having his body pressed against mine distracted me, and I didn't complete my thought.

"I understand. Your friends are just looking out for you. I'll tell him okay? I can't do it until I get back from Faerie."

"Faerie? Why are you going there?" I asked, looking up at his face. "Is everything okay?"

"There's nothing wrong. My father is receiving an honor at Court and our family's attendance is required. I received the summons this morning and need to make haste to the portal."

"When will you be back?" I asked.

"Sunday for our team breakfast, and I'll tell Cole that night. I promise." He caressed my cheek, and I leaned into his touch.

"Thank you," I whispered. A fae promise was as good as a blood oath.

"Anything for you, my love." We regarded each other, and our breath met first; puffs of white hanging in the cold air between us before Timber's lips sealed over mine. I sunk against him, seeking out his warmth. My hands slipped in the back pockets of his jeans, and he groaned when I squeezed his ass. His kisses grew more urgent. It was February, everything shrouded in winter, yet Timber tasted of summer—his lips carried the sweetness of watermelon or ice cream and were hot, like he burned with the warmth of the sun. His hands danced up my back, settling in my hair, cradling the back of my head. Voices carried on the air from near where we had secreted away, and I froze. Timber lifted his head and peered at me with his bright green eyes as we waited. The voices faded away as whoever was out walking continued on and we remained undiscovered.

"I don't want to, but I really must depart. I can't be late or the queen might demand my head," he said with a wink. Apparently he had read *Alice in Wonderland* over winter break, and it had quickly become one of his favorite books.

"Well, that can't happen. You have such a pretty head," I teased.

Timber gave me a quick kiss then turned and disappeared. He was just a blur as he used his full fae speed to run to the portals.

With Timber gone and my friends busy with Valentine's weekend plans, I spent that night listening to music and sketching, not in the mood to attend any parties. I slept in Saturday morning and wandered over to Halstein Hall for a late breakfast at Coffee Haven. Roxy was working, and her two mates, Vidar and Tyr, had taken up residency at the table closest to her. At first, I thought their behavior was possessive, but Roxy explained to me they had a hard time being apart since the mating bond was so new—almost like they all suffered from anxiety. Love was weird that way in the supernatural world.

"The usual?" she asked me, and I nodded, covering up a yawn at the same time. After fueling up, I used the afternoon to finish searching Modi for the artifact, but didn't have any luck. I did run into Eryx Stathos in the common lounge area on the fourth floor, though. Vanna told me he was the one on his team who found their artifact just a couple of weeks ago.

"Hey, Eryx, do you have a minute?" I approached the sofa where he was reading, his six-foot frame stretched out, taking up the whole length. Last semester he kept to himself a lot as he was kind of a loner, but lately he and Tempest Bell had been heating up campus, and he had recently discovered Calix was his twin brother. They had been spending more time together, too, so I was surprised to find Eryx alone.

"Sure, have a seat." He sat up and swung his legs down. His dirty blond curls were pulled back in a man bun, drawing attention to his dark brown eyes, which regarded me with curiosity when I sat down next to him.

"I'm just wondering if you can tell me how you found your artifact? The Hunt is what my team is working on now, and I have no clue what I'm doing."

"It's not straightforward, that's for sure. What's interesting is the crystal was in a place I'm very familiar with—almost like it was hiding in plain sight. The card is a map, but interpretation and intuition have a lot to do with it. Wish I could tell you more."

I thanked him and made my way upstairs to my room, frustrated at the lack of success. I was hoping to have something to report when we met for breakfast in the morning. When I got to my room, Fig was on her bed watching a movie on her laptop. She took one look at my face and paused it.

"What's wrong?" she asked.

"Be glad you're not taking ITF." I let out a dramatic sigh and plopped down on my bed.

"Maybe I can help?"

I turned my head and looked at my roommate. We didn't hate each other, but we never really hung out. She kept to herself and had her own circle of friends. We basically co-existed. At least she wasn't a neat freak bordering on OCD like Taylor. Perhaps she could lend some insight. Fig was an elf and connected to the earth element, like the fae.

"Okay, sure." I sat up and retrieved the tarot card from my bag then tossed it over. Fig caught it, and I watched as she studied the card.

"This is an eerie blue light surrounding the man and woman. I'm wondering if this is supposed to be their auras? They wouldn't be shared like that though. Hmmmm..."

"It surrounds those spheres with the pentagrams, too," I pointed out. "I thought it might represent some sort of energy transference."

"That's possible." Fig flipped the card over and read the poem.

Be careful what you seek
　Reward doesn't come without sacrifice
　And is not for the weak
　Instinct will guide you, beware of false advice
　All journeys lead to enlightenment;
　Transformation and truth lie ahead
　If that's your intent.
　A test of wills and strength at its core.
　What you unearth can destroy or restore.

Fig shrugged and handed the card back to me. "I don't know,

and I'm afraid my ideas might fall under the 'beware of false advice' category."

I thanked her and tucked the card away. Yet another day was drawing to a close, and I wasn't any closer to finding the artifact. With being the team leader on this task, it was up to me to provide direction and strategy, and right about now, I felt as directionless as a rudderless boat.

CHAPTER 7

The next morning my phone chimed, waking me up from a fitful sleep. I reached for the device, which was charging on the floor right by the head of my bed. There was a text message with a video from Timber, sitting on his favorite lakeside rock.

"Hi, my love. I'm back and here's the song I wrote for you. See you at breakfast."

His hair was tucked underneath a gray beanie cap, and his eyes closed when he started playing. He moved the bow across his violin's strings like a gentle caress, drawing each note out. When the song was done, tears were running down my face. It was so beautiful. I listened to it on repeat while getting ready for breakfast, grateful that Fig had left earlier to go skiing, leaving me with the room to myself and my emotions.

I arrived at Coffee Haven early and full of nervous energy. I was just getting ready to pay for my order when a deep voice from behind said, "I'll take care of it."

I spun around to find Timber smiling at me. He scanned his tattoo, and Roxy handed me my coffee.

"Are you still telling Cole tonight?" I whispered as we wove through a sea of tables in the dining hall to the one where Amaruq and Vanna were sitting.

"Yes." His smile faltered.

"Do you want me to be there when you tell him?"

"No. It would be advantageous if he hears it from me."

I wanted to give him a reassuring hug or take his hand, but there were too many people around. Cole needed to hear it straight from Timber and not via campus gossip. I could wait just a little bit longer. By this time tomorrow, we'd be public with our relationship.

Once seated, we quickly compared notes. Amaruq and Vanna both lived in Hel Tower, and they did a thorough search, like I did of Modi and Timber did the same in Muninn. That left Jory and Heimdall Towers.

"I think the word unearth is a clue," I said. "Maybe the artifact is underground, like in a cave or bottom level of a building."

"I can check the basements of the classroom buildings," Amaruq volunteered.

"Okay, Timber and I will spread out and check the caves plus Clifftop."

"Wait, before we spread out, I have a suggestion—well, it's a method that Natalie and Tempest suggested might help," Vanna chimed in. She explained it was like a meditation ritual and required a quiet place where we could meet without interruption.

Modi Tower had a number of smaller rooms that could be used for studying...or hooking up. After awkwardly stumbling across Destiny Nelson and her red headed girlfriend, Linnie, kissing in a room, we found an empty one and pushed the furniture against the walls, so there was a large opening in the middle. I unfolded the blanket I brought from my room and laid it on the stone floor.

"Natalie and Tempest gave me these candles. They said it will help clean the energy in the air." Vanna pulled four white pillar candles out of her bag and set one on each corner of the blanket.

Taylor had explained the significance of this formation to me at one of our sleepovers when we were in high school. The candles represented compass points or the four elements.

"This will help us clear our minds so we can focus on the hunt," she said and lit the candles before sitting down cross legged on the blanket. I turned off the overhead light and joined everyone else who was sitting. We had each memorized certain parts of the poem. As a manifestation technique, Natalie and Tempest had suggested this exercise to see if something jumped out at us, and if we were lucky, perhaps the artifact we sought would reveal itself. It was worth a shot.

"Okay, you ready guys?" I asked. Timber, Amaruq, and Vanna murmured in agreement, and we took a collective deep breath, exhaling at the same time. After a few deep breaths like that, the room took on a muffled quality. Any noise from outside was filtered out.

Be careful what you seek
Reward doesn't come without sacrifice
And is not for the weak
Instinct will guide you, beware of false advice
All journeys lead to enlightenment
Transformation and truth lie ahead if that's your intent
A test of wills and strength at its core
What you unearth can destroy or restore

With my eyes closed, I started chanting the poem over and over again in my head and thought about the object depicted on the card. I thought so hard my ears started to ring and a vein throbbed in my forehead, a steady drumbeat.

Suddenly Vanna gasped, and I opened my eyes.

"I think I know where it is!" she exclaimed.

"Where?"

"I saw a vision of the two Valkyrie statues that are positioned at the bridge. It makes sense. A test of wills and strength—Valkyries are known to be fierce warriors. Makes sense, right?"

"Yeah, and they determine who lives or who dies. What you unearth can destroy or restore. Fuck yes, Shaw! I think you're on to something." Amaruq held his fist out for a fist bump.

"It can't be that easy, can it?" I asked, scrambling to my feet.

"Any lead is worth exploring," Timber said. "Maybe it's been hiding in plain sight all along." He turned on the lights, and Vanna blew out the candles, filling the room with bitter smoke.

"You know, Eryx said almost the exact same thing when I asked him about his hunt mission—that it was hiding in plain sight." I folded my blanket and whispered my room number into the fabric then tossed it into the air. The blanket disappeared, and

I knew I'd find it back in my room. Hopefully it didn't land on an unsuspecting Fig. Magic was fucking awesome but unpredictable that way.

One of the advantages of being supernatural was that we all could run, like, really fast. We practically flew across the quad and stampeded over the bridge, coming to an abrupt halt when we reached the statues. They stood about eight feet tall, which meant I felt like a dwarf in comparison. They were almost identical, two sentries guarding the entrance to campus with their swords pointed down, wings pulled back as if ready to take flight at any time. I eyed them warily, expecting them to come to life like they did last semester. That was terrifying.

I noticed Vanna giving them the side eye too. The statues were made of stone, but their swords were iron, and I felt the effects of the metal even from five feet away. Breakfast gurgled in my stomach as a wave of nausea washed over me. Timber stood by my side and reached for my hand, pulling me farther away. The tightness in my chest loosened, and my stomach immediately settled.

"Uh, guys," I said. "We're going to have to sit this one out. Can you look for the artifact?"

"Sure. Vanna you check that one, and I got this one." Amaruq walked to the statue on the right side of the bridge.

I watched as they circled each statue, which were far more detailed than I realized and could easily conceal an artifact.

"I think I found something!" Vanna called. She was squatting down in front of the statue, her back to me so I couldn't see what she was doing, but her arms were moving and I could hear her scraping at something. Amaruq gave up his search and crossed over to help. There was a loud click followed by an "Oh, fuck."

"What happened?" I asked.

"Nothing." Vanna stood up and turned to face us. "It was like a button or something. I accidentally pushed on it, and now it's gone."

A tremor shook the ground and knocked me to my knees. Timber swooped in to assist me, and as I stood up, I looked over at Vanna and Amaruq to check on them and froze in shock. The

Valkyrie had come to life again, and the giant sword was slicing through the air, aiming for my teammates.

"Watch out!" I cried out. Amaruq whipped his head around, following my gaze, and moved in a blur of motion, shoving Vanna out of the sword's path. Hard. Her scream faded as she disappeared over the edge of the chasm.

"Holy faeries!" I rushed forward to try to grab Vanna's arm, but she was already falling toward the river water churning below. Suddenly a long vine burst out of the side of the chasm and wrapped around Vanna's waist, stopping her free fall.

"I have her, love. Go check on Amaruq," Timber whispered in my ear as he crouched down next to me and caused another vine to grow. This one Vanna grabbed onto with her hands. I spun on my heel to see Amaruq pinned to the ground, a pool of blood seeping out from beneath him. The sword had penetrated through his shoulder, and he writhed in pain, groaning against gritted teeth.

"Shit, hold on, Amaruq!" I rushed over, but the moment I drew close to the iron, my leg muscles started to tremble and a ripple of nausea threatened to purge my breakfast. Cold sweat broke out along my spine, and I dropped to my knees, panting. Iron to fae was like kryptonite to Superman, and the five foot sword was a large chunk of the toxic ore. I couldn't get any closer and never felt so helpless.

"I got this, Paisely," Vanna said as she passed by me. I stared in shock as she wrenched the pointed end out of Amaruq without hesitation. She snapped the blade in half with her bare hands like it was a toothpick. She tossed the iron away and then dragged Amaruq to me, leaving a glistening trail of blood on the dark stone. Yes, other supes had iron in their blood, but for some reason it didn't have as strong of an effect. I suspected supernatural biology had something to do with it and hoped to learn more about that distinction in my studies.

Shifters had the ability to heal faster than humans, but it still took some time. I placed my hands around the oozing wound on Amaruq's shoulder. His buffalo plaid flannel was saturated with blood that made the fabric warm and wet like a sponge. I took a deep breath and closed my eyes, focusing on the injury. Just like that, I could see inside Amaruq's body, and I concentrated on knitting the veins, capillaries, tissue, and muscle together. My hands grew hot as more energy spilled into his body. Finally, I closed the skin, sealing it with a scab that would slough off in a day or two.

"You're all set," I said and fell back onto my ass as exhaustion washed over me.

Amaruq sat up, wincing slightly as he moved his shoulder. "That's a handy gift, Underwood. Thanks."

"You're welcome. Are you feeling okay?"

"Yeah, but I'm beginning to think the ITF is trying to kill me, eh? First Wolfsbane and now this." Amaruq chuckled and shook his head, causing his hair to fall in front of his dark eyes.

"It's Totally Fucked, right? I told you that's what ITF stands for," I said with a laugh.

"Be careful what you seek," Timber said and held out his hand, helping me to my feet. "The riddle starts with a warning—lesson learned." He nodded in the direction of the statue, which had assumed its original position, the sword completely intact as if nothing had happened.

"And not for the weak," Vanna muttered as she dusted dirt off of her jeans. Her shirt was torn where the vine had wrapped around her waist.

Amaruq's stomach rumbled as we crossed over the bridge to return to campus.

"Are you guys hungry?" he asked, heading toward Halstein Hall.

"I could eat," Vanna answered. "But I need to change first. You might want to, also." She looked at Amaruq's bloody shirt.

"Do you guys still want to keep looking or do you want to call it a day?" I asked. "I understand if you don't want to since, you know, near death experiences and all."

"Fuck no. I'm pissed and more determined than ever to find this stupid thing. Let's hunt, bitches," Vanna said, dramatically pushing her white-blond hair out of her face.

"I'm with Shaw. Get some food in me and I'll be ready to hunt some more." Amaruq rubbed a hand over his flat stomach.

Amaruq and Vanna left to get changed while Timber and I continued on to the dining hall.

"Are you sure about continuing our search today?" Timber asked when we sat down with our trays piled high with food. My salad was loaded with olives and cheese, and I had a roll the size of a baguette slathered with butter. Healing used a lot of energy and made me hungry.

I looked over at him and saw the concern in his green eyes. "I'm sure. We need to take advantage of the weekends since we don't have much time during the school week."

"Okay, love." He placed a hand on my leg under the table and picked up his fork to start eating. I leaned in closer and caught a hint of his scent. I was getting a glimpse of what it would be like as a real couple out in the open, just sitting together enjoying lunch. I stole a pickle off his plate and popped it in my mouth. His eyes grew darker as he watched me lick the salty brine off my lips.

The scrape of a chair across the floor shattered our moment when Amaruq plopped down across from Timber, a knowing grin on his face. My cheeks felt like they were on fire as I turned my attention to my salad. Moments later, Vanna joined us. Her white shirt had been swapped with a black one, the short sleeves putting her tattoos on full display.

For the next phase of our search, we decided to go back to the original plan of splitting up. We all had a print out of the campus map, so we could mark off as we went, promising to send texts after areas were searched.

Timber and I decided to tackle Clifftop first. We went out the northern entrance of Halstein Hall, the one that led directly to the opening to Clifftop, and we emerged into a winter wonderland, a contrast of green from the pine trees and white from snow. In the near distance, sun reflected off of the glass greenhouse roof. I pulled on the hood of my parka to keep it from being blown by the gusts of wind that created little tornadoes, or snow devils, from the fresh powder. Timber stepped forward and sunk up to his knees in snow.

"Um, I think it's going to be impossible to find the artifact if it is in fact up here. It will be buried underneath all this."

"I agree," I said and shivered.

"We should check the greenhouse. Do you think it's as easy as being buried in the gardens?" Timber asked.

"It can't be that easy, but we should at least scratch it off the list. Let's go." We followed the treeline to the greenhouse, since it blocked most of the wind. I buried my nose in the collar of my jacket and noticed Timber's cheeks were an alarming red already from the cold.

A path to the door had been cleared, probably by one of the gnomes who maintained the campus grounds, and we stomped our feet to remove clumps of snow before entering. Inside the greenhouse, it was balmy and the air humid. I breathed a sigh of relief as my body began to thaw. The building was empty save for the plants.

"We're all alone in here," Timber said, moving in close to me. "And I've missed you."

"I missed you too," I whispered and tilted my head, opening myself up for a kiss. Timber immediately obliged. He cradled my chilled cheeks like I was a fragile teacup and he took a long drink of my lips. Our tongues met and slid against each other as the kiss deepened. My gloved hands gripped the back of his jacket, and I held on. We bumped against a table of flowering plants, which set off an eruption. Dozens of butterflies took to flight, and the sound of their fluttering wings filled the greenhouse. I broke off the kiss when I gasped at the sight.

"Butterfly!" I cried out. "Like on the card. We should be looking for the artifact," I said, stepping out of the circle of Timber's arms. "It's not fair that Amaruq and Vanna are actually working on the task, while we're here making out."

Timber sighed and reached up to caress my cheek. "You're right, as much as I want to stay here tasting your sweet kisses and holding you close to my heart."

I snorted and shook my head. Timber was a hopeless romantic straight out of a nineteenth century novel. Since he was born back then, it kind of made sense.

I pulled the tarot card out of my jacket pocket. I examined the image again, and Timber moved around to stand behind me. I automatically leaned back against him, and he rested his chin on my shoulder. With his closeness and his scent filling my nose, I was immediately distracted. It was like this whenever we were together—electric.

"What are we supposed to do, excavate the flower beds?" I asked.

"No, I have a better idea. I'll talk to the plants and find out if they're hiding anything."

I stood back and watched Timber as he closed his eyes and held his arms open wide, his hands facing palms down. Movement out of the corner of my eye drew my attention away, and that's when I noticed the plants were swaying, animated even. Yes, my boyfriend was the plant whisperer. A few minutes later, the plants stilled and Timber opened his eyes.

"Nothing unusual here. There is an aphid infestation brewing, though. That should be addressed."

"That's not our problem. Focus, Nature Boy," I teased and tugged on his arm.

Bracing ourselves for the cold, we stepped out of our little tropical paradise and retraced our footprints in the snow back to the entrance to campus. Timber reached for my gloved hand. This was our first public display of being a couple, but nobody was around to see it. Along the way, my phone buzzed, and I pulled it out of my back pocket. "Vanna just checked in. She searched the amethyst pools. I'll let her know we're finished at Clifftop and are heading to the caves."

We were almost to the campus when we passed a hole just large enough for a person to crawl through, in the side of the mountain. I stopped to take a closer look.

"I don't remember seeing this before. Do you?" I asked Timber, feeling drawn to the opening.

"No, I don't." He bent over to peer inside. "Let's take a look, shall we?" He got down on all floors and crawled forward. A shower of dirt was knocked loose when his head scraped the top of the hole. Dropping onto my hands and knees, I followed him. It was a tunnel, and the farther we went, the darker it became. The dirt was damp and soaked through my jeans at the knees. Suddenly Timber stopped, and I almost ran face first into his ass.

"What is it?" I whispered.

"The tunnel is widening and…glowing. I'm going to stand."

There was a scraping noise as Timber stood, and I quickly scrambled to my feet to stand beside him and look around. The tunnel had opened up to a cavern with moisture slick walls that glowed a neon green. The cavern itself was about thirty feet in diameter, and the ceiling was about as tall.

"What is this place?" I asked.

"Just some random pocket. The mountain is probably riddled with these things."

I pictured the mountain as a piece of Swiss cheese and shuddered at how unstable the rock we were living under must be. Timber moved farther into the cavern, his voice echoing in the chamber. "The bioluminescent moss is interesting, though, as it's not native to Earth."

"Where is it from?" I asked, following him and staring up in wonder. The entire cavern was covered with what looked like radioactive moss, from the jagged ceiling, down the walls and had even bled onto the ground.

"Faerie has bioluminescent plants, fungi and even trees. They're absolutely stunning at night."

"Wow, that sounds beautiful."

Timber looked over his shoulder at me and flashed a grin. "I want to show you a glimpse of my world."

With his hands open, palms facing the ground, he closed his eyes. Like when I use my healing power, his hands began to glow, surrounded by soft white light. The earth vibrated beneath my feet, and I stepped back as a tree erupted out of the cave floor. The tree continued to grow, only stopping when the top hit the ceiling. Wide leaves unfurled, creating a canopy of neon green. More trees erupted, some with flowers that emitted a softer light. Glowing vines crawled out of the ground, and bright pink, orange, and blue mushrooms popped up. They didn't look real, but like they were from a cartoon. A few of the mushrooms were enormous, and that's when I realized the fairy tales showing creatures living in mushroom houses weren't lore. Soon the ground was covered with a blanket of soft, springy moss that emitted a subtle hint of light.

"Holy faeries, Timber! This is incredible!" He was unusually quiet, so I stopped gawking to check on him only to find him watching me, his green eyes bright and shining. "What?" I asked.

"You." He took a few steps to close the gap between us. "You're absolutely stunning. Your hair and your skin, the way they capture the light."

I could say the same for him. There was no way he would pass for human right now. Timber lowered his face to mine and captured my lips. I tugged on his jacket, pulling him closer, and he slipped his arms around my waist. Opening my mouth, I teased him with my tongue, and he deepened the kiss. All thoughts about the tarot card and searching for the artifact slipped my mind at that moment. Not when we were alone in a scene straight out of a childhood storybook.

Timber's hands slid under my jacket and my shirt, his hands cool on my bare skin. He moved them from my waist, and up over my stomach, leaving goosebumps in their wake. My nipples hardened in anticipation. With a flick of his wrist, my bra was flipped up, and he cupped my breasts. I moaned and arched against him, pressing further into his touch. We had to break apart in order to take off our clothes. We could have used magic to become naked immediately, but I wanted to draw this out. Timber watched as my jacket fell to the ground and I slowly peeled my shirt up and over my head. My bra came off next and was added to the pile. Then it was Timber's turn, and I licked my lips as I watched him undress. We stood there regarding each other, before I bent down and took off my boots, so I could remove my jeans, which were damp from traipsing through the snow and crawling through the tunnel. Wearing layers sure was a pain in the ass.

Once naked, I stretched out like a cat in the sun on the moss that covered the ground as I discovered it was as soft as velvet and surprisingly warm. Timber kicked his jeans to the side and smiled down at me as I admired every muscle on display. Everything about him was thoroughly defined. His abs rippled when he lowered himself to lie beside me. His hand ghosted across my stomach and settled on the curve of my hip. I rolled toward him, pressing my body against his, bare skin against bare skin followed by a crush of lips. He eased me onto my back, and his eyes glowed like the plants around us as he looked down at me.

"Are you sure, my love?" he asked, and I nodded, tracing my finger along his full bottom lip. His blond hair framed his face and the ends brushed against my neck when he lowered his head to kiss me. He blanketed me with his body and my hips rose to meet his. Then we were fully joined, and I cried out as he filled me. We rocked together, creating a rhythm of our own. The plants around us flickered and grew brighter while petals from the trees rained down, showering us in brilliant flakes of color. When we finished, we both collapsed, and the moss cushioned our bodies as our hearts slowed from their gallop. Timber laced his fingers with mine, and I looked over at him with a huge smile that was mirrored on his face.

"I wish we could stay here forever," I said wistfully. "It's so peaceful and private."

"Mmmm, perhaps we shall. Just me and my fairy princess," Timber teased, raising my hand to his lips where he placed a gentle kiss. The movement drew my attention to his shoulder and the tease of color just beyond.

"What's that?" I pointed at a darker blue light that was visible from beneath a fern.

"I don't know." Timber rolled to his feet and walked over. I admired the view from behind. He had a perfect ass. He bent over and after a bit of rustling that caused the leaves to move, he stood and turned to face me, holding a glowing blue orb in his hands. "I think this is the artifact we've been looking for!" Timber exclaimed.

"What?" I started to stand when suddenly Timber's eyes rolled to the back of his head and he collapsed. The orb fell out of his grasp, and that's when I noticed blue light traveling up his arms, his veins glowing as whatever he absorbed was introduced to his blood supply.

"Timber!" I shrieked and rushed over to him. It took a second, maybe two, but in that time he had started to convulse. Foam bubbled up out of his mouth and spilled over the side of his face. His lips were turning blue, and his muscles twitched like he was being electrocuted. *Holy faeries, what do I do? Think. Think. You're a healer. You got this.*

I took a few deep breaths to get under control and knelt down so my thighs were like a cushion for his head. I placed my hands by each temple and closed my eyes. I connected my energy with his body and felt my hands warm as I started an internal diagnostic to determine what was wrong. Immediately a warning flashed in my mind. Allergic reaction! I located the toxin that was polluting his blood and already beginning to shut down organs. I had to act fast—faster than whatever he had come in contact with.

Narrowing in on the toxin, I focused on drawing it out of his body, but inadvertently started absorbing it into my own. My energy stuttered, but I held on and fought against the pain that was washing over me like I was being burned from the inside out. Still the toxin flowed from Timber into me, and I couldn't stop it. It became harder to breathe and shadows formed in the corners of my eyes. I blinked to clear them, but they only got worse until darkness swallowed me. Class had prepared me for blindness, and I used my inner sight, pouring everything I had into Timber to keep him alive. Then even my inner sight failed me, and a weightless sensation took over, like I had become detached from my body. I sighed, welcoming a respite from the pain.

I regained consciousness briefly when someone started violently shaking me.

"Paisley, wake up!" a woman's voice commanded. I managed to open my eyes into slits, and Vanna's face hovered over me. I could see! My pale reflection in her sunglasses peered back at me, and I opened my mouth to scream, but no sound came out. Vanna poured a bitter liquid down my throat and clamped my mouth shut before I could spit anything out. Whatever she gave me burned like hellfire and worse than the poison invading my body. I could feel the liquid as it traveled down and seemed to detonate in my stomach. I couldn't scream, I couldn't move, I couldn't breathe. I knew this feeling as I'd felt it before. I was dying.

CHAPTER 8

A gentle touch on my forehead roused me from my sleep, and my eyes flickered open to see my dad leaning over me. I breathed in his familiar earthy scent that reminded me of home. I tried to ask him what he was doing but couldn't speak. That's when I realized there was something in my throat. I made a harsh grunting sound as panic set in. I was choking on something!

"Easy, relax. You're fine. Hold on." My dad held me down by the shoulders and forced me to look at his eyes. "You were intubated, but now that you're awake and able to breathe on your own, we removed it, but your throat is still swollen and sore. Okay?"

I nodded and struggled to calm down. A flash of red drew my attention to the side as Scottlin Glover appeared, her red braids standing out against her white lab coat.

"Good to see you awake, Paisley," she said with a smile.

"Ready?" my dad asked Scottlin, who nodded and handed him a plastic cup with a straw. "Here's some water. Drink slowly, okay, peanut?"

I nodded and closed my lips around the straw, bracing myself for any discomfort. I had seen patients intubated before when I shadowed my dad at the medical center, but had never been on the receiving end. My muscles were slow in responding, and I almost gagged on the first sip, but soon got the hang of it. It became easier, and I released the straw with a sigh of relief. My dad released my wrist, where I thought he was checking my pulse, but saw his hands were glowing, letting me know that he had been pushing healing energy into me.

"Dad, what happened? Where's Timber?" I asked, not recognizing my own voice as it was so raspy.

My dad stopped fussing and placed his hand on my arm. "Timber is recovering in a room next door. From what I gather, he found an enchanted iron disk that was easily one hundred times more toxic than normal iron. Unfortunately, when you went to heal him, you absorbed the poison as well. Fortunately, thanks to the quick thinking by your teammates, who administered a detoxifying potion, you're alive." My dad's face crumpled and his professional medical demeanor vanished as he broke down into sobs. "This is twice I almost lost you, peanut. I don't think your mother and I can go through this again."

I placed my hand over his, using all the energy I could muster. That's how my mom found us a few minutes later when she walked in, carrying a canvas bag. When she saw I was awake, she dropped the bag and rushed over to sit across from my dad. She took my other hand, careful not to dislodge the IV.

"Thank the faeries you're so strong, honey," she said, her voice thick with emotion. "I know being a healer means putting other lives before yours, but can you at least get through school first?" She laughed through her tears, and my dad reached over me to place his hand on top of hers. I remembered my mom saying my dad's selflessness was one of the things that made her fall in love with him.

"I can't make any promises," I said. Timber was alive, and I healed Amaruq all in one day, which probably depleted my energy reserves, but I'd do it all over again, without hesitation.

Over the course of that afternoon, I grew gradually stronger. My fae ability for accelerated healing kicked in after the last traces of iron had left my system. I learned that Vanna and Amaruq had gone looking for me and Timber when we didn't meet them at the caves. Using their heightened sense of smell, they traced us to the opening and crawled through to discover us. Timber was weak and struggling to pull me toward the opening. Amaruq still had the rest of the detoxifying potion on him. After they got us out and to the campus infirmary, they went back for whatever had poisoned us. The enchanted iron was in fact the artifact we had been seeking. There weren't three pieces, as originally thought, but three medallions melded together to resemble the holy trinity and a pentagram was engraved in the center. Like with the crystal that Eryx's team found and the ankh Elliana's team found, the Board of Regents had collected our artifact for safe keeping. That was fine with me. I never wanted to be near it again. I also learned that it was Wednesday—making it my fourth day at the Havenwood Falls Medical Center.

I was sitting up in bed, drinking a coffee from Coffee Haven (hand delivered by my cousin, Willow) when I noticed the bag my mom had dropped on the floor.

"What's in the bag?" I asked her, pleased that my voice was no longer hoarse.

Her cheeks flared red, and she looked away, biting on her lower lip. She was clearly uncomfortable.

"Mom?"

"They're clothes for you, honey. You, um. . . " She cleared her throat. "You were brought in naked."

"Holy faeries!" My cheeks burned, and I buried my face in my hands. I had forgotten that Timber and I had just finished having sex and were both buck naked when we collapsed. That meant Amaruq and Vanna found us that way. How mortifying!

Just then Timber walked in, carrying an armful of lilies. He was wearing a hospital gown and beige skidproof socks. Cole followed him into the room. Of course, why not add another layer of awkward. Cole stood off to the side, far away from my mom, who glared at him, while Timber rushed forward and knelt down beside my bed, setting the fragrant flowers on top of the blankets before he picked up my hand and kissed it. His lips were soft and warm against my skin, which was still extra sensitive. He had faint smudges under his eyes, but other than that, he seemed to be fully recovered.

I glanced over at Cole, who was fiddling with the cuff on his right wrist.

"So now you know. Are you okay with this?" I asked him.

"Yeah." He let go of the cuff and looked me in the eyes. "I mean, I was pissed that Timber didn't tell me earlier, but I'm over it. You're a great girl, Paisley, and I want you to be happy just like I want my bro to be happy."

I laced my fingers with Timber's, and he gave my hand a gentle squeeze. We may have almost died, but I would do it all again to save the life of someone I loved.

All journeys lead to enlightenment.

Yes. Yes, they do.

THE DEVIL

JUSTINE WINTER

To my SMA author family; we survived 2020 long enough to get this done. Now bring on the cocktails!

PROLOGUE

There was this thing about life that had everyone taking it seriously. Why? What was wrong with a bit of fun? Hell, what was wrong with life being all about the fun? Why did we have to be serious at all?

Generally speaking, it was those draining adults that sucked joy from the world. They had a way of making serious situations so very, uh, serious.

Why did it matter who ran the country, or whether we grew up educated, or why we had to keep from revealing our true selves to humans?

Yeah, okay, I wasn't that much of an asshole, or an idiot. But you couldn't deny there were many rules in life that didn't need to be so stringent, or boring, or had to affect us on the daily. That was why I had to be the life of the party, bringing in a little mischief every now and then. . .

Or so I thought.

CHAPTER 1

"What happens when a beautiful red-headed Amazon agrees to be my girl?"

"You become the luckiest guy on campus?" Nadine quipped, batting those gorgeous eyelashes of hers at me.

"Actually, I was going to say *you* do." I grinned, pulling her toward me.

She frowned. "But I don't want to be the luckiest guy on campus dating an Amazon."

I shook my head, unable to stop the chuckle that escaped my lips as she pouted at me, giving me puppy dog eyes too irresistible to ignore. Fuck, this girl was going to be my undoing.

"Ugh, you two are determined to make me lose my lunch. What's with all the sappiness lately? A girl can't seem to eat at the table without battling nauseating, overbearing cuteness that is the two of you. I suggest you cut it out before I become skeletal." Tess, Nadine's roommate and best friend, whined. Her eyes tried to narrow, as though portraying she was mad at us, but the tiger shifter was softer than a cuddly toy. She was like a cub attempting to roar for the first time. Instead of being fierce and intimidating, it was a cute, high-pitched squeak.

"Blame Dylan. It's always his fault." Nadine winked, separating herself from me on the bench, returning to her mound of food. I had no idea where the woman put it. From what I'd seen so far, there wasn't an ounce of fat on her body. Though, as a trainee protector, I was willing to undergo a full body search to ensure there was no threat.

"Sounds like you need to find yourself a play mate," I said.

Tess rolled her eyes at me, huffing over her fork of mac and cheese. "Piss off, Dylan. You were starting to grow on me, but now you're like an unwanted mole giving me trouble." She stuck out her tongue like we were kids in kindergarten. Next, she'd be threatening to tell my mom on me.

"Geez, Tess. What's gotten into you today? You seem extra cranky," Nadine said, staring at her friend as though she could read her mind. Why did girls do that? Was it even possible? I mean, could they really know what the other was thinking from just a look? I swear, the other sex baffled us guys more often than we ever let on. They were like the eighth wonder of the world, all cryptic and puzzling and dangerous, yet we blokes couldn't get enough of them, playing with fire every day in an effort to set our eyes upon the jewels of beauty, grace, elegance, and utter madness that was women. Or in my case, woman. Singular. This man meat was off the market.

I glanced at my watch, noting the time. If I didn't leave soon, I was going to be in the shit with whoever today's professor was at the Interdisciplinary Task Force class. A module I hadn't willingly signed up for this semester, but appeared on my itinerary regardless.

Ugh, I was *so* not here for the education. . .

"Dylan!" Nadine punched my arm, using more force than was absolutely necessary. God, the woman had strength she wasn't even aware of. It was a major turn-on, but not when it was aimed at me. I bruised like a peach.

"What was that for?" I raised a brow, knowing full well I hadn't done anything wrong. I'd been sitting quietly talking to myself in my head like a crazy person. There was no way I could fuck up when my mouth was shut. It wasn't possible. Right?

"Don't you have that mysterious class to get to?" Nadine mocked, clearly pissed off. The woman got more and more frustrated every time I mentioned it, which was why I didn't anymore.

"Babe, what's with the animosity?" I inwardly cringed as the words left my mouth. I was sure to be dicing with death.

"Nothing. Go on, you don't want to be late." She waved her hand as though to dismiss me.

What the fuck? Nadine gave me more whiplash than any car crash ever could. I thought we'd gotten over the whole hot-and-cold vibe thing. Apparently not.

"Are you still upset you weren't included in the class this semester?" I frowned, unsure why she'd let such a novelty get her down. As far as I was concerned, she was lucky *not* to be included. The missions were proving to be harder each time, and a new one was on the horizon. I could sense it. That, and well, the fact my team had just completed another one.

"It's easy for you, Dylan. You're in the mix. Meanwhile, I get to go about my boring lessons alone." Nadine pouted, glancing down at her hands.

"A couple months ago you were screaming to be left alone," Tess interrupted. Better she said it than I. Somehow, I didn't think she'd take kindly to the truth, seeing it as more of a criticism coming from a guy.

"Yeah, well, you two spoiled me, and now there's no going back. So suck it up. My jealousy is your fault. You made me care."

"Aww, that was almost like a big, giant hug," I teased, wrapping my arms around her precious body. "You're getting good at these warm sentiments," I whispered in her ear, biting her lobe.

"Oh, sod off, Dylan, before I say something I'll regret."

I chuckled loudly, knowing she'd meant her feelings. After all she'd been through, she wasn't the kind to express anything that portrayed her as vulnerable. I didn't begrudge her that. Though we'd had different upbringings, there were similarities in the shields we protected our minds and hearts with. I just believed hers was stronger than mine, but I was sure she was close in telling me how ooey-gooey, melt-in-the-middle I made her feel. And when that day came, I wasn't going to let her forget it. It would be a feat that would live on in history. *How the worthless shapeshifter tamed the mighty Amazon.* I would inspire generations to come.

If only.

"Trust me, Nadine. When your turn comes to take this class,

and you're groaning about how much you hate it, I'll remind you of this day when you were jealous of us *going* to *this* class."

She scoffed, rolling her eyes dramatically. God, the woman was a tumultuous storm of emotions today. Whatever had gotten into Tess earlier seemed to rub off on Nadine. Was this a PMS thing?

"We don't even know that I'll get to take this class. It's not like you chose it either."

I shook my head. "No, but it's mandatory. Trust me, I'd much rather be hanging out with you, getting up to mischief. . ."

"You can't distract me from this, Dylan. I just don't understand what I did or *didn't* do to not be selected. Maybe I messed up with the hourglass challenge or something."

"Will you stop this pity party already? Everyone knows how awesome you are, and you completed that challenge. What's gotten into you?" Tess probed, scrutinizing her friend.

Nadine shrugged, offering no explanation. What was going through her mind? Why was this shitty class so important to her?

I didn't get it. A woman's mind was a plethora of tangled mazes, all interlocked with strands of unconnected thoughts and feelings. It was no wonder we men couldn't keep up. We were on entirely different frequencies.

"I tell you what, how about my next mission you help me figure it out? You won't get any credit for it, but you'll make me look good in the process." I raised my brows comically, attempting to ease a smile onto her beautiful face.

"Damn you, Dylan." She smiled, unable to stop herself. "Stop trying to placate me."

I feigned understanding. "I wouldn't dare." I cleared my throat. "Do I at least get a good luck kiss before I go?" I batted my eyes, knowing she couldn't resist my handsome charm.

"And here comes the vomit train again." Tess disappeared.

"Well, well, well, look who it is. A shapeshifter and his misfit bitch. Shouldn't you be locked away somewhere?" Harvey towered over my seat, his ugly face burning my eyes.

"Is there something you want, bloodsucker?" I gritted my teeth, clenching my fists below the table. I wasn't going to give him the satisfaction of losing my cool. Nadine, however, stared at him with such ferocity I wondered if she was about to break him in half. Not that I minded, though it wouldn't do my street cred much good either.

"The only thing I want from you, trickster, is to see you gone. Your kind don't belong here." He slapped my back and walked away, strutting like he owned the place.

"What the hell was that about?" Nadine pounced, frowning with anger.

I shook my head, unwilling to give it thought; it was what he wanted after all. "Nothing, just a dickhead slapping his cock around."

I glanced at Nadine, her eyebrows raised, quizzical.

"And what the bloody hell does that mean?" She smirked, making me think twice about what I'd said.

I shrugged. "You know, his mouth was doing the talking, but it was his dick on full display. He may as well have lobbed it out on the table."

Nadine remained perplexed so I continued. "That there was just him trying to prove he's better than me. Testosterone thing. You know, he may as well have flopped his cock out and asked to compare size with mine."

"Eww, gross. You guys are sick."

I laughed.

"So that wasn't him edging for a fight?" She frowned, clearly trying to understand the male dynamics at play.

I scoffed. "No, he was. He laid down his challenge, and when I didn't take the bait, he moved on. Guys like him are cowards. All talk."

"Dylan, you're really confusing me. I'm guessing this must be a Y chromosome thing."

"I guess." I shrugged.

"And what he said doesn't bother you?"

I paused, thinking how best to answer.

"It did, but not enough for me to do something about it," I said, unwilling to let Nadine see just how much Harvey's quips actually hurt. She didn't need to know.

She narrowed her eyes with suspicion, as though she were deciding whether to believe me or not.

"Okay, just one more question then." She smirked.

"Shoot," I replied, slightly apprehensive of what would come next. She snuggled in closer, batting her beautiful eyes at me. I was hooked.

"Can I have a kiss before class?" she crooned, pouting her luscious lips.

How could a guy say no to that?

CHAPTER 2

"*W*ell, well, well. Looks like it's the team's troublemaker to take a turn in the front seat and lead us astray." Harvey, the biggest douchebag flavor of the month sauntered into the classroom like he owned the place. The guy had a serious ego problem. I curled my lip and snorted in disgust at the vampire, knowing full well the girls on our team weren't buying his peacocking.

"Don't worry, Harvey. You've already taken the prize for worst team leader in this group. If I'm even half as bad as you were, I'll have to start watching my back. It would be too embarrassing to be kicked out of school for something so. . ." I paused for dramatic effect. "Well, let's just say I'd rather be kicked out for doing some mischief I shouldn't, than sucking so badly at something I *should* be doing." I returned the jibe, knowing there was more truth behind the jabs than actual banter. He was a bane of existence to the team. In fact, our precious supply of air was wasted on him.

"Any idea which task we should choose next?" Shay asked, no doubt trying to diffuse the tension. It was clear she was more of a peace keeping fae than a soldier. I'd bet if given the choice, she'd choose words over a weapon every time, no matter how dangerous and futile the situation.

"Team, if I may suggest, you may want to get The Hunt over with sooner rather than later. Dylan, do you have the card with the clues you chose at the beginning of the semester?" I glanced up at Professor Beltaine, the weight of his gaze resting on my shoulders, seeping into my skin like a black layer of responsibility.

I fumbled in my pockets, searching for the card I'd kept in my pants pockets every day since our first lesson, never knowing when we'd need it. Beads of sweat gathered on my forehead, the room quickly becoming a sauna. Why'd they turn up the heat so much?

"Got it!" I relaxed, yanking the crumpled bit of card from the depths of my trouser pocket. Hell, that was more stressful than any task to date!

"Nice to see you took great care of this, Mr. Wray." The professor raised his brow, pursing his lips with indignation.

I tried flattening the edges, bending them in the opposite direction, hoping for a quick fix. Instead, the card mocked my efforts and twisted out of shape even more.

"Will you just leave it alone already?" Winter pulled it from my grasp, magically straightening it out with a touch of her fingertips.

"Cheater," I mumbled, earning myself a scowl from the witch. Geez, you could feel the love emanating from my teammates today.

"This card will tell you everything you need to know." Professor Beltaine turned and walked away, proving to be as useless as the object itself. I'd already scanned the thing inside out—it was just a picture of the devil. What was so special about that?

"Come on then, shapeshifter. Lead on," Harvey probed, sniggering like a childish imp.

"So does anyone know anything about tarot cards? I mean, I'm guessing that's what this is, right?" I asked, looking at the three blank faces expecting me to lead. I was out of my depth here. Tarot was the thing fortunes were read from; I didn't need a psychic to tell me my past was what brought me here, and what will inevitably fuck up my future. I didn't need to waste money on a crazed loon giving me a half-assed attempt to read my mind, and hoping I'd fill in the blanks. You couldn't trick a trickster. Although, I'd had a few run-ins with "fortune tellers" before, all wanting to impart their wisdom on me. They'd been like lurkers, waiting in the shadows and pouncing on me when I was at my most defenseless.

"This ain't like no tarot card I've ever seen before. As The Devil cards go, this is a creepy version. I mean, just look at that wispy skeleton. It's almost fused to the devil, like he's drawing it into him," Winter offered, visibly spooked by the card if the whites of her eyes had anything to say about it. It didn't surprise me that she knew a little about tarot, as the witch of the group; I always felt like it was a part of their DNA.

I didn't know if the card was odd or not. I had no frame of reference to compare it to. All I saw was what was in front of me. The color scheme was mostly dark with hints of red outlining the shapes. A horned devil stood in the background, its long wings hung inches above the ground. Bright orange eyes glared from the devil's head, which was hidden in darkness. In front of him a skeleton was bound to a cross, bending toward the devil as though offering itself as a sacrifice, coins littered at its feet. Payment for the devil?

I had no idea what it meant. "You guys got any ideas?"

It seemed like I'd managed to become leader of the hardest task, a responsibility I was not grateful for.

"Maybe we're supposed to hunt the devil," Harvey chimed, clearly not taking this seriously. "Don't go pissing your panties now, cheater."

I clenched my jaw, willing myself to ignore the racial slur. How many times in my life had I been called that? My nostrils flared as anger raised in my chest, my beast rising to attention, desperate to take control of the situation.

"Why would they want us to hunt down the devil? That makes no sense. He's probably locked up in the Infernum anyway." Winter rolled her eyes at Harvey, instantly diffusing the volcano erupting inside me. I could almost taste the absurdity from Winter clinging in the air, and it was sour.

"Hey, what about this? Why didn't you tell us there was more, Dylan?"

I looked up at Shay, frowning with confusion. What was she talking about?

She picked up the card and turned it over.

"No way—that wasn't there before. This is new." Was the school trying to mess with me? What the fuck was going on? Was it making me out to be stupid on purpose? A weak link in the team? "How did you do that, Shay?" I asked, raising my eyebrows in wonder. The other two had fallen into silence, eyes glued to the card as though it were about to jump up and start dancing.

"I didn't do anything, Dylan. It was already there."

I bit my tongue at her patronizing tone.

"Well, it wasn't before," I said through clenched teeth, and stared at the words written on the card, doubting myself. Had I really paid that much attention to the bloody thing before?

In the depths
> *Of what you seek*
> *You'll find the shadows*
> *That make you weak*

The path will come
> *Where freedom is found*
> *Where chains are untied*
> *And lead below ground*

In pain there is grief
> *In love there is light*
> *Beware of the air*
> *Which comes with a bite*

Hidden in sight
> *Protected by lies*
> *The Devil sees all*
> *But in him truth dies*

CHAPTER 3

"*The Devil sees all, but in him truth dies,*" I repeated to Seb, my roommate, once I returned to the dorm. I felt honored to have his attention, that he was able to leave his Xbox alone long enough to talk.

"Wow, that's some fucked up shit, bro. What's it mean?"

I shook my head, completely out of my comfort zone. "No idea, man. I swear most days I feel like this place is messing with me. Now I know it is." I stared at my roommate, getting a read on him. He seemed just as perplexed as I did. I mean, it had to be a riddle, but for what?

"Dude, you sound paranoid. Why would this place mess with you? You got in, right? What's this place gonna have against you, man?" Seb spoke like he was high, but I'd come to learn that was his chilled-out, surfer-type personality. Most days he was easy to get along with. Other times I wanted to shove a flaming hot reality stick up his ass just to get him out of his whacky world and into this one.

"Seriously, bro. We're small fish here. Don't take things so personally." Seb returned to his Xbox game, readjusting his position in the large, bright green bean bag he always used. The thing was both a nightmare for the eyes and ears. He zoned out. Clearly I'd used up his quota for conversation. I swear the guy would've been better suited as a sloth shifter than a lion. I just couldn't imagine him as head of his pride someday. Crazy fucking world.

"You gonna get that, bro? In the groove here. . ." Seb's voice grated on my nerves, just as there was a knock on the door. Nadine's impatient tone calling my name followed. Harvey was an asshole big enough for everyone. I didn't need Seb's attitude on top of it. Thank fuck for small mercies. I grabbed my jacket off the bed and left the room, not giving Nadine the chance to come in. I desperately needed breathing space.

"You okay?" She immediately frowned, clearly seeing the storm written on my face.

"So much better now." I pulled her to me, wrapping my arms around her tight body, pressing my lips against hers and losing all my frustrations in her as our tongues battled. "Mmm, much better," I reiterated as she pulled away.

"Looks like you could do with letting off some steam." Nadine tilted her head to the side.

Fuck, she was adorable. How did I manage to trick her into being mine? More importantly, how was I going to make sure she *remained* mine?

"You wanna go spar?" Nadine's eyes lit up at the prospect of beating me up. There was no denying she would win. I didn't even begin to have the kind of strength that compared to an Amazon's.

"As much as I'd love to get sweaty and roll around the mats with you," I raised my eyebrows in suggestion, "I have another idea."

"You do?"

I tried not to let her disappointed face change the plans I'd concocted earlier today. Here at the academy we could spar all day long, but what I had in store didn't come so easily.

"Well, let's see. Two teenagers on a Friday night with no work schedule to wake up for tomorrow? What could we possibly do?" I pressed my index finger on my lips, pretending to look deep in thought. "There's only one possible answer, right?" I smirked, grabbing her hand as we rushed our way out of the tower and into the courtyard, where everyone else was having the same idea. Granted, it wasn't a unique idea, but fun nonetheless.

"Hanging out in the courtyard?" Nadine lifted an eyebrow as

though she couldn't believe I would choose something so mundane.

I shrugged, letting her stew on the idea. She shook her head, smiling. "Nah-uh. Mister full-of-mischievous-ideas doesn't do things this easy. Well, except for our first date when I asked you for something mellow and no action after I'd killed that draikana in the lake. Since then you've been full of . . ."

I covered her mouth with my hand in an attempt to stop the word-vomit spitting from her lips. Was she nervous tonight? That didn't make any sense.

"Breathe, please." I tugged her towards an empty bench on the outskirts of the courtyard, where few of the students loitered. "What's going on, sweetheart?" I held her hand in mine, resting it on my lap.

"Nothing," she started, before stopping herself. "I don't understand it. I'm all out of sorts today, and I don't know why." Her lower lip quivered, and I knew I was in trouble. Nadine wasn't the kind for emotions, and definitely not the kind for tears. She'd end up calling herself weak for even allowing a single teardrop to fall. I had to do something.

I was so not equipped for handling tears. No man was. Not really. All we could do was stand like lemmings and offer sympathetic pats on the back and a hug every now and then. We were rendered useless. Give us something physical and we would slay the problem. Give us emotions and we would drown alongside the ones we loved. We couldn't fight the pain that came from within.

"Are you still worked up about the stupid task force class?"

She winced. "You don't have to make me sound so pathetic, you know."

Now it was my turn to wince. I hadn't meant to sound so unsympathetic, but I couldn't understand why something I truly didn't want to be a part of, meant so much to her. Was it some kind of superiority complex? "Be grateful when it comes to your turn in this class that you won't get the douchebag on my team. That's a blessing in itself for you already."

She frowned, and I realized I'd said too much. I wanted to ease her pain; instead I showed her a glimpse of mine. Fuck, I had to be smoother than that.

I glanced around, noting the outdoor space was quieting down, students disappearing for their Friday night antics. The temperature had dropped a little, though the space was still dark, lit up by torches of flickering light.

A chill scurried along my spine, spurring my senses into awareness. What was going on? I looked around again, but saw no threat. I was clearly making something out of nothing.

"Dylan?" Nadine grabbed my arm, calling my attention.

"Sorry, sweetheart. Are you still in the mood for date night, or do you wanna call it a night?" I distracted her, knowing we were headed down a rabbit hole I had no understanding of how to burrow out of.

"Aha! I knew this wasn't it!" She jumped off the bench, dancing around in victory.

A glint in the light caught my eye as Nadine moved, and I noticed a couple of oval plaques on the back of the bench. I wasn't so sure why it interested me. All it said was 'Reed & Company,' clearly the manufacturer where they'd been made. How odd.

"Dylan, what's gotten into you?"

"Huh?" I swiveled my head around, forgetting what we were discussing before.

"The date?" she questioned. "Or was this all a joke?" She frowned, arms folded over her chest.

I stood immediately, forgetting the bench. "I would never joke about us, sweetheart. You know that." I pulled her into me, kissing away the doubt. "Come on, we're heading for the portal."

I held her hand in mine as we walked over the bridge, venturing toward the only portal that brought us in and out of the academy.

"Where are we going specifically?" She fluttered her eyes at me, trying her coy smile with me, the one she already knew made me melt in her hands. Like this, she knew I would give her anything she asked of me. It took sheer willpower to not give in every time.

"It's a surprise." I winked, and disappeared into the portal that took us back to Havenwood Falls.

CHAPTER 4

"So, any of you had some magical thoughts over the weekend? Any fantastic enlightenments you'd like to share?" I glanced at my teammates. All wore faces of sleep deprivation. I got it—Monday mornings sucked. There'd be no joy for us today. It was like the first day of the week was a mandatory suckfest. The gods had made it so.

"I've been analyzing the poem all weekend, and I just can't figure it out. I mean, this task is called The Hunt, but *what* are we hunting? I keep asking myself that same question, and my mind keeps drawing a blank when I look at these words." Shay huffed, exhaling her frustrations and blowing her mousy brown bangs in the process. "In all honesty, I'm not even sure these *are* words anymore. It's all one big blur to me." She sat back in her seat, folding her arms over her chest like a toddler throwing a tantrum.

"Okay, thank you, Shay. . ." I paused for thought. "We have two sides of the card. The picture and the poem. I'm imagining both are equally important, and that they correspond with each other."

"Duh, genius." Harvey scoffed, rolling his eyes as though he'd had better ideas, but I'd yet to hear any. I let it go, clamping my teeth together in an effort to keep my mouth shut. Shit, where the fuck did this zen version of me come from? I was impressing myself with this bullshit. My younger self would've destroyed him already. Just a funny look would've had me on a rampage.

"For five minutes, let's work on the basis that the poem makes the picture clearer. Let's see if we can find something from that. If not, plan B it is." I didn't have a plan B yet. They grunted in return, unhappy faces all around.

"You know what, we'll each take a verse of the poem to work on. Harvey, you take the first. I'll take the second. Girls, you take the last two—Winter the third, Shay fourth." I clapped my hands together loudly, trying to add some urgency into the team. If anything, it slowed them down.

Assholes.

The path will come
Where freedom is found
Where chains are untied
And lead below ground

I mulled the verse over, certain I was staring at hints to a location. It had to be on the campus somewhere. What were the clues?

Freedom . . . freedom . . . I frowned to no one in particular, using my thumbs to massage my temples. Where in the campus did we find freedom? It was like an oxymoron—as far as I could tell there was no freedom here. Not unless you counted the portal, which *led* to freedom, but that wasn't necessarily freedom itself.

"Hey, if I asked you guys where would you find freedom on campus, what would you say?" I disrupted the silence, my own thoughts too loud to quiet.

"Clifftop?" Winter answered immediately, and I instantly assumed it had been her own place of refuge. The answer seemed more of a reflex than a thought.

"Our dorm room?" Shay pondered just as Harvey belted out, "The dining hall." Winter and Shay expressed my thoughts on their faces, both frowning hard at Harvey, a quizzical glint in their eyes. Fucking idiot. Had I made it clear I didn't like the guy?

"You think The Hunt is going to take us to the dining hall?" Winter enunciated slowly, making sure to express every syllable slowly enough for Harvey's brain to accept and understand. If I wasn't getting so pissed off with it all, I probably would've laughed.

"Don't pretend it hasn't crossed your minds. Several of us supes call eating going on a hunt. The dining hall is the likeliest choice." Harvey shrugged unapologetically. "You're going to think about this later and realize I've hit the mark."

I needed a minute to think. Was the guy really being serious or just mocking this mission? Fuuckkk, what I wouldn't give for a new teammate.

The absurdity of my so-called team was making me grumpier by the second. A perfect way to spend the rest of the day.

At least you're not back home, my inner self reminded me, sitting like a pious guardian demon on my shoulder. Home was never a haven.

"I like your thoughts, girls. Freedom as in the outdoors, fresh air, not feeling so claustrophobic like it gets down here at times." It was the one downer about being on a campus deep within a magical cave. Between the constant darkness and vigorous schedules, it was easy to feel suffocated. It was a whole other lesson in itself—schooling the mind to endure the lack of natural light.

"And I guess our dorm rooms gives us our personal escape from classes and everything else. Almost a temporary comfort zone if you will . . ." I mused out loud, pacing to and fro between the desks, unable to sit still. It was a habit I couldn't shake—when my mind moved fast, my feet couldn't stay still either.

"And look, in the third verse it talks about the air biting. I'm thinking that's related to cold temperatures, perhaps snow and ice," Winter continued, suddenly feeling very energetic and enthused. "Clifftop is the only place you're gonna find freedom *and* fresh air. That's got to be it, right? Our hunt mission is on Clifftop."

"Hold on." Shay touched Winter's arm, stopping her from disappearing out of the room. "I don't think it is Clifftop. The last verse doesn't fit into the theory. *The Devil sees all.* If he's involved, then it can't be above ground. The Devil is notorious for ruling Hell, which is deep down below the earth's core."

My brain wanted to explode. One potential step forward, another retracted.

Shay's remarks stuck in my mind; a thought that hadn't even

occurred to me yet. The Devil belonged in Hell, perhaps even the Infernum, and I was missing a valuable source of information. What did I know of the Devil? Not much, but I was sure I knew someone who did.

It looked like I did need Nadine's help after all. Well, her connection to a well-known reaper to be precise.

I grabbed my jacket, leaving the group. I needed answers, ones I didn't want to share just yet.

And I needed them now.

CHAPTER 5

"It's a good thing I'm no normal girl. I mean, having your boyfriend ask to share your reaper friend is all kinds of weird even in this supernatural world." Nadine raised an eyebrow. "But you're lucky—" she winked— "that even in this world I'm still not normal."

"Yeah? Sounds to me like you're edging towards some kind of compliment . . . Or present," I added, pulling her toward me. The scent of her shampoo bombarded my senses, and it took every restraint I had in me to not react like an animal and dry-hump her leg in front of everyone in the dining hall.

"How is it I always find you in the canteen nowadays, baby cakes?" Shade appeared at her side as though popping out of thin air. The reaper had this air of coolness about him that I admired. He didn't seem like the type to let anything bother him, which was probably a trait of being a reaper, but still, there'd been many a time in my past where I'd wished I hadn't cared so much. And no doubt would again in the future.

"Well, you know I have years of catching up to do." Nadine smirked, shoving in another mouthful of her mac and cheese, cheeks puffed like a chipmunk's. The woman was going to kill me with her adorability factor. Just when I thought she couldn't look any cuter, she tops it.

"So, what life and death situation have you gotten yourself into

255

this time? Do I need to call out the cavalry?" Shade sat down beside Nadine, shirking off his leather jacket. I couldn't help the jealousy monster creeping up through my spine and into my brain. I envied their easy relationship, how quickly Nadine relaxed around the reaper. They had this easy banter that only came with time. I had a lot of years of catching up to do to be on par with Shade. Not that I ever could; there was just something unique about the way they interacted. It bothered me as much as I admired it.

"Actually, it's me who needs your help this time." I had to stop myself from calling him Sir, knowing the pair of them would have a field day of laughter. A trap I'd fallen into before.

"Trickster? What can I do for you?" He stared at me from over the table, curiosity glinting in his eyes. At least, I hoped that was curiosity and not hatred.

"Well, it's your knowledge on creatures. Does the Devil exist?" I blurted, finding no other way to sound smooth about it. I didn't care. I'd rather look like a fool in front of Nadine and gain some insight, than be tarnished with the kind of stupidity that came from Harvey. Whoever decided there were no stupid questions in life had to be an idiot themselves, and the phrase was a way to placate ridiculous behavior. Because seriously, common sense existed for a reason.

"The Devil? As in Satan, Lucifer, Beelzebub—"

"Yes, that's the one," I cut in, determined to not feel silly.

"Well," Shade sighed, rubbing his hands over his face, suddenly looking very tired. "He does, though his current whereabouts are a little sketchy. I was, in my spare time between taking souls, trying to track him down, but then I ended up in this skin suit, and my priorities shifted."

My eyes widened, as did Nadine's. Neither one of us had expected that answer.

"He's not in Hell?" Nadine asked, sucked into her friend and mentor's story.

"Not right now, no. Unless he returned over the last few months I've been away, although I'm sure Death would've summoned me by now." He paused, lost in his own thoughts.

Man, I had a lot of new questions I wanted to ask, but I had to stick to my goal. I didn't know how long I had until the reaper took off; he wasn't one to stick around.

"Why do you want to know about the Devil anyway?"

"It's part of a project. I pulled this card from a deck in the beginning of the semester, and I know nothing about it. We're thinking it's a tarot card, and my teammates got me thinking about whether the Devil is real, and I figured you were the likeliest person on campus to know." I rambled on, wishing Nadine would interrupt and shut me up.

"Let me see that." Shade took the card from my hand, glancing at the picture. He studied it for a few agonizingly silent minutes, giving away no facial expressions to his thoughts. "Well, he doesn't normally look like this. I mean, not unless he's pissed off or wants to scare the shit out of someone. The guy does love his games . . ." Shade spoke as though he admired the Devil. But maybe it was their similar taste in humor that had him smiling. For all I knew they could be best buddies. Imagine that!

"Okay, is he usually a pants kind of guy?" I joked, remembering the image on the card. There were no clothes, no accessories, nothing that could've possibly made him look human. Instead, he had large wings, massive horns, clawed hands and feet, and terrifying glowing eyes. He was every bit the monster written in fairy tales.

"Something like that, says silk is soft on his skin," Shade joked. At least, I assumed it was a joke. "His eyes don't look like this though. This depiction is completely wrong. Even in his pissed-off moods they don't glow orange," Shade finished, and I finally felt like I was getting somewhere.

"What are they usually like?" Nadine interrupted, picking up the thought I'd let trail away. There was far too much information to absorb.

"They're just black voids, usually. I wonder why they've done this?" Shade pointed to the eyes on the card, clearly perplexed. I didn't think there was anything more he could tell me. At least, none that he was offering.

"What's the project for?" Shade suddenly asked, pulled away from his momentary stupor. What had he been thinking about? Was he reminiscing on the good ol' days with the Devil?

I cleared my throat. "For my interdisciplinary task force class."
I winced, hoping I hadn't pissed off Nadine with the mere mention
of the thing that's had her acting crazy lately. "We've got a project
called The Hunt. As I understand it, this tarot card is supposed to
give us clues. For what, though, I'm not entirely sure." I shrugged,
depleted of energy again. The class was proving to be more of a
problem than helpful to my supposedly rich education at the
esteemed academy. I couldn't roll my eyes hard enough if I tried.
Despite what Shade had revealed, I still wasn't going to believe our
task was to hunt down the Devil. Even if he was missing. There
was no way he was hiding out here. I just couldn't picture it.

"Interesting." Shade stood without muttering another word.
He disappeared before I could thank him, which wasn't too
unusual for the reaper.

"That's something at least, right?" Nadine urged, holding my
hand from across the table. "I mean, I know it doesn't answer
everything, but it's a start."

I wanted to melt as she looked at me so earnestly. I wanted to
give in and believe everything was going to figure itself out now
that we'd started. But I knew it wouldn't, and I couldn't fool myself
into believing it would. That wasn't me. I didn't pin my hopes on
fantasies. I'd tasted reality too many times to know the truth.
Reality usually came with assholes like Harvey in the mix.

"I'm not sure how eyes fit into this whole thing," I expressed
honestly. "I must be missing something."

"Hey." Nadine shook my hand, jolting me away from the pits
of despair I was spiraling into. "Have you asked the other teams in
your class what they had to do? If we analyze theirs, we could see if
there's a pattern to understanding The Hunt and what to look for.
I mean, Paisley and Timber seem to be recovered now after their
recent trip to the hospital."

I leaped across the table, grabbing her face as I kissed her with
an urgency, showing my appreciation.

"You are a genius!" I laughed, disbelieving my own stupidity.
Why hadn't I thought of that myself? I knew for a fact there were a
couple groups who'd already completed the task. We were all
completing different projects each time. It just happened to be that

we chose The Hunt next. I was an imbecile. And so were the others on my team.

Nadine shook her head, laughing wildly.

"I can't believe you haven't done that yet. You need me on your team." She winked, seducing me with another kiss.

Fuck, she was irresistible. "Whatever you say, Amazon."

CHAPTER 6

"**G**ood news! The Devil does exist," I said to my teammates, kick-starting our meeting in the Jory Tower common room.

"And how would you know that, shapeshifter?" Harvey challenged, attitude in his tone, as he fixed me with his cold stare. Fuck, I was not in the mood to deal with his bullshit today.

"I spoke to a reliable source."

Harvey snorted. "Yeah, right."

"What's your problem, Harvey? You're constantly on Dylan's case." Winter said.

"The question should be why aren't you putting the mutt down, too?"

"Calm down, Harvey..."

Anger rose within me. I'd had enough. "No, Winter. Let him say whatever he wants. I bet it's nothing I haven't heard before!"

"There's a reason why the supernatural are against believing anything a trickster says. You're all liars and cheaters, getting what you want however you want it. You don't have any morals. Just take a skin, use it for what you need, and throw it away, not giving a shit about how it affects the real person and their relationships. And at this rate the only thing you'll be leading us into is expulsion!" Harvey yelled, standing and leaning over the small table, pointing his finger at me.

"You know what, mate. If I'm such a terrible creature to be around, then fuck off. I can't stand to look at your ugly face for a minute longer anyway," I retorted, getting on my own feet.

"Well, at least I came here by choice. My parents didn't ship me off to this boot camp as a way to get rid of me."

My eyes glazed over with a red hue, anger bubbling beneath the surface of my skin. I lost control.

I threw my fist at Harvey, connecting with his jaw, before throwing another punch. The girls screamed, leaving the table, and huddling in the corner out of the way. Harvey recoiled, gaining composure. His fangs extended, hissing at me as he lunged for my throat.

I landed on the hard ground, holding his weight in my outstretched arms, keeping him from biting me.

I called on every ounce of my strength and shoved him away, using the surprise to get to my feet and call on my inner demons.

"You're a disgrace to the supernatural community," Harvey roared, stalking toward me.

I thought of all the times in the past I'd heard the same thing. Over and over. There was never an original insult among them.

Anger. Hatred. Disappointment. They all raged on wildly inside me, and I snapped, shifting effortlessly.

Harvey stopped suddenly, surprise in his eyes.

"What the fuck, man?" His eyes widened, hesitating for a second too long. "Get out of my fucking skin!" He raged, tearing at me again. I didn't pause, using his momentary lapse to my advantage. I launched my fist, hitting him square on the nose. He fell backward, landing on the ground with a thud, out cold.

He'd never looked so good.

I turned to Winter and Shay, both looking on from a distance. "Ladies, *if* you still want to work with me, I'll be headed out to Clifftop for some fresh air." My bones cracked, organs shifted, and skin moved as I changed form back into myself. Becoming Harvey for as short a time as I did had my teeth on edge. Everything about him pissed me off. Along with the weeks of snide comments.

I cleared my throat, giving the slimy bastard one last disgusted look.

"If you wanted to find someone else for your team," I gave

both Winter and Shay a knowing look, "I'd understand, but we're all stuck in this together." I shrugged, almost as a way of apology. I turned and walked away, feeling lighter than I had in days.

There was only one person I wanted to see right now. Only one person who seemed to have an uncanny ability to make everything seem better with a simple smile.

I just hoped she wasn't too busy for me.

CHAPTER 7

I tossed and turned in bed, suffocating from the extreme heat in the room. My lungs struggled for oxygen, burning in my chest like a raging fire. What was going on with me? I was exhausted, desperate for sleep, while Seb snoozed his way through a peaceful night. Anger bubbled in me, pissed that I wasn't catching zzz's too. Why was it so hot in here?

I thought of Nadine, probably curled up like a sleeping baby, no worries or stress etched on her face. I thought of the sun in her beautiful red hair, of the way it always smelled like sweet coconut, and framed her gorgeous face.

My eyes felt heavy the more I thought of Nadine, and eventually I dozed off.

The wind howled, rattling the windows like it was trying to break in. Rain poured from the stormy sky, hitting the pavement like it was punishment for existing there. There wasn't enough music in my ears to drown out the horrendous noise. No amount of erratic drumbeats could silence the raging weather. And it was relentless. I was as bored as could be, desperate to be outside, my skin crawling with the need to be with my friends, away from this stupid house. This place lacked fun. There was *nothing* interesting going on here.

I heard the doorbell ring. Out of curiosity, I pulled my headphones from my ears, and glanced out my bedroom window. I didn't expect to see much beyond the trees bowing in the wind and rain droplets hitting the glass.

"What the…" I trailed off, loud voices booming downstairs, cutting off my train of thought.

"Where's that son of yours? He'll be paying for it this time, I'm telling you!" Anger tainted the atmosphere, its taste bitter in the air. I edged out of my bedroom door, trying to discern what was actually going on.

"I know he's in here, and I know he's the one to blame!" The male voice raged, and my father trying to placate the man with calming platitudes wasn't working. The guy sounded hell bent on seeing some kind of justice. Who was it? And why?

Across the hallway my little sister stepped out of her room, concern etched across her young face.

I raised my finger to my lips, signaling for her to remain quiet. She nodded and listened on just like I did.

"What's the problem, Frank?" I heard my dad say, now that the man had shut up long enough to listen.

"Dylan! That's my problem!" The man, Frank, growled.

I frowned, glancing at my sister whose eyes widened in fear. I shook my head, holding my hands out and shrugging. I had no idea what I'd supposedly done. I didn't even know who Frank was. I heard Dad sigh, and I imagined him shaking his head in despair.

"What did he do this time?" His voice was laden with disappointment. I clenched my jaw, anger burning my chest. My sister fixed me with an accusatory glare, shaking her head before turning away back into the bedroom, closing the door behind her. Clearly, she'd heard enough to understand.

"The pen to my chickens has been left wide open, and they've all gone. It's only a matter of time before the foxes get them! That boy of yours is always out skulking around, looking for mischief!" Frank yelled. I imagined a rotund man, his chubby face bright red as he struggled for breath between rants.

What the hell was this bullshit about?

"And last month I know it was him who rewired my stereo to the horn in the car so that whenever I wanted to use it, I'd have to continuously honk the horn, making it look like I'm full of road rage! I won't have it anymore! This ends now or so help me. . ."

"Don't worry, Frank. We'll see to our son's punishment," Dad interrupted, a cruel malice clouding his tone.

I edged back, stepping a little closer to my room. I didn't like where this was headed.

The front door slammed shut, and my father's footsteps thudded their way up the stairs. I wanted to cower back in fear, my every instinct on edge. But I stood still, staring at the anger contorting my dad's face, his hands bunched at his sides.

My sister never reopened her door.

"How many times do we have to go through this, Dylan?" Dad spoke softly, alarmingly patient and quiet. What was happening? Was he finally going to believe what I had to say?

"We have to be on our best behavior at all times. No trouble. No mischief. No entanglements with the community."

I opened my mouth to speak, but he pointed his finger out in warning.

"As shapeshifters, we've already got the supernatural community watching us with a keen eye, making sure we stick to good behavior."

"I know," I interrupted, nodding my head in agreement.

"So why do you keep defying our rules, Dylan!" Dad raged in an instant. Gone was the calm façade, and I realized too late it had all been fake. A show. To get me to believe they were finally trusting me. I shouldn't have been surprised. Why change their minds now after years of disbelief?

"I didn't do anything!" I blurted, trying to make him see sense. "Nobody ever has proof for a reason! It's not me!" I yelled in desperation, but I knew he wasn't listening. His eyes had glazed over, his feet moving on auto-pilot, his fist raised, making it perfectly clear he was done talking.

I watched his hand come to my face, and I yelled. "NO!"

I bolted upright, heart hammering away in the darkness.

"Dude, you need to chill, man." Seb, my roommate, spoke from his corner of the room, Xbox controller in hand, face lit up from the monitor. What time was it? Had I overslept?

"Sure. Whatever," I mumbled, needing a moment to reorient myself. Dad wasn't there. It was just a bad memory.

Right?

CHAPTER 8

In the depths
    Of what you seek
    You'll find the shadows
    That make you weak

The path will come
    Where freedom is found
    Where chains are untied
    And lead below ground

In pain there is grief
    In love there is light
    Beware of the air
    It comes with a bite

Hidden in sight
    Protected by lies
    The devil sees all
    But in him truth dies

"I don't see anything out here. At least, nothing that isn't usually here," Nadine called from one side of the

Clifftop area, her beautiful voice traveling across the playing field we often used for training and football when we needed a break.

My heart sank a little more. I hadn't found anything either. I was way out of my depth with this project.

"Can you tell me that verse again?" Nadine didn't need to specify which one—it was the same one we'd been focusing our efforts on all day.

"The path will come where freedom is found, where chains are untied, and lead below ground," I called out, just as she reached my side. By this point I practically had the verse memorized.

"You know, it's hard to know if this is all metaphorical or if it actually exists."

I nodded. "Theoretically, this here is freedom. We're outdoors, which as I understand it, is always considered freeing." I moved a little, nearing the walkway. "And here, this path quite literally takes us back down in the mountain cave, which you could argue is below ground."

Nadine agreed, head bobbing enthusiastically. "The only thing that doesn't fit are the chains. I can't find any up here, and I can't think of anything metaphorical that would fit the situation."

I pursed my lips, thoughts whirring in my mind. "Unless they relate to us, the students, being free from classes, no chains . . ."

"Hmm. I don't see it. We still have classes out here, so we wouldn't be *unchained* then."

"Fuck," I groaned, clutching tufts of my hair in frustration. "Why is this so hard to figure out?" I asked the air around me, my question rhetorical. Nothing was easy at this academy; every day seemed to be getting harder.

"What if the clues in the verse are more literal?" Nadine asked, her beautiful eyes lighting up with her fierce intelligence. Christ, my girl was the whole package. When did I get so lucky in life?

"We need to re-think your strategy." Nadine spoke just as her stomach declared war and growled relentlessly.

I laughed, grabbing her hand and pulling her in for a kiss. "Sounds like it's time for some food."

"Yeah, I am starting to feel a little weak actually." She kissed me again and led the way to the dark depths of our campus.

"I swear you only just had a feast for lunch." I shook my head in wonder. I couldn't get over how much the woman ate. She was probably single handedly costing the academy a fortune in food. She rivaled all the bigger shifters. If only there was a food eating contest here. Nadine would be my secret weapon, and she'd help me win the big bucks. If only!

Didn't the woman know by now that all she had to do was flutter her eyelashes at me and I was putty in her hands? Silly girl.

"What's happening, guys?" Tess pounced between us, popping up like a meerkat.

"Not much, just figuring out this project." I waved my hand as though to dismiss its importance.

"Oh, speaking of which, have you seen Calix recently? He's suddenly like a spitting image of Eryx, right?" She raised her brows, always the one full of gossip.

"Yeah, something about them being related?" Nadine mumbled, clearly not as interested as her roommate wanted her to be.

"A bit creepy though, if I didn't know better I'd say he was a shapeshifter." Tess winked at me. Was that supposed to be consoling or an insult? Either way it didn't make me feel good.

"You okay there, Tess?" Nadine frowned at her roommate's sudden quietness.

Tess smiled. "Never better. Now if you'll excuse me, I've got some important crap to do. Laters, losers." She bounced away, more jovial than I'd witnessed in days.

"You reckon she's got a leg over someone?" I raised my brows comically, willing to believe she hadn't meant to offend me.

"If she does, she's not spilled the beans with me yet." She sighed. "Oh, look. It's your roommate. We should go sit with him." Nadine yanked my arm as we stepped into the dining hall. What was this? Roommates R Us?

"Do we have to? I . . ." I trailed off as Nadine fixed me with a determined glare.

"You have to get along with him, Dylan. You share a room together!" Nadine raised her brows as though she dared me to poke holes in her logic. As much as I wanted to argue the fact her living arrangements with Tess hadn't been so friendly to begin with, I acquiesced. Grumpily. And grabbed food from the hot counter before heading toward Seb. Nadine urged me on with a fixed stare, following behind me. Ugh, she was cute but infuriating.

"What's up, bro? Mind if we sit?"

Seb glanced up from his plate, surprise on his face. "Sure, dude. Dudette." He nodded to Nadine. "What brings you by my sweet table?"

"Figured we'd say hello." Nadine shrugged like it was no big deal.

"Cool. You chilled now, man? After those nightmares last night?"

Nadine raised her brow, concern written all over her face.

"All good, bro. Just the shitty stress of my workload weighing me down." I skirted around the truth, though it wasn't a complete lie. I was pretty sure my skirmish with Harvey was what brought the memories back in my sleep, that and the lack of answers to this project.

"Anything I can help with?" Seb asked.

I shrugged. There was no harm in asking was there? "If I asked you to find freedom on campus, where would you say it is?"

Seb paused for a moment of thought before cracking a crooked smile. "Dude, I know exactly where it is. It's written down somewhere I'm positive ..."

"Where?" Nadine and I asked at the same time, hoping to put some haste into the guy.

"Get this, right . . ." He began, using his hands to emphasize his point. "It's in the courtyard."

CHAPTER 9

$\mathcal{I}$ stood in the center of the courtyard, students coming and going from every direction.

"I can't believe it's here," Nadine muttered, clearly distracted by something. "You know, because my big hourglass hung here for everyone to see. And now, according to Seb, this is where your task begins." Nadine shook her head, lost in her own world.

I headed toward the benches on the outer perimeter, where we'd been sitting the other day. I knew I'd felt something eerie that night that I couldn't explain. Was this it? A hint to the task? Some higher power pointing me in the right direction?

"Okay, what else did he say?" I asked Nadine, hoping she'd remember the latter half of his long-winded story. The guy couldn't tell a short tale if he tried, too scatterbrained and full of tangents to form one conscious thought.

"On the bench," Nadine answered, straight to the point.

"He said he'd seen it written on a bench, whenever he comes to hangout here." I glanced around the wooden seating, trying to find freedom. The more I looked, the more I was becoming certain the guy was actually more spaced out than I gave him credit for. We were on a wild goose chase.

"Did he say *which* bench? I can't remember. I lost focus the moment he said it was here."

"The one with the wooden legs!" Nadine called out, voice dripping in sarcasm.

"Cheeky git," I replied, glancing over all the benches. I saw the same gold plaque I'd spotted the other day, the one with the manufacturer's name on it. "Anything?" I asked, already knowing a silent Nadine meant nothing.

"Nu-uh." She shook her head, making her way toward me. "The only thing I can find is a gold plate on them all saying—"

"Reed and Company," I finished for her.

She nodded in response. "You think he got it wrong? Reed and Company could look a little like freedom if you look at it quickly?"

I thought it over. Were we reaching? Fitting in the scenario that best suited us, but if that was the case, we still hadn't found it. The freedom in the poem.

I exhaled loudly, putting my hands on my hips. "What now? If Seb was wrong, we need to start over. Again." I sat on the nearest bench, the one we happened to use the other night. I rested my arms on my knees, leaning forward with my head in my hands, massaging my temples. "I can't believe how much trust I put in Seb's story."

Nadine rubbed my back. "Come on, it's not like he failed us on purpose. He genuinely believed he'd seen it …" Nadine trailed off, her voice growing distant as though she were distracted.

I lifted my head, looking to see what had grabbed her attention.

"Wha—"

She cut me off. "I found it," Nadine whispered as though she couldn't believe it herself. "Dylan, get up!" She squeaked with excitement, and I immediately acquiesced. With hope bubbling up inside me again, I kneeled on the ground and stared at the wooden slats that had Nadine entranced, quickly finding my hope diffusing again.

"It's the same gold plate, Nadine. I already saw that one." I sighed, disappointed.

"Look again, you muppet. *Really* look."

I did as she said, internally rolling my eyes.

"No way…" I exhaled.

I touched the small plaque. Now that I knew it was there, I couldn't *unsee* it. It was so obviously clear. The letters shimmered and squiggled with movement. I rubbed my eyes, believing I'd been staring too hard and my eyes were playing tricks on me. Reed and Company suddenly became FREEDOM.

"Did you just. . ." Nadine's voice trailed off, and I knew I wasn't the only one who'd seen it.

The once solid gold plaque became a liquid goo, sliding along the bench as though it had a life of its own. I watched it descend to the ground and light up a path that ventured ahead, toward the stone wall.

My mouth gaped. "Fuuucckkkk."

I couldn't believe what I was seeing.

"Hurry. Before it disappears and we lose the way!" Nadine cried, pulling my arm in a frenzy.

We raced through the courtyard, ignoring the yells of "watch out!" around us, not giving much thought to the others in our way. The mission was too important. We were too close now.

"Now what?" Nadine huffed as we came up against the stone wall where the golden path ended.

"Where chains are untied," I whispered, running my hands along the wall, seeing interlocking rings imprinted on the structure. I followed the pattern, noticing them trailing downward to the ground. "Holy shit," I exclaimed, picking up metal hoops that connected to open cuffs.

"Untied." Nadine grinned at the object in my hands.

A jolt shuddered through me, and I yanked the chains. The force juddered an opening in the wall, and I pulled out the piece of stone that had shaken loose.

Seconds later, the wall crumbled in one distinct area, revealing an opening large enough for a body to squeeze through.

I shared a knowing look with Nadine, disbelief etched on both our faces. Surprising still was that no one around us seemed to notice what was going on. Completely oblivious. We could have been standing stark naked and singing loud like a gospel choir and no one would've batted an eyelid. Were we cloaked in some kind of invisibility? Why? How?

"After you." Nadine smirked, letting me lead the way. I cleared my throat and shrugged my shoulders. Nothing had better jump out at me. If I squeaked in surprise, I'd never live it down. Not in front of an almighty Amazon. Even if she was my girlfriend.

I stepped into the darkness, my eyes adjusting to the cramped space. I forced my way forward, my shoulders getting wedged in the tight space. I could feel my skin grazing against the sharp surface, opening wounds over and over.

I hoped this wasn't a mistake and we'd end up stuck halfway through, suffocating to death. I couldn't bear the thought of being responsible for Nadine's demise all in the name of a stupid *educational* task. Did we automatically succeed by proxy from dying? Was that the benefit here? Get an education or die trying?

I pushed harder, not knowing what was on the other side. *If* there even was one.

"Come on, Dylan. Put some bloody effort in, will you?" Nadine grunted, voice strained from the lack of oxygen reaching our squished lungs.

I struggled against the confines of the wall, stretching my muscles to the extreme as I called on all my energy and pushed against the stone.

A crack boomed in the dark silence.

I stopped, unsure what was happening.

Another crack like thunder clapped overhead. The noise reverberated around us, bouncing between the walls we were squished in. The ground vibrated, walls trembling.

"Shit, Dylan, what did you do?" Nadine yelled behind me, her voice barely discernible amongst the thundering ruckus.

Pieces of the wall fell around us, some small at first, but the longer the ground shook, the larger they became, filling up the restricted space even more.

I tried moving, dodging the larger chunks of stone as best I could, though I couldn't see very well. For all I knew I could've been ducking toward a meteor landing on my head.

"Are you okay?" I called out, not liking the silence coming from Nadine.

"Will you move your arse already?" She huffed, clearly unhappy. How could I tell her I was stuck? Wedged in by the debris filling the small space ahead.

"Sweetheart, I . . ." I trailed off as everything grew ten times louder. The ground shook relentlessly. "Oh, shiii . . ." My mouth fell to my stomach as the ground opened up, disappearing from under me. I scraped long gashes along my arms and legs as I tried to find a ledge to hold onto. It seemed like hours passed before I hit the ground, my body tired of fighting an unknown enemy, exhausted from the darkness.

I crashed hard on the ground, my bones snapping as they took the brunt of the force.

I couldn't move. Excruciating pain rang through my head like an out of control wildfire. I didn't dare move, afraid I'd make things worse for myself. I wanted to sleep.

My eyes were heavy-lidded, a blackness closing in on me. My breath was weak, it felt like I was losing more air than I was breathing in. Had I punctured a lung?

I was deflated. Beaten. After all the punishments I'd endured through my childhood, I was finally succumbing to death. I was too tired to fight it anymore. I'd lost the will.

I wheezed in the darkness, my last thought of the beautiful Amazon I'd shared my heart with. The one I loved.

I closed my eyes. Letting the pain melt away as darkness numbed me into oblivion.

"Oh my goddess, I'm going to kill you. You scared me to death!" I heard Nadine's voice as if from afar, like I was underwater and her words were muffled.

"Get up, Dylan! No more nap time!" she yelled as though her mouth was in my ear, startling me awake as her voice boomed on my eardrum. I jumped, sitting upright as I took in my surroundings, nothing making sense. Where were we?

"What happened?" I spluttered, throat incredibly dry.

"We fell . . ." She paused, and I glanced up to see her frowning. "Well, I don't know how many feet we fell, but it was a lot. Luckily for you, I recently started my lessons on how to transfer my strength and healing abilities to someone else." She smirked like she was my own personal savior. Was she? She seemed to save me in more ways than I could count.

Flashbacks whizzed through my mind, the sound of cracking bones. Gingerly, I moved my arm, then a leg, before getting to my feet. I felt absolutely fine, like I hadn't just broken every bone in my body.

"How is this possible?" I asked in wonder.

"I escalated your healing rate to the same as mine, and voila!" She held out her hands, smiling widely. Clearly, she was pleased with herself. At least one of us was getting something out of this school.

"Are you okay?" I asked, frowning. "*How* are you okay?" I amended, noting my earlier mistake. Though she had to be if she'd patched me up too.

"Amazon, remember?" She shrugged like it was no big deal that her biology gave her super-speed healing. She was one of the lucky types of supernaturals who healed almost instantaneously, never mind the fact she could somehow transfer that ability. She was practically a god. "Come on, we need to finish what we started." She reminded me of the reason we'd ended up down here in the first place.

"The stupid project," I said between clenched teeth. I noticed the space had opened up, and small balls of light lit up the jagged cavernous walls. "You looked around yet?" I asked, taking it all in.

"Too busy saving your arse," she snorted, moving ahead. "Maybe I should lead this time. I'm a little more indestructible than you." She winked, loving the power she had over me.

I let her lead, enjoying the view of her ass swinging from side to side in front of me, completely forgetting why we were here. A new desire pushed to the forefront of my mind, overtaking all my senses.

"Ooh, look at this." Nadine distracted me again, pulling my eyes away from her curvy ass and back to the room, which was different. An even longer space had opened up, revealing an empty cavern except for a small cage situated in the center of the room.

I moved forward, getting a better look, noticing the cage wasn't empty. Inside, a glowing orange stone rested on top of a black velvet cushion, as though it were displayed for ogling. The Devil card flashed in my mind, the picture clear with the glowing orange eyes. The ones Shade had said didn't belong. This was it! This was what The Hunt was all about! Finding this stone—but what was so precious about it? I didn't understand.

"Hello, freedom," I joked, and strode my way up to the cage, looking for a latch to unhook.

"Can you see an opening?" I asked as Nadine scanned the opposite side.

She shook her head. "How odd," she murmured.

I reached toward the cage, testing to see if my hand would fit between the metal bars. I didn't expect them to, but I had to give it a go. I outstretched my hand, skin touched the metal, and I was zapped backward by an invisible force field. At least, that was what it had felt like.

I landed on my ass. Nadine rushed over to my side again, searching for signs I was about to pass out.

I wasn't. Being knocked unconscious once was quite enough.

Instead, my eyes widened in fear.

"What's wro—" She began, but I forced her to turn around, unable to get the words out of my mouth. Ahead, where the stone sat in its cage, a large tornado appeared in front of it, smaller whirlwinds off-shooting from it, as though it was multiplying, filling the space.

"Any ideas?" Nadine called, the swirling wind coming closer, attacking us on all sides, blocking all exits.

I charged ahead, but an image of my dad's face appeared in the center of the biggest tornado, and I stumbled, unable to move.

I was thrown backward with such a strong force, I landed back in the courtyard, Shay and Winter staring down at me, arms crossed over their chests. I glanced around, looking for Nadine. She groaned behind me, clutching her head.

"What the hell was that?" she asked, frowning deeply, just as I uttered, "What the fuck is going on?"

Shay and Winter pursed their lips. Attitude hovered around them by the bucket loads.

"Yes, Dylan. That's what we want to know," the usually placid Shay yelled.

"What the fuck is going on?" Winter reiterated.

CHAPTER 10

"Y ou came back?" I snorted, shocked faces on both Shay and Winter. Neither one looked happy. What was it with women sticking together to face off with a guy? It was like they were indoctrinated to come in packs. Didn't they call it sister power and all that hokey crap?

"Dylan, we never left," Shay huffed, her peaceful ways long gone.

"You did!" Winter poked my chest with her accusatory finger, ignoring the fact Nadine stood by my side. Why wasn't she getting involved? It wasn't like her to miss an opportunity to flex her muscles. "We couldn't leave the team, remember? We were all chosen to be together for a reason. House rules!"

"Hang on now," I began, mouth hanging wide open as Winter thrusted her hand in my face, cutting me off.

"No excuses, Dylan. *You* left the classroom after your little fight with Harvey, not us!"

"Not that the semantics really matter. You look like you've found something worth sharing?" Shay pursed her lips, glancing at my no doubt disheveled appearance. It was impossible to come away from a beating by a big tornado without looking a little windswept.

"Actually, we found what your project is all about," Nadine answered, earning a side glance from Winter.

"Since when were you on the team?" Winter huffed, her snotty uptight attitude shining through.

"When I understood more about the poem than you did." Nadine stood in her face, squaring off with Winter. "Don't worry, though, you'll get *all* the credit," she hissed.

"Okay, we don't have time for this. We're pissed at Dylan, not Nadine, remember?" Shay interjected, tugging Winter's arm, trying to pull her away from Nadine.

I struggled not to laugh, amazed at how quickly their problem with me escalated to Nadine, almost forgetting me entirely. Women were strange creatures. They made zero sense.

"So did you get it?" Shay glared at me.

"Get what?" I asked, fully confused by the swing of conversations happening around me.

"Whatever it is we're supposed to be finding on The Hunt." Shay said with exasperation, looking at me like I was an idiot. It was the same expression she'd reserved for Harvey's stupidity. I despised the fact she was using it on me too. It was completely uncalled for.

I shook my head. "It's protected by some kind of enchantment. It kicked us out the minute I went to grab it."

"And what *is* it?" Winter spat, still unhappy.

"It's an orange stone, probably a crystal," Nadine answered, reminding the two she was still standing there.

"Like the glowing eyes on the card?" Winter questioned.

"Shade said the Devil's real eyes are black voids. The picture on the tarot was wrong," Nadine quickly filled in, and I remembered they hadn't gotten around to hearing what I'd found out from Shade after the bullshit with Harvey. Who, thankfully, had stayed away. He wasn't welcome around me anymore, and I'd happily repeat the process until he understood.

"Your source?" Shay raised an eyebrow.

I shrugged. "You wanna help me get this thing out, or do you wanna continue chit-chatting about it, using up valuable time?" I huffed, wanting this thing to be over. I was still rattled from seeing my father's face in the tornado. Had Nadine seen it to too, or was I hallucinating? A by-product of all the adrenaline rushing through my system?

"Go on, lead the way," Winter pushed, proving they hadn't gotten any closer to figuring out the poem without me.

"I hope you're ready," I exclaimed, showing them the key to the entrance, hoping we didn't have to go through the whole stuck-in-the-wall charade all over again. I was exhausted, desperate for my comfy bed. Hell, even the bench looked luxurious enough to rest my eyes and body on. Anything to get off my feet right now.

"This is insane," Winter muttered as I tugged on the chains once again. "How on earth did you figure it out?"

I shared a glance with Nadine as the wall opened up once more. I hoped the girls were ready, knowing they were in for a world of shock.

"Into the belly of the beast," I exclaimed, venturing forward.

"And out of the demon's arse," Nadine finished.

"Come on, bro. Just one more time. I'm bored here. This place sucks the life out of you."

I shook my head at my long-time friend, ignoring his pleas. Casey was absolutely incorrigible. Always had been.

"You know we can't. For starters my dad would have a fit. . ."

Casey stood, full of energy. "All the more reason why we should do it. You're already being blamed for everything that goes wrong around here." The air grew heavy with expectations. As usual, Casey was right. Why was I bothering to stick to rules they believed I was already breaking? I deserved to have fun.

"You know I'm right," he taunted. "You may as well do the deed you're being blamed for."

Everything spun around me, blurred movements of the two of us misbehaving. Breaking into shops. Changing my appearance to look like a local policeman, pulling people over as I took a cop car for a joy ride, impersonating my father to get whatever drink I wanted from the local watering hole. The room stilled, allowing me to witness my partner in crime disappearing before my eyes.

We'd infiltrated a bike gang, taking on the appearances of their president and master of arms. We stirred shit up until the real guys walked in on us. I wriggled my way out, but Casey was too slow.

They'd caught him in the yard outside their MC and beat the life out of him. I watched from a distance as my best friend lay dying, unable to step away from my safe hiding spot. I was a coward. I let him talk me into the dumbest ideas, and now I would forever carry the burden of his life on my shoulders.

I crashed back into the courtyard for the second time today, both winded and wounded emotionally. What was that? Why was my past haunting me? Seeing Casey again, even briefly, opened a wound in my heart the size of a crater. I couldn't deal with this pain, not again, not here in front of everyone.

"We're gonna need to find a way to remove that damn protection barrier on the crystal." Nadine stood, dusting off her clothes. "I do not enjoy being tossed around like a rag doll."

"This is what happened earlier? Why you were on the ground when we found you?" Winter asked, though it seemed like a redundant question. Had she thought we were rolling on the concrete in the courtyard for fun?

My nerves were rattled, and I was barely paying attention to what was being said around me. Had they all seen what I had? Did they know my darkest secrets too?

"That was crazy. We need to revisit the poem," Shay said, her hair standing on end as though she'd been electrocuted. Why weren't they saying anything? Where were all the questions? The accusations? The sheer disgust in me?

"Yeah," I murmured, all energy drained from my being. I didn't feel right. I was weaker than I'd ever been in my life. If I didn't know better, I'd say I was human. My heart was surely hurting like one.

"You guys go ahead. I'll meet you back here in an hour." I ran toward my tower, leaving Nadine behind before she could stop me. I didn't have answers for her yet.

I needed some quiet. A chance to heal my emotional wounds. Using my painful past against me was just plain cruel, a sign the academy had no limits. What kind of a lesson was this? Trauma wasn't to be toyed with.

I dreaded going down there again. Who knew what else would be thrown my way. I didn't know if I could handle more, and I wasn't eager to find out. The team could figure the rest out by themselves, I'd done my part.

Reliving Casey's death had destroyed me. All progress I'd made in healing and forgiving myself was gone.

I was broken once again; darkness would only surround me now.

CHAPTER 11

*E*verything ached—my heart, my head, my limbs. Physically. Mentally. Emotionally. I was wiped out, completely drained.

The school had finally taken everything from me. I sank further into the comfort of my bed, grateful for the empty room. I was definitely not in a sharing mood.

Why?

It was the same question I kept circling back to. Why was I made to witness Casey's death again? Why was it reminding me how much of a bad person I was?

A knock sounded on the bedroom door, but I ignored it, staring up at the ceiling instead, looking for answers.

"Dylan, it's me." Nadine's voice broke through the silence, muffled by the closed door. "What's wrong, Dylan? Talk to me …"

I closed my eyes, trying to ignore the hurt in her voice.

"Please, Dylan …"

I stood, letting out a sigh and shaking my limbs as I walked over to the door. "Sorry, dudette, he's not here."

"Oh," Nadine's eyes widened. "Sorry, Seb. I could've sworn I saw him come this way. Have you seen him?"

I shook my head. "Dude's been incommunicado with me."

"Oh, okay. I guess I'll keep looking then. If you see him, tell him I'm looking for him. He's got me worried." Nadine's lower lip quivered as though she were holding back tears. It took everything I had in me to not reach out to her, but my pain would only make her feel worse. I needed space right now. It was the best thing for her. She turned and walked away, making her way around the dorm rooms.

I closed the door and rested my head against the wooden frame, feeling the pull of my organs shifting around my body, bones cracking as I contorted back into my own skin. Lying to Nadine by impersonating Seb was going to cost me. But that was who I was. I pretended to be someone else to get what I wanted; wasn't that why Casey died?

I didn't deserve Nadine, and she'd probably figured that out soon.

My family hated me, blamed me for everything that went wrong. It was why they shipped me here to the academy, miles and miles and miles away from them so they didn't have to endure me anymore.

My best friend died because of me.

Inevitably, I would end up hurting and disappointing Nadine; it was all I knew. It was the only thing I appeared to be good at.

Harvey had been right. It was why I despised him so much. He knew I was worthless, and he had the guts to say it to my face.

I crashed back onto my bed, letting my thoughts fall deeper into darkness.

There would be no return to the light now.

CHAPTER 12

"*D*ude, I'm done with your depressing drama. Talk to me. This place is sadder than a damn funeral. It's messing with my head!" Seb cried out, turning off his Xbox completely and coming to stand over the edge of my bed like a worried relative visiting their sick kin in the hospital.

"I told you, Seb. I don't want to talk about it. Leave me alone." I turned over, facing the wall. With any luck, he'd get the message and piss off.

"Don't be so petty, Dylan. And don't feed me more of your 'I'm fine' bullshit. You're ignoring Nadine who, by the way, asks me every day where you are; she doesn't deserve this treatment. You're skipping out on every class. Dude, this isn't healthy!" Seb yelled, pulling on my arm so that I'd roll over on the bed and face him. "I've been lying for you, man, but not anymore. It's time to face your demons." He folded his arms over his chest. "I'm not moving until you start sharing." He fixed me with a stern gaze, a level of anger I'd never seen on my roommate's face before.

"There's nothing to share—" I blinked as Seb's fist connected with my nose, cracking bones.

"Fuck." I gingerly touched my face, eyes watering. "What was that for?"

"I told you I didn't wanna hear any more bullshit. And there you went denying …"

284

"Okay, I got it." I wheezed through the pain, wishing I had some of that super-speedy healing ability right now. Instead, I had to settle for normal supernatural speed healing. In comparison, it sucked.

"So, you about ready to open up, or do I need to give your face another go round with my fist? Either way I'm happy." Seb grinned, bordering sadistically.

"So much for your chilled vibe. Where'd that go?" I asked sarcastically, and I got the impression Seb knew it was rhetorical.

"Come on, man. You're making this way more painful than it needs be." Seb grabbed his bright green bean bag, placing it in the center of the room. Once he'd nestled in to a comfortable position, he held out his hands. "Proceed."

I sighed heavily. Where did I start? "It's the stupid Hunt project," I began, agitated. "There's this spell or curse, some kind of enchantment protecting the thing we're supposed to retrieve."

"What thing?" He furrowed his brows.

"Looked like an orange stone, but it's protected in a cage."

"And then what happens? You get your arm chewed off trying to grab it?" I snorted at Seb's attempt to figure out my problem. If only it was that easy.

"And then this magic hoodoo happens. It starts with a tornado that multiplies, and then it somehow replays your worst moments in life." I shuddered, remembering with clarity how awful it was. Even my skin was getting goosepimples.

"And that's what's got you moping, right? Saw something you wanted to forget?" Seb rubbed his eyes. "What you do that was so bad, Dylan?"

I shook my head, before realizing what I was doing. My nose wasn't recovered enough for round two with his fist.

"It's hard," I began, panting as though I'd just run a race against Nadine and won—it hadn't happened yet, but it was what I imagined I would feel like if I ever did.

"If it were easy then it wouldn't be a problem." Seb raised an eyebrow, putting his hands together.

"Yes, Zen Master." I bowed in jest. "I'm a shapeshifter, right? And with that comes a lot of instant negativity and dislike. I bet you weren't happy when you found out what I was?" I clenched my jaw, waiting for the hurtful truth.

"Why, because you can turn into other people? Like pretending to be your roommate and lying to your girlfriend at the same time?"

I winced; I knew I wouldn't get away with that one.

"Yeah, I know. And so does Nadine, by the way. She bumped into me on the way out of our dorm when I was walking in. Figured it out instantly. She's smart, you know."

Fuck, I really was in the shit. But how could I be sorry for doing something I believed was right at the time?

"Dude, I don't get it. She wasn't even mad, just concerned about you. You owe her an explanation, but we'll come back to that. I, on the other hand, am not happy you used our friendship like that." Seb stood, no longer able to sit still. He paced the small floor space we had in the room, eyes to the ground as though he were concentrating on something.

"I know it was wrong, but in that moment I felt like I had no other choice." I could hear the desperation in my voice, and it made me feel disgusted with myself.

"Is that what you did in the past? You impersonate someone you shouldn't have?" Seb stopped, staring at me, waiting with anticipation.

"Something like that." I sighed dejectedly. "And in turn I got my best friend killed. Like a coward, I hid, and eventually ran away, leaving him there." My voice grew hollow, distant. It felt like my chest had cracked open, and my heart was on full display for the taking.

"Everyone makes mistakes, Dylan. It's a part of life." Seb tried easing my pain.

"No." I shook my head. "I grew up being blamed for shit I'd never done just because I was a shapeshifter and a boy." I hopped off the bed, too worked up and agitated. I headed to the window, seeking some kind of solace. "I was always the troublemaker no matter where we lived. Down south, out west, no one ever believed it could've been anyone else the minute they found out a shapeshifter was among their supernatural community. Of course it had to be me. I wasn't even old enough to learn how to control my abilities and understand that everything was mine to take, depending on whose skin I was wearing."

"Your family? What did they have to say about it?" Seb interjected, and I'd almost forgotten he was there, too caught up in my monologue.

I snorted. "Dad believed every word that came out of a stranger's mouth. Why would he believe his own son who hadn't given him any reason to not trust him?"

I felt the anger build up in me again; it was the same sensation I felt burning my throat and stomach every time I thought of the injustices of it all.

"Did you ever confront him? Tell him your side of every story?" Seb relaxed back into the bean bag, stretching out his long legs.

"There was no point. I got a beating whether I did or didn't. So I just saved my breath in the end." I exhaled, anger giving way to depression again. "I don't know what the task wants from me. I don't know what it expects me to do when the tornadoes hit. I can't complete it, and by proxy the whole team will fail." I threw myself back onto my bed, sinking into the comfortable mattress.

"Have you ever met a pride of lions before?" Seb's change of topic had my head spinning.

"No, why? Is this where you tell me your kind would have me as prey?"

He laughed, a deep rumbling sound that seemed to come from his stomach. "There's not enough meat there, dude. But seriously, I know what it's like to feel responsible for the death of someone close to you."

I sat forward, intrigued. "How so?"

"Only one male can be head of the pride. The others either move on or fight for it. But sometimes, you come up against true evil and the rules of play change."

My mouth hung open. "What happened?"

He sighed. "Some families believe there should only be one male heir to lead the pride on. And when that doesn't happen..." He stood, needing to pace again. "If there's more than one male heir, they make an occasion of it, and have us fight to the end. Last lion standing is their true heir."

287

My jaw hit the floor. I couldn't believe what I was hearing. Surely I had misheard? "Did you... Were you a part of one of these families?"

He nodded slowly. "I was made to fight my brother. I was only a cub at the time." Tears sparkled in his eyes, pain just as present even now. "The thing is, Dylan, even though *I* killed him, the circumstances around it were not of my making. I was forced into it by some ancient sadistic ritual, and I know I am not wholly responsible for my brother's death. Just like you aren't for your friend's.

I shook my head, disagreeing wholeheartedly.

"Listen to me, Dylan. The only way you're going to get through this is if you learn to forgive yourself." He patted my shoulder. "It's time you accept who you are."

CHAPTER 13

In the depths
    Of what you seek
    You'll find the shadows
    That make you weak

The path will come
    Where freedom is found
    Where chains are untied
    And lead below ground

In pain there is grief
    In love there is light
    Beware of the air
    It comes with a bite

Hidden in sight
    Protected by lies
    The devil sees all
    But in him truth dies

I reread the poem one last time, hoping to feel more enlightened before heading back down in the secret cave below the courtyard. The once tight pathway between the walls had opened up and become a staircase after the first time Nadine and I had entered the space and the ground fell from under our feet. In theory, I had saved Shay and Winter from the same fate. They could've ended up in dire need of healing like I did, and I just didn't know if Nadine would've been able to save us all. I could've been facing another death on my shoulders.

As I stepped down the last of the descending stairway, I heard voices in the distance, all female, all familiar. No wonder I couldn't find them before, give them my apologies.

I made my way over to them in silence, expecting another tirade of profanities and abuse for disappearing again. Instead, they focused their efforts, trying to get to the amber crystal. Sparks of magic flew from Winter's fingers, though everything she tried failed to penetrate the barrier enough.

"You got any bright ideas, team leader?" Winter groaned, sweat beading on her forehead. Nadine sat on the ground, barely glancing my way. Shit, I was going to be groveling for days.

I scoured the cave. I felt like I was missing something. What was it Seb had said to me? Hadn't the protection barriers been showing me my problems this whole time?

"No way," I said, a crazy thought coming to my mind. It seemed too easy now that it was staring me in the face.

"What is it, Dylan?" Winter asked, following my line of sight to the cage.

"All this time I've been beating myself up for being who I am, what I've done in the past, allowing all of it to brand who I am today, when in fact it's all been way out of whack." I chuckled to myself, believing I'd been spending too much time around Seb. I was beginning to talk like him. Not that I really minded. I was beginning to understand him much more. He wasn't lazy or unsociable; he was chilled. It was his way of coping through what he'd endured as a kid. The guy was more of a genius than he ever let on. He saw so much when you thought he wasn't looking.

"Dylan, that all seems to be making a kind of sense that isn't." Nadine stood, coming to my side, putting whatever feelings she had for me aside.

"Listen to this," I began. "In the depths of what you seek,

you'll find the shadows that make you weak." I paused, expecting them to all jump to the same conclusions I had. They didn't.

"The depths are here, right, in this cave?" I waited until they nodded in agreement. "And it's my personal shadows, my past, that make me weak because I'm constantly holding them against myself."

"I don't know, Dylan. That's quite theoretical," Shay said.

I shook my head, not letting the negativity dissuade me. "The next verse was obvious. It led us down here. But then it says, 'in pain there is grief, in love there is light.' I've been letting the wrong things consume me! And then—" I waved my arms around, incredibly animated now that it was all adding up. "Beware of the air, it comes with a bite. It's the air-element protections we've been battling against. You've all seen how they've been showing the best highlights of my past." I cringed, not wanting to see their judgment of me just yet.

"What are you talking about?" Shay squinted. Was I growing another head or something?

"You know, the memory of my dad, the police joy ride, my best friend dying . . ." I trailed off as they all shared blank faces.

"I didn't see anything, just big scary-ass tornadoes coming for us, multiplying like they were rabbits in heat."

I glanced at Winter and Nadine, who both agreed with Shay.

"You hadn't seen anything else?" What did that mean? Was the whole mission somehow dedicated to just me? But that didn't make sense either. It was supposed to be a team task.

"What about the last verse, Dylan? How do you think that fits in to your theory?" Nadine asked, clearly curious. Did she think I'd gone crazy?

"'Hidden in sight'—on the picture the Devil's eyes are orange. This is an amber crystal. It was showing us what we needed to find the whole time."

They all nodded.

"We don't disagree with you there," Nadine said.

"'Protected by lies, the Devil sees all, but in him truth dies.'" I paused. "The lies are my past, at least how I've perceived them all these years. The Devil is my personal demons, misrepresenting the truth." I stopped to catch my breath. "All this time I believed I killed my best friend, because I'd grown up always believing that everything was my fault when it wasn't. People are so prejudiced toward me when they know I'm a shapeshifter, that any mischief, trouble, or even disaster is automatically pinned on my shoulders. You all saw how Harvey treated me just because of my species. I can't change that, and now I think my mum and dad were using their own experiences to put blame on me. They'd been treated the same way. How could they know any better?" I was on a whirlwind of revelations; there was no stopping me now.

Nadine sidled up to me, holding my hands in hers, concern etched in the creasing of her forehead. "If all of that is true, then how do we get the crystal out of the cage without being blown out of here again?"

I looked deeply into her stunning eyes, knowing I could lose myself in them for days.

"That's simple. All of this was a lesson for me to accept who I am, consequences and all." I walked up to the cage, full of confidence in my stride. I believed I'd figured it out, thanks to my discussion with Seb, and I'd forgiven my parents. I didn't blame them anymore. We were all surviving in a world that wasn't accepting of who we were.

"Maybe that's why you instinctively drew that card at the beginning of the semester with Professor Beaumont," Winter said.

I contemplated the idea. Had all of it been pre-destined?

I eased my hand toward the cage, slipping it through the metal bars without kick-back. So far so good. I closed my hand around the crystal and gently eased it out of the cage, unharmed.

"Well, shit. You were right," Winter admitted, though she didn't seem anywhere near as happy as the rest of us.

"You did it!" Nadine beamed, kissing me feverishly, forgetting the other two were still in the room with us. Or her anger and possible hatred of me.

"I'm so sorry, sweetheart."

She put her finger on my lips, shutting me up. "Just don't block me out of your battles next time. We're in this together, remember? That's what you told me." She raised her eyebrow, pursing her lips.

"Such a smart ass," I mocked, smiling widely. "I like it."

A loud cacophony of throats being cleared rang out, disrupting my blissful kiss with Nadine.

Regrettably, I pulled away to find both Winter and Shay standing with arms folded, amused expressions on their faces.

"Ladies," I sighed, exasperated. "Is there something else I can help you with?"

"The task isn't complete yet, Romeo," Winter answered.

I raised a brow. "What—"

"We have to hand this in to Addie Beaumont," Shay finished, both smirking widely like they were in on a big secret.

"Nah-uh. Pass." I grabbed Nadine's hand. "You girls can get the glory. I have a different form of satisfaction on my mind." I wiggled my brows suggestively.

"Ewww, we did not want to hear that." Winter's voice faded into the distance. "Oh wait, did you hear about Harvey?"

I paused, looking back at Winter, brows furrowed. "What about him?"

"Dude got disqualified. He's no longer on our team!" With that happy news, Winter walked away with Shay at her side.

I didn't know what that meant for Harvey, whether he was facing expulsion or on a temporary suspension, but I didn't really care. He'd proved himself an asshole from the moment I met him; I wouldn't be sorry to see him go.

"Now, where were we?" I whisked Nadine up into my arms, holding tight to the precious package in my hands. "What do you say, sweetheart? We've got a lot of making up to do." I winked, stealing a kiss from her poised lips.

"Oh, really? In that case, I may have a few more problems we need to hash out. Starting with your imitation trick."

"Oh, boy." I hurried my way out of the cave. I had a lot of forgiveness to seek.

EPILOGUE

*I*t was true. The world needed fun and joy to allow the more serious moments in life the gravity and weight they deserved. I'd been wrong. Adults weren't the ones sucking the fun out of everything to be cruel. They were busy wading through their own shit, trying to survive each day. If we didn't experience pain, then how could we appreciate laughter?

My education was proving to be more useful than I gave it credit for. Initially, I didn't want to be here. I didn't want to be a part of some paranormal army, another tool for others, higher beings, to use.

Instead, I found what I'd been missing. Love, from a beautiful woman. Friendship, from a caring roommate, and loyalty from those who didn't treat me like I was the scum of all creatures.

The academy was insane, long hours, hard work, strange happenings. But right now, I wouldn't trade my place with anyone.

Beware future criminals. I'll be coming for you.

WHEEL OF FORTUNE

VICTORIA FLYNN & TISH THAWER

CHAPTER 1

"*A*dd in your sweetener of choice and mix vigorously until the concoction is frothy and you begin to smell the pain resistance elixir. There will be a bluish tint, but the degree will vary depending on your choice of ingredients and magical signatures. It should make your sinus cavity rather tingly when you smell it. You all already have the grading rubric, so you know you have one hour. Use your time wisely."

Professor Parker stared out at the determined faces of her Potions students, skipping right over me, the one person in the room who was practically coming out of her skin with anxiety about this potion. It was simple. One I'd mixed on several occasions without incident ... but all of those attempts had been before.

Now I was broken.

No, not broken. Tainted. Like a castaway thing people no longer have use for. Being so far from home and in a land so different from the briny depths of Cancun's shores, I felt my otherness acutely.

My family line were outcasts and the primary reason I'd been sent to school in Colorado, but that was a very long and convoluted story for another day. All that mattered was that I needed a backup plan and to make myself useful to the supernatural community. For all its snow and mountains,

Havenwood Falls and the Halvard campus were inclusive communities. Sea witches were clannish people and never strayed from their own kind, except my family. I'd never liked the boundaries of the system, but since I'd tapped into the dark arts of my ancestors while helping Vanna defeat the Gjenganger last semester, I'd been clinging to boundaries like my life depended on it. Hell, I was beginning to think it just might.

My abuela had long warned me of the risks should a sea witch ever tap into the ancient dark arts, and I'd done it anyway. These last few months had been some of the hardest I'd ever experienced. So when it came time to book my flight home for spring break, I'd hesitated and then procrastinated. By that point, I'd convinced myself it was better to not go home. In part because I was afraid they'd see how different I was now, that maybe they'd know what I'd done. That shame and disappointment in my abuela's eyes would break me far worse than my magic imploding ever could.

I guess Professor Parker noticed my reluctance to begin the mixture because as I stared intently at the collection of ingredients laid out before me, a shadow darkened the edge of my apothecary table.

"Miss Del Mar, are you having any trouble finding the necessary materials?" Her eyes darted over the table, scanning for any item which might be missing.

"No, not really. It's more of a ... how do I say, a personal problem?"

The corners of the woman's mouth turned down in a slight frown, her gaze boring into me as if she was rooting out my darkest secrets, but I felt no intrusion. Still, I shifted in my seat, squirming like a worm on a hook.

"Marina, I won't say I haven't noticed a decline in your work, but I had hoped you could pull yourself out of whatever funk you'd stumbled into. I'm starting to think it might be a little deeper than that," she noted.

I couldn't even lift my eyes for the weight of my shame was heavy.

"My door is always open if you want to discuss this further. My suggestion—take a moment to compose yourself and channel all that energy into precise measurements and a solid attempt. I can't grade what you don't try."

She lifted a shoulder and let it fall before continuing on with her room-wide inspection. Her sage words were my only comfort, and that was fleeting. Taking a deep breath, I tried to shake the trepidation from the worry-filled creases in my face, but they persisted. Grabbing the pre-prepared mixture of salts and herbs, I emptied the vile of agave syrup into the bottle and sealed it with the stopper before the gaseous mixture it would emit could begin to vaporize.

Just as expected, the bottle warmed in my palm as I held the cork tighter, feeling the pressure inside growing with each jolt and shake. The bubbles began to form immediately, and it was the first good sign I'd had since Samhain. Hope welled up in my middle, however, just like every time I'd attempted to use my magic since that fateful day, my elation was short-lived. The frothy mixture went from light and fizzy to the consistency of primordial sludge. The white foam began to blacken in a single spot before the inky tendrils of its taint spread through the whole bottle until there wasn't a single speck of the concoction untarnished.

"No, no, no! Maldición!" I groaned, letting the bottle roll from my fingers, skittering across the table before it rolled into a smudge stick and came to a gooey stop.

I tried to ignore the odd stare or whisper, but I was shit for holding a tether on my temper and even worse at keeping my mouth shut. Professor Parker must've heard my outburst because she was beside my table in an instant.

"No luck, huh? You've got enough materials here to give it another shot. Do that and I'll give you full points for the day, so long as you promise me you'll get some help to correct this change, whatever help that may be."

When I didn't answer right away, her brows rose with an edge of warning. She was willing to be lenient, but that mercy would only go so far.

My lips pressed into a thin line with my growing irritation, and I gave the woman a single curt nod. What else could I do? My back was wedged into a corner, and the only way out was Professor Parker's offer. I'd do as she asked and try again, but there was no doubt how it would go. The woman didn't waste another moment on our interaction before she sauntered off to inspect the rest of the room's progress, leaving me to my own devices. Twice more I attempted the elixir and each time received the same disappointing results. It was beyond useless. Staring at the remnants of my materials and a pile of discarded vials, tears threatened as I noticed a shadow darken the table from behind me.

"You're not submitting that, are you, Del Mar?"

I glanced up, peering into the smug face of Catalina Vega. Her deep red shirt had a plunging neckline, displaying her ample assets. I was amazed she could even breathe with it on; I'd have thought it was painted on if it didn't occasionally gap to reveal a lacey black bra. Such a class act. Cat was one of those women who made it all too easy to hate them. She was a grade-A bitch and a hell of a conjurer, so it was hard to find fault with someone who was committed to being the best at everything. Just once I wanted to watch that *puta* fall flat on her face or let one of those spells backfire. Ix Chel forbid the wench have to deal with something truly inconvenient like a magical blemish!

"*Nadie puede ser correcto todo el tiempo, Cat.*"

It was a miracle I didn't choke on the words as they left my lips. Her grin was synthetic and mocking as she flipped her hair over her shoulder and strode away, taking her pound of flesh from my pride as her trophy. I couldn't stand the bitch as far as I could throw her, and I'd bet anything she was denser than she looked.

The mechanical clock on the wall chimed, signaling the end of the class, and everyone scrambled to collect their things, depositing their final elixirs on the table at the front. Every bottle was labeled with a student's name, and there were only a couple that were visibly wrong, like mine. Salt didn't burn or sting my wounds, as it was an integral part of being a sea witch, but I was sure it was the most appropriate analogy I could think of as I stared at the rows of flawless elixirs. Mine was a sure failure, all three of them. When the last student filed through the doorway, I made my way to the front of the room and placed all three bottles down. All I could do was shrug. Potions was one of my best subjects, yet my performance today was an absolute joke.

I opened my mouth to deliver some excuse, yet Professor Parker just held her hand up, silencing anything I might say.

"I'm going to contact Madame Roth and have her schedule an evaluation and a consult with Professor Lavinia. I won't ask any more about it, just please keep the appointment, okay? When we come back from break, I'll have a written exam for you to take to replace this score, pending your keeping that appointment."

So there was hope after all. The tightness in my chest eased only a little, allowing me to release a heavy breath.

"Thank you, Professor Parker. I won't let you down ... again." I rushed out, eager to get as far away from that room as possible. If she had more to say to me, she didn't get it out before I hit the door and ran away.

CHAPTER 2

$\mathcal{I}$'d been riding the high of Parker's reprieve when I found myself staring at Felix—looking just as fuckable as ever—with his arms wrapped around some random chick sitting on his lap. He'd held me like that once, not so long ago. Ironically, he didn't have a use for me now that I couldn't use my magic to help give his plants an extra boost anymore. Fuck, why was I even thinking about him? Why did I care? He clearly hadn't given a shit about me beyond a few hot weeks of lap time. Holy hell, who was I kidding, those weeks were scorching.

He'd moved on ... unlike me, who stood there staring at the pair of them with my emotions whipping into a frenzy. I felt out of control, like a hurricane had been unleashed inside me and was now threatening to tear me apart. As if the moment couldn't get any worse, his new rando flipped her hair and looked directly at me. I didn't bother trying to read her lips as I watched Felix's head swivel in my direction, his eyes locking with mine. My feet were rooted to the spot, and no matter how hard I tried to avert my gaze, it kept going back to the pair like a magnet along an electromagnetic field line.

"There you are! Oh shit, girl. You okay?" Tempest skidded to a stop beside me, following my stare to the retreating forms of Felix and his latest piece. "You dodged a bullet there, you know that, right? He was never going to be anything more than thirty seconds of fun, and that goes for anyone he tangles with. His type never settles, and it wasn't something you did or something you didn't do."

Tempest wrapped her arm around my shoulder and gave a gentle tug, urging me to keep moving and put an end to my self-inflicted torture session. "Come on, babe. Let's get out of here. It's spring break, we're done with exams, and it's time to get sideways. Natalie has a bottle set aside just for this occasion."

"What's that? Complete humiliation? Rejection? Being painfully single?" I groaned as she towed me behind her through the courtyard toward the bridge to Hel Tower.

"Screw all that noise. We're popping a bottle to finishing up the first half of the semester and checking our ITF card assignment off the list. At this point, the rest should be a breeze." The witch shrugged, tucking a stray strand of hair behind her ear.

The long lock fell right back where it had just been, but not before I noticed the barely visible hickey just under Tempest's ear. She and Eryx had been hot and heavy since I'd been tied up with Felix. It was a stark reminder of everything I could've had but didn't.

"Not all of us can raise our glasses to that feat. My team's gotten nowhere with our card assignment yet. Every time I've been to a team meeting, we all walk away without any ideas, and to be honest, I can't remember the last time we discussed the damn thing." I shrugged. "Got anything that might help me forget that I'm drowning and about to get sent home in disgrace?"

Tears came on hot and swift, welling up and spilling over my cheeks before I could muster the energy to stop them—this was happening a lot lately. I was just so tired. Why did everything have to be so damn hard? Besides Tempest and Natalie, it was like I'd become a pariah after embracing my dark magic. No one wanted anything to do with me, not my extended friends, not guys … not even some of my teachers seemed to care what happened to me now. Even Vanna and I weren't doing so well.

"Hold up, you mean you guys haven't come up with a game plan at all?" Tempest's question yanked me back on task.

I shook my head, confirming the shameful truth about my procrastination, but what else was I supposed to do? With my magic fuzzed up, it wasn't like I had anything to offer my group. "No. After pulling our card during the first ITF class, we haven't been able to come up with anything that resembles the image on the front, nor have we been able to decipher the clue on the back. At this point, we're royally fucked."

"What does your card look like? Maybe I could help, or at least keep an eye out for anything that might be helpful. Maybe?" Tempest gave me her quirkiest grin.

I pulled out the copy of the card I had in my bag and showed it to Tempest. Her eyes widened, and her goofy grin turned into a genuine smile.

"It's the Wheel of Fortune."

I huffed, not appreciating her joke. "Sure, I'll just ask for a vowel and a couple of consonants and give the wheel a spin to see if we can solve the puzzle."

"No. You don't understand. It's the Wheel of Fortune. It's a card in a tarot deck. That's the theme—tarots. Ours resembled the Hanged Man."

I stared back at the carbon copy of the card like it was the first time I was really seeing it. There were six spokes spreading out from the center of a wheel, each wedge crested by winged beasts. The background looked like stone, similar in color to the caverns of our campus. But the one thing that stood out the most, at least to me, was the man hiding in the shadows wearing a blindfold.

"So what's the clue on the back say?" Tempest asked, pulling me again from my internal thoughts.

I flipped the paper over and read my hand-scrawled version of the poem.

"Sunken deep under the mirror, a boon of the sea you'll find here. Surrounded by stone and power alike, the wheel of the gods may give you a fright. Ancient and cold in the depths you'll be, but brave the darkness and forever be free."

"Whoa. That sounds ... mysterious." Tempest's brows shot into her hairline. "You sure you don't want some help figuring it out?"

Goddess, she was such a good friend. I wanted so badly to say yes and very nearly did, but knew she had the rest of her projects to work on still too. And honestly, I suddenly felt like this was something I would need to figure out on my own.

"I can't let you do that. Not this time. This one I need to settle on my own."

She shrugged and linked her arm through mine, pulling me forward across the quad. "Okay, just let me know if you change your mind."

The shortest of the five residential towers came into view as we neared the bridge to Hel Tower, or what we affectionately called home. It didn't give me the same sense of peace I'd known when returning home to Cancun, though. The sea there would always greet me, and we'd never strayed too far from it when we traveled. But here, well ... Colorado was a long way from the salty seas, and I had to admit I was more homesick than ever.

"Offer's still on the table. No witch left behind." Tempest nudged me with her shoulder before bounding up the steps to the massive red door that greeted any who dwelled in Hel Tower.

If she said anything more, I didn't realize it. I was too lost in my own head, wondering how I'd ever dig myself out of this hole. I ambled behind her, keeping my eyes trained on the rouge carpet, avoiding anyone who might have a chance of seeing how much of a mess I really was. One thought stood out beyond all others.

I wanted peace and solitude, to shut it all out and find some solace with my creatures. They needed me, kept that connection with home alive. Okay, so perhaps co-dependent was more appropriate. The last door on the left was mine, directly across from the room Tempest shared with Natalie. We'd all become fast friends, more like sisters, when we'd moved into Hel. Aside from the tension between Tempest and Vanna earlier in the year, we'd become our own family. However, just like family, shit happened, and people came and went.

Lately, things had been rocky between Vanna and me, and I wasn't handling the changes very well. With Professor Asher Kincaid—aka Professor Hot Pants—in the picture now, she'd become a completely different hellhound. She didn't want to hear anyone's honest opinion on the pair of them unless it fell perfectly in line with her own views. I'd hardly seen her since she'd pressed me on how I felt about it. Still, I crept back into my dorm room daily with growing anxiety about fighting with her over the whole thing again. My stomach was constantly tied up in knots. I missed my best friend, but I couldn't ignore the fact that there was something to be said for those who felt like Vanna was skating by and getting off easy because she was sleeping with a teacher. But what did she expect? Just because it wasn't technically breaking rules didn't mean it wouldn't ruffle feathers. Whispers and rumors came with the territory.

Tempest let out a little squeal, and I looked up to find Eryx Strathos waiting for my friend at her door, which signaled Natalie must've been out. She, too, had been distant lately, but I knew she would come to us when she was ready to share what was going on. She hadn't pried or forced me to try any hairbrained spells with the hope of redeeming my magic, so I wouldn't ask more of her than she had of me.

"Nat didn't answer, so I waited," Eryx confessed.

The old me would've stuck around, slinging jabs and playful insults at the adoring couple, but not even that sounded like it would bring me any joy. Without giving either of them a backward glance or giving Tempest a moment to remember she'd talked about keeping me distracted, I turned the knob and slipped into the sanctuary of my dorm room. Tension eased from my shoulders, melting away like hot butter, but the reprieve was short-lived as a buzzing sound came from within.

A flurry of sudden movement caught my attention, and I saw the duvet cover on Vanna's bed settle into place, thrown haphazardly over herself.

"Shit, uh, hey."

The vibrating came to an abrupt stop, and my cheeks flamed with mortified embarrassment as the pieces of what I'd walked in on knitted together to weave a very vivid picture.

"Yo, V . . . and V's vagina." Unable to contain it, laughter erupted from me like a hysterical hyena. Every raw edge of my broken bits was hemorrhaging emotional fuel directly onto what was quickly becoming a raging inferno. Vanna's face screwed up tightly, and I could tell she was rolling her eyes despite the dark sunglasses she always wore.

Without a single shred of shame, Vanna tossed the covers aside and tugged her jeans over her nakedness. Not a single fuck was given that I'd seen what I had or that she'd been caught. Vanna just shrugged.

"Professor Commando not available to fill your needs?" I teased, trying to keep the bitter jealousy from my tone, but the twitch near the corner of Vanna's mouth was my only indication that she'd heard it.

"You know he hates it when you call him that."

"Then he should keep his ass covered," I snapped, harsher than I initially meant.

My guilt was immediate, yet Vanna's perfectly arched brows rose with irritation and challenge.

"How were we supposed to know you wouldn't know what a sock on the doorknob meant? It's the universal sign for *come back later*; everyone knows that. Obviously, if we would've known you were coming back to the room on a Friday night, we would've gone to his room at the Lilith Nest."

My lips pursed as I tried to contemplate why they wouldn't just go to Asher's room. After a second, I remembered Professor Kincaid mentioning something in passing about the staff.

"Where else would I go? This is where I live."

Vanna threw her hands up in the air like she couldn't take another second of me and stuffed her feet into her combat boots, not bothering to lace them up. She grabbed her leather motorcycle jacket from where it hung limply across her computer chair, clutching it tightly and marching for the door. As her hand closed around the doorknob, she paused and half turned to face me, the need to get the last word in written all over her face.

"We've all been trying really hard to give you space and searching for ways to get this whole fucking mess straightened out. Marina, you're my best friend and I can't tell you how sorry I am for what you're going through, but you can't keep pushing us away and going full on sea bitch to isolate yourself. If you keep this shit up, one of these days you're going to wake up and realize that we can't keep trying forever."

I know, I thought as she slammed the door in my face.

I looked around our room, desperate to find the solace it once offered, but couldn't see it anywhere. I had to get out of here, and it didn't matter where I went … I just couldn't stay here. Bolting for the door, I tore out of my room and down the hall. My feet barely made contact with the steps as I sprinted down them, desperate for an exit. If it weren't for his quick reflexes, I would've steamrolled Amaruq as I leapt from the last step, ignoring the curious stares and annoyed comments. It wasn't every day there was a lunatic running through the tower. That was usually reserved for Tuesdays and special occasions like full moons. Turns out, people didn't really like it when you upset the norms even when they were extremely abnormal. Living in Cancun among the humans had taught me that.

My family had been banished from the Campeche clan on the other side of the bay, forced to blend in as much as possible with the mortals. That had been before my time, so I'd always known and understood the necessity to look a certain way to not draw attention. Halvard was different though. No one had to hide who or what they were to fit into the molds humanity had set. It was vastly different here and yet so eerily similar—my running through the tower was evidence of that. The irritation my disturbance caused continued to elicit whispers and snide comments from the surrounding students with every step I took, and I obsessed over every single word until I pushed out the front door.

I didn't know where I was going; I just went, letting my intuition carry me somewhere I could find some damn peace. I'd never known anyone from my clan who'd taken on the taint of black magic, so I had nothing to refer to when it came to my own experiences. However, I'd begun to wonder if being barred from knowing peace was my true curse, even more so than losing the tight control I'd always maintained over myself and my magic.

I was now magically incontinent, spewing twisted magic all over without an ounce of restraint or the ability to mold it with my intentions. Control didn't exist for me anymore. I could turn it on and off, but what the outcome may be … there was never any telling. I'd recently transformed more potions into squid ink than I wanted to think about.

Tears again streamed down my cheeks, utterly destroying my mostly waterproof eye makeup—another sad downside to my magic being on the fritz. I'd never had to worry about my makeup running because water didn't quite affect me the same way, but now that wasn't the case. I'd learned that struggle the hard way, and my budget hadn't afforded me the option of better-quality makeup to fill in for my deficiency. I knew my friends wouldn't mind helping me out, but I hadn't found the right time to tell them how much I'd been struggling ... or even if I wanted to. Vanna knew. Hell, I think they all *knew* something was wrong with me, but I believed deep down that no one could help me. This was a solo mission.

Carried to the water's edge, I hardly even realized what my destination was until I'd arrived. Sobs racked my body, and I fell to my knees, straining to drag in enough air to quench the pain swirling within. The smooth pebbles felt like boulders as they bit into my flesh, undoubtedly leaving bruises behind. Gentle lapping waves washed over my hands as my fingers dug into the shore of the underground lake. With the arrival of spring break, the campus was pretty vacant. There were always those who didn't have a home to go to, but that had never been me—until now. Tears continued to streak down my hot cheeks as I tried to time my shallow pants with the lapping of the water against the stony shore. It was my own slice of paradise in a hell of my own creation.

Soon, the water had soaked through every layer of my clothes, but I didn't care. It was familiar, my only solace at this point. If I couldn't be worth a damn at the Sun & Moon Academy, then for at least a few moments, I would be at one with the water again. When the darkness would finally consume me, I hoped it would be right here in this spot. Stories of Avalon and the Lady of the Lake, King Arthur and the kind came to mind. To be legendary like that had been a dream since I'd been a child.

I wanted to be great, but all I'd managed was to ensure I'd join the sea sponges sooner than later. For now, I'd wait for the darkness to take me, praying Ix Chel would hear my cries and end my suffering.

CHAPTER 3

*L*ong after I should've meandered back to my dorm, I was still sitting lakeside, staring out over the calm waters. Somewhere along the way, my sorrow and despair had turned to something darker, angrier. It wasn't fair. I'd done the right thing helping to get rid of the Gjenganger, and still, I'd paid dearly for it. Like the tides, what you put out into the world will one day return to you, or so I'd always thought. That wasn't really true now, was it? Not for me anyway.

As much as I wanted to wail until my throat was raw and hoarse, screaming wasn't my style, but I still felt the need to lash out. Legs numbed with sleep, I ambled to my feet and wobbled deeper into the black waters of the cavern lake. Life was brimming in the steady depths; I could feel their essence in the currents as they brushed over my skin. I could feel the tiny barnacles clinging to the rocky surfaces and the pale and blind cave fish searching for their next unsuspecting catch. Algae bloomed plentifully, feeding the rocksuckers and crustaceans so small I could hardly detect their presence if not for their abundance. Wading deeper until I was submerged to my waist, I let the lake have my fury. It could handle it, of that there were zero doubts. I wouldn't have been surprised if the mountain had a magical backbone running throughout the stalagmite laden cavern.

The currents changed direction as I let my magic slip from my fingers, shifting around me. Unlike so many other times, my magic didn't fight me when I unleashed it. It surged forth, pouring from me and lighting the lake up like the Cinco de Mayo festivities in Mexico City. Bubbles surfaced as the waves began to churn over, spinning round and round and picking up force as if they were fueled by my tumultuous emotions. Letting it all go, the rotating spout stretched deeper below the surface and spun outward until nearly half the lake was encompassed by my whirlpool. It pulled water toward its middle, dropping ever lower and thrashing twelve-foot swells against the walls. I wasn't a stormbringer like my abuela had been, but I wasn't without my own talents either—when they actually worked.

Freshly ingrained into my memory, I saw Felix's face. He watched me with indifference and mild disdain right along with that little tart who'd been practically mounting him in front of everyone like one of those cougar shifters in heat. It was the cherry on top of my guano sundae. The roar of the crashing waves and misty spray would likely be heard all over campus; the sounds underground tended to echo and amplify, but I didn't care. Let them see. It couldn't hurt any more than it did to look myself in the mirror every morning knowing I'd failed everyone I loved and worst of all, myself. Being tainted by this dark magic was making me an outcast here at the all-inclusive Sun & Moon Academy, but even worse, it meant I'd be an outcast within my clan as well.

"*Marina,*" a voice whispered, breaking my melancholy.

The hold I had on the whirlpool slipped and with it, my control. The walls of the watery tornado became unstable, making increasingly oblong passes as the circle became an oval and then began to disintegrate entirely. In the distance, I could make out the curious hollers of a few onlookers from far above in Modi Tower, which had a view of the lake, but again, I didn't care. There was nothing more to see. It couldn't have lasted more than a few minutes, and even that hadn't gone the way I'd planned. I hadn't been able to maintain control after all.

Dragging in a deep, ragged breath, I tried to steady my frayed nerves. The lake had already begun to settle, and I cast my eyes toward the skylight at the pinnacle of Mount Alexa. It was too far to see clearly, and I wasn't so lucky to be blessed with perfect eyesight like some of my classmates. But right now, I didn't want to see anyone anyway.

"Marina," the voice whispered again. This time it was so loud I expected to see someone standing on the beach behind me.

Undeterred by being submerged to my waist, I twisted around. There was no one close by, but I knew without a single shred of doubt that I'd heard someone calling out to me. Uneasy, I took a step to the side, parallel to the shore, and instead of meeting the rocky bottom, my foot dropped almost half a foot.

My gut clenched as I plunged downward a few inches, and as a short woman, I didn't have a few inches to spare. Thankfully, my foot came to an abrupt stop on a sturdy rock, stopping me from dropping off into the deep. It took a second for me to realize my foot was on a completely level, flat surface, unlike anything I'd found elsewhere on the beach or along the shores.

For as heavy as the world had felt the previous few months, that single discovery had nudged my curiosity awake, giving me something else to fixate on. Whatever worked, right? Stepping down onto the ledge with both feet, I held my arms out in case it gave under my weight. I could tread water with the best of them, but that didn't mean I enjoyed it. Shuffling along the slab, my big toe kissed the face of a stone with enough force to make me inhale sharply and want to cry out every curse I could conjure, but instead I grit my teeth and dragged air in through my nose sharply, like it would somehow magically make the pain dissipate. I wasn't lucky enough to be a natural born healer. I could tinker and make a mean potion, but I struggled. That was where my studious nature came in handy. Reading was my stress reliever, and I'd devoured my textbooks. Where Vanna would procrastinate, I would have done the reading and started a project the very day it was assigned. I hated feeling left behind, especially in the classroom, so I'd taken my studies seriously while knowing it was the only way I'd be able to survive ... until recently, that is. Now, I barely had the urge to crack open a book at all.

When I regained my small thread of composure, I tried to feel out the rock and realized it was more than a stone, but instead, more like a short retaining wall that rose nearly half a foot. The ledge was just as straight and smooth as the one I was standing on,

leaving zero doubt it was a man-made or magic-made structure—
but what was it? Sliding closer to the edge of the slab, I slid my
foot over its squared corner and bent down so I could feel for
anything lower. Just as the tip of my shoe brushed another flat
surface, I heard the voice call my name again.

"Marina."

Bubbles in the distance caught my attention first. They began
small and so far away, I could hardly make out what they were, but
then they grew and started to move closer. Not fast, but quick
enough it was noticeable, and very obvious it was headed in my
direction. Anyone else might've panicked at the sight, but not me.
I wanted to see what was happening.

Rumor had it they'd hauled the lake monster off to the
Infernum, but right now, I wasn't so sure I bought that excuse. The
bubbles started to get bigger, spanning the space between the far
cave wall on the opposite side of the lake and nearly halfway
across, growing by the second.

Perhaps a sea serpent?

The lake had mostly calmed from the spout I'd created but was
churning again by whatever was lurking under the surface.
Squaring up to it, I stepped fully onto the lower ledge and scanned
the glassy topside. Ripples began from something lurking below,
sending rings stretching outward in every direction.

Smaller waves lapped at my navel, pushed along by the force of
something larger behind it. I stood stock still, keeping my eyes
trained on the water, scanning for the shadow that would herald a
beast's arrival.

Yet, no creature broke the surface.

Instead, the water directly in front of me began to recede,
much like one would expect before the arrival of a tsunami. I took
a step back, but my heel caught on the lip of the ledge behind me,
and I went tumbling. My arms flailed as I tried fruitlessly to right
my balance and catch myself. To no avail, I fell right onto my butt;
my elbow bit into the stone, and the flesh split like a ripe banana.

"What the—" My words died in my throat as what happened
in that moment dawned on me.

I'd fallen ... and no water had been there to cushion my
descent. My oozing elbow forgotten, I could feel the gritty

sprinkling of sand against the stone under my hand. Where had the water gone? It had been there one second and gone the next.

Swinging my head around to look out toward the lake, I couldn't believe what I was witnessing. I hadn't been standing on a ledge. Well, I had ... but not really.

It was a stairway descending under the lake.

"Whoa. Did not see that coming," I hissed.

The frothing waters parted several feet, creating a soggy pathway deeper under the lake. Scanning the vacant beach around me, I bit my lip as I waited anxiously for whomever had done this to step out. It surely wasn't me. I would've been able to feel the pull of the water, if it had been. I saw no one, and not a single person stepped out to claim credit for the trick. Ignoring that uneasy feeling, I took a careful step in the soaked sand, and the water receded a little farther, inviting me deeper into the lake.

Alarm bells should've been going off; somewhere in the recesses of my brain I knew that. I kept waiting for my better judgement to kick in and listen to those cautious warnings and doubts, but the bell towers of self-preservation were silent this day as I put one foot in front of the other and strode toward the approaching drop off, wondering with each step when the edge would reveal itself. However, when I got closer and the waters receded farther, it revealed smooth polished blocks almost a meter across. The pathway took an abrupt drop and then another to unveil more steps leading into the murky depths.

I glanced back at the shore. The waters remained parted, and there was not a soul in sight. Any apprehension I might've felt was snuffed out by the driving force of my curiosity. I just had to know what waited for me at the end of the path. Perhaps it was the owner of the voice I'd been hearing or maybe even another crystal cave like the amethyst thermal pool. Nimbly, I traversed the algae-slickened stairs for what seemed like forever. My ears popped as I descended deeper under Mount Alexa until the steps disappeared into what I assumed was the floor of the lake. There was a hole roughly five feet in diameter, and the stairs followed this direction. Without hesitation, I trudged lower still but the steps stopped shortly after my head cleared the entrance and leveled out into a cleanly cut hallway. Water dripped down the walls, and I could hear the sound of crab feet on rock as they skittered away from the dry air. It was pitch black, and I couldn't see much beyond the circle of light cast down by the entrance.

"*Accendo*," I whispered, hoping like hell my magic would rise to the occasion and work right for a change.

I really didn't want to go traipsing around when I couldn't see a thing beyond the confines of my illuminated circle. Holding my hand out in front of me, I felt the energy build, and a second later, a ball of light nearly the size of a bowling ball expelled from my fingertips and soared down the hall before me like a shot. It happened so fast that I was slow to respond and take off after it. It wasn't exactly what I was hoping for, but it was close enough I was going to mark it down in the win column; I needed more of those anyway.

The light came to an abrupt stop about fifty feet or so ahead of me, colliding with another stone wall. Carved into the rocky edifice was a symbol I was sure I'd seen before but couldn't place. However, as soon as I took a step to get a closer look, the light flickered out, leaving me in darkness, beyond the safety of the lighted entry behind me. In a panic, I reached for anything I could grab onto to find my bearings. It was a straight hallway, so it wasn't difficult to find the algae covered limestone blocks on either side. The second my fingers contacted the wall, its surface came to life.

It was a bright blue, glowing against the warmth of my skin. When I pulled my hand back, tiny specks clung to my fingers, rolling down with rivulets of condensation. I'd recognize those little buggers anywhere, but I hadn't expected to find bioluminescent plankton this far from the ocean ... or underground, for that matter.

One gift that hadn't dimmed with my tainted magic was my ability to understand sea life. It wasn't like I could speak dolphin; I'm no Doctor Doolittle. Yet, ever since I could remember, I just sort of knew what they wanted and how to get them to do what I wanted. It never mattered how small or seemingly insignificant the organism. Being so far from the sea, I'd missed having more than just my pet eel to talk to when people were too tricky.

Bringing my fingers to my lips, I whispered a command to my microscopic friends, letting the Latin roll off my tongue with ease.

When my whisper fell quiet, I pressed my full hand against the limestone and let my will spread like a blue wildfire. It was the most breathtaking sight to behold, watching the walls come alive with light. With a little more confidence and that familiar sass in my step, I rushed down the walkway, only pausing at the end to commit that symbol to memory.

There was another set of steps at the end of the space, going to the left. Only these steps started back up, reminding me of the underwater caves back home. Most of them weren't even accessible from the land. You had to go down before you could come back up. I didn't see any reason this would be any different and moved before I could think better of it and talk myself out of the whole venture.

Dios mio, what did I get myself into?

CHAPTER 4

*E*xactly two things went through my head as I stared at the majestic structure that lay ahead. One: I was absolutely certain no one at Halvard or Havenwood Falls had ventured this far. And two: only the most skilled architects could accomplish such a task, much less underground, but they'd done it in splendid fashion.

A modest temple guarded by statues of fierce winged beasts hovered atop a plateau in the middle of the cavern. It could've been Greek or Roman if it weren't for the Babylonian-styled tiers. Each column and carved fresco on the outer walls appeared to be different in origin, and that was even more puzzling. So many millennia of history and culture all fused into a single building to worship … what, exactly?

The temperature here, inside the cavern, was noticeably warmer than the outer hall section had been, and I tried not to think too hard about what made things hot underground. Magma wasn't my forte, and I had no desire to tangle with it, but I'd come too far to stop now. As I edged closer to the base of the stairs, I eyed the gap between the rocky outcropping where I stood and the beginning of the plateau. It wasn't massively wide, and for someone a little more athletic than me, it might not have been an obstacle, but for a sea witch who wasn't well suited for land endeavors, it looked like a goddamn bottomless pit. Heights and

Marina did not mix. But something wanted me here; it wanted me to go inside and find what was hidden. I didn't know how I knew that, but I did. I could feel it in my bones. The energy in the cavern was distinctly magical. The place was absolutely brimming with it. So many questions swirled, spurring me into action, my fears dampened by my need to know what lay inside.

The muscles in my thighs bunched tightly as I sprinted toward the edge and launched myself forward, grappling for my footing as I barely made it across.

I could hear small bits of rock pinging off the sheer façade I'd just cleared. I instinctively knew not to look down, keeping my eyes focused on the double doors of the temple and throwing my weight forward, a move that likely saved my hide. Taking a few more steps just to be sure, I numbly ambled toward the dais of the temple, my hands reaching for the door like it was my lifeline.

Flames burst to life in the long empty sconces, lighting the temple in all its glory. The sound of fire crackling echoed through the chamber, breaking up the silence enough to give the impression that perhaps someone was there with me. Yet, as I made a full turn to inspect the room, I noticed far more interesting figures than any hidden spy.

Six marble statues stood tall on individual pedestals, evenly spaced in a circle. I took stock of the deities, and it dawned on me the magnitude of what I was standing in. It wasn't a just a circle; it was more than that. So much more.

It was a wheel—the Wheel of Fortune, just like our card—and I was standing smack dab in the middle of it.

My inner geek was practically doing dolphin flips at the sight of the gods and goddesses perched on their daises. I'd spent so much time devouring every book on the gods and legends during my Pantheons of the World—Truth or Myth? class.

Each spoke of the wheel ended at one of the statues, which must've stood at least twelve feet tall. No two architectural styles or building materials seemed to match, yet every single spoke was balanced with a counter spoke. Slowly, I began my stroll around the space, inspecting each effigy with care. Trying to discern any notation of direction, my gaze was brought down to the floor where weathered symbols knit together to form words and then sentences, creating a spiral that ended at my feet in the center of the circle.

Fata caeca est. Levitate ambulant semita.

Fate is blind. Walk the path lightly.

As soon as I understood its meaning, my muscles tensed apprehensively, and I was instantly looking for possible booby traps. Temples back home were designed to prevent any who might disturb the peace of the temple from ever reaching their destination. Nothing stood out as my cautious eyes scanned over the temple, but no good trap was visible to the prey. I would have to be careful and watch my steps and my back; nothing was safe.

Dragging the moist warm air into my lungs, I stepped forward to the first statue. This one was easy to identify for his falcon head and mighty wings—Horus, lord of the skies. Around his neck hung a talisman, glowing from within to create a magical aura around it. The Eye of Horus was etched into the golden surface and glittered in the low light. There was something about it that made me want to reach out and take it, but I knew an enchantment when I saw one, and as I moved onto the next statue, I understood what was meant by walking the path lightly. The treasures each offered were more precious than the rarest diamonds, and I couldn't ignore the nagging sensation that one of these was what we were meant to find for the Hunt. The outstanding assignment had been a thorn in my side since the semester had started, given that I was elected team leader when I wasn't present. I'd been hard at work on an ulcer over that. Among so many other problems.

But which one? I would have to choose the token from the gods that spoke to me the most, maybe even break the enchantment to remove anything from the temple, because this was just too good to be true.

It can't be that easy.

A tight ball formed in the pit of my stomach as I watched a mental play-by-play of every possible wrong way my magic could ruin this task. Backfiring was a very strong possibility, but gazing into the supple petals of the goddess Flora's proffered mayflower, I was almost certain I would be willing to take that risk. Looking at her beautiful marble form, I felt as though I could clip the stem neatly without distributing the glow of its vibrant bloom. But still, Flora's flower wasn't truly calling to me so I moved on, stowing my curious fingers.

I continued past a great golden dragon that curled high above a small jade statue. In its clutching talons was an orb of water the size of a mango. Gazing into the liquid, I saw myself staring back, but older and regal. Age marred the smooth skin near my eyes, but the power within me radiated outward, exuding from my reflection. My arms seemed like they were moving of their own volition as I reached toward the promising liquid. It was almost painfully difficult to stop and keep moving, but the next figure was far more imposing and even more fierce.

Ogun stood tall and proud with his mighty hammer, ready to forge the strongest of weapons from the fires of his homeland. Dreadlocks hung down to his waist, only adding to the dashing ruggedness of his profile. From where I was standing, I could feel the fire within the hammer in his hand and smiled.

Next, Vayu rose high from a plume of marble smoke, holding his prized goad high, the hook curved to a wicked point, but I cared not for what he offered me. My eyes were transfixed to the next figure—one I knew all too well and had since I was three and first went to the temple with my abuela.

Mist gathered in my eyes, and I had to blink a few times to see the woman clearly. It was her—Ixa. Her kind, broad face was inviting and warm as she gazed down at the most magnificent pearl I'd ever seen. It was massive, and the luster was nearly pristine. There were a few imperfections I could see from where I was standing, but it was still the most impressive bauble I'd ever laid eyes on.

As I stared longingly at the woman's outstretched offering, I could feel the excitement well up inside me and awaken something I hadn't thought I would ever feel again. Like a light switch had been flipped, I could feel every cell come to life, bursting with magical potential like I'd been doused in water and was only now dry enough to truly take flight.

A tsunami of guilt washed over me, and I suddenly remembered myself, glancing around the temple quickly to see if anyone had witnessed my momentary weakness. Nothing had changed; I was alone. My abuela's voice whispered in the recesses of my thoughts, reminding me to always trust in Ixa and turn to the sea, for she will always provide. It was a thought that refused to be silenced as I cast my eyes back to the other gods like they'd been my silent judges.

Like you didn't fuck up in just about every story you've ever been cast in, I thought accusingly at the wheel of the gods. Oh yeah, I saw them; and I was calling them on their crap. They could stick their snooty celestial noses in the air all they wanted, but they acted more human than mortals did most of the time.

Suddenly, everything that had happened this semester, or maybe even this whole year, snapped into picture-perfect focus.

"Choose well, Marina."

It was the same voice I'd heard a hundred times and I knew I'd hear a hundred more in the nightmares that seemed to constantly plague me. It sent shivers down my spine, and I knew beyond all doubt that voice meant trouble. It was sound advice regardless. Choose well was exactly what I planned to do. Abuela Maris always said when I was troubled and needed guidance to first ask the gods. If that failed, to think of what my papa would do in my situation and do the exact opposite. He was no stranger to danger or finding something with bad intentions; deep down, I was half-convinced that was why my grandmother was as powerful as she was. The other reason being she was a Campeche pureblooded sea witch once upon a time, before she was banished for marrying a mortal. I'd seen that woman do things I could only dream of accomplishing one day.

When my faith had faltered, I turned on my magic and took more than I should've. I wouldn't make that same mistake again. As I reached for the pearl in Ixa's outstretched hand, pterodactyls felt like they were taking flight in my rib cage and could carry me away from her, so I closed the distance. My fingertips brushed the cool smooth surface of the plum-sized pearl in the goddess's cupped palms, and a warm zing ran up my arm.

The jolt halted me in my steps but not before I plucked the pearl up, cradling it against my chest in shock.

"Mierda!" I hissed, my fingers burning from the jolt.

Panic washed through me in waves, and I eyed every corner of the temple with terror and bewilderment as I anticipated any number of booby traps that might've been lying in wait. Drips of water and the thudding of my racing heart were all I could hear over the deafening silence. Every muscle was tensed as I held my pose, afraid any movement might set something off. Carefully and almost painfully slowly, I shifted my weight around to get a better look at the opulent gem.

Light swirled within it, enrapturing me. Around and around, one wave crashing over another as each swirl fought for dominance. It was like watching an intricate dance where you couldn't begin to anticipate the moves. I didn't know how long I stood there watching the tumbling lights, however my hands were numb with cold and my stomach felt like it was going to start eating itself if I didn't take my prize and high-tail it back to Hel and let the rest of my team know about the temple I discovered. I'd found the Wheel of Fortune and knew the pearl had to be the piece we'd been searching for all along. This had to at least be enough to cement my A on the project.

"If you're listening, I hope you know you won't regret giving me another chance," I whispered to the awaiting quiet, wondering if the source of the voice was watching from the shadows.

There was no answer and had there been, I'm not sure I would've had the stones to stay and hold a conversation with a disembodied voice. Sending up a silent prayer and appreciation to Ixa, I made my way out of the temple and through the soggy passage, which had remained open during the entirety of my visit. The pearl was warm in my hand, invigorating my chilled bones. I caught myself staring at it every chance I got, only looking up to watch my step and assure myself of the path. Glancing up toward the surface, I placed my foot on the bottom step and marveled at the sight of the walls of water still parted, awaiting my arrival. However, I didn't stick around to marvel too long. I needed privacy to examine my find further.

Each step carrying me up toward the beach filled me with raw energy, enough I was even beginning to feel the familiar call of the sea filling my belly. Every nerve was alight with sensations as magic surged through me, and I sent up another silent thanks to Ixa for granting me a second chance.

I extended my hand, my fingers dipping into the wall of water rising above my head, feeling the cool wetness under my touch. In the dark distance, I could make out a small school of fish as they turned and headed toward my hand. The silver of their scales shimmered in the blue light dancing from the watery walls. The fish were moving so quickly I thought they'd tear right through the water and jump the gap. Yet, they turned at the last minute and stopped. The school of nearly thirty silver-scaled cave fish hovered near the edge of the water, yet they had no eyes to speak of.

I'd never seen such a reaction from cave fish. Usually they were extremely shy and hesitant to approach with the sweetest of lures. Were they sensing the pearl?

Even the lowliest of creatures are drawn to power and those who possess it.

When I would take a step up, the school followed. I toyed with them, jumping up one step and back down two. They made sharp turns as they followed, and if I didn't know better, I'd have thought they could see. I was so caught up in the curious game and watching them flip around in a tight formation, I didn't notice a dark shadow moving up ahead, near the top of the stairs. By the time I turned my head to glance at it, it was already gone. The momentary distraction reminded me I should get back before anyone started looking for me. If the pearl could give me back my magic, it was valuable to more than just me, and it became paramount that I kept the bauble secret.

The Hunt be damned.

If word got out that I had a magical pearl, let alone one I found in a sunken temple, the Regents would be all over it and I'd be right back to square one. Squeezing my fist tightly around the pearl, I bolted up the stairs. The tiny silver fish swam alongside me as I went, their little fins breaking the watery wall and sending a tiny spray of mist against my arm. As soon as my head breeched the lake level, they turned away and darted back into the depths.

"*Adios, mis amigos,*" I whispered as I watched the silver streaks disappear from sight.

The cold stones under my feet were slick with damp silt, and I turned back toward the shore with more pep in my step than I'd had in months. I felt like a whole new sea witch. When I was close to the beach, the prickly rush of anxiety set in, and I became hyperaware of my surroundings. Reality came crashing down around me, and I spun, letting my magic fill me. Ixa was with me; I could feel her guiding presence. I stared at the water, waiting for it to release back into place, then realized it was waiting for me.

"*Reditus!*"

With a soft plop and splash, the azure waters crashed back together, splashing around my legs halfway up my calves, soaking my jeans twice as high. I didn't care, though. I was still reeling with shock and awe with everything that had transpired. The pearl nestled in my palm was the only evidence I would believe that it had really happened. On the tips of my fingers was the faintest glow of my tiny bioluminescent friends, so I plunged my free hand into the water, wiggling my fingers to shake them off.

The ripples spread outward, colliding with the tiny lapping waves approaching from the underwater currents. As I watched the flecks detach and disappear into the dark, murky depths, a shadow passed overhead, and I ducked in reflex. Whatever it was had moved so fast it was a blur and a miracle I'd seen it at all. Crouching low in the water, I eyed the cavern above me. I was sure I'd heard the sound of beating wings, yet as I scanned over the rocky cave walls and the empty shoreline, there was no one. Slowly, I turned, half-expecting to see another lake monster staring back at me from the deeper waters, but I'd just been down there and saw nothing of the sort. Like the peccary before the jaguar leaps, I froze as I could feel the studious watch of something or someone who was, by my first judgment, highly capable of lethal force.

"There's an object in your possession of great power, so I will assume you've been successful in your excursion. I'll take it from here," a deep voice purred from the shore at my back.

"And you must not know who I am, because if you did, you might not make the mistake in assuming that I'm some pushover who can be ordered around."

The words flew out of my mouth before I could stop them, and I spun in the water to meet my spy. I didn't know who or what I was expecting to see, but a tall man with broad, muscular shoulders was definitely not it.

CHAPTER 5

"*M*arina Del Mar. A sea witch with a background in chemistry and potions. I've done my research, my dear. I know who you are. Have you done yours?"

The bastard was cocky. If I was at the top of my game, I could turn this arrogant *pendejo* into a blob and add him to my tank with my collection of sea jellies. However, at the top of my game I was not, though he didn't need to know that. What was worse than being mocked was the knowledge he was right; I was at a disadvantage. I knew who the man was. In fact, he was the lone male on my ITF team—Caspar Yazdani. Cas to those unlucky enough to know the ancient-as-all-hell gryphon. However, my attendance had been less than stellar, and even when I had managed to drag my ass to class, my brain was in so many other places. When I'd try to buckle down and read the texts, I'd find myself rereading the same paragraph over and again. To be perfectly honest, the man was hardly on my radar, but with that attitude, he was edging closer to the bull's eye of my ire.

Ix Chel, he's annoying!

"Anyone with a computer and a working knowledge of hacking basics could've patched into the servers on campus and find that information out. If you told me something that couldn't be found in my file, then I might be impressed. You'll have to do better than my biographical basics," I challenged.

The cool current running under the surface of the lake embraced my ankles as if to give me the reassurance and support I needed to stand my ground, not backing down an inch.

"I know you don't go to many parties and for the most part have been a good student. You helped vanquish the Gjenganger before the entire campus was compromised, a feat worthy to be proud of, but since the event, your grades have started to slip and you spend an increasing amount of time by yourself, despite having a trio of women who seem to surround you at least most of the time. Is that personal enough or should I keep going? I know that the woman I see standing before me, while still as ravishing as Aphrodite's handmaidens, is only a shadow of the woman she once was, and as far as I'm concerned, it's a shame."

Every word was like a cut doused in lime juice followed by a kick to the balls ... or what I imagined it would feel like. Who the hell was he to hold my decline over me like a black mark? I filed away the comment about being beautiful, though. Flattery typically got people much further with me. Leveling the man with an icy glare, I strode out of the water and stomped ashore, tucking the pearl safely into my bra, without letting him directly see it. "Not so cocky now that you'd have to come and get it yourself, are you, tough guy?"

Damn it if he didn't crack an amused smile.

Mierda.

I didn't give myself time to second guess my confidence before trudging from the water and coming to a stop so close to the man, I knew he could feel the warmth of my breath as I shot daggers up at him with the sweetest grin plastered on my lips.

"You don't know me."

Four simple words. Each one was punctuated with the appropriate pop to let him know I wasn't fucking around anymore. His lips pressed into a thin line, and for a moment, he looked like he wanted to argue the point further, but I wasn't quite finished with him yet.

"If you think you can show up out of nowhere with some stalker-level knowledge and take me for a fool, then you clearly haven't been properly introduced to this sea bitch. I'm Marina Del Mar. Now who the fuck are you?"

The man took a single step, closing the distance between us until there was barely more than our clothing separating his body from mine, invading my space and overwhelming me. I think that's what he was trying to do, but I wasn't having any of it. My hand went up defensively, colliding with pecs that I was sure had to be chiseled straight from granite and not flesh and bone. I shoved him, meaning to push him away enough to give me some space, but instead, he folded both hands around mine and brought them to his lips.

"Caspar Yazdani, the pleasure is all mine."

His eyes were nearly black, lightening to a molten gold near the pupils and rimmed by impossibly thick lashes—and they were trained on me expectantly.

He placed my hands back on his chest. "Please, don't stop on my account."

Oh, so now he was mocking me?

Where a thousand questions should've fired from my mouth in rapid succession, I found myself shocked into silence, mesmerized by the dark stare of the handsome stranger.

"I wonder if you would be spying on me if you knew that I could turn your eyes into jelly just for looking at me the wrong way," I mused.

A single dark brow rose, and if I didn't blink, I would've sworn I even saw a ghost of a grin grace his full lips. Oh hell, it had been too damn long since a guy had even so much as paid me any attention. I couldn't get anything more than friend-zoned and asked for homework help from the opposite sex since I'd broken rank and mucked my magic up, so this particular one was looking extra delicious with a side of dreamy and a dash of smoldering sexuality. Even better, he was looking at me like he could eat me in only the best of ways, and I wasn't about to look a gift-Ix Chel in the mouth.

"I've seen many things in my lifetime, but I must say, that would be a first. If the shoe was on the other foot, I might even pay good money to see such a sight." Caspar stepped away from me, disappeared for a brief moment, then reappeared a few steps away, farther down the shore. It was a show-off move, but I wasn't going to call him on it. The male ego was a fragile thing, and he looked like the Achilles type. Maybe it was the muscles. I liked those, and they definitely added to his appeal.

"Parting the waters is no small feat. You'll have to let me know how you did it some time. I didn't think a demi-sea witch could harness that kind of control. It wouldn't be the first time I've been wrong, but that doesn't happen often." He smirked.

I winced at the way he'd said *demi*. It was a sore spot for me. My papa had been a human man, the son of a fisherman, and he'd loved my abuela more than life itself. It didn't change that it had torn the family apart, nor did it negate the fact that I, like my three cousins, would never be able to harness the power of the seas the way our grandmother and other full-blooded sea witches could. It was both a blessing and a curse.

Dammit! How did this spy know so much about me?

"Take a good hard look at me. There's no half anything here. I'm a whole woman and more than you can handle. Didn't your mother ever teach you it was rude to so brazenly point out blemishes in those you don't know from Adam?" My brow arched high in challenge.

He looked directly into my eyes. "No, she didn't. I never had a mother. Nor a father. None of my kind do. So I have no idea what such individuals might teach."

My stomach tightened into a lead boulder and practically dropped to my toes. Of all the things he might've said, I hadn't seen that one coming. Now I felt like complete shark shit. I swiveled my head back and forth, trying to find something, anything, interesting enough to hold my attention and avert my eyes from his now intense golden gaze. Yet, each time I looked right at him, my eyes widened in awkward shock, before I could look away again. The tips of my ears were burning; I was mortified. I had to get out of here, no other way around it.

"Right then, I'm just going to go now," I whispered, mostly to myself as I tried to make myself as small as sea-witchily possible.

Great job, dumb ass.

In the back of my mind, the wheels were turning as I wondered who this man was. What type of supernatural being had no parents beyond a celestial being?

Just as I made to step around him, Caspar's hand shot out at a blinding speed, and the iron vice that was his fingers curled around my bicep, locking me in place.

"Tell me, what exactly did you find down there?"

The corners of my mouth turned down in a deep frown as I glanced back and forth between his hand and his face. His eyes were fixed on me, burning through me like he was seeking out every secret I held onto. It was unsettling and certainly more intimate than I was comfortable with. Everything about the moment was just too close, too vulnerable, too ... much, but suddenly, I was desperate to share my secrets with him, as if I couldn't help myself.

After a pause, Caspar released my arm. Smoothing the nonexistent wrinkles from my sleeve like I was well and truly offended, I fished the pearl from my bra, noting the way his watchful gaze was locked on my fingers. I kept the bauble clenched tightly in my fist until it was right in between us. Unfurling my grip, the pearl rolled into the seat of my cupped palm, gleaming brilliantly in the low light.

Caspar's posture and demeanor changed in an instant, from relaxed but ready to rigid and waiting for doom and gloom to rain down. It was the most beautiful pearl I'd ever laid eyes on, and I wasn't exactly someone who was unfamiliar with them, yet he didn't seem to feel the same way about it. Bringing his face closer to my hand like it would help him see the gem better, he turned at the last second, tipping his head toward it.

"Can't you hear its whispers?" he asked, not looking at me, but simply shaking his head like he'd already drawn whatever conclusion he was searching for.

"Whispers? It's a pearl."

When he straightened, he crossed his thickly muscled arms over his chest and on a better day, I might've taken bets on whether his shirt would rip with a good flex, but today was not that day.

"The things that pearl has seen ... it's far too dangerous for someone so young and inexperienced to be walking around with. Someone is going to get hurt if you're not abundantly careful, and even then, there's no guarantees. Do the right thing and return the pearl—or give it to me now."

Something in me snapped, and I pulled the pearl back to my chest. "Pass. I'm pretty sure I've got it under control and haven't you ever heard of the phrase finders' keepers and all that jazz? Because that's real. We live by that shit where I come from." Stepping out of his reach, I peered deep into his eyes, so he'd feel the full weight of what I was about to say. "There is nothing you can say or do to make me hand this over to you, so fuck you very much."

His face darkened, looking somewhat confused, and briefly, I second-guessed poking the bull, so to speak. But my mind was made up, and there'd be no budging on it. Clutching the bauble tightly in my enclosed fist, I sidestepped and moved to evade the hunky speed bump, but he moved directly into my path every single time. By the third block, I was done and about to drop him with tricks dirtier than a brothel's bed knob, and I swear to Ix Chel, I wouldn't have felt bad about it. Not right away, at least.

"You want to dance?" I taunted.

There was a low clicking deep in his throat, my only indication I'd struck a nerve. *Good.*

"Don't start something you can't finish," he warned, his eyes again lightening to gold, which glowed in the low light.

Suddenly, there was a heaviness to the air emanating from Caspar.

"I'll admit, mistakes were made, but your biggest mistake was thinking this would end any other way than with me telling you to go fly a kite, which is exactly what I'm doing. So, see you later." I rushed past him, finally sidestepping him and breaking free of this awkward exchange.

There was no way in hell, I'd be giving this pearl to anyone ... especially him.

CHAPTER 6

*A*fter racing back to my room, I was beyond grateful to find it Vanna-free. I needed time alone to process this, and doubt she'd be back for the night. As soon as I knew I was alone, I pulled the pearl from my soggy brassiere and placed it carefully in my sea shell bowl like it was supposed to be there all along. My admiration for the lustrous orb was blinding. I'd never in all my years seen a pearl so enamoring.

Crossing to my closet, I reached in and felt blindly for my favorite silk sleep pants, then stripped down and slid on my sleepwear, scooping up my soggy clothes and hanging them out to dry over the top of the door. My stomach took that moment to rumble so loudly, it sounded like thunder from the heavens. Yet, when I really thought about the concept of eating, my stomach rebelled.

Shaking my head, I climbed on top of my bed and wriggled my way under the covers. I thought back to what happened today and hoped it was the first step in fixing my fucked up life.

I'd found the Wheel of Fortune related to our assignment, and it would be all too easy to conceal the discovery...that is, assuming Caspar didn't spill to the team. I shook my head. I couldn't believe that asshole Caspar had used a spell, or whatever it was, to make me show him what I'd found. He obviously knew I had something of power, but until that moment, he didn't know exactly what it was. But at usual, I screwed that up too. *Fuck!* Couldn't I catch a break?

Plucking up the pearl from the shell, I gazed into its swirling depth and felt Ix Chel's presence once more. She was calling me, and I was ready to follow.

Closing my eyes, I followed her whisper, recalling the day's events as the vision took hold. I watched, this time as if I was an outsider, and even though some things were the same, others were absolutely not ...

Taking a step into the cleared-out tunnel, I crept forward toward the secret door. The walls of water remained still around me, making the ringing silence seem deafening. It put me on edge. Still waters were traps, as far as I was concerned.

"Who's there?" I called out, not sure whether I wanted someone to answer or not.

"I'm glad you finally accepted my invitation," a voice rumbled from everywhere around me, yet still, I saw no one. "I've been expecting you."

A lump formed in my throat as my anxiety ratcheted through the roof, but I would give this thing nothing. My fear would be mine to control, even if it was the only thing I could exercise restraint over anymore.

"Answer my question, phantom. Or are you too afraid to face me? I bet you're not quite so scary in the flesh, probably more like Baby Yoda with a temper and an over-inflated ego."

A booming laugh rattled me to my core. Enveloping my being, it wrapped around me with its mocking taunt.

"You know not to whom you speak, and yet I know you, Marina Del Mar. In your heart, you've longed for someone who understands what it's like to be misunderstood, different, broken ... an outcast unwelcome by the narrowminded. Every wish. Every heartbreak. Your secrets are my treasures, cast unto the waves like forgotten flotsam."

Something about those words scratched at a distant memory, but it was too out of focus to recognize.

"You speak as though we've met, but I would surely remember someone I told all my secrets to. While I have many friends, there are few I would trust with that kind of information. You seem decidedly more ... penile."

That laugh came again, but this time it had a cold edge to it that unnerved me even more. Had it been my sharp wit or the fact that I didn't hold back when addressing him, even if his voice made every hair on the back of my neck stand at attention?

"*Just as the salt from whence you came, your sharp tongue stings my wounded ego, young one. Please deliver a message for me.*"

"Deliver your own message. I'm not a fucking secretary," I spat back, folding my arms over my chest to keep myself from doing something stupid.

"*As much as I would relish doing just that, our time has not yet come ... but soon. Please tell your team when the red tide meets the green flash, the maelstrom shall rise and all will be as it should.*"

Great! Another fucking riddle.

I jolted upright, grabbing onto anything I could to anchor me in the moment. The covers on my bed were twisted around my feet, and I was still alone in my room, feeling more than a little unnerved by my dream. Abuela Maris always said dreams were visions from the gods, possibilities and alternatives. No matter how unusual or mundane, every dream had a purpose, and sometimes when life blinded you to the correct path, dreams could guide the way.

Glancing at the clock, I realized I'd been asleep almost two hours, longer than I'd anticipated. It was a lot to unpack, and I was reeling at the second riddle I'd been posed. That didn't even address who the source of the voice was. The feeling that I'd heard that voice before hit too close to home.

Before I could shuffle any of this into a proper place in my brain, a jarring knock sounded on my door. The most unladylike yelp tore out of my throat as I jumped up and tugged it ajar in a single motion. Peeking wide-eyed around the doorjamb, I eyed Tempest suspiciously. The woman looked like she was ready for a night out, complete with the cutest strappy sandals I'd seen since I'd left Mexico.

"Don't tell me you're planning on backing out of this one too," Tempest accused, pushing the door aside, not bothering to wait for an invite.

"It's ... not really a good time for me right now," I stammered, the weight of everything that had happened seeming to grow exponentially as I stood in front of one of my best friends as though I was going before a judge and jury.

Tempest stepped closer, noticing my damp clothes hanging on the door for the first time since she'd entered my room.

"Spill it. Now. Shit. Wait. Hold that thought." She rushed out, darting around me.

My body stiffened as she tore out of my dorm room. In the distance, I could hear the door to her room open and the tinkering of glass before her footsteps came running back. Tempest came bearing one of her reserve bottles of wine from the cellar and two glasses.

"Okay, now spill."

With a wave of her hand, my door shut, and my friend found her usual comfortable spot sitting on the end of my bed. Pulling a corkscrew from her pocket, Tempest worked the bottle open and held it out at a distance, just in case it decided to get a little squirrely and splash my blankets. It had happened on more than one occasion, and I wasn't sure how much more magical clean-up the poor fabric would be able to withstand.

"I'm not sure what you mean," I answered.

It was dinner time and not just for me. Heading to the refrigerator, I retrieved a jar of fish bits. The briny aroma filled the air as soon as I cracked the lid on the glass container before the familiar scent of preserved fish followed.

"Mmm, dinner time," I groaned staring down at the salty contents as my stomach roiled.

Placing the jar on my nightstand, I knelt down and gripped the bottom ledge of my bed, pulling the compartment out. The sound of the tank sliding easily was a welcome sign. Asher had fixed the slides on Kukulkan's tank after a disastrous winter break had left my precious moray eel lethargic and half-starved while I was unable to get his tank out from under my bed. Kuku had been ravenous since, and I owed Asher big time.

Shit. There was that nasty feeling of guilt again. He'd done me a solid by saving Kuku, yet I'd only continued to give him and Vanna a rash of shit in return.

I peered through the water as I searched for the dark grey form of my beloved moray.

"*Ahí tienes!*" I crooned as a sleek shadow poked its head out from a crevice in the rocky coral. "*Te extrañé.*"

His slick form slid over my hand, Kuku's own special way of saying hello, and he nipped my fingers for keeping the fish too close to my palm. He was very particular, but that was why I loved him so. The two of us made quite the pair, Marina and Kukulkan, a two-creature school in a sea of weirdos.

"Playing coy only works when you're trying to do it with someone who didn't practically invent the game," Tempest said. "Usually, you have so many words for things that I end up tuning out. You're clammed up tighter than an oyster's ass and not saying a word. Obviously, something major has happened and as the only other member of the Fab Four present, I feel obligated, no … honored, to listen."

She batted her big blue eyes at me like it was supposed to convince me she was sincere. Every word dripped with sarcasm, and there was no pretense she wanted anything other than the honest and whole scoop. Every fear that had held me back from divulging more than I should came crumbling down as I sat across from my sister witch and she called me on my bullshit. We'd made a pact that no matter what college brought, the four of us would stay strong and never waver. It had been touch and go there for a while during the first semester, but Natalie and I were right. Vanna and Tempest had worked things out, and I knew me and Vanna would do the same this semester too.

"I cracked the location of my tarot card. Oh, and turns out, the lake isn't just a lake. There's a temple down there about thirty to forty meters, but it's strange. The markings are distinct, but none of them match a particular architectural or cultural style like you'd think it should. I think it might've been original to the campus, but it seems like they would've known the temple would flood, right?"

When I glanced up from my lap, Tempest was staring at me wide-eyed with her glass of wine frozen midair almost to her lips. The whole thing was farfetched, and I wouldn't blame her if she thought I had taken a dive off the deep end. Although, why any of us were still surprised by anything that happened at the Sun &

Moon Academy was beyond my comprehension. Its very existence defied reality.

"So just another Thursday, then?" my friend finally managed to squeak out, lifting her glass to her lips and taking a long sip.

I followed suit, barely registering the tart wine as I drank nearly half a glass with my first gulp. My hands shook the entire time, as I was coming down from the adrenaline rush, still blown away by what I'd witnessed, and the fucked-up dream that followed.

"If you've got the location of the biggest project of the semester checked off that little list I know you have, then there shouldn't be any protests about going out tonight then, right? It is spring break, ya know." Tempest smiled sweetly. "Eryx mentioned bringing a few of his, I don't know if I would call them friends, but guys. There will be hot, single dick by the plenty. But if it royally sucks, we can try to hit the slopes this weekend and snuggle up over at the ski resort instead."

"I don't really do the cold."

The witch pursed her lips as she mulled over my point. Seconds stretched into what felt like minutes as I waited for Tempest to say anything that might fill the anxious silence. Somewhere down the hall, I could hear other Hel residents bidding their farewells as they left for the break, going home to visit loving families or far off places. I could've, but I never would've survived seeing the look of disappointment written in my grandmother's face. Under the frozen mountain, I wanted nothing more than to feel the scorching sun and the cool waters of home. Winter had been long, dark, and harder than I'd ever imagined it could be. Every ray of sunshine that would brave piercing the thick cloud cover had students flooding out onto Clifftop, trying to soak it up like little sponges. I'd been the worst sponge, but the sun was always tainted with the bitter cold, a reminder of how far from home I was.

Needing a distraction, I nudged Tempest. "You're not going to ask about the temple or more about the story? I feel like that was kind of a big deal. Worth at least a few inquiries, *ooh's* and *ahh's*, something." I sighed, slugging down the rest of my glass and reaching for the bottle to pour another.

"Well, I figured if you wanted to elaborate you would. You know me, girl—I'm not one to push." Tempest slammed back another glass and winked.

Gods, I loved her. Alright, well, I guess if we were going to do the damn thing tonight, we'd do it the right way and start pre-gaming now.

CHAPTER 7

*B*y the time we made it out of the tower and down to the beach, the rager sounded like it was well underway. Lights bounced off the cave walls, dancing with the floating lanterns suspended over the crowd of students. Music was playing from somewhere, but I didn't see a band, nor any sound equipment set up anywhere. This was definitely not your average party.

Tempest and I wove our way through the crowd, and for the first time in forever, people were actually smiling and waving at me. I wondered how so many could be trashed already.

Torent Stark and his girlfriend, Mallory, were standing by the water's edge. Both looked up and waved as we moved past their group. I hadn't ever spoken to them and Tempest wasn't the closest with them either, but for some reason they now seemed drawn to me as they stepped away from their friends, acting like they wanted to follow me through the crowd. It was strange. Tempest shrugged and tugged me in the opposite direction, picking up her pace. I followed her path to find Eryx holding a plastic cup nearly empty of gods only knew what.

"Ladies, can I get you a drink? What are you having?" Eryx asked.

The warmth in my middle from the wine we'd drunk earlier

was beginning to wear off, and I wanted anything to chase it, hold onto it for a little longer.

"I've got two bottles of a damn good vintage. I'll be okay for a little while." Tempest grinned ear to ear, pulling a bottle from her bag.

"Marina? Can I grab you something while I'm grabbing a refill?" Eryx turned his sights on me, ever the charmer.

What I should've said was no; that would've been the smart decision. However, what left my lips was the exact opposite of what would've been the smart choice. "Sure. Grab me one of whatever you're having."

Eryx circled the crowd, departing with several other drink orders, though I hadn't seen a bartender on the beach anywhere just yet.

Swaying to the beat, I found myself extremely ready to get lost in tonight's frivolity. I needed this and was happy Tempest dragged me from my room. I was ready to let down my hair, so to speak, and word of the beach party must have spread like an algae bloom because before ten o'clock, the shore was fairly crowded. I'd even heard whispers the amethyst thermal pools were at capacity and there was a wait to get in. Even though the party wasn't as well attended as it would've been if most of campus hadn't gone home for vacation or was headed to the ski slopes in town, I was seriously impressed with the turnout. I had an inkling that Tempest and Natalie's private reserve wine had something to do with it; their shit was high quality and in even higher demand.

As for me, I was happy to keep swaying to the beat. Where the music came from, I still didn't know, but it had an ethereal quality to it that made me want to get lost in it, forgetting myself.

Forgetting. That's what everyone seemed to be doing when it came to me. After Samhain, no one gave me the time of day anymore. It was like I didn't even exist. Lovers dropped me like last year's fashions, and peripheral friends dried up like the Sahara, distancing themselves from the magic-challenged witch. Yet now … people were flocking to me, asking me what I thought about any given topic. Guys I didn't even recognize were making their way to me between throngs of dancing bodies to gain my attention, even just for a moment. Until I'd lost my magic, I'd never had difficulties in finding lovers, and that was paling in comparison to the attention being thrown at me tonight. The first couple times, I chalked it up to coincidence or the lack of inhibitions. But it soon became evident that it was much more than that. I rubbed the pearl in my pocket and sent a prayer of thanks up to Ix Chel. This had to be her.

I couldn't get higher in that moment. Pure bliss ... the only thing that might've made it better would've been to fly and feel the rush of air through my hair and over my skin.

Hands tightened on my hips as I ground against a hot, hard body before spinning around. I didn't know the man I was dancing with and I didn't care to find out his name either, but when he spun me, I froze at the sight I saw. A few yards away was Felix and his latest conquest locked in a loving embrace while they danced right along with the rest of the crowd. As if serendipity had nothing better to do than mess with my life, our eyes collided.

The pearl warmed against my leg, almost burning through my pocket. Maybe now was the time for this wrong to right itself too. The muscles at the corners of my mouth twitched my most seductive smile to life, and my heavy-lidded stare was trained right on him. Just like that, my warm and optimistic outlook turned arctic and bleak. In an instant, I was too far gone to be reasoned with, too. My anger was about to bubble up and over into a full-blown rage, and even Tempest's hand on my shoulder couldn't temper the storm brewing inside me.

It was in that moment that Eryx returned with our drinks, sloshing them all over me and Tempest, breaking my concentration.

Thankfully, the splash of liquor from the drinks cooled the pearl, and I took a deep breath and quickly realized Felix wasn't even that damn special. I knew it from the way he'd treated me, but even more so now from his current choice of trashy companions. So why in the hell had I wanted to make him mine again?

I lifted my cup to my lips, barely tasting what was left as hardly anything met my awaiting taste buds.

"Need another," I called back over my shoulder.

Eryx and Tempest waved me off and turned back to the

crowd as I headed somewhere a tad quieter. Stumbling through the sand, I made my way to the outer edges of the party toward the cave wall. My racing heart began to slow in my chest as I caught my breath, and the thin sheen of sweat began to evaporate. Probably should've quit drinking a few glasses sooner, but YOLO.

Leaning against the rocky cave wall, I let my muscles relax for a moment as I took in the scene before me. Eyes kept darting to me, and the occasional wave or friendly smile was still being thrown my way. Such a change...I could hard believe it was real.

Pinching the side of my leg, I winced as the dull sting shot up my thigh and put the fantasy of surrealness to bed.

Not a dream then.

Looking back across the lake, I caught movement on the far side. Squinting my eyes, I tried to focus against the buzzing in my head, which at present was a feat in and of itself. But there, on the far side of the water, stood Caspar, his watchful eyes darting between the stars in the sky high above our heads and then scanning the crowd like he was constantly searching for an attack. He was an enigma, and in that moment, one I had to learn more about.

A noise behind me pulled my attention from Caspar, and I turned around to see a cluster of four girls moving closer to me. If I remembered their faces correctly, I thought they were from Jory, but at the moment...I wasn't really remembering shit. I took a deep breath, and the ground finally started to feel a tad more solid under me, so I focused on the group to keep myself from spinning out of control. At first, it was almost impossible to make out what they were saying, but in my drunken stupor I'd stumbled a few feet closer and plopped down onto a rock. The girls cast a quick glance my way with friendly smiles marring their faces, but ultimately paid me no mind.

"Do you think she even has to turn in the assignments? Or does she just meet him during office hours and negotiate the old-fashioned way?"

"Guaranteed she's fucking him."

"Oh, yeah, they don't even try to hide it, and the Regents just look the other way. I heard Shelby say it's because Professor

Kincaid is pledged to the Lilith Nest; practically Regent Doyle's pawn. Is it nepotism if they're in a family group?"

I'd been listening, mostly for bits of juicy gossip to tell Tempest and Natalie later, but it very quickly became clear they were talking about Vanna and Asher.

The pearl warmed in my pocket again, and if I'd been sober, I might've given the words that flew out of my mouth more thought before I hurled them toward the group of women as I shot to my feet.

"The fuck you think you know about those lovebirds? Hmm? You're all just jealoussss because he didn't give your saggy asses the time of day. He wanted a real woman with personality and balls to match. Face it, hoe; you're not shit."

My hands were waving wildly through the air, and by the end of my tirade, I wasn't more than a meter from them with an accusing finger at the ready and an ass load of sass to back it up. They'd flipped my sea bitch switch, and with no inhibitions, I wasn't holding back. Each of the women looked me over with a mixture of confusion on their faces.

Wasn't it just their luck I was feeling feisty enough and emboldened by too many drinks and my goddess on my side? How could I go wrong? Squaring up to them again, I rubbed the pearl in my pocket and immediately saw red. My adrenaline was pumping, and my heart felt like it was sure to pound its way right out of my chest, fueling my rage. I let them have it. I threw every damn thing I could think of at the group, tearing down everything from their split ends to how their pores reminded me of barnacles. Albeit, it was not my finest moment.

Eyebrows raised at the confrontation, and we caught the attention of a lot of the party by that point. I hadn't exactly been quiet about it, but when was I ever? If any of them so much as opened their mouths one more time, I was likely to punch someone square in the face. But oddly enough, the group just sank further into each other, looking up at me with concern, but still wearing their weird-ass smiles.

Out of the corner of my eye, I saw Tempest and Eryx moving toward us. Shoving people aside, the pair made their way across the beach as if it were a race to prevent the apocalypse.

Energy and magic were bubbling under the surface within me, waiting to explode forth. The pearl was humming against my skin, and I could feel Ix Chel's blessing pushing me to defend myself and my friend's honor.

"What the hell's going on? Why were you railing these girls like that?" Tempest pointed to the huddle of females, cocking out her hip as she waited for my answer. I didn't think she was friends with them, but who knows. Maybe it was just one more boundary I'd lazily stepped over.

"Not that it matters to you, but they were talking mad shit about Vanessa, and I clearly had something to say."

Tempest jerked back like I'd struck her. She'd always been on Vanna's side and on my side...hell, she was on everybody's side, as far as I knew, but as I started to rail into her too, strong fingers wrapped around my bicep firmly, towing me away from the group.

"I need to talk to you." Caspar's deep voice sounded right behind my ear, his warm breath brushing against my neck.

Jerking my arm free of him, I rooted myself to the spot several feet away from the group and crossed my arms over my chest. I dared him to lay a finger on me again with every fiber of my being. All I needed was an excuse to turn the handsome jerk into a pufferfish. With how full of himself he was, that seemed pretty fitting.

"Not the time," I brushed him off, but apparently, he wasn't the type of man to be pushed aside. As soon as my mouth opened to unleash another venomous assault, Caspar made his move and swooped in, sweeping me off my feet.

I was upside down, and before I knew what was happening, he'd tossed me over his shoulder and pushed into the sky. Clapping, laughter, and cheers filled my ears as he flew back to the campus, hauling me away from the party like a sack of potatoes and back toward Hel. It didn't matter how much I protested or pounded my fists against his winged back, absolutely nothing fazed the gryphon who was now carrying me away from the crowd.

The realization of what he was struck when we crested the tallest tower and were still climbing. I'd never been this far up in all my life, and I held my breath, my heart racing with fear and exhilaration. The ground was fuzzy, blurring with the magically infused booze waging war on my system, and there was a brief second where I was fairly sure I was going to embarrass myself horribly all over Caspar and his black feathers. The ground grew farther from my feet, and I squeezed my eyes tightly shut to keep myself from completely losing it. Caspar didn't take the short way to Hel either. I drifted off feeling the rushing cool breeze over my face and the safety of his hands on my skin. There was no missing the rumbling coming from his center either.

Was he purring?

CHAPTER 8

I must have slept longer than I realized, for when I woke, a small crowd had gathered in my room, including Vanna. All of them were looking at me like I was the peanut butter to their jelly, or the salt to their sea. All except Tempest. The frown she wore was causing a deep crease between her brows, and I almost jumped when she ordered everyone out.

"The sea witch and I have some things to discuss, so move it! Everybody out!"

The crowd stumbled from my room, somewhat reluctantly, dragging their feet as they waved goodbye. What the fresh hell was going on with everyone? It was like suddenly the clouds had cleared from around me and everyone could see me again. Even the ones who'd spent the past couple months pretending like I blended in with the rocky walls, nothing more than just a piece of the scenery and not worth noticing—now, they saw me for who I truly was. Not even just saw me, but they clearly wanted to talk to me, and that meant more than I cared to admit.

Excited as all hell, I couldn't wait to discuss the sudden shift with Tempest—that somehow, people were taking notice of me despite the stain of my tainted magic. But before the words could spill from my lips, she was waiving her hand in front of my face.

"Hello? Earth to Marina? What the hell's going on with you?" she snapped.

It was clear from the accusation in her tone she wasn't affected in the same way all the others had been. And suddenly, I shared her question. What the hell *was* wrong with me?

"You lost your shit last night, and now all these people are acting like robots around you, wanting to get close to you for whatever reason. So, tell me…what's going on?"

Blinking once, then twice, I struggled to recall anything about last night, but when I ran my hand over the pearl warming in my pocket, I pushed from the bed in one swift move. Walking to where Tempest stood in the center of my room, I poked a finger into her chest.

"Oh, so now that people are paying attention to me again, you have a problem with that? What? Can't stand to share the spotlight?"

She jerked back. "What are you talking about? First of all, I don't walk around in a spotlight, and secondly… Well, secondly, I've always paid attention to you. Through the good and the bad, remember?"

I stood still, blinking, as the fog in my mind started to lift. I did remember, actually. I remembered that Tempest had always been there for me, especially after I'd chosen to embrace my culture's dark magic to help save us all when I helped Vanna. I remembered my heart breaking when I realized just how much it was starting to affect me. And I remembered the day when I started pulling away. Maybe it wasn't that everyone else had abandoned me, but the other way around. Yet, here stood Tempest, always a safe harbor in my storm.

The pearl cooled against my leg, and I finally understood. Ix Chel's blessing was what had drawn everyone else back to me, but since Tempest had never gone anywhere to begin with, she was unaffected by its magical pull.

A knock on the door interrupted us, pulling me back from the edge of another emotional breakdown.

My concerns and curiosity spiked, as Roxy, Kalani, and Caspar walked into my room.

Great. The whole damn ITF gang. They'd really thought of everyone.

I spun to Tempest. "What at they doing here, and what is *he* doing with them?"

The faint tinkling of bells filled the space as Kalani, the albino air nymph, fluttered around the room. "We're a team, of course. We're here to help you get through this and finish our assignment."

Roxy plopped onto Vanna's bed, as Cas's deep voice filled the room. "We need to discuss what you found, and how it's been affecting you."

My hand flew protectively to my pocket, my fingers rubbing the smooth orb. It was cool to the touch, which helped douse my rising temper.

"It's okay," Cas continued. "We need to work together, and everything will be okay."

I shook my head, frustrated by my inability to disguise my thoughts as they played out on my face. I told him I wouldn't give up the pearl before, and clearly, he could still see I wasn't planning to now either...but maybe I didn't have to.

"Okay, fine. Yes, I found the location depicted on our card. It's a temple at the bottom of the underground lake."

"A temple?" Roxy inquired, shifting forward on the bed.

I had her full attention now. Kalani's too. Cas, on the other hand, was staring intently at me. It wasn't breaking news for him, but he held his tongue, and I suddenly wondered why that was, and why he looked so damn serious. He had the male equivalent of resting bitch face as he stood there on guard, like the dutiful soldier he apparently was.

"Yes. A temple. Under the lake. It was unlike anything I've ever laid eyes on before. There was a single chamber, and at its center was the Wheel of Fortune, just like on the card."

Pulling the card from her bag, Roxy held it up then flipped it over to read the poem on the back, but before she could, Kalani interrupted her, her ethereal voice reciting the poem from memory. "Sunken deep under the mirror, a boon of the sea you'll find here. Surrounded by stone and power alike, the wheel of the gods may give you a fright. Ancient and cold in the depths you'll be, but brave the darkness and forever be free."

"The lake's surface is essentially a giant mirror. But what about the boon of the sea bit? You've been down there. Was there anything like that there?" Roxy's eyes were fixed on mine.

I opened my mouth to answer, but stopped when Kalani's soft voice interrupted again.

"What do you think it means by braving the darkness and forever being free? Sounds ominous, if you ask me," she whispered, shuddering like it was the worst possible ending.

"Your guess is as good as mine. We've been combing over the poem and the campus for weeks, and we're still no closer to figuring that bit out," Roxy groaned. The tight stress lines near her eyes were something I could easily relate to.

I glanced to the one person who had yet to weigh in, despite our shared knowledge on the subject.

"What do you think, *Cas*?" I inquired, raising a challenging brow. "You haven't been too keen on sharing your thoughts on this little project of ours. So give it your best shot, bird boy." Yeah…my memory had cleared, and I knew Cas was the gryphon who'd flown me home last night from the party.

Caspar crossed his arms over his broad chest, his face practically cast in marble with the ever-stoic expression he sported.

"The temple you speak of is the most likely candidate, given the card we were dealt. The clues fit. However, we shouldn't overlook the location of the temple. Hard to reach, impossible for some. Whoever built it did so with that specific purpose in mind. Why else would they build it so far beneath the surface?" His jaw flexed.

He looked down at my pocket, as if he could see through the material to the pearl in my hand. I wondered why he wasn't coming clean, or giving me up.

"Maybe it's like burying nuclear waste. Contain the danger and hope no one ever breeches the containment," Roxy surmised. "Look, I'm an okay swimmer for being a cat, but I don't think I've got the chops to make that kind of dive."

"Ditto, water is too confining," Kalani added.

I hadn't missed how both women's eyes kept going to the gryphon. Was that lust I saw in Kalani's eyes? I wasn't jealous. The uncomfortable tightening in my belly was nothing more than indigestion. Okay, fine, it was nerves.

My teeth worried my lip as a war raged within me while I figured out how much I wanted to tell them. It didn't feel right to tell them about the pearl. The beauty had been a gift from Ix Chel herself, and honestly, I didn't think it had anything to with our ITF assignment. Or at least, that's what I kept telling myself.

"What if it wasn't to contain a danger, but to hide a treasure so great it would draw the greatest hunters of all time to its doors?" I offered instead, the question spilling from me before I could stop it.

Blurting out exactly what was on my mind was a problem I would have to remedy very soon. I wanted to kick myself, sort of. Now, it would only be a matter of time before the proverbial cat was out of the bag, because for some reason, I felt my secret urging to be set free.

"You said that the dragon was made of gold, right? From the sounds of the wheel, there's a priceless trove of artifacts. The boon of the sea has to be one of them. If the gods and goddesses were chosen to represent the elements, our scope should be pretty narrow. That only leaves two options," Kalani pointed out.

My anxiety was increasing with each nervous thud of my heartbeat, and I wanted to crawl out of my own skin. Holding this secret in when I wanted to shout from the mountain peaks that Ix Chel had blessed me with her cherished pearl was killing me, infecting me from the inside out. I rubbed the pearl faster and faster, until I could contain my secret no more.

"Fine. I might've brought a boon of the sea back with me. But it's not a bad thing, I swear. Just trust me on this one."

Everyone's eyes locked on me.

"You know what they say about people who say they should be trusted," Cas pointed out.

My angry leer zeroed in on his stupid pretty face as I recalled the first time we met, and how I'd been drawn to show him the pearl then too. He either had some sort of magic way to make people reveal their secrets, or a death wish for taunting me in front of the group. Roxy's face was expressionless, fixed on me, but I couldn't get a read on what she might've been thinking.

"Oh, well, that is a new development," Kalani added, her

mouth turning down in an uncharacteristic frown, which she still managed to make look ethereal and stunning.

"There was this voice, and it told me to choose wisely from the Wheel of Gods and their offerings. How was I supposed to turn that down?"

Cas shifted, refolding his arms back over his chest.

"Have you ever heard of *just say no?*" Roxy finally asked, her tone less than understanding.

Indignation began to bubble in the recesses of my middle, and I wanted to tell her exactly where she could put her opinion. I mean, hello? It was a gift from the gods. That's nothing to turn down, ever.

"Did you not learn anything from fall semester? When you go rogue and take things like this into your own hands, people get hurt and things go south. This is no different. You need to turn that over to Addie, or anyone, for that matter, on the Board of Regents." Cas had drawn his line in the sand.

"Look, we're not even sure if the pearl is what we were supposed to find down there. Honestly, it called to me, so who's to say that if we go back, the other trinkets wouldn't call to any of you instead? Maybe one of those is what we're actually we're looking for." I spoke my dearest wish into the room, hoping they'd all buy it.

Unfortunately, they did not.

Roxy and Kalani just shook their heads, while Cas pierced me with his dark, ultra-sad eyes. Disappointment was written all over their faces, which somehow took the wind right out of my sails. I stared at Cas, fumbling for something else to say, but the candidness in his face stalled any further excuses or lies. I had no words to hurl at him. There was nothing to depress the ire I felt, but for the first time I wondered what he'd been through. The sadness in his eyes was the haunted look of someone who'd seen brethren lay down their lives for the mistakes of others.

I recalled what I'd heard the other students say about him and knew he was old enough to have lived a thousand lives or more. Undoubtedly, he'd seen some shit in his time. None of that gave him permission to act like my keeper, though.

"Thanks for your input. Next?" I dismissed him, looking to Roxy and then Kalani.

"I vote turn it over," Roxy answered.

"I'm with you, Marina. This was a gift, and we need to look deeper. We still don't know what the last part of the poem means. I vote to give it a week and reassess then," Kalani whispered in her sing-song voice.

Fuck yeah! Kalani for the win!

Popping my hip out to the side, I anchored my hand on the small of my waist and looked Caspar up and down.

"That's two to two. It's a draw. What now?"

Roxy's lips parted as she began to protest and reply with something undoubtedly sarcastic and frustrated, but Cas held up a hand, cutting her off.

"Nothing. We don't do a single thing. This journey is yours to take and yours alone. It's not by chance that you chose the pearl. Nothing is ever by chance. There is not a soul who can force that pearl from its host until the host willfully gives it to another."

There was an audible groan from Roxy, and I began to wonder if she would go full cougar if she got any angrier.

"It's given me my magic back. You can't ask me to give that up again." It was a plea more than anything. Desperation did funny things to a person.

"You've got to be fucking kidding me. I'm supposed to just sit back and hope she does the right thing at the end of all this and everything works out hunky-dory? I don't want any part of the havoc this is going to bring. I'm out." Roxy turned and stormed away, slamming the door to my room so hard, I thought it might break from its hinges.

"I'm rooting for you, Marina. Let me know what you might need from me, and I'd be happy to assist you," Kalani offered, her face solemn yet still somehow beaming with delight. The nymph disappeared into thin air, slipping away like a faint breeze and leaving me and Tempest alone with a stoic and frustrated gryphon who kept eyeing me like he was contemplating kidnapping and locking me up until I agreed to whichever terms he offered.

Tempest pursed her lips and glanced back and forth between

Cas and me. With a single nod, she gave me a strained smile and headed for the door.

And then there was one.

Anxiously, I peeked up at the hulking figure in front of me and wasn't shocked to find him watching me intently.

"I know you think you've won something here, but you don't have any idea what you're playing with. The pearl is dangerous, not a toy to be trifled with." Cas re-crossed his arms over his broad chest again, standing firm on his side of the proverbial line.

"And this is the part where I remind you that you can't tell me what .to do, and I can make my own choices," I sang out in sarcasm—my language of choice.

"Very mature." Cas blew out a frustrated breath and turned to the door, stopping to look back over his shoulder. "Don't say I didn't warn you."

His eyes flared a deep gold, and suddenly, the seriousness of the situation struck me—or maybe it was just all the unanswered questions I had tumbling around in my brain. Lunging forward, I went to grab him, but my feet tangled with one another, and in an instant, I was falling over. He was there in a blink, his strong arms cradling me like a newborn fawn. His skin seared me everywhere we made contact. I couldn't hold in the breathy sigh that slipped from me. Caspar's nostril's flared, and his jaw clenched like he was using every ounce of effort not to act on his baser desires. Time ground to a halt, and our stares locked. The room fell away until there wasn't anything more than just us in that moment.

My heart pounded, and my body felt like it was on the brink of boiling. His breathing was a little labored too. Could there be more to the man than the hardened warrior that I'd first seen?

Or maybe I had read him completely wrong. Damn, my skills were rusty. I wanted to be alone, so I could lick my wounds privately…but then again, maybe not.

"Do you know what the pearl you've been carrying around is even known for?" he whispered down to me, his arms still encircling my waist.

I shook my head.

"It's called the Pearl of Wisdom, and it's not because it makes everything better with knowledge and understanding," Cas confessed, his eyes boring into mine.

The heat between us was rising—rolling off him or me, I couldn't tell.

"So, it is a magical artifact, and it's somehow been affecting me?" Regardless of how he felt, I needed answers.

"Yes, it's an arcane artifact. To understand, you must know that my people, the gryphon, we are not born, but forged. Frankenstein's monsters pieced together by the best sorcerers' money and power could buy. We were built to seek and protect the arcane coveted by the warlords and emperors of the day. There were so many, and they changed so fast, you could never remember their names before a trusted vizier would plot a coup and stab the sultan in the back. This artifact is not one I've ever seen before, but I've heard tales of it from my brethren."

I finally pulled out of Cas's embrace and sank down onto my bed, my eyes still trained on his. "Cas? What have you heard?"

"The pearl has surfaced periodically all over the world, throughout much of ancient history. It's been considered a lost artifact for the last millennium. What I know is only whispers of stories from people who knew people. If there was ever one of my kind to guard the Pearl of Wisdom, I've never known him personally. And there's not too many of us left. If such an individual did exist, I don't believe he's still here today."

"Okay, so it's some sort of lost magical artifact. Why doesn't the pearl affect you like the others?"

"We were created by the same magic that forged many of these objects. Like a eunuch, the best guards are those who are not tempted by the objects they're charged with protecting. So when I'm near one of these objects, I can hear the arcane words it whispers, the things it's seen and done, the future, the past…a frequency you're all immune to, for the most part. Every once in a few centuries, one of you comes along who can hear their whispers too. And those who can hear the artifact's whispers never cease to surprise me, even after three and a half millennia."

"Okkayyy…" I drew out. "So why am I getting the impression those other forbearers didn't meet the best end? And how does it relate to me? Like I said, the only thing that's happened since I found the pearl is that I've regained my magic, which apparently improved my standing at the school as well. I mean, you said it whispers, and I haven't heard it make a peep."

Caspar shook his head. "Marina, you have to trust me, and believe me when I tell you, what you're seeing isn't real. The pearl will grow more lustrous as the days pass, and all those around it will see the beauty, but not the truth. Soon, you'll start to grow weaker and your magic will, too. Hair loss, memory loss, loss of appetite…it'll consume everything you are. It's bonded to you now, and unless you can break free of the illusion and give the pearl up on your own, I don't think you have much time left."

I shivered at the seriousness in his voice. "What are you saying? That the pearl is what…absorbing me?"

Solemnly, Cas nodded.

"Yes. And you have to give it up freely, before there's not enough of you left to withstand the separation.

Well, fuck.

CHAPTER 9

I stared down at the handful of dull hair—the latest to fall out—as it floated atop the water of the soaking pool and racked my brain to come up with anything else besides giving up the pearl that might counter the hair loss. Maybe if I took more vitamins, or hell, I could have Tempest brew me up a spell to stop its affects. That should work, right?

Yeah, right…

I wouldn't be able to hide my thinning hair much longer. If people saw I was going bald at my tender age, there was no way they'd still talk to me and welcome me into their circles with open arms. The dark rings under my eyes only accentuated the lines that had begun to form on my face, making me look more like my abuela with every passing day.

The gleam from the pearl caught my attention from the corner of my eye, pulling me away from my cares of premature aging, reminding me of how lucky I was to have such a gift. I held it up from the chain it now hung on, and slipped it over my head.

Caspar's warning had sat on my heart for two days, but when the pearl warmed in my pocket again, I'd pulled it out to judge for myself if what he said was true.

It was the most beautiful thing I'd ever seen, its luster so brilliant it could've easily been the crowning gem of a regal crown. I'd grown addicted to the look of admiration on the faces of those who were affected by the pearl's magic, and decided to encase it in an equally beautiful coral setting to hang around my neck. It was covet-worthy, and I wouldn't hide it anymore.

The water lapping around in the soaking pool had cooled, but it didn't bother me too much. Although, my pruned fingers disagreed with that assessment. I stared down at my wrinkled digits, a deep frown cutting through my cheeks. Never in all my memory could I recall another time when I'd suffered the affliction and decided that perhaps it was time to pull myself from the Hel Tower bathing pool and see what Cas was up to.

I hadn't seen him since he'd stormed off all huffy puffy because I'd refused to give him the pearl right then and there. As much as he desperately needed to pull the stick out of his butt, I missed his strong, reassuring presence. Besides, if I was going to keep it, he had the answers I needed to figure out how to stop its affects—at least that's what I kept telling myself to justify my desire to see him.

The image of him standing on that rock outcropping at the beach party had somehow been etched into my brain. He'd been staring up at the stars with the same boyish wonder I'd expect of someone far younger than him, and it endeared him to me even more than the way his thick corded muscles tapered nicely down his back into the most perfect guy-butt I'd ever laid eyes on. I stood, my skin chilled by the cool cavern air as I reached for my towel. It cooled my libido enough to realize that beyond the raw lust, the man underneath it all still made me want to listen to his deep voice, even if all he talked about was me giving up the pearl.

The terry cloth was soft against my soaked flesh, sopping up every drop of water and cloaking me in a warm embrace. The cloth itself seemed to go further around me than it ever had before, and the gap between my brows pinched at the realization. Instinctively, my fingers went to the pearl hanging around my neck. It was warm and practically buzzing with energy.

From above in the main section of the bathroom, I could hear the faint steps of someone approaching, but they were slow, deliberate.

"Vanna? Is that you?" I asked, knowing before I even finished the sentence it wouldn't ever be her.

When Vanesssa Shaw moved, she did so with the attention and care of the deadliest apex predator. She'd never make a sound, not even in her boots or her heels, which seemed to be a type of magic all its own.

"Hope I'm not too disappointing," Natalie answered, stepping out of the shadows into the low glow cast by the sconces.

A sigh rushed out of me at the familiar face, and I tossed my hand back over the bath, casting out my magic to turn the jets back on. Yet, I didn't hear the bubbling begin like I expected.

"Damn, I thought you'd at least tell me I was wrong," Nat groaned, her eyes never lifting from the ground.

"Sorry, momentary ADD. Of course, I'm not disappointed it's you. *Hermanas de lunas*, that's us," I rushed out, trying to reassure her.

Nat had been giving off some desolate waves, but we'd all hoped she'd come to us when she was ready. She hadn't, however.

"I thought I might find you here. You know…things have been hard lately, and I was hoping we could go for a walk and just talk about normal stuff. I need a slice of normal." The pleading in her voice left little room to refuse her even if I wanted to.

As the last of the water droplets fell from my body, I reached for my dress where it hung from a stone hook on the wall. I slipped it over my head and let the cotton fall in waves down to my knees, tossing the terrycloth towel into the dirty linen pile.

"Trust me, I get it. There's this spot down by the water's edge where I like to go when I need to be alone and think. Since it's you, I'll share." I winked.

Natalie smiled, but it didn't quite reach her eyes. Moving first, I stepped around her, and as soon as her image slipped from my peripheral view, I felt the touch of a hand at the base of my neck and then darkness swallowed me whole.

Fluttering open, my eyes were dry, and it was nearly impossible to bring anything into focus. In the back of my head, there was a constant pounding, throbbing in time with my heart. The only thing I could hear was the whooshing of blood through my ears. Squeezing my eyes tight, I pushed myself up so I was upright, and my stomach clenched at the sudden change, threatening to empty its contents onto the floor.

After a couple moments, it slowly began to subside, and I had enough of my bearings to know wherever I was, I was alone. Trying to think back, I couldn't remember what had happened or how I'd come to be here. The last thing I could conjure was soaking in the soaking pool.

"Marina," a masculine voice whispered from the shadows.

The voice seemed to morph from one to another, one syllable being the chilling call from the depths of the trenches I'd seen so many times in my nightmares, to Cas, and finally to Vanna. Casting my eyes as wide as they would go, I scanned the empty dark space, yet there was nothing there. However, when my gaze passed over the spot several paces ahead of me and where there had been nothing moments before was a large mirror. The woman looking back at me wasn't me, though.

It was my abuela.

Rushing closer, I reached out to touch her, not even thinking of the glass separating the two of us, and drew up short mere feet from the looking glass. From a distance, the woman was nearly identical to the woman I'd known my entire life, but there were subtle differences once I got closer. The eyes were the color of seaweed, the same color as mine. Her hair hung long and thickly braided, just like my grandmother's did. There were tokens of the sea distributed like fine jewels, bits of coral and pearls woven into the masterpiece.

The woman was me.

I didn't know how I knew it, but my intuition screamed it. As the understanding washed through me, the image in the mirror began to change. The old woman began to shrivel, withering away before me. Her form shrunk until she was nearly skeletal. Eyes sunken in until it was painful to behold silently cried out for help, but I didn't know what I could do to help the woman. Was she still me? That thought haunted me the most.

A second later, she was gone and nothing more than a pile of dust and bones. Staring down at the pile near my feet, I realized the mirror had vanished, leaving the degraded remains of a future me. There was a large round lump in the middle of the dusty pile, and I bent down, scooping it up, brushing the dirt and dust away from the small orb. With every pass of my fingers, the shimmery luster of a pearl *began to peek through. Furiously, I worked to clean the pearl off, angry that I'd let it get so dirty, but it was already growing brighter by the moment.*

Like a moth to a flame, I couldn't break my fixed stare on the blinding pearl. So intense I was sure I would burn up in it any second, I knew I couldn't endure another moment of the sweet torture, but I didn't know how to save myself from that horrid end.

A bright flash and I could've sworn I heard Caspar's voice calling my name again, anchoring me to something as I felt more adrift than ever.

Like a newborn being thrust from the warmth and comfort of the womb to the cold, harsh air of reality, I was awakened by the incomprehensible swirling mass of voices from those crowded around me.

"What if it doesn't work? You could kill her," Tempest pleaded.

"If we do nothing, we guarantee she will meet her end tonight," Cas urged, his voice raw and low, infusing his gryphon dominance into the statement.

I wondered briefly who they were talking about, but the thought was slippery and was gone just as soon as it came.

"Well, hey there, sleepyhead," Tempest teased from beside me.

Little by little, the ordeal came back to me. I'd been in the soaking pool and then Natalie had been there...she'd...she'd done something to me. One of my best friends, and she'd as good as stabbed me in the back as I looked down at the mixture of deep sea trench sludge and black volcanic salt forming a ring around me.

"That's cold, Nat. Why are you doing this to me? I love you guys like sisters," I pleaded, tears slipping down my cheeks as I sent up a silent prayer she'd wipe the line away and let me out.

"Because we love the shit out of you too much to let you keep doing this to yourself," Vanna answered for her. She shucked her jacket and seemed like she was loosening up in preparation for something.

Scanning the faces, I realized there was more than just the girls and Cas.

"I'm just here to make sure I can get a grade and have

something to show for this asinine assignment," Roxy piped up from behind Kalani.

Cas was on his knees, just outside the blackened border of my makeshift prison. His palm was open and facing up, waiting for me to give over every last bit of myself to him for safe keeping. I knew what he was asking; he wouldn't have gone this far and pulled an intervention if he wasn't asking me to give up something so vital to my being that I was sure I couldn't survive without it.

"You ask too much, Cas. You don't know what it was like before," I groaned, the ache in my middle unrelenting and beginning to intensify in waves. "Please don't ask me to do this."

"You have so much more to offer than what you're clinging to with that." He pointed at my necklace, the pearl shining so bright that I could hardly see the coral it was encased in.

My lips parted to object, but his gentle finger hushed me before I could utter a word. I was too stunned he'd actually reached past the circle to shush me to put up any more fight, not when the ache had grown to include my chest. What could've been a spiked lasso wrapped around my heart and tightened, until I was sure the organ was going to burst from the strain.

"You have to let it go, Marina. You can't give up on us now; we haven't given up on you. Look at them. They're all here for you. I'm here for you," Cas whispered, twining his fingers through mine.

Cas stood and fully entered the circle, then crossed his legs and sat in front of me, close enough to ensure our bodies were touching from foreheads to feet. I was sure it was the tainted magic playing tricks, but Cas looked like his eyes had begun to mist.

"You don't need the pearl, Marina. I've watched you from afar and know you've been struggling, but I can tell you honestly...in all of my years, I've never seen anyone as strong as you. You chose to do what was right to help your friends, not knowing the toll it might take. And while you may have felt lost and cast out, you know in your heart you can find that woman again." He placed his hands on either side of my face. "I need you to do that again now. Search your soul for who you truly are, and I promise, once you're free, I'll be here waiting for you to help pick up the pieces."

"Ancient and cold in the depths you'll be, but brave the darkness

and forever be free." Kalani's ethereal voice recited the last line of our poem, and in that instant, I knew it was referring to me.

This was a darkness that only I could face, but if I could push through it, push past the fear and shame of being tainted and alone, maybe…just maybe, I'd have something worth living for again, and I truly would be free.

I stared into the eyes of the mighty and proud gryphon who'd lived long enough to see civilizations rise and fall, and my heart broke. He was crying, and he was doing it for me. I pulled back and looked to the group outside the circle, finding their eyes glossed over as well. They nodded their encouragement, and I decided right then and there that if that was how I was going to go out, I would be happy. They really did care about me, and in the end, even when I had nothing left to offer, I was enough.

"It's time." Cas nodded to the pearl against my chest, and I remembered what he'd said. I'd have to give it up freely.

I looked down to the pearl shining brightly against my chest, and every breath felt like I was fighting the tightening coils of an anaconda. My clenched heart struggled to keep up. There was nothing more to give than my life.

My body was tired, and everything took so much energy to accomplish. A single breath felt like I'd just run a marathon, and I knew my time to cross over was coming quickly if I didn't do this. Caspar's words echoed, claiming that very beauty was draining everything from me, and the heaviness behind every action told me that was true. Yet, I still couldn't bring myself to cast it off and let it become another's burden. This was a gift from Ix Chel; it should be cherished as such.

If I was afraid, I couldn't feel it anymore. I couldn't feel much of anything other than the sadness for the situation I was leaving my friends in. It would be up to them to tell my story and get the authorities. My family would wait for my body to be brought home before they'd send me out to sea. Abuela Maris wouldn't recover from this loss. I didn't have to stick around to know this would change everything for my loved ones. Each glub of my heart made me more tired, and I wanted to close my eyes and let the heaviness go, let the sand slip through the cracks and be lost to memories and the pages of time.

As my eyes fluttered closed, I heard screams in the distance. Cries rang out, calling my name, but the only thing I could feel was the warmth of the pearl against my chest—until Cas's lips pressed against mine.

"Fight, Marina. I just found you, and I don't want to lose you now." His words whispered across my lips, and his soft kisses began to drag me back to the present, back to hope and back to a life worth living.

I squeezed my eyes tighter, thinking back to the temple and the underground lake. As I walked to the shore in my mind's eye, a tide as red as blood rushed over my feet, and in a spark of green light, I stood before Ix Chel again. Bowing my head, I returned the pearl to its resting place, then opened my eyes.

Back in the Hel Tower bathroom, the pearl sat warm in my hand, pulsing strong and bright. My fingers twitched, closing a little tighter around it, and I smiled.

"When the red tide meets the green flash, the maelstrom shall rise, and all will be as it should." I repeated back Cas's words from my strange dream, as he started at me with tears in his eyes.

I'd done it. I'd faced the darkness and was choosing to give the pearl away willingly so that I could be free. I stretched out my hand, but my muscles were still weak and jerky. Cas reached forward and latched onto it before I hurt myself trying.

He's one of the good ones.

I loosened my grip and let the pendant fall.

"Take care of this for me. I don't think I'm going to need it anymore." I smiled and felt immediately better once the pearl had left my hand.

A knock on the door sounded, and with a flick of her wrist, Tempest flung it wide.

Addie Beaumont walked in, easing up to the edge of the black salt circle. "Tempest notified me the second it was over, and I have to say, it doesn't look like a moment too soon."

She whispered under hear breath then drug her boot through the sludge and salt.

Cas stayed on the floor, his body, knees, and feet still pressed against mine as he lifted the pearl into Addie's waiting hands.

"I'm glad you're okay, Marina." Addie looked around the room. "We all are."

She bent down beside me and placed her hands over my heart where the pearl had rested. A warmth of a different kind radiated from beneath her fingers as her magic flowed through me. I could feel the pull of my memories rising to the surface, as she took stock on all I'd been through. With one last surge of her magic, Addie pulled away, and I felt better than I had for months.

"Thank you for your bravery, Marina. I know what a sacrifice this must feel like." She pocketed the pearl and stood up, waving everyone out the door as she too disappeared, leaving me and Caspar alone.

"How do you feel?" he asked, pulling me to my feet.

I was shocked to find I bounced up from the floor without any popping or cracking of my bones. I ran to the bathroom mirror and gasped. My hair was back to normal, and the dark circles under my eyes were gone too. I couldn't believe it. I felt amazing. Racing back into the soaking pool, I wiggled my fingers above the water and watched in awe as my magic spun a tiny whirlpool into the air. I was back, baby. Magic and all.

I turned and threw myself into Caspar's arms. "Thank you for believing in me."

He pulled back, piercing me with that sexy-ass golden gaze. "Thank you for believing in me. And I meant it, Marina—I really do want to be here for you."

"Well, good. Because like it or not, bird-boy, you're the one thing I'm not willing to let go."

ACE OF WANDS

AMY RICHIE

For anyone that is walking through their own nightmares right now,
know that you aren't alone. Take courage, my dear ones.
God grant me an angel to mend my broken heart,
Make his embrace strong, so that I don't fall apart.

CHAPTER 1

I was about eighty percent sure that I was dreaming. For one thing, it was bright outside. Not just any kind of bright either. It was the actual sun beating down on me. I was a vampire and not a Belladonna like my girlfriend, Linnie, so although the sun didn't burn me to ash thanks to my tattoo, it still gave me one hell of a headache.

This sunlight didn't affect me at all, though. *Weird.*

Also, my school— Sun & Moon Academy—was hidden inside of a mountain, a real mountain. We didn't get much light here. So it just didn't make sense to see the vast blue sky above me while I stood in the campus courtyard.

Another thing—the school was completely empty.

"*Destiny!*"

I whirled around at the sound of my name. There was no one there, though. As far as I could tell, I was alone.

"Hello?" My call whirled around me in a chaotic echo. "Is anyone there?"

The acrid smell of smoke suddenly filled the air. The once blue sky had turned a dark gray. A large cloud of thick smoke gathered above me, choking out the sunlight.

Not being a fan of sunlight, I wasn't sure why the disappointment hit me so hard.

Far in the distance, maybe where the forest started, I could see the flash of flames as they licked hungrily at the sky. The sight sparked fear inside my heart.

But wait. How was it possible for me to see the forest? How was it underground with us? What the fuck…

So far, I didn't like this dream.

I really hated fire.

I shuddered at memories that had no business trying to resurface. I needed to get out of here. Clearly no one else had been stupid enough to stick around.

"*Destiny!*"

I knew that voice. Why couldn't I remember who it was?

Just as I decided to go find other people, I saw movement inside the flames. My heart lurched into hyper drive when I realized it was a person. Someone was burning.

With the unnatural speed of my kind, I darted forward until I was face to face with the wall of fire. It was impossible to tell where the fire started, impossible to see where it ended.

The man writhed inside the fire, and I knew I had to help.

The heat was too intense, though. I couldn't get close enough to save him.

"Please," I screamed desperately, "try to come to my voice. Please!"

I didn't recognize the guy. He just stood there staring at me through the flames. The seconds that passed seemed to be hours as we stood there, shocked and afraid.

"I'll help you," I yelled, panic coloring my voice. As soon as I took a step forward, white hot pain licked at my arms, stealing my breath away completely.

My whole body was stiff as I woke up in a different reality. A scream still lingered on my lips as I sat straight up in my bed.

My bed.

I sucked in a quick, strangled breath. "I'm in my own bed."

It was all just a dream. There was no fire, and there was no guy burning alive in front of my eyes.

"Des?"

My body reacted to the sweet voice beside me. Even as my mind refused to calm down, my body relaxed at her call.

"Are you okay?" Linnie, my fire-haired girlfriend, peered at me through half slitted eyes. We had been through a lot the previous semester, the whole cursed hourglasses and statues coming to life thing. She had been chosen.

"I'm okay," I gasped.

"You don't seem okay."

"Bad dream." I shook my head firmly, as if trying to erase the memory. "Just a dream."

"What happened in the dream?" She pulled herself up so that she was sitting next to me.

"There was a man inside a fire. He was just in there, not burning." I only realized the truth of that now.

"A man was walking in the fire?" Her eyebrows twisted wildly.

"Yeah."

"That doesn't seem very scary," she scoffed.

"No, I guess not." I wasn't going to tell her I went all superhero crazy on him. Rolling my eyes at my own stupidity, I let out a heavy sigh that still shook slightly.

"I think you need something to take your mind off that dream," she purred.

"Oh yeah?" I grinned over at her. "Did you have something in mind?"

"Mmmm." She reached out to caress my face. "I do, actually."

Her mouth was already open when it met with mine, sending my senses reeling as soon as her warmth enveloped me. There was no need for thought—my lips parted instinctively, inviting her tongue to dance with mine.

As if we had become one person, we collapsed back onto the bed. Linnie had never had a girlfriend before me—no boyfriends either. She wasn't my first, but I knew she would be my last. It's like we were made for each other.

"There's something I don't understand, though." My eyebrows lowered on my forehead as I broke away enough to look up at her from my position under her slender body. "Why are you here?"

"Don't you want me here?" She pouted her beautiful lips, while her fingers traced my collar bone.

"Of course I want you here." Wanting to see her smile again, I pushed my mouth against hers again briefly. "But you said..."

After Tank barged into my room one night and found us in a

less than lady like position, Linnie vowed to never sleep over in my dorm room again. I wasn't complaining, but when did she change her mind?

"Well," her fingers fanned out along my inner thigh, "I missed you. Is that all right?"

"Yep." My back arched at her touch.

"That's...good," she whispered, bringing her face back to mine.

I ran the tip of my tongue across her bottom lip, eager to taste the sweetness that was her. A soft moan escaped her parted lips, filling my mouth and making my breath come faster.

Soon the sound of our kissing chased away any lingering thoughts of my nightmare. This was real. This was Linnie. My lovely Linnie.

Most days I couldn't believe how lucky I was to find her. And nights like this...

"Wow." A soft whistle came from a shadowed corner of the room.

"Wha...?" It was difficult to concentrate on anything except Linnie and what her tongue was doing to my skin, but I had definitely heard a voice. Years of living as a creature of the night taught me not to let my guard down.

"She's so pretty."

"Linnie." I pressed my palms against her shoulder to stop her from moving down any farther on my body.

"Yeah, Linnie," the voice replied to me even though I hadn't been talking to her.

"What's wrong?" Linnie panted, bringing her face up to mine.

"Someone is in here."

"What?"

"You two can just continue," the low voice teased.

"Did you hear that?" Twisting out from under Linnie, I rose up to crouch over her.

"There's no one there." Linnie pulled on my arm. "I have really good hearing," she reminded me. "I would know if we weren't alone."

My nostrils flared. Why was I hearing something that she couldn't? A soft giggle erupted from the darkness, making the small hairs on my arms stand straight up. It wasn't possible...

"Show yourself," I demanded. The shadows suddenly separated, and a young woman stepped forward. A girl who I knew very well. "Claire," I breathed, too shocked to get any more volume out.

"Well, this is awkward."

"You can't be here."

"And yet," she shrugged her pale shoulders, "here I am."

My stomach lurched until I was sure I would throw up...or pass out.

"Destiny?" Linnie asked.

I turned back immediately. I always reacted to her. I couldn't help it. She was my earth while I was the moon, needing her gravity to keep me in orbit.

"It's okay," I assured without knowing what I was saying.

"I feel strange." Her voice came out breathy.

"It's all right," I cooed. "I'm here."

"No. Something is really wrong."

The panic in her voice made me peer at her face more closely. Besides the fear in her eyes, she didn't look any different. She certainly didn't look like she was going to burst into flames and turn into ash next to me.

But that's exactly what happened.

Horror gripped my lungs and refused to let any oxygen in. Gasping painfully, I clutched at the ash on the sheet.

"Linnie!"

My eyes popped open again, tears streaming down my face. I wasn't in bed anymore, though. I was outside, and it was daylight again.

"Linnie," I sobbed.

Was it all a dream? What was happening?

Above me, the thick cloud of smoke still sat there. Did that mean there was actually a man burning, or was this the dream and Linnie was really the one burning?

I shook my head sharply from side to side.

"Wake up," I told myself. "Just wake up." But did I really want to? Not if it meant Linnie was... "Shit."

"If it helps," Claire was suddenly outside with me, "I don't know what the hell is going on either."

"You're dead," I threw at her.

"I thought so, too."

"So you can't be here."

"To be fair," she raised one eyebrow in an achingly familiar gesture, "I don't think either one of us are really here."

Here. "I'm at my school." I wasn't sure why I kept pointing out the obvious. "But it's different."

"And that was your girlfriend, before?"

My eyes widened then narrowed again just as quickly. "You don't have any right to say anything about Linnie."

"I didn't say anything bad." She widened her own eyes in mock innocence. "She's cute."

"Stop it."

"What?"

"You...left me." Insane that I was talking to a girl who had died years ago. I had met Claire when I first became a vampire. She was wild and beautiful. She taught me more than I could ever learn at a school. But then she left me alone.

"I died," she argued out loud. "I died, and you lived."

"Yeah." I pushed my chin out. "That means you're not my girlfriend anymore."

"You found someone new." Although she smiled, I felt the accusation in her words.

"I...."

"Hello there," a deep yell from the other side of the courtyard cut off any stupid thing I was about to say. Claire was dead. I had Linnie now. *Focus Destiny.*

"Hey."

A guy whom I didn't recognize rose an unsure hand into the air by way of greeting. "I saw you earlier."

Confusion wrinkled my forehead. How did he see me earlier? Where? Ignoring Claire, I hurried forward to meet him. "Who are you?"

"I'm Craig." He smiled awkwardly with all of his teeth. Several were pointy and out of place in his mouth. "You're Destiny, right?"

"How do you know me?"

"Everyone knows you." He started to smile again but gave up halfway through. "You have a hot girlfriend."

"Excuse me?" Looking at him, it was hard to believe he said that.

"Linnie." He let out a nervous chuckle. "All the guys talk about how hot she is, how hot both of you are."

"Do they?" I crossed my arms tightly over my chest, breathing back my anger. What kind of a jackass was this guy?

"I'm guessing that's why I'm dreaming about you right now. Is she here too?" He glanced behind me hopefully. "I kind of expected the two of you...me...a bed." He pulled slightly at the collar of his shirt.

"What the fuck?"

"Yeah," his face fell as he looked behind him. "This isn't exactly the kind of dream I would expect you two to be in."

"Linnie isn't here," I snapped. "And you better watch what you say about my girl."

Craig paled and balked away from my harsh words. "This is my dream," he tried to argue back. "You can't talk to me like that."

"This is not your dream." Everything was so confusing, though. "I woke up here, alone."

"That's weird. In all my other dreams about you, you're usually nice and dressed..." His eyes scanned the length of my body.

"Holy shit." Claire laughed loudly. "The little shit is braver than he looks."

"I already told you," I shoved one finger into his chest, "this isn't a dream."

His eyes narrowed as he watched me.

"Well it is a dream," I corrected myself. "I'm the one dreaming, though."

"Definitely not one of my better dreams."

I didn't want to know anything about those. "There was a man walking through the fire. Was it you?"

Normally I would have never bothered to talk to him for fear I would punch him, but there was literally no one else around.

"Not a big fan of fire." He crinkled his nose in distaste.

"Me, either."

"I often dream about being burned alive," he suddenly blurted out.

"So it was you?"

"I saw you, too." He nodded slowly.

"You weren't burning."

"The flames don't burn my skin like normal humans." He clicked his tongue against the roof of his mouth as if I should already know such basic information.

This kid was really starting to piss me off.

"What are you then, if you're not human?"

"Dragon shifter."

"A dragon who's afraid of fire?"

"Family get-togethers are a real blast."

"He's really weird," Claire pointed out dryly.

"Yeah."

"Should we just go ahead without Linnie?" Craig smacked his hands together and wriggled his eyebrows suggestively.

"It's like you want me to punch you."

"What I want is for you to take that shirt off."

Behind me, Claire giggled.

Before I could act on the rage that was flooding my veins, a loud scream filled the air, making us both crouch low to the ground. Anger momentarily forgotten, I let Craig duck behind my shoulder.

"What was that?" he hissed.

How would I know? I was exactly where he was—in a dream. I had no idea what was going on, either.

"Someone help me," a girl called.

She didn't seem far away, but I was quickly learning not to trust anything here.

"I think it's coming from this way," I told Craig in a low voice. I was trying my best to ignore Claire. She wasn't real, like really not real.

"Running toward danger is never a good idea," Craig croaked out, gliding his tongue across his bottom lip.

"How do you know it's dangerous?"

"Why else would she be calling for help?"

"We can't just leave her there." How did such a coward get into this school?

"Yes, we can, actually."

"Please," the girl called again. I could hear the tears that were just barely being contained. "Is anyone there?"

"She's not far."

"All the more reason to get the hell away from here." His eyes widened behind the thick glasses.

"I'm not leaving her."

"I'm not going."

"You stay here then," I yelled to him. "I'm going to help her." I wasn't even sure what she needed, but I knew I couldn't just turn my back and run away. It wasn't in my nature. It had never been in my nature, even when I was a human. It didn't surprise me that he followed when I started moving toward the girl and the mysterious forest that had just sprouted underground.

If it wasn't for Craig, I probably would have fallen into the large hole that just seemed to open up in the ground right where we were running.

"Watch where you're going," he half growled, clutching my arm right above the elbow. "Are you trying to get yourself killed?"

"I thought you weren't coming," I gasped, holding tightly to his scrawny arm.

"You're welcome."

"There's a—" I peered cautiously just over the edge of the hole— "a pit here," I finished lamely, scowling enough to wrinkle my forehead. "Where did this come from?" Craig shrugged. "It wasn't here before."

I would have noticed if there was a pit in the middle of campus. Just on the other side of it, another fire was roaring as if it had a life of its own. It was an impossible fire, of course—since there was nothing to burn. It was just rocks and dirt and the trees.

"The fire is following us," Craig whimpered. "It always follows me."

"Is someone up there?" the girl screamed from inside the pit.

"This...this is bad." I glanced over my shoulder where Craig danced nervously from one foot to the other.

"Let's just go," he hissed.

"Please," the girl cried out, "if someone is up there, please help me out of here."

"Just hurry up and save her," Claire called out, rolling her wide eyes. "You already know you're going to, so why the dramatic hesitation?"

"Whatever." I shuffled forward the few steps it took to see better down into the pit. A young girl stood there, her hair bushing out past her shoulders. She wasn't far down; she probably would have been able to crawl out herself if she tried. Maybe she was too scared.

Hell, I was scared, too. What if the ground gave way more if I tried getting her out? Jumping down there was out of the question.

"Be careful." Claire snorted. "Unless you want to join her?"

"Hey," I called down. "We're going to get you out of there."

The girl craned her head to look up at me. Her thick black curls fell away from her pale forehead and long neck.

"I knew you would come." Despite the tears choking her voice, she smiled wide. "Can you reach me?" She raised her arms up as far as they would go, almost reaching the top of the pit.

"Hang on," I grunted, dropping to my stomach in an effort to get closer. "I think I can reach you."

"I hear something," Craig yelled.

I took a few seconds to glare over at him.

"Is it the fire or the girl screaming for help?" I sneered.

"Neither." His nostrils flared wide as if he was sniffing out some unseen danger.

What a weirdo.

"Don't leave me here," the girl shrieked. Her dark eyes widened, pleading with me.

"I won't."

"That hero act, though." Claire whistled softly.

"I got you." I focused on grabbing the frightened girl, ignoring Claire who wasn't even really there. Probably.

Once my fingers clasped around her thin wrists, the rest was easy.

"Thank you," she breathed, resting her forehead briefly against my shoulder. "If you didn't come—"

"Guys," Craig interrupted, panic coloring his voice. "I think we have a problem."

CHAPTER 2

A second hole opened up just a few feet from where we stood. The earth just started swallowing itself until suddenly there it was.

Like magic—only scarier.

"What...?"

"Don't get any closer," the girl from the pit warned.

"Maybe there's someone else down in that one who you can save." Claire smirked.

"Don't be an asshole."

"I'm not," the girl misunderstood. "I really don't think you should go near it."

"I wasn't talking to you," I muttered. And I didn't need her warning. The hairs along the back of my neck were standing up, warning enough that something bad was down there.

"You hear it now, right?" Craig whispered.

Yes.

An eerie clicking was coming from the pit, along with a scratching that sounded like someone was digging. Only it wasn't a someone—it was a something.

A thick leg covered in spiky hair rose up out of the pit, followed by a second and third. Straight from a horror movie, the giant body of a spider flopped up next.

"Holy shit," Craig said for all of us.

"Agreed." I swallowed past the lump of fear that was lodged in my throat. I hadn't felt fear like this in such a long time. Not since...

My eyes darted briefly to where Claire stood. She watched the spider with mild interest but not fear. Anyone would be scared, I reminded myself. Claire wasn't real.

The spider reared back like a bucking horse onto its hind legs. The front legs dangled in the air above us for several long seconds —the world around us went strangely quiet, making the clicking sound so much louder.

"It's attacking!" Craig bellowed.

Clearly.

"What do we do?" he simpered, his thin lips pursing outward in fear.

"Just...stay behind me," I panted.

Although I had no real weapons, I grabbed a large bo staff that had rolled our way when the second pit opened up. I recognized the weapon from my combat classes, but I had no idea how it ended up here.

"You expect to fight that thing off with a twig?" Claire gasped.

"It's all I have," I informed her through clenched teeth. Maybe if I stabbed one of its eyes, I would hurt it enough to scare it off.

"It's going to eat us," Craig squealed. "We're all going to die."

"This is just a dream," I yelled back. "We can't die, can we?"

"Let's not stay and find out, okay?"

The spider crashed back down to all eight legs and scurried toward us. It hesitated when I swung the bo staff. But it was only a hesitation.

"Let's run," Craig suggested.

"Run where?" Claire asked.

"The spiders," the girl rasped out, not taking her eyes off the creature. "They don't like the fire."

"Okay." That was something. Maybe I could drive it back into the impossible fire that was still burning.

I lunged forward, brandishing my makeshift weapon. The spider grabbed it away from me and snapped it in half. From the pit, another leg was emerging.

"I don't think we can fight them." I hated the idea of just

running and hiding, but this was beyond what I knew how to fight. We didn't even have any weapons. If that thing could snap the staff that easily, we didn't stand a chance.

"Then?"

"Let's run, go toward the forest."

Craig was already several feet away before I could turn around. The girl we had rescued was right in front of me but moving quickly. For a wild moment of panic, I searched for Claire.

I didn't see her, though.

Maybe she was ahead of Craig or maybe she had disappeared again. Either way, I could only run now. My feet thudded across the bridge, echoing through my chest and hurting my teeth. Blind panic was not a sensation I enjoyed.

The trees all around us were on fire, burning hot. Desperation propelled us into the heat that burned all the saliva from my mouth and seemed to set my lungs ablaze.

I tried to look behind us as we ran, to see if the spiders were still coming, but I couldn't see much. The fire closed in as soon as we entered the forest. There was no going back now.

Not that we wanted to.

Whatever was happening around us, it was better than being eaten by a giant spider. As far as deaths went, death by spider didn't seem like a good way to go. Especially if the spider was the size of a lion.

"This way," Craig bellowed, leading the way through the maze of trees. How did he know where we were going? I had been in the forest many times before, and I had no clue.

My feet carried me forward even while my eyes searched out a possible hiding place. For being a forest, it was surprisingly bare. Trees grew up to kiss the sky, but they weren't big enough for the three of us to hide behind. My lungs were already hurting from the heat and fear—I wasn't sure how much longer I could run.

"Let's find a place to hide," I screamed.

"Quick, get behind here."

A young man was suddenly there, leaning around a large tree. I recognized him from one of my classes, but I couldn't recall his name. Straw colored hair lay haphazardly all over his head.

Craig obeyed immediately, ducking behind the tree where the guy was crouching. The girl and I were close behind. Her face stirred a memory, but I didn't think I knew her. Considering the spiders chasing us, I hadn't had time to ask her what her name was.

"Well," I panted, "this is cozy."

Also, it wouldn't exactly hide us—four people plus Claire standing behind a tree the size of a pole. This dream was getting weirder every minute.

"Good to see you made it," I told Claire. She wasn't winded; if anything, she looked amused by our plight.

"Yeah," the tall guy groaned, "made it for now. We need to get somewhere safer."

"Where?"

"Go into there," he pointed wildly to where a large bush obscured most of the forest floor.

It wasn't exactly warm and welcoming, but it offered more protection than what we had behind the tree.

One by one, we dropped to our knees and crawled into the middle of the bush.

"It's bigger on the inside," I noted, surprised by how much room we had.

"We can't stay here," Craig pointed out, his small eyes going briefly wide. "The fire will burn us up."

"The fire isn't spreading," the other guy, who was much larger than Craig, said. "I'm Matthew, by the way."

"Amelia," the girl from the pit grunted her own introduction.

"I'm Destiny; this is Craig."

"Well," Craig threw his hands up dramatically, "now that we're all best friends—can we go?"

"Go?" My mouth fell open and stayed slack. "How the fuck did the forest move? How does it grow underground?"

"Destiny." Craig clicked his tongue at me. "I know this is hard for you to understand, but none of this is real."

"Shut up." He wasn't allowed to talk to me like that, not after he almost pissed himself when he saw that spider.

"This isn't even our school." He shrugged. "Not really. It's merely a mass illusion brought on by the nature of the curse."

"What curse? What the fuck are you talking about?" If we had been in a larger area, I would have kicked him for sure. "There's a forest underground but it's not our forest; there's a school out there overrun with giant spiders but it's not our school?" We were all going to die here.

"It's okay," Craig cooed.

I angrily shook off the hand he had snaked up my back. "Don't fucking touch me."

"I was trying to make you feel better!"

"You didn't. At all." My narrowed eyes honed in on his hand, ready to attack if it made any sudden movements.

"Shh," Matthew hissed, pressing one finger against his pursed lips. "We have to be quiet or it will hear us."

"It?" My eyebrows lowered. "You mean the spiders?"

Were they in the forest, too? How did Matthew even see them? He wasn't out there when the pit opened up and they started crawling up from the middle of the fucking earth.

"I think they're gone," Amelia whispered close to my ear.

"The fire must have scared them away," I whispered back, not as quietly. "You said they didn't like the fire."

One side of her lip tried to raise up into a smile of sorts, but the rest of her face gave up long before the gesture was completed.

"Everyone be quiet." Matthew's wide eyes took up all of his face. His fear was making my own rise.

"They're gone." Craig assured him.

"They're never gone," Matthew breathed out, shaking his head back and forth.

"Have you seen the spiders in here?" I peered out of our hiding place, really hoping I didn't come face to face with any of them.

"Not spiders," he moaned, hugging his arms around his middle.

"Then...?"

There was a sudden gush of wind that seemed to come from nowhere and everywhere all at once. Since the guy who had sort of saved us was looking up, we all searched the sky as well. Clearly, Matthew knew something that we didn't.

The forest—which was my favorite place on campus—wasn't done with us yet.

"Fuck," I sputtered. "What next?"

"What is that?" Amelia half whispered.

"Is it the spiders?" Claire added, almost hopefully. A small smile tugged at the corners of her lips.

"Spiders can't fly." Of course, who knew what could or could not happen here? Dead girls could show up. Why couldn't spiders fly?

A high-pitched screech made Matthew whimper and cower down even further. "They've found us. They can smell our fear."

"There's nothing up there," I yelled, craning my head every which way to try to find the sound of the mysterious wind.

"Are we okay then?" As if he were a child, Craig sought reassurance.

"Definitely not okay," Matthew replied.

"Well," I shrugged, "we are in the middle of a burning forest which may or may not be infested with giant killer spiders." As far as okay went, we were a long way from there.

Matthew peered out through the bush leaves, scanning the trees and leaves. His breath came out fast and shallow. He was obviously terrified.

"It's like we are living in everyone's worst nightmares," I concluded out loud.

"We are." Amelia nodded her agreement. "I'm not sure how we all got here, but we are inside of a dream."

"How do you know?"

"I've been here before."

"So have I," Matthew panted, his lower lip trembling.

He looked at least twice the size of Craig. Muscles bulged along his arms and shoulder blades. I would have expected him to be a bit braver. He went to SMA—I really didn't realize they recruited so many cowards. Of course, I wasn't exactly out there being brave either. I was cowering in the bushes, just like they were.

"We should make a run for it," Matthew suddenly yelped.

"No way."

"We're safe here," Craig protested.

"No, we are not safe anywhere in this forest," Matthew was quick to argue.

"There's nowhere to go." Amelia seconded Craig's idea to sit tight and wait for the fire.

"We can go back to the school," he suggested.

"There are giant spiders back at the school," I reminded our small group. "Out here is just some phantom wind." If I absolutely had to choose between the two—it was a no-brainer.

"This is actually kind of cozy." Claire grinned, winking at me. "It reminds me of that camping trip we took up in the mountains. Remember that?"

Only all the time.

"Shut up," I hissed at her.

"It's not the wind." Matthew's grunt made me look away from Claire and the memories she was awakening.

"Then what is it?" Amelia asked, her eyes bulging again.

"A bird."

"A bird?" Was he really that scared of a bird? "Birds aren't scary."

"This one is." He swallowed thickly. "He tries to eat me every time I'm here."

"A bird can't eat a human." Craig scowled. "Unless it's Caspar or D, but they wouldn't. Besides, I think it's just the wind."

"No, it isn't," Matthew insisted.

As if to prove Matthew's words were true, a long screech sounded above us.

"Okay, that definitely wasn't the wind," Craig whimpered.

Maybe not, but I couldn't actually see anything. How could I fight something that I couldn't see?

"Can we outrun this thing?" Amelia asked, rising up slightly to look for it. "It's a long way back to the school."

"Shit," Matthew suddenly cried out, then flattened himself out on the ground. "It's found us."

"What has found us? I don't see anything." The bird still wasn't in sight.

"Don't go out there," he wailed, pulling me roughly to his side.

"I wasn't going anywhere." I glared down to where his fingers dug into my arm. "Just calm down."

"This is not a time to be calm." He spoke through his clenched teeth, his voice coming out thick and fearful to the point he sounded crazy. Spit gathered at the sides of his lips. "If we lower our guard for even a second, it will get us. Do you want that?"

"Not really."

"I'm not staying here," he burst out. "If you guys want to stay here and get killed, go right ahead."

"Killed by a bird?" I scoffed back.

"I told you—" he rose up slightly— "It's more than just a bird."

"Maybe we should listen to him," Amelia suggested nervously.

Craig looked ready to bolt, too. Maybe Claire was right—I should just take my chances on my own.

"All right." I held my hand out in the air between us all. "We'll head back to the school and see if we can find anyone there."

"You're inside of a dream." Claire's eyebrows slid low on her forehead. "How can there be more people here?"

"These three are here." I swung my arm to indicate the trio with us. "Why can't there be more?"

"What?" Craig looked behind him to where Claire sat, but to him it was only empty air.

"Let's go," I grumbled. Seeing my dead girlfriend wasn't exactly something to be proud of. It was probably best not to tell the others.

Still irritated, I backed my way clear of the bushes and stood up. Everything was strangely quiet again. My heart hammered inside my chest as the others came to stand next to me.

"This is kind of weird, huh?" Amelia asked, her voice lowering automatically.

"The air tastes different." Craig nodded.

I knew what he meant; I couldn't tell if it was fear that made it taste like that or if it was the fire.

"Let's move," I suggested nervously.

Before we could take a step away from our hiding place, the sky darkened above us.

As soon as I saw the bird, it became obvious why Matthew was so afraid. The creature was large enough to blot out the entire sky above us. Wings that looked like they were made of swords moved just enough to let the bird hover there.

Matthew opened his mouth, but no sound came out. I had always wondered what a silent scream would look like.

The bird moved his wings slowly, his beady eyes glared out at Matthew.

"Move!" I yelped. If he just stood there like an idiot, he was going to be bird food.

Everything slowed down until I could see each feather in the bird's wing. Matthew's neck throbbed where the blood was racing through his veins. My fangs should have been showing, but it was like I wasn't even a vampire anymore in this dream world. My reflexes were slow, the sun didn't hurt, my senses were dull, and I was afraid.

Still...

Instinctively, I yanked on his arm when the bird swooped down. We both dropped to our knees. I felt the brush of feathers against my face. This was it. There was no way I would be able to run away this time. What would happen to us in real life if we died here? Would it hurt?

"Out of the way." From out of nowhere, Craig shoved Matthew and me out of the way so he was facing the bird.

I wouldn't have thought he had it in him. Why wasn't he running while the bird was distracted with us? He didn't have any weapons. What exactly did he think he was going to do?

Craig opened his mouth wide, inhumanly wide, and made a growl-like sound deep in his throat. Flames of fire erupted from him, shooting right at the bird.

Screeching loud enough to hurt my ears, the bird flapped its wings harder. In response, Craig blew more fire from his fucking mouth.

"This is not real life."

"No," Amelia echoed my escaped thoughts. "It's a dream." Her fingers wrapped around my hand tightly as we stood and watched in awe.

After a few more seconds of Craig blowing fire, the bird gave up and flew away with a mighty screech.

My breath forced its way inside of my lungs and then whooshed back out of my parted lips. "What the hell was that?"

Craig—wimpy, perverted Craig—had just bellowed fire from his mouth to chase off a huge bird. What the actual fuck?

"How did you do that?" Amelia asked him. I was sure my face looked the same as hers; shock and disbelief warred with relief that the bird was gone.

"Old family trick." He shrugged. Instead of pride at having saved us, he looked disturbed.

"You could have let us know about that trick before," I growled. "Like when we were running from spiders."

"Holy shit." Matthew suddenly sank to the ground. He fainted. He actually fainted like a girl in a romance movie.

CHAPTER 3

I sniffed back something that felt like raw emotion. Would this dream ever end? All I wanted to do was wake up and make sure Linnie was okay.

While running for our lives, I had been able to put it out of my head that I had watched her burn to ashes in my bed. Now that we were sitting on the forest floor, waiting for Matthew to come to his senses, forgetting was out of the question.

So far we had been attacked by spiders, birds, and a raging fire that was burning everything and nothing all at the same time. Linnie had burned up, and Claire was following us. I was afraid to think what could be coming next for us; maybe thinking about something would make it come to life here.

"I'm okay now," Matthew assured Amelia, who was still mopping at his brow with her dainty fingers. "This is such a weird dream."

"The bird is gone now. You don't have to be afraid," Amelia cooed.

"I'm fine," he grumbled, pushing her hands away. "Let's just get the hell out of here."

I fell into step behind Matthew as we made our slow way back to the school. Had we really come this far into the forest? It certainly didn't seem like it.

In front of all of us, Claire danced merrily along, uncaring of all the dangers around us.

"Why were you so scared back there?" I tapped Matthew in his side. "I mean, I get that it was a big fucking bird, but you were *really* scared."

"I don't like the birds here," he grunted.

"Me, either." Craig shivered. Anyone would be afraid of a bird that size, but Matthew was terrified; he even fainted.

"I'm a shifter," Matthew began softly. "I change into a mouse in this place, and the birds chase me until..." He shuddered into silence.

"Did you say you shift into a mouse?" Amelia half snorted, her mouth hanging open.

"Only when I dream." He scowled back. "I'm a lion shifter."

"Cat and mouse." Claire giggled. "I get it."

A lion shifter who changed into a mouse and was chased by a giant bird until he died. Yeah, I could see why this was his worst nightmare.

"So ... what do you do?" Matthew asked Amelia from over his shoulder.

"Oracle." She shrugged. "Kind of."

"Meaning?"

"My abilities mostly come from dreams, my own and others'." She sucked in her bottom lip. "I'm trying to figure out how to control it better."

"When you say others'...?"

"I can walk in other people's dreams," she explained. "But I don't know how to control it. I just get pulled in randomly."

"Seems kind of cool." Craig smirked. "Watching dreams like that."

"Dreams are different than real life, though."

Obviously. Spiders and birds weren't that big in real life.

"Fears are irrational inside of dreams. Ordinary things can become your worst fears." Her eyes moved to take in Matthew's back. "So there is no need to feel ashamed of things you feel here."

"Who said anything about being ashamed?" Craig scoffed.

"How do we wake up from this dream?" I demanded. Amelia was the dream expert. She should know.

"We need to find the card."

"The card? What kind of card?"

"We were given an assignment." She spoke slowly, as if the memories were coming back to her one at a time. "A class assignment to find...something."

"A card?"

"A...an artifact. But not an artifact."

"You just said a card."

"The card is a clue."

"So....they trapped us here in the dream until we find this mysterious card or artifact or whatever?" Did they put Claire here, too?

"I'm not sure about that part."

"Where's the card then? Let's go get it." She said it was a clue, and looking for that seemed better than wandering around in this hellish nightmare.

"I don't know."

Her uselessness was really starting to get on my nerves.

"All you know for sure is that we're stuck here until we find some mystery object for a class project that none of us remember anything about?"

Amelia nodded.

"Perfect." That was plenty of information to get us out of here alive and well. How were we supposed to find a card or a mystery object here? The forest was huge, and the school wasn't exactly small.

"What are you guys afraid of?" Matthew asked.

"What?"

"The bird was my nightmare and we all saw it, so what do you guys usually dream about? We need to be prepared."

I hated how right he was. I wasn't sure what I was afraid of, but I knew what my dreams usually consisted of. *Claire.* She was standing right there with us, but no one else could see her.

I sucked in a quick breath through my nose and let it back out as discreetly as possible through my mouth. I needed to calm my breathing down before panic took over again. The familiar trees around us were so menacing now, despite the added light coming from the fire.

Anything could come out and attack us—anything. And we

391

still had no weapons to protect ourselves. We were walking targets out here.

"Everyone stick together," I warned as we quickened our pace.

"The forest stops here." Amelia unnecessarily pointed out when the trees abruptly came to an end.

"The school seems kind of far, huh?" Matthew's narrowed eyes turned to rest on me.

The ground between us and the campus was filled with large, spider-sized holes. "Shit."

"Let's stop here for a minute," Amelia pleaded.

"Why?" My nerves were stretched tightly, and I felt like I was going to explode any second. I needed to be doing something —anything.

"I want to try to see more of what is happening here." Without waiting for an answer, she dropped to the ground and pulled her legs under her.

"Are you going to start meditating?" My nose scrunched up at the thought.

"Be quiet so I can concentrate."

"Whatever." I could be quiet. I was good at silence.

Chewing hard at my bottom lip, I stared off into the distance where the holes would make walking to the school more difficult. As far as I could tell, there were no people inside the school or on the grounds. Although my hearing wasn't as good as Linnie's – she had the best hearing of any vampire I had ever known—I still could hear if people were around us.

All I could hear now was Craig's heavy breathing in my ear.

"I'll be right back," I told anyone who was listening to me. Considering the lack of response, no one was.

Maybe if I was away from the others, I'd be able to hear better. It had been a really long time since I had needed to try so hard. Being human wasn't easy. How did they manage with such limited senses?

Following the line of the trees, I moved far enough away so I couldn't hear Craig and Matthew muttering about birds and fire but still close enough that I could see if they were in any danger. Even with the absence of their added noise, I couldn't hear anything up at the school.

Weird.

"Do you think that means you're not a vampire anymore?" Claire asked, suddenly appearing again in front of me.

"Where did you come from?"

"I would assume from your subconscious." She shrugged. "You've kept me pretty well preserved." She grinned, admiring the curve of her pale legs.

"If I made you up, then...then I want to undo it." My eyebrows wrinkled at the stuttered words. Seeing her made it hard to think of anything else, things that were more important.

"What is that supposed to mean?"

"It means," I growled, leaning in close to her face, "that I want you to go away."

"Does this have anything to do with that pretty little redhead I saw you with earlier?" Her expression darkened; her lips pursed out.

"It has nothing to do with Linnie." Even though it should. "She's not here. This is just a dream."

"You've always liked long hair." She smiled sadly, fingering her own short hair by her neck. "You must be really happy now."

"I was happy with you, too."

"We did have some good times, huh?" Her eyes shone with unshed tears. Claire never cried. She was the strongest person I knew. I didn't know she would one day die on me and leave me alone with only my guilt for company.

We had gone camping with a few of our friends; far from home, far from where we were safe. Claire liked to live life like that —dangerous and free. She hated the rules imposed on us by the nest, and she often went out of her way to break them.

We didn't hear the hunters until it was too late.

I was the only survivor.

That was why I was seeing Claire now; she was my worst nightmare. Not being able to save her had haunted me ever since that night. I tried hard not to think of her, but when I was asleep, she creeped back into my mind. I had never told Linnie about her. I couldn't face the disappointment she would surely feel at me for hiding from the hunters instead of trying to save the one I was supposed to love.

"I'm sorry," I choked out. "Is that what you want to hear?"

"Why would I want to hear that?"

"We both know it was my fault that you died."

"Because you hid?"

I nodded miserably. I hid and left Claire and our friends to their deaths. If only I wasn't such a coward.

"I don't blame you."

"I blame myself."

"Blame yourself for what?"

I spun around at the sound of Amelia's voice. Evidently, she had come up behind me, and I didn't realize it. I really was not myself here. She stared at me intently with a lone leaf sticking out from her mess of curls.

"How long have you been standing there?"

"Just now." Her eyes narrowed. "Who were you talking to?"

"No one," I snarled. I regretted my tone almost immediately when her eyes widened as if I had slapped her. "I was talking to myself, trying to figure out where to find this card and how to get out of this nightmare."

My eyes slid to Claire. As much as I wanted her to not be dead, I knew she was. Seeing her only made me confused and angry. I loved Linnie, and I wanted to get back to her side where I belonged. What if she was in danger? I had already let Claire die; I was not going to let history repeat itself.

No fucking way.

"I think I can help with that."

"You know how to get out of here?"

"I think I know where to find the artifact." She wriggled her eyebrows vigorously.

"Where is it?"

"Well..." She flashed her forearm at me, wrist up. A tattoo was etched there, words in a rich brown ink swirled all the way up her arm.

"Why are you showing me your tattoo? What does that have to do with finding a hidden object here?"

"These words just showed up right now while I was sitting there." She jerked her thumb over her shoulder to where the boys still sat. "I think it's a clue."

Eyebrows scrunched, I pulled her arm closer to read the words out loud.

At the very top of the tower
where the Raven resides;
you'll find a treasure
that magic attempts to hide.

Beware the things
you fear in your heart;
they may end your search
before it can start.

But if you can master
the truth through the lies;
your own awakening
will be the prize.

Claire was still smiling wide when I finished reading. What was she so happy about? It didn't exactly give us very clear instructions on how to find this thing.

"It's a riddle." I scowled.

"It's more than we had before."

The words began to fade, but when Amelia ran her fingers lightly over her arm, they glowed brightly again. That was a good thing since we didn't have a paper and pen to write them down.

"On top of everything else, we have to figure this thing out." My eyes rolled dramatically. "Whose nightmare is puzzles? I need to have a few words with them."

Now it was Amelia's turn to roll her eyes. "It doesn't seem that hard. We just need to figure out where to go next."

I nodded my agreement. Knowing where to go next would be a good start on finding the way out. One step at a time, as long as you're moving forward. It's what I had been taught as a child from my grandpa who raised me. Of course, that was a different lifetime ago, and he couldn't know then that I would one day be trapped inside a shared nightmare, but the theory was the same.

"Let's go see if the guys know what it means."

Claire followed silently behind us as we hurried back to Matthew and Craig. I didn't want to ask her what she thought, not with Amelia there. She had already caught me talking to the air once; better not do it again.

"Obviously, this is Muninn Tower." Craig tapped the first part of the riddle.

"Why obviously?" I leaned around him to read the words again.

"The raven is the mascot for Muninn tower," Amelia noted.

"And Rhian is in Muninn," Matthew said.

Okay, maybe it was obvious, after they pointed that out. What did I know about Muninn Tower? My girlfriend lived there, but we didn't sit around and talk about the mascot. I should have realized the Rhian connection, though. She could turn into a raven, after all.

"All right." I smacked my hands against my thighs. "Let's go then. Muninn Tower is just over there. We have to go through the library." Of course, if it was still where it was supposed to be. The forest had moved, so...

"We can't just go." Craig opened his mouth wide in disbelief that I would suggest such a thing as actually going to where the clue directed us. If we ever got out of this thing, I was finding him just so I could kick his ass.

"This line here says to beware the things we fear." Amelia touched her arm. "Craig might be right; we need to be careful."

"The things we fear? It must be talking about that bird that tried to kill us." I glanced around our partial circle, waiting for the others to see that I was right. "That thing was scary, right?"

"That was my fear." Matthew poked himself in the chest.

"Mine was the spiders." Amelia shuddered.

"Spiders?" Matthew glanced around, searching the ground for them. I hated to be the bearer of bad news, but he wouldn't have to search for them if they were around.

"They came up out of those holes." Craig pointed toward a large building that I knew well. The armory, where the school housed weapons. "It looks like there are more than just the two we saw."

"When you say spiders...?"

"Big spiders." Craig held his arms wide.

"Awesome." How could Matthew look less afraid of giant spiders than he was of the bird? Amelia was right—dreams didn't work like real life did. I had never given it much thought before.

"I've never really liked fire." Craig sniffed. "So the fire must be from me."

"You breathe fire. How can you not like it?" Matthew snorted. I agreed with him, but maybe in life, Craig didn't mind fire so much.

Craig shrugged. "The fire isn't hunting us down though." He glared at Amelia. "So at least there's that."

"What about you?" Matthew asked. Three pairs of eyes turned to me.

"What about me?" I jerked back from their accusations.

"What is coming after us from you?"

"I'm not afraid of anything." My tongue darted across my bottom lip.

"Everyone is afraid of something."

"Nothing that can chase us." I shook my head back and forth. "No need to worry."

"Destiny."

A soft voice echoed across the ground and vibrated inside my chest. I had heard the voice before, when I was alone in here. I still didn't know who it was, but I felt the urgency in her call. Even if I wasn't sure why, I knew I had to find whoever was calling my name. And quickly, before it was too late.

"Waiting here isn't helping anything." I blew air roughly through my nose. "Let's start moving. We can figure shit out as we go."

"Shouldn't we have a plan?"

"Why? None of this is real, so we have no way of knowing what can come after us."

Matthew nodded in agreement, but Amelia and Craig remained unconvinced. Oh well, we weren't waiting any longer.

"The plan is not to get killed," I said.

"Good plan," Matthew muttered.

CHAPTER 4

We stood in a line, shoulder to shoulder, as if we were going into battle. I wasn't sure if I would have picked any of them to go into battle with or not, but they were what I had now. Against an unknown enemy. There were no spiders that we could see, and the sky was bird free. Maybe we would get lucky and the path would be clear to the library.

"Ready?"

"Nope."

"Okay, let's move it." I took the first step, and Matthew was right behind me. I didn't look back to make sure the others followed.

Suddenly, just a few feet from the imagined safety of the tree line, the world shifted. It felt like we had only taken a step, but we were, impossibly, right outside the armory. I heard the unmistakable sound of scurrying feet. Eight feet, to be exact. Matthew gasped loud enough to make me pause. A furry body rounded the corner of the armory, its pincers clicking loudly through the still air.

"What the hell is that?" Matthew screamed.

"Spider," I panted. "Craig, can you do that fire thing?" I yelled back to him.

"I...I'll try." A small puff of smoke came from his mouth, but no flames. My abilities were practically gone in here, too, so I couldn't be mad at him, but we really could have used some fire.

"How are we going to get past that thing?" Amelia hissed. "We can't outrun it."

"And we have no weapons." I tried not to glare at Craig.

"We need a distraction," Matthew concluded.

"What kind of distraction?"

"One that will make that thing run the other way."

"Like a bomb or something?" We were right outside the weapons building. If I could get in there, I might be able to find something we could use. But the trick would be getting in there without the spider eating me.

"I was thinking of something a little smaller than a bomb." Matthew took a shaky breath and rubbed his hand down his face.

"What are you thinking?" Did he have a plan that he wasn't sharing with the rest of us? Hopefully it wasn't too dangerous. The others weren't likely to go along with anything that could get them killed. I wasn't seeing a lot of options.

"I'll shift," he stated boldly. "I'll be the distraction."

"What will you shift into?"

"Either a lion or a mouse." He shrugged.

"You can't just blindly shift," Amelia protested. "For all you know, you could change into an elephant."

"Even better." He grinned nervously. "Then I can just stomp on that thing."

"I think this is a really bad idea," she whined fiercely. "Like, really bad."

"We don't have many other options." Matthew looked at me for confirmation. He was right, but I didn't nod or say anything. If he was going to risk his life to save us, that had to be his choice.

"If I turn into a lion, I'll fight the spider. If I change to a mouse, I'll run so it will chase me."

"Stupid plan," Amelia said stubbornly.

"We're in a dream, right?" His eyes searched her face. "Whatever happens here isn't real."

"It will feel real."

"You guys hurry up and get to the tower, find that damn

artifact, and get us the hell out of here. I can keep running for longer than you think. I'll be fine."

"But..."

"This is the best idea we have."

This was the only idea we had.

"As soon as the spider is distracted, you guys need to hurry."

I nodded for us. Amelia wasn't going to agree, and Craig was too busy gawking at the spider. "Lead it back out to Clifftop. We'll hurry and find whatever it is we're looking for."

With the morbid sounds of bones snapping and joints popping, Matthew's body twisted and turned before disappearing. On the ground, small and pitiful looking, was a small brown mouse with huge ears.

"We can't let him go out there alone," Amelia cried out. "He'll get eaten."

"This was his idea, and he knew the risks."

Matthew's whiskers tweaked a little and then he was off. He ran straight at the spider. At first, I thought he was too small for the spider to notice but then the enormous creature suddenly reared back and pounced at the ground.

Amelia squeaked a small scream but thankfully didn't rush forward to help. We all watched in silence as the mouse danced around the spider's legs before darting back toward the trees that shouldn't exist but were far away from us.

I was almost surprised when the spider followed. Maybe I didn't really expect the plan to work. The ground shook slightly when the spider thundered past us.

"Time to go." We couldn't waste what precious time Matthew had given us.

Crouching slightly, I took off as fast as I could go along the path that would take me to Halstein Hall. There were pits all around us, deep pits that seemed to drill down to the center of the earth.

Luckily, none of them held any spiders.

Once inside, it was easier to breathe. There was a moment of false security, like nothing could get us in here. But the absence of Matthew chased that feeling away. We still had to make it down a few floors to get to the library; from there we would be able to get to Muninn Tower. Hopefully, we didn't run into anything else.

Craig reached the door to the library first. He swung it open and ducked inside without waiting for Amelia and me. She moved slower than I did, probably because she was looking around more. I kept my eyes focused on that door as if it were the only thing that could save me.

Panting hard, I flung the door open and hurried inside after Amelia got in.

"Shit," I gasped, holding my side. "I had no idea that running could be so difficult."

"Were there any more?" Craig asked, scanning outside the glass doors. "Did you guys see any more?"

"No," Amelia told him. "I think we're safe."

Thanks to Matthew and his ability to change into a mouse, we were safe for now. Unless the spiders learned how to open doors. Outside, the fires continued to ravage the trees and the sun continued to shine down on all the holes in the courtyard.

Somewhere out there, a little brown mouse was running for his life. I could only hope that he didn't die.

"The library is really creepy when it's empty, huh?" Amelia took several steps into the poorly lit room.

I thought the library was creepy even when it was full of people. I tried to avoid it as much as I could. Of course, I came here more often than necessary to meet Linnie, but I seldom ventured past the first floor.

"Here's the passage," Amelia called out, pulling open a familiar door. "Come on."

"How do you know where it is?" I asked, following her through.

"I'm in Muninn."

"You are? Then you must know my girlfriend."

"Linnie Andrews." She nodded. "I know her and her friends."

"I know they seem snobby, but they aren't bad." I must really be dreaming, for me to say good things about Marcia and Molly.

"I don't remember this passage being so dark before," I whispered to Amelia, who was directly in front of me. I could hear

Craig breathing on the back of my neck, but he had never been in this passage before so what would he know?

"Me, either," she hissed back. I jumped when I felt her hand grab mine. I wouldn't have imagined myself girly enough to want to hold hands, but I tightened our hold anyways.

It was a breath of fresh air when we finally reached the end of the passage and burst into the Muninn Tower common room. Memories assaulted my senses: Linnie and me on the chair pretending to read a book but really just listening to each other's heart beats mingle, the two of us sitting at the table picking apart a cheese omelet that Molly had insisted on making us, tiptoeing up the stairs to her bedroom, thinking we were sneaky in a tower stashed with vampires and shifters and who knew what else. They knew exactly what we were up to.

I really missed her.

"These stairs will take us to the highest floor," Amelia announced, leading us to a narrow flight of stairs.

"It's okay that you held my hand back there," I told her. "I was scared, too."

"I didn't hold your hand," she said, her eyebrows bunched in the middle. "I'm not scared of that passage. Even in the dark, I know it well."

"You held my hand in the passage," I stupidly insisted. I'd felt her hand in mine. I even squeezed it back. Why was she lying? She couldn't possibly be embarrassed because of Craig.

"It wasn't me." She shrugged, turning back to the steps.

"If it wasn't you, then who was it?" I glanced down at Craig.

"It wasn't me," he muttered, ducking his head angrily. "You two just left me behind."

"You weren't that far back," Amelia grumbled, yet again. "We would have heard you if anything happened."

I definitely felt a hand in mine. If it wasn't either of these two... I shook my head roughly. Best not to think about that stuff. Just focus on the task at hand.

At the top of the steps was a small blue door that led out to the top of the tower. According to Amelia, this was the tallest point of Muninn Tower. It was hard to tell from here, with all the rough edges and the way the tower seemed to go on forever up into the dark top of the campus's cavern.

"There's nothing up there?" I asked, pointing to the rest of the tower above us.

"Nothing you can get to. This is the highest point. The rest is just old ruins."

"So the card must be here."

"Or the artifact."

"And once we find that..."

"Hopefully we'll wake up again."

Then we could find Matthew.

Peering over the edge of the tower, I scanned the ground below for any sign of the spider chasing a small mouse. I assumed the spider wouldn't give up without its prize. Would Matthew tire out first?

I didn't see anything moving below us. What was really strange, though, was that I didn't see any holes either. The ground was smooth once again.

"Hey, I found it," Craig suddenly exclaimed. "Here's the card."

Amelia and I both hurried to his side. Sure enough, he was holding what looked like a regular sized tarot card. I recognized it; I just couldn't place where I had seen it. There was a large stick that took up most of the front with objects swirling around it in blues and purples. There was a dragon and a moon, a lion, a raven, and several other objects that I didn't know. On the back of the card was the same poem that had etched itself onto Amelia's skin.

"Where did you find that?" I demanded, snatching the card from his fingers.

"It was just lying here on the ground." He pointed at a spot that was clearly out in the open.

"That doesn't seem right, though." Amelia's words echoed my own thoughts.

"Why not?" Craig asked, his voice going high. "We followed the clue to come to this spot and then we found the card."

"Seems too easy." My eyes narrowed. The riddle said that magic was trying to hide it from us. This card wasn't hidden at all. Something was wrong.

"If this really was what we are supposed to find," Amelia took the card from me, "then why didn't we wake up yet?"

"You said an artifact that wasn't an artifact," I pointed out, tapping the card in front of me. "This isn't it."

"You don't know," Craig growled angrily.

"We have to find...something else."

"Is there some kind of spell that we need to say?" Craig searched the card and the place where the card had been laying. "Do you two know any spells?"

"No."

"I don't think it's a spell," I said slowly. "There must be more to the clue than what we thought."

"So what do we do now?"

"Let's see the clue again." Bowing together over the card, I reread the lines of the riddle with Amelia and Craig.

"You're sure this is the top, right?"

"I'm sure." Amelia nodded. "There's no way to get any higher than this."

"The truth through the lies," Amelia murmured. "What do you think that means?"

"I don't know." I was never very good at riddles. Give me a weapon and a target any day. This kind of thing was for smart people.

Without warning, the wind started to pick up. It should have been warm wind with all the fire that was burning, but it was cold. The kind of cold wind that cut through my skin and chilled my bones. The sun was covered by a large gray cloud that came in from nowhere. We shouldn't have been able to even see the sky.

"It's talking about mastering the truth." Craig continued to read as if he didn't notice the wind.

I was the only one who could see Claire. Was I also the only one who could see the sky? Was one of my fears the sun? I didn't feel like I was afraid of it, but I was a vampire, after all. Maybe in my subconscious—where Claire lived—I was also afraid of the sun. Was it going to start attacking us next?

"Mastering the truth..." Amelia turned questioning eyes toward the sky. "Does that mean we have to face our fears?"

"Haven't we already been facing our fears?"

"Not really." I pursed my lips out. "We've only been hiding from them." If this really were an assignment given to us by our teachers, it made sense that they wanted us to face our fears instead of running. That was sort of the point of the school.

"Does that mean we have to go back down there?" Craig jutted his chin to the edge of the tower.

"Maybe. Matthew already faced his fears. I bet he already woke up."

"Hmm. . ." I wrapped my arm around my middle. It was a good theory, one that I might just be willing to test out.

"Destiny."

"What?" Dropping my hand, I spun around in a slow circle. It was that voice again, but I could hear it more clearly up here. "That's Linnie."

"Linnie is here?" Amelia also spun around, searching for her.

"I've been hearing someone call my name," I explained in a rush of words, excited now that I recognized who was calling to me. "It's Linnie."

"Destiny."

"I don't hear anything," Amelia said, shaking her head.

That was all right, though. My nightmares were for me alone. The others weren't a part of them like I was a part of theirs. I didn't know why, but it didn't matter.

Linnie mattered. She was here somewhere, and I had to find her.

"I think it's coming from inside the tower."

Without waiting for the others to believe me, I darted back into the tower where I fully expected Linnie to be waiting for me. The second my feet crossed the threshold, the door completely disappeared. I was locked apart from the others.

A thin needle of fear pricked my spine. It was difficult not to regret my hastiness, but I shook the feeling off. Linnie was in here somewhere. The others would just have to figure it out on their own. I didn't owe them anything.

The corridor on the other side of the door was pitch black. The only thing I could see were the steps we had come up; a small stream of light came from them. This was a dream, so it must be showing me the way to go. My subconscious had been in charge all this time. No sense in doubting it now.

With only a slight hesitation, I stepped down onto the first step.

I knew as soon as I dropped that it was a mistake, but it was too late. The step gave way under my weight, and I was falling through a black tunnel. *This must have been what Alice felt like when she was falling into Wonderland*, I thought stupidly. There was nothing to stop my fall, nothing to grab onto. I didn't feel afraid, though.

After a long time or maybe it was just the blink of an eye, I landed with a soft thump onto a hard stone floor. I checked my body for cuts or broken bones and found nothing wrong with me. Scrambling back to my feet, I looked where I had landed.

I was in a large room that I had never been in before. Although there were no windows, the room was well lit.

There was nothing in the room with me; no furniture, no people, no pictures, nothing. Four doors lined one of the dull gray walls. They were numbered one through four. *Wait a minute.* My eyes narrowed as I studied that impassable wood. Someone else had to face four doors too. Another ITF team. Who was it? Who told me about that?

Maybe that had been a dream too.

Swallowing thickly, I crossed to the door marked *One* and tried the handle. It was locked. I knew the others would be, too, but I tried them anyway. Just in case.

"What the hell is this?" I asked to no one. "Let me out of here." I pounded on door number four, the one I was standing in front of.

"It's not going to open just because you asked it to." Claire giggled. She was in the room with me, sitting on a high stool that hadn't been there a second ago.

"Then how do I get it to open?"

"Funny you should ask." She crossed her arms over her chest, smiling wide at me.

Fuck, this wasn't going to be pleasant.

CHAPTER 5

I took a deep breath.

"Tell me the riddle again," I requested on a sigh.

"You've already heard it several times," Claire grumbled.

"I know," I held up one finger, "but I need to hear it again. I don't want to get it wrong."

> *At the very top of the tower*
> *where the Raven resides;*
> *you'll find a treasure*
> *that magic attempts to hide.*
>
> *Beware the things*
> *you fear in your heart;*
> *they may end your search*
> *before it can start.*
>
> *But if you can master*
> *the truth through the lies;*
> *your own awakening*
> *will be the prize.*

Just like all the other times she had said it, it didn't make any sense to me. There were no clues in those lines about which door I should take. If I took the wrong one, I would be screwed. Lost or worse.

"What kind of a riddle is that?" I groaned, pushing my fingers into my temples.

"I'm just the messenger." She pressed her lips together in an amused line. "Can't really help you decide which door to choose. But I will give you this little gem."

"Yeah?" I looked at her hopefully.

"Don't pick the wrong door. That doesn't sound like it will be much fun."

"Gee, thanks."

"Happy to help."

"I don't like this place, Claire."

"The room?"

"This whole place," I corrected, shuddering slightly.

"Of course not. It's a world of your own nightmares. Who would like to come here and hang out?"

"It's full of riddles and monsters. I don't know which door to choose."

"You'll have to pick one of them."

Right; she was right. I had to make a choice.

Sighing deeply, I got up off the floor and approached door number one. There was nothing special about it from the outside; nothing made it better than any of the other three. I pressed my hand against the pale wood, hoping for some kind of clue.

What was behind there waiting for me? A terrible fate; but what did that mean? Were there more spiders or birds? Was it fire? Would Linnie be there waiting for me to come and find her? I had been hearing her all over the school. If I picked the right door, would I finally be reunited with her? Or was it all just a trick?

From behind the door came a soft cry for help. It was Linnie. My heart sped up at the sound. "Destiny," she called, "help me. Please Destiny, help me."

"Linnie," I pounded on the door. "What is wrong? Are you hurt?"

"Destiny!" Her screams grew louder and more panicked. "Open the door and save me."

My fingers hesitated just over the door handle. Why would she say that? If she really were in there, why would she ask me to open the door? She could just open it herself—unless she couldn't.

I shook my head. I couldn't let the room trick me so easily.

With great difficulty, I moved on to the second door and touched my hand against the wood. It felt hot, like there was a fire raging on the other side. We had been taught at school to feel a door, and if it was hot, don't open it.

This door was a lot easier to pass on.

Door three was something I didn't expect.

"Are you sure this is safe?" a boy asked in a nervous whisper.

"Of course it is, Jerry," came the girl's sassy response.

"I don't know, Des," Jerry whined. "Mrs. Dorance said to never climb out onto the roof."

"Are you a baby, Jerry?" I mocked him.

This was me, when I was like eight or nine years old. Jerry and I lived in the same foster home. Mrs. Dorance and her husband took in kids by the handfuls just to get the government checks each month. They lived in a great big house out in the country. It was an old house that was falling apart a little more each day. They weren't exactly mean to us, and they did feed us three meals a day. Who really needed a bedtime story every night or help with their homework? TV dinners counted as a meal; we shouldn't have complained so much.

"I'm not a baby." Jerry pouted.

I could practically hear the way his chin rose up in the air when he was trying to pretend he was brave.

Snotty little kid actually listened to me that day. I didn't know the roof was going to cave in like that. I was just a kid myself.

"I didn't know, Jerry," I whispered to the back of the door, moving on quickly. That wasn't a replay I cared to hear any more of.

When I placed my hand on the fourth door, I heard Claire's voice. She was sitting behind me, but I knew it was her behind the door, too. I would recognize her voice anywhere.

"You did this to me, Destiny," she hissed from the other side. "This is all your fault. You are the one who wanted to go camping and then you just ran away at the first sign of trouble. You did this!"

My hand fell limply back to my side. "No one is behind the doors." I came to the conclusion dully. "I'm in this room alone."

"Of course you are," Claire trilled. "Well, to be fair, you aren't actually in this room at all."

"Nothing here is real."

"A dream."

"I haven't been hearing Linnie, either, have I?"

"Dreams are funny sorts of things." Claire's forehead wrinkled. "Everything in here is in your head. It's just laid out more clearly so you can see it. Maybe Linnie is trying to tell you something?"

"What is she trying to say? She wants me to save her."

"Did she actually say that though?" Claire tilted her head dramatically to one side.

"I'm pretty sure she did." I peered back at the door. She was definitely asking for help.

"I don't mean here in this room." Claire rolled her eyes. "Try not to overthink things. You always do that and cause yourself more of a headache than you need to."

"I know which door is the right one." It was obvious, really. It was the only door that had something real behind it. Three of the doors were just part of my nightmares; they would lead me further into this crazy world. There was only one way out of here.

The riddle on the back of the card we had found said we had to face our fears—maybe this was what it had meant. It wasn't talking about the ones we had already gotten past; the card must have known there was more to come.

"Which one do you pick?"

"Number two," I stated with confidence. At my words, the other three doors turned black. "Did I pick the right one?"

"Only one way to find out."

"Right." I nodded firmly. "What's the worst that can happen?"

"Best not to ask questions like that," she scolded playfully. "You remember little Jerry, right?"

Why did she have to bring that up again? Hadn't I just heard enough of him?

Willing myself not to shake, I gripped the handle and turned it roughly, maybe a little too roughly. The door swung open.

Fire raged on the other side of the door, fire unlike any I had ever seen before. It was a miracle that the room was still intact at all. How had it contained such a ferocious blaze? I jumped backward so the fire wouldn't burn me up, but I already knew what I was going to have to do.

There was only one way out of this room, and it was through that door. I had already chosen this one. The others were gone now.

"The fire isn't real," I whispered to myself. "Fake fire cannot hurt you. Just close your eyes and walk through the door. Easy as that."

"Yeah, sounds really easy. Do you mind if I just meet you on the other side?" Claire winked, then disappeared.

"Can't blame you there," I muttered. Closing my eyes tightly, I took a step into the fire.

The heat enveloped me on all sides, so strongly that I thought I was going to stop breathing. Just as the panic was starting to rise, the heat faded away. I had come through to the other side, unburnt.

When I opened my eyes again, the fire was gone. There were no smoke or charred places to even suggest it had ever really been there. The door that I had stepped through was gone, too, leaving behind a stone-gray wall.

In front of me was a long hallway. It was so long that I couldn't tell where it ended—if it ended at all.

All along the hallway were doors of various sizes and colors. There had to be hundreds of doors along the wall. Wooden, stone, tall, wide, narrow, some with handles and some without.

"Shit, this is going to take forever."

"I doubt they all open," Claire sang out.

"You're awfully helpful today."

Her laughter rang out in the empty hall, echoing back to me and reminding me of a time long ago. A ghost of something warm tried to enter my heart. I hurried to push it away before I had time to think about it too much.

My footsteps echoed loudly in the hallway that never ended. No matter how far I walked, the hallway stayed the same. Doors upon doors and nothing else. It was the same as the room had been; there were no windows but the space was still bright.

Claire stayed right in front of me. Her walk was just how I remembered it; hips swaying like a cat on a fence. How I had missed those hips.

"I wonder if Amelia and Craig are still on top of that tower," she said, turning just enough for me to see her profile. Her soft jawline moved with her words.

"They're probably looking for me," I told her. My words came out raspy; I cleared my throat and tried again. "I must have just disappeared to them."

"Probably."

"How are we going to get out of here? This can't still be Muninn Tower, right?" I think we would know if there was a never-ending hall of doors in the tower. It wasn't a big enough building to hold that many rooms. Of course, the school was magical, so it was possible. Anything was possible.

And this was a dream. There was that, too.

"Maybe one of the doors is unlocked." Claire suggested the exact thing I had been thinking.

"Should we try?"

"Why not?" She sighed. "What do we have to lose at this point?"

The next door we came to was a wide door with blue hinges and a red handle. There was nothing that stood out about the door; it was just the next one we came to. I stopped and puffed out my cheeks.

I didn't feel fear when I touched the handle, so I took that as a good sign. The door opened easily, revealing nothing significant on the other side. In fact, it looked like another hallway. This one wasn't as brightly lit.

Once we walked through the door, the other one disappeared behind us, just like before. "You don't think this is some kind of maze, do you?"

"A labyrinth?" Claire's eyes lit up. "That would be so cool."

"Except, not really," I scoffed. "We'd be stuck in here forever. Do you feel hunger in dreams?" Or the need to go to the bathroom? Would I just have to wander around forever inside the school? What kind of bullshit was that?

The dark hall was a lot shorter than the previous one had been.

It ended in a T shape; I had to go either left or right. There were no hints—both ways looked exactly alike. On a whim, I turned right and ended up back in the never-ending hallway.

I was right outside the door with the blue hinges.

"Let's try another door," Claire said.

"There has to be a way out," I panted.

Despite my urging to stay calm, my breath seemed to be getting shorter and shorter. Each time I tried a new door, I ended up in a new hallway. Each hallway ended in some sort of decision to go one way or another. And each way I chose led me back to the never-ending hallway.

My lungs felt tight. Was the air running out in the hallway? There weren't any windows or anything. Maybe the air could run out and I was suffocating.

I tried to take a deep breath of the stale air, but it didn't fill up my lungs the way it was supposed to. Everything was getting blurry.

"Are you all right?" Claire asked from somewhere very far away. She must have gone farther down the hallway without me.

"I don't know," I gasped. "I can't breathe very well."

"Maybe you should sit down for a minute. We've been going in circles for a while now. You must need a rest."

"A rest?" But sitting down actually did sound like a good idea. My legs were starting to shake anyway. They probably wouldn't hold me up for too much longer. I slid down the wall until my butt hit the cold concrete. "I think I'll sit down for a minute," I told Claire. Hopefully she didn't think I was weak.

"You're the same as I remember you, you know." Claire put her hand on my arm. I was surprised that I could feel it. I thought she was a ghost.

"I'm not the same as I was before," I feebly argued, well aware of the way my breath was coming out in short little puffs. "I'm sure that I'm braver than before."

"You were always brave," she cooed, moving her hand so that she was rubbing my skin. "So much braver than I was."

"Are you kidding?" Tears suddenly sprang into the corners of my eyes. "You're the bravest person I know. You weren't afraid of anything."

Claire laughed a delicious sort of sound that sent a shiver up my spine. "That was all just an act to get you to like me."

"Well, it worked."

"You and I made a good pair," she said softly.

"Yes, we did." Claire taught me what it was to be a vampire, but even more than that, she showed me who I really was. She showed me how to love and be loved in return. I thought we would be together forever. We should have been together for so much longer.

"Our time was cut short," she agreed with my thoughts.

"Mmm. . ." I could only grunt my reply. My throat was too thick for words.

"Do you ever think about me?"

"I think about you all the time."

"Do you miss me?"

"All the time," I whispered.

Her face moved slowly toward mine. Even if I wanted to stop what was happening, I couldn't move. Some sort of gravity was holding me to that place and bringing us closer to the inevitable. My body knew hers too well for it not to respond.

When her lips finally touched mine, it was like I could breathe again after being under water for a very long time. I sighed into her and let my mouth open to receive her breath. Her kiss was what I needed to survive in that hallway. It was what I had been missing for so long.

As I hungrily kissed Claire, all my senses tuned in to her. I didn't let myself think of anything except her softness against me. Her tongue moved inside my mouth, finding my tongue and brushing against it. I moved my face so the kiss could deepen. My heart was racing.

But then...

Fire red hair exploded all around me. A gentle smile and dainty laugh filled my mind with an ache that I had never known before.

I pulled away from Claire so I could see her face. Although I had once loved that face more than anything else on the planet, it wasn't the one I wanted to see now. Guilt rushed in at me.

Guilt for kissing Claire when I loved Linnie and guilt for loving Linnie when Claire was dead.

"I love Linnie," I blurted out.

"I know."

"I'm sorry, but I do love her."

"You loved me first, though, right?" She touched her finger to my chin.

"I did love you first," I readily agreed.

"Do you love me more than you love her? I can forgive you for loving her if you at least love me more."

"I don't know if it works like that."

"It works however you want it to." She leaned forward and pressed her lips briefly to mine again. I was ready this time and not willing to betray Linnie, even in a dream.

"We should go."

"There's nowhere to go." Claire widened her eyes and flung her hands out. "Let's just stay here for a little while longer. Don't you like being close to me?"

"I do, but..."

"But nothing."

There was a flash of movement behind her. A small creature had just darted out from under one of the doors.

"What the hell was that?" I sat up straighter.

"What?" Claire turned to see what I was looking at.

"It's a mouse," I practically screamed. "It's Matthew."

"How is that possible?" Her nose wrinkled at the sight of his furry brown body.

I didn't know, either, but I was extremely glad to see him. The mouse shot back up into his human form. Matthew stood there, breathless and shaking but otherwise whole.

"Destiny," he gasped. "I'm so glad to see you here. I've been running in circles for days now."

CHAPTER 6

I pulled my knees close to my chest and looked over at Matthew, who was now sitting where Claire and I had kissed. Claire was across from us, still invisible to Matthew.

"I don't get how you got here," I muttered into my legs. "You were outside." Nothing here made sense.

"I don't really get it, either." He shivered. "I was out there running from the spider."

I remembered.

"It wasn't hard to outrun it, actually. I thought it would catch me and wrap me up in that web shit, but it couldn't get me."

"It wasn't your nightmare," I said out loud. "It wasn't scary to you because it wasn't yours."

"It was still scary," he argued.

"So what happened?"

"The spider disappeared." He shrugged. "One minute it was there, and the next it was gone."

"And then you just beamed up to this hallway?"

"The ground opened up, like one of those holes, and I fell through. When I landed, I was here."

I had fallen through a step to get here. "Does that mean the spiders are all here?"

We both glanced down the long hall.

"I haven't seen any." He shook his head. "I've been here for so

416

long. Pretty sure it's been days, at least. I would have seen something."

"You haven't been here for days. We just separated outside. That wasn't that long ago."

"I have," he insisted.

"It just seems like that long." His eyes were bloodshot, and huge circles were under them, making him look sick.

"The hallways just goes on and on," he said dully. "No matter which door I try, it leads back to here."

"There has to be a way out."

"Why does there have to be?"

It must have been awful to be alone for what felt like that long, losing all hope of finding an exit. "We're both here."

"So?"

"If we're both in the same place, it must not be completely in our heads. It's an actual place that we can both be in at the same time. That means we can get back out together, too."

"Do you really think so?"

"Yeah." I rubbed his arm, hoping that somehow offered comfort to him. "We'll get out of here and find the others."

"They aren't here with you?" He looked shocked, as if he only just now realized that we were alone in this hallway.

"I fell through a step on my own."

"Where are Craig and Amelia?"

"We were up at the top of the tower. We found the card, but it didn't wake us up. I heard something—" no need to tell him I had heard Linnie calling to me— "and went back inside the tower to see what it was. As soon as I went through the door, I was trapped here without them."

"We can keep trying doors," he suggested weakly. "Maybe we'll find them."

"Better than just sitting here and waiting for nothing to come save us." I smirked, standing up and pulling him with me. In my experience, if I wanted to be saved, it was best to do it myself.

It was hard to ignore Claire as we walked. She kept brushing her fingers along my arm and on the back of my hand, no matter how many times I tried to push her off. Kissing her had been a

417

mistake. Thankfully Matthew had shown up and reminded me what was real.

Claire was not real.

"Do you have a family, Matthew?" I asked loudly, darting away from Claire once again.

"Yeah." He sighed. "I have three sisters and four brothers."

"Wow, that's a hell of a lot of family."

"Adopted family," he grunted. "We've been together for so many years now, I can't remember what I was before them."

"Are they all shifters like you?"

"Yep."

"You must miss them."

"They're probably worried about me." His voice caught.

That was the worst thing about being in danger or being sick —the people you loved had to worry about you.

"To them, you're just sleeping. They don't know you're here." At least, I hoped that were true.

"Did you hear that?" Matthew abruptly stopped walking and turned to me with wide eyes.

"I don't hear anything." I couldn't hear like a vampire anymore. I had practically reverted back to a human. "What did you hear?"

"Someone is knocking up there."

"Knocking?" I sucked in my breath and held it inside my lungs so I could hear past my own breathing. Very faintly, up ahead of us, there came three sharp knocks. "I hear it," I hissed, excited.

"Where is it coming from?"

"This way." I darted in front of him and ran down the hall, ears strained to hear the knocking again. The farther we ran, the louder the knocking became.

"It's here." Matthew slid to a stop in front of a tall pink door. "There's definitely someone in there."

I pressed my ear against the door, listening. Behind the heavy wood came the muffled sounds of someone crying. I could make out the whimpering.

"Hello?" I screamed. The crying stopped.

"Don't do that." Matthew jerked me back from the door. "You don't know what's in there."

"I hear them crying. It has to be human."

"It doesn't have to be anything," he snarled, fear making his eyes go narrow again.

"I think we'll have to take our chances." Anything was better than walking this hallway for who knew how long. Maybe the knocking was a sign that this door was the way out.

"How do we know if it's dangerous or not?" His eyebrows furrowed, but he wasn't running away.

"Only one way to find out." I tried to sound light-hearted, but my breath was coming out too shaky to pull it off.

Hands trembling, I grabbed the small knob on the door. It was my idea to open it so I had to be the one to face whatever was in there first. Of course, if it was something unfriendly, Matthew would have no choice but to face it as well.

"Here's hoping. . ." I swallowed hard. Just as I was about to turn the knob, the knock came again.

I was shocked enough to let go. Maybe this was a bad idea after all. "I'm..."

"Scared?" He cocked one eyebrow high on his forehead.

"Yeah."

"Me too." The hand that had been on the door handle found Matthew's hand instead and pulled him close to me. "Let's try this," he suggested. Closing his fist, he tapped three times on the door, returning the knock.

The response was immediate. Whatever was on the other side of the door knocked again, only this time it was louder and more panicked. The knocking became more of a banging, over and over again.

"Is someone there?" I called out, pressing my face close to the door again. As scared as I was, I needed to know who was there and if they needed our help.

Maybe it was Linnie. It was hard to think of her being trapped somewhere and I was just standing here, too afraid to open the door.

"Help me," came a muffled reply. "The door is locked. I can't get it open."

"What should we do?" I asked Matthew, even though I already knew the answer.

"Let's open it." He pressed his lips tightly together. "Just hurry up and do it."

"Right." Without giving myself time to hesitate, I flung the door open wide. It wasn't locked on our side.

"Destiny?" Amelia stepped into the light cast by the hallway. "Is that really you?"

"Amelia!"

She stumbled forward until she was out of the room that she had been a prisoner of. It was dark inside, but I could tell it was empty. Amelia was eager to get out. How long had she been inside there by herself?

"I can't believe you're here," she sobbed, flinging her arms around my neck. "We were looking for you, and now you're just here."

"We?" Matthew peered around the two of us to see if anyone else would come from the shadows. "Is Craig with you?"

"Matthew." She turned tear-filled eyes to him. "You're here, too. I can't believe this is real. I've been inside there for so long. I didn't think anyone would ever come."

"Craig isn't with you?" I pulled away from Amelia but kept my hand at her waist. She looked like she might fall over if I didn't hold onto her.

"I don't know where he went," she cried, the tears falling freely down her face. "We were both trying doors; each of us took one side of the hall. And then...he was just gone." She shuddered hard. "I went in there," she looked behind her at the still open doorway, "and the door locked on me."

"If you guys were together," Matthew began, "then he might be close by."

Amelia nodded. "He probably got taken by one of the rooms, too."

"Most of these rooms just lead to more of the maze, though," I pointed out. "We didn't get stuck inside any of them."

"But Amelia did. Let's just try to find him." Matthew looked behind us, as if Craig was going to pop out from somewhere.

"Just knock on the doors, though," I warned. "Don't go inside."

"Let's stay close together," Amelia pleaded. "I don't want to get separated again."

Moving as one, we made our way back down where we had just come from. I doubted Craig was still in any of the rooms, but to make them happy, I was willing to try knocking with them.

"We tried to look for you." Amelia sniffled, watching me pound on cool wood. "We searched for days, but we couldn't find you."

"Days?" My steps faltered. She thought we were here for days too? "Why do you think it's been that long?"

"We've been walking and walking and walking. Then we'd sleep, get up, and start again. Most of the doors were locked, so we just walked and walked."

"How could you be down here for days and not feel hungry?"

"I don't know," she croaked. "It was awful, but not as awful as being alone."

"Hey, guys," Matthew called. He was two doors away from us. "I think I found something."

"Is it Craig?" I asked, hurrying to join him by a plain wooden door.

"Feel this door."

Confused, I placed my palm against the faded brown wood. It was hot to the touch.

"Fire," I whispered out loud.

"Could be him." Matthew swallowed loudly. "He doesn't like fire so maybe..."

I didn't need Matthew to finish the words out loud. Maybe Craig was trapped inside the room, burning all this time without actually dying. If he was in there, he was terrified.

"Stand back," I ordered the other two.

"You're going to open it?"

"Yep." I yanked hard at the door, expecting some resistance; it came open easily, though.

Fire spilled out into the hallway, but it wasn't like normal fire. It didn't hurt me. The flames licked at my skin, but it didn't burn me. It looked and smelled like real fire, consuming every space inside the four walls and yet burning nothing.

Craig was not in the room.

On the other side of the room, through all the flames and smoke, I could see the outline of a second door, or maybe it was just a doorway without the physical door there. He might have gone that way, since the fire was still burning. He might even still be there.

"Is that another door?" I asked pointing inside the room. "Do you guys see it?"

"I see it." Matthew pulled my arm back. "But there's no way to get to it."

"I think we can go through the flames."

"Are you insane?" Amelia spat, eyes bulging. "You can't walk through fire."

"It doesn't burn, though." I put my arm back into the flames, trying to prove my point.

"Don't do that," Matthew yelled, pulling my arm again. His fingertips were already turning red where the fire touched them.

My eyebrows dipped low in confusion. "It burns you?"

"It's fire," he scoffed. "What do you think it does?"

"But..." Reaching my hand out yet again, I let the fire graze against my skin. There was no heat, no red marks. I didn't feel anything. It was a little warmer than the hallway, but nothing I couldn't handle. "It doesn't hurt me."

"How are you doing that?"

"I have no idea."

"Does it burn you, Amelia?"

"I can feel the heat from here," she said. She was standing several steps back. "There's no way we can go through those flames."

"But I can." I peered through the fire, at the door on the other side. If he was really in there, I could just run across the room and grab him real fast. It wouldn't take long. They could keep the door open for me and watch the entire time. We wouldn't get separated again. "I'll go alone and see if Craig is in there."

"No way," Amelia was quick to protest. "We need to stick together. I don't want to be stuck alone anymore."

"I'll stay with you," Matthew vowed.

"You can't be sure that the fire won't burn you up," she

continued to argue. "What if it changes as soon as you cross into the room? I don't think it's safe."

"I wouldn't leave you in that pit, and I won't leave Craig alone either." Fear made cowards out of most people, myself included. I had lived for a very long time with the guilt of that cowardliness; I made a vow to myself after Claire died that I wouldn't hide ever again.

I wasn't a superhero, but I could wear a cape just like anyone else.

"Please don't go in there."

"I'll be quick."

"You're going to go alone no matter what we say, aren't you?" Amelia finally conceded. Sort of.

"I won't be long."

"Unless you are." She moved closer so she could wrap her hand around Matthew's arm. "We'll stand right here and wait for you."

"If you start to feel afraid, just come back," Matthew added. "The door will be open so you can find your way back to the hallway."

"If you don't see Craig in the next room, don't go any farther by yourself."

"I won't." I nodded quickly. "There's no reason to worry. I got this. You two just make sure you stay together." It would be a lot harder if I came back and had to find both of them.

Here goes, I muttered inside my own head. If they could see how scared I really was, they might make more of a fuss about me going in alone.

Somehow, although I couldn't explain how, I knew I had to go into this room alone. There was something I had to see. That's why the fire didn't burn me like it burned them. This was still part of my dream, the part they couldn't see. Claire was still with us, so I would have to face more before this was all over. I really doubted it would be anything as easy as spiders or birds.

"See you in just a second." I grinned, waving at Amelia and Matthew.

For the briefest of moments, just on the other side of the threshold, I turned back to the duo. They stood there holding onto each other tightly, watching me with fear filled eyes.

KRISTIE COOK

No matter what we were being trained for at SMA, we were all just scared children when it came to nightmares. Inside here, the clothes on the chair were actually monsters and that sound under the bed was someone waiting to grab our ankles. It was all real, and it was all scary.

"I'll be right back," I mouthed, then turned and ran into the fire.

As I expected, the flames didn't touch me as I crossed the room. It was like walking through a warm shower, quite pleasant in fact. If only I wasn't terrified of what was on the other side of the room. Once I made it to the other door, I glanced back at the way I had come.

The fire had grown tall enough to block out Matthew and Amelia and my way back to them, but I was sure that it was still there and that I could find it. There was no reason to borrow trouble—I had to stay focused on finding Craig. Then we could worry about getting back.

After one steadying breath, I ducked inside the open doorway. The flames disappeared immediately, like someone had turned the light switch off and it controlled the fire. I let my breath out in an audible whoosh.

"Craig," I choked out. "Are you in here?"

"I'm here!"

I jerked backward at the sound of his call. I hadn't fully expected to find him so easily. "Where are you? I can't see you."

"Destiny." His relief was unmistakable. "You're finally here. We've been waiting for you."

We?

Craig came into view then, but he wasn't alone.

CHAPTER 7

"Hey, Des," Claire purred, scraping one finger down Craig's arm. "I found your friend for you."

"H...how...?"

"Just say thank you." She smiled proudly. "No need for stutters and embarrassment."

"You can see her?"

Craig glanced beside him and then back at me again. "Of course," he gushed. "She said she knows you."

"Yeah." But I had left Claire back with Matthew and Amelia. How had she come ahead of me and found Craig already? We weren't apart for long enough. Here she was, all friendly with him. And how was he able to see her now when he wasn't before? "Why are you two here together?" I asked Craig. "We've been looking for you."

"I've been talking to Claire." He pushed his glasses up on his face.

"Yeah? About what?"

"We need to stay here."

"Stay where?" Was he talking about this room we were in? It wasn't a very big room. There were no doors that I could see, except the one I had come through—the one we needed to go back through to return to Matthew and Amelia. "We can't stay here. The others are waiting for us."

"I don't want to wake up anymore. I like it here."

"What are you talking about? Have you lost your mind?"

"This place is better than the real world," Claire spoke up. She let go of Craig so she could come closer to me. "Can't you see that?"

"We can't stay in a dream world." I looked past her to talk to Craig. "We need to wake up. There are giant spiders here and fire and an empty school." I was ready to get back to the people I loved. Mostly one person, but I had friends at SMA, too. Not to mention the school itself; I believed in what they were trying to teach us.

"We can be happy here, Destiny," Claire pleaded. "We can be together again." Claire held her hand out to me. "Don't you want to be with me anymore?"

"Of course I do." I had once loved Claire. Of course I didn't want her to be dead. But wanting it didn't make it reality.

"Destiny!" Linnie's voice called out, more clearly than ever before. "Destiny, wake up!"

"That's Linnie," I gasped. "Did you hear her?" I asked Craig.

"I didn't hear anything," he denied. Either he was lying or this place was making him crazy. Both were very real possibilities.

"Linnie," I screamed. If I could hear her, maybe she would hear me. The wall in front of me shimmered, and a door suddenly appeared out of nowhere. "That's our way out," I declared, sure of it. "Let's go, Craig."

"No!" Claire rushed forward and clutched her hand around my wrist. "You can't leave me here alone."

"You're not even real!"

"How can you say that?" she whimpered. "I'm real." She brushed her fingers across my cheek. "Doesn't that feel real?"

"I have to get back to Linnie."

"No, you don't." She shook her head. "She's fine. She has plenty of people back at the school. I have no one."

"I'm not staying here." I pried Claire off of my arm. "I choose Linnie. I want to be wherever she is. Please, Claire, you have to let me go."

"I don't want you to go." A tear made its way slowly down her pretty face.

"Why don't we go find Matthew and Amelia?" Craig suggested. "We can find them, and all of us can stay here."

"No." I took a step toward the door. "If we wake up, we'll be free of this place."

Amelia said to get out of here, we had to find an artifact. I wasn't sure what we were exactly looking for, but I knew for sure it was behind that door. It didn't make any sense that Craig was trying to stay here. He hated this place, with all the fires burning. He didn't want to stay.

Everything was starting to get foggy, like I was looking in the bathroom mirror after a really hot shower. My head felt heavy, and my hands were shaking. What was happening to me?

I tried to keep my focus on Craig, but he kept changing forms. One second he was himself and the next he had the head of a dragon.

"Are you all right?" he asked me, his voice warped and devoid of concern. "Let's go find somewhere to lie down."

"No." I pushed his hands away. "I'm going to find Linnie. If you don't want to come, I'll go by myself."

"You are not going to walk through that door." Claire's face changed from pleading to angry in a flash. "I'm not going to let you go that easily."

"Claire."

"It might have been easy for you to move on to some new pretty thing but how do you think I feel? I'm always going to be stuck here alone because you left me to die."

"I didn't..." Tears stung the corners of my eyes. "I didn't leave you to die. It wasn't my fault."

"Wasn't your fault?" she barked out cruelly. "I called your name when the hunters were burning my flesh. Didn't you hear me calling you?"

"I heard you." The tears fell one by one, tears that I had held back for so many years. "I heard you, but I was too afraid. I'm so sorry, Claire. I was afraid, so I stayed hidden."

"And now you're trying to run away again?"

"I'm not running away." I hurried forward and collected both her hands into mine. "I'm not running away from you. I'm running back to her. You have to let me go."

"No."

"You've been holding onto me for so long." It was time for both of us to let go. "I will *never* forget you, but I have found someone else who I love."

"I'm not letting you go." She twisted her hands free of my grasp so she could hold onto my wrists again. "I would rather you die here than go back to living a happy life with her."

Everything went quiet with her words. Craig was gone now, and it was just the two of us in the hallway, a few feet from the shimmering door. This was my nightmare come to life—facing Claire again, knowing she would be angry with me.

But then I realized, with an absolution that made me brave. "You're not Claire," I growled out through clenched teeth. "You were never her."

"Yes, I am."

I shook my head wildly. "She loved me, and I loved her, and I miss her so much but you," I took her hands off of me, "are not Claire." Using both hands, I shoved against her chest as hard as I could. She fell to the ground, her mouth opened wide in shock. Then she was gone. Just like that.

"What the fuck was that?" a small voice squeaked out. I looked up to see Craig rounding a corner. That opening hadn't been there just a second ago.

"If you've come to talk me into staying again..."

"Staying where?" He looked around us to the door. "Where did that door come from? I've been up and down this damn hallway, and there was never a door here."

"What?"

"And where did you come from?"

"Were you just here with Claire?"

"Who?"

That wasn't him. Of course it wasn't him.

"Listen, I think we should go through here. You think this might be the way out?" Craig hopped over to the door and examined it more closely.

"What about the others?" I had told them I would be right back. How long ago had that been now?

"No, we don't want to get lost again. Let's just wake up, and it'll save us all."

Is that how it worked, though? I felt numb, like I wanted to lie down and sleep. Who took a nap in their dream? "Yeah, you're probably right."

"I am right."

"I feel really weak all of a sudden." I put one hand to my forehead. "I don't know what's happened to me." I wasn't very good at being weak.

"I'll help you, don't worry." Craig put his arm around my waist and led me forward, one shaking step at a time until we were face to face with the door.

There was no handle that I could see. "Is there...like a magic word we have to say?"

I was forced to lean more heavily on Craig as a wave of dizziness washed over me.

"Do you know any magic?" he scoffed.

"I think we have to walk through it."

Craig turned sharply to look at me. "Are you sure?"

"No."

"Good enough for me." He shrugged, then pulled me through the door with him.

It was like walking through the fire again, all warm and cozy. I didn't have a lot of experience with magic, but this must be it. The riddle did warn us that magic would be trying to hide whatever it was we were looking for. I didn't think it would be so obvious though.

Once on the other side, my strength came back just as suddenly as it had been depleted.

"I think I'm okay now," I told Craig, pushing myself away from him. "Thanks for not leaving me back there."

"You would have done the same for me." He laughed nervously.

"Maybe."

We were outside of the tower, all hallways and hidden doors gone. There was no fire here and no giant creatures bent on killing us. It was just a clear sky filled with bright stars that seemed close enough to hold.

"We're up on a tower," Craig said, leaning over the edge and peering down. "But I don't think we're inside the school anymore."

"That door must have been some sort of hidden passageway." That's why the object wasn't on the other tower. It wasn't the highest point. But Amelia didn't know about this place. She wouldn't be able to find it on her own. Hopefully she would wake up with us.

"Here it is," Craig said softly, pointing to a ledge along the tower.

A thin metal object sat there, looking mostly like an ordinary candle stick. It didn't have a hole to put the candle inside of, but nothing here made sense. I was done being surprised.

"Are we just supposed to grab it then?"

"I guess." Craig shrugged his shoulders glumly. After all we had been through to get here, a broken candlestick seemed anticlimactic.

"All right." I sighed heavily. "I'll see you on the other side then?"

"That's the plan."

"On the count of three."

"One."

"Two."

"Three."

I woke up gasping and choking on the air. My chest burned like there was an actual fire inside my lungs.

"Wh...where am I?" I sputtered. I tried to sit up, but there was something tying me to the bed I lay on. Machines beeped next to my head, loud and annoying machines.

Over the sound of my own panicked breathing, I could make out other things around me—things that didn't make sense. Someone crying outside, a person sleeping in a nearby bed, the gentle drip of some sort of liquid.

I was in the hospital, I realized. And I could hear again. Did that mean...?

I turned my head on the pillow. Next to the bed were

machines that were attached to tubes—which were attached to me. My body felt heavy, but my mind felt clear. My eyes slid closed as a wave of nausea hit. There was something important I wanted to remember, but it was fading too quickly to hold onto.

When my eyes opened again, they fell upon a sleeping form in the chair next to me. Her head was resting on the edge of the bed and partially on my arm. Red hair billowed out all around her like a halo made of fire.

Linnie.

Was this real?

"You're awake." A woman walked briskly into the room with a clipboard in her hands. "We were beginning to wonder when you would wake up."

"I was sleeping?"

"You could say that." She glanced quickly down at the papers she had. "How do you feel?"

Of course I was sleeping. I scowled. I had been dreaming this whole time. I knew it was a dream; why was I so surprised now? "How long?"

"Destiny." Linnie woke with a start, my name already on her lips before her eyes even opened. "You woke up!" In her usual enthusiastic flare, she kissed my forehead, cheeks, chin—anywhere she could find skin. "I was so worried about you."

"I've already warned you," the woman wagged her finger at Linnie disapprovingly, "if you can't control yourself, you'll have to wait outside."

"She's fine." I giggled. "I don't mind."

"Nevertheless," she frowned severely, "she will have to behave if she expects to stay."

"How long have I been sleeping?" I asked again, looking at Linnie for an answer.

"Six days." She pouted. "I was so worried."

Six days? We were in there for six days? It only seemed like a day to me. But the others had said they were in the hallway for longer. That reminded me.

"What about the others? Are they awake now?"

The nurse raised one eyebrow sharply but didn't reply. She

didn't need to. Craig came in the room then, limping and looking pale.

"I heard you were awake," he said awkwardly.

"Who told you?" I had only been awake for ten minutes, if that.

"Thin walls."

"Matthew and Amelia?"

Craig shook his head. Next to me, Linnie squeezed my hand tightly in hers.

Two weeks later

"What do you think is happening to them?" I asked softly, brushing my fingers along the palm of Amelia's hand.

So far since I had woken up, the school's doctors and experts had been doing a thousand tests on Craig and me. Apparently, the artifact we had been assigned to find carried a heavy curse on it. Our team had both passed and failed the task.

We found the artifact but failed to break the curse completely.

I remembered now, getting assigned to work with Matthew, Amelia, and Craig in our ITF class. We'd been working on The Hunt mission. We were all four top students; the nightmare that we were trapped inside had made us weak but didn't defeat us.

"Do you think they're together in there?"

"They must be," Craig murmured.

"Do you think they'll find the door?"

"I think the curse must be broken from our end first. Addie has the stick now."

"We shouldn't have left them."

"We didn't leave them." He sighed. "We just found the right door before they did."

"Mmm. . ." I nodded slowly. However Craig chose to look at it, I couldn't see it as a happy ending. I was back with Linnie but with new guilt to deal with.

"See you tomorrow?" He moved his head to take in Linnie, who had just ducked into the room.

"Same time." I smiled tightly. Even if I couldn't help them

inside the nightmare, I could sit with their sleeping forms at the hospital. Maybe if they could hear my voice, it would help lead them out.

♠

"I can tell you're worried," Linnie scrunched her nose up. "I wish there was something I could do to help."

I studied our intertwined fingers, feeling the warmth that her touch gave me. "When I was stuck in there, I heard you calling to me," I told her. "I think that's what led me to the way out. I can't leave them there all alone."

"Try not to worry." She squeezed my hand. "There's a lot of people here who know magic. We'll figure it out."

I didn't have her confidence though. SMA wasn't the only place that knew magic; and some people didn't use it for good. Matthew and Amelia might be lost forever in that nightmare world.

"Why don't we get some lunch," she wiggled her eyebrows my way, "and then go back to your room?"

"My room?" I frowned down at her. "I thought you didn't like my room?"

"Yeah well..." She rose up on her tiptoes to press her lips to mine. "I'm feeling a little daring today."

"Whatever." I wrapped my arms around her waist and pulled her close to me. "I'm sure we can find some secluded place in the forest to make out."

"Who said anything about making out?" she cried in mock indignation. "You're so bad, Destiny Nelson."

I laughed out loud, the sound coming out and filling the air. It felt nice to laugh again, even for just a little bit.

"Destiny," someone called, running over to us. I recognized Eryx, who also lived in Modi, but I had no idea why he was seeking me out.

"What's wrong?" I immediately moved in front of Linnie.

"Addie wants to see you," he panted, holding onto his side.

"Why?"

"No idea." He shrugged, then was off again as quickly as he had appeared.

"Guess we'll have to make out later," I grumbled, dropping a kiss on Linnie's forehead before I, too, hurried away.

When I found her, Addie was perched on a window ledge, letting her long legs dangle in front of her. Although she invited me to sit next to her, I chose to lean against a sturdy table inside the room instead.

"Eryx said you wanted to see me...?" I started, hesitantly. It wasn't like Addie struck fear in my heart, but I hadn't talked to her very many times. In fact, the last time we spoke, it was to give her that cursed artifact and to tell her that Matthew and Amelia were still trapped. Did she call me here to expel me? I had failed to save them. What good was a guardian who couldn't get the job done?

"We haven't really had a chance to talk since you came back." She smiled gently in my direction. A warm sensation flowed through me. "You haven't been going to classes?"

"I've been at the hospital," I grunted. The idea of going back to that ITF class without half of my team was unbearable.

"Do you remember now, where you found that?" She nodded toward the candlestick type object on the table, the same object that I had been trying to avoid.

"Amelia called it a wand." I swallowed hard. I did remember now. We had been given the Ace of Wands card in our ITF class as part of a semester-long project. I didn't know what it was, but Amelia seemed to know a great deal about tarot cards.

"This card is so beautiful," she exclaimed, delight brightening her face.

"What is it?" Craig scowled, pulling the card away from her so he could peer more closely at it. "It looks like a candlestick to me." He shrugged. "And is that a dragon?"

"It's not a candlestick." Amelia clicked her tongue impatiently. "Don't you know anything?"

Fuck, this was going to be a long semester.

"Let me see it," I demanded. It was pretty enough, even if it didn't mean much to me. A stick that could have been a wand took up most of the card's face. All around it, in swirls of blue and purple, was a

tornado of seemingly random things. A dragon, a lion, a moon, a raven...

"Does anyone know what it means?" Matthew asked, turning the card over to read the back.

"It represents that the mind and body are closely linked. Or that a new spiritual influence is coming into one's life," Amelia said. She wriggled her eyebrows mysteriously.

"I meant the poem." Matthew jabbed the back of the card.

"We should pay attention to this," Amelia stubbornly continued. "It's definitely a clue."

"Our mind and body are linked?" Craig laughed out loud. "Do you want us all to sit on the ground and meditate?"

"You can laugh all you want, but there is a reason we got this card. It means something."

"Maybe." I read the words of the poem over Matthew's shoulder. "But I think we should focus on this part. It might lead us to the actual artifact that we're supposed to be finding."

I regretted being so hasty now, of course. If only we had taken the time to figure out the curse, maybe we wouldn't have ended up in that nightmare. Maybe Amelia and Matthew wouldn't still be suffering. Instead, as soon as our fingers slid onto the cool metal of that stick, we were lost in our own heads. Our minds and bodies were indeed linked—more than we realized.

"I've been thinking." I ran my tongue over my lips. "I want to go back and find Amelia and Matthew."

"I'm afraid that's out of the question," Addie said.

"I never should have left them."

"I don't know if that's true or not." Considering that two students were lying in a deep comma, maybe forever, she didn't seem concerned enough. "I don't think the curse works like that, though. If you were to touch the wand now . . . who knows where you would end up? I doubt it would be with Amelia and Matthew."

Before she said the words out loud, I knew it would be impossible. "So what do I do now?"

"Go back to class." Her lips pursed. "You and Craig can work on the rest of the missions alone until the others wake up."

"What if they don't wake up?"

"You did," she said bluntly. "Since you were able to save yourself, there is no reason to think they won't be able to do the same. It's not your responsibility to save everyone, Destiny."

"Ugh." I threw my head back and stared at the rocky space above our heads. True to my promise to Addie, I was heading back to classes today. But I didn't want to. "ITF is going to suck," I grumbled.

Between sips of her coffee, Linnie patted my knee affectionately. Across the crowded courtyard, Fin and her boyfriend Joe were wrapped up in each other as if no one else was here. As soon as I looked away from them, Cat came into my line of sight, but only for the briefest of moments. Timber Greenwood sauntered past, holding a cup with brown liquid sloshing around inside.

It was good to see that Timber and Paisley had recovered from the curse their own Hunt put on them. Maybe that meant we would be okay, too. And, I reminded myself, Elliana's team lost two people, but they came back. So there was a chance Matthew and Amelia would do the same.

Life was indeed moving on at SMA—with or without us.

Leaving Linnie there with her coffee, I got up and began that long walk to my first class. No matter what, I needed to get back into the swing of things. It was either that or drop out; and I was never going to quit. That just wasn't going to happen.

Just past the courtyard, Craig cut me off. "You have to come to the hospital," he said without preamble. "They're awake."

"It's a good thing you didn't come back from that room after you went to look for Craig." Amelia giggled brightly. For someone who had just spent the last couple of weeks in a coma, she had no right to look that happy. "We wouldn't have been there."

"What happened to you two?" Craig asked the question before I could.

"We were alone in that fucking hallway." Matthew shuddered. "One of the spiders got in, so we didn't have a choice but to run."

"Run where?" I squeezed Amelia's hand.

"We managed to get outside again," he started.

"And then we just ran back through the forest," Amelia picked up. "On the other side of the trees was a stream."

"As soon as we crossed the stream," Matthew smacked his hands together, "we were back here."

"Just like that?" Craig's eyebrows slid together on his forehead.

"Like Sadie Angrec." I nodded, as if I had known all along that they would be fine. "She was trapped behind that door in the library and then just reappeared in the woods."

"Well, we did have to run through a fake forest with a giant bird chasing us and fire burning everywhere." Amelia grinned. "But yeah, just like that."

"I'm so glad you guys are back." Craig reclined in his seat and propped his feet on the edge of Amelia's bed. "We have to do an entire presentation on weapons next."

"And I'm in charge," I growled.

"Wow." Matthew threw himself backward on his own bed. "So glad we were missed."

As the two boys bickered over which weapons we would use—which I would be the one to choose—I turned to Amelia. "You were right about the card, you know."

"Which part?"

"Mostly all of it." I rolled my eyes. "But I'm talking about the spiritual influence."

"Meaning?"

"While we were there," my tongue glided across my bottom lip, "I saw the ghost of my first girlfriend. She died because I couldn't save her."

"That's not true." Amelia's eyes twinkled.

"I know she wasn't actually there," I conceded, "but I did see her ghost."

"I mean, that's not why she died." Her eyes bore into mine, keeping me prisoner there. "She died because a hunter killed her. It had nothing to do with you. You wouldn't have been able to save her—no matter what you did."

"How do you know what happened to her?" I whispered.

"I'm a dream walker." She scrunched her nose. "I saw it all inside your dream."

"Destiny." Craig tapped lightly against my leg. "They're kicking us out."

Madame Roth stood in the doorway with her arms crossed and a pointed look on her face.

"We have to get to class anyway." I stood up quickly. "We'll come back to see you guys later," I promised before ducking back out of the room.

Linnie was waiting for me outside the infirmary, a huge mug in her pretty hands. "You forgot your coffee," she sang out. "Hurry up, I'll walk you to class."

"Your girlfriend is so…"

"Seriously, Craig," I warned him, "if you want to live, you better not finish that sentence."

"Nice," he finished lamely. "I was going to say she was nice for bringing you coffee."

"Mmm-hmm." Not sparing him a glance, I ran to join Linnie. "Thank you." I smiled widely. Acutely aware of Craig still watching us, I didn't kiss her the way I longed to. Instead, I laced my fingers with hers and let her walk me to my class.

TWO OF CUPS

ROSE GARCIA

When the world has you feeling not quite like yourself, remember to stay true to who you really are!

CHAPTER 1

The stillness in the library filled Infiniti's ears like wads of cotton, and she didn't like it. She thrived on sound and commotion, preferring it over peace and quiet because noise distracted her thoughts, but she had left her earbuds in her room. Without something for her mind to hold on to, she often got lost in worry, anxiety, and fear. Plus, the library freaked her out. Dark and mysterious, with floating orbs for light and moving shelves and walkways, the place gave her the creeps. She shuddered, forcing her mind off the spooky vibe, and tried her hardest to focus on her Interdisciplinary Task Force class.

She hated that class.

Instead of referring to it as ITF like everyone else, she had personally dubbed it WTF because half the time she didn't know what in the world was going on in there. With different professors teaching various subjects on different days and in different classrooms, she often found herself not remembering what to prepare for and when. Even her planner needed a planner. But the worst part of WTF was being randomly assigned to a team with lightning bird Dingane Gazini, or D; Unseelie fae Cole Silver; and fellow Transhuman Cat Vega. All type-A personalities with chips on their shoulders the size of Texas, they argued over every freakin' thing. Most assignments left her exhausted and drained, especially since she was still learning so much about the supernatural world and the people at SMA.

Like Cole. He had fair skin, making his black hair and sea glass green eyes pop in the most striking way. He was also quiet and observant but held his ground whenever something mattered to him. As an Unseelie fae, he was part of the dark and malevolent side of the fae, but he wasn't just a regular Unseelie. He was a Gancanagh and excreted a skin toxin deadly to human women. He had even killed a couple of girls and had almost killed his ex-girlfriend, Paisley. At first, Infiniti freaked about being in a group with him, but quickly learned that he wore a metal bracelet made from a special ore found only in Faerie to neutralize the poison. Still, she kept her distance, just in case.

D, the lightning bird, or Impundulu, had dark skin, with dark hair and eyes. His kind were known to be malevolent with vampiric and shape-shifting qualities. He had alluded to doing some horrible things in his past, but was working on pursuing a better life. During her hourglass challenge last semester, he had transformed to help her. Infiniti would never forget the sight of D spreading his magnificent black and white feathers and later careening to the ground and landing with a thud when her powers accidentally froze over half of the student body. That terrifying image was etched forever in Infiniti's brain, and she hoped to never have to go through something like that again.

The final person on the team was Cat. The Latina Transhuman had a killer bod and attitude for days. She had tried to steal Joe from Infiniti fall semester. But after Infiniti overcame her hourglass challenge, she and Cat had come to an understanding. Joe was hers, and Cat needed to back off. Even though they had come out of that ordeal on amicable terms, Cat wasn't exactly her favorite person. Overly competitive and full of herself, Cat didn't play well with others. In fact, the entire team lacked cohesiveness. Everyone wanted to take charge and prove their stuff, except for Infiniti. She just wanted to finish the class with a C.

"Cs get degrees," she mumbled.

"Babe, stop. You're gonna do better than a C in WTF. I know it," Joe whispered from across the table

He set aside his laptop and gave her his full attention. His blond hair had grown out some, hanging slightly into his sexy blue-green eyes. His shirt hugged his sculpted arms and chest in the most perfect way. And ever since they had returned to school for the spring semester as a newly engaged couple, they hadn't been able to keep their hands off each other. He was her biggest distraction, and she wanted to be with him all the time. And he with her. But with the end of the school year in sight, they had decided to focus on their classes. For Infiniti, that meant prioritizing WTF above anything else since it was her lowest grade.

She blew out, making a raspberry sound with her lips. "I don't know. Every assignment has been hell. And with The Hunt mission next, I'm not feeling all that confident. It's been so hard for all the other teams, and they're way more together than we are."

She let her head fall back as she stared at the darkness that shrouded the cave-like ceiling, thinking they'd never be able to find a hidden object solely with the help of a tarot card—the Two of Cups. She knew nothing about tarot cards.

"When are you guys starting the mission?"

"Tomorrow night after everyone's finished with class. We're supposed to pick our team leader and then come up with a game plan."

She brought her attention back to Joe, realizing that with the mission starting, she probably wouldn't be able to see much of him until they finished. And right there in that moment, she craved some time with her wolf shifter.

She slipped off her sneaker, stretched out her leg, and nestled her toes between his legs. Joe sprang to life under her foot while a look of surprise gave way to fiery desire. She loved the way he devoured her with just a glance.

She bit her lower lip while heat crept up her cheeks. "I think I need a study break."

He grabbed her foot and pressed it against himself. "I could use a break right about now, too."

"Good," Infiniti said, hoping her roomie might be gone for a while. "I'll text Taylor."

Joe whipped out his phone. "I'll text Kase."

Before either one of them could get a response, Cat strolled up to their table. Her hair was pulled up in her regular high pony, ruby red lipstick covered her lips, and her cleavage was bursting out of her tight V-neck leather shirt.

"Hey, Fin," she said in her thick Spanish accent, drawing out the *i* as if it were two *ee*'s. She barely looked at Joe, but gave a slight nod in his direction.

Totally busted with her foot on Joe's crotch, Infiniti lowered her leg ever so slowly and cleared her throat, hoping Cat hadn't notice. "Um, hey, Cat."

"I know our team is meeting tomorrow to start work on The Hunt mission, but I thought maybe we could talk about something really quick. Since you're here in the library and I am, too."

Joe placed his phone face down next to his laptop. He eyed Infiniti. "My idea isn't going to work."

Glancing at her phone, Infiniti saw that her plan wouldn't work either. Taylor had texted, saying she was in the room catching up on some reading.

"Same," she said to Joe.

With an eyebrow lifted, Cat looked from Infiniti to Joe. She placed her hands on her hips. "Well? Can I talk to you, Fin?"

"Yeah...sure," Infiniti agreed. "Of course."

Moving his things aside, Joe rose to his feet. "I need to stretch anyway. Be back in a few."

Infiniti pulled her long, wavy dark hair behind her ears and sat up straight as Cat took Joe's seat.

"What's up?"

Never one to beat around the bush, Cat got straight to it. "I want to be the leader for The Hunt mission, and I want you to back me."

"Oh," Infiniti said, taking a second to consider her request.

The team always had a hard time selecting their project leaders. Mostly because Cole, D, and Cat always wanted to be in charge. As for Infiniti, she couldn't care less. Plus, as things stood, they had each served as team captain equally so far. So why not throw her support at Cat and let the three of them duke it out? It might be fun to watch.

"Yeah, okay. Fine by me."

"Thanks, Chica."

"But you might want to be ready for a fight," Infiniti added. "This is our biggest project of the semester. I'm pretty sure the guys will want to take lead, too."

Cat smirked, muttered something in Spanish, then added, "Leave them to me."

"Okayyy."

Cat sauntered away from the table, and Infiniti eyed her swaying hips. She thought of Cole and D. Even though Cole and Paisley had broken up, Paisley had moved on to Timber, and Cole was single, something told her Cole wouldn't fall for whatever Cat had in mind. So the only guy Cat had any chance of manipulating was probably D. He was completely unattached. Infiniti chuckled to herself, thinking the lightning bird had no idea what was coming at him.

"What's so funny?" Joe asked, sliding back in his seat.

"Well, Cat is on the prowl, and I think D is her target."

Joe glanced over his shoulder at Cat. "Better him than me."

With their rooms unavailable for a "study break," she and Joe continued with their homework. But all the while, Infiniti kept thinking about the tarot card they'd been given for their hunt on the first day of class. When they first drew it, they had no idea what it was. Later, with Natalie Putman's help, they had at least figured out it was the Two of Cups. Even though the team had good intentions of working on the card the last few months, none of them had gotten around to it. But with the semester going by so quickly, they decided it was too big of an assignment to put off any longer.

"What is it now? You've got a frowny worried face."

She rubbed her forehead. "I'm thinking about the mission. That's all."

"Babe, you guys are gonna kill it. I know it."

She eased up. "You're right. I mean, nothing can be worse than last semester's hourglass challenge. Right?"

CHAPTER 2

A blaring buzz jarred Infiniti out of a deep sleep. She slammed her hand on her alarm clock and closed her eyes, slipping back into her dreams. She and Joe were swimming in a beautiful crystal-clear blue lagoon. The cool water lapped against their bodies. The brilliant sun shone down on them, caressing their skin with rays of energetic warmth. She wrapped her legs around Joe's waist and her arms around his neck, gazing into his seductive eyes that sparkled like priceless jewels.

"Your eyes illuminate like a kaleidoscope when the sun is shining on them." She threaded her fingers through his wet hair. "Like majestic emeralds with flecks of yellow and blue."

He kissed her lips softly. "And yours are like pools of amber with fiery sparks of gold." He held her closer. "Sparks that drive me crazy with desire."

She pressed against him and moaned. "I want you so bad right now."

"Then have me." He moved his hands up her back, undoing her bikini top, when something hard smacked her face.

"Fin!" Taylor hollered. "You're going to be late!"

"Wh-wh-what?" She cracked an eyelid and saw Taylor in her yoga gear. She must've just come back from her morning workout. And that's when stark realization set in. She had hit the snooze button and fallen back asleep! She bolted upright, and the pillow

Taylor had thrown at her slid down her chest. She whipped her head at her alarm clock. It was 7:30, and her WTF class that morning was in fifteen minutes. She wasn't gonna make it!

"Oh my god, Taylor! I can't be late!" WTF had strict rules on tardiness, and so far she'd been able to make it to every class on time. But this time, there was no way.

Taylor tossed her gym bag on the floor. "Here, let me help you!"

Infiniti scrambled to her feet, and Taylor grabbed her slim shoulders, holding her in place. "Be still, okay? This is a new spell."

"Yeah, yeah. Okay." And then she gulped. *A new spell?*

Taylor had been flexing her witchy muscles all semester with new spells. Sometimes they worked; other times they didn't. And even though Infiniti didn't want to accidentally be turned into a frog, or get obliterated on the spot, she needed help.

"You can do it, Taylor. I believe in you." She blew out and relaxed her shoulders. "Just get me ready. Easy peasy."

Taylor stepped back. She pursed her lips, wrinkled her tiny pierced nose, and held out her wand. She muttered a rhyming sentence under her breath, then flicked her wrist.

Infiniti's pajamas vanished, replaced with jeans, shoes, and a bra. But no shirt!

"Oh shit, sorry!" Taylor grabbed a shirt from a pile near Infiniti's bed and tossed it at her. "Here!"

She caught it with a swipe, pulled it on, and grabbed her backpack. "Hey," she added, thinking of the long trek to class. "Think you can you zap me to class?"

"That might be too risky."

"You're right. I got it. Thanks, Taylor!"

Infiniti bolted from the room. Taking the exterior stairs that wrapped around Jory Tower, she started running her fingers through her tousled hair when she realized it wasn't its usual crazy mess. Taylor's spell must've combed her hair for her. Then she ran her tongue over her teeth, realizing they were smooth and clean. She cupped her hand around her mouth and blew out. Her morning breath was gone, replaced with minty freshness. Damn, Taylor had skills! But Infiniti still had to pee. She thought she could hold it until she got to class.

She dodged around others who were also late, weaved her way around the stalagmites that dotted the path from Jory to Eirhal until she finally stumbled into the potion's lab of Professor Parker —the location for WTF that day.

The class looked like a regular science lab...for a supernatural college. Long metal tables lined both sides of the room and floating cauldrons hovered over each one. Shelves with all kinds of herbs and magical ingredients filled the back wall. The thick aroma of dirt and leaves permeated the air. She spotted her team right away at a table up front. Luckily, there was no sign of Professor Parker.

She slammed her stuff down with a kerplunk. "Gotta pee! Be right back!"

With her legs practically crossed, she made a beeline to the restroom, did her business in a flash, and then hurried back to class. Seeing Professor Parker still hadn't showed up, she let out a huge breath and slumped over onto the cold metal table, thinking it felt good against her flushed cheek.

"Oh my god," she rasped between gulping breaths. "I ran for like ten minutes straight."

Cole did a double take. "You can't run for ten minutes?"

She narrowed her eyes at the disapproving fae, trying to come up with something clever to say, when D chimed in.

"Fin, come on," D chided. "Ten minutes is nothing."

"Hey, my legs have to work twice as hard as y'all's because you three are abnormally tall. Like, circus freaks. So yeah, a ten-minute run is a big deal for me."

"It shouldn't be," Cat added with a raised brow.

Even though she knew they were mostly joking, she was starting to feel a little attacked. Luckily, Professor Parker glided in, silencing the class. She was a fifty-year-old looking witch with brown hair shaped in a perfectly sleek bob. She wore a short cropped pink jacket and a perfectly ironed black pencil skirt. She scanned the class with a twinkle in her eye.

"A lively bunch today, I see. Or, should I say, I hear." She placed her things on a small wooden desk at the front of the room. "Let's get started. As most of you know, I'm Professor Parker, and I teach Potions. Today I'll be condensing and highlighting important things for you to know as part of the ITF inaugural class. Those who've already taken Potions will have an advantage over those who have not. And the witches in the room, even more so. Therefore, I'm allowing open collaboration on the assignment you'll be receiving at the end of today's session. All work is due Friday. No extensions will be given, so I suggest you all pay attention."

Infiniti pulled her notebook out of her backpack as her stomach sank. "Great. The Hunt mission and now this."

Cole didn't seem worried at all. "We got this, Fin."

Picking up her pen, she noticed how close Cat and D were sitting, their stools practically touching. It seemed Cat's efforts to get D's support for team leader were working because he didn't seem to mind her long legs pressed against his. Then again, would any guy mind? Cat oozed with sexiness.

For the next hour, Infiniti took copious notes on herbs, recipes, ingredients, mixtures, brewing potions, storing potions, and even administering potions. Trying to wrap her head around the nuances and with her brain ready to explode, Infiniti tried to keep up as Professor Parker started talking about each team's assignment.

"Whoa," Infiniti muttered, dropping her pen. "Class is over?"

Cat stretched her arms and pulled her fingers. "That was intense."

"I don't even think Professor Parker stopped to breathe," Cole chimed in.

Right on cue, Professor Parker came up to their table holding a small black cauldron.

"I took a few strategic breaths," she said with a smile. She held out the cauldron. "Now, pick your assignment."

Cat, D, and Cole reached at the same time, their hands colliding midair. Keeping her hand held out, Cat eyed D and Cole until they gave up and lowered theirs. Cat sifted through the contents then pulled out a folded piece of paper. She opened it.

"Healing."

"Ah, very good." Professor Parker nodded. "The particulars are up to your team, so long as I have a healing potion by Friday. And before you ask, this is separate from the detoxifying potion you have to make for one of your missions."

The professor moved along, and the team started gathering their stuff. D eyed the paper Cat had placed on the table.

"A healing potion sounds fairly easy," he said. "How about we put it off until after we complete The Hunt mission?"

"I was thinking the opposite," Cat replied. "I say we knock it out tonight and then focus on the hunt."

Cole seemed disinterested. "I'm fine with whatever."

Infiniti's stomach grumbled as she thought of meeting Joe for breakfast. "Same, I'll do whatever. But let's hurry and decide 'cause I gotta go."

"I know," Cat offered. "How about we do both. We can work on The Hunt tonight, starting with picking our leader, and then we can work on the potion tomorrow. Back and forth like that until we finish. ¿Está bien?"

D nodded. "Sounds good to me."

Not really seeing why Cat's method wouldn't work, Infiniti agreed. "Sure, fine with me."

Cole slung his backpack over his shoulder. "Fine with me, too. What time are we meeting tonight? And where?"

Cat slipped her backpack on. The weight made her posture straighter than normal, forcing her boobs to stand at the ready. Armed and dangerous. "Ten o'clock. Heimdall study lounge. Top floor."

With the group dispersing, Infiniti's appetite kicked into overdrive, along with her desire to see Joe. From Eirhal, she took the sky bridge to the quad that connected to Halstein. Pulling open the doors, she walked through the archway. The aroma of all things delicious and savory filled her nose as she crossed the open area of the student union and approached the dining hall in the back. She spotted Joe waiting for her, and her heart fluttered. She slowed her pace so she could study him for a second. Tall, muscular, perfectly dreamy, and all hers, he was casually scanning the crowd when he shifted to face her direction. With laser focus, his gaze swept over to hers.

Her heart melted. She had no idea exactly how he sensed her, but he did. He always did. And she loved it.

He came up to her with a swift stride, his mouth formed into a perfect smile. "Hey, beautiful."

"Hey," she said, resting her hands on his chest and lifting herself up on her toes for a kiss. Everyone and everything around them faded away whenever they were together, and their small peck quickly turned into a make-out session.

"Get a room!" someone hollered.

She laughed against Joe's mouth. "Maybe I should use my powers and freeze everyone in here so we can do whatever we want."

"I wish. But I got class after we eat. Remember?"

She let out a soft groan. "Yeah, I remember."

He tugged her along. "Come on."

They sat close together side by side while they ate, and Infiniti filled Joe in on the potions lesson, confessing her worry over their team being able to handle the potions assignment *and* The Hunt mission.

"This week is gonna suck so hard." She sighed.

Joe pushed their finished trays away and angled toward Infiniti. "I know, babe. But think of it this way. When it's over, there'll only be about a month left of school. We'll be in the home stretch."

Infiniti could hardly believe their first year at SMA would be finished sooner than later. She wanted nothing more than to escape the gloom and shadow of the mountain and get back outside where there was fresh air and sunshine. Visits to Clifftop and occasionally to Havenwood Falls weren't cutting it anymore.

"The sun," she murmured, remembering her dream of swimming with Joe in a blue lagoon. Her eyes grew wide.

"The sun?" he asked.

She scooted closer to him. "Let's get away, Joe. After finals. Let's go somewhere tropical with amazing white sands and crystal-clear water and tons of sunshine. Just the two of us."

He traced her hands with his fingers, spinning her diamond engagement ring around her slim finger, and smiled. "I think that's an amazing idea."

"Really? You do?"

"Of course. But we can only be gone for twenty-eight days because of the memory wards around Havenwood Falls. But that's plenty of time for us to have a nice," he kissed her lips, "relaxing," he kissed her lips again, "romantic getaway."

"With *no* interruptions."

He leaned forward, nibbled on her ear, and whispered. "None. And I can ravage you all day and all night if you want."

She shivered with desire. "Oh, I want."

Kase, Joe's best friend and fellow wolf shifter, came up to them. "Hey, Joe. Hey, Fin." He clapped Joe on the back. "I'm heading for class. You ready?"

Joe pulled away from Infiniti and lowered his arms. Of course, Infiniti knew why, his bulge was back. Infiniti forced herself to not laugh out loud.

"Um," Joe said. "You go ahead, dude. I'll be right there."

"Okay. See you guys."

Infiniti leaned into him and whispered against his ear. "You want me that bad?"

He smiled and shifted in his seat. "Babe, stop."

She pulled away with a laugh. "Okay. Let's talk about something really boring for a minute while you, you know, forget about the ravaging me thing."

After a quick chat about the weather, Joe was on his way. But Infiniti's head stayed in the clouds as she drifted her way from Halstein Hall to her room in Jory Tower, daydreaming about being alone with Joe in a tropical paradise.

Flopping on her bed, she stared at the magical moon mural that sprawled across her ceiling. With her thoughts finally in check, she moved to her desk and dove into homework, looking up anything and everything on the Two of Cups. And when it was almost ten, she made her way to Heimdall for her first Hunt mission meeting. She hoped it would go okay.

CHAPTER 3

$\mathscr{H}$eimdall had the weirdest shape of all the towers—wide at the bottom, narrow at the middle, then wide again at the top. But the size of the bottom meant it also had a huge common room when you walked in. Probably the biggest of all the towers. With a dark and moody vibe with hues of soft yellow lighting, it was a great place to chill. Shelves filled with all kinds of books lined the perimeter. Chairs, couches, and tables were set up throughout, providing different areas for people to sit and read or study or whatever. Making her way over the stone floor to the stairs at the back, Infiniti saw several groups sitting around with their laptops. And way in the dark corner, she spotted a couple lip locked. She smiled. She and Joe knew that couch well.

"Hey, Fin." Cole came up to join her.

"Hey, Cole."

When they made it to the top floor, they found it empty. Cole took out his phone and started texting while Infiniti sunk down into the nearest leather couch. The dark lounge with leather chairs and heavy wood furnishings made her think of old-timey movies. The kind where everyone drank bourbon and smoked cigars. The scent of wood and spice mixed in the perfect way, reminding her of a cabin or a lodge. She liked the vibe, thinking she and Joe needed to spend more time up here. Especially if it was always empty like this.

After a few minutes, Cat and D showed up practically arm in arm. Infiniti spotted a smudge of red lipstick on the crease of D's mouth. Her eyes went wide as she stifled a laugh. She tried to catch Cat's attention so she could tell her, but Cat didn't notice. She was on a mission.

She took the Two of Cups tarot card out of her backpack and placed it on the coffee table. "Let's start with this. First, we need a team leader. And I think it should be me."

"Fine with me," D announced, taking a seat on an oversized red upholstered chair.

Wow, man down, Infiniti thought.

Cat whipped her sleek, dark brown ponytail around and turned her attention to Infiniti and Cole. "And you two?"

Infiniti wanted Cole to speak first, but he looked at her as if waiting for her to say something. She had already told Cat she'd support her, and there was no way was she going to cross Cat by changing her mind now.

"Well, I'm not interested. My plate is full right now. So I'm fine with Cat taking lead."

Making sure the guys weren't looking at her, she eyed Cat, tapped her finger on her lip then flicked her eyes in D's direction.

Cat tilted her head and furrowed her brow. "What, Fin?" She pointed at her lips in an exaggerating movement. "Why are you doing this?"

Geez, really? Girl couldn't take a hint. "I was trying to tell you that your lipstick is on D's face."

She huffed, strolled over to D, then rubbed the red away with her thumb.

"Cole," she said, not skipping a beat from her mission, "do you have a problem with me being team leader?"

He shook his head a little. "Nope. If you want it that bad, then have at it."

"Good."

With that settled, and surprisingly without any arguing, the four settled in around the coffee table and studied the tarot card.

On the first day of ITF class, Saundra Beaumont had magically displayed an arc of cards in the air, asking the teams to pick one. She and Cat had reached for the same card at the same time—the

Two of Cups. Claiming she was the best one to safeguard the assignment, Cat had kept it with her, and the others had taken pics of it.

According to the quick search she had done, most Two of Cups cards had a man and woman facing each other, holding chalices. The card represented some sort of partnership. But the card they had chosen was *way* different. Painted in dreamy, ethereal, yet haunting strokes, the card featured two fiery lions. Joined at the middle, they stretched away from each other at the head, as if forcing separation in the most agonizing way. With their teeth bared, she could almost hear their roars as they fought to tear away from each other. Their long, thick tail with blazing fur split into tiny strands. And nestled within the strands sat two chalices that burrowed into the dirt, connecting to thick bulging roots from a nearby decaying tree.

"So weird," Infiniti whispered.

"*Claro*," Cat agreed. After waiting for everyone to get a good look at the card, she flipped it over to the clue on the back.

Cole eyed it, then read out loud. "When the bluff is not a lie and all seems lost, you must brave the sky at any cost. Face the drum fire, confront your fear, the God of Thunder will hold you near. But should you shelter yourself away, the company will fail, the task will fade. Embrace the other, hold the tongue in hand, the prize will appear where you stand."

No one spoke for a while as they all considered what the words meant. Finally, D broke the silence. "That's messed up."

They exchanged clueless glances.

"Well." Infiniti cleared her throat. "How about we focus on the image first? Does anyone know about tarot? Did anyone get around to looking up the Two of Cups?"

Cat turned the card over to the picture of the lions. "I wanted to, but I got busy with my classes right away."

"Same," Cole added. "My classes have been insane."

"Me too," D tacked on. "Totally insane."

Infiniti picked up the card. "Well, I looked it up before heading over here, and usually the Two of Cups has a man and a woman on it and they're each holding a cup. The card means a relationship of some sort."

D swiped the card from Infiniti so he could take a better look. "A male lion has a prominent mane. But here, with the lions blurred together and pulling apart in a blazing blur, it's hard to tell if these are male or female."

"But we're definitely dealing with a couple." Cole swiped his dark hair away from his green eyes. "A couple that doesn't want to be together."

"A couple that doesn't want to be together?" Infiniti stitched her brows together but couldn't come up with anything.

"What about the other stuff?" D asked. "Why are the lions on fire? And why are the cups connected to the roots of a dead tree?"

Infiniti's head spun with ideas, but none of them were any good. "I don't know, but I hate fire." She shivered, thinking of the flames that had consumed her house and killed her mom. The fire Joe had saved her from. Forcing herself not to think of that horrible scene, she changed the subject. "Maybe we should go back to the riddle."

Cat flipped the card back over. "I think in Spanish, so these words make no sense to me. *Lo siento*."

D crossed his arms. "Don't feel bad, Cat. It may as well be a foreign language to us, too, because none of it makes sense to me either."

Cat smiled. "Thanks, D."

But then, D got up to his feet. "Wait a minute. This line sort of makes sense. Face the drum fire, confront your fear, the God of Thunder will hold you near."

Cole rose to his feet too, sparked by D's enthusiasm. "Yeah, how?"

"Drum fire means lightning. And I'm a—"

"—Lightning bird," Infiniti and Cat finished at the same time.

Excitement buzzed in the room while everyone's faces lit up with hope. Maybe their hunt mission wasn't going to be that hard after all.

"How do we get to the roof from here?" D asked, eyeing Cat since she lived in Heimdall. "I have an idea."

"Over here."

Everyone followed Cat as she zigzagged her way through the plush chairs and oversized dark furniture until they reached a large plain black door in the back. She opened it with a push, and the group emerged onto a simple and plain flat surface. A wide-open, empty space occupied most of the rooftop with seating areas and tables arranged at each corner.

Infiniti held out her arms and circled the area. "This space is huge. You could land a helicopter here if you wanted. Or a humongous dragon."

D peeled off his gray T-shirt. "Or set off a magnificent lightning storm."

Cat was peering over the edge of the tower when she backed up. "What? Right here?"

"Yeah," D answered with excitement in his eyes. "Maybe we'll figure something out."

"I'm all in for a lightning storm," Cole said, rubbing his hands together.

Watching D flex his impressive muscles, Infiniti thought it'd be cool to see him in action, but then she started worrying about getting struck by lightning. "Should we, uh, get back or something?"

"Yeah," D warned. "I'd say you guys need to get back."

She shot Cat and Cole a glance as they slowly moved away from the lightning bird. She scanned the space. They were inside Mount Alexa, surrounded by rock, stone, and dirt. Was it that smart to unleash a bolt of electricity inside? She wasn't so sure.

"Maybe we should go to Clifftop?" Infiniti suggested, wringing her hands together. "I mean, a lightning storm inside of a mountain might not be a great idea."

D paused for a few seconds before an idea came to him. "I know, how about this. I won't unleash anything crazy. Just a bolt, to see what will happen. We have to know if lightning will help us solve the mission."

Cole nodded "A bolt." He nodded his approval. "I think that will be fine."

"Yeah," Cat agreed. "A bolt should be okay."

"A small bolt," Infiniti tacked on.

"I can do that," D said, cracking his neck. He stepped away from the group, his back facing them, and stretched out his arms to the side. Every muscle in his back and arms accentuated in a display of strength and beauty as massive wings erupted from his shoulder blades in a sweeping flash.

"Wow," Cat breathed out with her hand on her chest. "You're incredible, D."

He turned to face her and winked. "Well, wait until you see this."

With his black and white plumes fully outstretched, D brought his wings up, then swooshed them down in a fluid movement. The force lifted him off the rooftop as a white crackling burst shot out of his body, forming a jagged lightning bolt that exploded out of him and streaked into the air. Larger than expected, Infiniti gasped as the spectacle soared high and crashed into a massive stalactite.

The hanging mineral deposit cracked, then split, hurtling to the ground. Seconds later, a booming crash reverberated through the mountain as if a bomb had detonated. Dust particles fell from above as the tower shifted.

"Fuck," Cole muttered.

Infiniti slammed her hands over mouth and muttered against her fingers. "Shit, shit, shit."

"What do we do?" Cat asked, her tan skin almost losing its color as fear drained the blood from her face.

With his wings outstretched, D eyed the group. "Meet me down on the ground."

He flew out then soared downward. Cole dashed for the door, and Cat and Infiniti followed.

"Please, don't let anyone be hurt," Infiniti repeated, struggling to keep up with Cat and Cole who were running so fast they quickly slipped from view.

With each step, her brain cluttered with the possible scenarios of what she'd find on the ground—structural damage to Heimdall, students injured. Or worse, students killed. And then she stopped dead in her tracks. Joe lived in Heimdall. Was he okay? She took off with more speed than she'd ever mustered, her heart caught in her throat. Rounding the stairs and dashing into the common room, she crashed into Joe. He swooped her up and held her tight.

"Infiniti, you're okay."

She buried her face into his chest relieved he was okay but still sick about what had happened and scared to death that someone had been injured. "Oh, Joe."

He held her close to him for a few seconds. "What happened?"

With no time to go through the whole thing, she looked up at him. "We accidentally," she bit her bottom lip, "caused a stalactite to fall."

"Oh, shit."

She shook with fear. "I know. Is everyone okay?"

"I have no idea. I sensed you were in danger and headed over here straightaway from my room." He slowly let go of her and took her hands. "But we should go check."

With Joe at her side, Infiniti joined the stream of students pouring out of Heimdall. Emerging into the dimly lit night, she tried to make out the scene while the smell of dank earth that permeated campus clogged her throat. People scattered about. Gasps rang out. Chunks from the fallen stalactite littered the small area in front of Heimdall. Infiniti craned her neck, trying to see if anyone had been hurt, when she spotted her team.

She made her way toward them with Joe behind her. When she got closer, she saw they were standing in front of an enormous piece of rock, the size of a boulder. And when she got even closer, she noticed small greenish colored legs sticking out from underneath it. One foot had a pointy brown leather work shoe on, the other foot exposed. She slammed her hands over her mouth and looked away.

"Is that..." She paused, not even wanting to verbalize what they had done. "One of the gnomes?" She gaped at D, Cat, and Cole. "Did we...kill him?"

Child-sized gnomes roamed SMA, largely unseen and hidden as they took care of the grounds. But this one had been in the wrong place at the wrong time, and the stalactite had fallen on him. Now he was dead. And it was their fault. She turned into Joe, unable to look at the tiny, motionless legs.

"Break it up," a voice commanded, coming their way.

It was Addie Beaumont. When she spotted the rock and the legs, her expression switched from pissed to shocked. She lowered her dark rimmed glasses as she scanned the area, taking in the scene. With the small group of onlookers turning into a sizeable crowd, she started barking orders.

"Everyone move out! Now!" Strands of long light brown hair spilled out of her messy bun. Crossing her arms, she added, "But if anyone here knows what happened, stay put!"

Cat, D, Cole, Infiniti, and Joe huddled together as everyone else filtered out of the area.

Addie held her hand to her forehead. "What in the hell happened here?"

Before anyone could answer, a small group of gnomes appeared. Eyes cast down, shoulders slumped over, they approached with caution. The oldest looking one with a full head of white hair stepped forward. A small shoe was in his hand. Addie went over to him, and the pair had a whispered conversation. She returned to the group when they were finished.

"They are going to take care of the body." She motioned for the group to follow her to Heimdall. "Let's give them privacy."

Tears spilled onto Infiniti's face as they followed Addie. They had killed an innocent creature, a keeper of the mountain, because they were careless and stupid. She wouldn't blame Addie at all if she kicked them out of SMA.

They deserved it.

CHAPTER 4

*I*nfiniti shivered as Addie cleared out the stragglers from the Heimdall common room. Guilt and fear clenched her gut tight. Scanning the faces of Cat, D, and Cole, she could tell they felt the same way. Cole was chewing his thumbnail while D paced about. Cat's features had hardened, as if waiting for certain punishment.

They were screwed.

"I'm assuming this is ITF-related as you all are on a team together?" Addie asked, circling the room with her arms crossed.

"Yes," D answered in a low voice.

Infiniti had never seen Addie mad before. Like really and truly furious. So furious she couldn't even speak. And then Saundra Beaumont showed up. Saundra was Addie's grandmother and probably the most powerful witch in Havenwood Falls. She wore a dark colored skirt suit with heels, and her silver hair was tied in a formal twist. She and Addie stepped to the side. After a hushed discussion, the imposing witches came back to the group.

"You'll be relieved to know the gnome has survived," Saundra said in a formal tone.

Infiniti squeezed Joe's hand while her tensed body eased up a tad.

Cat made the sign of the cross up and down and across her chest. "*¡Gracias a Díos!*"

D blew out, as if he'd been holding his breath this whole time. And maybe he had. "That's great news."

"But how?" Cole ran his fingers through his dark hair. "He was under that stalactite, right?"

Saundra stepped toward the fae. "Yes, a gnome was under there. And now he is not." She eyed each one of them in turn with her laser focused brown eyes. "There is no explanation, other than to say the gnomes that reside here are magical and mysterious. They can do things we cannot begin to understand."

"So…we didn't kill anyone?" Infiniti asked, needing confirmation.

"No, you all did not," Saundra answered.

"But you could have!" Addie huffed. "Anyone could have been on the ground when that stalactite fell! But a gnome was—a sacred creature to this mountain!"

The group moved together, as if closing in for protection. Addie studied them with a fierce stare, then zeroed in on Joe. She raised an eyebrow.

"Joe, you are not part of this ITF team, are you?"

"I'm not. I'm just here to offer my support." He released Infiniti's hand. "I'll, uh, go to my room now."

When Joe left, Addie and Saundra asked the group to explain what had happened. Taking turns with the details, Infiniti, Cat, D, and Cole shared how their study of their tarot card led them to believe lightning would help them solve The Hunt mission and how they had agreed to send a small bolt into the air to see what would happen.

Infiniti cringed on the inside with each word because hearing the account out loud made them sound like dumbasses. But what was done was done. Infiniti wondered what their punishment would be.

"We take safety seriously around here," Saundra admonished. "And while we understand the innate danger associated with some of our classes, and our degree programs in general, we expect all SMA students to conduct themselves in a manner consistent with prudence and restraint. You have behaved irresponsibly and dangerously, and the gnomes are demanding retribution." She rubbed the space between her eyes for a few long seconds. "I need you all to stop working on The Hunt mission while this is sorted out."

Infiniti's stomach dropped. Were they being suspended?

As far as Infiniti knew, no other team had been stopped from working on The Hunt mission. She wondered what the implication would be if they couldn't finish, especially since she needed a good grade in that class.

"Um, so . . ." Tears strangled her voice. She swallowed them down, trying to keep herself from bawling in front of everyone. "What will happen with the class? I really can't," she swallowed again, "fail."

Saundra's eyes softened a bit. "We don't want any of you to fail. But Addie and I need to report this matter to the Board of Regents. You each may stay in the class and complete your other assignments. But all work on The Hunt mission must cease until such time as you hear from us."

"And, please," Addie warned, "whatever you do, stay out of trouble."

"Indeed," Saundra reiterated. "No more mishaps. Not a single infraction. Understood?"

"Yes," the team muttered.

When Addie and Saundra left Heimdall, Infiniti could barely keep herself together. Shaking all over, and feeling like she wanted to barf, she needed to get out of there. With a swift turn, she headed for the stairs so she could go to Joe's room. And when she rounded the first landing, she collided into him with a crash.

"Oh, Joe," she choked out, tears spilling from her eyes as she held onto him. Even though she was relieved the gnome had survived, she was so mad at herself for being so dumb. She should've told the team not to do it. She should've been louder with her doubts. And now her grade in that class and her entire tenure at SMA was in jeopardy. Worse yet, she had let down Saundra and Addie. They, along with Lyra, were like family to her, taking her in when her house in Houston burned down and her mother died. She'd even had Thanksgiving dinner with them.

Joe rubbed her back. "It's going to be okay, babe."

She wanted to believe him, but in that moment she couldn't.

"Come on," he said. "Let's go to my room."

Once inside the safety of Joe's four walls, she curled up in a ball on his bed. Joe draped a soft blanket over her and dimmed the lights. The dark blues and grays made her feel at ease, and the smell of Joe's spicy and clean scent on the sheets calmed her. She and Joe had experienced some incredibly beautiful and intimate moments here. And in this space, with the man who loved her completely, she felt safe.

"What did Addie and Saundra say?" he asked after a while.

Her lip quivered again. Working to control it, she muttered, "We have to stop working on The Hunt mission until the Board of Regents is consulted."

Kase burst into the room.

"Guys! Did you hear that a stalactite fell right outside Heimdall and smashed one of the gnomes? And he somehow sprang back to life when the pillar was removed?" He tossed his backpack to the floor, excitement covering his face. "Someone from ITF was on the roof and caused the whole thing!"

Infiniti covered her face with the blanket and shrank into the covers.

"Yeah, we know, Kase," Joe said.

"Well, who did it? Fill me in!"

Joe stayed silent but must've mouthed something to Kase because she could feel a shift in Kase's energy.

"Ah, Fin. I'm so sorry," Kase said in a low voice. "I'll, uh, let you guys have your privacy."

After more tears, and a whole lot of feeling awful about what happened, Infiniti started feeling better. An hour after that, when Kase returned, Joe walked her back to her room. It was well past midnight, and she was exhausted. All she wanted to do was sleep. That, and talk to Taylor. Taylor always made her feel better.

She entered her dark dorm room and stood still, waiting for her eyes to adjust to the soft glow from the salt lamp in the corner of the room.

"Hey, Fin." Taylor's sheets crinkled as she moved around in bed. The overhead light illuminated from the flick of her wand and then dimmed to a soft glow.

Infiniti set her stuff down. "I guess you heard?"

"Yeah, I heard. Are you okay?"

"I am, but only because that gnome survived." She kicked off her sneakers. "I don't know what I would've done if he had died." She flopped down on her bed.

"Like, how did that little guy even get out of there?" Taylor asked.

Infiniti sighed. "I don't know. I'm just glad he did. And now my team has to stop working on The Hunt mission while the board tries to figure out what to do with us."

Taylor gasped. "Oh, Fin."

They sat there for a while in silence, each of them caught up in their thoughts. And when Infiniti's eyelids grew so heavy she thought she'd fall asleep, she got up to get ready for bed. Luckily, the bathrooms were empty, and she was back in her bed in no time.

"You ready for sleep?" Taylor asked.

She crawled into bed feeling pitiful and defeated. "I'm ready."

Taylor used her magic to turn off the overhead light. Only the hazy glow from the salt lamp remained. Even though she was dead tired after what had happened, she couldn't fall asleep.

"Hey, Taylor," she whispered.

"Yeah?"

"Have you seen the Wizard of Oz?"

"When I was little," she answered in a low voice.

"Well, it was like that. The stalactite was like Dorothy's house, and those little green legs sticking out were like the witch's. Except the gnome wasn't wearing ruby red slippers. He was wearing pointy brown work shoes."

"No way."

"But one of his shoes had flown off."

Somewhere between whispering with Taylor about the ordeal, and yawning giant yawns, Infiniti fell asleep.

CHAPTER 5

*W*aking up, Infiniti told herself everything was going to change. Her day was going to be awesome. Her classes would rock. The administration would be lenient on her team. So yeah, everything was going to be cool.

It had to be.

With Taylor gone early as usual, she stretched in bed before reaching over and checking her phone for messages. There was a text from Joe checking on her, and five messages from her WTF group.

With a groan, Infiniti read them. Apparently, they wanted to prove themselves by working on their potions assignment and producing a kickass healing potion. Not a bad idea. Infiniti texted back, and everyone agreed on doing as much research as they could on their own, and then meeting later that evening at the lab. Determined to turn things around, she got to work. After paying attention in all her classes, she spent the rest of her time braving the spooky library to look up healing potions. And when it was time to meet the team, she brought her positive attitude with her. But when she stepped into the lab, the tension in the air hit her square in the face.

Cat's arms were crossed tightly across her body. Cole perched on one of the stools with his face buried in his phone. D stood at the back of the lab, eyeing the supply of herbs on the shelves.

Infiniti thought it weird how none of them were standing together, but decided to ignore it. They needed to nail their assignment.

She set her stuff down on the nearest table. "All right. Let's start."

Everyone moved together, taking papers out of their backpacks, except for Cole. He had nothing.

"Cole," Cat barked, placing her hand on her hip. "Really?"

He shoved his phone in his back pocket. "I didn't have time."

Infiniti shook her head. "Let's just please do this, okay?"

Comparing notes with Cat and D, the group decided to do a rub. Debating the ingredients, they compiled a master list of what they needed.

Infiniti handed the written list to Cat. "You call out the ingredients and D, Cole, and I will gather everything."

Excited to get going, Infiniti, Cole, and D went to the back of the room. They eyed the jars as Cat started reading the first ingredient.

"Rah-noon-coo-loos ree-choor-vayt-ahs…" Giving up on her slaughtered pronunciation, she threw the list on the floor. "Okay, no. I can't read this."

D sprang to her rescue, scooping up the list. "I got it." He peered at the word. "Ranunculus recurvatas."

"Ra—what?" Infiniti laughed, understanding why Cat butchered the name. "That sounds like a disease, not an ingredient."

"Here it is," Cole said. He moved a glass jar off the shelf and placed it on the metal table.

D continued rattling off the list while Infiniti and Cole plucked each one from the shelves and lined them up. When they were finished, they got to work on the recipe.

Measuring out each item needed, they placed everything in a small stone mortar. Cat palmed the pestle and started grinding. After a while, she eyed the mixture. "I think it's ready."

Cole peered over her shoulder. "Let's test it out."

They had already planned to use themselves as test subjects, but now that it was time, Infiniti grew nervous. They had agreed to cut someone and use the concoction to heal the wound. But what if something went wrong? What if their mixture was off and didn't work? Or what if it caused the opposite? What if it made the wound worse? Like, a lot worse. Images of those lifeless gnome legs sprang to mind.

D pulled a small pocketknife out of his back pocket. He whipped it open in a flash.

"I volunteer," he said, ready to cut himself.

"Um… I don't know, y'all. Maybe we should rethink this," Infiniti warned, feeling like they needed to work on the recipe more. They couldn't afford another disaster.

"Fin, it'll just be a small nick, that's all," D scoffed.

"Exactly," Cat agreed. "It's no big deal."

"Tell that to the gnome and his people," Infiniti whispered.

"The gnome survived," Cat spit out.

"Yeah, well, what if he hadn't?"

Infiniti could feel heat rising up her neck. If she had been more assertive on the rooftop of Heimdall, the whole near-gnome-death-experience wouldn't have happened. And if that were the case, they wouldn't be in trouble with the school.

Cat leaned over. "He did not, and that's all that matters."

"Other things matter, too. Like us being in trouble with the school, Cat. And I don't know about you, but I like it here."

Cat flared her nostrils. "What are you saying?"

Infiniti paused. Truth was, she didn't exactly know what she was saying. Other than, Cat needed to show more restraint. "You need to be more careful and considerate."

"You are weak and helpless and should be more like me," Cat seethed. "Bold and fearless."

Infiniti's mouth dropped while she considered a comeback. She was terrible at comebacks. "Well, I-I NEVER want to be like you in skintight clothes!"

With a sweeping arm motion, Cat launched into a tirade in Spanish while at the same time knocking the mortar and its contents all over herself and Infiniti.

"Cat! What the hell!" Infiniti hollered.

The room quieted. D and Cole looked at each other, trying to figure out what to say, when Cat solved the problem. She dusted herself off and flipped her ponytail. "I can't take you right now."

She shoved her papers in her backpack and stomped out of the room.

Staring at Cole and D, and feeling awful inside, Infiniti whispered, "That didn't go over very well."

D shook his head. "Let me go after her."

Staring at the mess, and feeling like shit, Infiniti started cleaning up.

Cole reached in to help, but she stopped him with a wave of her hand. It was her mess, not his. "I got it, Cole. Thanks."

He slipped his backpack on. "I guess I'll see you tomorrow, then."

"Yeah, see you."

Finished with cleanup, and with all her positivity drained, she put on her backpack and headed home to Jory Tower. She texted Joe, hoping he wasn't busy and could come over. She really needed him.

Infiniti: You home?

Joe: No, sorry. At the library with Kase. Working on this dumb paper. I can come by later, tho

She wanted to tell him about her fight with Cat, but stopped herself. He needed to focus on his paper. Drama with Cat could wait.

Infiniti: Ok

Joe: See you then. Love you

Infiniti: Love you

She meandered her way to Jory, lost in her melancholy thoughts. And when she got to her room, she flopped on her bed and stared at the ceiling. The semester had started off great but had turned into a shit show. Like, a huge shit show. She and her WTF team had almost killed a gnome and were in huge trouble with the Board of Regents. And now Cat hated her. They weren't the best of friends by any means, but she couldn't stand to have anyone hate her. It made her feel awful inside.

A knock sounded at the door.

"Come in," Infiniti called out.

Tyr, who also lived in Jory, stuck his head in. His long dark hair hung loose, and his ice blue eyes danced with excitement.

"Hey, Fin. Roxy, Vid, and I are mixing drinks in the media

471

room for a viewing of The Shining. Show starts in thirty minutes. Spread the word."

As quick as he popped in, he popped out, leaving Infiniti perked up. Drinks and a movie sounded perfect. She texted Joe and then Taylor, letting them know, and then headed to the first floor for some social therapy. One hour in, and slamming drinks with her Jory friends, Infiniti was feeling good. Fight with Cat? So what! A gnome almost died? But he didn't! Life was good.

"Another shot?" Roxy asked, passing by with a tray of small plastic cups filled with a blue liquid.

She hiccupped, took a drink, and slammed it down. Two seconds later, an arm slipped around her waist. She grabbed the hand, sensing the familiar muscular hold, and spun around to see Joe.

"There you are." They hadn't had any alone time in a while, and she was ready to be with him. Just him. Doing amazing things to each other.

Joe pulled her close. "Yep, here I am." Roxy had come back and handed him a shot. He downed it, then grabbed another. "You been missing me?"

Quoting one of her fave movies from the eighties, she threw her arms around his neck. "Take me to bed or lose me forever!"

Joe laughed, then whispered in her ear, "I most certainly don't want to lose you forever."

She pulled him closer. "Then let's go."

Hand in hand, they left the party and did their best balancing act on the narrow exterior stairs of Jory as they made their way to Infiniti's room on the second floor. As luck would have it, Taylor still wasn't back.

Their lips locked as they tore off each other's shirts and shuffled over to the bed. But as soon as Infiniti's body hit the sheets, the room started spinning.

"Oh shnap," she slurred with a groan. "I'm shpinning."

Joe held her steady. "Babe, did you have any dinner?"

She gripped the sides of her head, as if trying to keep herself in place. "Uhhh...no?"

Joe slipped her shirt back on over her head, then threaded her arms through the armholes. He stacked her pillows against her headboard and propped her against them.

"Hold steady."

He left her on the bed, rifled through her snack drawer, and brought her some crackers and an electrolyte drink.

"Here, take this."

She nibbled on the dry snack, took a sip of the drink, and snuggled up next to him.

"I'm shorry I drank sho mush," she slurred out. "But Caash and I had a ffight."

He hugged her close, rubbing her arms. "Cat? What happened?"

"She's a..." Her sentence trailed off as she searched for the right word through the slosh in her brain. "...meanie."

He chuckled. "I guess she is. But it's over now. Just rest."

She babbled on about potions class and the herbal mixture that scattered everywhere while she closed her eyes and continued nibbling on crackers and drinking her purple drink. Eventually, her speech slowed down. Her head stopped spinning. And she slipped into a hazy sleep.

Lying face down with her eyes closed, Infiniti slowly started to awaken. The more awake she was, the more she remembered the details of the night before. She had gotten hammered, but miraculously wasn't feeling all that bad. And then she remembered Joe taking care of her.

"Joe?" she whispered.

Figuring he'd left for class, she wondered if Taylor was still there.

"Taylor?"

Deafening silence expanded between her ears. With her eyes still closed, she reached out for her nightstand for her phone, but didn't feel anything. Stretching her arm as far as it would go, she patted the smooth wood surface of her nightstand, but didn't feel anything. She pried open her eyes. Instead of her usual cluttered nightstand with her phone, clock, tissue box, phone, and assortment of lip balm, she saw a simple lamp with a clear base and white shade.

Huh?

She blinked. Forcing her eyes into focus, she noticed her room with its usual ethereal and peaceful vibe of white and purple hues had been replaced with a stark red, black, and white color palette. And across the way was a bed all decked out in pink and white.

"What the?"

She sat up. Had one of Taylor's spells gone haywire? The timing couldn't have been worse.

She remained motionless for a while, then swung her legs off the edge of her bed and slowly stood up. She made her way to the door when she caught sight of Cat in the room.

"Cat?"

Cat looked busted. Her eyes were wide, her expression almost confused.

"Um, Cat, what are you doing here?"

Cat looked like she was talking, but nothing was coming out of her mouth. And then Infiniti saw that she was only seeing Cat from the waist up. The lower part of her was a...desk? Infiniti screamed. She noticed Cat screaming too, but again there was no sound.

"What the hell?" she shouted. And then she detected something strange in her own voice. Like she wasn't exactly sounding like herself. "What is wrong with my voice?"

She raised her hand to touch her throat and noticed her hands were super tan. She gaped at the still stunned Cat before her when the horrible reality set in. She was looking at a mirror. And her reflection *was* Cat.

Her hands shot to her chest. Her normally modest breasts were well rounded and voluptuous. Her arms were long. Her legs strong and muscular. And she was wearing a sexy red nightie.

"I-I-I'm Cat?"

CHAPTER 6

*S*tomping away from the potions lab, Cat flung the grains of herb from her shirt and spit out the few that had ended up in her mouth, the earthy and bitter flavor heavy on her tongue. How dare Fin blame her for the accident with the gnome and tell her to have more restraint! Who the hell did she think she was?

She burst out of the building, enraged and ready to explode.

"Cat! Slow down!"

Hearing D's pleas behind her only made her quicken her pace. She didn't want to talk to him. She was a loner who prided herself on being self-sufficient. She didn't need him meddling in her life. If he knew what was good for him, he'd back off.

"Cat," he huffed beside her. "Are you okay?"

Crackling energy sparked at her fingertips. She fisted her hands at her sides, struggling to keep her powers in check. Last thing she wanted to do was hurt someone. But sometimes, her anger exploded out of her.

She halted in place and stared him down. "Leave me the hell alone!"

Not giving D a chance to respond, she spun around and continued to Heimdall when D stopped her with a grab of her arm.

"Cat, come on. It's me."

Me? Pfft. Just because she'd had sex with him, he thought he was important to her? She didn't think so. All guys were assholes and proved themselves to be eventually.

"Me? Me who? I don't know you, and you don't know me. Get that straight."

She jerked away from him and stomped away. Finally making it to Heimdall, she rushed through the entrance and hurried across the common room to the steps. Taking them two by two to the seventh floor, she reached for her door when it swung open from the inside.

"Oh, hey, Cat."

Makenna Walsh, her Seelie fae roommate, came out of their room. A petite girlie girl with long, straight auburn hair and brown eyes, she was the opposite of Cat. Despite their personality differences, their living arrangement worked perfectly. Mostly because Mak was a social butterfly and was hardly around, allowing Cat to hide away in solitude when she wanted to get away.

"Hey, Mak."

"I'm heading to Jory for drinks and a showing of The Shining. They're making a bunch of their yummy Slithering Serpent drink. Wanna come?"

Cat didn't have to think twice. That's where Fin and D lived. "No, thanks."

"Okay. See you later, then."

Mak trotted on while Cat retreated to their room. She sat on her bed, her heart beating wildly and her mind racing. She couldn't let anyone know how badly she felt about what had happened to that gnome, or how desperately she needed to stay at SMA, or how furious she was at D for thinking sleeping with him meant anything.

Forcing her thoughts away from her troubles, she slipped out of her black leather pants and shirt and put on a sports bra and training shorts. She stood in front of the oversized floor to ceiling mirror, blasted some Reggaeton music, and started lifting weights. After an hour of working her upper body, and drenched in sweat, she took a shower down the hall. With her anger settled, she climbed in bed, telling herself her worries could wait until tomorrow. Everything was always better after a good night's sleep.

The pounding of Cat's head demanded to be heard. Like a needy sledgehammer. With a groan, she kept her pillow on her face as she rolled over to her back. Why was her head hurting so badly? And then a harsh beeping sound jarred her. She rolled over onto her stomach, issuing a series of choice Spanish phrases under her breath. Had Mak changed the tone of her alarm? And put the alarm on her nightstand?

"Mak!"

With no reply from Mak, Cat scooted to the edge of her bed and fumbled around for the source, knocking over an assortment of things that thudded to the ground as her hand swept across her nightstand.

She froze.

She didn't have anything on her nightstand except for her lamp and the phone she placed there at night. So what had tumbled to the floor? Wide-eyed now, she rolled over to her back and saw a mural of the moon on her ceiling. She sat up with a start, her head pounding. *A moon mural?* Her gaze swept the room. Her usual sleek and modern decor of red and black were replaced with a messy and bohemian scheme of purple and white.

She jumped to her feet, hands up, ready to fight, when she noticed how small and slender her arms were. And pale. She patted her upper body. Her boobs had shrunk. Her muscular physique had given way to slender softness. She spotted a vanity with a mirror and dashed over. There before her appeared the reflection of Infiniti Clausman. She slammed her hands over Fin's mouth, then stretched out her cheeks, realizing from the pain that she *was* Fin. Or, her body was.

"¡*Que chingados!*"

Shivers raced down her spine. Her mind scrambled. She was trying to figure out what had happened when the movie where the mother and daughter switched bodies sprang to mind.

"*Cambiamos,*" she muttered.

She needed to get a hold of Fin right away. She darted back to the bed, looking for a phone. She got on her hands and knees and sifted through the contents that had fallen—lip balm, hair ties, a tissue box, a bottle of ibuprofen, an electrolyte drink, and a note from Joe.

Babe, went to class. Take 2 ibuprofen and text me when you're up. Hope your head doesn't hurt too bad. Love you.

With her throbbing headache, she realized Fin must've had a night of drinking. It would explain the pain and the fact that she awoke fully clothed. Eyeing the small white bottle of pain pills, she opened it and downed two. Then she stretched her arm under the bed in search of Fin's phone. Finding it, she held it up to her face, and it sprang to life. She typed in her number, but the call failed.

"¡*Estúpido!*"

She needed to get to Fin, pronto. She tucked the phone in the back pocket of her jeans and tore out of there. After a quick pit stop at the restroom, she headed straight for Heimdall. With her head down, she avoided eye contact with passersby, praying no one would try to talk to her. She may have looked like Fin, but she certainly didn't act like Fin.

To get to Heimdall from Jory, Cat had to take the skybridge to the library, connect to Halstein Hall, then take two separate sky bridges from Halstein to Heimdall. Usually an easy walk, Cat found herself out of breath by the time she got to Halstein. She slowed her pace, practically gasping for air as her head pounded from fresh pain. So this was what it was like to be petite and out of shape.

With Heimdall in sight, Cat dug deep and powered through. She needed to hurry so she and Fin could figure out a way to switch back before anyone noticed.

"Hey, Fin," said Kase, wolf shifter and best friend to Joe, coming up beside her.

Cat hid an internal gulp. "Hey."

"I heard you were wasted last night." He laughed. "How ya feeling?"

Um, should she laugh or be embarrassed? If it were her, she'd tell him to mind his own business, but what would Fin say? She wasn't sure, so she settled on the simplest of responses.

"Yes. I was."

They kept walking, almost coming to the entrance to Heimdall.

"You know Joe's in class, right?" Kase asked with a curious glance.

They stepped inside the tower. "Yes, I know. I'm here to see Cat."

"Cat? Why her?" he asked, as if she had mentioned the name of the devil. She was ready to tell him off but forced herself to stop. She needed to keep her cool. Climbing the stairs, Cat said, "She's in my hunt mission group."

"Oh, yeah. That's right. Lucky you," Kase said sarcastically. "That must suck."

Cat had had enough. She stopped on the steps and turned to face the tan-skinned, muscular wolf shifter. "Shut the hell up, Kase."

Taken aback, Kase's mouth fell open. He offered a quick apology. "Geez, sorry, Fin. I thought you and Cat were, well... Never mind."

She moved closer to him. "What? You thought we were what?"

Kase rubbed the back of his neck. "Nothing. I didn't know you two were...uh...close or anything. I mean, you know."

"Yeah, I know," she huffed. Then, getting herself in check, she added, "Cat's not that bad."

"Yeah, of course," he said.

Even though her petite thighs were burning, she trudged ahead of Kase. When they got to the sixth floor, he split off with a quick wave. Finally, at the seventh floor, she reached her room and hastily knocked.

"Fin, I mean, Cat," she said in a hushed voice. "It's me."

The door jerked open, and there was Fin, in Cat's body. Still dressed in Cat's red nighty. Fin grabbed her arm, pulled her in, and slammed the door shut. Once inside, the two stood face to face, eyeing each other.

"Oh my god." Fin gaped. "I'm you. You're me. It's Freaky—" She stopped, as if trying to recall the day— "Wednesday."

Cat started spewing in Spanish, arms gesturing, voice loud and heated.

Fin started laughing. "Holy shit, I look so funny yelling in Spanish. Like, wow."

Forcing herself not to give in to the absurdity of the moment, and terrified to be stuck in Fin's body, Cat huffed. "It won't be funny if this is permanent."

Fin bit her lip. "Yeah, you're right. We need to figure this out."

Cat went over to her bed and sat down. Fin joined her. They didn't say anything for a few minutes.

"I think we should tell Taylor. Maybe she can help," Fin suggested.

"No way," Cat practically yelled. "We can't. We're already in big trouble because of the gnome, and we were told to stay out of trouble. I think this qualifies as trouble. We need to figure this out ourselves and not tell anyone. Not even Joe."

"You're right," Fin whispered. "If we tell others they could possibly get in trouble, too."

She pushed Fin's long wavy hair out of her face, wishing she had it pulled up. "We need to figure out how this happened so we can fix it."

"Okay. Figure it out." Fin walked around the room, stretching out her legs as if getting used to how long they were. "Well, last night after our, you know, fight over the healing potion mixture I—"

Fin stopped.

Cat sat up.

"The herbs," Cat said.

"Got all over us," Fin finished.

Cat drew her phone from her pocket. "The guys. We need to see if they're affected like us." She stared at the phone, which was Fin's, and held it out. "This is yours."

Fin took it and gave her the one she had. "And this is yours."

Before she could text the guys, a message flashed on Cat's phone. She sucked in her breath. "It's Professor Beaumont."

Fin eyed her phone. "Shit. Me too."

It was a group message addressed to Fin, Cat, D, and Cole.

Prof. Beaumont: Please meet immediately in my ethics classroom. If anyone is unable to do so, let me know ASAP. Thank you. Prof. Saundra Beaumont

Fin's mouth fell open. "Oh my god. She knows we switched."

Cat considered the possibility. Professor Saundra Beaumont was indeed a powerful witch. But could she have figured it out so quickly? She wasn't sure. "I don't know, Fin."

Fin's eyes opened wide. "If that's not it, then it must be the decision on The Hunt mission."

"You're right," Cat agreed. She rubbed her head, the pain still throbbing. "We need to get going."

"But what about the guys? We need to see if that herb mixture affected them in any way."

"Don't worry," Cat offered. "I can text them on the way. And I'll be sure to be subtle about it."

Fin glanced around the room, then looked down at herself. She was still in the red lingerie. "You dress like this for bed?"

Cat opened her dresser. She took out a pair of jeans and a shirt and threw them at Fin. "Yes, I wear nighties like that because I like them. You can't just turn off sexiness. Now put this on. Hurry." Then she gave Fin a hair tie. "And if you're gonna be me, you need to pull your hair up. Oh, and by the way, thanks for the hangover."

"Oops, I forgot about that. Sorry."

Dressed and ready, agreeing to act as normally as possible with very little interaction with others, they took off in their new bodies.

Professor Beaumont's ethics class was in Halstein Hall, two sky bridges away. Plenty of time for Cat to text D and Cole. Luckily, the guys were still themselves. Now all they needed was the school to go light on them with the gnome thing so that she and Fin could figure out how to swap back. No way did she want to be stuck in Fin's soft, petite body forever. That would suck.

CHAPTER 7

*C*at stayed close to Fin as they walked into the ethics classroom. Professors Saundra and Addie Beaumont were standing at the front, talking in low voices. The four exchanged silent nods while an uncomfortable feeling hung in the air. Cat was used to walking into a cold-shouldered room, so it didn't bother her. She took a seat in the front row of the class, held her head high, and crossed her arms confidently. Fin sat next to her, fumbling with her hands like she didn't know what to do with them. Cat thought for sure the professors would see right away that she wasn't acting quite right.

"Cat," Cat whispered to Fin in a barely audible voice. "Relax."

Fin folded her hands on her lap and took a deep breath. "Relax," she repeated.

"And sit tall."

Fin straightened her back.

Addie raised an eyebrow at the pair over her dark rimmed glasses. She opened her mouth to say something when D and Cole came in.

"Sorry if we're late," D said. "We got here as soon as we could."

Saundra waved them over to the seats. "You're right on time, gentlemen."

The guys settled in next to Cat and Fin, looking slightly unnerved.

The elder witch eyed each one in turn then cleared her throat. "Addie and I have consulted with the Board. We recognize that some matters are inherently dangerous on this campus. We are also grateful that the gnome came out, miraculously, unscathed and that we have been able to smooth things over with the gnome leaders."

Cat had been holding her breath. She let it trickle out slowly as her shoulders relaxed some. She detected an exhale from Fin, too.

The stately witch continued. "You may resume work on The Hunt mission immediately. However, you must exercise extreme caution with the assignment, as well as all assignments. Understood?"

"Yes," the four said together. "Understood."

Cat wasn't sure what to do next, and neither did Fin, D, and Cole. They all just sat there.

"Well," Addie said, shooing them out of the room. "Get busy!"

The four gathered their things and shuffled out of the room. They were down the hall when Cat noticed an empty classroom. "Let's duck in here."

With the door shut behind them, Cole and D high fived each other. "Damn," D exclaimed. "We got lucky!"

Cat kept her arms crossed, her mind processing what they needed to do so she could get her body back. "We sure did. And with that behind us, here's the plan. Our first order of business is that healing potion. We need to knock that out of the way ASAP before we do anything else. Then we can focus on The Hunt mission."

The guys looked from her to Fin. "Sounds good to me, Fin," Cole said. "But isn't Cat supposed to be in charge?"

Crap, that's right. She looked at her body, at Fin. "Cat, is that okay with you?"

"Yes, that's a great idea. How about we meet in the potions lab at—"

"Now," Cat cut in. "If we're all free. The sooner the better." She leaned toward Cat. "So we can fix this thing."

Fin nodded. "Right. We need to fix this."

With everyone's schedules open, and ITF not until later at nine p.m., the team headed for the potions classroom and thankfully found the room empty.

Cat directed the group to a table in the back. "I think we should recreate exactly what we did yesterday."

She reached for her backpack because she had stuffed the ingredient list in there when she stopped. She was Fin now, and Fin would never reach into Cat's backpack.

"Um, Cat—" she motioned at her backpack— "Your list. I think I saw you put it in there. Can you get it?"

"Oh, yeah, that's right." Fin opened Cat's backpack and rifled through the papers. "Here."

The group took the list to the back and started gathering the ingredients. When everything was set out on the table, D retrieved the mortal and the pestle. They measured out everything carefully, adding the ingredients to the stone mortar one at a time. Cole took the pestle and started grinding.

After about a minute, he eyed the contents. "Looks good to me."

"So, Fin," Fin said to Cat. "What do we do *now*?"

Gazing into the mortar, Cat thought about their next move. Last time they were there, she had knocked the mortar and the grains flew all over herself and Fin. She needed to do the same thing with the grains. "Well, we do exactly what we did before, I think."

"The exact same thing?" Fin asked.

"Yes. Exactly."

Cole tapped his finger on the metal table. "Is there something going on with you two? You're both acting really strange."

"Yeah," D chimed in. "I've been noticing that, too. What's going on?"

Ignoring him, Cat scooped out some mixture. She flicked it on herself and then on Fin's face.

"Whoa! Ladies!" D exclaimed.

Cat stared at Fin, waiting for something to happen.

"Let's hold hands," Cat said.

They reached out and held hands. Still nothing.

Cole leaned back, as if watching a performance. "Whatever's

happening here is some weird shit. Do you two want to fight or make out?"

They dropped their hands. "Shut up!"

Cole's expression went from amused to exasperated. "D, cut your finger."

D pulled out his pocketknife and opened it. He balanced the tip over his finger and sliced deep.

A line of blood sprang on his skin and oozed out. Putting the pocketknife on the table, he got a pinch of the herbal mixture and rubbed it on the spot. He eyed the clock.

"Let's give it a minute."

Dusting herself off, Cat watched D's thumb, hoping the mixture wouldn't work so they could continue with other recipes. There had to be a way for her and Fin to change back, and the answer had to be in one of the ingredients. When the minute lapsed, D blew the powder away. He rubbed at the dried blood, exposing perfect skin.

D gave Cole a fist bump. "We did it!"

Cole smiled. "Yep, now let's put the mixture in a clean jar and turn it in."

With the guys busy with their task, Cat pulled Fin to the side. "Now what do we do?"

"I don't know," Fin said. "But I'm freaking out. This is *so* bad."

Cat pushed Fin's long hair out of her face. "The guys will want to start working on The Hunt."

Fin chewed on her bottom lip. "Well, maybe we should? And then after we're done, you and I can come back here and try different measurements?"

Cat nodded, thinking the plan sounded pretty good. And really, they didn't have much choice.

Going back to the table, Cole was scooping the contents into a clean jar. He screwed the lid on tight.

"Done and done," he said.

"I'll go turn this in to Professor Parker right away," D offered. "Then we can focus on that tarot card. Where do you guys want to meet?"

Thinking of Heimdall brought images of those lifeless gnome legs. Cat didn't think it a good idea to go back there.

"What about Jory," D suggested. "Fin and I live there, and I can tell you nobody really uses the study rooms."

After they agreed on the location, D took off. Cat, Fin, and Cole cleaned up their mess, then started off for Jory. With Cole busy on his phone, Cat and Fin dropped behind him and moved in close.

"I was thinking, maybe we have to wait for the morning for the switcheroo," Fin whispered.

"Good idea," Cat said, matching her low tone. "There must be a delay. We didn't exactly switch bodies right away."

"Exactly. We woke up like this. It wasn't immediate."

Cole stopped. He turned around. His green eyes pierced them with a knowing gaze. "What's up with you two?"

Cat's heart thrummed out of control. She and Fin needed to keep their switch a secret so they wouldn't get in any more trouble, but Cole looked as if he knew the truth. She had no idea what he could do as a fae, but wondered if it included mind reading.

"Hey, guys." Joe came upon them. He grabbed Cat's hand and squeezed. "Hey, beautiful." And then he kissed her. A quick peck with the softest lips.

Cat froze. Her mouth dropped. She glanced at Fin who looked as if she'd just lost her puppy. She closed her mouth, remembering that as far as anyone knew, she was Fin. And she needed to act like it.

"Um, hey." She dropped his hand and backed away, playing with her hair.

"What are you guys doing?" Joe asked.

Cole shot the girls a piercing glance. "Yeah, what are you guys doing?"

Scrambling with what to say or do and knowing she needed to get away from Joe, Cat moved even farther away from him. "We're working on our hunt mission. And I, uh, really can't be with you. We have to go. Now."

"Oh," Joe said with a wounded and confused look on his face. "Um, yeah sure. See you later."

Looking in shock and almost on the verge of tears, Fin said, "Um, yeah. We're busy. Sorry, Joe."

Practically spinning on her heels, Cat rushed away, and Fin

followed. They moved into Jory quickly and hurried to the first-floor study room with Cole trailing behind them. Once inside Cat closed the oversized thick, wooden door.

"That was close," she said to Fin.

"What was close?" Cole asked. Crossing his arms, Cole stared down Cat and Fin. "You two gonna spill?"

Cat was trying to figure out what to say, when Fin started crying.

"I need a second," she said, leaving the room.

"Whoa," Cole said. "Cat is *crying*? Never thought I'd see that. I thought she was heartless."

Cat was stunned. She was tough and didn't take shit from anyone, and she knew she was guarded, but heartless? Is that how everyone saw her? "She is *not* heartless!"

"Come on, Fin. You know she is."

Cat crossed her arms and walked away. Being stuck inside Fin's body was proving way more difficult than she had imagined, and it hadn't even been long. How dare people think so little of her. If only they knew what hell she'd been through, maybe they'd understand. But they didn't need to know about her life. That was her business and hers alone.

A knock sounded on the door. It swung open, and D stuck his head in. Seeing the group, he came in and closed the door behind him.

"Package has been delivered." He scanned the room. "Where's Cat?"

"She had to take a minute," Cat said.

D flashed her a look. "Is she okay?"

Not two seconds later, Fin returned. Her eyes were bloodshot and puffy. The tip of her nose red.

"Hey, Cat, you okay?" D touched her shoulder, leaving his hand there for a moment.

It was so weird for Cat to watch D display emotion for her. Concerned filled his eyes. Tenderness softened his dark, handsome, and chiseled face. Was it possible that he really and truly cared for her?

Fin squeezed his fingers. "I'm okay. Thanks, D."

Finding the whole scenario too much, Cat did what she did best. Moved the focus to a task. "How about we get to work?"

Shaking his head as if he didn't know what the heck was going on, Cole took the Two of Cups card out of his backpack and placed it on the table. Everyone leaned in, as if eyeing the image would reveal something new from the last time they examined the card at Heimdall. And for Cat, it did. The fiery image of the two lions tearing apart in agony screamed out a new meaning for her. She grabbed Fin's arm.

"Fin, it's us."

Gasping, Fin placed her fingers on the card. "Oh. My. God. It is."

"Fin?" D gazed from Cat to Fin. "Why are you calling Cat...Fin?"

"Holy fuck," Cole blew out. He slammed his hands on the table and rose to his feet. "You two have switched bodies!"

"Huh?" D did a double take. "They've switched...what?"

"Bodies," Cole said again.

Cat eyed Fin, and the two exchanged a defeated look. They may as well confess.

"Yes, we've switched. This is Fin's body, but it's me. Cat." Making sure she got her point across, she rattled off some Spanish phrases.

"Shit," D whispered, rubbing his face.

Fin stroked Cat's long ponytail. "This hair and body belong to Cat, but inside it's me. Fin."

Cole let out a long whistle. "Son of a bitch. How did that happen?"

"That mixture we made in the potions lab. Not the one today, but the one yesterday. Somehow getting those grains on us made us wake up this morning like this," Cat said. "Or, at least, we think that's what did it."

"And we tried to switch back at the lab today, but it didn't work," Fin finished.

"So that's what that whole throwing herbs at each other was all about?" Cole asked.

"Yes," Cat answered. "And now it looks as if reversing us is linked to this tarot card and our hunt mission. I mean, it must. Right?"

A feeling of fear and uncertainty hung in the air as Cat and the others eyed the card with newfound perspective.

"Now there's more reason than ever to solve this hunt mission, and fast," Fin whispered. "And before you ask why we didn't tell y'all, and why I lied to Joe, it's because Addie and Saundra warned us to stay out of trouble. We figured switching qualified as trouble."

Still looking shocked, D agreed. "Yeah, switching bodies definitely qualifies as trouble."

Cat picked up the card. The separating lions were pulling apart so violently, with so much pain and effort, she didn't know if she and Fin could really switch back. "But if we fail," Cat added in a serious tone. "If we can't solve the mission, then we'll have no other choice but to tell the professors."

Completing The Hunt mission had turned to so much more than a class assignment. Their futures at SMA depended on their success, as well as their very lives.

CHAPTER 8

*R*elief washed over Infiniti because now, even though she was in Cat's body, she could act like herself. At least around the team. Yet she couldn't shake her guilt over not being able to tell Joe. But telling him might put him in jeopardy. No way would she risk his future at SMA. She loved him too much to do that to him.

Cat cleared her throat. "Well, since the four of us know who Fin and I really are, I'm getting this hair out of my face." She pulled Infiniti's long wavy locks up into a ponytail and tied it with a hair band she had stuffed in her pocket.

"Well, I'm doing the opposite." Infiniti took her hair tie out, letting Cat's long, thick, straight hair drape over her shoulder. She massaged her head a few times, then glanced down at her impressive cleavage. "I wish I had a sweatshirt and leggings instead of this super tight cat woman outfit."

Cat raised her eyebrow. "It's not exactly you, is it?"

"Uh, no," Infiniti said with a chuckle. And then everyone joined in. For the first time in a long time, maybe in forever, the four laughed. The kind of laughter that stretched out for minutes and brought tears to everyone's eyes.

Fin wiped her cheeks. "Wow, I really needed that."

"Me, too," Cat agreed.

With the air cleared and everyone feeling better, they huddled around the card again.

"So everyone agrees the lions are me and Cat. But what about those cups going into the ground and connecting with the roots of that dead tree?" Fin asked.

D rubbed his chin. "I spend a lot of time out on Clifftop. Maybe there's a dead tree out there."

Excitement sprang in Cole's eyes. "Of course! With all the trees out there, surely there's a dead one like this. Right?"

"Great idea," Fin said, thinking of all the trees on Clifftop. "But let's finish with this card first. We can go out there later." She went back to studying the card. "What are those cups all about? What kind of tree roots connect to…cups?"

"I don't know. Maybe that'll come to us later," Cat said. Still eyeing the card, she asked, "Are we finished looking at this side?"

When everyone nodded, Cat flipped the card to the riddle. She nudged it toward Infiniti, and Infiniti started reading.

"When the bluff is not a lie and all seems lost, you must brave the sky at any cost. Face the drum fire, confront your fear, the God of Thunder will hold you near. But should you shelter yourself away, the company will fail, the task will fade. Embrace the other, hold the tongue in hand, the prize will appear where you stand."

Grappling with the words, Infiniti tried to understand what the riddle could mean, when a growling stomach cut through the silence. Cat slammed her arms over her stomach. "Was that me? Or, I mean, Fin?"

With a nod, Infiniti smiled. "Probably. You wouldn't know it from my petite frame, but I'm not one to miss a meal."

"I'm actually pretty hungry, too," D chimed in. "I haven't had anything to eat since breakfast. I don't mind getting food for everyone."

"That would be great," Cat said. "Some food will help my, I mean, Fin's hangover."

"Ah, I know the perfect thing for a hangover," D said. "Be right back."

D went out and brought back a stack of pizzas for the team, and when he returned, they stopped for a break. With her stomach getting full, Infiniti kept eyeing her phone, expecting Joe to text, but he never did.

"He'll be okay," Cat offered. "He's probably just giving you space."

"I know," she answered. "But I feel so bad about it."

"Hey," Cole said, pulling Infiniti from her thoughts. "I have an idea. Let's write out each line of the clue on a separate paper and write down what we think it could mean."

"Good thinking, Cole." Infiniti opened her notebook. She wrote at the top of a clean piece of paper, *When the bluff is not a lie and all seems lost, you must brave the sky at any cost.*

"That part is easy," D said. "When the bluff is not a lie is you two." D pointed from Infiniti to Cat. "You were lying to us about who you were. So, it was a bluff. It wasn't a lie."

Infiniti thought it sounded like pretty good reasoning. With a nod from Cat and Cole, she scribbled out the theory.

"But what about the sky part?" she asked. "Brave the sky? What could that mean?"

D shrugged his shoulders. "Now that part, I have no idea."

With nobody able to come up with anything for the sky part, Infiniti went on to the next line.

Face the drum fire, confront your fear, the God of Thunder will hold you near.

"Well," D said, looking a little embarrassed. "I thought that part meant lightning, but after what happened up on Heimdall, I'm thinking not."

Infiniti tapped her pen against her lips. "If drum fire isn't lightning, then maybe it's...."

"¿Música?" Cat asked, as if unsure of the idea. "As in, actual drums?"

Infiniti's mind raced as she thought of music. "Maybe. Are there any actual drums on campus?" She envisioned the different buildings, wondering if any of them were designed for music.

Everyone thought for a minute. "I don't think so," D said.

"Okay, then. I'll make a notation to look for drums," Infiniti said.

"I have an idea on the next part," Cole chimed in. "The God of Thunder holds you near part."

"Oh yeah, what?" Infiniti asked.

"Well," he said, "the God of Thunder is Thor, right? Maybe if we research Thor, we'll come across something about cups and a dead tree. Or, even, switching bodies."

"You might be onto something, Cole," Infiniti agreed. "Norse mythology is filled with all kinds of weird shit."

"Let's go to the library then. *Vamos,*" Cat urged, getting to her feet. Even though Cat was in Infiniti's body, her sheer badass attitude came across through Infiniti's petite form. Her shoulders were pulled back, her small chest jutted out. Cat was ready to charge, and Infiniti kinda liked seeing herself like that. But she also thought they needed to think things through a little more.

"Before we tear out of here, let's finish the riddle," Infiniti cautioned.

Cat eased back down on her chair while Infiniti wrote the next part.

But should you shelter yourself away, the company will fail, the task will fade.

Cole scratched his head. "Shelter," he mumbled. "I got nothing on that."

With no one having a clue what that meant, Infiniti let out a sigh. "Let's move on to the last part."

Embrace the other, hold the tongue in hand, the prize will appear where you stand.

If the part about shelter was confusing, then holding the tongue was even more so. Everyone flashed each other befuddled glances as they all sat around. And then an idea sprang into Infiniti's mind.

"This is going to sound crazy," Infiniti said, "but let's all stick out our tongues and hold them."

Cole pushed his chair back. "You're right. That does sound crazy. And I'm not doing it."

D echoed Cole's sentiment. "It does sound crazy, but then again, why not try it? I mean, this whole fucking thing is crazy, right?"

"I'm in," Cat said.

Cole reluctantly scooted his chair back in. "Fine, let's do it. But we will never speak of this to anyone. Deal?"

"Deal," they replied.

Scanning each other for a few seconds, they slowly stuck out their tongues.

"Holth eath otheth's thonths," Fin managed to say with hers dangling.

She reached out to her right and pinched her thumb and forefinger down on Cat's wet tongue. Cat did the same to D, and then D to Cole. Cole was about to pinch Infiniti's tongue, when she flinched and pulled back a smidge, thinking of his deadly touch.

"The bracelet, remember?" Cole said.

She let out a nervous chuckle. Then moved closer to him. He pinched Infiniti's tongue with a roll of his eyes.

They sat like that for a while. When nothing happened, they dropped their hands.

"Ew," Cat said, eyeing her fingers.

"That was dumb as shit," Cole said, wiping his off on his sleeve.

And then they busted out with laughter.

Infiniti dabbed at her eyes. "OMG, y'all. I can't even!"

Cole's laugh quickly faded. "But we're still not telling anyone."

"Right, no way," Fin agreed.

With that behind them, they eyed their notes. They only had two ideas to pursue. First, go to Clifftop and look for a dead tree with cups, or whatever, at the roots; and second, go to the library to research Thor. Oh, and they also had class. She had almost forgotten. They couldn't go to Clifftop after class because it would be too dark. So that left the library. And Infiniti hated going to the library, especially at night. It was creepy and dangerous, and some students were even rumored to have been lost in there. As in, never seen again. Ever.

"I guess we're library bound after class," Infiniti sighed.

"Guess so," D agreed. "And then Clifftop in the morning."

After a very boring and uneventful WTF lecture, and a quick bite after, the group headed for the dreaded library. They made their way across the narrow sky bridge with slow steps, the dimmed lights of the orbs only casting enough glow for them to barely see their own shoes. Focusing on keeping one foot in front of the other, the team held hands with D in the front and Cole bringing up the rear as they walked single file across the skybridge.

As they got closer to the looming stone structure that rose from the ground toward the skylight above, they moved faster, as if they couldn't wait to get off the bridge and inside. And when the grand arched entrance came into view, they practically dashed through the doors, almost bumping into Rhian.

"Whoa, Rhian," D said.

The Celtic goddess of the moon, night, and death had her braided hair pulled up high in a bun and held a stack of books in her arms. "Hey, D. Hey, guys. You all heading to the library at this hour?"

"Yeah," Infiniti answered. "We've got research to do on our hunt mission."

Rhian flashed Infiniti and Cat a knowing look, studying them with curiosity. If she knew about their switch, which of course she knew, she didn't say anything. "Well, I think I'm the last one in there. Though perhaps there's a librarian lurking around. Not sure. But you should all be careful. The orbs seem frisky tonight."

"Thanks," Cole said. "We will."

The hive-like interior of the library spiraled up as far as the eye could see with at least a dozen levels with halls, tunnels, and caverns branching off in various directions. Like the rest of the campus, orbs and torches provided the only source of light and had reduced way low in the evening.

Infiniti swallowed. "I really don't like this," she said. "Especially the frisky orbs part."

Peering about with sharp eyes, D muttered, "I don't like this either, so let's get what we came for, and fast."

"Let's look for the librarian," Cat added.

A circle of light floated down from above, stopping at eye level.

"Shit," Fin whispered. "I've heard of these librarian orb thingies, but I've never seen one."

"They're no biggie," Cole said. He got up close to the light. "Hey, we need books on Thor. Whatever we can find about cups and dead trees."

"And people switching bodies," Infiniti blurted.

495

The orb swayed back and forth and up and down, as if thinking. The indecisive movement wasn't a good sign.

"Anything on Thor, God of Thunder," D added, as if the light needed clarification.

"T-H-O-R," he spelled in an exaggerated voice.

"Really?" Infiniti said. "I'm pretty sure it can spell."

The supernatural glow stopped moving for a few seconds, then floated past them.

"Um, okay," Infiniti said.

The four followed the cryptic light as it wound around the stacks, flicking left and turning right, like a speedster. Without warning, it came to a full stop. Infiniti, Cat, D, and Cole skidded to a halt, colliding into each other like an accordion.

"What the hell, orb," Infiniti murmured.

The light sat on a shelf, its glow brightening up the book titles. D peered at the spines. He read one title out loud. "*Understanding Almighty Thor.*"

He pulled the book from the shelf and dusted it off at the top. It was a black hardbound book with the title etched on the cover in gold print.

"I guess this book has our answers," Cat whispered.

The supernatural light faded out with a snap, plunging the group in darkness.

A yelp shot out of Infiniti, then a snap sounded, and a flame burst before her face. She hollered, backing up, her fear of fire taking her over.

"It's me—it's my flame," Cole rushed out. The fire reduced to a finger-sized flicker. "I can produce fire with a snap of my fingers."

Fin pushed Cole's chest, but not knowing Cat's strength, he flew against the shelves, and a tower of books fell down on him.

Everyone sucked in their breath and froze in place because bad things happened when the books were disturbed. Eyeing the space all around them, and with nothing happening, everyone relaxed a little.

"Sorry, Cole," Infiniti whispered. "I didn't know my strength, or, er, Cat's strength. But also, don't do that again. Fire freaks me out."

Cole stood. With his flame snuffed from the fall, he pulled out his phone and turned on the flashlight. He matched her low tone. "Well, now that I know how you feel about fire, I most definitely won't do that again."

D was still holding the book, and in his other hand he held Cat's hand. It was so weird for Infiniti to see her physical body so close to another guy, and her hand in someone's other than Joe's. And even though it wasn't her, she still felt a pang of guilt. She was about to jokingly say something to them about not getting too close when a creaking moan floated in the air. And off in the distance Infiniti thought she heard a sinister cackle.

A chill raced down her spine. "Can we please get out of here?"

"I'm with Fin," Cat declared, sounding ready to fight anyone who opposed her.

Cole and D did a quick scan of the shelf for other books. Not finding anything else on Thor, the four left the library in double time and were back safe and sound in the Jory study.

"I will never get used to this school," Infiniti said, flopping her head on the desk.

CHAPTER 9

*I*nfiniti stayed up as late as she could with Cat, Cole, and D as they painstakingly picked their way through the massive Thor book. But when it hit five in the morning, and with no answers in the tome, she decided to get some rest. She was exhausted.

"I'm really sorry, y'all, but I've got to sleep."

She shuffled over to the oversized, green and gold fabric-covered couch on the far side of the room and crashed down face first. The stiff cushions made her body ache all over. She turned from side to side, trying to find a comfortable spot, when her phone dinged. She hoped it was Joe. After seeing him on the skybridge outside Jory, she had texted him a lame excuse about how the team was taking all her time and that she was sorry if she wasn't acting herself. It took him a while to respond, and when he did, he said he understood and for her to text him when she was finished. But something in the way he paused with his message told her he knew something was up.

She pulled her phone out of her back pocket. It wasn't Joe, but Taylor.

Taylor: Hey, roomie. Checking on you. Everything ok? Up early for yoga and I see you're not here.

Crap, she had forgotten to tell Taylor she'd be pulling an all-nighter, working on The Hunt mission. They had a rule to let each other know when they'd be gone like that.

Infiniti: Sorry! Working on this dumb mission and lost track of time. This assignment is literally ruining my life

Taylor: I know girl

Infiniti: I'll probably be gone all day today and all night. Ughhh

Taylor: You've got this, but let me know if you need help

Infiniti: I will. Thank youuuu

Infiniti scrolled to her message thread with Joe. Her fingers hovered over the screen. Her heart ached for him, but now that she was in Cat's body, she needed to avoid him. She shoved her phone back in her pocket, angrily punched one of the throw pillows on the couch, then snuggled into it. Finding the best spot, she closed her eyes. She could hear Cole, D, and Cat talking about different theories regarding Thor. Then Cole's voice faded. After that, all she could hear were Cat and D. Their voices were low and their tone intimate, and even though she didn't want to eavesdrop, she couldn't help it.

"What happened to you, Cat? Who hurt you so badly that you ended up like this?"

She didn't answer.

"I understand, you know. I understand hurt and betrayal. And when you're ready, you can tell me. But I need you to know that I will never hurt you. Not ever."

Cat whispered something back, but Infiniti couldn't hear it. But she hoped, as they talked in low voices, they'd find a way to each other. They deserved love and happiness. Everyone did. Finally, every sound in the room faded as she drifted to sleep.

With Fin snoozing on the couch in the far corner of the study lounge, and Cole asleep on an oversized chair, Cat moved in close to D. She had always been attracted to the lightning bird, and her feelings for him had slowly magnified over the semester while they worked together as a team in the ITF class. And even though she had

499

turned on the heat to get him to support her as team leader for the mission, she secretly just wanted to get closer to him but didn't know how. She thought she should come clean if they were to ever be anything to each other. She wanted him to know how she really felt.

She traced his muscular arm with her fingers. "I know I came on strong to get you to support me for team leader, and you probably think it was all fake, but it wasn't."

His lips curled up in a sexy smile that was equal parts surprised and relieved. "It wasn't?"

"No. It wasn't."

They sat like that for a while, their eyes locked while heat and longing radiated deep within her body. She could feel the same oozing from D. But she wasn't herself. She was Fin, and she needed to bring it down. D must've been thinking the same thing.

"If you were you, I don't know if I'd be able to keep my hands off you," he confessed.

Forcing herself to keep her distance, she said, "If I were me, I wouldn't *want* you to keep your hands off me."

He leaned forward and pressed his forehead against hers. He closed his eyes. "We really need to solve the mission," he said with a groan. "So I can get you back."

She laced her arms around his waist. "Back?"

"Back as in, I want you to be mine. And if you'll have me, I want to be yours."

Resisting the urge to kiss him, she kept her forehead pressed against his and closed her eyes, too. Envisioning herself with him, she whispered, "I will most definitely have you."

A creak sounded as the heavy doors of the study lounge swung open and in walked Joe. In a flash, Cat remembered she was Fin, and she was dangerously close to D. She pushed away from the lightning bird while her mouth fell open.

"Joe!"

Joe stumbled back, as if he had taken a blow. "Infiniti?" he asked, not believing what he had seen. "What the hell is going on?"

Cat swallowed hard, not knowing what to say. "Joe," she muttered. "I, uh, um…"

"Joe, dude," D said. He raised his hands, as if busted in a raid. "It's not what you think."

Joe jabbed his finger in D's direction. Every vein in his neck throbbed with anger. Cat thought he might shift. "Get the fuck away from her before I kill you."

D stepped away slowly, then said again, "Joe, I promise, it's not—"

"I said, get the fuck away," he warned. Then he looked at Cat. Anger gave way to pain. "Infiniti," he said, struggling to find the right words. "What are you doing?"

Cat glanced at Fin, the real Fin, so dead asleep, she didn't hear Joe's voice. Cole was nearby, slowly rising to his feet, watching the unfolding scene with shocked surprise.

"Joe," Cat pleaded with desperation, bringing her attention back to the wolf shifter. The last thing she wanted to do was cause trouble between him and Fin. "D is right. It's not what you think."

Joe shook his head and backed up. He ran his fingers through his hair while deep pain etched all over his face.

"I gotta get out of here," he mumbled as he took off.

Cat remained frozen in place as the door slammed. Her mind raced as she tried to figure out if she should run after Joe, but she knew she'd only make things worse. She stared at D. "*Dios mío.* What do I do?"

D rubbed his face for a few seconds. "We need to wake Fin. She needs to know, and she needs to make the call."

Cat slowly crept close to the slumbering Fin. She placed a soft hand on her shoulder. "Fin, you need to wake up." Cat shook her a little. With no response, she said louder with a hard nudge, "Fin."

With a groan, Fin rubbed her eyes a bit before opening them fully. She sucked in her breath when she saw Cat in front of her, but then remembered the whole switcheroo thing.

"Geez, it's not me. I mean, it is, but it's you." She sat up and wiped the drool at the corner of her mouth. "I had almost forgotten."

Trying not to sound alarming, Cat let out a weak laugh. "Yep, it's you, but it's still me." She paused for a long second. "And there's a problem."

Fully awake now, Infiniti sat upright. "Yeah? What is it?"

Feeling like she needed to say it quick, like pulling a band-aid, Cat rushed out, "Joe came in and saw me sitting really, really close to D."

Infiniti blinked. Her mouth fell open. She looked from Cat to D and then back to Cat. "What?"

In a lowered voice, D explained. "He came in, and we were talking, but leaning in and kind of hugging. And he got really pissed."

"And then he took off," Cat finished.

Fin's hands shook while a look of dread spread across her face and tears sprang to her eyes. "No, no, no."

"I'm so sorry, Fin. I really am, and I promise it wasn't intentional."

"Not at all," D added. "We were just talking," he paused, "in close proximity."

Infiniti sprang to her feet. "I have to go to him." She dashed for the door, but then stopped. She spun around. "But I'm not me!"

She paced in a circle, wiping the tears that poured from her eyes. "I know. I'll call him." She raced over to her phone, but stopped. "I don't even have my voice," she said between sobs.

"Text him," Cole suggested.

"Yeah, I'll text," she muttered, moving away from the group. She returned a few seconds later, looking devastated. "He's not answering."

Crushed at what she had done, and wanting to make things right, Cat sat in front of Fin. Even if it meant they could all be in some serious trouble if their mishap leaked to the Board of Regents, Cat needed to do whatever she could to help Fin. "Let's both go to him and explain the whole thing."

"I'm involved and should go too," D offered.

While Fin processed Cat's offer, Cole had his own idea. "I'm all for going to Joe and explaining, and I'll go too, but let's do that *after* we go to Clifftop and look for those dead trees and cups. I'd like to avoid trouble with school if at all possible. But I'll stand by whatever the group wants to do."

Nobody said anything as everyone waited for Fin to speak. She looked up at them with a tear-streaked face. Cat had only cried like that once, and it was a long time ago. She had hardened herself to such an extreme, she barely recognized herself looking so heartbroken. It was a strange sight and made her uncomfortable, even though those feelings were Fin's. Sensing her emotions, D placed a reassuring hand on Cat's shoulder.

"Today," Fin finally said. "We look up on Clifftop today. But if we don't find anything, then we tell Joe. And then Addie and Saundra."

Cat nodded, thinking it was a good idea. She just prayed they could complete the mission before the end of the day.

CHAPTER 10

*A*greeing to skip their classes for the day, the four made the trek from Jory to Clifftop. Once they emerged from the mountain and into the outside world, Infiniti drew in a deep breath, erasing the musty and humid cave air from her lungs and replacing it with crisp, fresh mountain aroma. Usually, Infiniti loved springtime in Colorado because it was still cool, but not too cold. Thin layers of snow dotted the ground in patches. White clumps hung to the highest tree branches. Birds crisscrossed from the sky while puffy clouds strolled across the blue backdrop. She loved coming out here where everything was alive. But after learning Joe had seen Cat with D, thinking it was her with D, she felt hollow inside. And he still hadn't answered her texts.

D scanned the area. "I think we should start to the right and circle back to here."

"Sounds good," Cole said.

They made their way across the open area where the combat classes and outdoor sports took place. They were about to slip into the woods when Infiniti spotted Natalie Putman. She was sitting on a blanket, her head pointed up at the sky. Natalie was a super cool witch, and she and Infiniti had gotten close when they battled the Valkyries last semester. She also knew Natalie had lost her mom that semester. Infiniti understood that kind of loss. Her mom had died when their house burned down, and she had been saved by Joe. She shivered while the pain of that moment worked through her. She hated that Natalie was suffering.

"Is that Natalie?" Cat asked.

"Yeah, that's her," Infiniti said. "I'm gonna check on her real quick."

Stepping off in Natalie's direction, Cat stopped Infiniti with a tug on the arm. "Uh, are you forgetting that you're me?"

Infiniti stared down at the long legs of the body she inhabited, Cat's body, almost forgetting about their switch.

"Shit," she murmured. "I'm getting used to being you. That can't be a good sign."

"No," Cat admitted. "It can't. And I'm feeling the same. Like I'm comfortable being petite and soft."

Infiniti gazed into her own face, almost feeling detached from it. "I wonder if the longer we're like this, the further we are from being able to change back."

"Whoa," D cut in. "Are you saying the longer you're like this, the more likely it is that it's permanent?"

Infiniti shook her head, dismissing the idea even though deep down she thought it a possibility. "Nah, no way." She let out a nervous chuckle. "Right?"

"No way," Cat added quickly, but Infiniti saw the doubt in her own eyes.

Natalie started getting up, taking their attention from their conversation. She dusted herself off, then folded her blanket. She spotted the group and headed their way.

"Hey, guys," she said, tucking her long brown hair behind her ears.

"Hey, Natalie," Infiniti and Cat said at the same time.

Natalie shifted the blanket in her hands. She eyed the skies. "Rain is coming. You guys may want to head back in."

Infiniti scanned the skies. The wind had kicked up. The white puffy clouds had multiplied, forming a blanket of gray.

"That was fast," Infiniti said, thinking it weird how the weather had turned so quickly. She eyed the team. "We will. We just need to do some investigating for our hunt mission."

Natalie wrapped her arms around herself. "I see. Well, be careful. I sense something coming in the wind."

"Something coming?" Cole's piercing green eyes swept the skies. "Like what?"

She shrugged. "I'm not sure. Could be something, could be nothing. Just, don't stay out here too long." With a nod, Natalie headed back to campus.

The team moved in close together. "April showers," Infiniti said. "But worse? I mean, nothing can really be worse right now, right?"

"Right. Plus, rain never hurt anyone," D declared with determination. "Besides, it hasn't even started. I say we do what we can for as long as we can."

"You're right," Cat agreed. "It's not raining yet. And we're running out of time."

With the temperature plummeting, Infiniti started shivering. Her mind cluttered with thoughts of not finishing the mission and being stuck in Cat's body forever. What would happen between her and Joe then? She pushed away her fears and forced herself to focus on the task at hand—finding a dead tree that had something to do with cups.

"Okay, let's do this," she said to the group, mustering her courage.

The group roamed through the forest, crisscrossing in and out of clusters of various sizes of pine trees. Some loomed high and thin, others were short and thick.

"There," D announced, pointing at a grouping. "Those trees are dying. See how they look grayish brownish. They're supposed to be evergreens. And they don't even have that many leaves."

A fat droplet of water splashed on Infiniti's forehead. She wiped it away. "Oh no, I felt a raindrop."

Cat held out her hand. "I feel it, too."

Dismissing the weather, Cole approached the cluster of trees, and the others followed.

"Everyone look for something resembling a cup," he said.

Infiniti circled the trees, studying the trunks. She pressed her hands on a few chunks of bark, hoping a cup would magically appear, but nothing happened. Moving around and trading positions with the others, she examined the branches. She tugged here and there, but still nothing.

She sighed. "I don't see anything that looks like a cup."

More droplets started coming down from the skies. The wind whipped through the trees, kicking up leaves and sending waves of rustling through the air. The temperature plummeted a few more degrees.

"We should go back in before it gets worse," Cat cautioned, pulling on a strand of long hair that had blown into her mouth.

"Agreed," D said. "Let's go back."

Wrapping her arms around her body and tucking her chin down with her shoulders up, Infiniti hurried to the entrance back into campus. And when the rain started coming down in sheets and the winds turned frigid, she kicked her stride into full speed. Cat's long legs catapulted her forward with ease, and she was the first one back at the entrance to SMA.

"Wow," Infiniti said, realizing she wasn't even winded. "So this is what it feels like to run really fast." Cole filed in after her. And then she saw her petite frame trucking along with D at her side, holding her hand.

"D really has it for Cat."

"Only all semester," Cole added.

"Really?"

"Really."

Now that they were together inside the opening that led down to campus, they huddled together for a few seconds as they tried to figure out their next move.

"Now what?" D asked.

"Now we wait for the rain to stop, I guess," Cat suggested, gazing over her shoulder at the buckets of water coming down so hard you couldn't even see the forest."

Infiniti watched the showers, too, wondering if they'd pass quickly or not. "Let's go back to our rooms and change clothes."

She wondered if she'd see Joe, and hoped she would. The longer she held the pain of him "seeing" her with D, the worse she felt.

"I could use a change of clothes," Cole agreed. "And then we can come right back. The rain will probably pass by then."

Walking down the surface of the slick cave, a massive crackle of thunder shook from Clifftop. Infiniti pressed her hands against the cavern walls, her heart lurching from another, even louder crackle that followed. Her mind immediately went to the tarot card, the part about the drum fire. D had said drum fire meant thunder.

She turned to face Cat, who was right behind her.

"Face the drum fire," she uttered, her mouth hanging open while droplets fell from her wet hair.

"Confront your fear," Cat whispered, her soaked clothes stuck to her frame.

"The God of Thunder will hold you near," D said, finishing the line.

Cole's face set in determination. His stare intensified. "But should you shelter yourself away, the company will fail, the task will fade."

Another thunderclap exploded overhead, followed by a burst of lightning that illuminated the space all around them. Infiniti clutched the top of her shirt and pulled the soaked fabric, realizing that by leaving Clifftop and escaping the storm, they were sheltering away.

And then a light bulb went off in Infiniti's head. "When the bluff is not a lie! That's not me and Cat. It's Clifftop. Bluff is another word for cliff. And we're in here, sheltering away!"

Cat held Infiniti's arm. "We have to go back."

Cole and D peered at the opening to Clifftop. The view revealed dark skies and streaks of light that showcased thick rain hammering down from the heavens. Infiniti gulped. She was from Houston. She had braved monstrous hurricanes and floods. But in that moment, steps away from a mother of a storm, knowing she and her friends needed to face the onslaught, terror gripped her.

"We need to go back out there, don't we?" she asked in a quivering voice.

D kept his stare on the pounding storm. "I got caught in a storm like this once when I was out running. The rain was so thick, I couldn't see more than an inch in front of my face. Even with my enhanced sight connected to my abilities." He paused as more thunder erupted overhead. He rubbed his forehead. "And one of the guys I was with got struck by lightning."

Infiniti gulped. "What happened to him?"

Amid another streak of light and booming thunder crash, he said, "He didn't make it."

Infiniti punched his shoulder. "Really? You have to tell us that story right now?"

"Sorry, Fin," D went on. "I just want us to be prepared. Our visibility might be low and that lightning could hurt one of you."

The team moved in close as they considered their next move.

Imagining trying to walk through a massive storm with rain pounding her face, water streaming into her eyes, and lightning bolts everywhere, Infiniti said, "We need this storm to stop..." Her voice trailed off as her mind processed what she had said. "Stop," she repeated, thinking of her time freezing abilities. She'd been working hard all semester at honing her skills. Maybe she could freeze the storm.

"What is it?" Cat asked.

"Maybe I can make the storm stop."

Cole moved around to fully face her. "Can you do that?"

Shit, could she? She'd been able to advance her supernatural abilities over the last few months, but could she stop a storm? She didn't know. But she knew she had to try. It was either that or fail The Hunt mission and the WTF class, possibly get kicked out of SMA, and risk staying stuck in Cat's body forever. And then there was Joe...she needed to complete the mission so she could go to him and explain things. Completing the WTF mission had become everything.

CHAPTER 11

*I*nfiniti stared down at Cat's olive-toned hands that were long and strong, the hands that were now hers. Could she wield her power in Cat's body and control the rain? Surely, she could. Her power came from her mind, not her body. And her mind was still hers.

"I think I can do it," she said after a while.

"That's good enough for me," D said, pulling his phone out of the back pocket of his jeans. "Unless your phones are waterproof, we should keep them here."

He tucked his phone on a ledge that jutted out from the pathway. Infiniti, Cat, and Cole handed him their phones, and he put theirs away, too.

With another rumble from the heavens, Cole asked, "So we head to that cluster of dead trees?"

"Yes," Infiniti answered. "I do my thing and then we head to the trees. Unless anyone else has a better idea."

With no one else offering an alternate idea, the four made their way back to the opening. The angry skies continued their onslaught of rain as thunder and lightning warred in an epic battle of light and sound.

Just before stepping out into the deluge, Infiniti called out.

"Wait!" All eyes turned to her as doubt clouded her mind. Eyeing the endless rains, she gulped. "This is a lot bigger than I thought. I mean, you know, standing here and looking at it." She shook her hands and took deep breaths. "Give me a quick second."

Cat rubbed her chin. "Rain is pretty big. But can you do maybe a small patch? Like the area around the trees?"

Infiniti thought about it. "Good idea, Cat. I can manage that way better."

"Then let's link hands and get to those trees as quick as possible," Cat said.

"Sounds like a plan," Cole said. He took his place in the front of the group and held out his hand to Infiniti. She took it with a firm grip.

"Let's go," Cole said, stepping into the storm.

Infiniti kept her head down and eyes closed as torrents poured down on her. Thunder boomed. Lightning snapped. Sloshing through the saturated ground, she kept telling herself she'd be fine, that she could freeze the rain and the lightning. That they'd finish the mission. That she and Cat would switch back. And she'd see Joe again and explain everything.

Cole stopped in place. "We're here!"

Infiniti dropped his hand and pressed her hands across her forehead, shielding her eyes as she cracked them so she could see the trees. Cat and D huddled around her.

"You ready?" Cat hollered.

With a nod, Infiniti widened her stance. She held out her hands, closed her eyes, and focused on the trees. She envisioned an invisible shield around them, a shield big enough to include herself and her friends, like a giant umbrella. Massive, thick, and clear, it stretched out far and wide and blocked the rain and lightning from getting through. With the picture clear in her mind she said, "Stop."

The rain pouring down on them halted. Opening her eyes, she looked all around. Just as she envisioned, the storm hammered on all around them, but she and her friends and the trees around them were spared as the droplets from the heavens hovered over their heads.

Cat smiled. "You did it!"

Infiniti smiled, too, because she had! And on her first try! But now what were they supposed to do?

As if Mother Nature had read her mind, an ear-deafening crack exploded all around them, followed by a blast of light that sparked red in front of Infiniti's eyes. Cole and D knocked Infiniti and Cat to the ground, shielding them. And when the last reverberation of the phenomenon faded, Infiniti sensed crackling warmth. She jerked her head up with a start to see flames erupting as the dead trees burned with fury. So she wasn't able to freeze the lightning after all, and now they faced an inferno!

"Oh shit, shit, shit," she uttered, while fear gripped her.

"The rain!" D hollered. "Release it."

"No! Don't!" Cole yelled. "Remember the riddle? Embrace the other, hold the tongue in hand. The prize will appear where you stand." He pointed at the flames. "Tongues of fire."

Infiniti covered her mouth with her hands while her spine tingled, and her gut clenched. "Oh, shit," she mumbled against her fingers. "*Actual* fire is part of our mission?"

Cole ran his fingers through his wet, dark hair. "Seems so. And it looks like someone has to go in there."

The fire crackled and popped. The heat intensified. Infiniti wanted to unfreeze the rain and douse the fire, but Cole was right. The answer to the riddle was in the fire. Somewhere in those red-hot trees.

"I'll go," D offered. He tore off his T-shirt, ready to summon his lightning bird.

Cole stepped forward. "No, I'll do it. I'm connected to the element of fire. I've got this."

"The card," Cat warned, stopping Cole in his tracks. "There are two in flames. Not one. Two that are joined."

Tingles of panic and dread raced across Infiniti's skin as dawning recognition set in. "Holy hell," Infiniti whispered. "It's us, Cat. *We* have to go in there."

A wave of despair came over her as her eyes watered over. She was deathly afraid of fire and didn't know if she could charge into a blaze. Not after what had happened to her mom. And then she remembered how Destiny and Craig said they had to face fire in their mission. Theirs had been in a dreamscape and not exactly real, but they'd been brave and done it. Could she and Cat?

Cat took Infiniti's hands. She squeezed. "I've got this, Fin. I've got nothing to lose. I'll go in."

"The hell you won't," D cut. "You've got me, Cat."

Infiniti's mouth dropped. Cat was willing to sacrifice herself for her? Even at D's expense? She didn't know a lot about Cat, but she knew Cat had a future to live for. One that included D.

"No way, Cat," Infiniti declared. "We're in this together."

D tugged on Cat's arm. He pulled her around and planted his mouth on hers. Infiniti blinked, thinking it was so weird to see someone kissing her like that. Especially someone other than Joe. But if she was charging into certain death, she understood the gesture. If Joe were around, she'd kiss him too.

"Three seconds," D said when he pulled away from Cat. "You both go in. And if you don't holler that you're okay in three seconds, I'm coming in."

"*We're* coming in," Cole added.

Cat lifted herself up on Infiniti's toes and kissed him again. "Three seconds."

Hand in hand with Cat, Infiniti eyed the growing inferno. "We run in fast," she whispered to Cat. "Like, really, really fast."

"*Muy rápido*," Cat agreed.

Closing her eyes and sucking in her breath, Infiniti yelled, "Now!"

Charging forward with Cat, a spray of heat blew against her, then faded. She stopped in place, her heart pounding out of control.

"Are we...alive?" She asked.

Cat yanked Infiniti in close. "Yes!" Then she yelled out to the guys, "We're okay!"

Slowly separating from their embrace, they examined their surroundings. They stood in a space with no fire, no rain. In fact, there wasn't even any sound. It was only the two of them and before them a small, white-barked tree with no leaves. Infiniti placed her fingertips on it and found the surface smooth and warm. The texture reminded her of sanded wood. And there at the base of the tree sat a bowl-shaped glowing red object.

"I don't know what that is, but it must be what we're looking for," Infiniti whispered, as if they were in a holy place of magic or something.

"It must," Cat agreed, her hands now on the tree too.

Taking a closer look, Infiniti bent down. "Do we get it?"

Crouching next to her, Cat said, "I think so."

"Together?" Infiniti asked, peering at her own face.

"Yes," Cat said. "Together."

Eyeing the small, glowing bowl, they extended their hands. Their fingers moved closer to the object. Slowly, they touched it. Barely making contact at first, they waited a few seconds before cupping it fully and lifting it off the ground. They stood, clutching the warm bowl.

Infiniti glanced about, waiting for something to happen, but nothing did. Touching the bowl did nothing. Facing her fears and stepping through the fire did nothing. They were still the same. In each other's bodies, trapped, and maybe forever. She and Cat sank to their knees.

"We're still stuck," Cat choked out, as a lone tear streaked down her face.

Infiniti's hopes of returning to her true self dashed away while the hot sting of tears filled her eyes. "Look at us," she said to Cat. "Still switched and both of us crying."

They each kept one hand on the bowl, but reached out with their other hand, wiping each other's tears away.

"We'll make it work," Infiniti said. "It's not so bad being you."

Cat nodded. "Okay." And then she smiled. "You're not so bad either."

The ground beneath their feet shook. A rumble filled their ears. And out of nowhere, a white flash blinded them. Infiniti held her breath and braced herself, waiting for a bolt of lightning to strike her to the core, but it didn't. Instead, a warmth started in her belly and spread throughout her, like hot chocolate on a cold day. She waited a few seconds before sneaking a peak and saw Cat in front of her. The real Cat. Long, wet, dark hair. Skintight soaking clothes. Cleavage for miles. She looked down at her petite frame. She patted her small chest and tugged at her wet hair that Cat had pulled up in a ponytail.

"Oh my god! I'm me!"

She lunged for Cat and gave her the biggest hug.

"And I'm me." Cat laughed with a tight squeeze.

Cole and D stumbled into the space, nearly colliding with Infiniti and Cat. A sweeping burst of fire followed them but evaporated with a whoosh.

"You're both okay," D said with a sigh of relief.

"And celebrating," Cole added with his brow raised. "I assume that means—"

"We're back in our bodies!" Infiniti finished quickly. She lifted the bowl. "And we've got this!"

D eyed the shallow bowl. "That's our object?"

"Has to be," Cat said. "There's nothing else here."

"Well done ladies!" Cole exclaimed. "But now we need to figure out what to do next because outside this supernatural space, a fire is raging." Cole eyed Infiniti. "And miraculously, your shield is still holding. You need to drop it so the rain can douse the flames."

She handed the bowl to Cat and widened her stance. Holding out her hands, she caught a glint of the engagement ring Joe had given her, thinking how much she had missed having it on her finger and how she couldn't wait to see Joe.

"Okay," she whispered. "Release the rain. Here goes."

She envisioned the shield she had placed over the trees, the clear umbrella that stopped the rain, freezing it in place. She didn't need the rain then, but she needed it now. With the image clear in her mind, she uttered, "Release."

With a rush, as if a heavenly floodgate had been opened, torrents of water fell around them. The sizzle of dying flames floated in the air. And just as quickly as they were doused, the rain stopped. Standing with Cat, D, and Cole, she looked around. The mysterious white tree had vanished. Only the dead bark and branches from earlier remained.

"We did it," Infiniti said.

The four gathered in and hugged. Their smiles turned to laughter as the relief of having survived what they had been through set in.

"Infiniti!" Joe ran over to them. But before he swooped in, he stopped, remnants of betrayal clear in his eyes.

"Joe!" She rushed into him and held on for dear life, thinking how she could've died, and how grateful she was that she hadn't. "It wasn't me that you saw with D in the study lounge. It was Cat. We had switched bodies somehow, but now I'm back to being me again."

The others chimed in, backing up Infiniti.

Joe buried his face into her neck and squeezed her tight. "Babe," he whispered. "I knew you couldn't do that to me, but I was scared as hell. I had no idea what was happening."

She pulled back and cupped his face, kissing him over and over. "I would never ever hurt you, Joe. Not ever."

"Oh, thank Goddess!" Natalie called out, rushing up to them with a group of other students. "You guys are okay!"

"We are," Cat said. "Thank you, Natalie."

With her hair tied up in a messy bun, Addie came into view. She cut through the group and pushed her dark glasses up the bridge of her nose. "I see the four of you can't stay out of trouble." Her scowl turned to a smile. "But I'm happy to see no one was hurt."

"Yeah," Infiniti laughed. "We're happy about that part, too."

"And we're also thrilled to have found this," Cat added, extending the bowl to Addie.

"Ah, you've found the object for your hunt mission?"

"Yes," the four said in unison.

"And you were the team leader, right, Cat?"

"Well, I was, but not really. We all kinda were."

Addie smiled and nodded. "Very well." She tapped the bowl. "I'll be sure to get this to Saundra." She looked over the object carefully with both hands, then tucked it under her arm. "Good work, team. Now, get back to campus and get out of those soaked clothes. Don't want you guys catching a cold out here."

With everyone celebrating their victory, Infiniti tugged Cat to the side. "I think you're amazing. Being you was pretty fun."

Cat smiled. "And so was being you."

They hugged long and hard. Pulling apart, Infiniti said, "And I really like you and D together."

Cat eyed D, who was patiently waiting for her. "I really like him, too."

After a long hot shower, Infiniti slipped on her robe, wrapped her hair up in a towel, and headed for her room. And when she stepped inside, she found the space transformed. Rose petals covered the floor. A small fire crackled in the fireplace. Candles cast a soft white glow around the perimeter. And Joe was sitting in her chair, holding a long-stemmed rose. He stood and walked over to her.

"Taylor texted me. Said she was spending the night with Clay."

She took the rose and smelled the sweet fragrance. "She is?"

"Yes, she is. So tonight, it's just me and you."

She placed the rose on her nightstand, took the towel off her head, and shook her hair with her hands. "I love it when it's just me and you."

She tucked her hand in his jeans and pulled him close. He bent down and kissed her softly, tenderly, as if it was their first kiss. "I love you so much, Infiniti."

"I love you, too, Joseph Greg." She pulled away and stared up into his dreamy eyes. "So much."

He slid his hands behind her head and into her hair and kissed her neck. "Can I make love to you all night?"

She tingled all over, her heart racing with excitement and desire. She loved it when he asked her that question. "Yes, you can."

He scooped her up, placed her on her bed, and stripped off his clothes nice and slow, his hungry stare never leaving hers. And as their bodies became one, her heart and soul soared with his to magical and sensual places knowing everything in the world was right.

THE MOON

TISH THAWER

"Only a *true* witch may enter here."
—Unknown, Halvard Campus

CHAPTER 1

*E*vergreens swayed ever so slightly up on Clifftop, their pine scent drifting to my nose on an *almost* warm breeze. I zipped up my jacket, yanking its hood over my long dark hair. At this elevation near the end of April, warm was a relative term.

"Hey, Putnam. Why up so early? Bird watching again?"

"Bird watching, bear watching ... you know, something like that."

"Bear watching? Wait, what?" Caleb, our resident bear-shifter, emerged from the woods, pulling a sweatshirt over his head and down his lean chest and chiseled abs.

"Yeah, I saw you lumber off this morning. Find anything good to eat?"

Caleb folded his long legs beneath him and sat down beside me on my blanket-covered log. "Don't tell anyone, but I found a great berry patch and a bee hive just off one of the side trails. It's like my own personal breakfast buffet."

"Nice!" My mouth watered as an awkward grumble from my stomach filled the air. "Maybe I should've grabbed something to eat before heading up too. Note to self," I joked.

Caleb laughed as he leaned down to tie his boots, his dark, angle-cut bangs hanging slightly over his warm brown eyes that mirrored my own. "So seriously, what are you doing up here? I've seen you pretty much every morning this semester. Is your first class up here or something, or do you just like chatting me up?"

I shook my head. "Nope. Just hanging out, enjoying the company."

I shrugged and pushed the worn tarot card under the edge of my leg and let an uncomfortable silence fill the air between us. I didn't want to discuss our shared assignment at the moment.

The end of the semester was quickly approaching, and with finals coming up—plus all the damn extra interdisciplinary projects we were given—I knew these last few weeks were bound to fly by. Problem was...I didn't care about any of it—finals, helping with everyone's team assignments, whatever the latest impending doom was; none of it mattered to me. Not since Mom.

Tempest, my best friend and roommate, had tried her damnedest to pull me back to being myself, throwing out all the stops and tossing every cheer-filled and frivolous event my way since Christmas break, but nothing worked. I wasn't mad at her for trying, but I had to admit, spending time alone up here on Clifftop mostly started as a way to avoid her latest attempts. I'd even considered requesting to move into the empty dorm room next to our current one, just for some alone time. But that would break her heart, and I couldn't do that to her. I loved fun; I loved Tempest, but sometimes I didn't think she truly understood what I was really going through. The relationship with her parents was so different than my mom's and mine. I just didn't think she could relate to the soul-deep loss I felt—or more so, the overwhelming guilt.

"Well, I'm headed in." Caleb's voice brought me back to the moment. "Guess I'll see you tomorrow. Bye, Natalie." He pushed from the log and jogged to the spot where the skybridge led back down onto campus.

I needed to get going too, but...

I pulled the card from beneath my leg, looking at its worn image again. We'd first pulled it during our ITF class, and I immediately recognized it for what it was. The Moon card. I'd read enough tarot growing up to know the symbols of the eighteenth major arcana, even if this card's imagery was a bit darker and somewhat specific to our campus. A silver orb shone brightly in the top center, resting lazily between two pillars carved to look like part of our castle walls surrounded by a backdrop of evergreen forest, but its beauty mocked me. I'd tried everything I could think of to decipher the clue on the back, but to no avail.

The forever shimmering moon, hides what you seek. Travel as you may, you'll never find where I lay. Shillelagh from blackthorn are meant for thee, but hidden in the depths forever I'll be. Illusion or deception, for you will have to choose, but make no mistake, transformation's the ultimate ruse.

I tilted my head back and closed my eyes; the wind whistling through the pines created a song that helped lull me to my center, which lately, was a feat in and of itself. I took a deep breath and whispered the blessing I'd repeated every morning since Mom's death.

"*Remain free, Mom. May your soul forever soar with the Goddess.*"

A soft wind brushed my cheek, and I was as ready as I was going to be to face another day.

I looked around for my backpack, its olive-green canvas blending into the grass behind the log. Once spotted, I tucked my blanket inside, tossed it over my shoulder, and sprinted inside the mountain. The campus was buzzing with activity as I made my way to Eirhal Hall for my first class of the day. Waving to Madame Roth outside the Infirmary, I continued to the staircase that would carry me up to the second floor and Professor Knox's Alchemy class.

After playing "Secret Santa" with him over Christmas break, I was happy to have him as a teacher, but dang—his class was hard. As a true witch, I never needed to know much about Alchemy, since most of what I accomplished was done with a spell. But, since coming here to the Sun & Moon Academy for Supernatural Guardians, all sorts of new information was required for the tasks we were being trained to face. Especially since my major was Healing Arts—there were a lot of creatures who didn't respond to magic like you'd expect. It was also why I was taking Supernatural History with Professor Fairchild this semester and Intro to

Supernatural Cultural Relations with Professor Admundson. I had a lot to learn about the other species surrounding me.

"Good morning, Natalie," Professor Knox acknowledged me as I slid into my seat.

"Good morning." I pulled out my notes, eyeing the symbols and scratches along their edges. I was familiar with a few, but had no idea the history or the intricacy behind what most of them meant.

"Today, we'll be continuing our study of one of the most basic but most important elements in the sacred science and royal art that is Alchemy—Mercury. Please turn your books to page 693."

I flopped the heavy leather-bound tome that was my Alchemy textbook open to about half-way. The page I landed on contained an image of a filigree border surrounding some text. The border was formed by intricate scrollwork filled with multiple phoenixes along its edge with an elaborate crest at its top. I squinted and read the text inside.

> *"Now I will teach and describe the secret of the arts, which secret is at the heart of all secrets hidden in the art of Alchemy; since one will here understand the wonderful works that God has accomplished in all things he has made out of the four elements... For I shall here teach you to know the spirits of herbs, trees, and all growing things; how to separate them from their bodies, and also how to purify the four elements and restore them to their first being and their perfect power; that is, that when the elements are purified, how they can be put together again and make a perfect and fixed body of them, which is then glorified and has a miraculous effect."* — Issac Holland, *Opera Vegetabilia* (15ᵗʰ century)

Drawn to the words, I leaned closer, running a finger over the page. I wanted to re-read the passage again and again but didn't have time. Following Knox's instructions, I continued to flip through the book until reaching the number he'd called out...693.

The alchemic symbol for mercury, or quicksilver as it was also known, was centered at the top of the page. A circle sitting atop a cross with a crescent moon at its peak. It looked familiar to the astrological symbol for the planet Mercury as we learned last week, and apparently, the element could also be represented by a stylized snake or serpent.

"Today, we'll discover why the quicksilver is thought to resemble a snake. Your labs have been prepared with the proper ingredients, but have a care." Professor Knox's voice dropped to a serious tone. "You must follow the directions exactly."

I glanced around my station to see a Bunsen burner, a couple Erlenmeyer flasks, and two beakers containing liquids—one silver, and one clear—and a whole measure of safety equipment.

I looked to my book and read the recipe for the assignment:

Creating Mercuric Oxide:

    1. Put on goggles, gloves, and mask. (Do not skip, as final substance is highly toxic)

    2. Mix two grams of elemental mercury with two grams of nitric acid in flask.

    2. Heat over burner for one minute.

    3. Remove from heat and notate your results. (Warning: Do not inhale)

Wow. Sounded easy enough.

Lifting the charcoal-lined breathing mask to my face, I took a deep breath and struggled not to laugh. The urge to call out *"Luke, I am your father"* filled my head. The same thought must have occurred to a few other students as a couple of fake lightsaber fights broke out around the room. Following the rest of the instructions, I placed the plastic safety goggles over my eyes and pulled on the rubber gloves.

Rereading the next step, I noticed it didn't specify which liquid to use first, so I assumed it wouldn't matter. Measuring out the thick silver mercury, I poured it into my flask—the nitric acid came next. Now that the two materials were combined, I lit my Bunsen burner.

The reaction was instantaneous.

A thick red vapor rose from the surface, hovering over the top and writhing like a snake. The mercuric oxide precipitated and fell through the liquid in the form of bright red crystals. It was amazing. Magical.

Professor Knox's voice filled the room again. "Mercury was believed to transcend the liquid and solid states, and that belief carried over into other areas such as life and death, heaven and earth."

I bent down closer, inspecting the fallen crystals now resting on the bottom of the flask.

"The element has a feminine quality, so it can also be common for the mercury alchemy symbol to reflect female influences." Knox's voice was now directly behind me. "As you can imagine, its transformative properties can be very alluring."

The foggy *snake* continued to writhe atop the solution, and I became lost in its dance.

"This is why alchemy is considered the Sacred Science or Royal Arts, for not only have you created something that is truly new in nature, but transformative at its very core."

I stared at the crystals, shining brightly in the liquid and totally got what he was saying. There was something about them that seemed to draw me in, and I wasn't the only one.

In the next lab over, Dillys, a witch from Modi tower, had a glazed look in her eyes as she reached her hand toward the flask.

"Ms. Sprokes, I would advise against that. As I mentioned before, the fumes are toxic, and so is the liquid itself," Professor Knox warned.

Dillys pulled back her hand and shook her head, as if breaking free from a trance.

With all of our attention back on high alert, we spent the rest of class learning how to safely sift the crystals from the solution and dispose of the bio-waste. It was a little precarious, but all-in-all, pretty easy. Once the crystals were sorted, we were asked to deposit them into a basket at the front of class when we left for the day.

Once my station was clean, I stuffed my textbook back into my pack and headed for the door. As one of the last to leave, I stopped to admire the basket of beautiful red crystals collected so far. There were large and small chunks, each uniquely facetted, but all sharing the same vibrant hue. I extended my hand, ready to add mine to the pile, when Professor Knox grabbed my wrist.

"Want to keep one?" he asked, lifting the largest crystal from my palm.

"Really? Can I?" I turned my hand over, dumping the rest into the basket.

"Sure. Just don't tell the others." He winked and placed the jagged chunk of stone back in my hand, snagged the basket, and walked away.

Cool. I rubbed my finger down a smooth edge of the ruby-like crystal, noting its perfect shape and sheen. Shoving it into my pocket, I headed out the door and back toward the food court. My next class was in half-an-hour, and at this point, I was absolutely starving.

CHAPTER 2

"*B*lock, pivot, chant, cast! Block, pivot, chant, cast! Faster!"

Addie Beaumont was a tyrant. A sweet and caring tyrant, but a tyrant nonetheless.

Her instructions rang out over Clifftop for everyone to hear. "Make sure you have a defensive spell ready to protect yourself. You never know when you'll come up against another skilled witch."

I had plenty of spells in my repertoire—offensive and defensive —but learning how to weave them skillfully into combat alongside other guardians was a completely different story. One witch would move left while another moved right, walking directly into the path of the magic. To say we were nowhere close to being a true "team" was a total understatement. Then again, I thought we worked pretty damn well together last semester against the Valkyries and zombies.

"Ouch!" A sizzle of magic zinged my shoulder.

"Stay focused," Addie snapped, her brown eyes sparkling with magic.

Addie was usually the coolest witch around, but these drill-sergeant-like tactics had me smarting back, "Yes, sir."

She turned and leveled me with a withering glare. "I'm only trying to prepare you for the worst, Natalie. Letting your mind drift during a fight won't only get you hurt, but could lead to others being killed. Is that something you want on your conscience?"

I gritted my teeth and shook my head. How could she say that to me? I was already carrying enough guilt over my mom. "No. You're right. I'm sorry. I lost focus. It won't happen again."

I stood there, frozen in anger as she walked back across the field.

"Hey...are you all right?" Taylor whispered from over my shoulder.

"I'm fine," I replied, not turning around.

"I heard what Addie said to you in class today." Tempest sighed. "I'm sorry. I almost said something, but didn't want to make things worse."

I lifted my face from my pillow and smiled at my best friend. "It's okay."

"Maybe we should practice some spells to impress her. See if she lets up a bit. Besides, I know you're holding back." Tempest winked, excited by the potential of working magic together again.

I'd helped her and Eryx with their hunt mission, and that had gone fine. But she was right—even then, I was holding back. My magic had been bolstered by Tempest, Marina, and the others, but to be honest, if I'd had to do it alone, I'm not sure the outcome would have been the same. I just wasn't at the top of my game lately.

I sat up and swung my legs over the edge of my bed. Mystic was there, weaving between my feet, ready to go as well.

"I don't know. I think we can practice all we want and follow all her lessons to a T, but it's just not the same as being in a real fight, ya know? It's not like you can choreograph your opponent's reactions and skills." I shrugged.

"Yeah, I get that, but you know what they say...when you're in a stressful situation, you automatically revert to your training. I think that's what Addie's trying to drill into us—so we'll automatically react the right way when things go south."

"I'm sure you're right. I just hate the idea of things *going south* again so soon." I pushed from the bed, tip-toeing around our shared familiar, and hit the power button on our Keurig. The idea of facing another round of challenges had worn heavy on me since the first day of our Interdisciplinary team missions. My team had thankfully blown through all so far, but it was my turn to take point on the final one. And as expected, The Hunt was proving to be the most difficult.

I knew most of the other teams had already found their magical artifacts, mainly because I'd helped out with a few. Combining my magic with others, I was able to help solve their issue, but for some reason, I couldn't get past my own clue.

"Do you mind if we work on something else instead?" I returned to my bed with a cup of hot cider in hand.

"Sure. What'd ya have in mind?" Tempest folded her legs beneath her.

"I need help deciphering the clue for my ITF hunt assignment."

"Yeah, sure. You know I love a good mystery." Tempest rubbed her hands together.

I pulled the card from the side-pocket of my backpack and read it out loud. "The forever shimmering moon, hides what you seek. Travel as you may, you'll never find where I lay. Shillelagh from blackthorn are meant for thee, but hidden in the depths forever I'll be. Illusion or deception, for you will have to choose, but make no mistake, transformation's the ultimate ruse."

"Wow! That's a mouthful." Tempest crawled up onto her bed, her legs now dangling over the edge like play toys for Mystic to bat at. "Let's break it down line by line. What was the first one again?"

"The forever shimmering moon, hides what you seek."

"Okay. The forever shimmering moon...that could be..."

"Anything with a reflective surface is what we initially thought," I interjected.

"Right. So let's figure out a few options." Tempest tapped her forefinger against her chin. "Obviously it could be the moon, or a round mirror, or a piece of glass. Maybe one of the witch's balls that hang in the potions room?"

"Oh, wow. I hadn't thought about those."

"But how could something that's see-through hide what you seek?" Tempest questioned her own theory.

"With magic, of course." I sighed.

"Well, duh, but let's think about the next line. Read that one again."

"'Travel as you may, you'll never find where I lay,'" I repeated.

"Hmm. That makes it sound like it's lying down somewhere. So a place low to the ground, maybe?"

"Maybe."

"What's the next line?"

"'Shillelagh from blackthorn are meant for thee, but hidden in the depths forever I'll be.'"

"Okay, see, that one gets me. I have no idea who or what Shillelagh is, but again, hidden in the depths, makes it seem like lake or pool. Something ground level, or beneath."

"Yeah, that's what we thought too, but none of the pools or lakes around here look like a shimmering moon."

"True, but maybe it's outside of the campus."

"The instructions we were given was that the objects were hidden around the campus, so I don't think it can be anywhere else but here."

"Dang. Okay, what's the rest?" Tempest had begun to gnaw on her thumbnail.

"'Illusion or deception, for you will have to choose, but make no mistake, transformation's the ultimate ruse.'"

"Aren't illusion and deception kind of the same thing?" Tempest quirked her head to the side, questioning the obvious.

"Yeah, we don't think that part's relevant, though, but the last bit that hints about transformation seems important and has us all stumped."

Tempest reverted back to tapping her finger to her chin. "Maybe it means whatever you're looking for has been transformed."

"Yeah, maybe. I just don't know. If I had an idea of what Shillelagh meant, maybe I'd understand the transformation line better, but we have no clue. Mallory and Min are heading to the library tomorrow to search for the word, or at least some mention of it, so I guess I'll just wait to hear back from them."

"Yeah. Dang, this is hard. Sorry I'm not much help." Tempest gnawed on the side of her thumb.

"It's okay. You want to go grab some lunch? My next class isn't until two."

"Sure thing." She jumped from her bed and grabbed her favorite quilted shoulder bag off the chair. As she crisscrossed the strap over her chest, I caught sight of something shiny sticking out of the top.

"What's that?" I asked.

"Oh, um…" Her cheeks started to turn red. "It's just something Eryx gave me." She pulled out a large crystal wand. A smooth shard of crystal quartz was wrapped in what looked like copper or bronze filigree that held a smaller round piece of labradorite. It was absolutely gorgeous.

"Wow. That's amazing. Does this mean things are good between you guys, then?"

She smiled shyly. "Yes. At first I thought maybe it was just his way of apologizing, but before I could ask him about it, he said that when he saw it, he instantly thought of me."

"Aww, that's so sweet," I teased.

"Shut up."

"No, really. I'm happy for you. Since we don't have many classes together this semester, and I've definitely been more withdrawn this year, I'm glad you have someone who cares about you and who's watching your back."

She followed me into the hall, pulling the door closed behind us. "Me, too. Speaking of…how's Caleb?"

I spun around to face her. "What?"

"Caleb…I've heard you've been hanging out with him a lot."

"Well, yeah, I guess, but mostly in passing, or just having to do our ITF stuff. There's nothing going on between us."

"Hmm…" Tempest raised her left eyebrow, mocking me.

"What do you mean, *hmmm*?" I asked, not sure if she was pressing me for more information, or if *she* had information *I* needed to know.

"I heard he goes up to Clifftop every day before breakfast because he knows you'll be there." Tempest's cheesy smile spread even wider when she caught sight of the sheer shock plastered on my face.

"You've got to be kidding me. I know for a fact that's not why he's up there." I refused to spill the secret of his hiding place, but dang, I wish he hadn't told people this lie to cover his tracks. Thankfully, Tempest let it drop as we made our way to the food court and finished our lunch. Oddly enough, I found myself rubbing the ruby crystal in my pocket like a damn worry stone the whole time, thinking about what she said.

Caleb and me? I don't know—*maybe.*

CHAPTER 3

I released the crystal and pulled my hand from my pocket as I entered Ansgar I for my two p.m. Basic Weaponry class. Professor Beltaine was one of my favorites, but lately, our lessons had been conducted by Caspar Yazdani.

Cas was a gryphon and student from Modi Tower, but being a 3,500-year-old Guardian of Olympus made his talent with a spear and sword invaluable to us all. Professor Beltaine had arranged for special lessons with him, and while I wasn't bad with the sword, the spear was proving problematic—as in, it was heavy and super long and I could barely control the damn thing.

"Natalie, widen your stance and slide your left hand further down the shaft …"

A round of laughter broke out behind us.

"It will help you gain control of the spear when thrusting." Cas ignored the snickers and continued his one-on-one lesson with me. "You have great instincts, and your speed will improve the more comfortable you get with the weapon."

"Thanks, Cas. I'll keep practicing." I smiled and repositioned my hands as instructed, but was grateful when he moved on.

"Wow. I think he likes you." Caleb walked up behind me and nodded toward Cas.

"Nah. I just think he doesn't get the double entendre of pretty much everything he says. He's way more mature than the rest of us. Plus, he's with Marina now."

Caleb's deep laugh reverberated around me.

"Hey, can I ask you something?" I lowered my spear and turned to face him.

"Sure. Hit me... Well, not really, but you know what I mean." He winked.

"Yeah, um...I was just wondering if you told someone that you go up to Clifftop every morning to see me?" I shook my head and rushed on. "I mean, *I* know why you're up there—your hidden breakfast buffet—but I was just curious why you told them that instead."

Caleb shifted on his feet and shoved his hands into the front pockets of his well-fitting jeans. "Okay. Well, yes. I did tell someone that. Quite a few someone's, actually."

I blinked in confusion. "Why?"

He swallowed hard and looked at the ground. "Because it's true."

Whoa. I did not see that coming. I was definitely comfortable around Caleb and had grown fond of his company this semester, but I hadn't realized it'd become something more for him.

"Um...I don't quite know what to say," I stammered.

"You don't have to say anything." He picked up the closest sword. "But how about you let me help you with your stance and grip?"

I smiled—grateful we weren't going to have some awkward exchange right here and now. "Sounds great."

The clang of steel and wood filled the armory for the rest of class. By the time it was over, I actually felt more confident and in control than ever before.

"Hey, you're a really good sparring partner." I bumped Caleb's shoulder as we replaced our weapons in their designated holders.

"Thanks. So are you."

Summoning my courage, I asked, "So, um, do you want to get some coffee or something and...talk?"

I wasn't sure if I was ready for this, but I felt like it needed to happen. I didn't want to lose Caleb as a friend, and it's not like I was against seeing if there could be something more between us.

Caleb's eyes lit up. "Absolutely. I have one more class today, but I could meet you in the food court as soon as I'm done, if that's okay."

"For sure. I'm done for the day, so whatever's convenient. Just let me know."

"How about six o'clock in front of the Coffee Haven kiosk?"

"Perfect. I'll see you there." I smiled and gave him a little wave as I left the armory.

Booking it down the path to Halstein Hall, I couldn't wait to tell Tempest she was right and to get her take on what I should do. Usually she was already there, hanging with Eryx, but I didn't see her as I walked through the open space of the food court. A cacophony of voices filled the space, one in particular piercing my ears.

"Natalie. Hey, Natalie!"

I turned to see Mallory Dorian and Min Lee strutting toward me through the crowd. They were the other members of my ITF group, and from the grins on both of their faces, they had something to share.

"Hey, what's up?"

Mallory smiled and looked to Min, her golden locks swinging with the motion. "We had some extra down time this afternoon, so we went ahead and popped into the library today. It took some digging, but we finally found mention of Shillelagh." Her purple eyes sparkled with the news.

"Great! What'd ya find out?"

"Any reference made to it states that it's a long wooden stick or staff of some sort, usually made from knotty blackthorn or oak. Some of them have a large knob at the top, but others don't. But in every case, it's associated with Ireland and Irish folklore."

"Wow. Seriously? That's…interesting. But how does it relate to the clue?" I asked.

I pulled the tarot card from my bag and read the passage out loud again. "Shillelagh from blackthorn are meant for thee, but hidden in the depths forever I'll be."

Min hooked his thumbs through the beltloops of his black skinny jeans. "If everything we just found tracks, it sounds like we're looking for some sort of staff."

"Sure, I guess so. But where? *Hidden in the depths* sounds like a pool or lake of some kind, but the previous line talks about a forever shining moon, so it can't be the lake here on campus. Besides, Marina already found the Temple of the Gods there, so if the staff was part of that, she would have seen it down there," I surmised.

"True," Mallory added. "Still, I think we need to keep searching for other bodies of water."

"Okay, but you said it didn't have anything to do with Peacock Lake, and we've already ruled out the Falls. What other bodies of water are there in Havenwood Falls? Remember, Mallory, I'm not from around here." I smiled, trying to lighten the mood that was dwindling fast. They'd come to me with a piece of useful information, and now, it seemed like we were sliding back toward square one.

"Let Min and me do a little more digging. We'll get back to you." She smiled and linked arms with the vampire, sauntering off in their matching kicks toward the quad. They'd become fast friends, especially after she'd explained to her boyfriend, Torent, that he had nothing to worry about because she wasn't Min's type. Then again, no *girl* was. Honestly, if she hadn't set Min up with her best friend Beck already, I figured it was coming soon. The shifter and vampire would make an adorable couple.

I glanced around the food court one more time, and still didn't see Tempest, so I headed back to our dorm. The room was empty, but as expected, there was a note laying on my bed: *Ran to town with Eryx for dinner. Be back soon. XOXO - Temp*

I was truly happy she'd found her person. Looking at the clock, I realized I had an hour to waste and decided to lay down for a power nap. I'd need all the energy I could get if I was going to talk feelings with Caleb. Perhaps at six o'clock, I'd be on the cusp of finding my person as well.

Speckled light drifted in through the open window to our room, casting fractured shadows across my already dark duvet. Sprigs of lavender and juniper dangled from my headboard, offering relaxation and protection as I slept. I snapped my fingers and lit the end of an incense stick propped and ready on my altar. Unfortunately, as peaceful as our room was, I couldn't sleep.

Tossing and turning, I continued to worry over the info Mallory and Min had provided.

Why would an Irish staff be hidden somewhere on our campus, or was I thinking about this all wrong? Maybe the item itself wasn't a big deal, and this was just another way to throw us off during The Hunt and to test our team-building skills. Who knew? Either way, I was still at a loss as to what our next move should be.

I laid my head back and closed my eyes, desperate for inspiration.

"Goddess of night, shine your light. Provide me with some needed insight. Show me the path on this day, for I will follow if you lead the way."

My eyes remained shut as flashes of light pulsed behind my lids. The full moon shone brightly in the sky, straight ahead of me, while my wings skimmed the tree tops below. My wings? Was I flying? Tilting my head left and right, the fractal vison confirmed I was viewing the scene as some sort of bird. What type, I had no idea, and whether that was important or not remained to be seen. What caught my attention, however, was the heavy pull of magic pulsing far below me, beneath the thick canopy of trees. Swooping down, I angled my wings to carry me lower and lower, until I saw a clearing directly in front of me. Gliding closer, I recognized it as one of the fields of Clifftop. Pulling my wings in tight, I landed on the familiar log where I'd spent most of my mornings for the past several months.

The pull of magic from deep within the woods continued to ruffle my feathers. I'd never gone into the woods while human, and I wasn't sure I wanted to now, either. Unfortunately, we needed clues, and this was the first I'd received since starting our hunt assignment.

Flapping my wings, I took flight again, reaching the air current just below the tree line. Riding the wind, I followed the path laid out before me, weaving my way through the evergreens and aspens. About a half-mile in, the pulse of magic pressed me to a stop. I landed in a nearby pine and studied the forest floor below.

Dappled light shone on the grass and ferns in a speckled array of shadows and moonbeams. It was beautiful—almost ethereal, and so very peaceful. My bird eyes blinked and focused closer, catching on a particular shiny section off the beaten trail. I fluttered down to the ground and hopped into the underbrush. The calls of crickets, cicadas, and katydids surrounded me as I explored forward, inch by inch.

A strange light shimmered just ahead as I jumped up on a fallen tree trunk. From this level, it was hard to see, but something was moving in front of me. I pumped my wings and rose a couple feet into the air, landing on a low-lying branch.

Directly below me was a silver pool filled with what looked like liquid metal. It pulsed and warbled as if it were alive, throbbing to a beat I could not hear. I watched, entranced, as it heaved and retracted like the pool itself was taking a breath.

Suddenly, a silver hand pushed up through its surface and I heard, *"Only a true witch may enter here."*

The message repeated in my head at least three times before I was pulled back into my own form. Blinking rapidly, I awoke safe and alone, back in my dorm room. *Holy crap!* This was the clue I needed; what we were looking for was up on Clifftop! I shook myself free of the vision and quickly gave thanks to the Goddess. "Thank you, my lady."

Shoving from the bed, I grabbed my coat, ready to go meet Caleb and share the good news.

I ran down the spiral staircase to the ground floor and out the front door of Hel Tower. Skipping across the bridge to the quad, I turned right and jogged toward Halstein Hall. Taking the steps two at a time, I entered the food court and shimmied my way between the crowd toward Coffee Haven.

Caleb was nowhere to be seen.

"Hey, have you seen Caleb come through here yet?" I asked Roxy when I reached the front of the line.

"Um, yeah, he was here a while ago, but didn't seem too happy when he left."

"Why? Is he okay?"

"I'm not sure. He just kept looking at his watch then finally stormed off."

Weird.

"Okay, thanks." I veered from line and walked to the closest table. Pulling out my phone, I flicked the screen to life, ready to enter my passcode but froze. The time on the screen read 8:30 p.m. *WTF?* I'd only lain down for a second and came straight here right after my vision. How in the world could I have lost three and a half hours? *Damn it.*

No wonder Caleb was pissed. He thought I'd stood him up.

CHAPTER 4

I sank down onto the bench behind me and typed out a text in a rush.

Me: Caleb. I'm in the food court right now. Please come back so I can explain.

I pressed send and hoped he'd return.

Thirty seconds later, those three damn dots began to flicker and pause, then flickered and paused again.

"Come on…please respond," I begged out loud.

I watched the screen with bated breath, almost surprised by how much I cared. Finally, a message came through.

Caleb: Let's talk tomorrow morning. I'll meet you on your log.

Dammit. I hated how you couldn't distinguish tone via a text message. I had no idea if he was mad, sad, or could truly care less. I decided to respond with as much enthusiasm as possible, and hoped my flamboyant use of exclamation marks relayed my excitement and sincerity.

Me: Sounds great!!! Can't wait! I'm sorry I missed you, but can't wait to tell you what happened!!!

I hit send, realizing it was all true. I couldn't wait to see him tomorrow and tell him about my vision and how it related to our team's assignment. Now, I just had to figure out what the rest meant, and where we should go from here.

Sprinting from the food court, I crossed the quad again and headed toward Hel Tower when I spotted Tempest and Eryx, arm in arm, walking back onto campus from the main bridge.

"Hey, you two! How was dinner?" I wrapped my arm around Tempest's shoulders as soon as she was within reach.

"It was great. We went to Napoli's. And can I just tell you, I *love* me some Italian food." Tempest giggled.

"Yum. That sounds great, but I really need to talk to you. Are you coming back to the dorm now?" I hung onto her, my arm draping heavily across her shoulders.

Tempest looked to Eryx. "Um, yeah...we can call it a night."

Eryx smiled and placed a light kiss on Tempest's cheek then whispered something in her ear that I couldn't quite hear. Tempest smiled and shook her head, clearly excited by what he'd said.

"Okay. All set. Let's go have some girl time." Tempest wound her arm through mine and pulled me back toward our tower. Obviously, she was just as eager to hang out, and suddenly, I felt like a complete asshole. I spent most of my time this semester occupying myself and practically hiding away from my best friend...until I needed something.

"Hey, Temp. I'm sorry for being so absent this semester. It's taken me a while to process Mom's death. And honestly, I'm not even sure I'm fully there yet, but still...I haven't been a good friend, and for that I'm truly sorry."

Tempest leaned her head on my shoulder as we passed through the red door of Hel Tower. "It's okay, Nat. Eryx helped me understand what you need is space and time, and I'm okay with that, as long as we keep doing this—always being able to count on each other."

"Of course. You know it. I love you, girl."

"I love you, too."

We scaled the spiral staircase and entered our dorm room arm-in-arm.

Tempest dropped her things onto her bed then turned to face me, ready to work. "Now, let's brew some tea and get down to business. Whatcha need my help with?"

"I had a vision that has to do with our hunt mission, I think, but I need help deciphering it all."

Tempest perked up. "Awesome. More mysteries. Let me change out of these clothes and grab my pendulum. Hopefully this time, we'll actually get somewhere."

"Great. I'll start on the tea." We may use our Keurig for a quick cup of coffee or cider, but when it came to our tea, only our black kettle would do. Steeping atop the small burner in our kitchenette, fragrant peppermint and lavender filled the space, along with our preferred additions of cinnamon and orange. Two minutes later, we were both in our pajamas with cups in hand.

"Okay. So, spill. What was this vision about?" Tempest sat cross-legged on her bed, slowly sipping her tea.

"I asked the Goddess to provide me with some insight, and I think she showed me where our piece from The Hunt may be located." I blew into my cup, stirring the steam up around my face. "The thing is, in the vision I was a bird, and I don't know what that means."

"Whoa. Crazy. What type of bird?" Tempest asked.

"I'm not sure. And I don't even really know if it matters. That's one of the things I need to figure out."

"Okay. So what did you see as the bird?"

"I was flying over Clifftop, and then into the forest to where I think our piece is hidden."

"Really? Like, hidden where? In a tree trunk or something? I thought your clue hinted at *the depths*."

"Yeah, it was weird. It was like this strange silvery-metal pool hidden deep in the forest."

"Wow. That does sound strange. Are you gonna go check it out tomorrow?"

"Yeah, I plan to. Hopefully Caleb will be speaking to me again and go with."

"Wait. What happened between you and Caleb? Did I miss something?" She scooted to the edge of her bed.

"Um, yes and no. Apparently you were right. Caleb has been coming to Clifftop every morning to see me. And tonight, we were supposed to meet up to talk about things. But instead, I got sucked into my vision and basically stood him up." I took a sip of my tea. "We're supposed to meet up again tomorrow morning, so I can explain."

"Dang. Off to a bumpy start, then." Tempest crinkled her nose.

"Yeah, seems so. Anyway, let's see if this bird thing is an important factor. I kinda want to know before I have to explain everything to Caleb."

"You got it." Tempest rose from her bed, placing her cup back in the kitchenette before walking to our shared altar. It was littered with crystals and herbs, but also had a tall wooden box pushed to the back edge that held our important tools. Lifting the lid, Tempest gently pinched the silver moon charm at the top of the chain between her finger and thumb and pulled out her favorite fluorite pendulum. The pieces of citrine we stored in the box kept it energetically cleansed, but she still paused to gather a few more items; a smudge stick that sat to North, and the feather that sat to the East of the metal pentacle in the center of our altar. Returning to our fluffy black rug, she lowered herself to the ground and crossed her legs. "All set."

I smiled and joined her. "This is so nice," I gushed. "I miss doing magic together."

"Me, too." Tempest raised the smudge stick, and I snapped my fingers, setting the end of the sage bundle alight.

"In the name of the God and Goddess, cleanse this space, so that only beings of the highest light may communicate with us this night."

Tempest repeated her chant, wafting the smoke around our informal circle with the feather, then passed it over her pendulum for good measure. Laying the smoking bundle back in the abalone shell, she picked up her tool. "Good to go. Now let's get you some answers."

She winked and launched into her first round of questions.

"Did Natalie's vision show her the location of the hidden piece she's looking for?" The pendulum immediately swung back and forth. "That's a yes," Tempest confirmed.

"Does the bird in Natalie's vision play a significant role?" Again, it swung back and forth. "Yes again."

She shifted in her spot on the rug. "Is there anything else Natalie needs to know about her vision?" This time it spun in a wild circle. "Oh, boy. Looks like that's a crazy yes, slash no, slash maybe."

Tempest's mouth pulled into a frown.

Of course. "Can you ask if there's someone specific I need to talk to for answers?"

Tempest repeated my question and smiled when the tool swung back and forth, indicating a yes. "Let's try to figure out who it is."

She raced on with a bunch of names, tossing them out like an auctioneer. No after no displayed from the swinging stone, until we finally had to give up.

"Sorry, Nat. Obviously, we just don't know their name." Tempest cleared her pendulum, swinging it through the smoke of the still wafting sage. "Maybe after you talk to Caleb in the morning, you two can go check out the pool and get some answers together."

"Yeah, maybe." I helped her clean the space then climbed into bed disheartened, discouraged, and woefully disappointed.

CHAPTER 5

*W*aking from a fitful sleep, I immediately looked to Tempest to make sure I hadn't woken her with all my tossing and turning. Today was Friday, and I was feeling a bit better. Hopefully, after my morning conversation with Caleb, I'd have some answers. I wanted to continue planning—and with any luck at all—finishing this hunt mission by the time the weekend was over.

Moving as quietly as I could, I gathered my things and headed for the showers. The lavender and eucalyptus scent that permanently wafted through the bathroom was a welcome tonic to my morning fog.

Following the stone hallway that spiraled inward, I entered a private shower and twisted the knobs set into the wall. Hot water slapped the floor, filling the space with steam. I closed my eyes and leaned back against the rounded wall, thinking about my vision and all it had shown me.

Clifftop was the obvious place, but the liquid metal pool still had me stumped. Where had it come from, and why hadn't anyone else seen it before? With the number of shifters that ran the forest, I'm surprised no one had stumbled across it. And the fact that Tempest's answers indicated that someone had more information on the matter set my teeth on edge. Who was this mystery guy, or girl for that matter? And where the hell should I start looking for them?

Showered and dressed, I redeposited my things in our dorm, and left Tempest a note thanking her for her help last night. It wasn't major magic, but it definitely guided me in a direction of sorts.

Following the sky bridge past the weapons building, I emerged on Clifftop with my usual backpack in tow. My stomach grumbled, and I realized I'd forgotten to grab breakfast...again. But honestly, with everything else on my mind, food was the last thing I was thinking about.

I looked around, but Caleb was nowhere to be found. I assumed he'd already lumbered off to grab his own breakfast from his hidden patch. So, braving the forest, I zipped up my hoodie and stepped into its embrace for the very first time.

Birds chirped and tiny feet skittered around me as I walked farther into the trees. Ferns created an almost carpet-like effect on either side of the rough trail. Dead logs lay haphazardly where they fell, crisscrossing themselves into a dangerous, yet beautiful maze. The morning light barely found its way through the branches and thick leaves, casting deep shadows as I pushed forward into the unknown.

Caleb's name was on the tip of my tongue, longing to be shouted out. But the idea of disturbing the peace of this forest, or rousing any unwanted attention, quickly nixed the thought. Instead, I trudged on aimlessly, having no idea where I was going. He'd said the patch was off one of the side trails, but where exactly? I hadn't seen any off-shoot paths just yet.

The snapping of wood jerked my head to the left and out trotted a small wolf. *Crap.* I knew other shifters roamed these woods, but I hadn't thought about running into them until this very second.

"Hey," I said lamely, raising my hand in what I hoped would be taken as a friendly gesture. The wolf raised its head in a quick nod, then ran past me into the thick brush on the other side of the trail. Following its direction, I scanned the waking forest for any other visitors that may be emerging from its depths.

Its depths. I pulled out the tarot card from my back pocket and read the third line again.

Shillelagh from blackthorn are meant for thee, but hidden in the depths forever I'll be.

Maybe *depths* didn't mean a pool of some sort after all.

Refocusing, I squinted, trying harder to see beyond the first layer of foliage. I couldn't make out anything of significance, but as I turned back to the main trail, a strange pull tugged at my chest, yanking me farther down the path.

I walked forward, the pulse of magic calling to me. Oblivious to any other sounds or sights, I continued toward the beacon's source. Coming out of a daze, my body stopped of its own accord in a small clearing off the opposite side of the trail. A fallen tree trunk blocked the ground just ahead of me, while the overhanging leaves and surrounding underbrush here almost seemed familiar. Stepping over the dead branch, I heard a high-pitched screech above me and looked up to find its source.

Perched in a tall pine sat a hawk on the lowest branch. To be specific, a red-tailed hawk with one blue eye and one green. *Holy shit!*

Everything else faded, and all I could see was the hawk. Its reddish-brown feathers speckled with white helped it blend into the forest, but its contrasting eyes sparkled brightly, lighting up its face. I had no doubt this was the bird I'd become in my vision. Focusing on its eyes, I wondered whether or not Mystic had anything to do with it, seeing as their eyes were exactly the same—one blue and one green. Was she able to project herself into other animals now, as another way to guide us? Or perhaps this was a new familiar she'd sent to me with help. Only one way to find out.

I held out my arm, creating a mock perch, and called to it with my mind.

"*Bird of prey, calling to me, friend or foe, what shall it be? If my familiar, come to thee, or fly away, so mote it be.*"

The beautiful bird flapped its wing and drifted slowly down to rest upon my outstretched arm. The moment its talons touched me, I heard its voice inside my head. *"Mistress. My name is Malyki. I am yours."*

I dipped my head in reverence. To have one familiar is a blessing, but to receive two was almost divine.

"It's nice to meet you, Malyki. Thank you for leading me here."

He squawked and flew back up into the tree. *"The magic you seek is just ahead. I'm here to watch over you, but be careful."*

His clipped instructions pulled me back on task. This was the place, the clearing where I'd seen the glistening pool in my vision. Turning again to face the log, I crept forward, carefully minding my steps. A silver flash caught my attention, and I pushed on, weaving my way through twisted vines and fallen limbs.

There it was.

A silver pool, the size of a small pond, pulsed on the ground. It was thick—almost clay-like—and undulated of its own free will. I took a step forward, scanning the area for any malintent. The energy radiating from the pool felt magical for sure, but not in a bad way. I bent down near its edge, my combat boots barely clear of the thick liquid, and listened. A low hum buzzed softly once I concentrated hard enough. Reaching out, I stretched my fingers toward the liquid, curious to see if contact would alter the frequency. Malyki screeched from above, stilling my hand.

"I would advise against contact until you're certain you can meet the price."

"What price?" I sent back through my thoughts.

The memory of a silver hand reaching up, and the message I'd received from my vision replayed in my mind. *"Only a true witch may enter here."*

The pool started to churn, swirling violently into a thick mercury mix. I jerked my hand away, feeling nervous and unworthy. Images of drowned animals and rotting fish filled my head, spiking my panic even higher. Crab-crawling backwards through the brush and leaves, I scurried away as fast as I could.

What the hell?

"I thought this is where I'm supposed to be, but it's like the damn thing doesn't want me anywhere near it," I called out to Malyki, hoping for an explanation.

"You are in the right place, just not in the right mind."

Shoving to my feet, I brushed the dirt and debris from my jeans. "What the hell is that supposed to mean?"

"While I am here for guidance, mistress, I cannot help solve the riddle or what ails you." Malyki took to the sky with one final screech.

Well, crap. Guess I needed to regroup and re-read that damn clue again.

Returning to the trail, I realized I still hadn't seen Caleb yet or found his hidden berry patch. Noting the time, I couldn't venture much farther without risking a late arrival to my first class of the day: Intro to Supernatural Cultural Relations with Professor Admundson. She was an angel…literally, the second one I'd met since coming to the Sun and Moon Academy, and I was truly enjoying her class.

The sun had risen higher in the sky, illuminating more of the main path as I backtracked toward the open field. About half-way down the trail, I heard someone shouting my name.

"Natalie!"

I turned around to see Caleb scrambling down the path as he fumbled with his pants.

"Hey! I was looking for you." I shoved my hands into my pockets and looked anywhere but his zipper. I knew most shifters usually transformed naked, but it wasn't something I'd actually thought about until now.

"Yeah, I came up early to grab a bite to eat and stretch my furry legs," he joked.

"I couldn't find the trail that led to your patch, and I didn't hear you rooting around out there, so yeah…I just turned back."

"Do you want me to show you where it is?" His expression brightened. "I'd be happy to share it with you."

Oh, man. This was going to get awkward fast. Yes, we were supposed to talk about things this morning, but being faced with it now had me backpedaling hard.

"Um, it's okay. Maybe some other time. I, uh…don't want to be late for class." I jerked a thumb over my shoulder, already two steps into my retreat.

"All right. Sure, but I thought we were going to talk about

what happened last night." The smile on his face faded. "You stood me up, remember?"

I yanked at the collar of my hoodie, pulling it away from my throat. "Yeah, I'm really sorry about that. It's not what you think, though, I promise. But can we continue this later? I really do need to go."

I didn't wait for Caleb's response before sprinting down the rest of the trail. *What in the world's going on with me?* Snagging my backpack, I raced toward the skybridge. Malyki was right. I wasn't in the right mindset for any of this.

CHAPTER 6

$\mathcal{M}$y senses dulled and all conversation stilled as I sat in Professor Admundson's class, thinking about what had happened. I'd been looking forward to telling Caleb about my vision, and the fact that I'd found the pool today. But when confronted by him, I completely froze. Why had I become so damn hesitant to share?

"Natalie?" Professor Admundson called my name.

I looked to the board, searching for the question she probably wanted answered.

There was nothing there.

"Yes?" I replied hesitantly.

"Are you all right?" she asked, pausing the entire class and causing every pair of eyes to focus in on me.

I slid a little farther into my seat, happy my hoodie was still pulled tightly around me. "I'm fine. Is there a problem?" I wasn't trying to be snarky; I honestly didn't know.

"Well, yes, there seems to be." She pointed to my backpack which was sitting next to my chair on the floor.

Oh, my goddess! I sucked in a shocked breath as I stared down at my bag. Red smoke was rising from it, slinking like a serpent and coiling into a small cloud by the side of my desk.

"Um…I don't know what's happening. I'm sorry. I've got to

go." I grabbed the straps, holding the pack away from me, and ran from the room.

The crimson fog trailed behind me as I raced out of Halstein Hall. The only thing I could think of was Professor Knox's class yesterday, and how he'd given me the red crystal that was currently tucked into my bag. I ran across the quad to Eirhal Hall and straight to my Alchemy class. Bursting in, I stopped only to catch my breath.

Everyone stared.

"Natalie? What is it?" Professor Knox walked toward me, clearly concerned.

"The crystal...it's smoking again..." I panted out.

"I'm sorry. What?" Knox gently placed his hand on my shoulder. "Natalie. Tell me what's wrong."

I looked up to meet his gaze, my brows pinched in confusion. "Can't you see it?" I held up my pack, the plumes of red smoke now encircling the entire thing. "I think the crystal somehow reverted to its previous state, causing this reaction."

My panic continued to rise.

Knox placed his other hand on my other shoulder, holding me in place. "Natalie. Calm down. Explain what you see."

Every pair of eyes in the class were laser-focused and boring into me. A sea of smirks and sneers was all I could see. I leaned forward, lowering my voice so only Knox could hear. "Can you not see the smoke coming from my backpack?"

Knox looked down at my bag and shook his head. "Natalie, I don't see anything wrong."

Laughter erupted, and even Professor Knox grinned, barely containing his amusement.

I looked down and gasped. The smoke was now coiling up my hand. I dropped the bag and shook out my arm, but it kept climbing. I swiped at it with my other hand, attempting to somehow push it off me, but it continued to rise. Now past my shoulder, the crimson fog crept higher and higher, encircling my neck. When it started to tighten around my throat, I screamed.

"Natalie! Are you all right?"

I looked up into Professor Admundson's sweet face, her eyes full of concern.

Struggling back to reality, I shifted in my seat. "Oh, my goodness, I'm so sorry. I must have fallen asleep. I'm truly sorry, Professor."

I dipped my head and met the gaze of everyone else in the room. Luckily, they, too, all seemed concerned. Obviously, I'd been dreaming, but I took a quick peek down at my backpack to confirm. Thank the Goddess, there was no smoke.

"Are you sure everything is all right? I can send you to the Infirmary to get checked out if you'd like?" Professor Admundson smiled and dipped her head—her way of letting me off the hook. Dang, she really was the sweetest angel I'd ever met.

"Actually, yes. That would probably be best. Thank you." I gently picked up my bag and left class. I didn't think she really expected me to go to the Infirmary, so instead, I headed downstairs to the main floor, hoping to grab a bite to eat. Maybe my lack of food was seriously becoming a problem here.

Sliding up to Coffee Haven, I ordered my usual: a blueberry muffin and large caramel-apple cider.

"Actually, make it two muffins," I amended, handing Roxy a few extra dollars.

Returning to the same bench where all this started last night, I sat down and plopped my backpack next to me. *What the hell is going on with me?*

Gasps and yelps of surprise rang out through the dining hall, and the next thing I knew, Malyki was dive-bombing me from out of the sky, landing on the bench beside me.

"What are you doing here?" I looked around, nervous we'd get in trouble.

"I sensed your confusion and frustration and came to help." His words drifted into my mind.

"Oh, like you helped me earlier when you just flew off into the forest?"

If a bird could *tsk*, that's what I heard, followed by, *"I may not be able to help you solve the puzzle, but I can help you find yourself again."*

"What does that even mean?" I sat down my drink, not wanting to spill hot cider onto his feathers, and spread my arms out wide. "I'm right here. Not lost, and not going anywhere, so why do all these vague statements make it sound like there's something wrong with me? Why can't you just tell me what I need to know?"

Malyki hopped up onto my leg, and everything else disappeared. *"Physical contact will allow me to communicate like this."*

Within my mind's eye, I watched as my beautiful new familiar transformed from a hawk into an equally beautiful man.

"Whoa."

Maintaining his coloring, he now had short auburn hair but kept his mis-matched eyes of blue and green. He wore black canvas pants and a deep aubergine loose-fitting shirt. The strong shape of his jaw and broad shoulders helped portray his role as my protector. I felt an overwhelming sense of safety and wondered if this was something he could do within the real world. A flesh and bone bodyguard could prove invaluable around here.

"Yes. Given the right circumstances," he answered my internal question.

"What circumstances?"

"If you are ever in grave danger, look for me in my human form."

Well, crap. That didn't bode well.

"Okay, now that you're transformed. Let's talk. What do I need to know?" I asked.

"Just that."

"What?"

"Transformed."

"Come on, dude. I thought you being in this form was supposed to help us communicate. Stop speaking in riddles."

"It's not a riddle. It's the word you need to recognize and understand. Transformation can mean many things, and in this case, it will."

"Well, gee, I'm sorry, but I don't understand. Are you saying I need to learn to transform like you to complete this hunt? Or are you saying that what we're looking for has transformed somehow? Come on, I need a little clarity here!"

"Clarity will only come once you've transformed your thinking."

"Okay, fuck this! I'm done. Go on, get out of here." I waved him

off in my mind's eye. *"If you're not actually going to help me, I need some time to think this through by myself."*

Malyki retreated from my mind's eye, and we were returned to the food court with him still sitting on my leg in his hawk form.

"I'm sorry, but I don't have time to deal with unspoken BS. I need answers, and if you can't give them to me, then..." I cut off the hurtful words poised on the tip of my tongue.

"You will have the answers when you need them. Until then, I'll be watching over you." Malyki flew off, disappearing out the double doors of Halstein Hall, and I was left sitting alone, feeling like a complete jerk.

Unfortunately, what I'd said was true. I needed time to think this through. Especially since our next ITF class was today at three p.m. I'd be seeing Caleb there, too, and hoped with my explanation to the team, he'd understand why I missed our initial date as well.

One could only hope.

CHAPTER 7

$\mathcal{M}$in, Mallory, and Caleb were all huddled together around one of the library's large round tables. Every ITF class shifted its location, and luckily, today was a research day. All the teams were scattered throughout the lower level with notes and tools laid out before them for whichever project they were working on. As you could guess...our table was empty.

"Hey," I greeted everyone lamely.

"Hey, yourself." Mallory looked up with her usual smile on her face. "You ready to get started?"

"Yeah, I guess so. How about you guys? Have you found anything new?" I slid into the chair opposite of Caleb, who had yet to cast a single look my way.

"Not really. The major bodies of water around Havenwood Falls have all been accounted for and checked out, so unless there's a hidden one that nobody's ever discovered, we've kind of hit a brick wall," Min quickly explained.

"Actually, I think I found the place."

Everyone's eyes snapped to me, even Caleb's.

"Do tell," he said, leaning back in his chair, his arms crossed over his broad chest.

"Well, last night, I had a vision that led me into the woods up on Clifftop and to a silver, mercury-like pool hidden off the main path. I think it's where our piece is hidden. Unfortunately, when I tried to get close, a weird silvery hand reached out, and I heard the message, *Only a true witch may enter here.*" I shifted uncomfortably under the weight of everyone's gaze. "Obviously, I didn't do anything else."

"Why not?" Caleb asked. "You're a true witch, and clearly like to do things on your own."

Taken aback, I realized that he was still hurt and not understanding the timing of what happened.

"Look. When I was supposed to meet you was when I had the vision. I thought I'd only been asleep for an hour or so, but when I woke up, it was already past eight. That's why I missed you. Then, this morning, when I found the pool for real, I was warned off again, and it left me shaken. That's why I bolted, okay? It has nothing to do with me wanting to do stuff alone. I'm just not sure what we're supposed to do next, and everything so far is pointing to this all being on me." I threw my hands in the air.

Everyone was silent for a moment until Min spoke up. "Nat, I get why it must feel like everything is being dumped on your shoulders, but we're a team and want to help however we can."

I sighed, slouching down in my chair. "I know that, but until I figure out all these damn clues and how they relate to me and what I, or *we*, need to do, I just don't know what kind of help to ask for yet, if that makes sense."

"It does, but just know we have your back." Min smiled.

"And we're here if you just want to bounce ideas off us, too," Mallory added.

I looked to Caleb, whose silence had me squirming even farther in my seat.

"If you can give me a few days to work through this, I'll try to have a plan in place by Monday's class. Does that work?" I asked the group.

"Sounds good. See you then." Mallory jumped up, pulling Min with her as she eyeballed Caleb and me from across the table.

Finally alone, Caleb leaned forward, propping his elbows on the hard wood surface between us.

"You could have told me all that in a text, or this morning before you ran away. I would have understood." His jaw flexed with each word.

"Really? Because right now, you still seem kind of pissed."

He shrugged. "Not pissed, just hurt. I thought we'd gotten close enough over the semester to at least talk to each other about this kind of stuff. Or anything really. It's one of the highlights of my morning actually—seeing you and having our little morning chats."

A slow smile crept across my face. "You sound like a little old lady; enjoying our morning chats...next we'll be drinking tea and having crumpets by a fire."

"Whatever it takes to get you alone." He winked. An ornery smirk marred his lips as he reached for my hand across the table. "How about we start over? Meet me tonight for dinner. We'll talk about the pool you found, the clues for The Hunt, and...us. What do you say?"

"That sounds great to me. Where do you want to meet?"

"How about we venture into Havenwood Falls? Try something new for a change?"

"Sure. My last class gets over at four-fifty p.m. How about I meet you in the quad around five-thirty?"

"Great. It's a date," he confirmed.

I smiled as his thumb rubbed a gentle circle over the back of my hand. "I guess it is."

Professor Herne Fairchild was one of the oldest fae I'd ever met—besides his grandfather, Elsmed, of course. I think Herne said he was turning one-hundred and thirty-seven later this year, so his take on Supernatural History was utterly intriguing. However, I spent my final class of the day engulfed between stories of the Dark Fae and their recent battles, and getting lost in my own personal thoughts about Caleb and our upcoming date.

The final bell rang, and I booked it from Halstein Hall, across the quad toward Hel Tower, and up to my dorm room to get ready. Shadows crept across the campus as the sun from the skylight made its retreat. Our room was dark and empty, which I assumed meant another dinner date for Tempest as well. Maybe we'd run into them in town. *That'd be cool—a double-date with my best friend*, I thought to myself.

My cheeks hurt from all the cheesy grinning I was doing. It felt strange to care about a boy, let alone what I looked like. But tonight, I wanted something different than my usual jeans, T-shirts, flannel, and boots. I wanted something...special.

Rifling through my closet was a waste of time, but I knew Tempest wouldn't mind if I took a peek inside hers. Shuffling past her day-to-day attire, I quickly found a few dresses in the back that I thought might work. Pulling the third one out, I slid the soft material over my head and smiled as it floated down over my curves, dropping to mid-calf. I turned to the mirror and gasped.

Interwoven blue and white flowers created a pattern all their own, making the sundress bright and festive and the perfect choice for a Spring evening meal. It was fitted but not tight; flirty, but not sexy. It was perfect. I spun around, wondering where we'd end up going tonight: Napoli's like Tempest and Eryx had, or perhaps something more low-key like the Burger Bar? Either way, the dress worked.

I returned to my closet and snagged the only pair of heels I owned, sliding into them with rising excitement. Heading for the door, I stopped to take one last look in the mirror.

My reflection wavered.

In its place stood a woman that looked like me, but was not me. Wrapped in rags, her hair was disheveled and her face mud-smeared. I tilted my head, and her long brown hair moved in unison with mine. I raised my hand, and hers mimicked the motion.

What the fresh hell is this?

I stepped closer but stopped short, weary of her forward movement as well. Reaching the mirror, I stared into the woman's eyes—my eyes. Twisting side to side, I watched in amazement as she did the same. Our arms were outstretched reaching toward one another, ready to touch.

My finger tapped the glass, and everything went black.

CHAPTER 8

*T*he darkness was suffocating, enveloping me from every angle. Desperate to break free, I reached out but felt nothing. I did, however, sense something—or *someone* close by.

"Hello? Who's there?"

"You are," a breathy voice sounded back.

"What are you talking about? What's going on? Where am I?" My panic rose to a fevered pitch.

A shuffling sound shifted to my left, and I snapped my head in its direction. My eyes began to adjust, and I could almost make out the silhouette of another person.

"Are you the person I saw in the mirror?" I asked.

"If you mean you, then yes."

I took a tentative step toward her.

"How can that be? I'm here, and you're there, so there's no way you can be me." Just saying that out loud made my head hurt.

"Yet, I'm here, and you're here, and together we are we."

What in the world? It was obvious I was getting nowhere with her, so I changed tactics. "Okay, if we are we, then tell me where *we* are."

"You've entered the realm of the witch," she replied.

I took a deep breath. If that was true, why didn't I feel safer? More connected? And what the hell was the realm of the witch?

"Can you tell more about it?"

Her form moved through the darkness, encircling me as she talked.

"Long ago, there was a sacred place. A place only true witches could enter. A place apart. It held our secrets and our power, but through the evolution of man and the disconnect of spirit, it became sealed for all time. And with it, the power you seek."

"I seek no special power," I snapped back.

"Yes, we do. The power you've been searching for is within your reach. You just have to enter the realm and claim it."

I had no idea what she was talking about, but I asked the question anyway. "And how do I do that?"

"Transform."

Oh, for fuck's sake. There was that damn word again.

"Transform, how? And please, be specific. Do I need to learn to transform my shape? My thoughts? What?"

Her breathy voice rattled near my ear. "You only need to transform your heart."

I spun around, grasping for anything to hold on to as my eyesight cleared. I was in my dorm, still wearing the sundress I'd picked out for my date. The mirror stood across the room, reflecting me as I was. No haggard doppelganger, no realm of the witch visible on the other side, just me looking back at myself, terrified and clueless.

I glanced down at my phone, oddly still in my hand as if I'd never left the room. 7:30 p.m. *Dammit!* I'd missed Caleb again.

Kicking my heels to the floor, I donned my boots and raced from Hel Tower directly to Jory. I took the stairs two at a time and wound my way around the outside of the building until I reached the entrance. Taking a deep breath, I pounded on the door.

Theo Murray, a wolf shifter—and Caleb's roommate—yanked it open and snapped, "Yeah, what?"

He was clearly annoyed with the intensity of my knocking.

"Sorry, I'm looking for Caleb. Is he here?"

"Yeah. He's in the commons." Theo waved me in.

I strode through the door, taking in the new-to-me space. The stone that made up our campus was still present here, but less so than in Hel Tower and way less gothic in nature. Jory had been modernized with sections of painted drywall and high-end amenities. I walked past the laundry room and moved into the common area where the first thing I saw was a massive clock jutting out from a stone wall. It was impressive, and from the size of the damn thing, I imagined its gong shaking the entire tower when it rang.

"What are you doing here?"

My head snapped to Caleb who was splayed across a lavish tan sectional that faced the fireplace. I walked past the hearth, noting its massive, almost walk-in size, and took a seat on the other end of the couch.

"I'm so sorry," I started. "I was all ready to go and on my way out the door but got sucked into another vision." I scooted a little closer. "I promise, I didn't mean to stand you up again." I held my tongue, waiting for his response, but continued when none came. "I was really looking forward to our date." I stood up. "Look, I even put on a dress."

A small smile pulled at his lips, and he released the orange pillow that had been suffering from his tight grip. "Well, I'm starving, so how about we pick up where you left off, and you can tell me about this vision over some grub in the food court, okay?"

"Yes. I'd like that very much. Thank you for understanding."

Caleb stood and led me in the opposite direction from which I entered the tower. Moving through the commons, we passed through a study lined with bookshelves, then made our way across the skybridge that connected Jory to the library. Descending floor after floor, we finally exited and entered the main area of Halstein Hall.

"How about something from Hog's Dogs and Blazed Burgers?" Caleb asked.

"Sounds perfect."

We ventured to the Student Union, grateful for the grab-and-go joint that supplied all the fried comfort food a college student could need. With a fully loaded New York-style dog and an order of fried pickles in hand, I followed Caleb to the nearest table, still a bit nervous for this conversation.

"Thanks for suggesting this. I was afraid you'd be so mad you wouldn't want to see me again." I picked up a pickle and tossed it into my mouth.

"You're not getting rid of me that easily." Caleb winked. "Besides, I'm really starting to worry about you and all these visions you're having. If they *are* to do with The Hunt, then why aren't the rest of us getting them, too?"

"Actually, I think this last vision might help explain that." I took a swig from my water bottle, readying myself for the tale. "So I was kind of sucked into a mirror, and within it was told I'd entered the realm of the witch, and that that's where the piece is hidden for our hunt." I lifted my shoulder, trying to be nonchalant. "I'm the only witch on our team."

Caleb nodded and took a bite of his burger.

"That, plus the message I received from my earlier vision that '*Only a true witch can enter here*,' definitely has me thinking it's something that only I can do. Not that I want it to be that way," I rushed on. "But I simply don't think we have a choice."

Caleb took a long pull from his soda and returned to his burger, still not saying a word as I rambled on.

"I think if I can figure out what the transformation part of the clue means, and how the witch's realm is connected with the silver pool, I'll be ready to take the next step. I just haven't gotten that far yet."

Finally finished with his meal, Caleb weighed in. "How about you take me to the pool tomorrow morning, so I can get a look at it? Maybe while we're there, I'll get some sort of vision too, or at least be there in case you have another one." He smiled. "I think it's a good step to take as a team, don't you?"

I smiled back. "Yes. I think it's a very good idea."

I lifted my hot dog, finally ready to start my dinner, but caught sight of Mallory barreling into the food court.

"Oh my god, here you two are." Mallory gasped, struggling to catch her breath. "I've been looking all over for you."

"What's wrong?" Caleb demanded, already on high alert.

"Min's missing. He went looking for your mercury pool, and I haven't seen him since."

Well, shit. So much for waiting and doing things as a team.

CHAPTER 9

*C*aleb lumbered through the trees in bear form, cutting a path through the thick underbrush beneath the night sky. Mallory and I jogged behind, hoping we weren't too late. Images of dead fish and that silver hand kept flashing through my mind.

"It should be just up ahead," I yelled to Caleb.

Crashing over the fallen log, he barreled to a halt, his paws inches from the edge of the silver pool.

Min was lying face-down, his left hand submerged in the mercury liquid.

"Oh my god!" Mallory ran to his side and bent down, checking his breathing. "He's alive."

Caleb rushed out from behind a nearby bush, pulling his pants into place. "Let's get him over here." As gently as possible, he pulled Min's body away from the pool, rolling him over onto his back. "Come on, buddy, stay with us."

I stared at the pool, its surface calm and serene, unlike the last time I'd been here.

Min coughed, drawing all our attention.

"Oh my god, Min. Are you okay? What were you thinking?" Mallory's balance of concern and reprimand was impressive.

Min sat up, rubbing his head. "Dang. I umm... followed Natalie's directions and found the pool after a quick sprint around the forest." He looked past me toward the pool, his brows knitted together tightly. "I remember bending down near the edge, but after that, everything went blank."

Mallory leaned down and gently lifted his forearm into the air. "So you don't remember putting your hand in there?"

Min gasped at the sight of his silver-coated hand. "No, I don't."

"Well, that's scary as hell." She released his arm and directed her next question at me. "So this thing really does have a mind of its own, then?"

"Seems so." I almost rolled my eyes. "I told you about the hand that reached out in my vision and the message I received. The pool probably tossed Min out because he isn't a true witch."

Caleb looked down at Min. "Well, thank God that's all that happened, because dude, this could have been so much worse. What if you'd been pulled in? You shouldn't have gone off alone."

Min held his tongue; any answer he could give was too horrible to think about.

"Well, it definitely sounds like you were right, Natalie. It does seem like this is something only you can do," Mallory stated flatly. "But I still wish we could all figure out how to help you."

I sighed, well aware I was on my own here. "It's okay. Hopefully I can figure out what I need to do in the next few days, and we can get this done and over with." I looked at the pool and instinctively knew it wouldn't be that easy. "For now, let's get Min to the Infirmary to make sure he's really okay."

"Nah, I'm fine. I'll just grab a little snack before heading in." Min pushed up from the ground, smiling at first, but sobered again at the sight of his left hand. "Do you think this will go away on its own, or am I gonna start a new trend here?" He wiggled his silver-coated fingers, catching the moonlight like some metallic, mechanical glove.

"I'm not sure," I answered honestly. "If you're not going to the Infirmary, at least try to wash it off when you get back to your dorm. I have no idea if water or heat will work, but it's worth a try." *And the only thing I can think of to suggest, since my magic's still not up to par,* I thought to myself.

Min shoved both hands into the front pocket of his red sweatshirt. "It's all good. I'll figure it out. It doesn't hurt or anything like that, and like Caleb said, it could have been a lot worse. I'll be fine."

With no other ideas between us, we all made our way out of the clearing, climbing over fallen trees and through the thick brush until we reached the main trail. Just before emerging back onto the open field, I caught sight of Malyki perched in the tree above me.

"You all go ahead. I'll be just a minute."

Min and Mallory nodded and continued on, but Caleb paused. "Everything okay?"

"Yes. I just need a minute to," I hesitated, "communicate with one of my familiars." With so many witches on campus, the mention of familiars was a pretty regular thing, but I wasn't sure he'd ever witnessed it firsthand. I hoped he'd understand.

"Gotcha. Do you mind if I wait for you up ahead?" He motioned over his shoulder with his thumb.

"Of course not. That would be great, actually. Thanks." I watched Caleb walk off, then turned my attention to Malyki.

"Did you see what happened to Min?" I sent through our mental bond.

"I did."

"And?"

"And, as you suspected, it barred him from entering because he's not a true witch."

I sighed. *"And why does it have to be a true witch that does this? There are plenty of magical beings here that could get the job done, I'm sure."*

"Correct, but none may enter Cailleach's cauldron."

"I'm sorry…the what?"

"Cailleach's cauldron. It's the birthplace of magic, the womb of transformation, and the realm which you seek."

"I thought the realm of the witch *was what I seek?"* I sent, frustrated by all this cloak and dagger bullshit.

"It is. For they are one and the same."

"Okay, wait. So you're telling me that the realm of the witch is just some old woman's cauldron?"

"Not just any woman's—The Cailleach. The Mother of all gods and goddesses."

"Holy shit." Caleb's response mirrored my own when I relayed the news.

After Malyki informed me what, or more so, who, we were dealing with, I ran straight to Caleb and told him what happened, and asked if we could stop by the library before calling it a night. A stack of Irish lore and Scottish mythology books now littered our study table.

"It says here that on the west coast of Scotland, the Cailleach ushers in winter by washing her great plaid in the Gulf of Corryvreckan, or the cauldron of the plaid. I guess the process is said to take three days, during which the roar of the coming tempest can be heard as far away as twenty miles. When she's finished, her plaid is pure white and snow covers the land," Caleb read from his phone—probably from Wikipedia, or some Celtic-specific version of it.

I continued to flip through the pages of an old Celtic tome, the name of which had long been worn away from the aging leather. "It says here, she carries a hammer for shaping the hills and valleys, and personifies winter by herding deer, fighting the Spring, and that her staff freezes the ground." My eyes snapped to Caleb's.

"Her *staff?*" he drew out the obvious question.

"You think all this is connected to our piece for The Hunt?" I exclaimed.

"Seems likely. Let's keep reading." Caleb grabbed the next book from the stack, while I returned to my current one.

Forty minutes later, we'd found more references to Cailleach's cauldron symbolizing the womb of magic, a place of transformation and abundance. It was linked to the divine feminine, the cycle of death and rebirth, and the act of creation as most cauldrons were. There was also an odd practice of Cailleach emerging to rule the land once the last stalks of wheat had been harvested. It was once common practice for the first farmer who finished their harvest to create a corn dolly from their very last stalks. The doll represented The Cailleach and was also sometimes called the Hag of the Harvest. Apparently, the farmers would pass it from one to the other, as they finished their work for the season.

The last farmer to finish their harvest would be the last to receive the doll and would be tasked with caring for it through the winter months. How poorly or well they cared for the doll would be reflected in the crop yield of the following year, as The Cailleach would blight or bless them, depending on their efforts. We also read that The Cailleach was tied to the triple moon, which echoes the phases of the divine feminine and the cycles of life and death it represents.

I closed the cover of the thick tome, and rubbed my head. "Okay, well, that ties in the moon part of our clue, and all this is great information, but it doesn't exactly explain what I'm supposed to do to get into the cauldron, or the realm of the witch, or whatever it is, to retrieve the staff."

Caleb placed his book on the pile. "Maybe you could ask Professor Fairchild about The Cailleach. Isn't that something he should know about, being the teacher of Supernatural History and all?"

"Maybe, but my next class with him isn't until Monday afternoon. And honestly, I don't think we can wait that long. I'm not sure why, but I feel a sense of urgency creeping up on me."

Pushing from the table, Caleb and I gathered the books and placed them at the return desk before heading out of the library. It was late, and Halstein Hall had fallen quiet.

"Thank you for tonight. I'm sorry it didn't go as planned." I smiled up at Caleb as my stomach growled.

"Speaking of, you didn't even get a chance to eat your dinner. Do you want to get a bite to eat before bed?"

"Is there anything still open?"

We looked around the food court and quickly realized everything was closed.

"Dang. Well, how about I cook you something back in my tower?" Caleb offered.

"Um, sure." I wasn't ready to go to bed—not with this much on my mind. And I didn't want to wake Tempest up by rooting around for food in our room, so I agreed. Besides, through all this, Caleb and I still hadn't addressed what was going on between us.

We backtracked into the library, climbing several floors to the skybridge to Jory. Looking down, I had the oddest thought, suddenly wondering if everyone in this tower had some way to fly or shift as a way to remain safe. If not, one wrong step could prove fatal. Clearly distracting myself, I listed off everyone that came to mind.

Vidar was a Valkyrie hybrid. Tyr, a Scandinavian demigod, and their mate Roxy, a cougar shifter. Fin was a Transhuman with the ability to freeze time, and my girl Taylor was a badass witch. Bryony was a Druid with wicked powers. Caleb, of course, was their mighty bear shifter, and his roommate Theo, a wolf shifter. Clay Washburn was another powerful witch, and then there was Dingane who was an Impundulu or lightning bird.

Ah ha! I thought to myself, confident in my assumption.

"Did you know that there are more witches in Hel Tower than any other, but apparently Jory has the most fliers?" I rambled out of the blue.

"Um, okay, yeah. I guess I never thought about it before. That's cool."

"I wonder if the other towers have a certain concentration of one species or another?"

"Yeah, um, I don't know." Caleb pushed open the door to his tower and led me through the commons into the kitchen. Here, too, there were upscale modern touches like stainless steel appliances and quartz countertops. I took a seat on one of the barstools at the massive island and watched Caleb go to work.

"Do you like fish?"

"Of course. I grew up in Massachusetts, so we ate a lot of seafood."

Suddenly bombarded with memories of Mom in the kitchen, I lowered my head. "When I was young, I would sit at the kitchen table and watch my Mom prepare her famous lobster rolls." I chuckled softly. "She always tied her hair back and wore this ugly green apron while she cooked. That was, of course, until I grew up, and things changed...until she'd changed. I was on my own then." I looked up to meet Caleb's concerned gaze. "I suppose looking back, I can pinpoint the shift in her, but when you're living with the only person who's ever loved you, I guess it was just too hard for me to see, ya know?"

Caleb set down the plate he was holding and reached for my

hand. "I'm so sorry for what you've been through. I know we all faced a lot last semester, and this one's not shaping up to be much better, but seriously, Nat," he paused and leaned in, looking me directly in the eyes, "I can't imagine what you've been dealing with."

Tears filled my vision, and my heart tightened in my chest. Those few words were all it took; my walls came crumbling down and sobs racked my body as I gasped for air. Embarrassed, I crossed my arms atop the island and laid down my head, hiding my face. Why was this happening now? I'd been processing my mom's death all semester long. Hadn't I?

Suddenly, Caleb's hands were gently rubbing my back, and I realized, no, I hadn't. I'd pushed Tempest away at every turn, telling her I was fine. I refused to talk to Saundra Beaumont who'd been repeatedly checking up on me. And I'd avoided Dr. Lavinia and her request to stop by her office multiple times this year. Caleb had been the only person I'd found myself comfortable around, and finally, I knew why. He hadn't pushed me in any way—even despite having feelings for me. He'd kept his distance, but was always there. More so than I ever realized. Time was what I needed, and that's exactly what he'd given me.

I spun in my seat and buried my head in his chest.

Pulling me closer, he lifted me from the stool and wrapped me in a bear hug—no pun intended. His arms were strong and comforting, and in this moment, it was the only place I wanted to be.

"Let it out, Nat. I've got you." He carried me to his room.

Unable to hold back, I cried and cried while he held me tight. He stroked my hair and whispered soothing words into my ear, allowing me to finally let it all go. The guilt, the sorrow, the anger—all of it poured out of me while he held me in his arms.

Finally cried out, my soft whimpers filled the room as I pulled back from his embrace. I wiped my eyes and caught sight of his ruined shirt. "I'm sorry."

Caleb shook his head and grinned. "It's okay. I never liked this shirt much anyway." He reached up and tucked a piece of my hair behind my ear. "Are you okay? Do you want to talk about it?"

I sniffled and shrugged my shoulders. "I'm not sure what there is to say. I've basically hidden myself away this whole semester—from my friends, from my feelings. That changed me somehow; I can feel it now. It's like my emotions have been stifling my power. I've been hiding inside of myself, and you are the only person who's seen the real me lately, so thank you for that." I leaned in and placed a soft kiss on his lips.

Lingering, our lips pressed softly together, and I scooted closer.

Caleb's shoulders tightened, but he didn't pull back. "Are you sure you're okay with this? I mean, we haven't even talked about things yet."

Damn, he's such a good guy.

I wanted this connection—needed it, in fact. So I answered his question with another kiss.

CHAPTER 10

I woke up a sweaty mess, my hair plastered to my neck and chest. Bear shifters were hot—in more ways than one. I tossed off the covers and pulled away from Caleb and his natural warmth. It was like an oven in here.

"Good morning," Caleb whispered, his voice deep and groggy. Sexy.

"Hi." I smiled. Quickly whispering a spell to freshen my breath, I leaned in for a kiss.

"Mmm, I could get use to this."

"Me, too," I answered honestly.

Caleb stretched out, linking his hands behind his head. "So I had an epiphany last night."

"Oh, yeah, and what was that?" I lay across his chest.

"That I think you're right."

"Well, that's a given, but right about what?" I teased.

"About your emotions blocking your powers."

I sat up, sobered by his words. "What makes you think that?"

"Because you said it yourself. You've been hiding away from everything, including your feelings. But last night, you were free. You opened your heart up to me, and I could feel your power rising."

Whoa.

Sex magic *was* a real thing, so maybe he was right. Maybe my magic's been blocked this whole time, and I hadn't even realized it. *Holy shit!* I recalled the words of my doppelganger in the mirror... *"You only need to transform your heart."*

I jumped out of bed and scrambled to get dressed. "Come on. I think I know what I have to do."

Caleb and I raced down the spiral stairs that encircled the outside of Jory Tower and ran into the quad. Min and Mallory were waiting for us on the nearest bench.

"This better be good. I haven't been out of bed this early on a weekend in years." Min grinned.

"I think I...well, we," I took Caleb's hand, "figured out what I need to do to gain access to the pool."

Mallory looked back and forth between Caleb and me, waggling her eyebrows while smiling ear to ear. "Well, it's about time."

I smiled back, not caring to dive into the fact that apparently everyone was aware of our budding relationship but me.

"Yeah, well, since we're a team, I figured we should all be there together. So, are you ready?" I nodded in the direction of Clifftop.

"Sure, but what do we have to do?" Min asked.

"Nothing, I hope. Like I said, this is something that only a true witch can do, and now...I'm finally ready." I squeezed Caleb's hand.

We made our way up to the skybridge and out onto Clifftop. The morning was calm with a few puffy clouds littering the blue sky. The sun shone warmly on my face.

Following my lead, we all walked down the main path into the forest, veering off toward the pool once we reached the appropriate spot. Caleb made it easier to reach this time by mashing down the overgrowth that covered the area. When the now-familiar fallen log came into view, I straightened my shoulders, ready to do this, and stepped over the trunk.

"What the hell?"

Everyone slammed to a stop behind me.

"Where did it go?" Mallory asked.

"I have no fucking idea."

CHAPTER 11

I spun around, looking over every fallen branch and twig, but the pool was gone. It was nowhere in sight, and I had no idea why or how it could have been moved. Then again, it's not like I understood the dynamics of a magical Celtic cauldron that led to a realm outside of our own, so yeah, why not? Why couldn't it just hop locations whenever it wanted to? *Fuck me!*

"Okay, so what do we do now?" Caleb asked, taking my hand.

I closed my eyes and took a deep breath. I needed to calm down, relax, and ground myself before I could think clearly. Actually…

"Can you give me a few minutes alone? I mean, can all of you just stand over there while I try to concentrate?" I pointed to the nearest evergreen bordering the area.

"Sure. Just be careful whatever you're planning to do." Caleb lifted the back of my hand to his lips, then sauntered off with Min and Mallory to give me some space.

I sat down in the grass, exactly where the pool used to be. Crossing my legs, I laid my hands over the knees and placed my fingers in a Shuni mudra, touching my middle finger to my thumb. The middle finger represented courage to hold duty and responsibility, and the thumb represented fire and divine nature. When the two fingers were placed together, it symbolized and encouraged patience, discernment, focus, and discipline—all the things I needed right now.

Grounding myself like my mother taught me, I imagined roots growing out of my skin, penetrating deep into the earth. The energy ebbed and flowed, pulsing as I reached for my magical center. My roots sank deeper, passing veins of gold the farther down they went. There, near its center, I felt it—my magic awaiting me. It beckoned me, warming the closer I got.

"You've shielded yourself away for too long," the Goddess's voice sounded in my head.

"I'm sorry, my lady. To be honest, I think my grief took a toll I wasn't prepared for, which left me numb and disconnected."

"As most grief does," she comforted me.

"But I'm here now. Ready to open my heart fully again and release my magic."

"Yes, but are you prepared for what that means? For what you'll have to do?"

I paused, scared and uncertain. *"I cannot lie; I'm not sure what has to be done, so fear of the unknown has a tight grasp upon me."*

"You know, they say FEAR can have two meanings: Forget Everything And Run, or Face Everything And Rise. The choice is yours."

"I will always choose to face everything and rise. In your name, my lady."

"Then you have nothing to fear. Embrace your true magic again, and you'll know just what to do."

Warmth radiated around me, and I smiled as I opened my eyes. Centered and at peace, I knew my true, hereditary magic was all I'd need to complete this task.

Screams erupted from my team as the ground opened up below me.

Sucked down into a pit, I realized the mercury pool hadn't disappeared, but had solidified beneath the surface. The energy of me reconnecting with my magic had heated it back up, and I now understood the urgency I'd previously felt. Our chance to access the pool had been fading—it was disappearing back into its own realm.

Panicked, I held my breath and struggled against the thick

liquid as I reached for the surface. Falling deeper and deeper, the mercurial substance surrounded me until I could no longer move.

Floating in stasis, I opened my eyes.

The substance was thick in viscosity but also somehow thinner here—clearer and easy to see through.

Even though I knew I was in the silver pool, the image before me transported my thoughts to a time long ago. Squinting, I made out a small village of huts surrounded by massive fields. Stone pathways wove between the buildings, and harvest animals and farmers could be seen working in the distance.

Lost in the moment, I took a breath. Thankfully, my lungs accepted the liquid as if it was air, and I was once again able to breathe.

The door of the nearest hut swung open and out stepped a woman, carrying a large cauldron in her arms. She walked toward me, her black woolen cloak and long white hair loosely blowing in the wind, shielding her weathered face. She set the piece at my feet and raised her head, staring straight into my soul.

"You're here for my staff, then, aye?" Her Celtic accent hung thick in the air.

"Yes," I replied on instinct.

"To prove you're worthy, you must transform the contents of my cauldron with your magic. But beware. Only those who are pure of heart can succeed."

I nodded, acknowledging her challenge, and closed my eyes. Taking a deep breath, I thought about my mom and all she'd taught me. I thought about Caleb and how he'd help me move past my grief without me even realizing it. I thought about the Goddess's words regarding fear and smiled to myself.

Opening my eyes, I looked down into the cauldron. It was full of liquid mercury—just like the pool. I frowned, confused for a moment, but was relieved when an immense sense of calm washed over me. Able to move again, I reached into my pocket and pulled out the large red crystal I'd been carrying around with me.

The stone warmed and buzzed softly in my hand.

Knox's lesson taught us how to separate elemental mercury and create something entirely new. Reaching out, I dropped my crystal into the cauldron and set it alight with a snap of my fingers.

Flames flared, and a cloud of red smoke rose from the depths, swirling and coiling over the top of the cauldron's surface.

Through the fog, I saw a large branch push its way up from the base, rising like a sprouting tree. Its wood was cracked and intertwined with a thick silver and blue liquid. *Quicksilver and aether*, my mind supplied—the transformation was almost complete.

Reaching out, I took ahold of the staff. Power slammed through me, sealing the cracks and solidifying the magical liquid into its core.

"You've done well, little witch. The Cailleach blesses you!"

With that, the Celtic goddess picked up her cauldron and strode away.

Hands gripped me, pulling me upward against the force of the thick mercury clinging to my body.

"Get her up! Pull!" Caleb's voice rang in my ears.

"Wait, what's that?" Mallory's voice pierced my consciousness.

"She did it. It's the staff," Min shouted.

Heaved free, I was pulled onto solid ground, the staff falling beside me, still in my grasp.

"Natalie, can you hear me?" Caleb's soft hands ran gently along my arms.

"I can hear you," I sputtered, coughing out the liquid in my lungs.

"Oh, thank the Goddess," Mallory sobbed.

Everyone took a step back as I sat up, struggling to expel the quicksilver from my mouth. The staff pulsed in my hand, and a warmth radiated through my body, healing me from within. I looked up to my friends and smiled.

"We did it."

Caleb lifted me to my feet and pulled me into a tight hug. "You did it."

"Woohoo!" Mallory exclaimed, joined by Min's surprised gasp.

"Holy crap, look..."

We all turned to see the silver on Min's hand liquify and drop to the ground—slithering its way back into the pool. The ground shook, and like a sink being drained, the mercury pool was sucked back down into the earth.

"Whoa." Caleb shuddered and pulled me close.

"So does this mean we're done?" Mallory stepped forward, looking at the ground.

"I think so." I held the wooden stick at arm's length, studying it fully for the first time. It was thick and made of smooth, black wood with cracks spiraling half-way up the shaft. The cracks glowed with the silver and blue mix of quicksilver and aether. It was magic incarnate. Powerful and ancient. And I couldn't believe it'd been gifted to me.

"Now what? Are we supposed to turn this in to someone?" Caleb asked.

"I'm not sure. Our next ITF class isn't until Monday at 8:00 a.m., but honestly, I don't think I want to hold onto it until then. The pull of magic coursing through it is kind of intense. Almost overwhelming," I admitted honestly.

I refrained from adding that this was in no way some random trinket to test our team-building skills through a class-assigned scavenger hunt. It was exponentially more than that, and obviously, something the Board of Regents wanted desperately. Especially if they were willing to put their students at risk to retrieve it. Suddenly, I wondered what other secrets they were keeping from us…again.

CHAPTER 12

We strode onto campus, concealing the staff between our bodies, and made our way directly to Halstein Hall.

"Is Professor Beaumont available?" I asked the receptionist behind the front desk of the Administrative Offices.

"Which one?" She sighed. "We currently have two teaching here, remember?"

"Yes, I remember, and either will do," I snapped, recalling a similar conversation the two of us shared last semester.

Before she could pick up the phone, Addie Beaumont appeared from around the corner.

"Hi, guys. What can I do for you?" Her tone was friendly, but the set of her jaw wasn't. She already knew something was up.

"Um…I have something for you. Can we head to your office?" I smiled nervously, hoping she'd take the hint.

"Of course. Follow me."

We all shimmied around the desk together, concealing our prize. The moment we walked through her door, Addie spun to face us. "You found it, didn't you?"

We all tensed up, not knowing what would happen when someone else touched the staff. So far, I'd been the only one who could. The shocks the others received continued to confirm that only a witch could wield it. Taking a deep breath, I pulled it out from behind my back and held it up for Addie to inspect.

With a smile on her face, she bent closer, examining every inch.

"This is amazing. Well done, guys." She held out her hand without hesitation and grabbed the staff.

We all held our breath.

"Oh, wow. That's powerful." She gasped. "I'll be looking forward to your team report."

"Report?" Min stuttered.

"Yes. We'll want to know how you solved your clue and how your selected card related to the task at hand. We'll also need a detailed account of how you actually retrieved your piece. Say about…a thousand words or so."

Everyone looked to me.

Addie was an amazing witch—a member of the Board of Regents, as well as a future member of the Court of the Sun and the Moon, not to mention someday she'd be taking over as high priestess of the Luna Coven. But, for whatever reason, I didn't think I was supposed to share what I'd learned…with anybody. The Cailleach was ancient—primal, and now personal to me. I didn't want to lie about what happened, but the feeling radiating in my gut told me I wouldn't be able to share my experience with anyone, even if I tried. And honestly, I found myself wondering if this report was required by all the teams or if it was something she was asking of just me.

"We'll do our best," I said.

Addie smiled, and the door opened behind us. We all shuffled out into the hallway and made our way from the Administrative Offices down to the food court a few floors below.

Gawking at each other, we stood there silently, still trying to process.

"Wow. Okay, so the staff is definitely a witch thing," Min stated first.

"Yeah, and how are we supposed to report what happened when none of us really did anything, besides Nat?" Mallory shifted from foot to foot, her hands wringing the hem of her sweatshirt.

"Guys, relax. Honestly, I'm not sure I can even describe what happened, but I'll try my best. This was my project, being the lead and all, so I'll take care of the report, too," I offered.

"Wow, okay. Thanks, Natalie. Do you want our notes from the library?" Mallory asked.

I did, but not to include them in the report. The urge to hide them away was overwhelming. "Yes, actually. That'll be great. Can you bring them by my dorm tomorrow morning?"

"Sure thing." Mallory bounced off after giving me a quick hug. Min flashed a peace sign and headed toward the quad. "Later."

"So," Caleb reached for my hand, "it's Saturday afternoon. What do you want to do now?"

The idea of following him back to his dorm and crawling into bed warmed me in all the right places, but the urge to be alone was pulling at me hard. "Actually, do you mind if I go clean up and take a nap? I'm exhausted."

"Of course not. Text me later if you want to grab dinner. Maybe we can try heading into town again."

"Sounds good," I replied.

He leaned down and placed a soft kiss on my lips then turned and walked away. I watched him head toward the library and grinned as the old adage popped into my head—*I hate when he leaves, but I love to watch him go.* Giggling like the fool I was, I turned around and spotted Tempest and Eryx coming up the front steps.

"I saw that." She winked, nodding in Caleb's direction.

"Yeah, yeah. You were right."

"Of course I was." She smirked playfully, rocking her hips into Eryx's. "So where ya headed? We just came from the beach." She lifted her rattan swim bag so I could see.

"Nice! I'm actually headed to our dorm. I'm in desperate need of a shower and a nap. Can I find you later?"

"You betcha! We'll either be here getting food, or in Eryx's tower just hanging out." Tempest stepped forward and gave me a hug while whispering in my ear, "Hey, are you okay?"

I nodded yes and squeezed her tight.

"Okay, catch you later." Tempest winked and walked off in the direction of Coffee Haven with Eryx in tow.

With no further distractions, I headed straight to Hel Tower. I had to figure out why I was being drawn to keep all of this a secret. Besides myself, Caleb was the only one I'd told about The Cailleach, and even that, for some reason, wasn't sitting right with me.

Pushing through the red gothic door of our tower, I sprinted up the spiral staircase, and raced to my room on the second floor, clicking the lock behind me. I quickly gathered my tools and sat alone on our fuzzy black circular rug, setting my candles around me. Snapping my fingers, I set them ablaze and reached for my selenite wand. I needed to connect with the Goddess, and this was usually the fastest way.

"Goddess of light, Goddess of night, show me if what I feel is right. Provide the reason, to walk alone, in the knowledge I now do own."

The crystal wand warmed in hand.

"You did well, facing your fear. I'm proud of you." The Goddess's voice floated around me, enveloping me like a warm hug.

"Thank you, my lady. I only did what came naturally, once my magic was fully flowing again."

"And what is your magic telling you now?" she prompted, already knowing the reason I was seeking her out.

"That I need to keep the knowledge of the Cailleach and the realm of the witch to myself."

"And why do you think that is?"

"Because it's sacred, and only meant for those who are touched by it directly."

"Your instincts are right again. It's also why the pool had begun to disappear. If those who are worthy do not present themselves in time, the chance to access the realm is removed. It's also the only reason you were able to find those books in the library. They don't appear for just anyone."

"I understand, and am so grateful you helped me reconnect in time."

"Time will always be on your side, Natalie, as long as you remain true to yourself and follow your heart. Grief and guilt are valid emotions; and while they're obstacles that hinder and hurt, they cannot change who you are at your core."

"*Thank you, my lady. Speaking of my heart, Caleb knows about The Cailleach. And while I trust him, I feel protective of the knowledge, and wonder if I'm to remove his memories?*"

"*What does your heart tell you to do?*"

I took a grounding breath. "*Thank you for your counsel, Goddess. I know what has to be done.*"

"*Blessed be, Natalie.*"

"*Blessed be.*"

CHAPTER 13

J texted Caleb as soon as I was showered and dressed. We were meeting in the quad and had dinner reservations at Napoli's for eight. But first...

"Hey, do you mind if we take a detour?" I asked. "I wanted to check out the beach before we left. Tempest and Eryx were down there yesterday, and it sounded like fun."

"Sure." Caleb took my hand in his, and we walked over the main bridge together, taking a right to follow the trail that led to the underground lake.

"I haven't been back down here since spring break." Caleb laughed, probably recalling all the chaos that ensued when Marina lost her shit and was hauled off over Cas's shoulder.

"Yeah, me neither."

As I hoped, the beach was empty. Being a Saturday night, most students were either at the party taking place on Hel Tower's roof, or out and about in town.

"It's peaceful down here when no one's losing their mind," Caleb joked.

"Yeah, I think so, too." I walked to the edge of the water and sat down in the sand, pulling him with me.

Shadows enveloped most of the area, except where the gnomes had hung fairy lights through the cavernous space. The flickering orbs sparkled on the water's surface. I stared at their reflection, thinking about what I had to do. I hoped my potion and spell would target only the memories I needed them to, or else this date—and any other—would become the shortest in my relationship history. I took a deep breath. *Here's goes nothing.*

"Hey, can I ask you something?" I turned to face Caleb, looking him straight in the eyes as I pulled my hand free of his grasp.

"Of course." He scooted closer.

Reaching behind me, I uncorked the stoppered vial and poured the powder into my hand.

"Do you…" I trailed off, lifting my palm and blowing the potion straight into his face.

"Goddess of old, mother of all, remove the memories so he doesn't recall. Cailleach now, wiped from his mind. Preserved only for witches, throughout time."

I waited with bated breath, as Caleb coughed and sputtered.

Blinking, his eyes finally cleared, and he shook his head and asked, "Do I…what?"

"Do you remember the other day in the library…" I started.

His brows drew together in a tight V. "Um, you and me? We were at the library together?"

Oh, thank Goddess, it worked.

"Hmm, maybe it was me and Tempest. I don't remember." I shrugged dramatically, a nervous giggle bubbling past my lips. "Anyway, when I was in there, I couldn't help but notice there seemed to be even more floors than there were last semester." There wasn't, of course, but I was struggling for a bit of random conversation to wrap this up.

"Really? I guess I never counted. The only one I ever kept track of is the one that leads to Jory." He laughed, and I joined in wholeheartedly.

"Yeah, I can see that. Well, it's almost eight. Should we head out for our date?" I stared at his handsome face, gauging his reaction, hoping he didn't jerk back in surprise or worse, wrinkle his nose in disgust.

"Hell yes, we should." He bent forward and gave me a kiss, as if nothing had changed between us.

I closed my eyes and leaned in. His lips were gentle against mine, but I needed more. I was so thankful we still had time to learn about each other, and what this could be. I pushed off the sand and crawled into his lap, deepening our kiss.

Eight p.m. passed, and our reservation with it, but neither of us minded as we rolled around in the sand, exploring each other and our developing feelings. My heart beat heavily in my chest, and I welcomed it. I was ready for this. I wanted to feel again.

Waking up on a Sunday morning, tucked in bed with my newly claimed boyfriend, was the best feeling I'd had in a long time. Unfortunately, I had a report to write.

"I'll find you later." I kissed Caleb and left Jory Tower, heading straight for my dorm room. I knew Tempest stayed at Eryx's again last night, so I'd have the place to myself. With a little magic, I'd have this baby done in no time.

Grabbing my laptop, I placed it on my desk and scattered my crystals around it. Labradorite for a boost to a writer's magic and psychic abilities; tiger's eye for directing thoughts and focus; carnelian for its boost to creativity and imagination; jasper for its help in calming emotions and nerves; and moonstone for its connection to the Goddess. With my power flowing, I blew out a cleansing breath, closed my eyes, and gave thanks to The Cailleach out loud.

"I'm so grateful for my magic and for this experience, and will keep this secret per the witch's pyramid: To know; To dare; To will; and To keep silent. It is part of our creed, and now I am a part of you. The ancient witches, the Gods and Goddesses who keep magic alive. Blessing to you. So mote it be."

And with that, I let the automatic writing begin.

Thirty minutes later, a knock at the door pulled me from my trance. I opened my eyes and smiled. The required pages for my report were done, and with only the appropriate details as guided by the Goddess. "Coming," I called out.

Unlocking the door, I pulled it open and gasped.

There before me stood Malyki in human form.

"What are you doing here?" I grabbed his arm and pulled him inside.

"I could not reach you mentally, or gain access through your window." He looked around the room on high alert, as if searching for someone or something.

"Thanks, but I'm fine. I just sealed the room so I could get some automatic writing done. I didn't want anyone to interrupt me." I tilted my head and gave him a quirky smile.

Malyki's breathing relaxed, along with his shoulders and the twitch in his jaw. "While I understand, may I ask that the next time you decide to do so, you warn me in advance? We are connected now."

"Okay, about that. Can you tell me how you came to be my familiar? Obviously, it has something to do with this little sweetheart." I reached down and picked up Mystic, who'd emerged from under my bed and was winding her way between my legs. I gave her a scratch behind the ears—just how she liked it, but oddly, she jumped from my grasp.

A purple light swirled around the black feline, and the next thing I knew, a beautiful woman stood in her place. Malyki reached for her hand.

"Mystic?" I stammered.

"Hello, Natalie." She blinked her mis-matched eyes and cocked her head—all feline and feminine-like—revealing ginger highlights beneath her long dark hair. "While you think it is I who led Malyki to you, it's actually the opposite. We've been searching for one another for centuries, and it was the magic of this place that called to us both, leading him here to me." Her white blouse and flowing multi-colored skirt ruffled around her as she pressed closer to Malyki's side.

"Are you…" I fumbled with which question to ask first.

"We are witches of a sort, we are partners, and now we are both your familiars. Our story is a long one, and one we'll happily share, but after we help find the next piece."

"The next piece?" I asked, worried there was more to the staff than I originally thought.

"There is a specific piece being searched for by another group.

However, they do not embody the element needed to be successful."

"And which element is that?"

"Air, to be exact." She smiled up at her partner. "For Malyki rides its currents, and I traverse its hidden realms. Without us, they'll never be able to find what they seek, for it is specifically connected to us."

Holy cow! I guess the Sun & Moon Academy just gained two more students.

THE MAGICIAN

TISH THAWER & BELINDA BORING

"Only when sacrifice is made, can true love endure."
—Unknown, Halvard Campus

CHAPTER 1

Finishing the telling of our story to our two favorite witches, I stretched my arms above my head, nuzzling into Malyki's side. It was strange wearing clothes and being in my human form again after spending so many years as a cat.

"So there you have it. We've spent centuries cursed to serve as familiars, searching for one another and a way to break the curse," I explained to a very shocked Tempest and Natalie inside their Hel Tower dorm.

The girls looked to one another, stunned expressions marring their faces.

"Wow, Mystic. That's a hell of a story. How did you end up here with us?" Natalie finally asked, gesturing around their room.

"Malyki disappeared into a demon realm the night we were cursed, but I spent my first three years bound to a witch in another village close to where our home used to be." I lowered my head, thinking back through the horrible memories and all I'd done. "I'm not proud of it, but I used her and her magic to exact my revenge on the man who cursed us." I lifted my chin and held the girls' gazes. "There is none of his line left."

"Good. That bastard deserved it," Natalie snapped, surprising me. Out of the two young witches, I thought she might not understand my need for revenge. Especially after spending so long shaping her path as a white witch, despite her mother's influence.

"When Danor was destroyed, his magic left a trace—one I followed all the way to Havenwood Falls," I continued to explain. "It turns out Marcus St. James was cursed by another clan from our region, and following that energy I wound up here, unable to leave."

"What do you mean, unable to leave?" Tempest asked.

"Well, perhaps *unable* isn't the right word. The wards around the town are so powerful, and after hearing about the memory loss they cause if you're beyond their limits for too long, I simply couldn't risk it. As long as Malyki and I are apart, I am stuck in my cat form without access to my true magic. It was also the first time I didn't have a witch to serve, which left me vulnerable as well. That was back in 1883."

"*What?* You've been here since 1883?" Natalie exclaimed.

"Yes—I've stayed hidden, living in the forest or up on the mountains while continuing to search for the object that would break our curse. It wasn't until the campus opened this year that I was finally able to pinpoint its location."

"What do you mean?" Tempest piped up. The girls looked ready to join in the search, and it touched my heart to think how strong our bond already was. They weren't just witches. They were family.

"One of the ITF teams has been assigned to find a vessel—the very demon vessel that's the source of our curse. If we can locate it, we can finally break the binding magic and be free."

Silence descended, blanketing the room, until Natalie, always the practical witch, asked her next question. "How do you know that's what their assignment has them looking for?"

"Because I've gotten very good at sneaking around. You can't imagine all the things I've seen and heard while here. Being ripped away from my husband centuries ago forced me to scratch out an existence all on my own, and you can't do that as a cat unless you become very good at living in the shadows."

Speaking of scratching...

I stretched my arms into the air again, lengthening my back like I'd done as a cat for so long. "Dear, could you get that spot behind my ears again?"

Malyki chuckled, the low rumble in his chest sending chills up my spine as he reached under the long curtain of my dark hair, past the ginger strands, and tickled my favorite spot. His touch sent goosebumps racing across my skin. Oh, how I'd missed the way my body reacted to him.

"Thanks, babe." I squirmed back into his side.

"All right. I understand Mystic's story, but what about you?" Natalie lifted her chin at Malyki. "How did you end up here?" I was proud of her inquisitive nature, the way she delved into discovering the truth. It was a characteristic that would serve her well as a guardian.

"Honestly, I'm not one-hundred percent sure. When Danor cursed us, I disappeared back into whatever demon realm he'd conjured the artifact from. Then, a few days ago, I was able to sense Mystic's magic again and rode its currents here. I materialized in the forest where my familiar bond attached itself to you." He nodded toward Natalie.

"Wow." Tempest linked arms with her bestie, smiling wide. "It's all so romantic. Cursed lovers, separated through space and time, only to find one another again in a magical college hidden under a mountain."

"Yeah, it's a real Disney moment," Natalie quipped. "But seriously, we're gonna need to talk to the Board of Regents now that you two are back together and can keep your human forms. They'll want to question you, and it'll be up to them as to whether you can stay or not." Her tone was somber; she was clearly worried they'd say no.

"But you're still our familiars, right?" Tempest questioned. "They can't make you leave if you're connected to us." Her brow furrowed deep with panic. "I mean, I know our relationship has changed since you're both in human form, but the Regents can't just kick you out. We won't let them." The anxiety that had previously filled her eyes was now replaced with bold determination. I had no doubt that both of them would fight to keep us here.

"That's my hope," I admitted, "though I do think we should ask for a separate room." I smiled up at Malyki who responded with a kiss to my cheek.

A knock on the door interrupted us, causing the girls to jump.

"Who is it?" Tempest called out.

"It's Addie. May I come in?"

"Oh, shit!" Natalie whispered, her eyes scanning the room for places we could hide until we were ready with a game plan. Tempest stood by the entrance, her body poised to stop the Regent member from entering should she try.

"I'm aware we have some new visitors. That's why I'm here. Please open up," Addie stated flatly from the hallway.

Tempest eased open the door with a quirky smile plastered on her face. "Oh, hey, come on in."

Addie Beaumont strolled into the room with her light brown hair plaited in low pig-tail braids and the diamond stud in her nose glinting under the light. She stared at Malyki and me sprawled atop Natalie's bed.

"These two tripped the wards, and we traced them to your room. Would you care to introduce us?" She nodded at Natalie, her magic sizzling just under the surface.

I pushed to stand, causing all three women to take a step back. "Allow me."

I motioned for Malyki to join me. It would be easier to show her instead of offering some long-winded explanation. The air shifted around us, and we both transformed into our familiar selves.

"Oh my Goddess, Mystic, is that you baby girl?" Addie cooed. "And, Malyki, right?" She turned to Natalie. "He's your new familiar, yes?"

"Yep. That's them," Natalie replied with a slow nod.

"Well, this is…surprising." Addie bent down and picked me up, placing me back on Natalie's bed with a gentle pat to my head. "Can we talk?"

Malyki and I both shifted back, casually sitting in our human forms again. "We're not here to cause trouble, I can promise you that."

I smiled, hoping it reached my mis-matched eyes and convinced her we meant no harm.

Addie nodded—a little too hesitantly for my tastes, though, so I continued to explain.

"Malyki and I were cursed and separated long ago, bound to

remain in our familiar forms until we recently reunited. Now, with access to our magic again, not only are we the girls' familiars, but also their human guardians as well. The bond we all share is even stronger now, but our curse requires us to remain close to our charges. If we were to be separated from them, or from each other again, we'd revert back to our animal selves permanently."

Addie took a deep breath and tilted her head. "Trust me, with all the familiars I have, I'm completely aware of the odd ways that bond and connection works. But I still need to get a read on things, if you don't mind." She held up a hand, and I immediately understood. Nodding, I welcomed her request for a physical connection. We had nothing to hide, and I was happy to prove that here and now.

Laying her hand on my forearm, she closed her eyes. A light sizzle of magic sparked against my skin as she skimmed through my memories, magically verifying our story and the reason for us both being here. She was basically the Court's version of a magical lie detector.

I pushed my memories through our shared connection, letting her see everything we'd been through—all the way back to our original curse. She witnessed our time separated from one another, as well as my time spent here in Havenwood Falls.

"Holy fuck," Addie whispered under her breath. Opening her eyes, she pulled back and smiled. "Oops. Sorry for the language, but that was . . . intense. I'm so glad to see you two have been reunited, though. Shifting into your human forms must have tripped the ward. We'll have to get you tattooed so it doesn't continue to be a problem." Dropping into her more business-like demeanor, she muttered a spell under her breath, and her portable tattoo-kit appeared. "You'll have to get one for the campus and one for the town. The campus one will be the same as everyone else's, but the one for town, you can choose the design yourselves. But please understand, until you meet with the Court, these will only be temporary."

"We understand. And as far as the design, can we just have something added to our clan marks here?" I leaned forward, flipping my curtain of dark hair over my shoulder to reveal the Mark of the Romani.

"Of course. Actually, that's exactly what my friend Callie did too. She's Romani, as well."

I sat up and smoothed my hair back down. "Really? I'd love to meet her sometime."

"I'm sure she'd love that as well." Addie pulled out her tools and got to work.

Malyki and I both agreed to have matching crescent moons added to our clan mark on the backs of our necks. Then we each took turns receiving our campus tattoos on the insides of our left wrists.

"Okay. All done. I'll contact my grandmother and let her know what happened here. I'll arrange a meeting for you to meet with her in the morning, if that's okay." Addie started packing away her tools.

"Actually, we were hoping to be assigned a room here in Hel Tower. Is that possible now?" Malyki asked.

I turned to my husband, feeling his anxiety spike. He wasn't usually much of a talker, unless our circumstances required it, but I could sense his urgency...and his needs. It'd been so long since we were alone, and the fact that we'd need to remain close to our charges was weighing heavily on him as well. He was such a good guardian.

"Well, let's see. Excuse me for just a moment." Addie stepped outside of the room, closing the door behind her. We heard a pop then the whispered tones of two distinct voices. With a quick wrap on the door, she reentered with her grandmother, Saundra Beaumont, in tow.

"Hello, Mystic. Malyki." Saundra dipped her head in greeting, her hair remaining flawless in a civilized updo. "Adelaide has explained your situation, and while I will still have to convene with the Board as well as the Court of the Sun and the Moon tomorrow morning, I think we can go ahead and grant your request on a probationary basis. However, there will be some restrictions placed upon you, until your stay here is officially approved."

"Thank you, Ms. Beaumont." I addressed her formally, even though I'd lived here long enough in my cat form to feel like I already knew her. "We completely understand. Actually, thank you both. May we take the room next door?" I nodded toward

Tempest's side of the room, already knowing the room on the other side was free and unoccupied.

Ms. Beaumont snapped her fingers, producing a set of silver keys out of thin air. "You'll be assigned the room next door for now, but once you enter, you won't be able to leave until it's time for our meeting in the morning. You also cannot leave Hel Tower until then as well. Enjoy the rest of your day and evening. I'll see you two in my office first thing tomorrow." She raised her chin in my and Malyki's direction then followed Addie back out the door.

"We'll be there," I called out, "and thank you again." I was excited to have gained her semi-approval. Out of all the Board members, I knew Tempest and Natalie liked and respected Saundra the most. That would make things much easier to navigate, than say if we had to deal with that vampiric-dick, Gabriel Doyle instead.

"Girls, if you'll excuse us, we'd like to go get settled in." I reached for Malyki's hand. "We'll see you tomorrow after our meeting with the Board." I smiled at Natalie and Tempest, happy we were able to remain so close.

Natalie nodded while Tempest just grinned, starting at our interlocked hands.

"No rush on our end. I'm sure you both have a lot of catching up to do." The lilt in her voice made her insinuation obvious, and I instantly became nervous.

Having been separated for so long—and forced straight into our explanations here—the idea of finally being alone sent chills up my spine. Had he constantly thought of me as I had him? Was he even cognizant within the demon realm? There were so many unanswered questions...even between the two of us.

"Shall we?" Malyki gestured to the door.

"After you." I purred, smiling as I followed *iubita mea* to our private room.

CHAPTER 2

*M*y sudden case of butterflies threw me for a loop.

I'd dreamt of this moment a bazillion times, having fantasy after detailed fantasy of what our reunion would be, but here I was . . . oddly nervous.

Peering at Malyki through my dark lashes, I was proud to see that my memory hadn't failed me after all these years. I had scorched his image into my very being, careful not to forget even the slightest of nuances about the man I loved more than my own life. Ignoring the way my stomach knotted in nerves, I took a moment to appreciate the miracle that had happened.

We were together again.

I was no longer bound in feline form, and for the first time in forever, I didn't have to rely solely on my mind. He was here—in the flesh, and within reach. My heart thundered so loudly in my chest that I could feel it pulsating throughout my body, even down to the soles of my feet.

"Malyki," I whispered, my voice sounding huskier than usual. What was I saying? I'd spent so long as a cat, it was exciting to be able to utter words. Part of me was still surprised I wasn't purring with contentment or meowing my approval. "Is this real?"

I still stood by the door as if closing the distance between us might prove that this was actually a dream, and I was currently curled up into a ball of black and ginger fur in my witches' room, snoozing. I saw the second of hesitation flash in my husband's eyes. Even now, we were still connected—a good sign that that magic in the curse hadn't destroyed the bond we both cherished.

His eyes twinkled, and a slow grin curled his lips. My god, how I had missed that smile.

"Would you think less of me if I confessed that I'm scared to breathe in case you disappear before my eyes, *iubita mea*?" Malyki let out a ragged breath as he reached for me. "Do we dare hope?"

My gaze dropped from his face to his outstretched arms, and I didn't waiver. I ran for him, throwing my arms around his neck as he picked me up easily, twirling me about. No words were needed—our shared joy and laughter spoke volumes. We were together again, and this time, this time nothing would ever keep us apart.

I would pull down the heavens and lay waste to the earth before anyone held that kind of power over us again. I wouldn't foolishly dismiss any threat to those I love. Time had taught me that brutal lesson well.

Malyki's deep chuckle rumbled in my ear. "Breathe, Mystic. Trust that we are together and safe." His mouth brushed softly against my cheek, and I leaned in to his touch. "Now that you're in my arms, I won't ever let you go."

Without words, he'd sensed my thoughts and the intensity of my emotions and instantly knew how to soften them. He'd always been the yin to my yang—the one to temper the fire within me and not be afraid to embrace the darker parts I kept hidden.

"You know me so well," I murmured as I peered up into his eyes, my fingers playing in his hair. Goddess, I missed this. "I have been so lost without you, as if half of me was missing." He lowered me to the ground, but I kept on my tiptoes, nestled against him. "The better half of me. Always the better."

He gently cradled my cheek, and a shiver of desire skated over my skin as his thumb brushed back and forth tenderly. "Sssh," he crooned, and like magic, my agitation instantly settled beneath his attention. "It has always been you. I thank the goddess that I lived long enough to be here in this moment. That our love proved stronger than jealousy and the cruelest magic." Slowly, he inched us backward, one step at a time. "I have so much to tell you, Mystic."

All I could do was nod. There was no way I could trust my voice with the large lump of emotion that was now lodged in my throat. Tears formed in my eyes as the love I felt for Malyki—the devotion I'd let fuel my determination to find him—finally broke free.

The backs of my legs hit against something. The bed. He'd maneuvered us skillfully, and my heart started pounding in my ears for a different reason. There were no more nerves. This . . . what was about to happen . . . this was as easy as breathing.

"More importantly," he murmured, staring down at my mouth, both of his hands cupping my face, "I have so much to show you."

Yes. I needed him to wipe away the loneliness and longing I'd felt for him—filling up those hollow spaces with his light and goodness. Hell, I needed to do the same and banish the shadows I saw hidden in his eyes.

His hands trembled—the movement almost undoing my barely contained patience. In the past, our lovemaking was explosive as our passion for each other took over, making it hard to savor each taste and measured touch. Judging by the energy that thrummed between us, he was also remembering the countless nights we spent intertwined together as our mouths hungrily explored our bodies. I wanted it all—every stroke, dip, and agonizingly slow thrust, but I couldn't deny the equally powerful yearning for our souls to commune. It was never just sex for us.

Our intimacy bordered on sacred—another reason why the curse had been so devastating in its intentions.

But that was over. We now had the chance to begin wiping away that trauma and replacing it with beauty—with our own personal magic. We were soulmates, and we were eternal. Each kiss and healing touch would work wonders in undoing that heartache.

"Malyki," I half-moaned, half-begged. "Please."

I murmured a quick spell, and my multi-colored skirt and white blouse disappeared. I moved to do the same to him, but he captured my hand with his and raised my fingers to his mouth.

"Tsk," he murmured as he shook his head, his dark hair falling across his desire-filled eyes. "Do you dare deny me, wife, of the pleasure of stripping you bare?" His tongue darted out to wet his bottom lip, and I mirrored the action without thinking. "It's been so long, Mystic . . ." His voice trailed off, but I was struggling to concentrate because he was already reacquainting himself with each curve of my body.

A hunger that had long been buried rose up like a furious tornado, and I snapped my fingers again, removing his black canvas pants and deep-purple shirt. He was finally naked. There would be a time for slow deliberation and blisteringly unhurried touches. I needed my husband—my lover and soulmate—inside me. Now.

"You talk too much," I countered, pulling him down upon me as my back hit the top of the bed. I was already kissing him, devouring his taste as though I'd been starved for a lifetime. As far as I was concerned, that's exactly how long our time apart had felt and no amount of days or years could quench how ravenous I was.

Words fell away, but in its place rose the beautiful symphony our souls created. We still remembered how to make our bodies sing together—the quiver that resulted in a trembling wave of pleasure or the rising to welcome each glorious thrust of Malyki's hips that made me moan.

I was home. We were home. We had overcome the hatred and jealousy of man to find our way back to each other.

As each second crescendoed and evolved into the next, we didn't look away—our gazes locked. Even if we were stripped of our powers this instant, we would still hold the most incredible magic together, and it showed in the way the air sizzled and sparked as we raced toward our joined climax.

This was something no one could ever steal from us—this feeling of complete and utter oneness. It was a sensation that had robbed me of breath the first time he took me, and it did the exact same thing now.

"My love, together," Malyki's husky voice snapped me back to the precipice he'd driven us to, and with one last thrust, I began to freefall—crying out his name, my nails gripping his shoulder tightly as I felt my energy detonate inside me.

Over and over my own name echoed in my ears as he stiffened

for a moment, then crashed on top of me, the weight of his body welcome. Everything else faded away. The past no longer pressed against my mind nor the future that awaited us. Whatever might come—in this moment, I knew that we would not only face it, but kick its ass.

"Am I dead?" he finally whispered, still motionless on top of me. A delicious warmth permeated through me, and with what little energy I could muster, I curled my leg around his, anchoring him in place. I wasn't ready for him to move. I wasn't ready to separate.

"If you are, then I am too." I chuckled, the sound a little shaky and croaky. "I'm quite content to stay in bed for the next few centuries, lover." He shifted his torso, and I groaned a little, slapping his behind in protest. "Stay put. I'm nowhere near ready for this to be over."

Malyki rested up on one elbow, and I tenderly brushed the curtain of hair that swooped across his brow. Sweet goddess, this man was beautiful.

"And you think I am? *Iupita mea*—" He grinned before feathering the lightest of kisses over my face. "We have a lot of catching up to do, and I've only just begun."

CHAPTER 3

*M*y body tingled from head to toe.

Our entire day and night had been spent reconnecting—mind, body, and soul. And if it was left up to me, we'd be starting all over again right now. Unfortunately, Malyki and I had an appointment with Saundra Beaumont and the Board of Regents first thing this morning—as in 7:30 a.m. this morning.

Rolling away from my lover's warmth was the hardest thing I'd done in years, but the sooner we got this over with, the sooner we could climb back into this bed.

"Good morning, husband. It's time to get up." I littered kisses across his torso then jumped to my feet. With a snap of my fingers, I refreshed my clothes and hair, settling on a burgundy sundress with a handkerchief hem instead of one of my usual flowy skirts. My dark hair hung loosely past my shoulders, its waves framing the talisman draped around my neck. It'd been so long since I'd felt its energy against my skin. I looked down and ran a finger over its threaded web. The necklace spanned the entire breadth of my chest, its charcoal strings and vibrant beads holding my stones of power in place. Each stone hummed under my touch, blazing a neon turquoise or a vibrant purple hue, and I was grateful to feel its power pulsing against my chest once more.

Malyki followed suit and dressed with a snap of his fingers. Ready in his canvas pants and black T-shirt, he looked like a soldier preparing to go to war. Damn, the man made my mouth water.

"You ready to do this?" I asked, confirming the door had unlocked this morning as Saundra indicated it would.

He nodded and followed me from our room in Hel Tower, down the spiral staircase, and out the main door.

"I know it's not necessarily how I want to be spending our first few days together again, but we have work to do." The threat of the curse loomed even more over our heads because of our reunion. I refused to be separated again.

"Of course." He squeezed my hand as we crossed the bridge. Malyki's eyes roamed back and forth as he studied our surroundings. He was curious about our new home. "I'd follow you anywhere, my love."

My heart melted at his words, and I gazed down at our entwined fingers. This was all so surreal—being here in this moment, the feel of his hand in mine, perfectly fitted together as we climbed the stairs to Halstein Hall and made our way up to the Administrative Offices.

"Good morning to you both. Please follow me," Saundra instructed, already poised and waiting at the front desk in her crisp navy suit and sensible heels.

There was no small talk, or 'how's the weather?' banter this morning. It was time to get down to business. We entered the boardroom, and every pair of eyes surrounding the long, polished table bore directly into ours.

"Mystic, Malyki, please take a seat." Saundra gestured to the two open chairs in front of us, then sat down beside me. "I've already explained your situation to the Board, and while everyone agrees that you'll be allowed to stay on a probationary basis, a few of us would appreciate more clarity on how you're connected to this particular hunt assignment."

I looked to Malyki, who dipped his head in a 'you've got this' gesture.

"The short of it...we were cursed by a rival clan leader who summoned a talisman from a demon realm. It contains powerful binding magic that holds the key to our curse in place. It's that talisman that is being searched for by one of your ITF teams now."

"And how exactly do you know this is the item being searched for?" From the tilt to Elsmed's head, I knew he was listening to my thoughts as well as my words. With nothing to hide, I left my inner defenses lowered so he could be free to probe.

"Because, as a familiar, I've been able to roam the campus and have kept track of all the teams and their hunts so far, even aiding in a few." I lifted my chin. Eryx, Tempest's boyfriend, liked to think he discovered the geode that contained their item, but I knew who'd really done the heavy lifting—or should I say, heavy scratching. I'd been instrumental in the discovery. "But this particular piece is hidden in the astral plane, protected here under the mountain. It's also clearly displayed on the card one of the teams selected."

"Which team?" Saundra asked as she scanned the notes in front of her. I couldn't quite read what was written there, but I assumed it was the list of students from the ITF class.

"Byrony's."

"The druid?" Mr. Doyle piped up, his fingers steepled in front of him as his brow piqued. "I'm sure her magic will prove powerful enough to succeed. Why exactly do you two need to be involved?"

I knew he could read minds, too, so I purposely let my thoughts flow as I explained. "While, yes, she is a druid and her magic is powerful, she nor any other member of her team are able to traverse the astral plane in the same way I am. Not to mention, they won't be able to retrieve it without Malyki—for he is bound to the artifact as well."

Silence descended as they murmured among themselves and made their final assessment. Part of me had already decided whatever their ruling was, Malyki and I would still pursue the item. There was too much resting on its retrieval—breaking our curse trumped any educational assignment.

"Well, it seems we have no choice but to assign you both to the team." Mr. Doyle pushed from his chair, his impeccable suit and piercing blue eyes both sharp as ever. "While we don't like the unorthodox manner in which you've arrived at Sun & Moon Academy or approve of human familiars, your words ring true. Our priority is providing a safe environment to teach and push our students to their limits magically. Be sure to know that we'll be watching you, and should you both pose any unnecessary danger, your staying here will be reevaluated, and no doubt terminated." He glanced at the other members, who nodded their agreement. "Do you understand?"

"We would expect nothing less." I met his gaze pointedly, making sure my thoughts resonated with the fact that he didn't scare me in the least. We were only here to help and free ourselves.

Elsmed then cleared his throat, drawing the room's attention. "I hope should you be presented with the choice over saving your token or protecting the lives of our students, that you would make the correct choice."

His voice then filled my mind. *"Freedom should never be achieved through the death of the innocent."*

It was Malyki who then spoke up. "I can assure you we will act with integrity and honor. You have no cause to fear or mistrust us."

The tension in the room seemed to reach a smothering crescendo—words being measured and weighed against the facts we'd shared. It was almost as if everyone held their breath, unsure.

Saundra was the first to dismiss the Board's apprehensions. "The teams are meeting shortly for their class. Follow me, and I'll make the proper introductions." She stood, cutting off any further questions or posturing from the other Regents in the room. I was happy she was on our side.

Malyki and I followed her from the conference room and down into the open area of Halstein Hall. I could feel the eyes of every student in our wake—staring, wondering who in the world these two new students were. Funny thing was, I probably knew most of them already. Their favorite foods, their preferred hangouts, even some of their deepest, darkest secrets—privy only to an innocent kitty wandering the campus at night.

"Do you want them to know your familiar status, or would you prefer to be considered new students?" Saundra whispered, probably feeling the shift in my energy.

"They should know who we truly are. Lies serve no one." Malyki spoke the truth, his words cutting sharply through the air. We were here to earn their trust and provide help in a task that only we could perform. Hiding who we truly were would surely only complicate things.

"Very well, but you must realize, the students may not take kindly to the fact that you've been present this entire time. Hiding, though not by choice, will still seem like a deception to some."

She had a point, and I personally wasn't looking forward to explaining ourselves over and over again. Malyki hadn't been here as long as I had, and therefore wouldn't fall under the same scrutiny.

This was not going to be fun.

CHAPTER 4

*O*ur introduction to the class took every ounce of control not to revert back to my feline instincts and randomly swat items off the desktops of those staring at Malyki and me. There was a sense of arrogance I'd held as Mystic the cat that I couldn't get away with now that I was human again.

My pride prickled, however, because just as Saundra Beaumont had warned, we were met with open curiosity and a healthy dose of skepticism. What irked me more were the few brazen grins from those who remembered stroking my furred body as the kitten familiar and were now appraising my new, slender form.

Pervs.

"Easy," Malyki whispered, squeezing my hand reassuringly. "Retract those claws, beloved. They're young, and from the stories Tempest and Natalie have shared, these students have been through a lot already with their education. We're here to help, not hinder."

I didn't answer, and instead, held my head high, offering a few smiles as we followed the Regent through the classroom before she stopped by a group of three—a young woman and two guys. What a motley crew they were. Bryony, as we were introduced, wore a long flowing dress of deep blues and gold. Her long dark kinked hair was pulled back into a loose bun with a stray strand that hung to the side of her face.

Next, Gable stood and extended his hand in greeting. Shaking it, I took his measure, noticing how the sun had streaked his hair and the muscles in his arms. The fact that he was even here warmed my heart. After Vidar broke the spell on him last semester, it locked him in his human form, unable to shift. *How ironic.* Still, he'd been left with his scorpion attributes of strength and poison, which I had no doubt would prove invaluable as we faced our team assignment. I returned his flirty wink with a smile, and continued looking around the table.

Finally, someone I recognized smiled up at Malyki and me, his hazel eyes twinkling as Ms. Beaumont continued speaking—Vidar, one of the students who worked here at the campus library, and secretly left out treats for me whenever I came to visit. The guy had an ancient kind of energy that I found comforting.

"I know this is somewhat unorthodox, but I trust you will all rise to the challenge and work as a team." She said it in such a matter-of-fact way as though she expected everyone to agree without hesitation. "Both Mystic and Malyki bring important skills to your group, so please make them feel welcome." Ms. Beaumont held eye contact with each of us for a few seconds before nodding her head briskly. That was that. The Regent had spoken, and we were to follow her instructions.

There was an awkward silence that followed her departure as the three of them eyed us dubiously. It was hard not to squirm beneath their scrutiny, but as Malyki squeezed my hand again, I let out a pent-up breath and gave them the sincerest smile I could muster.

"So," I drawled, the word stretching out while I searched for something else to say. "Any questions?" It was hard to imagine what they might be thinking so I figured why not get it all out on the table and then we could get started on the assignment.

Bryony was the first to accept the offer. "You're really Tempest and Natalie's familiar?" She cocked her head to the side, her gaze going up and down. "Their cute little ginger and black kitty?"

I answered quickly. "Is it so hard to believe? We're all magic users here. Is it that much of a stretch to think that Malyki and I were in different forms?"

I tried to keep my surprise out of my voice.

Bryony shook her head as Gable chimed in. His gaze darted back and forth as he bit on his bottom lip nervously. "I just want to know one thing . . . um, do you like. . . um—" He dragged his fingers through his hair and straightened in his seat. "You know a lot of our secrets, don't you?"

Ahh, so that explained why he was fidgeting. The poor guy must've realized that as a cat, I'd taken advantage of the free rein I'd had of the campus, and wondered whether I'd seen students getting into mischief.

I grinned at him and shrugged. "Any secret in particular, Gable?" Malyki elbowed me in the side, understanding what I was doing. I couldn't resist teasing my fellow team members, and reluctantly, I decided to put them out of their misery. "Don't sweat it, guys." I mimed zipping my lips and tossing it over my shoulder. "We're not here to cause trouble."

Vidar nodded, his dark dreads swaying softly. "You can understand why we'd ask, right?"

I liked the vibe of this guy, and there were many days when I visited the library that he'd leave me treats to enjoy before retreating to one of my many favorite nap places. He also didn't mind whenever I rubbed my body against his legs, scratching my ears until I purred.

Malyki held out a chair for me before sitting down, his leg resting against mine under the desk. "I also wanted to thank you for being okay with us joining your group."

Bryony snorted and murmured beneath her breath. "Did we have much of a choice?"

I understood her comment. It's not like anyone could really refuse one of the Regents without meeting their disapproval.

My beloved looked my way before giving her a sympathetic smile. "I can't speak on behalf of the school's administration, but I will for both myself and Mystic. We have an interest in the copper bird included with your task assignment's card and believe we can mutually benefit from working together. However, we'll both understand if you choose to go on without us."

His statement was met with all three of the students raising their eyes in skepticism.

"What's the catch?" Gable asked, slouched back in his chair. I

had the odd urge to lean forward and swipe at him with my claw .
. . hand.

I loved watching Malyki address the group—the way he made
sure to meet each person's gaze and the even tone of his voice. He
was always the best person to act as a mediator during conflict and
had this amazing gift of smoothing over ruffled feathers when
needed. I was too impulsive and sharp tongued.

Clasping his hands on top of the table, Malyki didn't falter.
"No catch. I don't believe in forcing people to do things contrary
to their better judgment. I will say this, though: regardless of
whether we work together as a group or separately, Mystic and I
will be searching for the copper bird. It holds the key to our
freedom." Suddenly his voice chilled, and goosebumps pebbled
over my skin. "Nothing will stop me from breaking our curse . . .
nothing and no one."

His declaration was both a warning and a promise.

Vidar cleared his throat, tapping his fingers against the desktop
like it was a drum. "I can only speak for myself, but if I can help
you both as well as getting an A for this class, I say hell yeah." He
looked over to Gable and Bryony. "Guys?" When they nodded in
agreement, Vidar flipped open his folder and slid out the
assignment from the plastic sleeve protecting it. "Here it is."

The card instantly reminded me of the Magician tarot card,
only this one had a noticeable difference—the copper bird that sat
on the wizard's shoulder. Even after all this time, I couldn't drag
my gaze away from the object, wishing it was as simple as reaching
into the image and pulling the item out. Magic was meant to make
life easier—aiding the wielder—but all I'd seen was how in the
wrong hands, that kind of power was a detriment.

"So," I said, wetting my lips, "what have you tried doing so
far?" From what I knew through Natalie and Tempest, the class
was already well underway, and the students had been given these
tasks from the beginning of the semester. "What have you found
out?"

Silence.

There were very few times where this kind of quiet signaled
anything but good news.

Malyki could feel my uneasiness when no one spoke up. His

arm had been propped behind me on my chair, and when I tensed up, his hand gently touched my back, his fingers softly brushing up and down. The gesture did little to calm my anxiety. All these weeks and they'd come up with nothing?

"Seriously?" I spat out, impatient. "Not even the smallest of clues?"

Gable was the first to get defensive. "Well, in all honesty, we figured this would require the most time and effort, so we were leaving it until we'd finished the other assignments."

Bryony chimed in, hoping to show solidarity. "That way we could give it our undivided attention." Her gaze felt like she was challenging me to get angry so she could put me in my place. Something whispered that maybe, just maybe, the young druid still viewed me as a kitten familiar and not the human sitting in front of her. "Of course, we've discussed the card and what it might mean."

"And what did you all surmise?" Malyki asked, his voice softer and without the intensity mine had held. "Please, don't think we're angry with you. We're just eager to remove the curse, and that eagerness sometimes comes across as aggression."

His eyes met mine, all but pleading for me to bite my tongue and breathe. For whatever reason, both he and Ms. Beaumont felt we needed these youngsters, and I trusted my soulmate. I took in a deep breath, closed my eyes, and then slowly exhaled.

"I'm sorry," I whispered. "I guess I'm not used to being in this form." I offered them a crooked grin. "I didn't need words as a cat." I didn't add that most times all I needed were my sharp claws to drive my point home. "Please continue."

Bryony picked up the card. "We talked with some of the other groups and discovered they also viewed their cards like tarot. By trying to understand what the image symbolized, it gave them enough hints toward finding their objects." She flipped it around, showing everyone the man in the center. "We're confident this represents the Magician."

"Which," Gable interjected, "is reassuring because it implies we'll have success as we work together and trust in the skills we each bring to the team." He gestured over to Vidar who was doodling on his blank notebook page. "With Vidar working in the library, he'd been using his spare time to research more about the nature of the Magician and how that pertains to us."

In other words, the three of them had pretty much zilch when it came to leads. All this time and I was pretty sure Malyki and I knew more about their task than they did.

I couldn't help myself. I took the card from Bryony and began pushing back on my chair. "Today's your lucky day. Malyki and I will take this from here and you guys can focus on your other assignments. We'll locate the copper bird and tell the Board it was a group effort."

Standing now, I looked down at Malyki, his eyes wide with surprise. Surely he didn't intend to work with them, not when we were obviously the better choice.

I may have been a cat for years, but Bryony's reflexes were impressive. I didn't even have time to register that she'd moved before she snatched the card back out of my hand.

"That's not how this works, Mystic." She remained standing, her feet shoulder-width apart, staring at me defiantly. "While I respect that this bird means a lot to you, I'm not about to be dictated to . . . especially by someone who only days ago was a cat."

Called it. I knew the druid wasn't totally on board when Malyki and I joined them.

"Mystic." By the Goddess, my beloved was using his calm voice, hoping that it would infuse a little of that peace onto me. That's all he said. My name. I tuned him out. I didn't have time to waste sitting about in a group while the curse was still in play. Every second that ticked by made my fear grow exponentially, the thought always in the back of my mind that magic would interfere and we'd be returned to our animal forms forever.

"I've made the decision, and that's final," I stated again, glowering at the lot of them. "Besides, if it's a matter of magic and power, Malyki and I hold the most." I leaned forward to take the card, but Bryony stopped me. Vidar and Gable now stood on either side of her, and somewhere in the back of my mind, I knew I had crossed a line, but I was committed to this path now. "You have no idea how much danger you could be in." I threw that last sentiment out as if it might soften my declaration.

It didn't.

Vidar scoffed openly. "You were here last semester, Mystic. You saw the chaos that was happening. If that's your selling point for taking over, I'm not convinced. People died. You can't treat us like we're starry-eyed kids who are completely clueless. You were here. We deserve more respect than that."

Silence descended over the group again, and I realized I'd made a grave mistake. I had forgotten to take the drama from last semester into account and dismissed the three of them. I'd seen everything Tempest and Natalie had endured going through their trials—the strength and courage it had pulled from them.

But before I could share that, Bryony gathered up her belongings and directed Gable and Vidar to join her.

"I think it's obvious now that we can't work together. How about we take it from here, and once the assignment's complete, we'll let the Board know it was a group effort."

Damn, she'd basically thrown my words right back in my face.

"Bryony," Malyki began but paused when the young druid raised her hand for him to stop.

"You both might be powerful, but we hold one advantage over you—we're not burdened by a curse that's kept us bound as animals. We don't have to readjust to being human and the use of our magic. You do. Perhaps that's what you should be focusing on now. Leave all the heavy lifting to us."

Sometime during our heated discussion, the class had ended, and the room was slowly emptying. With all their notebooks and folders packed back in their bags, they sadly smiled at Malyki before leaving us to stand there alone.

"Well, that went well," I murmured, knowing that I had royally fucked up. "Why didn't you stop me?"

There was no humor in Malyki's voice when he replied, "Would you have listened?"

I tried not to flinch at the truthfulness in his question.

"Probably not." I rubbed my face with my hands, suddenly exhausted and in dire need of a nap. "I forgot how hard being a human could be." I rested my head against his upper arm, craving his touch.

He instantly pulled me into his embrace. "Diplomacy was

never your strong suit, *iubita mea*." Malyki feathered a kiss on top of my head. "Give them a chance to think, and we'll approach them again."

I stared at the door they'd left through. "Do you think that will help?"

As much as I hated relying on others, I felt horrible over how I'd behaved.

He shrugged. "Only the Goddess knows, although I'm sure it wouldn't hurt . . ." He paused.

"What wouldn't?" I pushed, wanting him to finish his thought.

I could feel the beginning of his chuckle rumbling through his body as he held me tighter. "It wouldn't hurt if you kept quiet and let me do all the talking, beloved. For the good of the team."

I buried my face into his chest as I drew from his calming energy.

He was right.

Malyki would fix it.

If not, I had no problem with us being a team of two.

CHAPTER 5

I followed Malyki back to our room and closed the door
behind us. Tipping my head back, I stared at the ceiling
then dropped to the floor—stretching out on our gray and white
area rug. The dangling crystals floating above me held my
attention for a split second, while I tried to clear my mind.
Processing the kids' reaction was one thing, but there was
something else that kept nagging at me—a question I'd yet to ask.

"Malyki, what was it like when you were trapped in the demon
realm? Were you able to see or touch the talisman?"

My husband bent his long legs and lowered his imposing frame
to lay beside me. "I never saw it, but could feel its magic close by. I
tried to reach it, both physically and mentally, but never could. It
wasn't torturous in any way, just…a big void. It was like I was
floating inside a cloud with no grasp of time or space, if that makes
sense."

I closed my eyes and fought back tears. Thank the Goddess. I
couldn't imagine how horrible it would have been if he'd been
aware of the time passing. I rolled onto my side, draping an arm
and leg over his body and snuggled close. "We just need to figure
out precisely where the artifact is located here under the mountain.
Obviously, I haven't been able to enter the astral plane as a cat, so
although I know it's here, I don't know exactly where just yet."

Malyki hooked his arm around me and began to stroke my

hair. "It's been years since you've entered the astral realm. Are you sure you're up for such a big task right off the bat? Like it or not, the kids were right…we haven't used our true magic in a really long time."

"Do we have any other choice? I understand your desire to work with them, but realistically, this task concerns only us. And I don't know about you, but it's going to be difficult to be considered a student and have a schedule we're expected to adhere to." I craned my neck to look up at him. "I'm done waiting for this curse to be over. I want us to be free and able to live our lives again—unhindered and unbound from the bonds forced upon us for so long."

His broad chest lifted beneath me as he took a deep breath. "As do I. But the Board of Regents know who we are, so I doubt we'll have to follow any schedule, per se, but we will have to coordinate our efforts with the team and their classes. Saundra said so herself. The semester is nearing its end, and we all need to work together."

"Do we, though?" I pushed up from his chest, still hesitant and stubborn. "You and I are the only ones who can do this, so why should we wait and put ourselves on task according to someone else's idea or assignment, in this case?"

"I don't know, Mystic—call it a hawk's intuition, but I don't think we should fly at this head-on. We need to be careful, test our boundaries, slowly and methodically." He sat up, propping himself on his elbow. "I can't lose you again, my *iubire*. Promise me, we'll coordinate our plans before you do anything rash."

A knock interrupted my response—probably for the best.

"Come in," I called out, already sensing my two charges on the other side of the door.

"Okay, you two," Natalie started, "the Board of Regents may have given you permission to have your own room here in Hel, but that doesn't mean you can just lay around in the sun, groping each other all day." She looked out the window, noting the dark shadows that blanketed the campus as usual. "Actually, how are you laying here in the sun?"

I pushed the rest of the way up from the floor, hopping deftly to my feet. "With our combined magic of course." I batted at the crystals hanging from the ceiling we'd infused with our magic.

"They radiate whatever kind of light we want, depending on our mood. And we weren't groping each other...we were discussing plans for our mission." I smiled widely. "What about you two, what are you doing here at the start of a Monday?"

"It's our first break, and we wondered if you'd like to join us for some food?" Tempest answered for them both.

I looked to Malyki—still lying on the floor. I wanted to get a read on his thoughts and feelings about going back out into the student population. As expected, the V to his brow and the drop in his energy confirmed he'd rather remain in our room—alone.

"Actually, we're still in the middle of working out our plans. So, thank you, but I'm afraid we'll have to pass." I lifted a shoulder, shrugging nonchalantly in hopes they'd understand and let it go.

Tempest dropped her head, unable to hide her disappointment, but Natalie spoke up—probably sensing my need to honor Malyki's silent request.

"No worries. We'll catch up with you later." Natalie pulled Tempest from the room with a forced smile and tiny wave goodbye.

"Thank you." Malyki stood and wrapped his muscular arms around me from behind. "You've been here a lot longer than I have. Getting used to this many people again is going to take some time for me."

I spun in his arms and laid my head against his chest. "I understand, and despite my earlier behavior, it's like you said...we're here to help, and we can't stay holed-up in our room forever. We need to let them all see us interacting, especially with Natalie and Tempest. I think once they realize the bond with our familiars hasn't changed, they'll be quicker to accept us in our true forms." I reached up and placed a kiss on his cheek. "At least that's my hope."

Malyki's body stiffened under my lips, but not in a good way. I pulled back and gasped.

His eyes were glossed over—coated in a pure white fog. Nothing like this had ever happened before we were cursed, and I hadn't known him long enough in his familiar form to know whether this was normal or not. I eased my hands down the side of his arms, moving slowly, and whispered his name. "Malyki? Are you all right?"

"Dammit, those foolish kids!" His response startled me, but I quickly realized he was having a vision.

"What do you see, my love?"

"The druid girl has located the energy signature of our piece." He lifted his chin, concentrating deeply as his eyes continued to swirl a milky-white. "They're in her dorm room and are attempting to enter the astral plane using her magic, but it won't work." His vision cleared, and he stared at me in horror. "We need to stop them…now!"

CHAPTER 6

*R*acing through campus felt more like trudging endlessly in fields of thick, cloying mud. No matter how quickly Malyki tried to pull me along, my magical energy kept tangling my limbs.

Something wasn't right. Every cell in my body screamed for us to stop . . . for me to protect the man currently weaving through students. Damn, why wasn't everyone in class like they were meant to be? Didn't anyone value their education anymore?

My anger was red hot and growing by the second, and I swallowed the growl that danced at the tip of my tongue. It wasn't their fault my patience was no longer a virtue, and that the group of children performing magic way out of their league had snapped what little calmness I'd managed to nurture.

"Fools," I spat out through clenched teeth. "Whatever happened to listening and honoring your elders?" I stumbled over my feet, the act in complete defiance of my catlike agility. Oh, how things were simpler when all I had to worry about was dodging and averting whatever mischief Natalie and Tempest were brewing.

Malyki didn't even skip a beat, although he had slowed his pace considerably.

"Help first, scold second, my love. We need to ensure they survive and then we can arrange for a suitable punishment." He threw me a half-hearted smirk over his shoulder, and that's when I noticed the beads of sweat dripping from the side of his temples.

I jerked on his hand, doing my best to bring us to a stop. His magic tingled against mine, proving further that there was something more at play here than a simple vision.

Cradling his face with my hands, I scanned his features, peering into his eyes for answers. "What's wrong? And don't you dare lie to me."

He tried to hide the slight tremble and shook his head. "Priorities, *scumpa mea*." When I refused to let him go, he grimaced. "I would ask you not to kill me once I confess, but I know how much you relish torturing me."

Despite the pain I could see him feeling, his gaze heated with desire. The damn fool was teasing me.

I didn't wait for him to continue or offer an explanation. Time was already of the essence, and I felt like I had somehow entered a movie halfway through where everyone knew their parts but me. Annoyance flickered inside me, and in my mind's eye, the tip of my feline tail bristled and twitched in the air.

Men.

"Show me."

To his credit, Malyki drew in a deep breath before surrounding my thoughts and carefully drawing them into his mind. It was a technique we'd done countless times in the past—our own kind of shortcut when talking took too long to explain something. I kept my body as relaxed as I could, and I closed my eyes so I wouldn't get distracted by his discomfort.

It was those damn kids. Not only were they the reason for the panic that vibrated off Malyki's lean frame, but it also flooded through our psychic link, sending adrenaline-laced fear through every inch of my body.

"Shit," I uttered beneath my breath. Out of habit, I shook my head, knowing it wouldn't stop the images rapidly flashing behind my closed lids, but all I wanted to do was scream no over and over. "Why didn't they listen?"

Malyki squeezed my fingers tightly, and when I popped my eyes open, he was staring deeply into them. Urgency filled him. "We must hurry, Mystic."

When I went to ask him to keep our connection open so I could continue to see, he nodded before tugging me along. We ran now as though the demons were hunting us, their hot, blistering breath scorching our heels.

I still couldn't believe what I was seeing. Bryony, the young druid who had defiantly challenged us earlier, was currently sitting cross-legged inside a candle lit circle, meditating. I'd seen Natalie and Tempest meditate like this often, a sad reminder of when I'd been human and able to summon the strength of the Goddess.

Bryony's lips moved slowly, her voice barely above a whisper as her brow crinkled in concentration. The more I studied the vision, the easier I could see that she was inside her dorm room and had surrounded herself with the tools of her craft. Earth, air, water, and fire were all represented, but still that wasn't what terrified me. Any witch or magic practitioner worth their salt could summon the protection of the four elements. No, what had both Malyki and me pushing onward with everything we had was the fact that both Gable and Vidar stood near her—frozen by the tornado-like wind that whipped about them—holding them above the ground. Both of the young men's faces were distorted in agony, and to my absolute horror, slashes began appearing across their skin that left small trails of blood.

"Malyki!" I exclaimed, struggling to talk around the large lump that now felt lodged in my throat. "They're trying to access the realm! The fools are going to get themselves killed!" Tears burned my cheeks, but I let them fall. We were almost to Jory Tower, and there just wasn't enough time.

Malyki cussed out loud as he accidentally banged into a group of students, earning a round of "what the hells" and "watch its" from them. An irritated pulse crossed through our link, and I almost snorted at the glimpse I caught from my impatient lover.

"What was it you told me? Help first, scold second?" Damn, I sounded out of breath. We'd somehow managed to cross the entire campus in record time, but my screaming muscles would need to wait a little longer for relief. "Not that I wouldn't mind watching you knock a few teenagers on their asses with a blast of your magic."

Approaching the tower, we took the stairs two at a time, and as

I raced through the door he opened for me, I grinned at him winking in return. When we weren't facing curses and danger, it was often entertaining watching Malyki trying to rein in his temper whenever provoked. The man was beautiful to behold.

"What room is she?" I called out over my shoulder. I didn't really need to ask, however, because the magic being pumped into the air was so electrifying, it bordered on explosive.

More students were milling about, curious about what they were feeling, but we didn't stop. From the moment we'd entered the tower, a strangling sensation had settled around my chest, making it hard to breathe. The scary thing was that the majority of that energy was coming from Malyki. Sure enough, the closer we got to the source, the harder it was for him to maintain our connection until suddenly it snapped closed like a rubber band that had finally been stretched beyond its limits.

"Mystic!" he yelled before crumpling to the floor. His body began to contort beneath an invisible assault, but he refused my help. "Keep going! They need you. Break the circle. Stop the magic. Save them!"

I knew I'd found the right place when wave after wave of nausea hit me. Hard. With bile already in my mouth, I struggled to open the door because of the howling wind I could hear. And that's when I knew that if the evil forces at work within the realm didn't kill them, I would. They'd put themselves in this situation, and because of their stupidity and inexperience, they now threatened everyone's safety.

"Goddess, Blessed Mother, hear my plea. Grant thy strength to enter me." I recognized the instant my prayer had been heard because with only the smallest of pushes, the door flew open, and chaos was revealed.

Bryony was still chanting within the circle, oblivious to the destruction her spell was causing. Gable and Vidar now appeared to be crying blood, their bodies weakened as they hung limply in the air. There was a shocking amount of blood in puddles beneath them—rippling from the air being blustered about.

Shit.

I could feel it—the sickening presence of the astral realm where the copper bird had been hidden. The cloying tang of menace filled my mouth, defiling my taste buds, as I tried to scream for Bryony to stop. But still she continued uttering words of magic in her trance.

The wind wasn't letting me move, and in my mind's eye, I could see the inevitability of being caught up the same as the boys. I couldn't be rendered helpless. Not again. Never again.

Summoning all of my own power, I felt the first tingles of transformation before my world dramatically changed perspective and I dropped to all fours. I was too big as a human. What I needed was my feline form.

The second I could, I bounded over to the circle and began swiping at the candles, knocking everything over with paws and swishing tail. I didn't care about the candle flames as they died out, or the energetic kickback from not closing the circle properly. I would accept the price willingly—all complaining aside. I'd seen enough death and horror to last my nine lifetimes. Hades would have to wait for these three a little longer.

With each extinguished candle and toppled crystal, as I batted Bryony's elemental tokens away from her body, I could feel her spell weaken and lessen. The oppressive ambience within the room diminished until finally the boys crashed to the floor and the young druid slumped over to the side, unconscious.

Electricity crackled in the air, a residual from the realm they'd tried to enter. Meowing the words needed for me to shift back to human, I watched as my black furred paw turned into the soft subtle skin of my hand. I lifted it toward the shimmering rift and banished the magic. I demanded that it relinquish its grip on the three students still passed out on the floor, and as the realm blinked out of existence again, I let out a sigh of relief.

With enough time to thank the Goddess, I braced myself for the pain that came—accepting the price for misused magic.

The room began to spin, and my vision blackened, but we were safe.

Crisis averted.

As I crumpled to the floor as well, one thought called out: *For now.*

CHAPTER 7

*T*he first thing I saw when I woke up was Malyki's concerned face peering down at me.

"Welcome back, *iubita mea*," he whispered as the pad of his thumb gently brushed over my cheek. Tenderness flooded his eyes, and I pulled him in closer for a kiss, grateful to see he'd survived the ordeal.

Which reminded me . . .

I punched Malyki in the arm as hard as I could, which wasn't much because I still felt the effects of breaking the circle. The panic that had flooded my heart came rushing back with the realization that he'd done something incredibly stupid.

"You risked us. You put yourself in danger and didn't bother to tell me, your beloved about it!" Fear mixed with the threat of tears left my voice sounding ragged. "I've only just got you back . . . are you in that much of a rush to leave me again?" A violent sob shattered my resolve to keep my cool and I pulled him to me, crushing my lips to his.

This was what I needed—that connection as a reminder that Malyki was awake, alive, and responding to my urgent kiss. All I could focus on was the heat from his mouth and the warmth of his gentle touches—the way he instinctively knew how to soothe away my pain. I wanted to get lost in him again—in us—and forget the fact that we were buried beneath a mountain, attending a supernatural academy.

Which reminded me further . . .

I broke the seal of our lips and pushed myself up so I was sitting. Behind Malyki I could see the anxious and remorseful expressions of Bryony, Gable, and Vidar. At least that helped slake off some of my frustrations because nothing would've pissed me off more than seeing arrogance instead.

Lifting my finger, I pointed at the three of them, and shook my head. "You have some explaining to do, but fortunately you're at the end of my short-list of grievances." My annoyance returned back to the man staring at me, that perfectly gorgeous, irritating-as-hell grin of his working hard to soften my anger. "You." I prodded his chest with my index finger. "Explain yourself." I sat back and folded my arms. "I'm waiting."

Malyki, to his credit, didn't begin posturing or giving me some bullshit excuse. Just from the tone of his sigh, he realized how badly he'd scared me. We were used to flying by the seat of our pants and getting into magical mischief, but that had been pre-curse. Our recklessness now felt different, the consequences almost too much to bear.

I laid my hand lightly over his, and matched his exhale. "Please."

He took a few seconds to graze my cheek with the crook of his finger before beginning. "I suspected that they wouldn't listen and would try to perform some spell or ritual to access the copper bird. So I took precautions and placed a magical marker on each of them."

He was pretty genius with having the foresight to do that, but I wasn't ready to admit that just yet. "So when they called the elements and made the circle sacred . . ."

Malyki nodded. "I knew the instant Bryony began to meditate and ground herself." He cast a glance over his shoulder at the young woman. "Your power is impressive for someone so young." His gaze returned to me, his head ducking so he could look me straight in the eyes. Goddess, I loved him so much, which made the terror of losing him again worse. "I know how that felt and this task was too important to be making stupid mistakes."

He must've sensed the moment I accepted his explanation. "I'm sorry, *iubita mea*. I should've taken the time to explain my plans and include you in them. Although, in my defense, I'd forgotten how rebellious the youth can be." Malyki stood from where we'd been sitting and addressed the quiet group watching this all unfold. "I assumed that you'd respect your elders and obey our wishes."

Gable looked down at his shoes, avoiding eye contact.

Vidar ran his fingers over his dark dreads, keeping them from falling over his face.

It was Bryony who snorted, wetting her lips. "You're not the boss of me, despite how old you are. I thought you understood that when we last spoke, but obviously there's a lack of trust between us all."

Everything about her body language screamed defiance, but I recognized it for what it truly was . . . defensive.

My magic tingled beneath my skin, itching for me to release it. I'd become so used to being in my feline form and the freedom that came with it, that I wasn't quite adjusted to being human again. What I wouldn't give to be curled up in Natalie and Tempest's room right now on one of the soft, fluffy pillows, oblivious to the world.

I returned Bryony's snort with my own. "So you figured a sure fire way of us all bonding and working together was what? Ignoring our experience and knowledge of the item so you could be heroes? Rushing head first into danger without a damn clue about what you were doing?" She started to interrupt me, her eyes sparkling with indignation, but I wasn't ready to concede. "Way to build trust, guys. I don't know about you, but I'm filled with all the warm fuzzies right now."

I shook out my hands as electricity crackled from the tips of my fingers. I needed to calm down and find my center again. I had a sharp tongue at the best of times, and right now, I knew I was teetering dangerously close to saying something I might regret.

I stood finally and slowly stretched out my sore body, allowing my muscles to bend and twist. The room remained quiet like everyone was waiting to see if I'd snap and keep ranting. Instead, I did the opposite and took hold of Malyki's hand. "I'm glad you're doing okay, lover. Try not to give me a heart attack next time, okay?"

He squeezed my fingers before kissing the back of my hand. "I promise."

Now that I'd voiced some of that frustration, my mind cleared so I could refocus on what was important. The assignment. "So did we at least learn something from this fiasco?" Malyki nudged my shoulder slightly, and I quickly added. "I'm glad to see you're all in one piece, as well."

Truth be told, I was surprised Gable and Vidar were standing, and not hooked up to monitors and IVs getting blood transfusions. Seeing them hovering in the air, contorting, blood dripping, was a memory I hope I'd quickly forget. They'd been a gruesome mess.

"I only got a quick glimpse of something before the spell was broken, but I'm not sure if it means anything," Bryony confessed, her hands fidgeting in front of her. "I could sense the energy from the other realm. The force was unlike anything I've ever experienced, and frankly, I'd be happy to never tap into it again. It felt . . ." She struggled to find the words.

"Cold," Malyki answered, barely above a whisper. Then in a louder, stronger voice he added, "Malicious. Oppressive." He offered the young druid a sympathetic nod. "There's no shame in admitting that. Even the smallest minute is enough to cripple the most confident practitioners."

My heart instantly sunk. He'd been adamant with me that he'd felt nothing in his imprisonment, yet here he was confessing that he'd experienced it all. I must've gasped out loud because suddenly Malyki's eyes were on me with a pleading look for patience in them. There was the slightest shake of his head.

Not now.

I quickly wiped away my tears, my chest tightening with each breath. He'd known. My Goddess, he'd been aware the whole time he was in the demon realm.

"Yet you survived that," Vidar quipped. There was a look of respect on his face.

"I had the perfect incentive to endure my imprisonment." My stomach was suddenly filled with fluttering butterflies hearing

Malyki's admission. "But I'd also be a fool to say there weren't days where death seemed a tender mercy. Which brings us back to the fact that we need to work together. No more solo mission."

Vidar nodded. "Teamwork makes the dream work, right?"

Gable rolled his eyes over the cheesy platitude, but there was no denying that the three of them were woefully unprepared and under-skilled to go it alone—at least in this particular instance.

"Okay, tell us what you learned, Bryony, and we'll see whether what you saw is relevant." The air was finally cleared, and it was time to get back on task. "Whatever comes next we'll do together." I glanced around at everyone. "Trust."

We each agreed in turn.

Here I was, learning to play with others. Natalie and Tempest would be proud.

CHAPTER 8

*T*oday definitely had me on a hell of a wicked learning curve.

First, I realized that my word meant shit when I felt I was right.

Second, I couldn't believe the answer had been under my nose all this time.

"What the hell," I murmured beneath my breath. "How could I have been so freaking stupid?" I looked over to Malyki as he tentatively touched the large wooden door in front of us. "All this time and the answer has been under my very nose."

I groaned in embarrassment. All my magic and I hadn't even realized. I'd simply assumed what I'd been sensing was the academy and all the power being thrown around by the students. With the hourglasses and chaos last semester, it never occurred to me to explore what hid beyond the door.

What was that saying? Don't borrow trouble?

Malyki's hand trembled.

"We were closer than we thought," he whispered, stunned. It filled me with shame that my ineptness had caused him to suffer needlessly.

"I'm sorry, my love." Tears rolled over my cheeks slowly at first, but as the weight of this new knowledge crashed over me like waves during a storm, I crumbled, and I began to openly sob.

Burying my face into my hands, all I could do was apologize over and over again.

The brief glimpse Bryony had caught during her meditative state hadn't been useless at all. The second she'd described the door she'd seen, I'd known. I'd sent them off to the library for research as I bit my tongue and swallowed the truth. Malyki had looked at me questioningly as I began leading him through campus until we eventually stood where we now were.

Hel Tower.

To be more specific, at the very end of the wine cellar that Tempest had discovered last semester. I couldn't count how many times I'd followed her and Natalie down into the not-so-secret room behind the bookcase whenever they wanted to sample the magically infused alcohol. Thinking back, I'd even felt the same magic that now pulsed angrily from the wooden barrier. I'd deemed it unimportant—just another weird anomaly that was the Sun & Moon Academy campus and Havenwood Falls.

All. This. Time.

He'd been within my reach, and I had ignored the signs.

I slowly became aware of Malyki's strong arms encircling my body, offering me forgiveness and shelter. I didn't deserve him, not now that the truth was revealed and my failure exposed. He'd always been the better one between us, and another wretched sob exploded from me as I imagined his torment.

"Sssh, *iubira*. Calm your heart. We're together, and that's all that matters." He gently patted my back with the hope the rhythmic touch would somehow soothe away my guilt. "Most of all, I love you. From the beginning of time until this world takes its final breath. Nothing you could ever do will change that."

He meant his words to act as a salve to my broken heart, but I chose to use them like salt. I didn't want his forgiveness and patience. I refused to accept his generosity and grace. I'd listened as we laid in each other's arms—within the protective shroud of darkness—him giving me a glimpse of what his life had been like. I remembered the pain and the way he stumbled with words, the way his body flinched from unspoken memories that filled his mind.

He'd told the students that there were times he believed death would be a tender mercy. I'd been close enough to save him.

The front of his black T-shirt was drenched. I closed my eyes, my face buried in his chest. I couldn't bear to look at him . . . to let him see me.

"Forgive me, Malyki," I stammered, trying to slow my breathing down. "I hadn't known. I should've, but . . ."

This time he refused to let me hide from him. "No buts. No should haves. No what ifs. All we have is now, and in this moment, we are reunited and have a chance to finally be rid of this curse. That's all that matters. We've been given an incredible gift—the opportunity to make things right and reclaim our lives. Do you really want to waste time drowning in shame and guilt?" He tilted my chin upward when I tried to duck to the side. His loving eyes pierced my soul. "Do you?"

I shook my head. Despite the need to hold a vicious pity party for myself and lick my wounds, I couldn't deny the truth . . . reality. No matter what it took to bring us to this moment, we were here and there was still more to do.

"So what now?" I asked, a soft hiccup escaping through my lips. Most of my tears had dried over my cheeks, but it didn't stop Malyki from brushing a few away with the pad of his thumb. "I want this to be over. Truly over."

Cradling my face between his hands, Malyki tenderly brushed his lips over mine. "We'll do whatever we must. We always have. We won't give up until we can claim our freedom."

He believed in us so strongly that it was impossible not to get swept up in his optimism. Knowing the doorway to the other realm had been hidden under Hel Tower had been a crushing blow to my psyche and ego, but Malyki was right. We had work to do.

"I suppose this is where you remind me that we need to call the others and start strategizing." I offered him a crooked smile that almost reached my eyes. It would take time to heal and process all this, but for now, my mistakes needed to be boxed up inside my mind and shelved.

He cocked his dark eyebrow and smirked. "If we want to make the dream work." He laughed. "I know it's hard being part of a group when it's always been just us, but everything happens for a reason. And standing here on the other side of this door, I know with all my heart we won't be able to do this without them."

I tried to hide my shock at hearing him say that. I didn't argue with him, however. Bryony, Gable, and Vidar might still be somewhat strangers to me, but I trusted Malyki implicitly.

"Then lead the way before I change my mind. If we hurry, we should still catch them at the library." I chuckled beneath my breath. The poor guys were looking for a needle in a haystack there because the odds were slim there was a book about doors on campus.

"You're going to need to apologize again when we see them. You lied to them."

Ugh, he was being the voice of reason again.

I shook my head. "Is it really a lie if it's given with the intention to protect them?" I gave him the side-eye and saw that he wasn't buying my excuse. "Or how about it's better to ask forgiveness than permission?" That was a line I'd heard Tempest say often, and it seemed to work well for her.

We'd made it a few steps away from the door and to one of the many displays of bottles when Malyki doubled over, staggering backward, gasping in pain. Shock filled his beautiful features.

"Disconnect your magic from Bryony," I yelled, struggling to keep him still. I was nowhere near as strong as Malyki, but no matter how hard I pulled, he kept stumbling. "Cut it off!"

Those damned kids. Why wouldn't they listen?

He shook his head. His face was now dripping with sweat, yet as I blinked, the droplets took on a reddish hue. Blood. He was sweating blood as his jaw clenched tightly, his eyes bulging.

"No," he uttered. Wildly, he looked about for something to hold on to—anything that would stop him from returning to the door. "That. Connection. Is. Gone." His fingernails carved scores into the wall, his fingers bleeding from injury.

My mind raced with what to do. Tempest and Natalie were too far away. We'd come down here alone because I'd been a prideful jerk and hid the truth from the others. Something was happening to Malyki right before me, and the strain from the presence was literally trying to tear him apart.

His screams—shrieks—filled my ears and reverberated through

the air. His clothes were now stained from both blood and sweat, and with one vicious jerk, he flew back against the door—hitting it with such a force that I heard bones break.

"Mystic!" he yelled, reaching for me in slow motion. "The curse! It's trying to take me back!"

The horror of his words pulled my mind to the past...

Romania, 1879

Fires raged, tearing through the village as I searched for *iubita mea*—my beloved. "Malyki?" I called out, my throat raw and bare. Screams rent the air as a hateful smoke blanketed the night sky. "Malyki, where are you?" I shouted from the back of our caravan as our Romani brethren ran for their lives.

"I'm here, my love. Come, come, we must leave." Malyki reached for my hand, pulling me from our home. "They've found us, and I'm afraid none of us will survive."

With panicked eyes, I searched the scene, desperate for something—anything that could save our homes and our people. Dyed curtains in vibrant colors turned to dust as flames devoured them. Wooden wheels and caravans burned to the ground, leaving behind nothing but steel beams and charred spokes. Children screaming in their mother's arms wailed throughout the trees as the rival clan swept through the forest, destroying everything in their path.

And it was all my fault.

"*Handfast to me, Mystic, and you'll never have to worry another day in your life.*" I recalled the proposition Danor repeated to me daily as we neared the Summer Solstice no more than one year ago. But as always, I denied him; for his proposition was no more than an invitation to serve him and his family for eternity.

"*Danor, as I've told you many times, my heart lies with another.*"

"*Malyki,*" he spat.

"*Yes, Malyki. We are meant to be.*" I turned back to my threads, shells, and beads and continued to weave, whispering my magic into their strands. A magic he wanted all for himself.

"*You'll regret denying me.*"

Those were the last words I heard from Danor until he shouted my name earlier tonight—right before the attack. "Mystic! You made your choice. Now suffer the consequences."

I blinked through tears as Malyki pulled me farther into the woods.

"Wait. This is all my fault. We have to do something," I pleaded.

Malyki stopped and wrapped his arms around me, resting his chin upon my head. "My love—my *iubire*, this is not your fault, and there is nothing we can do."

My teeth ground together as I watched our village burn. "No!" I pushed from his embrace. "I refuse to run and hide. I will save our people. Now, please...help me!"

He let me go and followed me to the hilltop overlooking our tribe below. Reaching around my neck, I lifted the heavy necklace that hung across my chest like a spiderweb—the strings and beads, threads and webs, all holding my stones of power in place. Weaving my fingers through the openings, I stretched it out and nodded for Malyki to join me.

Our hands intertwined, and magic pulsed through the strands, lighting up each stone in a variety of deep blues and vibrant purples.

"I call upon the ancestors now, lend me your strength so powers abound. Fight the evil upon our land, give us your gift, your children of clan."

Our combined magic seeped out of my web, spreading down the hill and over the forest like a self-healing blanket. Fires diminished, and the forces threatening our caravans now found themselves stuck behind an invisible wall. Cries of anger and anguish mixed with those of relief, as the clans stared at one another through a hazy bubble of protection.

I sighed and smiled up at *iubita mea*. We'd done it. Malyki met my gaze with love and pride shining in his eyes—then screamed.

His knees buckled as he fell to the ground, pulling me with him through our still entwined fingers. I worked quickly to free my hands from the web and grabbed his face. "No, no, my *iubire*, what's wrong? Talk to me, Malyki."

"He can't respond, for I've bound his magic, and yours." Danor's voice dripped with hate from just over my shoulder.

I stood to defend myself, but it was too late. My body convulsed, twisting and snapping as my bones dislocated and reformed. I blinked as I fell, my vision blurred and tinted through two different tones—one a blue haze, and the other a sharp green. I was frozen, lying on my side while Danor hovered above me, holding something shiny in his hands. I tried to move but couldn't, realizing why a moment later. Danor stood inside a demon gate— one he'd drawn in the dirt in his effort to stop us.

"You will never see your precious Malyki again." He held up the small statue—a bird of some sort pulled from the demon realm, then shouted to the heavens...

"Take this link and bury it deep, within a distant magical keep. Separated for all time they'll be, bound to serve as others see. This otherworldly vessel's complete, take it now and hide it discreet."

The statue disappeared, and with it my beloved.

Yanked from the memory, in the midst of the chaos, clarity came, and with it my magic surged outward. Calling on the Goddess with everything inside me, I chanted words of power, begging for help. I uttered every spell that entered my mind. My fingers drew sigils and runes in the air so quickly that the energetic pulse that flared into existence began to tangle together above us.

"You cannot have him, you asshole!" I shouted as I tried to pry Malyki from the door. He was limp now with deathly white flesh that terrified me to see. His life force was slipping away, and all I could think was not again. Somehow the curse had sensed him on the other side and had reached out to reclaim him.

I was running out of energy and ideas. I'd thrown everything I could think of in my magical arsenal, but it wasn't enough. So I did the only thing I could think of.

I would offer myself up instead. Somehow I would pry open

the door and close it behind me. Malyki would live and I would be the one to endure the curse's brutal punishment. It was only fitting, considering this was all my fault.

I reached for the handle but despite my best efforts, there was no turning it. The copper metal heated up so quickly that it burned an impression into my palm. I didn't let go, though. There was no way Maylki would die.

With the smell of frying skin filling my nose, I slammed my shoulder hard against the barrier. Over and over, each jarring strike ended with the same results—nothing. I was running out of time. Screaming in agony, I released the door handle and stepped back.

Malyki was barely breathing. The curse had all but won. We'd dared to fight back, and it had stretched out and bitch-slapped us. As I felt the hope inside me drain away, I accepted reality. My soulmate was being taken away to somewhere I couldn't follow. His eyes that were once so full of vibrancy were now lifeless.

All I could do was help ease his suffering and make his last few moments as comfortable as possible. As gently as I could, I stepped up to him, my body fitting against his one last time. His arms that once held me tightly hung limply to his side. It was almost over.

Lifting his head up, I didn't hesitate. I leaned in and kissed his blue lips. I kissed him with every ounce of love I'd ever felt and would feel until the day I died. Not only did I infuse my kiss with magic, but also with the purity of our connection. Every sacrifice we'd made for each other flowed out of me into him. I gave him all of me, knowing that despite the curse winning, this final moment held triumph. We loved each other to the very end.

It was with that last thought that I feathered a second kiss over his mouth before letting go.

"I love you, my beloved," I whispered.

Malyki was almost dead as my heart screamed with how unjust this was and my soul vowed vengeance.

A tiny ripple flowed through our jagged connection—small enough that I almost missed it.

Malyki took in a deep breath, and then toppled forward onto the ground. Whatever the force was that had tried bringing him through the door had disappeared, and he was free.

I didn't waste time. I dragged him as fast as I could, ignoring how tired I was. There was no knowing when or if that power would come back and try to steal Malyki away again. I needed my girls.

By some miracle, I was given the chance to save him, and I'd be damned if I was going to fail him this time.

CHAPTER 9

I wiped my eyes with the back of my hand, desperate to clear my vision through the curtain of streaming tears. "Malyki, please come back to me. Let me know you're okay."

Natalie and Tempest helped me ease Malyki onto our bed, but remained silent. They hadn't been there when Malyki was struck down, but immediately heeded my call for help.

"Girls, please join me in casting a protective shield around him."

We linked hands, intertwining our magics, and I let my heart bleed into my words.

> "Goddess of love, Goddess of light, protect him with your awesome might. Within this bubble keep him safe, surrounded by your healing grace."

A barely visible forcefield surrounded my beloved and his chest began to rise.

I fell to my knees, my shoulders shaking as waves of anguish and fear wracked my body.

"Thank you, both. I...I just can't lose him again," I stammered through uncontrollable sobs. The loneliness and desperation of the years we spent separated came rushing back—crushing me in their villainous grip. I couldn't go back to the way things were. I wouldn't survive it again.

Tempest and Natalie dropped to the floor, wrapping me in their arms.

"We're here for you, Mystic. Whatever you need us to do, just say the word," Natalie whispered, squeezing me tightly.

The thing was…I didn't know what to do, or what to ask for. My mind was blank, and all I could feel was my heart withering inside my chest. I shuddered underneath the girls' comforting hug and shifted into my feline form—my instincts taking over. I couldn't process what was happening. The emotions of it were all too much. The image of Malyki being held against that wall and falling lifelessly to the ground tore a yowl from my throat. *Iubita mea*—my beloved. Now that we were reunited, I wouldn't survive if we were forced apart again. I couldn't go on without him.

Tempest raised me to her chest—like she'd done so many times when she was in need—but tonight the tables were turned; these two wonderful witches would be taking care of me instead. I nuzzled into her neck and closed my eyes.

"Rest, sweet girl. We'll keep an eye on him." Tempest scratched behind my ears and held me close, lulling me to sleep with the gentle stroke of her hand.

I woke to silence and darkness, still in my feline form. Reaching out with my senses, I surveyed my surroundings. The comforting heave of Malyki's chest rose behind me, and I realized the girls must have tucked me into his side before returning to their room. I craned my neck ever so slightly to peek over the edge of the bed and made out their prone forms, wrapped in blankets and lying on our floor.

Of course, they wouldn't leave us.

I pushed to all fours, arching my back to stretch as I turned to check on Malyki. Our protection was still in place, and luckily his coloring had finally started to return. With featherlight steps, I climbed onto his chest and curled into a ball just above his heart. Sleep would benefit us all right now, and until he woke up, I wasn't leaving his side. The rise and fall of his chest and the thump of his heartbeat beneath my paws was the most glorious thing I'd ever felt. He was okay, and I knew he'd recover given a little more time. Purring in contentment, I closed my eyes again, ready to stay here as long as it took.

Black shadows swirled in my mind, yanking me into a vision that wasn't my own. Smoke rose in the distance, a hot breeze fanning its thick plumes straight into my face. I opened my mouth to scream for Malyki, but it was my name that came spilling out instead.

"Mystic? Can you hear me? Please, my love, send me a sign you're okay."

The vision shifted, filling with flames and screams that transported me back to the moment of our initial curse.

"Please, Mystic, reach out and find me. I'm here. I'm right here!" Malyki's voice echoed in my mind as the wavering image showed me in my cursed form—a black and ginger cat lying on the forest floor all alone.

I watched myself through his eyes, rising on all fours and slinking away into the night.

"No!" Malyki screeched. "Mystic, please don't leave me. You have to find me. I'm right here!"

The forest grew silent, filled now with only smoke and flames and the insidious laughter of Danor as he sealed his curse that would separate us for centuries.

"No!" I woke up screaming in my human form, held tightly in Malyki's arms.

"Just breathe, Mystic. It's okay. You're safe."

Gasping for air, I took a few deep breaths and looked around the room, processing all I'd seen. The girls were gone, and it was just me and Malyki, lying atop our bed. I closed my eyes again and regretted it immediately.

I'd witnessed the night of our curse, only from Malyki's point of view. He'd been stuck inside the demon realm, just like he'd explained, but this was different. He was aware and able to see beyond his prison; a prison that was nothing close to the cloud-like void he'd previously described, but instead like the hellish nightmare he'd recently admitted to the kids: Cold. Malicious. Oppressive.

I twisted on the bed until I could see his face. Gazing into his mismatched eyes, I searched for the words to help explain what I'd seen and felt—to help me understand. Unfortunately, when I opened my mouth the only thing that spilled out was an accusation. "You lied to me."

Malyki shifted, sitting us both upright. "Yes, I did. But like I stated before, what good would it have done to tell you the truth? Just as you couldn't imagine me there…suffering—I couldn't imagine you here, hurting or dealing with the misplaced guilt I know you would have carried." He took a deep breath. "What happened to us was neither of our faults. It was all Danor, and you exacted our revenge a long time ago, so please, Mystic… While you may be upset that I lied to you, know that it will never happen again. You know the truth, in all its gory detail, but it doesn't change anything…we're together now, and that's all that matters."

I stared into his eyes, peering beyond his words, and saw the truth. He would always save me…even from myself. Easing back down, I rested my head against his chest and gave in. "You're right, my love. That is all that matters."

CHAPTER 10

*M*y eyelids felt heavy as I relaxed into the silence. It had taken a week for Malyki to recover, and despite what was about to happen, I savored the brief respite.

We were finally going to retrieve the copper bird. Many hours had been spent in researching and triple-checking information. Arguments were had about waiting a little longer—opinions that deep down I agreed with, but surprisingly Bryony was on board with the team pushing forward and not losing momentum.

We wanted to put an end to this so we could all finally breathe. Tensions were at an all-time high, which made this ceremonial bath even more appreciated. There were so many things that could go wrong, but sometimes the best-laid plans fell short as well. We would never feel one hundred percent ready.

We were determined, however. That counted for everything.

I heard Bryony approaching behind me, and sure enough, she was carrying in the herbs and flowers to add to the bath. We'd gone over every syllable of the magic required for us to perform the dangerous ritual, and judging by the crease in her brow, she was silently reciting her part in the spell. She reminded me of myself at her age—headstrong and full of confidence. Now that I'd had a chance to witness her in action, I could also admit that with that cockiness came the familiar talent when it came to working with the Goddess and manipulating energy. She was a natural.

"I quickly checked to see how Vidar and Gable are doing with Malyki," she mentioned before kneeling beside the heated bath in Hel Tower. "They've got everything under control so we're good to go whenever you're ready."

Natalie and Tempest had been adamant that we use the bathroom, hiding their disappointment that they couldn't be involved. They understood the stakes and had a personal investment in the outcome. I loved the two witches with all my heart, and it pained me to exclude them. Unfortunately, my anxiety was already at an all-time high, worrying over Malyki and what would happen once he got close enough to the gateway again. I couldn't bear to see anything happen to my beloved witches. I considered them my coven, and to ease their own apprehensions, I accepted one of the crystals that they kept on their altar. From the way Natalie explained it, the quartz would alert them should anything go wrong so they could come and help.

Rubbing my thumb back and forth over the stone now, I could feel their love and support pulsing out from it. For centuries I'd always believed the only person I needed in this life was Malyki, but now I knew differently.

I needed them. They gave me something more to live for.

I slipped beneath the fragrant water one last time, holding tight to the quartz, and as I reemerged, I allowed any doubt or fear I felt to melt away. There was no more room for second guessing. With one last check over the details, it would be show-time.

"Then let's do the next step," I announced, stepping out of the tub. To Bryony's credit, she didn't look away or blush at my nakedness. With a small bowl filled with ceremonial ink, she got to work at drawing sigils over my body. Malyki was having the same thing drawn on him—the logic being that together we would open the gateway—a connection linking us so I could enter through and retrieve the copper bird. Bryony, Gable, and Vidar would anchor Malyki while my beloved secured me to this reality.

My gaze fell to the card that had been given to them at the beginning of the semester. The more I looked at it, the more I felt like we were missing something. Maybe it was nerves, but this was too important to ignore.

"Bryony," I asked, my gaze trained on the tarot card. "Doesn't the Magician also symbolize the possibility of overlooking something?"

She placed the bowl down for a moment and stood up from where she'd been crouched, ink on her index finger. "What's on your mind, Mystic?"

In the beginning, she might have mocked my question, feeling that I was belittling her and the work she'd done. The young druid had spent long, tiring hours researching every detail of this ritual. We'd all crammed inside her dorm room, leaving only for coffee and food runs to the cafeteria. The experience had created a solid bond between us all, and I viewed the woman—friend—before me differently.

I drew in a ragged breath. "I don't know. Have you ever had a feeling like the obvious is staring you in the face but you're too blind to see it?" She brought the card to me, and I stared at it hard. "Maybe it's just me overthinking, but I swear the man is mocking me."

Her gentle laugh broke the tension. "Let's go over the plans again. Maybe that'll shake loose whatever's bugging you. I'd rather you astral project with a clear mind and focus."

She resumed painting the symbols as I slowly began reciting everything.

Bryony would represent earth as all druids do.

Gable would tap into his scorpion side and represent fire.

Vidar would represent air with his Valkyrie wings.

Malyki would represent the remaining element of water, and was the key to unlocking the doorway to where the bird was hidden.

Together they would maintain the powerful circle that would protect not only Malyki and keep him safe, but that would tether me to this world. Their energies combined would make it near impossible to defeat and undo.

At least that was the theory. We were following the guidance of the tarot card by combining our knowledge and gifts as a team. True, our start had been rocky with mistrust and vanity, especially on my own part, but this was bigger than us.

I fiddled with the card, trying to look at it from different perspectives. Nothing.

"Done," Bryony chimed in. She stood again and studied her artwork, scrutinizing every sigil to ensure they had been drawn with precision. "Other than last minute jitters, we're ready."

I nodded and handed her the card. "Then let's meet with the others and get started. I'm looking forward to a week-long nap once this is all over." With the markings dried, I carefully slipped on a robe and tied the sash in a knot. "Thank you, Bryony. I know I wasn't always the nicest, but I really do appreciate you."

She began to snort, but stopped, her eyes wide as saucers. Her gaze was focused on the card, and my stomach sunk. She'd seen something when I hadn't.

"What is it?" I asked.

Bryony ignored me. Instead she turned the tarot card back so it was upright and then switched it to the reverse. "Of course," she uttered softly beneath her breath. "Why didn't I think of that?" Finally she looked up and grinned. "Come on, let's go see the others, and I'll tell you all together."

I let her drag me by the hand. She'd stumbled across something, and instead of fear, all I felt was trust.

Trust in her.

Trust in us.

Bryony was brilliant.

By chance, she'd noticed something about the Magician himself, and the results would make all the difference. Once we'd gathered back under Hel Tower where the gateway was hidden behind the door, she revealed her last-minute inspiration.

"To the average practitioner, those markings look like scuff marks, which, let's be honest, makes sense because they're shoes. But I recognized this." She pointed to the soles of the man's shoes, and I squinted again to see what she meant. Damn, she had eyes like a hawk. "Sigils. Spirit whispers that these are just as important as the ones we've meticulously drawn on you and Malyki," Bryony explained. "In fact, I'd even say had we not included them, it would've spelt disaster."

Malyki lifted his foot to see what Bryony had drawn there. "So explain to me again why we need these?" It wasn't like him to be skeptical, but after the last time he came close to the door, he wanted to make sure. "They fortify my link with Mystic?"

She nodded. "Yes. Think of it as with each step she takes, you're there with her symbolically. You both can't go through the gateway or you'd be trapped in there and who knows where the curse will send the copper bird. In order for this to work, either one of you must stand on both sides . . . together yet separate.

I threw my arms around her neck and hugged her. "Thank you," I whispered, meaning it with all my heart. "I hope once this is over with, we can remain friends. I feel like I have a lot to learn from you." My admission was genuine. So was my newfound respect. "We couldn't have done this without you." Breaking apart and looking at Vidar and Gable, I smiled. "With all of you. Malyki and I both owe you so much for all your help. To you, it's simply a task assigned by the academy, but—" my voice cracked with emotion— "for us, this means everything." I took hold of Malyki's hand and squeezed it.

"I don't always believe in the concept of luck—if you're prepared, then success follows—but I don't think it would be wrong to wish us luck," Gable said as he let out a steadying breath. "There's nothing left to do but work the magic."

We all nodded.

"Let's get started," Vidar announced, and everyone began moving to their places. We'd brought down all the magical paraphernalia required and etched the pentacle and sigils onto the floor. Candles graced every surface in the room. The air was sweetly perfumed with burning herbs and incense.

Warmth from my necklace spread over my collarbone, and it softly vibrated against my skin from the web of crystals that held my magic. I'd be relying on every talisman I cherished and used. Checking my pocket for the quartz the girls had given me, I gestured for Malyki to follow me so we could speak privately. There were things I still wanted—needed—to say that were for his ears only.

Rubbing the side of my arms with his hands, he drew me into the comfort of his embrace. We stood there for what felt like a lifetime, hoping that was what we'd be rewarded with in the end.

We'd gone through so much—faced heartache and challenges together—but this felt like everything was on the line, and it was. This curse had hung over our heads for far too long.

Malyki pressed his lips to the top of my head. I inhaled deeply, drawing his scent into my lungs, cherishing the peace his presence brought me.

"I love you, Malyki. There hasn't been a second where I haven't thanked the Goddess for you." My words trembled, but I didn't care. This man was my everything, and I would risk it all to save him—save us.

"Sssh, *iubita mea*. This isn't goodbye so wipe away your tears. You won't be alone, remember. Bryony has ensured that I'll be there with you in spirit. We can finally bring this whole wretched curse business to an end." He crooked his index finger under my chin and raised my face. "Then we can make plans for how we'll spend our forever."

"Together," I said, smiling back at his tenderness. "You are my rock, Malyki."

"And you are mine. Now kiss me before we start. Let's remember what it is we're fighting for."

I didn't need to be asked because I was already pulling him closer, standing on tiptoes so my mouth could meet his. The second our lips touched, a surety and conviction solidified deep within me. His faith in me kindled a fire in my gut, and I returned his kiss with a passion and determination of my own. We would overcome this and come through it victorious. As he gathered me tighter in his arms, our energies merging so we became one, I knew that we'd done all we could.

His lips hovered over my mouth for a brief moment before we finally broke apart. It had only been a minute or two, but a lifetime of promises and words had been spoken.

"Let's get started, everybody," I declared, moving away from Malyki so I could stand by the door. "When you're ready, Bryony."

When she began to chant and the magic from each of us began to swirl about in the air, I nodded.

It was almost over.

CHAPTER 11

I was lost.

Time seemed to stand still here, stretching on endlessly as I stumbled through the oppressive terrain. How Malyki survived this stood as a testament to his strength and resilience. I conjured his face in my mind, but with each slow step I took, his features became blurrier and opaque.

Before our curse, I'd travailed the astral plane countless times, but this place was unlike anything I'd ever experienced. My surroundings were dismal without any kind of distinction—just barren trees and rocky landscapes. Dark clouds hung in the sky while shadows danced about, hiding dangers in their depths.

Malyki had warned me before I'd stepped through the portal that this realm would wear me down and play tricks with my mind. I'd given him the same kind of bravado I usually did that nothing would stop me from fulfilling our duty, but that courage was steadily eking away into the damp and chilled air.

What I needed was to regain my sense of direction. I followed the visual map that Malyki had me memorize during our week-long research and preparations, but even now those memories were hazy at best.

The copper bird was here somewhere—the key to ending our curse and helping Bryony, Gable, and Vidar pass their class. The Regents couldn't have chosen a more complicated assignment, and it made me wonder whether they held some kind of agenda when it came to testing their students. Last semester it had been the hourglasses that had filled the campus with terror, and now it was the mysterious cards and items to collect.

An icy blast of malicious magic struck me, forcing me forward until I crashed to my knees on the ground. The curse. I could all but taste the rancid magic of the witch who hated Malyki and I. It didn't surprise me that even though he was long dead, he'd conjured a presence to safeguard the bird. That dark shadow loomed over me now.

Give up. You have failed in your quest, and your misery will feed me for many lifetimes.

I shook my head, desperate to block out the voice that seemed to fill me from the inside. All I needed to do was hold on tightly to our plan and find the artifact. Malyki had promised me that as I grew closer to where it was hidden, I'd be able to sense its essence, but all I could feel was the bone-chilling emptiness of this place.

I dined on your beloved, the voice spat out next. *I believe you will prove the more delicious and succulent dish. Yes,* it hissed mockingly, *you will do wonderfully.*

Invisible hands roughly caressed me. Bile rose into my throat just as I doubled over and vomited to the ground. I caught sight of the sigils still marked over my body and took courage from them. This was all just an illusion—a cruel spell to break me. If my beloved could survive this, I would, too.

"You hold no power over me!" I yelled out into the void. I wiped my mouth with the back of my hand and rose slowly to my feet. "Your jealousy and wrath were pitiful then, and they are weak even now. I refuse to let you win!"

With surer steps, I closed my eyes and took a deep, fortifying breath. All I needed to do was regain my center and ground myself in the magic that tethered me to my world. I had people there who loved me and were fighting for our mission to be successful. They were smart and vibrant, the very best magical users of their time. They hadn't failed me, and I wouldn't repay their faith and confidence in me by buckling beneath this realm's cruelty.

A small tug at my spirit gave me my first real sign that I was in fact on the right path. I could sense the coppery metallic taste of the bird and knew it was a few hundred yards ahead. A cry of relief escaped through my lips, and I rushed forward, eyes scanning for the prize.

Noooooooo. The anger within the voice was almost deafening, and it echoed throughout the air. *You are mine.*

I was knocked to the ground again as a force pressed down hard against my chest, suffocating the very breath from my body. Dark spots filled my vision, and I thrashed against the weight, uttering spell after spell in desperation. I reached for my necklace, and in horror, felt the crystals crack and shatter beneath my touch. The power I'd stored in them filtered out into the air like fading colorful mist. It was a brutal blow to lose them, but luckily we had ensured I entered the astral plane with other talismans.

I wasn't defeated just yet.

"Enough!" I grunted through clenched teeth. "You will not destroy me. I will not bow down or yield."

Even as my muscles screamed and bones shook, I clawed my way forward to where I felt the bird beckoning me. That was all I could focus on. One step . . . one hand filled with sharp gravel after another. Retrieve the artifact and then face the next obstacle —returning home.

The ground began to thrum and radiate power beneath me. I was close, so close, and I gasped in relief when I finally spied the coppery surface. The next few seconds were vital, and I had to time it right. The presence would do all in its ability to stop me, but I'd come prepared.

The instant my fingers wrapped around the statue, I uttered the words of enchantment and fused the surface to my skin. I screamed out with agony as the fiery, blistering pain surged through my body. I couldn't risk dropping the bird or having the presence spirit it out of my reach. This way, as Bryony had explained, I could focus solely now on making my way home.

My skin ached and throbbed, but I pushed the pain down and buried it beneath a lifetime of memories. Malyki's smile and loving gaze pressed it into the recesses of my mind—the places we'd seen, the experiences we'd shared, and the countless examples of how greatly we loved each other. It only took a moment and my focus returned.

I could do this.

All I needed was to retrace my steps and recite the magic that would reopen the doorway.

I stumbled forward with determination, picking up the pace despite the presence constantly yanking at my body. The shadow whipped me about, trying to disorient me again, but this time I trained my thoughts and energy on the magic of my team. Water, air, earth, and fire—they were faint in my mind, but I cleaved to them nevertheless. They were the light in my darkness, and I knew I could trust them to guide the way.

Foooool, hissed the voice. *You fight in vain.*

I ignored the vicious threats and pressed onward through the oppressive mist. The trouble was there was something different in the air now—something that cloyed at my skin and battered over me. Hatred. Apathy. A bone weariness that threatened to crumble my resolve to move. A mocking laughter filled my ears that left me sobbing.

It was Malyki—or what sounded almost identical to him. Over and over he scorned me and railed over how disgusted he was in me, how furious he was to spend forever together. Vile complaints pierced my heart, but I knew better. This wasn't my beloved —*iubita mea.* He would never speak such things, so I did the only thing I could.

I laughed. Even as tears of pain trailed over my cheeks and wet my shirt, I laughed until I was hoarse. All this time trapped in the darkness, and the witch still didn't understand what kind of man my Malyki was.

He didn't understand us.

Hope swept over me in blessed waves when I finally recognized the familiar entry point of the realm. I had the artifact, and soon, I'd be reunited once more with everyone.

A shadow enveloped me, however, chilling me to the bone. My breath came out in white puffs, and that momentary feeling that I was in the clear disappeared with each shudder of my body.

What. The. Hell.

My skin began to prickle from the icy sensation, and I cried out in pain. Something was happening to me—something that was at war with my magic.

"The sigils!" I cried out, tugging at my clothes as I watched them disappear one by one. Nothing I did stopped the witch's energy from undoing the magic that tethered me to the other side. The power was trying to trap me to the realm like Malyki had been —the shadow growing bolder with each vanishing mark. I frantically rushed forward in an attempt to save myself, but I stumbled, growing weaker and weaker with each passing second.

"Nooooooo!" I screamed, fire blazing through my ragged throat. "Release me! You cannot keep me here!"

When I dropped to the floor, exhausted mentally and physically, I knew I was almost beat. After everything we'd endured and done to prepare, it wouldn't be enough.

I hadn't been enough.

I was moments from becoming trapped and separated from Malyki, and I could barely feel him. More pain stabbed at me, this time from the soles of my feet. The presence was breaking my connection, and if it succeeded, then all was lost.

There would be no more words of power to speak. I tried uttering the spell that we'd written to close the door behind me, but I wasn't close enough to leap through the portal before it shut for good.

I reached for my quartz, and it turned to sand in my hand, blowing away into the air. Each talisman I'd brought had been destroyed so all that remained was the bird fused to my body and the athame I'd slipped into a thigh holster just in case. The problem was the shadow wasn't corporeal, so no amount of slashing would deter it—let alone kill it.

That's when a thought came blasting into my mind—as Gable would say, a Hail Mary of an idea.

Pulling the athame out and ripping my shoes off, I didn't hesitate. I pressed the sharp blade against the tender skin of my sole and began carving the sigils back into my foot. There were no marks to unravel. These would be etched to the bone and filled with blood. I clenched my jaw against the pain and steadied my hand. I had to do this. This would be my sacrifice.

As I finished the last sigil, I heard the presence howl in distress, the sound so loud that I felt my eardrums burst. I was beyond feeling the agony, though. Blood flowed along with my tears.

Staggering forward once more, I sensed the shimmer of the doorway open before I could actually see it.

Shadowy arms scratched at me, shredding the clothes from my body and leaving deep welts across my skin. I screamed from strength—plead with my Goddess to help see me through this. I felt her warmth infuse me. I dug deeper than I ever had, and when I finally saw the underground hallway of Hel Tower glowing before me, I raced forward. They were there—Gable, Bryony, and Vidar. Malyki stood at the opening with his arm stretched forward, ready to catch me. Beside him, crowded by the entrance, was also Tempest and Natalie. Of course, the moment the quartz had been destroyed they would've come.

I wasn't alone anymore, and I could finish this race.

"Start the spell," I croaked, my throat dry. I was delirious with exhaustion, but I had enough magic left to recite the words.

Malyki's voice floated to me in a whisper, his deep timber mixing with the voice of the Goddess—no, the voices of Natalie and Tempest. Our girls were there, helping us as always. As the words formed in my mind, I opened my mouth and let the spell spill from my lips.

"Cursed demons, let me be. For you are no more than an illusion to me. Gone forever, by my own hand. Trapped and sealed in this tortured land. Release the hold, and stay within. Never to harm another again."

A powerful surge burst outward as I felt the shadow shriek with defeat, recoiling from the onslaught of the spell exploding through the realm. It slashed to grasp me, hoping to drag me deep into the darkness with it where no one would ever find me again. Its icy cold fingers wrapped around my wrist, but it had underestimated the strength of Malyki. Despite being told to stay out of the realm, he'd reached through the doorway, and with one sharp jolt, tugged me tumbling through the gateway.

"Now!" he yelled as he wrapped me tightly in his arms. All around me I heard the spell being spoken boldly—Bryony, Vidar, Gable, and my beloved witches, Tempest and Natalie. They'd linked hands and now faced the shadow that was rapidly diminishing in power.

There was a whooshing sound that whipped about and then a loud explosion. The gateway was closed. I was safe. The artifact had been rescued.

Silence descended over our small group as if we needed a brief respite to process the overwhelming task we'd just accomplished. It might've been Vidar or Gable who spoke first, but soon everyone was talking all at once. We'd done it.

Even though I could hear their questions, I only had eyes for Malyki.

"We did it, *iubita mea*," I whispered, relaxing into his warmth. "We finally found it."

The last thing I felt before surrendering to unconsciousness was his tender kiss against my bruised forehead, the heat from his breath calming me.

It was over.

CHAPTER 12

$\mathcal{H}$olding the bird in my hands felt completely surreal. I almost couldn't believe we'd done it, after all we'd been through. Our team had pulled together—all five of us, and I was so very grateful. Working together served as a good lesson—while this curse was always individually ours, the sacrifice to end it was not. It had taken all of us, and that was something I wouldn't soon forget. The chore now, however, would be to convince myself to give it up.

We all agreed Malyki and I would present our artifact to Addie tomorrow morning, but looking across the room at my lover—his back shirtless with muscles flexing as he bent over to make us some tea—gave me pause. This vessel held our happiness within its copper shell, and I could preserve that happiness here and now with a simple flick of my wrist. If this cursed object was destroyed, we'd finally be free. But that, too, held a lesson within itself.

While we needed the bird to end our curse, the school needed it too. The kids had fulfilled what they thought was another ITF assignment, but I knew there was more to it than that. Addie hadn't let anything slip, in particular, but I could tell there was something special about all the artifacts the teams had gathered so far. The magic of each piece called to me, subtly radiating out from wherever she kept them hidden. There was definitely a bigger picture at play here—one important enough to make me question my and Malyki's future after all the struggles we'd faced.

He had suffered for centuries, lost from me and tortured within the demon realm—my chest still tightened at the thought—but I tried to remember his words. "We're together now, and that's all that matters." But it wasn't that simple. Yes, for the moment, we were together, but without the curse being fully broken, that could change in a heartbeat. If we were separated now, we'd revert to our familiar forms, unable to shift back or use our magic. We'd be trapped apart…again.

The sound of the kettle's whistling pulled me from my thoughts.

"Tea's ready, my love." The deep timber in Malyki's voice soothed my nerves more than any cup of tea ever could. The honor in this man—the love and devotion—it was a magic all its own that pulled at my very soul. I reached up, taking the cup from his hand with tears in my eyes. "Mystic, what's wrong my dear?"

I took a sip of the lavender and chamomile tea—my favorite—then shared my selfish thoughts. "I know this is needed for the school, and I can tell it's important, but honestly…I'm not sure I care. This was our burden for so long…our curse, and we shouldn't have to suffer some unknown fate by handing it over after all this time."

I inhaled sharply, stifling a sob.

Malyki set down his cup of tea then sank to the floor in front of me, reaching out to caress my sore feet in his hands. The warmth of his aura enveloped me like a blanket, but his words sent a chill up my spine. "If we destroy this now, against their wishes, we'd have to leave—run away from Havenwood Falls, and that means leaving Tempest and Natalie behind." He scooted closer. "And as much as I want to finally be free of this curse, I couldn't ever do that to them. We're still their familiars, Mystic, and the Sun & Moon Academy is a dangerous place. They're going to need our help."

Honor. Sacrifice. Love…the words echoed loudly in my mind.

I lowered my chin to my chest, ashamed of my selfish thoughts. "You're right, of course. I could never leave the girls—they're our family now." I sniffled again, but this time it was to fight back tears of joy. "We'll stay…for them—for our family. We'll turn in the bird tomorrow, as planned."

Still seated below me, Malyki ran his hands up my legs, lifting the bottom of my skirt as his fingers crept higher and higher. "You are a selfless, loving woman, and I'm not going to pretend that doesn't turn me on."

A giggle boiled up and out of me as I let the joy of our reunion truly sink in. Sure, a part of our future might always remain unknown, but wasn't everyone's? What mattered was that Malyki was no longer trapped in the demon realm, and we'd made sure it could never happen again. So, yes, I'd take this for the win it was, and finally allow myself to be free.

Slinking to the floor, I straddled Malyki's lap and wrapped my arms around his shoulders. His hands, now on my hips, feathered my skirt out of the way as he positioned himself between my legs. Staring into each other's eyes, our gazes locked as our bodies and hearts became one.

This was all I needed—my husband, our magic, released and together in this world again. His strong hands glided up my back, easing my shirt over my head before grabbing a fist full of my hair as we both held on.

Lost in the sensations, euphoria overtook us. Our moans filled the room as we sank into a familiar rhythm—each movement measured yet wild as the energy between us continued to rise.

Honor. Sacrifice. Love. Magic… the words built within me the more and more I continued to let go.

"Mystic," Malyki groaned, his voice rough and tortured.

"Malyki, yes!" I cried out his name in return. "I'm yours, my love."

"Forever, mine…*iubita mea.*"

My beloved. Those words falling from his lips sent me over the edge—crashing into the wonderful unknown that was our new life here at the Sun & Moon Academy.

CHAPTER 13

"*A*re you sure you want to do this?" Natalie asked, voicing the concern she had with tear-filled eyes.

I stared at the copper bird resting in my lap, still struggling with our decision and all it meant. "Yes. We're sure."

I wanted to confess my own doubts, but all it would take was a syllable uttered by me, and my resolve would crumble.

"But that means your curse will remain in place." Tempest's breath hitched on a sob. "You'll never truly be free." She looked so forlorn and helpless as she watched her romantic notions of happily ever after fade away.

I took a deep breath and scooted closer to Malyki. He was my rock. "Yes, that is true. But it's a choice we're willing to make—for the greater good." I let my head fall against his shoulder, needing his steadfast strength to help get me through this. "By staying here on campus, at least we'll be together and able to shift into our human forms and use our magic freely."

It wasn't the perfect solution, but we would make it work. Being shackled by the curse would be bearable simply by being together.

Tempest wiped tears from her cheeks, her eyes blurry. "So you're okay with staying here...forever? You'll be bound to serve as familiars for a rotating set of witches as we all continue to graduate and leave." She glanced at her best friend, who nodded her encouragement. "Now that we know who you are, Natalie and I see you as our partners in magic, members of our small coven. We won't ever force you to do something against your conscience or will."

I knew both Tempest and Natalie were suffering at the thought of leaving us behind, and while I agreed—it would be my preference to leave campus with them when the time came—it just wasn't possible. Not until the bird was truly and utterly destroyed. "Yes. We will forever be bound to serve the witches here on campus as long as the talisman remains intact, but again...at least we'll be together. I hope you can understand that after centuries apart, it's the most important thing to us."

"Of course we understand." Natalie hugged Tempest, offering her bestie some much needed comfort. "And we'll do our best to ensure those who follow don't take advantage of your familial bond or taint your magic with bad intentions."

It was a fear Malyki and I had talked about, bouncing back and forth between wanting to be freed from the curse and our fear of being forced into magical slavery. Familiars were creatures to be honored and revered. We felt blessed to be tied to Natalie and Tempest because we knew their hearts. Part of me wondered if that was why Addie and the Board of Regents hadn't balked more over us being human.

Malyki brushed away one of Natalie's tears with the pad of his thumb. "We appreciate your worry on our behalf. If this assignment has taught me anything, it's that there is always a way to rise above a challenge no matter how insurmountable. We'll be okay because we have each other."

"Will they let you stay here in the dorms, or do you think they'll move you to the Administration Tower since you'll be here permanently—more like teachers instead of students?" Tempest sniffled and rubbed her nose.

"We're hoping we'll be allowed to stay here, in Hel Tower. Kind of like the mascots of the house." Malyki huffed out a laugh.

"That makes sense. Maybe when we graduate and leave, you could move into our room. We have the open window. Malyki could fly out, and it's where you—" Tempest lifted her chin in my direction— "spent most of your time here." No longer able to hold it together, Tempest's tears broke free, and with them, my heart.

Handing Malyki the statue, I pushed from the bed and wrapped her in my arms. "Oh, my sweet, sweet girl. Please don't cry. We still have plenty of time to spend together here. You don't graduate for a couple more years, and who knows...maybe eventually, the talisman will be destroyed, and Malyki and I will be able to join you on one of your missions as guardians out in the real world."

She pulled back and smiled, a spark of hope shining in her eyes. "That would be so great."

"Well, regardless. Whether we're your official familiars in the future or not, we'll still always be here to help you. You can reach out to us any time," Malyki added, melting my heart.

Hail to the Goddess, I hoped he was right—that we'd still be able to maintain contact with our charges of the past. Just because they'd be moving on didn't mean our connection was severed. From my lessons as a cat familiar all these centuries, the only time that a bond was truly broken was when one of our witches died. I shivered at the thought and gave Tempest another squeeze.

"Whether we're charged with other witches or not, we'll still be able to feel you here." I placed a hand over my heart, willing my words to be true.

"Okay, well, that makes me feel a little better." Tempest shrugged out of my embrace and moved toward the door. "I guess we'll let you get to it, then. I don't imagine the Board will want to wait too much longer for their prize." She nodded to Malyki and the copper bird in his hands.

"No, you're probably right," I agreed. Seeing the girls out with a kiss to each of their cheeks, I returned to the bed, taking back the statue once more. "I can't believe it's ending like this."

"I know, my *iubire*. But at least it is ending, and we're together."

"Forever," I stressed. I met Malyki's loving gaze and stared deeply into his eyes. I needed him to feel my words—my commitment to us never being separated again.

Setting the bird aside, I crawled into my husband's lap, straddling his waist and wrapping my arms around his neck. After all we'd been through, we could take this time for us—to claim our victory, even in this measured way. We may not be getting our true freedom, but sinking into Malyki's waiting arms was victory enough for me.

Lifting me in one fell swoop, Malyki spun and laid me back on the bed—his imposing frame towering above me as my lower legs dangled off the side.

"I'll never forget what we've been through, Mystic." He lowered himself to his knees. "But moments like this are helping to erase the bad." His lips touched my skin, trailing kisses up the inside of my thigh.

My head dropped back, and I closed my eyes. Everywhere his mouth touched, magic sparked—along my skin, in my heart...all the way down to the depths of my soul. This was our version of freedom now, and I wouldn't trade it for the world.

The time had come.

Hand-in-hand, Malyki and I walked into the Administrative Offices, ready to turn over the copper bird to Addie and Saundra. They were the only two board members I trusted, and even though parting with the source of our curse was going to be hard, I got the feeling they would be needing it for an even greater purpose soon, and that helped...a little.

Sometimes doing the right thing sucked, but it didn't change the truth that sacrifices were often needed for the bigger picture. The fact that Tempest and Natalie looked up to us both helped ease the sting.

The receptionist showed us into the same boardroom we'd been in before, but thankfully, only the two Beaumont witches were waiting inside.

"Malyki, Mystic...thank you so much," Addie started. "I know it's not easy for you to give this up."

"No. It's not," Malyki stated flatly, not bothering to sugarcoat things.

I put a hand on his arm and forced a smile onto my face. "It's not easy, but we understand there's a greater purpose here—one we won't hinder by being selfish."

I gave Malyki's arm a light squeeze then moved behind him to retrieve the bird from his pack. Unwrapping it slowly, I let the burlap covering fall away.

The statue hummed beneath my hands, its copper shell shimmering brightly despite the low lighting in the room. Dark energy radiated from it, and I could still feel pieces of our own magic held hostage within. Taking a deep breath, I set it on the polished wood table and lifted my chin.

"I don't know exactly why all these artifacts are being collected, but like I said...I can tell there's a greater purpose meant for them here." I nodded to the copper bird. "Since this isn't being destroyed, it will continue to hold our curse in place, making it so that if we were ever to be separated again, we'd revert to our familiar selves, no longer able to shift into our human forms."

Addie and Saundra both bowed their heads, confirming my suspicion about the artifacts was right. These missions were a ruse, and their need for the various objects stemmed from something that was far more important.

"We understand. And Mystic...your sacrifice won't be forgotten. I can promise you that." Saundra smiled, and my heart eased a little. "You have a home here with us now. Safe and together."

Stepping back, I reached for Malyki's hand. His touch helped to sooth me further, but it was his words that truly settled my soul.

"You know what the elders say, 'Only when sacrifice is made, can true love endure.'" He kissed the back of my hand and guided us out the door.

We walked in silence back to our tower. Looking at it from afar, it sat on a slight hill but wasn't overly noticeable—blending into the cave walls behind it instead. Its round stone façade was only five stories tall, topped with a flat roof surrounded by battlements—strong and fierce —just like all the inhabitants within. Grabbing the metal handle, I pulled open its gothic red door and walked into the great room.

"Home sweet home." I smiled and flopped onto one of the red velvet couches, pulling Malyki down with me.

Chuckling, he wrapped his arms around me and whispered in my ear, "Yes, my *iubire*, we are home…together in Hel forever."

I burst out laughing, welcoming a lightness and joy that I hadn't felt for a really long time and let it seep into my heart. I guess the elders were right—our sacrifice had been made and now our love could truly endure. Havenwood Falls was my home, and the Sun & Moon Academy, but more so, it was Malyki… He was my home, and I'd be happy to never leave.

DEATH

KRISTIE COOK, E.J. FECHENDA, ROSE GARCIA,
BELINDA BORING, JUSTINE WINTER & AMY
RICHIE

CHAPTER 1

*T*he underground river whooshed by about a yard from my feet, the thunderous sound exceptionally loud here as it echoed off the stone bridge spanning overhead. Perhaps because it drowned out all noise from the campus above was what kept drawing me to this place, or maybe it was the solitude. Don't get me wrong—I loved being at SMA and with all of the students and faculty. After lifetimes of quite grim experiences, this one was refreshing. But after I'd been forced to reveal my true identity— Rhiannon, a goddess of the moon, night, and death—at the end of last semester, I'd suddenly become Miss Popularity. Which just wasn't me. Before, I'd always been able to blend in, becoming unnoticeable almost to the point of invisibility. Now, especially when most everyone here had supernatural senses, I couldn't seem to pull that off anymore. So when this place under the main bridge to campus drew me to it, I'd found respite.

I lay back on the riverbank, staring at the bridge thirty feet or so above me, at the symbol carved in the center of the bridge's stony underside. Two fish chased each other in a circle—quite often seen to depict the Pisces zodiac sign. I wondered who had carved it there. My old friend Zandra a/k/a The Collector? The one members of the Court of the Sun and the Moon also knew as Kialah, but didn't know she was one and the same as their very enemy? It was quite likely. After all, she'd brought them here to

673

Halvard, and this entire campus had likely been her lair at one time long before their founding families ever discovered the box canyon that became Havenwood Falls.

I was more intrigued with the why—why carve the symbol in a place where nobody would ever see it? There had to be a reason, though after coming here all semester, I still hadn't figured it out. With finals starting next week, it might be a mystery that would have to remain unsolved, at least until next year.

For now, I had one more class before I'd be buckling down to study for exams. Transforming into my raven form, I flew up to the side of the bridge and over the archway that opened to the quad. With a flap of my wings, I soared over the expanse, a couple of students waving up at me. Yeah, they knew this part about me, too—that I could shift into a raven. Landing on the ledge of my window in Muninn Tower, I hopped inside and shifted back to my human form. A young woman with freakishly large blue eyes and a head that looked too big for her thin body, especially with all the blond braids and dreadlocks piled on it, stared back at me in the mirror.

After dressing in black jeans and a black hoodie with the purple and silver SMA logo on it, I grabbed my backpack and phone, noticing a text message.

Addie: Swing by my office ASAP?

I glanced at the time. I had longer than I thought before class started.

Me: OMW

I jogged down the stairs and through the tunnel that connected Muninn to the library, bleating a few "Heys" as I passed Marcia and Molly, belladonna vampires, and then Mallory Dorian, who was accompanied by her boyfriend Torent. Passing through the door into the library, I slowed to cross the mezzanine and descend the steps into Halstein Hall. Addie's office was in the administrative area on an upper floor.

"Addie?" I said to the receptionist at the front of the admin offices. "Uh, I mean, Professor Beaumont?"

The receptionist barely glanced up at me. "She's expecting you."

She flicked her hand in a shooing gesture, waving me off. I'd barely begun down the hall when Addie met me.

"I hope you called me here for good news?" I asked her as we continued walking. I slowed as we approached the door to her office, but she kept going.

"Maybe? And also no. Come with me."

We went to the end of the hall before she opened a door into a room that was larger than her office but not quite as big as the conference room where the Board of Regents met. As we crossed the threshold, powerful magic zinged through me. Shelves lined the walls, though most were empty. I recognized the items that were there, each one sitting on a separate shelf, each one far away from the others. A different kind of magical energy pulsed from them.

"They don't play well with each other?" I asked, bemused. "They're supposed to create a weapon, though."

"Exactly what I thought," Addie said.

Shit. Had we been wrong all this time? Did the Board of Regents send the ITF students out on ridiculous "missions" for no reason? Was this another of Kialah's games?

"It's not that they don't play well together," Addie continued. "It's just that their power is so strong when they're too close together that it's palpable. With all the supes under this mountain, many of whom can detect even the slightest shifts in energy, I didn't want anyone getting concerned—or nosy."

That made sense. These pieces were supposed to somehow work together to create a weapon powerful enough to be used against a god—specifically, Hermod, who wanted to destroy all magic. None of the students knew that part, though, that they'd been searching for its pieces as part of their ITF class. It was best to keep it that way.

"So I've noticed something," Addie said as she began to walk around the room. "Each piece, as well as its clues and what the students had to do to retrieve them—it's all related to an element."

"That sounds witchy." I followed her, though more slowly, pausing to study each one before moving on to the next. She'd shown them to me as each had been found, but we'd had no clue how they were supposed to become a weapon.

"Witchy or not, it's true." She ticked off her fingers as she continued. "Water, fire, earth, air, and even spirit are all represented here. That goes along with the tarot cards and how tarot symbolizes the elements. Plus, each team had to fight or somehow overcome at least one of the elements to claim their piece. Walking through walls of fire. Diving into pools or parting water. Destroying pieces of the earth—or being destroyed by the earth, in the case of the two fae who were iron-poisoned. Being attacked by magical tornados..."

"So what does it mean?" My eyes studied the symbols engraved into the ankh Elliana's team had found at the beginning of the semester. The icons represented various religions of the world, as well as others beyond this realm—symbols of spirit. "How do we use this information?"

Addie shrugged. "No idea," she said on a sigh. "The theory I'm leaning toward is that we have two sets of the five elements, if the staff is supposed to be linked to spirit, which I think it could be. I'm positive it's not a coincidence. I don't think the doors are, either."

"Doors?"

"Doors. Portals. Discovering new parts of campus. There was a lot of that going on, too."

"So the five elements and doors or portals. Hidden places." I looked up at her, tilting my head to the side as our eyes locked. Hers began to narrow, and I wondered if she was thinking the same thing I was. "Maybe the pieces somehow open portals?"

"Hmm ... Like the two elemental sets somehow make a portal ... Maybe one set on each side of the portal to create a connection?" She nodded as she considered this, then pulled her lips to the side, the stone in her nose catching the light with the movement. Her shoulders sagged. "Fuck. What if these aren't even the right pieces? Maybe they just open portals to find the actual ones."

I mentally went over the message delivered to Elsmed by Kialah over winter break.

"Entombed in stone, Difficult to find, Is the weapon of the gods, Broken in nine. Together with their staff, The nine become ten, And hope for our world Will be restored again," I recited aloud. I shook my head and lifted my arms, gesturing at all the pieces. "This *has* to be them. There's even a staff here."

She blew out a breath. "Yeah, okay. I hope you're right, because this whole thing has been stressful as fuck already. The students have been through hell again."

"For a good cause, though," I reminded her as I squatted to study a metal stick. Were there two staffs? There was a wooden one, found by Natalie Putnam and her team, and this one, found by Destiny Nelson and her team, if I remembered correctly.

"Right. There's just one problem, though."

I already knew and looked over at her with a raised brow. "That it's almost the end of the semester and there are only nine pieces here?"

"Yep." She popped the *p.* "That's where the bad news comes in. One of our teams is about to fail the class. They can't seem to find their piece. Are you still willing to help?"

"Of course! There's nothing I want more than to know we have a weapon that will destroy that asshole." I'd offered to help in the beginning, but because these had been class assignments for a grade, the Board wanted me to be available as a resource to all class members rather than assigned to a specific team. So far, none of the teams had needed me.

"There's one other, hopefully minor problem," Addie hedged with a grimace.

"What's that?"

She retrieved something out of the back pocket of her jeans, glanced at it briefly, then handed it over. "This is a copy. The team has the real card."

Taking it, I looked down at the creeptastically beautiful image of the tarot card. A hooded skull with glowing turquoise eyes stared back at me. Its dark red robes flowed from the hood down over a skeletal body, bony arms and hands sticking out of the wide sleeves, one gripping a golden cup at its side, the other lifted and holding a glowing orb that looked a lot like the moon. But there were no bony legs and feet. Rather, what looked like the bones of a fish's tail swept out of the bottom of the robes and curved upward. Not a fish, though. It was the skeleton of a mermaid or a siren, with the blues and greens of water creating the background and an expanse of light tan under the figure—the sandy floor of the sea or a lake. In the figure's center, just below the hand holding the orb, the robes appeared to be torn in several places almost all the way across the body, tattered ends drifting on the current. No bones were revealed by the rents in the cloth, as if they, too, had drifted away.

"You've got to be fucking kidding me," I whispered as I realized which tarot card this was: Death.

"Maybe it doesn't mean anything," Addie piped up, uncertainty filling her voice. "It could be coincidental and have nothing to do with your power over the dead."

I suppressed an internal shudder. My power regarding the dead was all wrong now, thanks to Hermod, and a danger to society. It'd almost gotten several students killed last semester when I awoke those zombies, which in turn enlivened the Valkyries.

This was her again. I just knew it was. Zandra messing with me once more. It had to be. Of all the teams that hadn't needed my help, the one that did just happened to have pulled the Death card?

"You really believe that?" I asked the witch.

Addie grimaced. "Uh ... no. Not really. In fact, I'm pretty sure it means all kinds of things, which is why I called you for help."

"They can't do it on their own?"

"Once you know who's on the team, I'm sure you can figure out the problem. Besides the fact that you're apparently needed for this one. The good news is, though, my cousin Gallad is on it. He's not supposed to be leading this mission, but he's kind of taken charge."

"Isn't he a future high priest of the Luna Coven?"

"Yes, and he'll take the Augustine seat on the Court. He and I are pretty much equals. Unfortunately, his team is...well, not the easiest to lead."

"Awesome," I muttered. "Fine. I don't really have a choice, do I? We need to find this last piece."

"Yes, if we want to save our school and our town and, well, the world. Gallad's already asked my advice about talking to you, but he's a little intimidated by you, I think. I'll let him know you're down with it."

Later that afternoon, after we were all done with classes for the day, I met Gallad's team, and when I saw them all gathered at a table in the Student Union, waiting for me, I silently snickered to myself. I totally understood now what Addie couldn't come out and say, being a professor and a Regent and all that. How Gallad had survived the semester this far was beyond me. Besides the Augustine male witch, there was Brooklyn, a water nymph, and Maria, a wolf shifter and a member of the Kasun pack. All three were local to Havenwood Falls, and I'd heard plenty of rumors from other locals—and seen a few instances myself—of the girls who made me think of the phrase, "On Wednesdays, we wear pink." Not exactly team players. And the fourth member was known as Tank, a big, burly vampire who was as sweet and loyal as he was strong, but not the sharpest cheese in the drawer.

"I hear you need a little help with The Hunt mission." I glanced at each of them as I took the seat next to Gallad.

Brooklyn's raven-black hair hung in curtains around her face as she stared at her phone, completely ignoring me. Maria couldn't look any more bored, twirling a lock of brown hair around her finger as she looked at me blankly. Tank, at least, grinned.

"Yeah, we just can't figure this out." He pushed the card across the table.

"You're the leader on this?"

He sighed. "Yeah. We're each supposed to take a turn, and I admittedly let the others lead on all the other missions. So I guess it's my turn."

That explained a lot, too. I picked up the card and flipped it over, reading the clue on the back.

Sisters in life
   Sisters in death
   Feed on the living
   Take their breath
   Sweet is the song
   To right the wrong

   To gain safe passage, repeat times three
     Once parted by death, a union made

In the wrong hands, pain will await
Tread carefully to avoid a mortal fate

"I've researched the hell out of Death—the card, the state of existence, whatever I could think of—and feed on the living and take their breath? That could be just about any supernatural creature in existence." Gallad groaned. "That one part to repeat three times sounds like a spell, but it's all just so ambiguous that I couldn't get a lock on any specific ideas. Tank and I searched everywhere, but we couldn't find anything on campus that seems relevant."

"We went to the cemetery, too," Tank added, "even though the artifact is supposed to be under the mountain. Thought we'd check anyway since there's, you know, death there. But we didn't find anything there either."

"And you two?" I asked the girls.

Brooklyn muttered something unintelligible without lifting her eyes from her screen.

"Same," Maria said. "No time with homework and everything."

"All the other teams managed to do it all," I said, trying not to snap at them. I had to remind myself that to them, it was just a grade, not the end of the world, as I knew it to be. Of course, it wasn't exactly fair that they'd dumped all the responsibility for the team's grade on Gallad and Tank. Biting back any further admonition, I flipped the card over and studied it again. "Hold on." I peered at it closer—at the cup in the skeletal hand. "No wonder you couldn't find anything." I tapped a finger on the symbol on the side of the cup: two fish chasing each other in a circle. "I know exactly where we can start the search."

CHAPTER 2

"*W*hat are we doing here again?" Maria yelled over the rushing water as the team gathered under the bridge.

I pointed at the stone spanning overhead. "Look familiar?"

Gallad, Maria, and Tank all craned their heads back. Brooklyn, however, crouched down on the bank, the water nymph drawn to the river.

"Ah," Gallad said, rubbing his dark, closely cropped beard.

"What's it even mean?" Maria asked.

"What even is it?" Tank tilted his head side to side.

"It's the same symbol on the cup on our card, you moron," Maria said. She dropped her hands on her hips and glared at me. "So? What do we—"

"Aye-eep!" Brooklyn squealed, jumping back from the water and shaking her hand, water droplets flying.

"What is it?" I asked.

Slowly, she moved forward and crouched again, gingerly trailing her fingertips into the water. "Something's in there."

"Like what?"

She shrugged. "A strange energy. This water is fed by the falls outside and goes to the campus lake, but I've never felt this power anywhere else."

She inhaled a breath, and as she exhaled, the river's movement slowed—enough that we could see under the surface. The other three gathered around us, crouching as we peered into the depths.

"Shit," I muttered. Bones. There were bones embedded in the riverbed. No, not just bones—skeletons. Full skeletons, like the one on the card, sans robe. I could see four of them from here.

"The power of death," Brooklyn whispered.

Well, now I knew why I'd been drawn down here all semester.

"Is one of those the artifact we're supposed to find?" Gallad asked. "They're just like the one on the card."

"Oh, yeah, I get it," Tank said, finally catching on. He began unlacing his shoes.

"What are you doing?" I asked.

Using his feet, he shucked his shoes off while at the same time pulling his shirt over his head, revealing an impressively muscular torso. "I'll go in and get it."

"Whoa. No. Hold on." I threw my hand out at him. "We don't even know what you're supposed to get."

"The skeleton, right?"

"There are four down there," Maria snapped.

He shrugged. "I'll get all four."

"No, just wait," I insisted. "I'm pretty sure it's not that easy."

We all stared at the water as the river's strength started building against Brooklyn's power.

"Let it go," I told her as I grabbed a handful of dreadlocks on the top of my head, as though they could help me focus.

"You're going to have to raise them, aren't you," Gallad said, not even making it a question.

My shoulders sank as I blew out a breath.

"Stand back," I ordered. "I don't know what will happen."

Three of them skittered almost halfway up the bank. I hadn't meant for them to go that far, but I guess I couldn't blame them. Last time I raised the dead, they'd had to fight for their lives against zombies and stone statues. Only Gallad stayed nearby, although he did take a few steps back.

Dropping to my knees, I closed my eyes and inhaled deeply. I held the air in my lungs, internally swearing up a storm because I really did not want to do this. Now that I acknowledged it, though, the power within me that I tried so hard to suppress awoke and stirred, then rushed toward the surface. Its strength became intoxicating, nearly overwhelming, as it zinged through my veins, making my whole body buzz with power. Trying to maintain control, I finally exhaled as I lifted my hands outward and released a slow trickle of the energy.

"Hold the water, Brooklyn," I ordered. "We don't need this power going downstream."

"I'll help," Gallad said from behind me, and the river immediately quieted.

Within moments, four skulls and collar bones popped through the surface, and as we watched, they quickly began to flesh out. As soon as their throats and lips formed, a hauntingly beautiful song filled the air.

"Fuck. Not mermaids," I muttered.

"Sirens," Gallad said. "I guess the Alversons aren't the only ones in Havenwood Falls."

"My bet is that these pre-date the Alversons by a few centuries —possibly longer," I said. "Long before any Old Families like the Alversons ever set eyes on these mountains."

Hair flowed out of the creatures' newly formed scalps—black, brown, red, and blond—at the same time their stunning facial features formed. Stunning except for the razor sharp, quite dangerous-looking teeth on full display as they sang. They began to move, bobbing in the water as they formed a circle, their song continuing, though all notes and melody, no words at all. My hands remained raised toward them, and I focused on maintaining control, allowing them to do their thing but prepared to pull back my magic if necessary. *These* zombies would remain under my power, unlike last time. As they moved faster, their hands lifted above the water, reaching upward toward the bridge. At the same time, a glow shone down on the whirlpool they were creating.

Shit. The last thing I wanted was any more students getting involved with yet more zombies. But when I looked up, there was nobody looking over the side of the bridge and shining a light down this way. No, it was the Pisces symbol glowing a bright blue in the stone of the bridge's underbelly. As its glow grew brighter, I looked back at the sirens and noticed the light had become like a spotlight, illuminating the circle of riverbed within the whirlpool, where the sand and pebbles were swirling, though the rest of the riverbed remained still.

The sirens' song grew louder and more urgent as they moved faster and faster. As each one came around to face my direction, they glared at me with lowered brows over glowing turquoise eyes—angry and expectant. What did they want? Faster and faster they went, that one spot in the middle of them swirling as though trying to reveal something.

"The spell!" I gasped. "Gallad, say the spell."

Gallad stepped up and recited the spell three times:

Once parted by death, a union made
In the wrong hands, pain will await
Tread carefully to avoid a mortal fate

As he finished the third repetition, the sand swirling in the center began to fall inward, creating a hole in the bed. As it widened, the sirens slowed, their song settling into more of a ballad. Now when they came around, their expressions were still expectant, but inviting.

"Our artifact must be in there," Gallad said.

"On it." Tank was suddenly by my side and once again undressing.

As one, the sirens rushed toward him, red bleeding into their turquoise eyes, their teeth lengthening into fangs. I strengthened my hold on them, keeping them back.

"You'd eat a vampire?" he asked. Their mouths stretched into wide grins as they continued singing, their only answer. His eyes glazing over, he shuffled forward, as though in a trance.

"Didn't expect that," I muttered. Maria grabbed him and pulled him back, holding his biceps tightly. Didn't expect that, either. "Gallad, you definitely don't have a chance. Brooklyn?"

"Hell no!" she screeched. "I'm not going anywhere near them."

"You're a water nymph. Practically like a sister to them. You can stay under longer than Maria, and I can't do it. I have to keep control over them."

She let out a few swear words before finally agreeing. As she waded in, their song silenced, and they stopped their circle dance, parting to let Brooklyn through, hissing as she passed them but not attacking. She looked back at me once before diving down, toward the opening.

As I watched her go, I began to reel in my power from the sirens to return them back to death. At once, the hole began closing up around Brooklyn, and the creatures spun on me, baring wicked teeth and hissing and growling even as the color leached from their hair and skin. The sounds they emitted became an angry rhythm as they glared at me with glowing red eyes.

"What the hell?" Maria gasped.

I immediately pushed my magic back into the sirens, but I'd already pissed them off. The hole widened around Brooklyn, but as soon as she slipped from sight, the river began to flow again, her power released from it. I could no longer see her, and the opening became nothing but a dark blur in the rapids.

The sirens' mouths stretched into those terrifying grins again, their eyes glowing brighter with hunger and bloodlust. Their heads bobbed and their shoulders shifted as they aligned with each other, creating a barrier between us and Brooklyn. A tail flicked up out of the water and slapped the surface. All four began singing again, a different tune now, and I thought they would come for me, but their eyes shifted to the two males. They swayed in unison as though they were one being, inching their way toward the bank. Their bodies came higher out of the water, exposing bare breasts hardly covered at all by their long hair.

His face still blank and his eyes empty, Tank broke free of Maria's hold and moved toward the water. Gallad's eyes glazed over, too, and he also stepped forward, humming under his breath to match the sirens' tune.

"Hey, no!" Maria yelled, trying to grab at both men, but they easily avoided her grasping fingers, their feet now at the water's edge.

They appeared to be completely unaware as the sirens' song grew louder, luring them in. Tails swished and flicked above the surface as their excitement grew.

"Hurry, Brooklyn," I murmured under my breath, keeping an eye on the dark smudge behind the beautifully dangerous creatures while trying to maintain control on my magic. Waiting to see any hint of the water nymph so I could release my power from the sirens and make them dead again.

Water splashed, and my gaze cut toward Tank. He was waist-deep, pushing against the current to reach the closest siren. The blonde reached out for him with webbed fingers that ended in long, needle-sharp nails. He smiled lazily as the raven-haired one swam his way, as well. The other two watched and sang as Gallad waded toward them.

"Gallad! Tank! Wake up!" Maria ran into the water after them.

Straining against my power, the sirens rushed toward the males. They were becoming stronger, fighting against my hold on them. If they broke through it, the battle of last semester would repeat all over again. I was a bit surprised the Valkyries hadn't already re-awoken, though I supposed this time, Zandra and the magic she'd imbued throughout campus wanted me to be doing this—as long as I could maintain control.

Maria reached out for Tank, but the blond siren curled her fingers around the shifter's wrist and yanked her closer. Maria's eyes glowed yellow, and fangs slid from her mouth as she began to shift, but the siren dove for her throat.

"No!" I yelled, and a bit of my power slipped from the loss of focus.

The siren's eyes locked on mine, and she lifted her head from Maria's throat, smiling to reveal blood-stained teeth. Maria's head lay back in the water, her mouth pulled in a lazy grin as crimson leaked from her throat and clouded the water around her even as the wound began to heal itself. The girl already boring her, the siren's attention returned to Tank. I didn't worry too much about the vampire, who could heal faster than the shifter. Gallad, on the other hand ... The brunette swam up behind him, singing softly as her hands pushed into his dark hair, cradling his head as the redhead trailed her fingers down his arm.

I tightened my hold on the undead water creatures before they went for his throat, but they strained harder against me. Every muscle in my body tensed, but this power was not my strong point. Ever since Hermod ruined it, I'd kept it locked away, never using it. The whole debacle before winter break started because I wasn't experienced enough to rein it in—I didn't know it intimately like I did my other abilities. I couldn't let it overwhelm me again.

Damn it, Brooklyn. Hurry the fuck up!

The redhead lifted Gallad's arm by the wrist, bringing it to her mouth at the same time the brunette curled in over his neck.

"No!" I shouted, rushing into the water.

At the same time, movement in my peripheral caught my eye, and then Brooklyn's head broke through the surface. I immediately yanked my power free, sucking the life out of the sirens. But it was too late. Even as the sirens' hair and flesh dissolved into the water and their bones sunk back toward the riverbed, Gallad's blood flowed quickly from his throat and wrist.

"No, no, no." I hurried for him while trying to push away the thought of having to tell Addie that I'd allowed her cousin to be killed.

One last piece of song burst from the water: *"Find our sister beyond the wall…"*

Then the song fell silent, only the rush of the river filling the space now, and Tank and Maria snapped out of their mind-hazes, lifting their heads from the water and looking around with bemusement.

"Get Gallad!" I shouted at them, since they were closer. Two pairs of eyes widened at the sight of their classmate floating in the crimson-stained water. They each hooked an arm under Gallad's shoulders and hauled him to the riverbank. Tank's fangs let out, and he bit into his own wrist before holding it over Gallad's mouth to heal him. Natural instinct, I supposed, though I was sure Gallad would have been okay without it.

He sat up, gasping for breath, as Brooklyn and I collapsed to the ground next to them.

"Did you get it?" I asked the water nymph.

"Well … I got something." She reached into the front pocket of her soaked hoodie and pulled out two handfuls of small bones.

"Finger bones?" I asked, bewildered.

"It's all there for a full hand and wrist," Brooklyn said. "It was embedded in the sand of a tiny cave. It was the only thing down there, so I figured it's what we're supposed to get."

"Why did you break it?" Tank asked as he leaned in for a better look.

Brooklyn rolled her eyes. "There's nothing left to hold them together, moron. No ligaments or anything. Don't you know how anatomy works?"

Gallad flicked his fingers at the bones while muttering something under his breath. The pieces floated upward and came together, forming a hand in the air.

"There. Now magic's holding them together," he said.

The last word had barely left his mouth when a feral snarl came from next to him. We all snapped our attention to Maria, whose eyes glowed yellow, fangs filling her mouth as claws shot out of her knuckles.

"What's...happening?" she asked around the teeth that were too large for her mouth. "I can't ... control it."

The bones fell to the ground in a heap, and Gallad groaned, his hands grabbing at his head. "I don't feel right, either."

The air tasted like burnt metal as shouts and curses floated down from the campus above.

"What the hell?" Brooklyn cried out. "My magic. I just felt it leave…"

I did, too. I felt *mine* leave. *Oh, no.*

"Hermod." I jumped to my feet and tried to take my raven form, but it was like slamming into an obsidian wall, no magic to make the transformation. So I gathered the bones and sprinted up the bank, for Halstein Hall and the administrative offices.

CHAPTER 3

Somewhere along the way, my power once again flowed through my veins. The others gasped behind me, and I looked over my shoulder to see Maria's face had returned to fully human, so it seemed magic was back to normal. For now, anyway. Had that been a strange fluke? Perhaps part of the ward on the bones? Several of the other artifacts had been cursed, our classmates nearly losing their lives or their minds after finding theirs. So it was possible. I liked that idea much better than the alternative—that Hermod was already here.

"You found it already?" Addie greeted me halfway up the steps to the administrative floor in Halstein, the team running up behind me.

"How'd you know?" I asked, patting my pockets where the bones rattled against each other in a macabre rhythm.

She opened her mouth to reply, but then looked over my shoulder and clamped it shut. She grinned at the others, though it didn't quite reach her eyes behind those dark-rimmed glasses. "Excellent job, team. You won't fail, after all. Remember—it's not a weakness to ask for help. You've completed The Hunt mission. Now go study for finals."

"Can you give any hint about ITF's final?" Gallad asked. "We have no idea what to even study."

"You'll know soon enough," Addie replied cryptically.

He narrowed his eyes, then shook his head before following the rest of his team. Addie turned, and together we went up the stairs and back to the room with the artifacts. I retrieved the bones from my pockets and laid them out on the table in the middle of the room. With a flick of Addie's fingers and a murmured spell, they arranged themselves into a skeletal hand.

"I figured you'd found it because weird shit started happening not five minutes before you came running up the stairs." She lifted the hand as one piece, as though invisible ligaments and tendons held the bones together. "These are real bones. Do you know from what?"

"A siren, I believe." I told her the full story.

"Their sister beyond the wall, huh?" Addie asked when I finished. "Maybe that's our first hint for where these all go once we put the weapon together."

"What weird shit happened?"

"First, my magic glitched for a few minutes. And not just mine. I was down at Coffee Haven, grabbing a Witch's Brew, when Bale almost burned down the whole student union when he sneezed a blast of fire, if not for Brielle Knight, who opened her mouth to yell a warning and vomited water over the flames. A bunch of shifters were losing control, too. I ran back up here as smoke poured off my own skin. I've never shifted fully—my witch genes overpower my hellhound ones—but I was beginning to panic that I just might do that. By the time I got back up here, I was fine, though. For the most part—" She cut herself off, rolling her shoulders and her neck. "Anyway, I found this."

She dropped the skeleton hand and stepped sideways to the leatherbound book on the table. It was spread open to a page of writing.

"This is new." She tapped a finger on the text.

Two by two
  Four from eight
  Like attracts like
  To find its mate.

Point by point

Plus three and a ring
Can be found on the gift
Of the wee folk of Spring.

Ten become six
Six become one
With a staff in the heart
Of the moon and the sun.

With all in place
You have a shield
And a twist and a thrust
For a weapon to yield.

"Awesome. We have to do fucking *math* now?" I muttered.

Addie snorted. "It'd be nice if not everything had to be a damn riddle, wouldn't it? I'm not liking this Kialah chick at the moment."

I suppressed my own snort. If she only knew who Kialah really was—pure hatred would be a more appropriate feeling.

Pressing my fingers to my temples, I rubbed circles as I tried to make sense of the new clue. "Can I sleep on it? That magic zap has me drained."

"Same. I need to get to town and meet with the Luna Coven in twenty minutes anyway. I'll let you know if we come up with any ideas, though."

Two days passed, and it was the Sunday before finals week when I heard from Addie again. I sat on my bed, headphones on with music blaring when the piece of paper came out of nowhere and drifted down before me. I snatched it from the air.

Tried to text. Wasn't going through. Need your help ASAP! ~ *Addie*

When I pulled the headphones off, all kinds of noise out in the halls bombarded me. Pounding on doors, people yelling at each other... I grabbed my phone, which showed no incoming messages, and shoved my feet into my Doc Martens before heading out.

"Don't let your door—" Linnie's shout was cut off by the snick of my door. "Close," she finished lamely. "You might not be able to get back in."

She flashed her wrist at me, where the school's tattoo should have been dark and obvious, but it was faded, almost unnoticeable. I looked down at my own, also barely legible.

"They're not opening the doors," Molly, another belladonna vampire, said from my other side. "Like the magic's stopped working."

"It's not the only magic that's not working right," Winter, a witch, piped in, wiping a bright green smudge of slime across her cheek as she came out into the hallway. What looked like neon pink ashes had settled in her hair. "A spell I do every day just exploded in my face! I just wanted some damn tea."

Shit. This wasn't good. My own power stirred in my blood, but at least I felt it, unlike the other day. What was going on now?

I left Muninn's residents to debate that answer and rushed over to Halstein Hall, where I hoped I'd get real answers. Addie waited at the top of the stairs.

"Muninn is freaking out," I said as I jogged up to her. "Something's wrong over there."

"It's not just Muninn. The Regents are meeting now and wanted you there."

We hurried to the conference room, where about half of the Board sat around the wooden table. The constant trickle of water on the far wall couldn't be heard as they all talked over each other. They fell silent and turned to us when we entered, their expressions expectant at first as they watched the door behind us, but eventually falling when nobody followed us in.

"We'll have to start without the others," Saundra eventually said. "They can't get into campus," she added as an explanation. Her gaze locked with Addie's, and the younger Beaumont witch frowned. "The portals aren't working properly. Nothing magical seems to be working properly." All eyes now turned on me. "Is this Hermod? Is he here already?"

I struggled to swallow, my mouth suddenly feeling as though

I'd inhaled the Sahara Desert. But after consideration, I shook my head. "I don't think so. I think I would feel him—my power would. But he could be testing us. Our strengths and weaknesses."

Saundra scowled. "Well, our biggest strength doesn't seem to be passing his tests. Our wards over Havenwood Falls and the entire canyon are failing."

"I knew I felt something," Addie growled under her breath.

"Failing?" I said, fear shooting through my veins. "The wards are *failing*?"

This wasn't good. The wards around Havenwood Falls and the surrounding area were everything. They kept the residents inside safe from intruders. They kept the secrets of the supernatural from leaking out into the human world. These wards were what prevented another massacre like the one of the 1870s from happening again.

"They're not completely down," Saundra said. "Yet."

Elsmed banged his fist on the table, startling me. "We have to put this weapon together *now*. There's no more time to waste." He gestured at Addie. "Tell us about this new clue."

She set the book on the table, already open to the page we'd been reading the other day.

"I think I have part of it figured out," she began. She started by telling them what she'd told me already—about the elements and the doors. "Before, I thought we had two sets of elements that somehow worked together. But I think that theory's wrong." She pointed to the first verse. "I think that *two by two* and *like attracts like* parts mean the two pieces for each element go together somehow."

"Yes!" I blurted. "Two halves make one. That would make eight of the pieces become four—four from eight."

"Exactly." She nodded enthusiastically.

"And the rest?" Elsmed demanded. "There are ten pieces, not eight."

She made a face, not having an answer to that, and he frowned in return, but before either could say anything, Gabriel Doyle, the vampire, strode into the room with two other Regents right behind him.

"The portals are working?" Addie asked him.

"Intermittently. Let's figure this out before it gets worse."

We went over the entire clue, everyone tossing out ideas but none sticking completely except for Addie's new hypothesis. After hours of arguing and theorizing, Gabriel shoved a hand through his dark hair.

"Let's start with the pieces," he said. "Make sure we're on the right track there."

"I have an idea." I hurried out of the room. It seemed so obvious now. I returned a minute later holding the skeleton hand and the Pearl of Wisdom Marina's team had found. "These are the two water pieces. They were both on the Death card one of the teams had pulled. Well, the skeleton definitely was, and I think the pearl ...well, I'll show you." I dropped the pearl in the bony palm, and its glow immediately brightened, while the energy pulsing off of the pair intensified. Together, they closely resembled the image on the card, of the siren skeleton holding the moon.

A melody drifted through the room, bouncing off the stone walls—the same song of the sirens.

"Find our sister beyond the wall," the voices sang on the last few notes.

The room fell silent, and the pearl rolled out of the hand and dropped to the floor. We all stared at it expectantly for a long moment before looking at each other when nothing else happened.

"It's still a good theory," Saundra said. "Perhaps they all need to be joined before we know more? Maybe the others have something to say, too."

She, Addie, and I retrieved the other pieces, keeping them at arms' length from each other until we returned to the conference room because of that energy pulsing off of all of them. But the precaution hadn't been necessary. The rest of the pieces didn't pair up as obviously as the hand and the pearl had.

"We've wasted enough of our time here. The ITF class now has a new final exam," Gabriel declared.

Elsmed nodded. "I also have an idea regarding the bit about the wee folk. Though not all of us fae are *wee*, we've often been called that in the homelands. And we have one in town who is, indeed, wee."

"Siobhan," Saundra said, and he nodded in reply. Siobhan

McFeeney, also known as Teeny Weeny, Madame Tahini, and as of this semester, Professor. I didn't know what they had in mind, but hoped they were right, whatever it was. If the failing magic was any indication, we were quickly running out of time.

Further plans were made before we all finally left. It was already dinnertime, which meant a whole afternoon of studying was gone. I wasn't even in the ITF class, but it just might be the only final I could possibly pass.

CHAPTER 4

$\mathcal{I}$t was impossible to slip into a classroom full of supernaturals unnoticed. Eyebrows were raised and questions were murmured when I entered the room the next morning. I'd been standing outside the door, waiting as Addie instructed the ITF class about their final exam, explaining how the artifacts they'd found matched up by element and then pairing off the teams accordingly. By the time I walked in, they were already gathered around five large tables, chattering away.

"Guys, can I have your attention?" she asked. Everyone looked up at her. "As I explained before you started this final exam, time is critical. We've all experienced inconsistencies with our magic and on campus. Rhian has been recruited by the Regents to help."

She went on to explain that I wouldn't be part of any specific ITF team, only providing support when needed. After she finished, I glanced around the classroom, looking for the team that seemed to need the most help. They all looked equally clueless, so I went to the closest table, which had the two earth element pieces—a tear-shaped gemstone found by Eryx's team and an iron relic unearthed by Paisley's that consisted of three medallions melded together, forming an engraved pentagram in the center.

Nowadays, the symbol of three entwined circles was most commonly known as trinity rings, but the icon had many names like the Celtic Knot or Triquetera. Borromean Rings was another.

Throughout time, among various civilizations, cultures and religions, this joining of three circles had always been powerful.

In my lifetime, I'd seen multiple variations of it, but never with a pentagram in the middle. How did it tie into the other earth artifact? I couldn't see how yet, and it bothered me more than I liked to admit.

The crystal that Eryx currently held in the palm of his hand with deference called to me like the sirens had called to the guys under the bridge, and it wasn't because it was a shiny object that sparked my curiosity, making me want to claim it for my own. I wasn't some common raven who liked collecting baubles as treasure. No, I sensed death, and that was why my stomach felt like a heavy stone had lodged itself there. What was it with the Sun & Moon Academy and the ever-present threat to mortality?

"Catch me up—what's the deal with your artifact?" I asked Eryx, his twin brother Calix also looking up at me. Their similarities were striking.

Eryx set the crystal down and wiped his hands on his jeans. "Well, it basically held the spirits of several women who claimed to be victims of the gods and their heartless antics."

He glanced over to his brother, and something unspoken passed between them. I'd heard the rumor that their mother had been none other than Medusa, herself. If there was ever a woman who'd suffered at the hands of a deity, it was her.

"Yep, the poor women were caught by the cruel and deceptive webs of the gods to be used and discarded as playthings." Felicia spoke up, using air quotes. "That's what the one spirit said when they were freed from the crystal. She also stated that it will be their tears for vengeance and justice that will fuel the power remaining in the crystal."

"Interesting," I murmured as I eyed the innocuous looking crystal with renewed respect. With that kind of power, it wasn't an item to be trifled with. "Any luck connecting it with the other piece?"

"We thought it would be easy because see this notch here?" Eryx pointed at a groove carved out of the center of the pentagram, which also happened to be the center of the overlapping circles. "It's the exact shape of the crystal." He traced the furrow lightly with the tip of his finger and let out a baffled sigh. "Well, I placed our piece in that spot, and it fit perfectly, but nothing happened." To prove his point, he dropped the crystal where he'd just touched, peering up at me. "See?"

Addie and I had tried the same thing in the conference room with the Board, and like then, nothing happened now. The crystal rolled off the iron rings and landed on the table with a thud.

Eryx dragged his fingers through his curls, frustrated. "Nothing's ever easy."

"That's for damn sure," Vanna agreed.

"I was monitoring the energy, and there was zero change," Tempest added, leaning forward on her elbows. "Do you have any suggestions, Rhian? We're running out of ideas."

"Maybe? Let me see."

Calix stood, flashing me a shy smile as he gave me his seat. I returned the smile and sat between Amaruq and Paisley, pulling the two artifacts toward me. Paisley jumped from her seat, and she and Timber shuffled several feet back, which was smart, considering the last time they came in contact with the relic, they almost died. The pieces still gave off that low hum of energy, the vibration traveling through my fingers and up my arms. The iron piece glowed like it was radioactive, generating the slightest presence of heat.

"I tried a binding spell, thinking that would forge a connection between them," Tempest said. She absentmindedly plucked out the hair stick that she'd stuck in her high ponytail. She then twirled the stick between her fingers like it would somehow help her think clearer—the clear quartz attached at the end pulsing. "Maybe there's another piece missing or we need to glue the stone to the iron?" she added.

Amaruq interrupted quickly with a barked laugh. "That or try good old-fashioned duct tape. I'm not opposed to being creative, eh?"

"That's a modern solution for something older than most of us in this room." I picked up the stone, which was heavy, like it was made of lead, and set it in the notch. As it had every other time, it fit perfectly but remained lifeless. Tempest leaned forward and brushed her finger along the opposite side of the disk from where I held it, and the stone pulsed briefly. A jolt shot through me, causing me to recoil. She gasped and jerked her hand away.

That captured everybody's full attention, and the group instantly quieted.

"What just happened?" Amaruq demanded, moving closer. He inhaled the air above the group. "Do you smell that? It's like after a bolt of lightning strikes." Still sniffing, he lowered his head to the table, following the scent, his inner wolf taking the lead. The moment he touched the iron, the stone pulsed again. I placed my fingers back on the artifact, intrigued by the sudden activity but also puzzled by it.

"It's getting warmer," Amaruq said, placing his entire palm on the bottom left circle, covering one of the pentagram points. He must have sensed the same heat I had, and excitement began to bubble amongst the group. I wasn't the only one who realized we were on the verge of uncovering something important.

"It is?" Vanna perked up and placed her hand opposite of his, over the bottom right point of the pentagram. The moment she made contact with the iron, the stone lit up brighter than ever, and the pulse sounded like a beat from a bass drum.

Shit. That was it. I knew how to make it work!

"Don't move," I shouted and looked across the table at Felicia. She was a psychic and communicated with the dead. "Spirit."

As each second passed, I became more and more certain I'd figured it out.

"Huh? Where?" She whipped about, scanning the room for a ghost.

"Oh, my goddess, now I get it!" Tempest bounced in her chair. "I'm water." She practically slammed her hand down on the pentagram point facing her. The moment she touched the iron, the energy increased significantly and actually made my teeth ache. "Felicia, you represent spirit, the last element. Vanna is fire, Amaruq is earth, and Rhian is air."

"Um, okay." Felicia made a face that scrunched up her freckle-covered nose before hesitantly placing her hand on the top point of the pentagram. The moment she did, there was a bright flash of light and a pulse resonated like a bomb going off. We all flew backward, stunned by the artifacts' combined power. A groan escaped my lips as I landed on top of Calix, his hands instantly gripping my hips as if to keep me from toppling over.

Realizing our compromising position, he quickly released his hold and ran a hand up my back, while his other hand tucked a stray braid behind my ear. My body betrayed me, and it took everything I had not to react to his touch.

"Are you all right, goddess?" he asked gently. As he peered into my face, I hoped he wouldn't detect the blush I felt creeping across my cheeks.

"Yes, thank you," I muttered, trying to regain some sense of decorum. I didn't have time for flirting with gorgeous young men. I met his brown eyes before quickly looking away and scrambling to my feet, unable to ignore the muscles I felt underneath his tight black T-shirt.

Damn. How long had it been since I'd taken pleasure in the arms of another? Judging by the way my throat felt dry like sandpaper, too long.

"Is everyone okay?" Paisley called out as Timber helped her to her feet. Her hair was a riot of pinks, purples and blues—a recent glamour change she'd made to celebrate Spring.

"I'm getting used to almost dying," Amaruq joked and ran his hand through his dark hair. Everyone chuckled.

That's when I noticed all of the other teams had stopped what they were doing and gathered around our group.

"Holy faeries, you guys have to look at this!" Paisley shouted, pointing at the artifacts on the table. They were now completely joined, the iron molded around the stone. Any rust that had previously clung to the ancient iron was gone, and the metal gleamed as if newly forged. The stone shone from within.

"Well done, earth teams." Addie stepped through the small crowd that had gathered and picked up the artifact. "One piece of the puzzle is complete."

But we were far from done.

The earth teams shouted in celebration before rushing out of the classroom, free for a while now that they'd aced their ITF exam. I waited for the other teams to settle down and get back to work. Closest to me, the fire group gathered around their table, but seemed completely unconcerned about their final exam.

Infiniti had her arms crossed and a worried look on her face, as if she wanted nothing to do with the metal stick and the small bowl. Cole was texting someone on his phone, while Cat and D sat close together, legs touching, eyes locked, as if they had no cares in the world.

From the other fire team, Amelia pushed her thick, black curls away from her forehead and exhaled loudly. Dark shadows still hung heavily under her eyes; she must not have been sleeping well yet. She wasn't even looking at the two pieces. Matthew held his jaw tightly, his hand resting on the back of Amelia's chair.

"How is this supposed to work?" Craig growled, his narrowed eyes glancing to Destiny.

"How would I know?" she bit back. "This is supposed to be teamwork, right?"

"Um, hey," I interrupted before tempers flared higher. "Can I help?"

Cole put his phone down quickly, and Fin offered me a sheepish smile. Cat scooted away from D.

"Oh, hey, Rhian," she said in her thick-laced Spanish accent. "We're just, um, observing the objects."

"Observing?" Skepticism edged my tone. They all looked at each other guiltily. "The longer you *observe*, the longer you'll be sitting in this room, you know."

"Well, ándale. Let's do this thing," Cat said impatiently.

She, D, and Cole reached for the bowl at the same time, their hands colliding mid-air. Cat kept hers held out and eyed the guys until they dropped theirs. Fin muttered something about them always doing that while Cat lifted the small bowl, eyeing it like a prized object.

At the same time, Destiny grabbed the stick. No one else from her team moved. "I guess these need to go together somehow."

"Maybe we touch them," Cat suggested to Destiny.

The others agreed that was a good idea, and everyone watched as Cat and Destiny moved the pieces around, seeing if they somehow went together. Impatience crackled through my veins as they tried every position and every angle, as if the pieces would snap and click. As if we hadn't already tried that. I knew it wasn't going to be easy, but because they didn't know what I did, I had to give them a chance, in case they figured out something we'd missed, like the earth teams had done only moments earlier.

"This is stupid," Cole whispered under his breath.

Craig snorted. "Sure is."

"*Claro que sí*," Cat agreed, flipping her long ponytail. "But we have to keep trying."

Fin mentioned needing a good grade in the class, pointing at different ways the objects might be connected, but nothing was working.

"Ladies," D suggested calmly to Cat and Destiny, "let's start at the beginning."

"Okay, the beginning. Well, this is clearly a candlestick," Amelia announced, touching the cool metal of the stick. "Candle … fire… You know, since we have the fire objects? Obviously."

"Okay, but it has to join with the bowl, right?" Cat kept her own piece in one hand while reaching for the stick Destiny held. "May I?"

"Sure." Destiny watched Cat as she took the stick and held the objects side by side, as if eyeing them for inspiration.

"How can they join?" D moved in closer, studying the pieces. "There are no grooves or notches or anything. Both pieces are perfectly smooth."

"It has to go in here somehow." Cat picked up the stick and placed it inside the bowl. "If it's a candlestick like you think, then a bowl is meant to catch the fire? Or hold the fire? Or something like that?"

Cole slammed his hands on the table. "That's it. Fire! We need fire."

D nodded and rubbed his hands together. "Okay, then. Fire in the hole. Do your thing, Cole."

Cat eyed D. "Fire right here?" And then Cat leaned in and lowered her voice. "What if there's an accident? Especially with how messed up magic has been lately?" She eyed Fin, D, and Cole in turn. "Don't forget we were in big trouble when we almost killed that gnome with the whole lightning thing, so I don't know if fire right here is a good idea."

I almost interrupted them to tell them we had already tried fire, but I wanted to see if they could produce a different result.

"Let's try it and see what happens." Craig lunged forward and grabbed the pieces in both hands. He took a deep breath, as if he were some kind of heroic character in a comic book. "Set them on fire."

"¿Qué?" Cat asked. "You want to set it on fire...in your hands?"

"Yeah, I'm a dragon shifter," he explained. "Fire doesn't burn me. I can take it." And then he looked at the others. "If that's okay with everyone."

Destiny shrugged and eyed Cat. They exchanged a similar "why not" look, then said at the same time, "Okay."

"I know you can breathe on that thing, but mind if I join the fun?" Cole asked with a grin. "Since I'm connected to fire, I can totally light that up."

"Fine with me," Craig nodded.

Fin shot up from her chair and stood back from the table while Cole moved his fingers together. He snapped, but instead of fire shooting out, a stream of water sprayed Craig in the eye.

"Uh, wrong element, dude," Craig said, wiping his face.

"What the shit?" Cole asked, staring at his hands.

"Messed up magic," Cat uttered in a low voice. "I knew it."

Cole's brows stitched together while a look of determination spread across his face. "Let me try that again." He snapped his fingers once more but again only water came out. "Son of a bitch."

"Let me give it a go." Craig blew out, letting loose a stream of fire. The flame intensified until it enveloped his hands and both objects.

Everyone, including me, stared in amazement as the smooth metal pieces flared to life and seemed to move on their own, molding and melding so that the edges were fluid, like someone creating glass out of liquid sand and a torch. Craig kept his fire streaming as the stick and the bowl shifted, joining together and forming into a new piece. A low humming sound emitted from the object.

"Well, look at that," Cole said.

After extinguishing the blaze, Craig set the new singular piece on the table, smiling with satisfaction.

"Is that a goblet?" Destiny eyed the object.

"Wow," Cat murmured. "It is."

Fin shifted closer, peering over Cat's shoulder in amazement.

"Huh," Amelia huffed, sitting back in her seat, but still keeping her distance.

"Guess it wasn't a candlestick after all." Matthew shrugged.

"Or a bowl," D added, rubbing his chin while studying their handiwork.

I admired the new object, a simple yet elegant chalice, while considering why Craig's fire worked and not Addie's. And that's when it hit me—the objects needed dragon fire, not hellfire. *Interesting.*

"Good work, guys," Addie said, coming up to join us and plucking the piece off the table. A vibration of energy pulsed in the air, and everyone stopped and stared at Addie. We exchanged a look. The objects were definitely communicating.

Like the earth teams before them, the fire group hurried out of the room, talking excitedly about being done with WTF.

Then a shout came from across the room. "What the fuck was that?"

CHAPTER 5

I whipped my head around at the sudden outburst. I caught the school's only shapeshifter with his hands in his hair, face ashen.

"Problems, Dylan?" I moved toward the table where he, Shay, and Winter were joined by Mystic, Malyki, Bryony, Gable, and Vidar.

"How are we supposed to fuse these pieces together?" he demanded. "I'm tired of getting whiplash every time we try something new. You got any ideas?"

I bit my lip to suppress a chuckle at Dylan's over-dramatic reaction, emphasized by how his hair shot out in various directions from all the pulling he'd obviously been doing.

"What have you got?" I asked.

"An orange gemstone and a copper bird. Got any magic tricks we don't know about?" Dylan raised a brow.

"I'm not sure," I pondered. "Your element is—"

"Air," Mystic chimed in, eyeing me curiously. Her soul mate sat close enough for their legs to press together, a quiet strength in both of their eyes. These two held power, and a lot of it.

Dylan huffed. "On the Devil's card, this gemstone represented his eyes. It makes sense that we should put the stone in the bird's eye too."

"Maybe it matters more *which* eye we put it in?" Winter

offered, making it sound like they'd been concentrating on one socket. Taking the stone in one hand, Winter lifted the bird with the other, and delicately placed the gem in the right eye.

They all held their breath, just as the gem slid into the gap and dropped inside the bird's body, unattached.

"Shit," Winter uttered.

"Well, I guess that answers that question," Shay said, rubbing her temples. "Maybe it's the crazy magic in the air. You can feel how unstable it is in here."

"You mean that's why this isn't working? Like the magic in the two pieces is being suppressed by something?" Dylan frowned.

I watched as Winter shook the bird with frustration, waiting for the gem to pop out like a coin in a piggy bank. I inwardly cringed, hoping the stone wouldn't shatter into pieces. Finesse seemed to be disappearing as frustrations took over.

"Okay, okay!" Mystic interrupted, snatching the bird out of Winter's hands, and holding it close to her chest.

I didn't blame her. According to Addie, that bird meant much more to Mystic and Malyki than anyone knew.

"Do you have any ideas, Mystic?" I asked.

She shook her head slowly, chewing on her bottom lip as she gingerly set the artifact back on the table. Glancing over at Malyki in some unspoken call for help, Mystic hovered her fingers lightly over the copper bird.

"I wish I knew the answers to this puzzle. It feels—" She tilted her head, and a deep crease angled across her forehead. "It's on the tip of my tongue. My intuition whispers not to overthink this, that the solution may be a simple one, but . . ." Her words trailed off. Malyki wrapped his arm around her shoulder and pulled her in.

"We'll figure it out," Vidar said, wearing an optimistic expression and smile. "I think Mystic's right. Don't overthink it. Listen to what our gut is telling us."

Gable snorted. "My gut's saying I need more snacks if I have to sit here much longer."

He let out a long and heavy sigh before plonking forward onto the table, his head resting on his arms.

Like the faintest of breezes on a stifling hot day, I felt a tiny spark of magic. I wasn't alone in feeling it either. Malkyi and Bryony bolted up in their seats, their eyes wide with surprise.

"Did you feel that?" Bryony exclaimed, excitement spilling out as she looked at each member of her group. "It was kind of a blink-and-you'll-miss-it sort of thing, but it was there."

We all stared down at the artifacts to see if anything had changed.

Nothing.

"Sure you didn't imagine it?" Dylan asked. "I didn't feel a thing. Anyone else?"

"I felt it. A magical spark." I nodded toward Malyki. "And I'm pretty sure you did as well. So that's three people. I'd say that's enough proof to show it wasn't a coincidence."

"What did you do, Gable?" Malyki asked, leaning forward in his chair, eyes locked with his fellow team mate. "Other than grumbling about being hungry. Any thoughts?"

An almost palpable anticipation hung in the air as everyone sat up a little straighter.

Gable cringed. "Um, that I'd pretty much sell my soul for a pizza right now." He had the grace enough to look ashamed as everyone else, me included, groaned at his confession. "Hey, you can mock me all you want. Tell me if I didn't set a twelve-inch pepperoni, sausage, jalapeno, and olive pizza in front of you with extra cheese and red pepper flakes, that you wouldn't be drooling and begging for a slice!"

"I pity your digestion system, dude," Shay quipped.

One by one, everyone let out a frustrated sigh or groan. Magic flared again, and this time, it jiggled the jewel against the top of the table, roughly jutting it an inch or two closer to the copper bird.

Holy shit.

Something had made the damn thing move!

"Do it again!" Mystic ordered. When Dylan groaned, his face scrunched with confusion, she shook her head and pointed toward the relics. "Exhale into the air, as big as you can."

There was no need to ask again. As one, we all leaned forward and blew. The jewel moved faster this time as the copper bird jerked—like two polar opposites desperate to be reunited.

Of course! The fire pieces had needed fire. The pentagram on the earth team was connected to the elements. I should have known.

Before I could open my mouth, though, Mystic began laughing and clapping her hands. "Why didn't we see this sooner? We're dealing with the elements, and what better representation of air than the very breath we breathe?"

To prove her point, she blew directly on the jewel.

"Yes!" Bryony shouted in excitement and jumped to her feet, joining Mystic. As each person stood and blew, I watched as the jewel inched up the bird until it nestled in its rightful spot.

"Our breath is needed to fuse the pieces together," I said. "Our breath and intention. Focus all your energy and magic into each exhalation—willing the jewel to meld with the copper and become whole."

As we did, the copper began to heat, the parts that touched the jewel bubbling slightly to anchor the stone in place. Then with a soft chink, the process was complete, a strong energy wafting off it. We had our relic for Addie.

"I don't know about you, but I think we've all earned a slice of pizza," Gable bragged. "Extra olives for me, considering I was the genius who figured it out."

Winter snorted, and her lips parted to correct him. Leaving them to celebrate, I took that as my cue to move on to the next group.

The only two teams who hadn't figured their pieces out were the water and spirit teams. I started for the spirit table, expecting that one to be the hardest and needing the most help. I still believed we'd had the water objects right yesterday with the Board, and I thought the team members would be able to figure it out. The ankh and the staff, however—I just wasn't sure about those. As I headed toward the table where Natalie, Caleb, Elliana, Sadie, and the rest of their teams were gathered, shouts rose from the other group. I hurried over there.

"Marina, love," Cas cooed as the water witch clawed at his raised arm, his fist lifted high above his head. "Please be reasonable. You know what happened last time."

"I promise ... I won't ... let it," she panted, the edge in her words betraying the lie. "Just please—I just want to hold it one more time."

"Cas, over here," Gallad said, reaching for the gryphon's raised hand.

"Hell, no!" Roxy McCabe snapped. "You're a witch, too. You're going to end up like her. Give it to me, Cas. Let the shifters over here handle it."

She was quite a bit shorter than the men, so instead of trying to grab for it, she simply held her hand out. Cas stretched out of Marina's reach to drop the Pearl of Wisdom into Roxy's palm, Marina's eyes glowing greedily as she watched it. I half expected her to start whispering, "My precioussss," but she crossed her arms over her chest and stepped back.

"So what the hell are we missing?" Maria asked as Roxy rested the pearl between two bones of the skeleton hand. The song drifted from it again, more of a whisper now, though, only faintly heard by those of us nearby. As though it were losing power. Shit. What did that mean? "It can't be more obvious that the pearl goes here. It's just like on our card. Are you sure it's supposed to do anything else besides sing?"

All eyes turned toward me.

"I'm pretty sure it should at least stay put," I said. "The other three teams found a way for their objects to fuse together."

"Maybe we need to add water," Gallad suggested. "I saw the fire teams use flames on theirs, and it worked."

"And blowing on their artifacts worked for the air group," I said with a nod. "Brooklyn?"

The raven-haired girl had been glued to her phone again, but finally looked up. She blew out a sigh and stood. "Fine. Whatever I need to do to be done with this already."

"I'll help," Marina chimed in, stepping back up to the table. Cas eyed her warily, concern filling his face. She gave him a small smile. "I'll be fine. I promise. I also just want to be done with this."

We all watched as the girls worked together, Marina chanting a spell as Brooklyn called on her own powers. After what felt like a long, drawn-out moment, water sprinkled from their fingers over the pearl and the bones.

Still nothing happened.

709

"I have an idea." The words came as a quiet tinkling from the opposite side of the table. Gallad and Tank parted to reveal Kalani, the air nymph, behind them. She shifted forward, her body even slighter than my own thin frame. Her light blue eyes fell on me. "Maybe the bones also need the right kind of magic."

Several people cursed under their breaths. Including me. Once again, all of their gazes turned my way.

"It makes sense," Gallad said.

"You controlled it last time," Maria added, and I lifted a brow.

"Gallad almost died," I reminded them.

"But I didn't." The male witch cocked his head. "You can do it. Just a tiny bit of your power."

I groaned. "Fuck. Fine. It's just a hand, right? How much damage can just a hand do?"

"Well. . . it could strangle us," Tank piped in. "Throw things. Poke its bony fingers through our eyeballs and into our brains—"

Maria punched his arm.

"Not helping," she growled.

I feared he could be right, though. With magic acting all wonky, a tiny push of my power could easily become a blast, not only strong enough to reanimate the hand but all of those sirens in the river—and who knew what else was buried under this mountain. And let's not even consider the fact that the cemetery was nearby ...

"Just do it already," Brooklyn groaned.

"Okay, okay." I sucked in a deep breath while rubbing my hands together. "Try the water again at the same time, in case they need both."

Closing my eyes, I drew on that power I hated so much, pulling it through my veins, then opened up a pinhole-sized outlet to allow the tiniest bit to seep out. I directed it toward the bones at the same time more water droplets fell on the pearl. The hum of the sirens floated on the air around us, quiet as a whisper at first but growing louder.

"Find our sister beyond the wall ..." they wailed as one.

Then their tune fell silent, and noticing a hiss for the first time, I leaned in toward the two objects on the table. So did everyone else. We watched closely as the water sizzled on the pearl and dripped down the sides. When it hit the skeleton, thin tendrils of smoke rose, and the bones twitched … jumped … the fingers curled upward. The smoke thickened as the bones drew on my power. I cut it off with a gasp, jumping backward. Almost instantly, the smoke cleared, revealing the bony hand perfectly cupping the brightly glowing pearl.

Tank's hand darted out, and he poked a bone, then the pearl. They moved as one. Gallad picked it up and tipped it over. The pearl remained lodged within the cage of the finger bones.

"¡Ay chingados!" Marina gasped. "I think we did it."

I could only nod, internally fuming at this whole situation. Zandra … Kialah … whatever the fuck name and face she went by the next time I saw her … I was going to poke my own fingers through her eyeballs and into her brain. Not once. Not twice. But three times now she'd forced me to use that power she knew I despised. The power that had been changed by Hermod himself. And I was sure it was no coincidence.

Addie came over to congratulate the teams while I settled my mood before heading over to the only group that remained.

They'd been watching us, and as I walked over to them, they all turned to stare dejectedly at the ankh and staff lying on the table.

"It's hopeless," Natalie groaned, flicking her hand toward the pieces. "Elliana's already tried her angel power, and then Torent even tried some demon magic—the closest things we could think of to the spirit element—but neither worked like it did for fire and water."

I frowned. That was going to be my suggestion, the only real one I had for this pairing.

"Let me see the ankh?" I said, thinking I needed to study the symbols etched into it once again. I must have missed something important about them.

As Sadie reached for it, the floor trembled under our feet. It was a brief shake, at first, forcing all of us to tense. But then it really started shaking, and we all grabbed the table to brace ourselves.

Just as that fucking gong went off again.

711

CHAPTER 6

"That can't be good," Torent muttered when it fell silent, while Elliana swore up a storm, her hands frosting over as her anger leaked into her powers.

Bewilderment with a touch of fear filled everyone's eyes. I couldn't blame them. Those gongs were probably a PTSD trigger for half of the student body, after last semester. Luckily, there had been only this term, on the first night we'd returned to campus. We'd chalked it up to being a "welcome," especially as time wore on and the campus had remained silent in that regard. Until now.

"What does it mean?" Mallorie asked.

The only answer came as a growl—from where Caleb had been standing only a second ago. Now there was only a huge-ass bear. Next to him, where Slaine has been, stood a horse with a shiny black coat. Just like that—no bones cracking and twisting or muscles ripping. They were human one moment and in their animal forms the next.

"Holy fuck!" Natalie gasped, her nails shredding the flesh of her own arms. A bluish light zapped out of her fingertips. "I can't … control my magic."

Caleb the bear growled again, and I couldn't tell if it was from concern—or as a threat. Slaine reared back, kicking powerful legs in the air, only inches from Mallorie's head. Torent jumped in front of her, demon fire lighting up his hands and arms. Min's fangs let fully out, sliding over his bottom lip, and his tongue swept out as he glared at Sadie with bloodlust glowing in his eyes.

The floor trembled again, then a huge piece of ceiling fell where the water teams had been gathered not five minutes ago.

"Run!" I shoved my hand against Natalie's back, urging her toward the door. "We have to get out of here!"

That seemed to snap everyone out of it. Elliana and Sadie were right on Natalie's heels, with Mallory, Torent, Min, and I behind them. The beasts brought up the rear, whether following or chasing, I couldn't be sure.

We hit the stairs as the floor continued to rumble and shake, tilting toward the side. I slammed against the wall while trying to take two steps at a time. We flew out of the building, into the quad of chaos.

Chunks of stone rained down from the cavern's ceiling, pelting students and faculty in the heads and shoulders. Pieces of buildings began crumbling away. Bangs sounded from their interiors, what sounded like doors slamming shut.

"The portals!" somebody screamed.

I found Saundra and Addie and other Board members gathered in front of Halstein Hall and ran over to them.

"We're under attack!" I blurted, but by their expression, they already knew this.

"All of Havenwood Falls is," Saundra said.

Several students who'd been running by slid to a halt.

"What's going on?" Tyr Skollson demanded, Vidar and Roxy, his mates, at his side.

The members of the Board all exchanged a glance before Saundra lifted her chin.

"It's time for you to use what you've been taught," she said as all of the students crowded around us. Her voice rose as she spoke to what may have now been the whole student body. "There is a god who is hell-bent on destroying all magic." Several gasps and murmurs traveled through the crowd. Saundra nodded. "You understand what this means. As magical beings, we could all cease to exist. And it seems that he is here now, right outside our borders but close enough to do harm. He wants to end us all. Our school—our town—perhaps our whole world is under attack. It is time for you to become the supernatural guardians we all need."

The students rapid-fired a volley of questions, all of them talking over each other.

Addie stepped up next to her grandmother and shot a shower of sparks from her fingers and into the air, silencing the crowd. "You have unknowingly been building a weapon precisely for this moment. The ITF class has been working on a bigger mission than you realized, and now it's time to finish what we've started. I have full faith in you all! We can defeat this fucker!"

The students erupted in cheers, and roars came from the shifters, the cacophony drowning out Saundra's admonishment of her granddaughter's language. But the cheers were quickly cut off when the ground shook harder than ever, knocking many to their knees, and a crack formed across the courtyard, making several students jump backward.

"Evacuate the campus before you all get trapped down here," Saundra ordered.

Students ran every which way, many fighting against the wave toward the portals to get back to their towers to grab precious belongings or their familiars. I was glad I had my own enchanted backpack with me already, my few valuables hidden deep within. Especially when I found Marina walking with Cas, who lugged her eel's huge tank.

"Here! In my bag," I called out to them, pulling my backpack off. "It's practically bottomless."

"Thank you!" Marina gasped. "I couldn't find Tempest and Natalie to help me spell my own."

Their burden lighter, we jogged toward the portals.

"Rhian," Addie called out to me as soon as I passed through to the other side, leaving Halvard Campus for what I hoped wouldn't be the last time. "Come with me!"

I hurriedly followed her out of the portal room and across the Falls Campus, which was SMA's private school for the younger supernatural students in Havenwood Falls. We entered the library, the exact opposite of Halvard's sinister one—bright and airy, elegant and luxurious. No dark corners here or sentient books with teeth and claws. On the table closest to the doors was Kialah's tome with the clues, and next to it, what looked like an architect's model of the town and surrounding mountains, which covered the rest of the table.

"They're gathering the students in the auditorium, so we need to hurry," she said. "I just wanted to go over this with you first, make sure I'm not missing anything. So the clue says 'point by point plus three and a ring'—five points and a ring is a pentagram, right?" She didn't wait for an answer. Pentagrams seemed to be a theme with this weapon, much like the elements were. "Then I noticed these symbols on this town map Teeny Weeny shared. The gift of the Spring fae."

The gift was the model—a complete, miniaturized replica of Havenwood Falls, including every building and home, the forests and mountains, rivers and lakes, everything.

"It's enchanted to magically update whenever there's a change," Addie continued as I studied it. "So I don't know if these are new or Teeny never noticed them before, because they look like part of the landscape, just slightly darker in color, but look." She pointed to five symbols on the map, naming off their meanings with each one. "Air, fire, earth, water, and spirit. And watch." She moved her finger from symbol to symbol, creating a star in the air over the map, then drew a circle around it. The pentagram covered the entire canyon.

"Five points and a ring," I murmured in awe.

"Right. So we have six pieces—the four pairs, plus the ankh and the staff that are still left over because they couldn't figure out how they fit together. Maybe because they're not supposed to yet— because now ten have become six. Are you with me?"

I nodded. "You think the ankh and the staff don't go together at all. Elli will murder you, you know, after all the frustration she had trying to figure that out. And if she doesn't, Natalie might."

"Yeah, well, they'll still get their A—if we live through this. Besides, the two pieces might still go together but we have to take them to their position first."

"And you're thinking we have to place each elemental piece where their corresponding symbol is? But these symbols cover, like, *acres* in real life. These pieces are small in comparison. It could take forever to figure out the exact spot."

She nodded. "I know, but we have to do it. The students will split up by teams again, taking along whoever wants to help them, and they'll have to find where their piece goes. They're smart and clever. They can do this."

The earth shook under our feet, the bookstacks swaying.

"We have to hurry," I said.

"So you think I'm right?"

I studied the map and the symbols, going over the clue in my head and trying to think like Zandra. "I think you are. And at least water should be easy again—the great falls and its pond is in that section of the map."

"So is Peacock Lake," she pointed out.

"My gut tells me it's at the great falls. And the sirens said to find their sister beyond the wall. The falls are just outside campus —the other side of the stone wall."

"Okay, then, you take the water teams. I'll take spirit. We might have to find *two* spots for that element."

I helped her carry Teeny Weeny's town model down the hall to the auditorium, where SMA's entire student body and many of the faculty were gathered. After setting it on the stage, Addie used her magic to project the model into the image of a two-dimensional map against the stage curtains, then dove into her explanation of everything. Hermod, the weapon, the artifacts and their assignments, and now her theory of what to do with them—she laid it all out for the student body.

This hadn't been the plan, of course. Some people, including some of the Regents, might have thought the students weren't ready yet. They hadn't completed their first year of training. But every time a challenge had been thrown at them—from simple to life-or-death—they stepped up and conquered it. We defeated zombies and Valkyrie statues last semester. Surely we could take on Hermod. They had me, they had each other, and they had the weapon. Well, if we could figure out where the pieces belonged and how it all worked, anyway.

"I can't tell you exactly what you're looking for," Addie admitted to the students as she continued her explanation, "but in each element's section of the map, there will be something that fits with your object perfectly. Use your heads, but also your intuition.

Remember my class at the beginning of the semester? Feel out for what can't be seen, for what's beyond the physical. An energy current. A pull in your gut. Symbolism that may or may not be exactly like the symbols on the map. I am positive you'll know it when you find it. Your school, this town—the whole world and all of the magic in it—are counting on you. You can do this!"

Everyone started gathering their things and leaving the auditorium when the building was rocked by a nearby explosion. Bits of plaster rained down on us as cracks formed on the ceiling.

"Go, now!" Addie yelled.

We rushed out the front doors and into a scene from a disaster movie. Giant fireballs were pummeling the landscape. Smoke spiraled up from multiple structures. Two lions ran past in a blur of sandy fur, and a dragon flew overhead, its shadow stretching across the campus grounds. Looking up at the dragon, I noticed glowing symbols or runes that seemed to be suspended in the air high above town.

"Shit, those are part of the wards! They're not supposed to be visible," Gallad said. He had stopped in his tracks next to me. "Rhian, do you know what the hell is going on?" We watched as Addie ran down the stairs and over to Elli's team. "I haven't seen my cousin look that stressed since…" His eyes widened, and a look of panic washed over his face before he pulled himself together.

"Since when? What were you going to say?"

"Since the Collector. You weren't here for that attack, but it was bad."

"Well, this is going to be much, much worse. We need to get your team and the other water element team. I know where we need to go."

Within seconds, Marina, Cas, Roxy, and Kalani joined Gallad's team, and I quickly explained our mission. Fortunately, the academy was close to the falls, and we didn't have far to go. Before we left, Gallad handed me the conjoined artifacts, and I dropped the skeleton hand clutching the pearl into my backpack. The energy pulsed between my shoulder blades in sync with my heartbeat, and as we ran up Alverson Road, closer to the falls, the energy grew stronger.

We passed a few vehicles. One minivan practically ran us over.

The human driver and the man in the passenger seat wore identical terrified expressions. I briefly wondered what they saw. Was it the giant fireballs falling from the sky that scared the shit out of them or did they see a neighbor shift into a mountain lion or perhaps they saw the dragon? If we survived this, there were going to be a ton of memories to wipe.

We ran down the path and through the trees until sparkling water came into view, and the roar of the falls became so loud that it drowned out all other noise. Spring meant the lakes and rivers were surging from snowmelt. Treacherous rapids formed where the falls spilled into the lake, creating such force that boulders were tossed about as if they were made of air. Rocks crashed against each other, rumbling like bowling balls. No, this was more than just the normal force of the falls. The aether in the water—one of the main sources of magic in the canyon—was acting up.

We stood along the shoreline, staring at the imposing wall of water that dropped 295 feet from the side of Mount Alexa.

"Find our sister beyond the wall…" Maria whispered.

"Do you guys hear that?" Kalani asked. I could barely hear her soft, tinkling voice over the roar of the falls, so I closed my eyes and listened. There, carried on the wind, was a cry so laden with sorrow that I wanted to weep. My backpack jerked, and like I was being yanked on a leash, I was dragged into the water.

"Rhian!" Gallad shouted, and several large splashes followed. Before I was completely submerged, I looked behind me to see everyone jumping in the lake except for Cas, who flew over me. I was being pulled against the current, and instead of fighting, I relaxed and let the artifacts lead. I was dragged through the rapids, my body knocking against the rocks, and I emerged on the other side of the falls, bruised, battered, and coughing up water, but I was alive. Here, the water was calm, almost serene, and the roar muted. Heads popped up around me as my classmates came up for air, looking worse for the wear, even Marina and Brooklyn who could usually control water.

"We tried to help," Marina explained, tossing her wet hair over her shoulder. "My powers are super glitchy right now."

"Same," Brooklyn said.

"That's okay. It looks like we all made it through." I stared up at the rock wall facing us.

The outlines of three archways were carved into the stone, looking very much like the portals to school—and I realized we were on the exact opposite side of the wall from those portals. Above the arches the word H A L V A R D was engraved.

"We're definitely beyond the wall," I murmured.

About ten feet farther up was a ledge, and just beyond that, a cave. The artifact started to hum louder and rattle against my back.

"Uh, I think it's trying to tell us something." Tank removed the backpack and held it out to me. The front was sticking straight forward, as though a finger tented the canvas.

Letting the artifact lead again, we followed the pull to the left of the arches, where a narrow set of steps was carved into the rockface. Putting the backpack on my chest, I went first, and we climbed the stairs in single file, leaving waterlogged shoeprints in our wake. There was a gap between the top step and the ledge, so I grabbed onto the edge of the ledge and pulled myself up. I cautiously approached the cave entrance, which was a black hole not even five feet high. I ducked and peered into the darkness. Mold and decay wafted out at me, and my nose wrinkled. My power rippled, responding to death that called to me from the depths.

"Are we going in?" Roxy asked, and I almost jumped. She'd approached so quietly, like the cat she was.

"We have to." I pointed to the shifting backpack.

"Let's go then." Together we entered the cave, hunching over to avoid hitting our heads. Tank found out the hard way when he stood up and almost knocked himself out.

The pull of death grew stronger. Gallad whispered a spell that illuminated the space, and on the back wall was a giant scallop shell, secured sideways. Above the shell, symbols were etched into the rock. First there was a series of three circles swirling—the Celtic symbol for water.

"That's the alchemic symbol for water," Gallad said, pointing to an upside-down triangle. Another etching consisted of three squiggly lines that could have been interpreted as mountains, but were actually waves: a tribal symbol for water. The hand in the backpack began moving, like it was trying to crawl free.

I approached the giant shell warily. The energy from the artifacts was beginning to hurt, a slow burn that had been steadily building to an inferno. The crying Kalani had brought to our attention earlier suddenly filled the cave at a volume and pitch that would shatter glass. Maria howled, and Roxy hissed at the assault. They both dropped to their knees, covering their ears, blood seeping between their fingers.

Removing the artifacts from the bag, I touched the hand to the shell, and the symbols above flashed a bright blue right before the shell swung out, revealing a large opening. The shrieking cry mercifully stopped. We were silent as we took in what was on the other side of the opening. It was like peering into a fishbowl. Only there weren't any goldfish, just a single skeleton. Like the ones in the riverbed, the skeleton was human on top, but with a fishtail. Blond hair floated around the skull like kelp.

"Shit, not sirens again," Gallad groaned when he saw the sharp teeth grinning at him.

"Yup," I said with a pop. "And do you see what that skeleton is missing?"

The skeleton was perfectly intact except for one thing—it only had one hand.

CHAPTER 7

"*I* think we found the sister beyond the wall," Brooklyn said.

Energy vibrated up my arm from the artifact. My power tugged at me in response. It wanted me to restore life. I hoped that wasn't in the plans again. Marina eyed the artifact longingly, her gaze focused on the pearl. I started to hand the artifact to her, and she stepped back.

"I can't." She licked her lips. "I don't trust myself."

Cas wrapped his arm around her waist.

"I trust you, love," he said, but she shook her head.

"We'll do it together." Brooklyn took the artifact. The water nymph and water witch stepped through the doorway and into the water, not a single drop spilling when they broke the surface. Magic held the watery tomb in place.

The women swam toward the skeleton. As they drew closer, the handless arm extended forward, and the skull pivoted as if watching the approaching women with sightless eyes. The moment Brooklyn connected the hand to the ulna and radius bones, the pearl flared, resembling a tiny full moon, and the symbols above the doorway lit up again. With the skeleton intact, the eye sockets flickered with blue flame, and with a swish of the siren's bony tail, Marina and Brooklyn were knocked backwards. They came tumbling out of the doorway, landing on the floor.

I sensed an energetic shift of sorts, as if something in the universe had settled into alignment, and the seashell door swung shut on its own.

"That wasn't as bad as I thought it was going to be," Marina panted as Cas helped her to her feet. "Once I was in the water, that compulsion to possess the pearl disappeared."

"Actually, this task was pretty easy," Brooklyn said.

"Almost too easy," Gallad added.

I hated to agree with him. Triumphant that our task was completed, we quickly left the cave, taking the ledge to dry land instead of passing through the falls again.

"Look at that!" Tank pointed at the sky. A greenish barrier glowed above our part of Mount Alexa and toward the west. Either activating just one piece of the weapon was enough to start protecting us or the Lunas had been successful in their attempts to restore the wards. Either way, as long as they held, it bought us more time to complete the weapon before Hermod wiped us off the map.

My gut went with the weapon theory, considering the new glow was only overhead while the ward's symbols and runes still glittered the sky in the distance. We needed to get to the next team to help them.

I slipped my backpack to its normal position. "Guys, I'm heading to find the fire teams. They're somewhere south of here, on the other side of Main Street. Take a short break and meet me over there, okay?"

With everyone in agreement, I hurried down the rocky path amidst the thick pines, thinking of the area assigned to the fire team, visualizing the structures and landmarks. As far as I could recall, that part of town included some of the ski resort, the Blaekthorn Lumber Yard, the unicorn stables and fields, and the Farnsworth Mining Co. Mine & Museum. My mind immediately went to the mines. Knowing Cat and her team, they'd gravitate to the most dangerous area. As for Destiny and her crew, I thought they'd go along pretty willingly.

"Off to the mines," I muttered.

I still couldn't take my raven form, so keeping my senses on high alert, I ran the straightest path possible south and west. And when I came closer to the mines, I spotted the fire teams.

As I ran up to them, Cat had her hands on her hips and a foot on a rock, looking like the Queen of the Mountain. "I can't believe you guys need a break already."

Destiny glared at Craig. "She's right," she snarled. "We're wasting time." She pinched the bridge of her nose. "You know what, let's just leave him here."

"What?" Craig rocked back on his heels. "You can't leave me. We're under attack!"

"And you're not helping!" Destiny poked her finger into his chest.

Fin agreed they should keep on when a shower of sparks rained down from the sky.

"What the fuck?" Cole shielded his eyes as he peered upward.

I didn't even have to look to know we were being attacked again.

"Get to shelter!" I shouted. "Now!"

Cat spun around, searching for a spot to hide, when the sparks came down thicker and faster, like miniature bolts of lightning. "¿Dónde? There is no shelter!"

Fin hollered that she had it under control. She planted her feet wide, determination sweeping over her petite frame as she held her hands out, commanding the sparks to freeze. But instead, she froze. Her body went stiff as a mannequin while the sparks from above continued their onslaught.

"¡Ay, no! Messed up magic!" Cat cried out. "Fin!"

With Infiniti out of commission and those blasts coming down, Cole started barking orders. "Someone get Fin, and follow me! I know where to go!"

"I got her!" D dodged the sparks as he ran for Fin, lifting her in one swoop and placing her rigid form on his shoulder as if she were a plank of wood.

"Go!" Matthew yelled, wrapping his arm around Amelia's shoulder and urging her to hurry.

With Cole in the lead, we all bolted, and it became clear that some of us were faster than others. Cat and Destiny blurred after Cole, stopping short before they overtook him. I kept one step behind them and stayed in the middle of the pack, ready to help if anyone needed me. Eyeing the thick trees and brush, I wondered where Cole was leading us. We were nowhere near the entrance to his family's mines.

"There," Cole yelled, pointing toward a small opening between what looked like a wall of shrubs. As he gestured, a careening spark hit his hand. "Son of a bitch!" he hollered, just as he broke through the tangle of leaves and branches and stumbled beyond it.

Cat and Destiny exploded through the opening next.

I lunged in after, ducking into the hole in the nick of time as a spark came dangerously close to singeing my eyebrows off my face. Catching my breath, I spun around to watch the others as they approached.

"We're going to die," Craig moaned, pumping his arms as he ran for us.

"We're not gonna die!" D yelled at him with an impressive grunt. With Fin on his shoulder, he slowed down just a tad, letting Craig go in first, and then he and his cargo followed.

"Move aside!" Matthew called out as he and Amelia brought up the rear, panting as they ducked inside.

"Shit," Amelia breathed out, leaning over and placing her hands on her knees. "Let's not do that again."

Staring out the opening of the cave, I watched the sparks raining down and wondered what would be next. The attacks would only get worse from here on out, until Hermod succeeded in destroying our magic and all of us as a result—or we killed him. One or the other was the only way this was all going to end.

D gently placed Infiniti on her feet. Her legs were still wide, her arms still out. "What do we do about Fin?"

I waved my hand in front of her face, then tried to push some of my power into her. She didn't even flinch. I lowered her hands to her sides. "I think she'll be fine here. At least for a little while."

I moved over to Cole, eyeing his hand. "You okay?"

He lifted it, revealing a superficial red scratch. "It'll take a lot more than that to hurt me."

"Well, what now? Craig asked.

"Now we explore the area," Destiny answered.

"You think the cup goes somewhere in here?" Amelia asked, looking around the dank area with disgust. "It's dark and gross."

"Well," Cole said, "I know this place. It's an abandoned section of the silver mines that my aunt and uncle own. I used to work here, so I know all the paths. We may as well look around."

"We need to hurry, though," I urged. "Before shit gets worse."

Cole nodded. "Yep, but first we need light. I'll be right back." He disappeared farther into the cave, returning a few seconds later with a long and rusty metal toolbox, which he set on the ground and opened. "My aunt and uncle have one of these at the entrance to each mine, just in case." He pulled out two flashlights and turned them on. "I'll take the front with one. Who's got the rear?"

"I got it," I said, taking the flashlight and moving to the back of the group.

"This way," Cole called out. The beam of his flashlight hit the top of the cave ceiling and danced around the walls as he led us in at a quick pace.

"How deep do the mines go?" Destiny asked with a slight tremble in her voice.

"Deep," Cole answered. "But we don't have to go all the way through them."

"Yeah," Cat agreed with Cole. "If we can't find where it goes right away, then we should go look somewhere else."

Suddenly, the walls shifted. Or—I *thought* they shifted. I stopped and studied my surroundings, wondering if my eyes were playing tricks on me, but Cole must have seen the same thing. His bouncing light halted in place as our formation came to a full stop.

"Did you guys see that?" Cole asked in a hushed tone.

"*Ay, Dios mío*," Cat muttered. "I saw that. Or, uh, I think I saw that."

"The walls moved, right?" Cole asked.

My light bobbed around as I peered about, waiting for more movement. I was about to tell Cole to keep going when I heard a low rumble.

I held my hand up. "Did you guys hear that?"

As one, the entire group moved their heads to the side, searching out the noise I'd heard. It sounded like someone was moving the ceiling above our heads. But that was impossible.

Right?

Without warning, a rock the size of an apple tore itself from the wall and pelted straight at us. It struck the side of Destiny's head, then smashed into the wall on the other side of the narrow tunnel.

"What the hell!" she cried out.

"Destiny, are you okay?" The words were barely out of Amelia's mouth before another rock made a second attack.

"Cole!" I commanded. "Get us the hell out of this tunnel!"

Our conga line moved forward at an awkward trot as we held our arms over our heads to protect us from the debris and chunks of wall showering down like rough hail.

"Here we go," Cole announced, rounding the tunnel.

The rest of us barreled after him and stumbled into a spacious area taken up mostly by an eerily still pond.

"This place doesn't feel right to me," Destiny said.

We were huddled together now, and Cole and I flashed our lights around, taking in the strangely silent space.

"Same," Amelia said, turning around to face Destiny fully. And then her big dark eyes grew even wider. "Destiny, you're bleeding." She pressed her fingers against the vampire's temple, where a thin ribbon of blood dripped down her pale face. "Does it hurt?"

"It hurt less when you weren't touching it." Destiny jerked herself out of Amelia's reach. "Everyone spread out and look for a place for this cup so we can get the hell out of here."

We broke up, searching the entire cavern. Nothing stood out as an obvious place for the cup to be placed. With each passing second, the knot in my stomach grew. We needed to hurry.

"There's nothing here," Matthew finally said with a frown.

"We should keep moving," D responded, glancing at the different tunnels we could take.

"Let's go this way," Cat said before anyone could argue, taking the lead as always.

Destiny nodded. "At least for a little longer. And if we don't find something soon, we turn around."

We hurried around the pond and followed Cat through an archway. The second my feet crossed the threshold into the new tunnel, I knew something was terribly wrong. What little bit of light from the spacious cavern and the pond was snuffed out completely. Even the flashlights barely shone. And then I realized it was because the walls were closing in.

"What the fuck!" D gasped.

"Turn around!" Cat yelled, spinning toward me. "Go back!"

I reeled around, ready to bolt out of there, but the tunnel was closing in. No way we could all make it through.

"We can't go back!" I shouted. "We have to keep moving that way!"

We charged forward in desperate silence as the walls tightened from all directions. The air thinned out, making every breath a struggle.

"We have to find a way out of here," Destiny groaned, stopping to push at the stone with all the impressive strength in her body. "Help me!"

Everyone shoved against the walls, grunting and groaning with effort. I focused on my power, commanding it to break through the cavernous walls, but it wasn't working.

"Cat! Can you move forward?" I yelled.

"No!" she hollered back over the grinding and shifting of stone against stone.

"Everyone push on three," Cole called out. "One, two…"

With a deafening rumble, a waterfall of rocks crashed to the ground a few feet from where we stood, revealing a new pathway.

"Was that us?" Destiny asked.

"Who cares? Just go!" Amelia pleaded.

The walls had closed in so much, we had to shuffle sideways toward the new opening.

Practically tumbling into the space, Cole raised a hand toward us. "Um, guys, I don't recognize this place."

"That's just great," Craig moaned.

We were in another large cavern. Etchings sprawled along the rock walls and ceilings. I spotted a raven on one and some weird letters on another.

"Hey, look." Cat pointed at a flat rock situated in the middle of the space with carvings all around it. "Those markings look like flames."

Craig tilted his head to one side. "It looks more like a tree to me."

"It's not a tree." Cat didn't wait for a group vote. She slipped off her backpack, took out the cup, and placed it on the middle of the rock.

Everything began moving all at once. The emblems scratched into the rock walls sprang to life, whirling around us like a tornado. Rocks crashed down from the ceiling. One of them hit Craig, sending him flying back against the wall. Another pelted Matthew.

"It must go somewhere else!" Amelia screamed.

"No," Cat argued. "That's the symbol. This is the right place—I know it. Those are flames, and we are the fire teams."

It made sense, but why wasn't the cup doing its thing?

"It took fire to join the pieces together." Destiny swatted away a rock that flew by her face.

"So fire is what it's missing," Cat agreed, finishing Destiny's thought as she nodded her head. In that tiny space of time, the two shared a small smile.

"Someone needs fire?" Cole asked, knocking down a flying rock with his flashlight.

Craig stepped forward, palming his forehead where he must've been hit. "We can double-up on the flame. In case one of our flames doesn't work."

The fae and the dragon shifter moved closer to the cup. Craig pulled his head back and roared deep in his chest as he opened his mouth and let loose a huge jet of flames. Cole flung out his hands, his fire working perfectly this time as it added to the stream.

"Wow," Cat uttered, wide-eyed as she watched the flames shoot at the chalice.

The cup rose several feet into the air, glowing bright orange. It floated back and forth gracefully, burning like a small sun, before returning to its spot on the rock with a click. When it touched down, the walls around us hummed and vibrated, as if signaling satisfaction. We all watched in awe as the earthen onslaught that had all started so abruptly stopped.

Cole and Craig extinguished their flames as a hush fell around us. Nobody spoke for a long moment as we all stared at the now glowing cup.

"I told you those etchings were flames." Cat nudged Craig in the ribs.

"Whatever," he grumbled back, but then added a playful nudge of his own.

"I vote we get the hell out of here," Matthew added.

D wrapped his arm around Cat's. "I second that."

Back in our conga-line formation, we weaved our way out of the mine and to the entrance. The water group was huddled together, surrounding the still stiff Fin. When they saw us, a million questions flew.

"Fin is okay, but frozen," I explained, giving them the simplest of answers because I didn't have time to go through the entire scenario. "And the fire team has put their object in its place. Now on to the next team. Let's hurry!"

Just like before, the sky directly overhead was clear of the glowing symbols of the ward's spells when we emerged, the reinforced shield shining in their place. From what I could see, the shield stretched almost like a crescent over the west side of the canyon. While Hermod's magic couldn't reach us here, flames licked from buildings all over town, an orange glow lighting up thick columns of smoke. Directly opposite our corner, in the northeast section of the canyon, a larger fire lit up part of the mountains—what was quickly becoming a full raging wildfire.

"We need to head over there!" I yelled, urgency ripping through my body. With the shield in place, I tried again to take my raven form. And holy fuck, it worked!

I didn't wait.

I launched into the air and flew over town, trying not to focus on the devastation below me. This beautiful town ... the people ... I cawed in anguish, refusing to let it bring me down yet. I could mourn later. Right now, we had to save what we could.

I heard the yells coming from ahead, a sense of panic filling the air with its sour taste. I found the group near Bels Creek, not too far from the vineyard of Stone Falls Winery, and dropped to the ground, returning to my human form.

"Shit! Come on, it's got to be here somewhere!" a deep voice said.

"Dude, leave the creek behind! We're air, not water, remember?" Winter barked in exasperation right before noticing me. "Thank the goddess you're here. I mean, you are the goddess, but, well, anyway. . . Will you talk some sense into these idiots?"

Before I could reply, a gust of wind blasted through the area, slashing at my face. I gasped a at the sting, gingerly touching my cheek. My fingertips came away bright red.

CHAPTER 8

"What the—" I began then realized what was happening. "GO!" I thundered. "We have to get out of the wind's path!"

I wasn't quick enough. Others cried out around me as the next attack came, slicing at our flesh as the breeze howled with a painful bite. Hermod's onslaught was not without creativity. I had to give him that.

"Over here!" Shay screamed, her voice small amongst the ruckus. "We need to head through the vineyard!"

We sprinted her way and darted into the rows of grapevines, escaping the wind. Though I couldn't see it, I felt it die down at the vineyard's borders as though we'd crossed an invisible barrier.

Continuing farther in, I glanced around, noting the tall vines and the grapes hanging off them. I had no idea if everyone had made it. The rows of fruit seemed to go on for miles, and it felt like we were trapped in a maze. Where were the buildings? There were at least half a dozen structures at Stone Falls Winery, but I couldn't see a trace of any of them. I wished Gallad's fiancée were with us—Macy's family owned this place.

"Is everyone okay?" Mystic's voice traveled through the twigs, murmurs and groans answering in reply.

"Who has the bird?" I asked.

"I do." Malyki's voice rumbled from ahead. I remembered the

very brief discussion we had about who would transport the relic. The older witch refused anyone's input, electing himself and refusing any other offers. It was too important to the curse that still held him and Mystic hostage for them to trust it to anyone else.

I strained my gaze to see through the darkness to find him. Was he in the next row ahead of me? There was no way he'd stray too far from his soulmate in the midst of all this chaos.

"I found something!" Dylan called.

I immediately rushed ahead, not knowing whether it was the right direction. A loud grumble came from above, like thunder roaring through the skies.

"That can't be good," I muttered, apprehension coursing through me.

Winter burst into the row ahead of me, sparking a red and green bomb as a section of the vines dispersed destructively. Twigs, grapes, and leaves scattered on the ground. Her fingertips still glowed from the magic she'd used.

A new gust of wind pushed me forward, and I tripped over my feet. I started dusting myself off when a full-blown tornado smacked me in the face and sent me skyward. I twisted left, then right as the mighty air threw me around like a ragdoll. It gained in strength the more I tried to fight it, hurling me harder in every direction. I couldn't see much beyond the stars in my dizzy head, darkness cloaking my heavy eyelids.

Was this it? After everything we'd been through, were we going to fail? Was Hermod going to win after all?

I tumbled through the air, again unable to call on my raven. I was ready to throw up, to blow chunks everywhere when the wind lost its grasp, and I was free-falling toward the fast approaching ground.

I caught a glimpse of the rubble on the ground right before I smacked into it, face-first. My limbs contorted, melding to the hard dirt. Bone-crunching agony swept through me, my body firing signals from every single nerve ending. I felt paralyzed, unable to move, the pain muting any attempt at a scream.

"Shit, is she okay?" Dylan's voice sounded as though it came from afar, yet I was sure I felt his presence near me.

"Rhian, can you move?" Mystic came close, and I could see her petite shoes in my sightline right before she knelt beside me with a look of concern.

"Winter, get over here now!" Dylan yelled. "There must be something you can do?"

"Why? Because I'm a woman?" Winter answered sarcastically. She clearly didn't enjoy being hollered at.

"No, because you're a witch, dumbass. Weave some magic to help heal Rhian already!"

A deafening silence encapsulated my mind. What was going on? Why wasn't I healing myself? I shouldn't have even been hurt in the first place. I was a fucking goddess! I was jostled around, pain darting through the worst parts of my broken body as Dylan and Gable lifted me into the air and onto Dylan's shoulder without finesse. Mouths moved around me, but I still couldn't hear anything. What were they saying?

The world's noises came rushing back to my ears, a loud commotion coming from ahead.

"Come on, this way. We know where we need to go!" Shay yelled. "Malyki found a cave just ahead."

"Put me . . . down," I panted, finding my voice. "It hurts … too much." The jostling was doing more damage than good. I could feel the magic inside me finally healing me, but with every jolt on Dylan's shoulder, the progress I made was being undone.

"Winter, give me a boost," I croaked, sliding off the shapeshifter's body and slinking to the ground. Winter furrowed her brows, clearly unsure what I meant. "Energy," I panted. "Zap me awake with your tingling fingers."

Electricity bolted through me, giving my body the go-go juice it needed. I stood, slowly, testing each one of my limbs. I wasn't perfect yet, but it was enough to get me mobile again.

"What the fuck is that?" Dylan's eyes widened, pointing to something behind me.

Dread filled me. Slowly, I turned around, watching the rows of vines rattle from side to side, wind shaking them violently. Leaves, grapes, and sections of vines swirled in the air.

"We need to—" Mystic began just as the blowing debris hurled at us like missiles.

"This way!" Malyki yelled above the din, leading the way to the cave he'd found. My aching body couldn't take many more hits. I needed a break. Winter came to my right and looped her arm through mine, Bryony copied with my left, and together we followed the crowd into the darkness.

The cave's entrance was larger than I anticipated, wide enough for the three of us to continue walking side-by-side. The air was damp, growing colder the farther we ventured.

"What are we looking for? How will we know it's the right place for this bird?" Dylan asked, from a few feet ahead.

"Pet—" I started when I was interrupted.

"Wait, what's this?"

The others ahead had stopped, leaving no room for the rest of us to see.

"What can you see, Mystic?" I called to her.

"There's some markings on the wall here."

"Petroglyphs?" I asked hopefully.

"Yes! Exactly!" She was soon surrounded by the others, everyone trying to figure out what they meant.

"Describe them to me," I said, a tingling sensation traveling up my spine.

"There are three swirls, the tails each pointing toward the same way."

"It's a symbol for air," Bryony said. "Not quite the same as the one on Addie's map, but that's definitely air."

"Then that's it! The bird has to be placed somewhere there," I yelled, frustrated that I couldn't do it myself.

"Look! There's a perch above the symbols!" Dylan shouted with excitement.

I heard some tinkling and rustling ahead, bracing myself for another booby trap. But without so much as a falling pebble, a bright orange light filled the cave, and I knew it was done.

We all breathed a sigh of relief, taking just a moment of respite before following the path back to the cave's entrance. The light continued to glow, and even illuminated the sky and destruction of the vineyard.

The shield overhead, though, was now in place over this part of town. Three sections down, two to go.

My body was strengthening, but not enough to take my raven form. Leaving the vineyard behind, we walked down Fourteenth Street, headed in the direction of Danzan Park. I appreciated being able to walk on a paved surface. My body had been taxed enough and not having to navigate through rough terrain helped my injuries heal faster. Some homes had been abandoned, their owners not bothering to close the front door. Some were burned down to their foundations. Charred craters from the previous onslaught of fireballs disfigured once manicured front lawns. I spotted a curtain move, and the barrel of a gun appeared in the dark window. It was trained on us. *Humans and their guns*, I thought to myself and shook my head, feeling my braids shift. By the time we reached the intersection of Blackstone Road, I was back to one hundred percent, and the fire and water teams were walking toward us.

"We came to help," Marina said.

"Well, the air piece has been activated, so we're on our way to find the earth teams. I'm going to shift and see if I can spot them from above. Anyone care to join?" I asked.

Cas and D stepped forward.

"Follow me." I spun on my heel and shifted in one movement, taking to the skies. I heard the rush of wind breaking over wings when Cas and D joined me, flanking me on each side as we headed south. From this angle, we had a clear view of the entire town. A line of taillights from cars trying to escape dotted Burdorf Pass and backed up onto Main Street. Smoke hung heavy in the air, and the smoldering remains of structures smudged the skyline.

Movement through the trees ahead, in the direction of Mount Mae caught my attention, and I sped up. We passed over Mathews River until we were above a group of people moving quickly, too quickly for humans, with a wolf running alongside them. A blur of bright pink, purple, and blue hair—Paisley's—confirmed we'd found the two teams responsible for the earth element part of the weapon. I called out to them, my caw echoing through the canyon.

Eryx, or maybe it was his twin, Calix, peered up at the sky and saw me. He came to a sudden stop, forcing the others to do the same.

"We'll circle around and bring the other teams," Cas said right before he and D banked to one side and turned around. They flew back toward the others, and I began my descent. As I closed in, I shifted into my human form, mid-flight, and landed in a crouch on top of a boulder.

"That's one hell of an entrance, Rhian," Vanna said.

"Thanks?" I shrugged, jumping down. "Any luck yet?"

"Yes, we believe so," Timber answered, stepping forward. "Trees have been marked with carvings of Borromean Rings, and the carvings in the trees are almost as old as the forest. They tell me to follow the trail."

"They?" I asked.

"The trees," Paisley replied. "Timber's like a tree whisperer. He can communicate with all plant life. Pretty sweet, huh?" She stood up on her tiptoes and kissed Timber's cheek. He grinned and wrapped an arm around her waist, tucking her up against his side. "Now that we know what to look for, we've been following the trail as fast as we can."

The large, gray wolf sniffed the perimeter of where we stood. The beautiful creature had to have been Amaruq—the lone wolf shifter between the two earth teams. He abruptly let out a low growl of warning, his fur bristling as he crouched to the ground.

We dropped into silence, and I searched for the threat. A lion appeared on the boulder I'd just vacated. His amber eyes glittered like stars as he stared down at us, lips curled up to reveal long, sharp canines.

"Holy fairies—Orion?" Paisley called out in surprise. The beast turned his head, his mane rippling with the movement, and zeroed in on her. Releasing a loud roar, it pounced toward the fae couple, knocking them apart. The lion and Timber went rolling while Paisley ran after them screaming.

As soon as Timber was on his feet, vines rushed toward the approaching lion, entangling him instantly. No matter how much the animal thrashed, the greenery held.

Timber's shirt was torn, and he was bleeding from a gash on his side. Despite being clearly outweighed by at least four hundred pounds, he seemed okay.

"What the fuck, Orion?" Paisley shouted, her hands on her hips, eyes fixed on the subdued lion. "Unbelievable." She shook her head and turned to face Timber. "Oh, babe, you're hurt." She rushed to his side, and after a rather uncomfortable display of affection, which caused the lion to lose his shit even more, Paisley tried healing her boyfriend. Nothing happened, though. She tried again, her hands beginning to glow with a soft white light before her power flickered out.

"Magic is still being affected. You need to hurry," I urged.

"What do we do with the cat?" Eryx asked, nodding toward the thrashing lion. Judging by the way he gave the creature a wide berth, he didn't want the job of feline sitting.

"Leave him. He needs to cool off," Vanna answered. "I just texted my brother, and some guys from the MC will come fetch him when they can. Apparently there's lava running down Petran Street, and they're trying to save the clubhouse."

"Lava? Seriously?" Tempest shook her head, her blue eyes wide. "I didn't think this semester was going to be as insane as last term. Shit, was I wrong." The witch crossed the clearing to Paisley and Timber, her hands already beginning to glow. "Let me try healing him, okay?" Hopefully her magic wasn't affected like Paisley's.

Paisley nodded and wiped away tears from her violet eyes. Her cheeks were smudged where dirt had mingled each time she swiped at her face. "Thanks, Tempest. I'd appreciate it."

Minutes later, Timber was healed, and the group was on the move again.

With no trail to follow, we wove our way through trees and underbrush, treading across the uneven terrain. As the terrain started climbing at the base of Mount Mae, the stronger the smell of smoke became, the stinging haze already making my eyes water. Popping and cracking in the distance put me on high alert.

"This is bad," Timber muttered, holding his hands up as tree branches stretched out to touch him.

"What is bad? You can't just say that and not follow up!" Vanna snapped. The flames of Hellfire blazed a little brighter behind the sunglasses she wore.

"There's a wildfire, and the plants are hurting. It's coming this way."

Not another one.

"I'll check it out," I said and morphed back into my raven

form. As soon as I broke the treeline, I saw the fire to the east. Flames and embers shot up toward the night sky, made brighter by the ominous backdrop of smoke. The fire formed a U shape on this side of the canyon, and Timber was right—it was closing in on our location. But where did it come from? When we'd been flying to meet them just minutes ago, we hadn't noticed this level of chaos. Just within the few minutes I was airborne, I witnessed the line of fire advance faster than normal. No doubt it was magical in origin.

Fucking hell!

I quickly rejoined the group, and by the time I landed back in my human form, a flicker of flames was already visible through the trees. Smoke stung my eyes and throat, making my lungs feel tight. Our group erupted into a series of ragged coughs and gasps for clean air.

Only Vanna seemed to be unaffected by the encroaching fire. She casually wiped at the layer of ash that had accumulated on her sunglasses. "Hey, Tempest, see if you can put this out so we can keep going."

She waved her hands like she was trying to freeze something, and between coughs, Tempest snorted.

"Stand aside. I'll show you how it's done." There was definitely confidence in the young witch's words. Her lips began moving in a soft chant, her entire focus on the growing flames. "So mote it be!" she roared, shaking her hands to direct the flow of her magic.

The fire intensified, clearly unaffected by whatever spell Tempest had performed.

Eryx came up beside his girlfriend, reassuringly stroking her back. "Try again. I know you can do this, sweetheart."

Something silent exchanged between them, and she nodded, struggling not to double over in a coughing fit, the smoke growing thicker.

"Give me one more chance. I can do this."

This time, Tempest crouched to the ground, planting her hands firmly before her, her fingertips piercing the soil. She was trying to call upon the water that resided within the earth, to tap into an underground spring.

Puffing a strand of hair from her face, her features stilled in concentration. "Blessed Goddess, hear my plea. Bring thy waters up to me. Through the earth, An arrow through the air, From these flames, thy servants spare."

I murmured so mote it be along with her, hoping against hope that we could eliminate at least one threat. We were running out of time.

Nothing. Tempest's magic hadn't been enough, and from the look on her face, she was already berating herself for the failure.

"We need to go. Now!" I yelled, which was followed by a coughing fit.

Amaruq led the group, his nose close to the ground. Occasionally Timber would call out and point at a tree that was marked with Borromean Rings, indicating we were on the right path. The air grew increasingly hotter, and sweat dripped down my back, causing the fabric to cling to my skin.

Soon the ash falling around us like snow was accompanied by glowing embers that reminded me of fireflies. Smaller fires sprung up by our feet as some of the cinders landed on the layer of dry leaves that blanketed parts of the forest floor. We needed to move faster before the fire completely surrounded us—trapped us.

Suddenly Amaruq bayed, bringing us to a complete halt and then he started to shift. I winced as he struggled to return to his human form. Bones snapped and realigned; a hand appeared briefly before it became a paw again. It went on for agonizing minutes. Finally, he stood before us, panting, and in all of his naked glory. His olive skin glistened with perspiration and dark ash, accentuating his muscles. I coughed and looked away.

"Here you go, bro." Calix tossed Amaruq a change of clothes he pulled out of the backpack he'd been carrying. "You're making me blush." He winked at me, having seen me turn away.

"Thanks." Amaruq quickly pulled on jeans and a gray T-shirt. He bent over at the waist as he let out a relieved groan. Dark hair fell over his face but didn't hide his facial bones rippling under the surface of his skin. He clenched his jaw, fighting the change. "I've been trying to shift back since Rhian first joined us," he explained once he had exerted enough control.

"Everything is so fucking whack right now," Felicia exclaimed.

"I used to think talking to the dead was boring, but if this is the shit you all deal with, I say drop me off at the nearest cemetery."

Calix squeezed her arm affectionately. "What, you don't like our very own Apocalypse?"

His words came out broken, and in between gasps. The air quality was rapidly deteriorating.

"Why did you stop?" Paisley asked, focusing back on the task.

"Follow me, and I'll show you." Amaruq straightened to his full height and pushed through an overgrown hedge, where he disappeared, swallowed up by leaves.

CHAPTER 9

With the flames licking at our heels, we followed and emerged on the other side of the hedge into the opening of a cave.

"I'm not sure how far back it goes, but we should be safe in here." Amaruq patted his hand against the side of the cave. "There's nothing here to feed the flames."

"Yes!" I blurted. "A cave. All of the other pieces have been placed in a cave."

"Wait, what the hell is that?" Vanna gestured toward where Amaruq's hand had been.

We crowded around her, peering up at the ceiling where she was pointing. Petroglyphs, faded with age, depicted a scene of Indigenous people facing what appeared to be a stone altar. Sitting on top of the altar was a tear-shaped rock that looked a lot like the artifact Eryx's team had found. Symbols decorated the base of the altar, including more Borromean Rings.

"We have to be getting close. The other caves had petroglyphs, too," I said.

Vanna followed the artwork farther into the cave to an opening for a tunnel that was dark and narrow. Dusty cobwebs draped across the entrance and swayed in a breeze that came from deep within the mountain. At least that's how it smelled—damp, musty, and ancient.

Tempest moved past us and formed a ball of light in her hand, which she released into the tunnel. It illuminated the jagged walls, and insects scurried away from the brightness. Just past the light, I could make out Vanna's white-blond hair as she moved farther into the tunnel.

"This reminds me of an Indiana Jones movie," Paisley murmured as the rest of us hesitated at the entrance to the tunnel. "Holy faeries, I hope there aren't any booby traps."

I thought of the rockslides and moving walls in the mine and started to yell, "Stop!"

As if on cue, a flash of blue light flared in the tunnel and surrounded Vanna. She immediately stopped moving, frozen in place.

"Vanna?" Tempest shouted and ran into the tunnel. The hellhound didn't respond. "Vanna!"

Tempest's shriek echoed out of the opening.

Eryx ran in next, and Calix started to go after his twin, but I grabbed his arm, holding him back. He turned to look at me with an eyebrow raised.

"We don't know what we're dealing with, and if we run in there, we could make matters worse. A lot worse." I gestured to the walls.

"Fuck. There *are* booby traps," Paisley groaned. She stepped closer to Timber.

"What's going on?" Felicia called to those inside the tunnel.

"I can't get her free. It's like she's frozen." Tempest's voice shook with desperation. We watched as she tried spell after spell, exhausting her power to save Vanna. "There's a force field or something around her that deflects any kind of magic."

"Is she injured?" Amaruq asked.

Tempest quickly checked her friend again. "No, I don't think so."

Paisley moved forward, nudging her way past Calix, Amaruq, and Felicia. Timber was right behind her.

"I'm going in. We know it's safe up until that point," she announced before entering the tunnel. Smoke was beginning to fill the cave, and just beyond the mouth, the hedge had begun to smolder. We all had to move, and I was beginning to worry the other teams wouldn't be able to reach us.

"I don't know about you, but I don't want to become barbecue," Amaruq said with a half-hearted laugh. A few members answered with their own.

With an unspoken consensus, we proceeded into the tunnel. Felicia and Amaruq went first, enough room for them to walk side by side. Calix walked beside me. Vanna was frozen only about thirty feet in, so it didn't take long to reach the others.

Tempest had been busy and sent balls of light ahead into the tunnel, illuminating the damp rock walls.

"Any change?" I asked, tentatively reaching out to touch the glowing blue force field that surrounded Vanna. I could see every muscle in her body was rigid with tension and imagined she was struggling to move, to fight whatever imprisoned her. Grabbing one of Tempest's balls, I crouched down to the ground, to see if maybe Vanna stepped on something that acted like a trigger, a snare for the trap. A fine silvery thread, almost translucent like a spider web, but thicker, lay on the ground. It was broken by Vanna's feet.

"What's that?" Calix asked, crouching down next to me.

"A magical tripwire."

"Wait, let me see that." Tempest held her hand out, and Calix dropped the thread onto her palm. Tempest sniffed it first, and her nose crinkled. "Magic for sure, but I think I can figure out the spell from the traces clinging to this strand." She pulled at her hair stick that doubled as a wand. "A girl never leaves home unprepared."

She wet her lips, nervous. Nothing she'd tried had worked, but the witch kept giving it her all, refusing to give up. We watched as she worked her magic and finally unraveled the spell.

The blue light disappeared in a mist, and Vanna moved, pulling her friend into a hug. "You're a badass witch, Bell," she comforted.

Just then I spotted tendrils of smoke curling around everyone's feet, like shadowy snakes. Thankfully, I wasn't the only one who noticed.

"We need to keep going," Paisley ordered, pointing at the

smoke, which was suddenly gone, as though sucked out of the tunnel. Seconds later, Bryony, Gable, Vidar, Mystic, and Malyki stood at the entrance. Behind them, Marina, Cas, Roxy, and Kalani appeared.

"Took care of the fire problem," Marina said, stepping around Bryony and walking toward us. "I extinguished the flames while Mystic whipped up a spell to take care of the smoke. So what have we missed?"

Eryx filled them in as they joined everyone else in the tunnel, which was beginning to feel cramped.

"So my amazing girlfriend just figured out how to free Vanna when you all showed up. That's what's going on," he finished.

"And we need to get going, but proceed with caution," Paisley said. "We don't want to activate any more traps, and I would like to be done with this and out of here as soon as possible." She eyed the narrow passage, her violet eyes glimmering in the light.

"Where are the others?" I asked Cas.

"They went to help the spirit team. Figured splitting up would speed things along."

Good. It was already shaping up to be a long night, and I had a feeling the spirit group was struggling, even with Addie's help.

Progress was slow as we moved deeper into the mountain, the temperature dropping as we went.

"Stop!" Eryx held his arm up. He and Calix had volunteered to lead the group and were paying attention for any more traps. I peered around Vidar's shoulder to see better. Tempest and Vanna huddled with the twins in deep discussion.

"What's going on?" I asked.

"Apparently there's a large crevice ahead that we have to cross," Vidar answered.

"Okay, listen up," Eryx called out. "Anyone who is able to fly or jump at least fifteen feet, come to the front of the line."

There was some shuffling from behind me as Cas moved forward, Vidar with him. Timber pressed his back against the tunnel wall so we could pass by him. When we reached the front of the group, I could see why we had stopped. The crevice wasn't just a crack that could be easily stepped over. No, it was at least ten feet across, and when I stared down from the edge, solid darkness rose up to meet me. Aside from Cas, Vidar, and myself, who were the only winged creatures in the group, Roxy had joined us as well as Maria, Vanna, and Amaruq.

"I can make the jump," Maria said, "but there isn't a lot of ceiling clearance. It will have to be a straight lunge."

She was right. There wasn't a lot of room to run and get a head start, either. Also, the tunnel opening on the other side of the crevice appeared to be narrower.

"I'll go first and make sure there aren't any surprises on the other side," I said before shifting forms. I flew over the gap and landed on the other side, which did in fact have a narrower opening. Those making the leap needed to do so with precision.

"I don't like this," Cas growled when he landed on the edge next to me. "I'll be right back." He was gone with a snap of his wings, the wind from his departure causing me to blink. Moments later, the griffon returned with Marina riding on his back.

Before anyone could attempt a jump, Timber emerged from between Amaruq and Vanna. He knelt down, placing his palms flat on the ground, and his fingers curled around the edge of the crevice. He closed his eyes and bowed his head, assuming an almost reverent pose. A glow emanated from his hands as a low rumbling came from below and the mountain started to vibrate. Suddenly, giant roots burst from the crevice wall and came shooting toward us. We jumped back, and I watched in amazement as the roots braided together before drilling into the ground right by my feet. Timber had created a bridge.

We made good progress from that point on, and somewhere along the way, we let our guard down. One minute we were moving along at a steady pace, and next there was a whoosh as something silver passed right next to my head, followed by a scream. A splash of warm liquid hit my face. The metallic tang of blood filled the narrow tunnel, and Amaruq, who had been in front of me, was hunched over, cradling the side of his head. In the dim light I saw crimson leaking between his long fingers.

"Holy faeries, what happened?" Suddenly Paisley was there, prying his hand away from his head, causing him to growl. Timber stood behind her and glared, daring Amaruq to move. "Relax. I'm not going to harm you."

Paisley winced when she examined Amaruq's head, and only when she moved his dark hair out of the way, did I see what was wrong. His entire right ear was gone.

"What the fuck happened?" I asked.

"That happened," Calix said from behind me, and I looked back to find him pointing at the tunnel wall next to him. A curved blade was embedded in the stone, with Amaruq's ear still attached.

"Hold still, you idiot. Let me heal you." Paisley's bedside manner was gone as Amaruq kept swatting her hands away whenever she got close to his wound.

"Oh, for fuck's sake." Vanna appeared beside me and grabbed Amaruq from behind, wrapping her arms around his chest, effectively pinning his arms to his sides.

Just as Paisley set her palms on Amaruq's head, her hands began to glow and grew steadily brighter. Her abilities were working again. Amaruq's ear began to regenerate in front of my eyes, unfurling like a bud beginning to bloom. Within seconds, aside from the soft pink of new skin, he looked unscathed.

Tempest cast a sanitizing spell that absorbed all of the blood, including the droplets on my face. Amaruq's old ear vanished, and I tore the blade out of the wall. It was heavy and tarnished, but marked with a symbol. Using the edge of my shirt, I wiped away some of the tarnish, and the symbol that emerged made my blood run cold. An old Asgardian symbol. Taking measured breaths to not betray the panic breaking loose internally, I tucked the blade in the waist of my pants, the metal pressed against the small of my back.

With Amaruq healed and the blood cleaned up, we continued deeper into the mountain. Every fifty feet or so, Borromean Rings appeared etched into the tunnel walls. Any small talk and nervous chatter from earlier had been silenced after Amaruq lost his ear. I didn't know how long we had been walking. There was no concept of time along this passage. The only light was created by magic. The only sound was our breathing, our footsteps, and the occasional rumble as something shook the mountain. The Havenwood Falls supernatural community had their hands full dealing with Hermod's attack. I worried there wouldn't be a town left when or if we ever emerged from Mount Mae. The odds of destruction were in Hermod's favor, unless we finished assembling the weapon. Tension hung heavy in the musty air.

We rounded a bend, and the tunnel started to widen. Soon we were standing at the entrance to a cavern. Stalagmites rose up from the floor to meet stalactites that hung from the ceiling, and it was like we were standing within the jaws of a prehistoric creature. It also reminded me of campus. Bryony, Tempest, and Mystic cast a flurry of light balls into the cavern, illuminating the entire floor that was submerged under water so still, it resembled a mirror. In the middle of the glasslike pond, the stone altar depicted in the petroglyphs stood like a lone island.

Brooklyn and Marina walked over and came to a stop at the edge of the pond. My intuition told me to expect the unexpected. Brooklyn knelt down and dragged her finger across the top, shattering the smooth surface. She yelped and jerked her hand back, cradling it against her chest.

"What is it?" Marina asked, kneeling down by her side.

"That's not water. It's acid." Her lower lip trembled when she held her hand out, and Marina gasped. The tip of Brooklyn's forefinger was a bloody mess, resembling a piece of hamburger. Tears ran down her cheeks. "I'm not healing."

Within seconds, both Tempest and Paisley joined them and went to work.

"Why don't I fly over and take a look at the altar—get a better sense of where the artifact needs to go?" I offered.

"That's a good idea," Eryx said, which was followed by murmurs of agreement.

Shifting again, I launched into the air, flying over the group that had gathered at the pond's edge. I was about halfway to the altar, when I slammed into an invisible barrier. As soon as I hit it, there was shimmer in the air followed by a loud boom that echoed off the cavern walls. I was thrown back and forced into my human form as I soared over the acid pond. I knocked into Cas and Gable, bowling them over. Stalactites broke loose from the ceiling and splashed into the pond, creating a shower of acid droplets. Right before the acid rained down on us, it froze in midair.

"Yes, Mystic!" Tempest cried out, cheering on her former familiar who slowed the acid to allow the other witches enough time to cast a spell, placing us all in a protective bubble. As soon as that was secure, Mystic released her hold, and acid drops pelted the shield, but didn't penetrate. Instead the acid evaporated upon impact.

"Is everyone okay?" I asked, looking over at Cas and Gable, who had cushioned my fall. No one appeared to be injured.

"How the hell are we supposed to reach that damn altar?" Vanna snapped. "We are so fucking close." She crossed her arms over her chest with a huff.

"What is impervious to acid?" Felicia asked.

"Stone," Tempest answered. Calix and Eryx shared a significant look, one that caused Eryx to frown and shake his head.

"It's the only way," Calix said to his twin before scanning the other students as if looking for something. His gaze landed on me, and he walked over to stand in front of me. Placing his hand under my chin, he tilted my head back, bringing my lips closer to his, and I thought he was going to kiss me. "Will you help me, goddess?"

"With what?" My voice was laced with disappointment when I realized he wasn't going to kiss me, and I didn't know how much I longed for a connection, to be touched in that way, until the moment presented itself before abruptly fading away.

As I stared into his eyes, they began to change. First the soft brown morphed into a greenish yellow and then his irises became black slits. I stood transfixed as I gazed into his mother's eyes. The infamous Medusa, who could turn people to stone. A sharp intake of breath broke me out of whatever hold he had on me. Calix's plan was to turn me into stone?

"Please," Calix pleaded, and that's when I realized his intentions. His skin took on a gray pallor and gritty texture, like sandpaper. He placed his hands on my shoulders, keeping me in place, and our eyes locked on each other again. "Someone hand me the artifact." His voice had become rough and gritty too.

Calix had activated his ability, but on himself.

Eryx appeared behind his brother, removing the backpack strapped to Calix's back. Calix held out his hand, and Eryx handed him the artifact.

"You don't have to do this. We can figure out another way."

Eryx rested his hand on Calix's forearm, which was now almost entirely stone. Tempest came to stand next to her boyfriend, offering quiet support.

"It's the only way, brother. I have centuries of sins to atone for. I need to do this. I'm so glad to have found you. Perhaps we'll meet again." Calix released his hold on me to pull Eryx into a hug before he let go and moved toward the edge of the acid lake. His steps were stiff and awkward, and I was reminded of a knight in a new suit of armor. In a way, his stone exterior was armor. He took his first step into the acid, and I held my breath, expecting the worst. Nothing happened, and I exhaled in relief.

With each stiff step, Calix waded farther into the acid until it was up to his waist. His shirt eroded as the acid slowly ate away at the material, revealing a smooth stone back and broad shoulders. A shimmer in the air indicated his passage through the magical barrier. Calix's movements slowed, and we all gasped as he stumbled. He struggled to move, fighting the change, or perhaps the barrier was affecting him after all. He was so close to the altar, and only a few more steps remained.

"You got this, Calix!" Felicia shouted, breaking the intense silence. He didn't turn to acknowledge her, but the encouragement registered as with a gargantuan effort, he pushed on. Time stretched out before us as each step seemed to take an hour. If he could sweat, I imagined he'd be drenched from the exertion.

Finally, he closed the distance to the altar. As soon as the artifact was placed in the center, there was a massive shift in energy that registered deep in my bones. The magical barrier that protected the altar shattered. All of the hairs on my body raised in response. Everyone seemed to rock back on their heels as if hit by a wave. All of the shifters cried out, the chorus of animal sounds incongruous with their human forms. Calix didn't react at all. He remained frozen at the altar, the transformation to stone complete.

CHAPTER 10

*E*ryx fell to his knees and sobbed as Tempest knelt beside him, pulling him against her, whispering words of comfort. I had to look away, the pain of loss too much to witness. You'd think after thousands of years, I would have grown numb to grief, but I never did.

A flutter of activity captured my attention, and I turned toward it. Cas had shifted into his griffon form and was flying toward the altar. With the barrier gone, he reached Calix without incident and plucked him up with his giant talons. He lowered the statue to the ground, and Marina conjured water out of the air, enough to rinse the acid from Calix's stone form.

"Eryx," Felicia said and approached the grieving twin. She crouched down to be at eye level. He wiped his eyes and looked at her. "Your brother isn't dead. I would have sensed his spirit leave his body."

Her comment made me focus, and I approached Calix. The dead usually called to me, and I didn't experience any pull toward the statue. He was made of stone, but he wasn't dead.

"She's right," I said.

"Wh-what?" Eryx stood up, wiping dirt from his jeans. "Then we're taking him with us." Determined, he strode to the statue. "I'll find a way to bring you back, brother," he vowed and bent over to pick Calix up. He struggled with the weight, and Vidar rushed to help. His dark braids swayed when he lifted the statue, hoisting the bottom half onto his shoulder, while Eryx balanced the top half, carefully cradling his brother's head.

Calix had sacrificed himself, but there was a chance to bring him back. He wasn't lost to us, and that gave us hope. What could have been a solemn march through the tunnel and back to town with Eryx and Vidar as pallbearers, was fueled by optimism. We were exhausted, shellshocked, and still not done with assembling the weapon, but we had made it this far, and our training was turning us into a force to be reckoned with. Hermod would rue the day he messed with SMA.

"I'm flying to Mount Alexa to find the spirit group," I said to the others once we escaped the mountain. It was instantly clear we weren't done yet. The shield overhead still wasn't complete, a large gap from the center of town and north. The spirit teams apparently hadn't found their mark and needed help. "Who wants to come with me? The rest of you can go help the Court and the Luna Coven in the center of town."

Cas and Vidar joined me, and the fastest runners of the group said they'd meet us over there. As I lifted into the air, I was just glad I could transform again. We hadn't reached Whisper Falls Inn at the edge of town square when the shield over the northern part of town filled in. I cawed with relief—the spirit teams must have placed their piece.

Yet...a huge hole still remained in the center of the shield, directly over town square.

With another caw, I led the way, and we swooped down into the square, where a large crowd was gathered. Magic spells flew, and I had to dart out of the way of one that buzzed by my head. I circled around to see the target, and expecting to see Hermod, I nearly sank to the ground at the sight.

That was not Hermod.

In fact, as I reached my senses outward, I couldn't feel his telltale energy at all. Had he never been close? Never even came to this world at all?

I took my human form as I dropped to the ground in town square, right in front of Saundra Beaumont and Roman Bishop, who were shooting the strongest spells through the opening in the shield, toward the formation high above the canyon. Their fire was returned, blasting into the town hall and sheriff's office behind us.

"Those are Zandra's creatures," I yelled at the witches.

Shock filled their faces.

"Zandra is working with Hermod?" Saundra shouted.

"I don't know. This might have been her all along."

Roman, a powerful witch and a member of the Court, glared at me with dark ocean blue eyes. "How do you know Zandra?"

"It's a long story. We have to stop her!"

"No shit." Addie dropped to the ground beside us, seemingly out of nowhere, then Natalie landed right next to her. I looked up to see the purple and black wings of the Knight twins as they soared back upward, toward Zandra's army, Vidar and D with them. Cas flew up to join them just as a bolt of D's lightning shot for one of the enemy creatures. Elli and Brielle both blasted fire.

"But we couldn't figure out where the staff goes to finish the weapon," Natalie said, bringing my attention back to earth. She held the long piece of smooth, black wood entwined with ribbons of quicksilver and aether protectively against her.

"It never fused with the ankh and apparently didn't need to," Addie added. "The ankh worked all on its own. Elliana and Brielle had seen the spirit markings in a cave near the top of Mount Alexa one night when they'd been out stretching their wings. It's not too far from Clifftop, actually. So it didn't take long to find the *where*. We just wasted a bunch of time trying to make the staff fit, too."

"Then Elli just placed the ankh on the pile of stones, and it worked." Natalie shrugged.

"So where does the staff go?" I wondered aloud as I stared at the open sky overhead. The hole in the shield spanned the town square, stretching just beyond it in all directions. I recalled one of the last lines of the clue. "The heart of the moon and the sun... Do you think it means the Court? The heart of the Court of the Sun and the Moon?"

"We're not the heart," Roman snapped. "We're the brains."

Addie rolled her eyes. "Maybe it's referring to the town—the heart would be town square. It's also the geographic center of the canyon."

"And at the heart of the square is the fountain," Saundra added.

I turned to gaze at the three-tiered fountain sitting in the center of Town Square Park. The park itself was full of students and remaining townspeople—all supernatural, of course—fighting for their lives, so they probably didn't notice that the water had turned blood red. I tilted my head to the side.

"What was there before?" I asked. "Before the fountain or even the town was built?"

I looked over my shoulder at the elders of the town—most of them had been around way back then. Many of them had been part of the travelers who had discovered the canyon and settled it as their haven from humans and those who meant harm to the supernatural kind.

"An ugly boulder," Elsmed answered. "It was an eyesore. We couldn't get it to budge or break with any amount of magic. That's why we put the fountain there."

"Were there any petroglyphs on it?" I hedged.

Roman's dark brows pinched together as he looked at me. "How did you know?"

My heart jumping, I snatched the staff out of Natalie's hold and bolted for the fountain as she yelled after me. Just when I reached it, the water disappeared, and the entire concrete fountain slid to the side as though a phantom hand moved it. Just barely visible under a layer of dirt were the etchings of two people holding a stick shoved into the ground. I brushed the dirt away from the rock, looking for a place for the staff—a groove, a hole, *something*—but I found none.

"Fuck," I muttered out loud. Where was this thing supposed to go?

"Let me try," Natalie said. She hovered her hands over the boulder and chanted, "Heart of hearts, hidden near, revealed to us, without fear. Show us where Shillelagh belongs, combining the magic, our power so strong."

The air froze in my lungs as we waited for a long moment, and just when I thought nothing would happen, the boulder took on a strange glow that pulsed—like a heartbeat.

Shouts and screams came from all around me as a shower of

spells rained down on us like lava. Thinking through the last lines of the clue once more, I could only come up with one idea. With a deep breath in, I stood to my full height, grasped the staff in both hands, and lifted it up.

"What are you doing?" Natalie cried out.

"Hoping for the best," I said before thrusting the very valuable and ancient artifact downward. I braced myself for the connection, for the reverberation I expected to feel—or worse, the smashing of the staff into splinters—but there was none.

Rather, the staff sank about a quarter of its length into the rock, as though the boulder were made of clay.

Cheers erupted all around me, and I looked up to see the shield had filled in completely. Zandra's creatures tried a few more spells, but they ricocheted off. They disappeared into the night sky.

The celebration immediately fell silent, though, and the crowd parted.

"Well, that was fun," a female's voice rang through the air. "I expected better from all of you, but at least you came through in time."

My spine locked as I stared at my one-time friend and now my nemesis, who walked for the center of the square.

"I was beginning to think I overestimated you, Rhiannon," Zandra continued as her gaze slid over me from head to toe.

"The Collector," someone from behind me whispered, recognizing her from their battle over a year ago.

Voices shouted from behind me, the cacophony growing louder by the word.

"The weapon!" Addie yelled above them all. "Rhian, activate the weapon!"

A thrust and a twist ... a weapon to yield

I looked down at the staff, my hands still wrapped around it, but hesitated. Addie suddenly appeared next to me, pushing me aside. Her own hands grasped the black wood—

"Wait!" Elsmed and Saundra called out in unison.

We both looked up, and Addie gasped. I, however, wasn't surprised.

Zandra's facial features had changed, the angles softening, full lips thinning, blue eyes becoming brown, and a dark red bleeding into her blond tresses.

"Kialah?" Elsmed's voice carried a level of shock I'd never expected from the ancient fae.

She smiled sweetly at him and tilted her head. "My old friend."

I glanced over as he strode up level with me. "Friend?" he bit out. "Is this a joke? I don't even know who you are. What you are. *Who* are you—the real you?"

She shrugged as her features morphed again, back into the cold appearance of Zandra. "I am Zandra, goddess of Vanir." She changed again. "And I am also Kialah. Still a goddess of Vanir, but also your friend."

"Friends don't do this!" Saundra snapped, gesturing toward all the destruction.

"Is Hermod even coming?" I demanded, anger bubbling from deep within. My power licked along my veins, wanting to break free. If she made the smallest wrong move, I'd certainly go full goddess on her. "Or was this all a ruse? Just a game to you?"

Zandra's features returned as her ice blue gaze traveled over all of us. Her voice rose, ensuring all could hear her. "It is not a question of *if* Hermod is coming. It is a question of when. There is too much magic in this world for him not to. But when he does, we are now prepared to fight."

"*We?*" Roman snarled.

She rested her attention on the handsome high priest of the Luna Coven. "Me and all of you—my army."

Addie growled from my side. "You expect us to fight for you after all you've done to us?"

"You mean after all I've done *for* you?" Zandra growled back. She strode several steps closer, her gaze sweeping over the members of the Court. "I *awakened* you. You had become *complacent*. Even arrogant, thinking nothing could harm you or your people. I made you realize there are bigger threats to your town and your world." She turned and gestured at the crowd around us. "I gave you a school and everything necessary to build and train an army." She motioned at the staff in front of me and the shield overhead. "I gave you this protection for your town, stronger than your own wards had ever been, that will also serve as a weapon against

Hermod!" Then she turned back toward us, to the leaders next to and behind me, and her voice fell. Quiet. Calm. Threatening. "But it's your choice, Elsmed, Saundra, Roman, and the rest of you. When the time comes, you can fight *with* me against Hermod—" She rose into the air, wind whipping around her as she lit up with her full power. "Or you can fight both of us."

And with that, she disappeared.

CHAPTER 11

"*H*ow in tarnation did she escape? I thought she was trapped in a bottle in the Infernum." The angry whisper captured my attention in the shocked silence that followed Zandra's departure. I turned in the direction of the voice to find Lawrence Mills, a crotchety old member of the Court and frost dragon shifter. His bushy eyebrows seemed to have a life of their own as he spoke to Saundra Beaumont.

"I don't know, Lawrence, but we will find out."

"We must! That has to be a priority. Someone made a grave mistake. Look at our town, the damage, the clean up this breach entails. Unacceptable." The older man made a sweeping gesture with his arm, pointing out the buildings that were still on fire and the bodies strewn across the town square. "Unacceptable!" he said again before storming off to speak to Sheriff Kasun.

At least there was time to be angry, to look for blame, and to breathe. The immediate threat was over, and the town was now in possession of a fierce weapon. I couldn't believe Zandra was behind this attack. Wait—yes, I could. I'd given her the benefit of the doubt for too long, but I should have known she'd go this far to get what she wanted. As much I hated to see the destruction before us, I kind of understood. After all, I alone knew Hermod like she did—what he was capable of.

And it was so much worse than this.

I caught Roman Bishop watching me, his blue eyes narrowed in speculation. He was going to want an explanation about how I knew Zandra, but that wouldn't be today or tonight. I wasn't even sure what time it was. I only knew I was bone tired, and there was still work to be done.

A triage tent had been assembled near the gazebo, which was missing its roof. A flurry of doctors, nurses, and healers ran back and forth from one cot to the next. Fin sat on one, but appeared to be back to normal, hugging Joe tightly. The restoration of magic must have broken the spell on her. Unfortunately, the same couldn't be said about Calix. Tears stung my eyes as I glimpsed his stone form between several witches trying to fix him. There were so many casualties. The sheriff's deputies and EMTs were draping sheets over those who were beyond saving. My power pulsed, urging me to restore life, but I resisted.

With the wards in place, the covens had come together to begin the clean-up. I joined a group of witches who had gathered on the southwest corner of the square, slipping in next to Clay Washburn, Taylor and Harlow Augustine on his other side. Taylor gave me a relieved smile. Ash clung to her dark hair like snowflakes, and her clothes were covered in soot. Harlow's shirt was torn, and Clay sported a bloody, swollen lip. He, too, was covered in soot.

Saundra Beaumont stood at the front of the group, providing instructions. "You need to go building by building and wipe memories. You have the spells to repair damaged structures, too. Don't bother with those that have burned. They will need to be rebuilt. The mayor will be holding a press conference, as soon as the media has been located, explaining the town experienced a series of gas explosions." Saundra paused and scanned the group, her gaze landing on me. "Rhian, you, Taylor, and Clay come with me. Everyone else, split up, and please report any problems immediately."

The witches dispersed, and Harlow gave her sister a hug before she left. Taylor, Clay, and I walked across the scorched grass to meet Saundra. Her silvery white hair had escaped from its signature twist and stuck out in all directions. Her shirt was untucked from her skirt that was smeared with dirt. This was the most unkempt I had ever seen her.

"I'm glad to see you all unscathed. Now." She spun on her heels and started marching across the square, continuing to talk to us over her shoulder. We immediately fell into step behind her. "I need all students to return to Halvard Campus. We need to do a head count and those who are able will assist with clean up. The portals are working, and Addie is already over there with the faculty, supervising efforts." She turned to face us again. "Things got, what do you kids say, 'very real' today, and I think we all learned a valuable lesson about becoming complacent. Zandra, whether she's friend or foe, has reminded us of threats to our kind. In the meantime, you will continue your training to become the elite guardians who will save this world."

"Yes, Mrs. Beaumont," Taylor said, and I nodded my head in agreement. I'd leave it up to the Court to decide how to categorize Zandra.

"Like, you weren't even in the ITF class this semester, right?" Taylor asked as we ran toward the Falls Campus of Sun and Moon Academy. Other students were making their way back too.

"No, I got roped into it at the end, but at least I'll get graded."

Taylor's ponytail swung when she shook her head. "Do grades even matter at this point? Like, basically pass or fail can mean life or death."

We arrived on campus to what looked like ruins from an ancient civilization. One of the Valkyrie statues at the main bridge was toppled over, and smoke had stained the side of Modi Tower black. Halstein Hall was still on fire, and we ran over to help. Tempest, Marina, Natalie, and Charleigh were pouring water onto the flames from the courtyard while Elli and Brielle Knight were above, their wings stretched wide as they blasted water from their palms to the roof.

An unexpected wave of emotion washed over me as I watched the twins, remembering what they'd told me over Spring Break: this would likely be their last semester here. Here at SMA and here in this world. Not only would their abilities be missed, but I would sorely miss their friendship.

I wondered who else wouldn't be returning next year, but also looked forward to the new faces that would be joining us. Because I most certainly would be back. This was home.

I had started out as an observer, an outsider, but as I joined in the effort to save Halstein Hall from total ruin, I looked around at everyone working together and realized my fellow students had become more than allies. They had become my friends, my family. We had also become a powerful, united force. I thought about what Saundra had said earlier, and I believed her.

We would become the elite guardians who will save this world.

Read *The Collector: Awakening* by Kristie Cook, Belinda Boring, R.K. Ryals & Nadirah Foxx

Discover how it all began with a collection of 10 bonus short stories from the authors of Book One.

Want more of these characters, their families, and friends? Read these books!

HAVENWOOD FALLS SHORT STORY ANTHOLOGY 2018
HAVENWOOD FALLS SHORT ANTHOLOGY 2019
HAVENWOOD FALLS SHORT ANTHOLOGY 2020

ROXY McCABE
Shift of Fate by Victoria Escobar

TAYLOR AUGUSTINE
Fata Morgana by E.J. Fechenda
Stray With Me by E.J. Fechenda

INFINITI CLAUSMAN
Saving Infiniti by Rose Garcia
Finding Infiniti by Rose Garcia
The Final Life Saga by Rose Garcia

THE KNIGHT TWINS
Soul Savers Series by Kristie Cook

ADDIE BEAUMONT
Forget You Not by Kristie Cook
Lose You Not by Kristie Cook
Break Me Not by Kristie Cook
The Collector: Awakening by Kristie Cook, Belinda Boring, R.K. Ryals & Nadirah Foxx

GABRIEL DOYLE
Stolen Wishes by Victoria Flynn

SHADE STORMIRON
Damned Allure by Justine Winter

THE HOWE WITCHES
Lost in Time by Tish Thawer
The Witches of Blackbrook Series by Tish Thawer

ABOUT THE AUTHORS

Kristie Cook—Award-winning, bestselling author of the Soul Savers Series, the Book of Phoenix trilogy, and creator, author, editor, and publisher of the Havenwood Falls universe. KristieCook.com

Belinda Boring—Bestselling author of tThe Mystic Wolves Series, Damaged Souls Series, *Loving Liberty*, *Broken Promises*, *Enchanted Hearts*, and Havenwood Falls. belindaboringauthor.com

E.J. Fechenda—Bestselling author of *The Beautiful People*, book one of the New Mafia Trilogy, the Ghost Stories Trilogy, and Havenwood Falls. www.facebook.com/EJFechendaAuthor

Justine Winter—Bestselling author of the Nature's Destiny series, Wanted series, *Wicked Sunshine*, and Havenwood Falls. justinewinter.wordpress.com

Victoria Flynn—Award-winning author of the Voodoo Revival series, Rescue Squad Shifters series, *Ravaged* (A Voodoo Revival Universe Novel), *Warrior's Kiss: Mountain Mermaids* (Sapphire Lake), and Havenwood Falls. victoriaflynn.com

Amy Richie—Bestselling author of the Blood Vine Series, When Leslie Cries Trilogy, The Girl from Ortec Trilogy, Speak No Evil Trilogy, the Immortal Love Series, the Aella Duology, and Havenwood Falls. authoramyrichie.com

Rose Garcia—Award-winning, best-selling author of The Final Life Series and Havenwood Falls. RoseGarciaBooks.com

Tish Thawer—Award-winning, bestselling author of the Witches of Blackbrook Series, the Women of Purgatory Series, the Rose Trilogy, *Handler*, the Ovialell series, the TS901 Chronicles (co-author), and Havenwood Falls. TishThawer.com

ACKNOWLEDGMENTS

When the world is burning around you, it can feel impossible to create. This year has been difficult for all artists, including us. Often times we wondered if we'd ever be able to finish this book— or any others, ever, for that matter. We know it's necessary to find escape from reality for a while, especially in stressful times. That's why we love to read. That's why we love to write. It's a conundrum we authors find ourselves in not infrequently—knowing that writing soothes our souls, but not being able to write when our souls hurt so much. This year, that torn feeling has been stronger than ever. Even when our hearts and souls begged to be lost in a fictional place, the weight of the real world was too much.

But we also heard the cries of readers' souls needing their own escape. It's because of you, dear reader, that so many of us have been able to push through the muck and keep writing, keep creating. You inspired and motivated us to deliver delicious characters and stories to feed and soothe your own souls. We are so grateful for you, this year more than ever.

We hope people will remember that they turned to art when the world went dark. Art is necessary in all its forms. Let's never forget that and be sure to support artists of all kinds in the way they deserve.

As always, we thank our families, but more than ever right

now. Even those we've been locked up with for months on end. We still love you. Mostly.

Many thanks to our cover designer, Regina Wamba. To all of the other Havenwood Falls authors who helped create the magical universe of our school. To Jessica Ramirez who kept up with us and didn't balk at our crazy deadline at the end.

Of course, we have to acknowledge each other. The first SMA book was probably one of the most challenging projects any of us have ever worked on. Yet, we jumped in to do it all over again—and then came 2020. Every single one of us gave everything we possibly could to make this project happen. Well done, yo! Someday we'll get to meet in person again and share those drinks and hugs.

Last but not least, we love you, Havenwoodies! See you in the club!

Made in the USA
Las Vegas, NV
19 December 2020